Port Honor

TS Dawson

Acknowledgments

Thank you to all of my friends and family who have aided in the process of writing this book. Without you I likely would have never started this process and I certainly would not have continued past chapter one without your love and encouragement. I really appreciate each and every one of you.

I would like to thank my husband and son for allowing me the time it took to be able to write this book. I love you both very much and appreciate all that you do for me.

I would also like to thank my parents, Linda and John Bryan, for their love and support in this process. A special thank you goes out to John for working so hard on my website and entertaining all of my special requests.

I would like to personally thank Donna M. Goss for being my first editor. Were it not for your encouragement and interest in the story, I would have continued to think I was writing complete crap. Thank you for all of your reading, re-reading, editing and spreading the word about the book all through this year long journey.

As for Annette Saunders, I know you were hesitant to read it to begin with, but I am so glad you did. I also appreciate your reading, editing and spreading the word as well. Your encouragement and support have meant the world to me.

Scott Meeks, thank you so much for your suggestions to the content especially to the beginning. It seems odd to say, but you made a funeral better. Thanks!

Susanne Smith, thank you so much for not being afraid to critique my work. I think your contribution was invaluable as well.

I would also like to personally thank all of my first readers; Jill Marriott, Dottie Harper, Susie Taylor, Phyllis Aycock, Greg Dinsmore, and Bett Smith. Thank you all for reading, providing feedback and helping to spread the word about the book.

Thank you to Bryan Garrett for the job at the club. Were it not for that job, I might not have gained the knowledge about golf and country club life to have been able to write this.

I would also like to send out a special thank you to all of you who have and will give my book a chance. Thank you for giving of your time and I hope I will be able to entertain you with my stories of romance and life in the South.

While some locations referenced in this book do exist, the characters are based solely on my overactive imagination. Any similarities to actual people are due to your own imagination.

Thank you for reading and enjoy!

Sincerely,

TS Dawson

Prologue

June 10, 1995

The smell of roses in the chapel of the funeral home was stiflingly strong. It was meat locker cold in there and the smell was suffocating. I knew I would never be able to tolerate the scent without thinking of a funeral again.

I cleared my throat and wondered how I was going to get through this as I scanned the faces of those in attendance at my grandfather's funeral. All eyes were on me, Aunt Gayle in the front row with my grandfather's sisters, Aunt Dot and Aunt Ruth; their children seated on the row behind them, and then well over half of the town consisting of Granddaddy's friends. I was quite sure that tears had already streaked my make-up before I took to the podium.

I tried to distract myself with thoughts ranging from what was cousin Dixon thinking wearing a Grateful Dead t-shirt to a funeral, let alone his uncle's funeral, to what was cousin Dixon ever thinking. What was Aunt Ruth thinking when she named her two children Dixon and Dixie? I let my mind wander for just a moment to try to squelch the tears so I could recite the poem. The distraction was working, but all eyes were on me and they were waiting.

I had memorized this poem in ninth grade and had yet to forget it, but could I get the words out? I cleared my throat again and began as I had rehearsed; an introduction and then the poem.

"I dare say everyone in this room knew my grandfather, George Anderson; the business man, the farmer, shipmate in the Navy, friend, brother and father, but to me he was Granddaddy. You probably don't know that he had quite the imagination, but I did. It was that imagination that got me through some of the toughest times of my childhood.

Unfortunately and fortunately, I remember Christmas 1978 with crystal clarity. I was four and my mother was on a cruise with her new doctor boyfriend. She left me with Granddaddy and Grandma two days before Christmas as she passed through on her way to board the ship in Florida. No presents. Not much in the way of clothes. No nothing really. Of course my Grandparents never made me feel as if I had been dumped on them, but that's exactly what had happened.

I did not know it then, but Granddaddy rushed all around town trying to find presents to put under the tree for me from Santa. As you can imagine there wasn't much left; you know, dolls or dollhouses on Christmas Eve without driving all the way to Augusta. My grandmother insisted that he drive to Augusta and he did, but there was not much left there either. He came home with just about the only doll that was left on the shelf at the K-Mart on Gordon Highway. The doll was Peter Pan and it was about as big as I was at the time.

Now, you all know George Anderson was not a man to be defeated and defeated is what he felt coming home with only a giant Peter Pan doll. So, that night, after everyone had gone to bed including Grandma, Granddaddy unwrapped the refrigerator that he had gotten Grandma for Christmas and from the refrigerator box he created a pirate ship for me and Peter Pan. He spent half the night painting the big box black, cutting port holes in the side, even made a flag out of some old bed sheets and fashioned a flag pole out of a broom stick.

That was the best Christmas ever and it wasn't because I got a Peter Pan doll or the most awesome pirate ship. It was because Granddaddy spent the rest of the week as Captain Hook with me and Peter Pan.

To the list of things George Anderson was, he was also my captain so I apologize if I get the words wrong or if I don't quite make it through this poem that I chose for him today."

I paused to wipe the tears from my eyes before I began. As I brought the handkerchief that Aunt Gayle had given me just before I went to the podium to my face, I noticed Granddaddy's initials stitched in the corner, G.A. The pause became more of a moment, but finally I choked back the tears and began my recital of Walt Whitman's "O Captain! My Captain!"

By the end of my reading, there was hardly a dry eye in the place, including my own. George Anderson was the closest thing to a father I had ever known and now I had to say a final goodbye. It just did not seem possible that life could go on without him.

CHAPTER 1

As I got dressed for my interview, I reflected on the events of the night before.

"I can't believe you are not coming with us," said Jay as he gathered his keys and headed toward the door of the apartment with Emma. My new roommates, Jay and Emma, were regulars at all of the college bars in Milledgeville, Georgia: The Opera House, The Brick, Cameron's and probably some of the not so college bars, Cowboy Bills and Lucy Coopers, in Macon as well.

"It's just not my thing. You all go on without me and have a good time," I responded. I sat on the couch and planned to continue reading my chapter for World History of the Twentieth Century for the remainder of the night.

Emma returned with a roll of her dark brown eyes, "That's fine Jay, leave her. It just means less competition and more boys for us!" I was no competition for Emma. She was here on a tennis scholarship from England and the accent really set her apart from most of the girls at Georgia College, but the fact that she was built like a brick shit house really put her in a league all her own.

Just when I thought they were out the door and with one hand on the handle pulling it behind her back, Emma turned back to me and made as sincere of a plea to join them as I would get. "If I can tolerate the pathetic bars in this God forsaken place, so can you. Now, get your ass up and come on!"

I did not budge from my spot on the couch, barely lifting my eyes from my text book; I declined the offer once more. "As enticing as that offer is, I just can't. I've got classes starting at eight in the morning and my interview tomorrow afternoon. Thanks anyway."

"Suit yourself," Jay yelled as they flitted out the door in their bar hopping best.

Emma shouted back with one more reminder that compared to them I was no fun at all. "Over achieving stick in the mud!"

The door closed behind them and I could hear them banging down the stairs, him in his Nikes and she in her stilettos. The door did not budge again until Jay returned around 2:15 a.m. I barely noticed except I was awakened by the creaking of the stairs through my bedroom wall as he ascended. The door never opened again during the night for Emma.

***

This is quite possibly the longest I had been without a job. After all, I had been working since I was fifteen, but here I am at the ripe old age of twenty having been unemployed for only three weeks and knowing that I am not cut out for doing nothing. I could scarcely imagine that between the change in residences and the full load of courses and making new friends, I had become bored, but I had. I needed a job and it wasn't just about the money. I needed something to occupy my time and unlike my roommates, being a student by day and a bar fly by night just was not enough.

Although this was the interview that I had lined up first, it was the last of three and I could only hope that it was more promising than the other two had been. The first had been for a position as a brew master at a coffee house named Brewers. Maybe it was obvious that I did not take brewing coffee seriously enough or perhaps I did not have enough piercings or perhaps what really sealed the fate of that one was when I told the owner, "No, thanks. I don't drink coffee." Apparently, one had to at least like coffee to work there.

The second interview was with a clothing store called Merry-Go-Round at the smallest mall in America, the mall in Milledgeville. The music was too loud, too fast and I could not get on board with the unwritten company motto of "Spandex looks great on everyone!" It doesn't. I failed at my test sale when the look on my face so clearly told the three hundred pound Mariah Carey wanna-be, "Yes, you are too fat for that skirt." That was unfortunate, since despite the fact that I could not hear myself think, I was really killing that interview up until that point.

Here it was nearly the sunniest and hottest day of the year, early September 1995 in Middle Georgia, and this was the day I would get a job. Everyone was in class so neither of my roommates was home to aid in my wardrobe selection. I had to go this one alone.

I chose the burgundy suit that I had worn to my grandfather's funeral a few months before. It was form fitting and short. In all honesty, it was indecently short for a funeral, but just right for an interview with a man, especially with the four inch high black heels that I had paired with it. This gave me another opportunity to wear the suit since I had only just purchased it for the funeral. It was probably my most prized, but useless outfit at the time. This suit was most definitely not something I would just throw on and wear to class. The jacket matched the skirt perfectly and the sleeves on the jacket had satin cuffs of the same color. It was exquisite. I felt damn near sexy in it, which was a foreign concept for me.

My make-up was about the same as I usually wore it with the idea of less is more. My hair on the other hand looked like the Cowardly Lion after he had been to the beauty salon in Oz. It was about the same color and just as big, curly and as long as his. It was not exactly the comparison I would like others to make, but looking in the mirror at myself all I could think as "Put 'em up! Put 'em up! I'll fight 'cha with one paw."

I had initially called regarding the job posting well over a week ago, but this was the first opening the manager of the club had for me to come in. The opening was for a server at a golf and country club near Greensboro on Lake Oconee called Port Honor. It was approximately forty miles from Milledgeville. I had had this scheduled so far in advance there really was no excuse for my being late, but who allows time for a cattle crossing?

How could I have known that the farmer owned pastures on both sides of the road and would choose today of all days, Wednesday at 1:45 p.m., to move his cattle from one field to the other on the opposite side of the road? Honestly, I was driving along making good time until I came to a screeching halt while, "one, two, three... forty-five, forty-six, forty-seven..." I counted aloud in my car as I waited while they passed. "One hundred sixty-nine, one hundred seventy..." The dairy cows just kept coming. I even counted one that looked like a double stuffed Oreo.

I waited thirty minutes for two hundred head of cattle to cross and cows clearly have no concept of time or hurrying. Behind the last cow the man who had stopped traffic with his antique looking tractor, tipped his hat to me and I restrained myself from flipping him the bird as I squalled my tires and sped off. There were ten cars that had accumulated behind me, but by the time I hit seventy in under about thirty seconds they were barely visible in my rear view mirror. My car might have been old, but it was reliable and it could still get up on it when I demanded.

I was now running considerably late and all I could think was there really should be some sort of Les Nessman Hog Report type thing on the local radio stations for such events. After all, the radio in my 1973 Corvette worked just fine. It was the air conditioner that does nothing unless I am moving at speed limit pace or faster.

The air conditioning was virtually non-existent while waiting on the cattle and all rolling down the window accomplished was letting the cow stench in. Unfortunately, I had not thought to take the T-tops off and the sun was really cooking me through those things. By the time the last cow crossed the road, I had sweated my ass off. My suit was likely pitted, my hair was flat and any trace of make-up was now dripping from my neck and it was quite possible that I smelled of manure.

I was officially thirty minutes late when I crossed over the Lake Oconee Bridge on Highway 44. I could barely see to the left across the lake in the distance a large white building of what appeared to be all windows tucked up in a cove. I could also see a smattering of houses dotting the wooded lawns along the shore. Everything was so small in the distance.

Before reaching the bridge, the scenery along the drive had been mostly pastures and woods with the exception of passing through the town of Eatonton, but here by the lake things were more modern. One could clearly tell the area was on the rise. The houses and businesses all appeared to be new, shiny and well maintained. I counted four real estate sales offices in the mile between the far side of the bridge and the gate for Port Honor.

Just before the turn in for Port Honor, the woods that were butted up against the side of the road were cut back. The break in the forest allowed for a white split rail fence and pristine landscaping consisting of azaleas, boxwoods, flowering cherry trees and Leland cypresses. Then there among the landscaping was a beautiful tower. It was nothing huge, no more than twenty feet tall, if that high. It had a wooden shingle roof on it of a natural stain color, white trim around the area where one might climb up and stand, and then the bottom was arched columns of stacked stone. Across the front were the words "Port Honor" with three squiggles underneath. I would later find out the squiggles were the logo which were supposed to be waves.

Just beyond the tower by about twenty yards was the entrance and the guard shack was set back off of the road by another thirty yards. It was a slight structure that very much resembled the tower by the road, same architectural style and colors, just a bit smaller.

Officer Ed, a friendly man of about sixty, was manning the gate. "Like the car, honey. Is it a Stingray?" he said as I pulled up to the gate.

"It is indeed a Stingray," I replied.

"327 engine or 350?" Officer Ed seemed to know a thing or two about cars.

"327, original too. Engine, transmission and body all original." I liked to brag a bit about the car, after all, it was my most prized possession.

Officer Ed was visibly impressed, but moved along from car talk. "Are you the one here for the job interview?"

"Yes, sir. My name is Millie Anderson and I was supposed to meet with Mr. Hewitt at 2:30. I know I am late, but you have to let me in," I begged.

"Did you just drive out here from Milledgeville?" he asked while still not using my name and again referring to me as "honey".

Once more, I responded with a polite, "Yes, sir."

"I bet you got stopped by Bill Randall and his damn cows, didn't you? Well, don't you worry about anything. I will call down to the club and tell them you are on your way and explain about the cows. I have lived next to that man for thirty years and I haven't been able to get in or out on a Wednesday afternoon because of those wretched animals." Officer Ed seemed to know all about the cow situation and was as thrilled about it as I was.

"Since I am already late, I don't suppose you have a restroom in there that I could borrow to tidy up a bit, would you? I promise I will only be five minutes." Officer Ed was more than happy to oblige as long as I agreed that if I got the job I would give him a ride in the Corvette sometime. I agreed. Unfortunately, before I finished the assessment of my looks in the bathroom, my thoughts sprang to life and before I realized it, the words, "Kiss me fat boy!" had escaped my lips. Immediately following my words was a flushing in the stall that adjoined the wash room. Just when I thought my day could not have gotten any worse, I lost all dignity. How could I have known that it was shift change at the guard shack and the other guard was in the stall changing clothes and relieving himself? It seems like something Officer Ed should have warned me about. Oh, well. Within five minutes I was back in the car, looking a little more like the girl who had first left her apartment that afternoon and a little less like Pennywise the clown, from the movie *It*.

The final directions to the club consisted of proceeding a quarter mile down Port Honor Parkway before turning onto the second street to the left and continuing past The Honor Inn and to the clubhouse at the bottom of the hill. Once in front of the clubhouse, I was certain that this was the building I had seen from the bridge. From this vantage point in the parking lot, the building seemed considerably smaller only because you could only see the upper level and the roof, but I just knew it had to be the same.

I parked in the parking lot for what was obviously the front door of the building, but there was another parking lot farther down a hill to the left by the tennis courts. There was also another lower level parking lot to the right near a driving range where various vehicles were parked and men continually zipped through on golf carts.

It was a great deal to take in and hard not to waste time doing just that, taking it all in. This place was unlike anything I had ever seen before. Although I grew up near Augusta, home of the Masters, I had never seen beyond the gates of Augusta National and the clubhouse for the sad country club in my home town was little more than an old brick ranch house with four golf carts parked under the carport. The greens there wished they were green like this, but instead they were a dry brown that surely crackled and crumbled beneath any ball. Not here though, everything was kept up and the greens were lush and called for me to run barefoot over them which I promised myself I would do should I get the job.

After parking the car, I took one last look in the mirror telling the flat haired girl looking back at me that she better wish me luck and then I headed to the door carrying only my keys. Upon entering the double doors I was greeted by a lovely woman of about fifty years. She was thin and ash blonde. She stood from her desk revealing her attire; the whitest of all white tennis skirts and a hot pink and green floral tennis shirt and her wedding ring was blindingly big. At that point I became unsure as to whether she was a secretary of sorts or the club tennis pro.

When she spoke she sounded more Southern than I did, it was refreshing, like hearing one of the church ladies from back home. "Dear, may I help you?" she inquired.

"I sure hope so. I am Millie Anderson here to see Mr. Hewitt." I responded.

"Right. Right," she said as she picked up the desk phone and dialed with one hand while holding up the other and gesturing for me to wait a minute. I could only hear her side of the conversation, but it went as follows: "Gabe, Joan here. I have Millie Anderson waiting for you...yes, the 2:30 appointment...yes, the same one that Ed just called about...sure. I will send her down."

While waiting for Mrs. Joan to hang up, I glanced around the room. The area that we were in, on that level of the clubhouse, clearly was meant to resemble a loft in a great lodge, with the exception of Joan's desk which was just tossed in there like a sore thumb. To the left behind the desk and a good ways across the room was a sitting area furnished in what appeared to be high end, but comfortable, living room furniture. The carpet was a navy color with gold lines forming diamond patterns through it. There were two leather hob nail couches across from one another and parallel to Joan's desk, sitting perpendicular to a large floor to ceiling stacked stone fireplace. The stacked stone fireplace was the only break in the railing that looked over into the great dining room below. At the opposite end of the sitting area from the fireplace were two striped accent chairs of navy blue and gold which perfectly matched the carpet. Aside from the fireplace, the most impressive thing in the room was the massive chandelier hanging in the center of it all. A countless number of deer had surely lost their antlers to form this intricate and extravagant fixture. The base was easily five or six feet wide and tier after tier, each smaller than the one below, rings of antlers and small candle-shaped bulbs rose toward the ceiling before being strung up by a brushed nickel chain.

Farther beyond the sitting area and near the far wall was a grand piano, not a baby grand, but a full sized grand piano. It appeared to have been freshly waxed as even though it was completely black the reflection of the floral arrangement of yellow roses and daisies shown in it like a mirror. It was amazing, the kind of piano that every girl who ever took a lesson dreams of owning, the kind of piano that I had always dreamed of playing. I would add that to the list of tasks that I would accomplish, along with running barefoot on the greens, should I actually survive the interview and get the job.

Ahead of the doors and near Joan's desk was another break in the balcony railing allowing for stairs leading down to the dining room. I could not see from my position near her desk anything beyond a hostess stand at the very bottom of the stairs next to the wall of windows.

The visual tour of my surroundings was cut short with the hanging up of the phone. Mrs. Joan turned back to me and instructed me to go down the stairs, make a right at the bottom and wait for Mr. Hewitt at one of the tables in the bar area. She said I could pick whichever table I liked. I did as she instructed: down the stairs, through the door to the right and into the bar I went, taking a seat at a table facing the windows overlooking the course outside.

As I waited for Mr. Hewitt, I sized up my surroundings and aside from the view of the cove and the green, the bar was rather lackluster. It had the same general décor as the loft upstairs: same carpet, same stacked stone fireplace, just on a smaller scale, and same paint hues on the walls. The only difference was it was a bar with about six four-top tables and the standard set up of stools around the actual bar.

About the time I was beginning to count how many types of liquors looked exactly the same color as tea, a swinging door just to the end of the liquor cabinet suddenly thrust open and a tall blonde man came bursting through it. I am not sure what I was expecting, but this was not it. This guy was definitely younger than what I had in mind.

The door made quite the commotion swinging back and forth. Clanging and squeaking all at once in desperate need of WD-40 on the hinges. This went on until he turned and went back to still it. I could faintly hear him curse at it under his breath as he grabbed it, "God damn it! Stop!"

My pulse had quickened at the sight of him and the sound, the demand in his voice urging the door to bend to his will. The blond hair, the blue eyes, the build, the height; he could have been Hitler's wet dream. He was the very definition of easy on the eyes.

The door was not the only thing that might have been about to come undone. I was incredibly nervous with being late and then the agony of sitting there waiting and now the sight of him. My mind had roamed to the thought of whether this was a test or punishment for being late: if I waited then I had the job or had he just hoped to keep me waiting until I gave up and went away. Had I not taken the hint and now I was just wasting more of his time? Was he pissed? He had just cursed at a swinging door. I gathered my nerve and stood as he came toward me. I was still trying to decide whether to make my apologies and run or to stay when he started to speak.

"Miss..." he trailed off snapping his fingers trying to recall my name. Right, I suppose a man that looks like this has never bothered to remember a woman's name beyond that of his mother or perhaps even his grandmother, but that may be stretching it.

I extended my hand to shake as he approached. "Anderson, Millie Anderson," I said as he took my hand. When our hands touched for the shake, I could feel a current run through me. My heart pounded and the room was suddenly hotter. Our eyes locked for a moment and he suddenly broke the connection, eyes and hands. Had he felt that as well?

I could hardly stand to look him in the eye as he was quite possibly the best looking man I have ever laid eyes on in person. I had watched "Cat on a Hot Tin Roof" countless times with my

14

grandmother while growing up and in that moment I knew I was looking into the eyes of young Paul Newman. Mr. Hewitt was beyond the marvel of Technicolor, he was the fulfillment of my imagination as I had watched in black and white.

I was intimidated to the thousandth degree. I looked down for as long as I could before it occurred to me, what loser gets a job when they are too sheepish to look their potential boss in the eye. All of my insides are screaming, "WOW!" and I think hives are beginning to sprout on my chest. Thank heavens I had decided on a short skirt for the interview instead of a low cut top. I am extremely pale and when I am flushed, pissed or embarrassed, the hives tend to take over my chest and give me away.

"Gabe Hewitt, general manager and executive chef. Please have a seat." He pulled the chair back out from the table for me to return to it. He then took the seat directly across the table from me. There was no one else in the bar, but the two of us and suddenly I was extremely aware of that.

"It says here on your application that your name is Amelia Anderson," and when he said my name I could not help but look up at him. Although no eye contact was made, it was singed in my memory from moments before that Mr. Hewitt had eyes that are so blue that you can nearly see through them. My eyes shift between blue and green with flakes of yellow, depending on what color I am wearing, but his appeared to be permanently blue.

For a moment my mind strayed while taking in the sight of Mr. Hewitt. He was wearing a chef's jacket with the sleeves rolled up nearly to his elbows, a pair of baggy black and white checkered pants with black clogs. The clothes did nothing for him, but he did everything for them.

As he walked to greet me, I had noticed the checkered pants were a little too thin. The way they gave away absolutely every inch of everything reminded me of creepy Ron Delano. Even though I had only just laid eyes on him, I knew without a doubt that Gabe Hewitt was no Ron Delano. I spent many days since our introduction on campus trying to avoid Ron and his pelvic hugs. Ron always wore the thinnest of thin sweat pants and from the looks of his pecker swinging in the breeze beneath them that was all he wore. Worse than just the view was that he insisted on giving hugs; hugs during which he squatted just a little and you could feel it slide between your legs as he hugged you. On the rare occasion when I thought of Ron Delano, I tended to cringe, but this time it occurred to me that I might not mind the pelvic hug so much coming from Mr. Hewitt. He was so much taller than me that the pelvic hug would likely be awkward in a whole other way; he would have to do more than bend his knees a little.

Regardless of my Ron Delano comparison, Mr. Hewitt was nothing like the college or high school boys to which I was accustomed. The way he had moved when entering the room exuded confidence and sophistication beyond any that a college boy could muster. He was every bit a man and I suspected about ten years older than myself. If he were older than thirty, I would have been shocked.

I had heard his question and despite my thoughts, I answered timely. "Right, my name is Amelia, but no one other than my grandmother has ever called me that," I stuttered. "Everyone calls me Millie."

"Well, *Amelia*, it also says here that you have experience waiting tables. Is that another half-truth or do you have experience?" he asks with a bit of impatience to his voice.

"Yes, sir," I answered.

"Yes, sir,' I have experience or 'Yes, sir,' I have just told another half-truth?"

I nearly cut him off with my response, "I have experience," I answered and continued by rattling off so many jobs that it made me sound unstable and of course he seemed to notice the instability. I immediately stopped and began to explain. "I have been working since I was fifteen. I know I have had a lot of jobs, but when I went to college in North Georgia, I had several of the jobs at once and that was while I attended a full load of classes."

I continued on. I was like Alice spiraling down the rabbit hole as he sat there staring at his clipboard reading my application. He did not look up at me once as I had gone on and on about my qualifications. I knew why I could hardly look at him, I was horribly nervous and he was frustratingly attractive, but what was he thinking? There really was not that much to read on my application and goodness knows I had just verbally vomited up everything that was written there and more.

Finally, he stopped me from my rambling. "Look, here's the thing," he started. When I did work up the nerve to look, I could not help but look at his mouth. His teeth were so white and like mine they weren't entirely perfect, but probably close enough that he either never had braces or he had braces and his teeth shifted slightly after their removal.

Mr. Hewitt continued, "I have interviewed five of you girls for this position, each a bigger waste of my time than the next. You all have experience bouncing from one job to the next. I will just be honest with you, Amelia. I am not hiring someone to hock food. I am looking to hire someone to sell the lifestyle here. Port Honor members can buy food anywhere. So tell me, what makes you so special that I should hire you?"

I thought for a moment. My first thought was, "Oh snap! He's an asshole!" But, the most prevalent thought was wondering if this was a challenge to impress him and regardless, I wanted to impress him. I rarely gave consideration to what others thought of me. I wanted to be a good person and all, but the only people I was ever interested in impressing were my grandfather and my aunt. What was it about Mr. Hewitt that put him in the category with the most important people in my life within five minutes of meeting him?

Quickly I thought about all of the women I knew from the country club growing up. Their noses were all so high in the air that had they been caught in the rain they would have drowned. They led a life that screamed, "I'm better than you." Perhaps that is the lifestyle he needs to be sold. I accepted the challenge.

I asked myself, what would Jessica Wren do in this situation? She was the biggest country club snob in our town. I knew the answer! Jessica would rise to the occasion and let him know that she was better than all of this. In her own way and without stooping to use the words, she would tell him to screw off. She was so accomplished at such tasks that she could do it with just a look. I was above being talked to like this, but I knew better than to think I could prove it with a single look.

I raised my head and ignoring all else, I looked him in the eye. I could feel that I was giving him that look that often got me into trouble with Aunt Gayle when I was angry with her and it showed on my face. One of my eyebrows arched and my nostrils flared. "That's a Fazioli piano upstairs, correct?" I asked him.

Seeming annoyed and sounding stern, he responded, "I really would not know."

"If you would indulge me just a moment and follow me," I said as I stood and he actually followed me up the stairs. I had no right to expect he would follow, but he did.

When we approached the door of the bar, Mr. Hewitt picked up the pace slightly to open the door for me. This was the second time he had displayed evidence that someone had trained him in the lost art of being a gentleman.

As we topped the stairs, Mrs. Joan rose from the seat at her desk as if to offer assistance. Mr. Hewitt waved her off as we passed toward the piano. About five feet from the piano, I stopped and asked him to wait where he stood.

I proceeded to the piano and asked if I may remove the floral arrangement from the lid. He continued to indulge me and I lifted the arrangement and placed it on the coffee table between the two leather couches. I returned and lifted the lid of the piano and propped it open. I then proceeded to the piano bench, but before I sat I slipped off my shoes, and strategically, in his direction, I bent over and picked them up and placed my shoes neatly next to the bench. I even looked back while bent over to make sure he checked out my behind as I had intended and he did. My insides jumped at the thrill of him having looked. I then took a seat at the piano bench, straightening my skirt and stretching my arms before I slid back the cover over the keys and began to play.

I started with something classical that surely anyone would recognize; "Beethoven's Fifth Symphony". All the while I played I explained, "This is a Fazioli piano. They are made in Italy and although the company has only been in production for about twenty years, they are the best of the best. This piano deserves to be played like this and regularly."

I knew all of this because when we went to buy my piano when I was ten, I picked out a shiny Fazioli and the salesman went on and on about it until my grandfather stopped him and explained that he was not spending *that* on a piano. I ended up with an upright which was cheaper and took up far less space, but did the same job.

I could tell from the layer of dust over the piano bench that the piano was rarely played if ever. The thought of this piano never having been played almost made me sad.

I went on as I played, "What I am playing now is "Beethoven's Fifth", in case you do not recognize it."

With little effort I wound off from Beethoven to the next piece and I continued to play effortlessly while I spoke. "This you may recognize as the theme from Young and the Restless, but the true name of it is 'Nadia's Theme'."

By this time, Mrs. Joan had joined Mr. Hewitt in watching me at the piano. I was really making it sing especially when I tapered off "Nadia's Theme" and busted loose with the Jackson 5's "I Want

You Back". The piano was really commanding attention and women were flocking from the back offices of the club to see what was going on.

A small crowd was already gathering when two gentlemen came through the front doors of the club. They appeared to be fresh off the course and one was dressed in a University of Georgia golf shirt so I went into the UGA alma mater. The one stopped in his tracks and the other followed. The UGA fan knew immediately what I was playing and began to chant the song and even screamed the end along with the piano, "All hail to dear old Georgia!"

Not to be offensive, but still aiming to impress with my variety of knowledge and demonstrating what the piano could do, I fired up the Georgia Tech Rambling Wreck song. Although not in the same manner, the UGA fan was still engaged. Toward the end of the Tech song, I noticed Mrs. Joan mouthing the words, "and a heck of an engineer!" She knew the words. Perhaps she too was a Tech fan.

I concluded with "Rocky Top", the Tennessee song. Although there probably wasn't a Tennessee fan in the house, everyone knows the words to "Rocky Top". Once finished, I slipped my hands from the ivories and gently closed the cover to the keys. The room erupted in applause.

Mr. Hewitt shook his head as if he did not quite know what to make of me. I believe I had succeeded in impressing him, but I was unsure if I had impressed him in a manner that would achieve my goal of getting a job. After all, a job requirement of a server did not include concert pianist. Regardless, I was not necessarily done. As he approached the piano, I began to stand and he held out his hand to help me up. I mustered all of my confidence and my inner diva and taking his hand, I again looked him directly in the eye. In a whisper so only he could hear, and as not to embarrass myself in front of all of the women, I said, "If you want a lifestyle, I am where it's at!" His mouth fell open and he immediately broke eye contact, but he still had my hand from helping me up. The look of annoyance on his face had been replaced while I was playing by a poker face laced with amazement, but now even the poker face was gone and replaced by sheer shock.

The clapping had wound down and I could hear Mrs. Joan explain to the other ladies that I was one of the girls the college had sent out for the server position. I also over heard one to say that if Gabe did not hire me he was a fool. I believe he may have heard that comment as well as that is when he realized he was still holding my hand and released it. The conversation was all so quick, but another added that if he did, he was a fool as he would not get any work out of the rest of the boys with me around. Another added that if I took the job I was the fool as the men would eat me alive here and the wives would hate me.

The office ladies soon disbanded and returned down the corridor across from Mrs. Joan's desk. Mrs. Joan then walked over to us. My shoes were still off from working the pedals on the piano and that needed to be rectified. Luckily, Mr. Hewitt was standing close to me and without thinking I reached for his arm to steady myself. Contrary to the ass he seemed to be earlier, he was now appearing to be a perfect gentleman. He only moved slightly to hold my arm for support while I slipped on my heels.

"That was absolutely wonderful, Millie," Mrs. Joan complimented me.

"Thank you," I said modestly. It was not in my nature to show off quite like that. It was also not in my nature to bend over and invite a guy to check out my behind. I hope I was not too obvious about that.

The look on Mr. Hewitt's face was as if he might be proud of me while Mrs. Joan paid her compliments. "How long have you been playing?" he asked.

"I began lessons when I was five," and as the words escaped my lips I realized I had not exactly answered the question. "So, fifteen years," I added in an attempt to clarify.

"Millie, you may be the best pianist I have ever heard," Joan went on. "If you can do all of that from memory, I shudder to think what you would be able to do with sheet music in front of you."

"And she wants to be a server. What do you think Joan, should we hire her?" Mr. Hewitt smiled.

Joan laughed and I suppose she was recalling the conversation with the other office ladies. "I think you would be a fool not to hire her."

Mr. Hewitt glanced at his watch as Joan was answering. It was rocking on toward 4:30 p.m. at that time.

Mr. Hewitt started toward the door and ushered me along. Joan followed returning to her desk. "Joan, I am going to walk Amelia out. I will be right back," he said as he held the door for me. Joan looked a little surprised as if this might be unusual or inappropriate for him.

Once safely outside and out of Joan's earshot he touched me on the arm, stopping me to look at him before he asked, "Are you sure you want a job here?" He was very serious and his eyes burned through me. The tension was back and I was hot again, smoking hot like the end of a date, but this was no date. My mind drifted to imagine the end of a date with him. What would it be like? Butterflies flipped in my stomach at the thought of a goodnight kiss from him.

Before answering, I took a moment to study his face. The butterflies flipped fiercely, but I had to remember every detail as I would be expected to recount all of this to Emma and Jay once back at the apartment. As I looked at him and my imagination ran away, I could again feel the hives rising on my chest. He really was something to look at.

I barely thought about the answer to the question. It seemed strange for him to ask at this point. I know I initially tanked the interview, but I really came from behind and aced it, not to mention the earlier lecture about his time being wasted. Where did this question come from?

I quickly decided to analyze it later, but to just answer. I reigned in my imagination and the butterflies and I answered, "Yes. I really want the job."

"Call Joan after 2:00 p.m. tomorrow and she will have an answer for you," he stated. We shook hands and I turned to head to my car. I was half way to the car when he yelled to me, "Hey, Amelia!"

I turned and took a few steps back toward him before yelling back, "If you expect me to answer, call me Millie."

He took steps toward me and we were less than shouting distance when he said with a little force in his voice as he said my name, "Amelia, the recital was great!"

Was he flirting? I am the world's worst at telling if a guy is flirting. The insecurities were creeping in, but I responded in kind, "Thanks, Gabriel!" I really hope Gabe is short for Gabriel or that just failed miserably. I then turned and walked to my car as he watched. I glanced back at him for one more look. Even if I did not get the job, I was certain I would remember the sight of him forever.

Once in the car I made my way back to the guard gate where I stopped and thanked Officer Ed for his assistance earlier. He could not have been nicer and again I promised to take him for a ride in the

Corvette if I got the job. I then proceeded out of the gate and back onto Highway 44 toward Eatonton and back to Milledgeville.

Although it was not original to the car and did not keep with the whole perfectly original theme I had going with the Corvette, I did have a CD changer and was able to listen to music all the way back. I picked upbeat music to keep me pumped from the way the interview ended. I jammed to "Paint it Black" from the Rolling Stones, one of my favorite songs. I know if you listened to the words it really did not fit with keeping up the mood, but the beat sure did. At the other end of the spectrum, I rocked to Montel Jordan's "This is How We Do It" and others. Aside from me singing in full concert, the ride back to Milledgeville was uneventful.

Surely I had the job. I was singing and singing and my mind was wondering and spinning. I hardly noticed the scenery on the way back. I was completely lost in my thoughts and daydreams. What would it be like to work there? What would it be like to run barefoot over the greens? Would it be like tickly, prickly carpet? Was Gabriel going to be my new boss? Was it alright to have called him Gabriel? Did I have a crush on my new boss? Heavens, yes! And, was that inappropriate? Of course! Oh, the anxiety of it all.

***

Back at the apartment, I found my roommates had returned from class. Emma was getting dressed to go to tennis practice and Jay was watching his stories. I let myself in and went straight to my room unnoticed. I changed out of my suit and into some college girl type clothes, tank top and shorts.

Emma left for tennis and Jay continued on with *General Hospital* in his room while I went into the living room and kitchen area of the apartment. I sat down on the couch to read over this week's assignments for Art History class, the Greeks and their pottery. I really couldn't have cared less.

Finally Jay emerged from his room to find me and inquire as to how my interview went. "You know I live for Jax on *General Hospital*," he started. I knew he lived for watching his soaps worse than any little old lady other than his grandmother.

"Have you already made your daily call to Grandma-ma to discuss today's episode?" I asked him. Jay was actually addicted to *General Hospital*, which he taped and watched religiously every day. He was a real "B" the week before last when lightning struck the house during a storm and wiped out the VCR. Luckily his Mother drove down to see her sister at the end of the week and brought him another recorder. Emma and I were afraid that he was about to drop his biology lab so he could stay home to watch.

The reason he was addicted was quite sweet. Jay grew up in the town next to me and we had known each other since we attended kindergarten together. In the summers when he was little and his Father went to work, his Mother, even though she never worked, sent Jay to stay at his Grandparents' house. Jay's favorite place in the world was wherever his Grandparents were. They were each retired so every afternoon the three of them would sit down after lunch and watch *The Young and The Restless* and then *The Bold and The Beautiful*. They would all take a nap during "As the World Turns" and when they got up they would watch *General Hospital*. As soon as *General Hospital* was over Jay's Dad would arrive from work and take him home. Here he was now in college and still nostalgic over the times with his Grandparents. The real hoot was that he did not miss a day calling his Grandmother to discuss the characters as if they were real people.

"Yes, I already made the call and she is just beside herself that Brenda has gone back to Sonny again and left poor Jax broken hearted, but enough about that. How was your day? Did you get the job? Tell me everything!" After getting himself a drink from the refrigerator he flopped down on the couch right up on me with no regard for personal space.

Jay was salivating for details and I gave them all to him with full analytical commentary. "I need to see what you wore to the interview," he demanded. I sprung from the couch and retrieved the suit to show him. "This is the same suit you wore to the funeral?"

"Yes, the very same," I answered as I held it up for him to imagine how it looked on me.

"Very good, Miss Anderson, and I could not have dressed you better, at least not from your closet. Well done." Jay was very complimentary regarding my outfit.

"Now tell me again," he went on, "He addressed you as Amelia each time he spoke to you? The entire time?"

"Yes, the entire time."

"That's a little hot. Don't you think?" Jay fanned himself.

I thought for a moment before I answered. "It made me hot, but I really had not thought about his intentions. I just thought he was being formal. Seriously, what if suddenly someone you really did not know chose to call you Geoffrey?" That was his actual

23

name. His father was named Jeffrey and his mother thought she was being clever, but every good old Southerner called him "JEFF-ree" instead of "Joff-ree", which he hated so in middle school he skirted the whole name issue and thereafter would only answer when called "Jay."

"I see your point, but I still think you are just oblivious," Jay said with exasperation. "You wore a skirt that short to an interview. Plus, just look at you! You can roll out of bed in the morning and stop traffic. You are so pretty and you have no idea."

I could feel myself starting to blush, but he went on. "You rarely brush your hair, yet you walk around looking like a live shampoo commercial. If I looked like you, I would definitely use my powers for evil. Then there's you, who does not even know she has powers let alone how to use them, but the flashing your butt to him as you bent over was a good start. You are still oblivious though!"

Definitely blushing, I professed, "You have no idea what you are talking about!"

"You think so? You told him to fuck off with a piano and then he walked you out and even held the door for you. Then he watched you drive away. You fool, they don't do that unless they are interested. If you don't get the job it's because he wants to get in your pants. You really should look up the word oblivious."

"Why when he walked me out did he ask me, 'Are you sure you really want a job here?' He touched my arm and stopped me and asked. Looked me right in the eye and asked all serious. Yet he had given me the lecture about wasting his time."

"He was warning you. Heck he was warning himself, you know, forbidden fruit and all. Seriously, you should thank God you have me. Would you like for me to explain to you why he called after you to tell you that you rocked the recital?"

I nodded my head yes and Jay said, "He wanted one last look at you so it could inspire him later. You know, aid in revving his own engine."

I got up from the couch and I could not believe all of this. "You are disgusting, Jay!" I said as I took my Art History book and went to my room.

He called after me, "Ask Emma when she gets here! She will tell you the same thing."

I had only just emerged from my room and started dinner when Emma returned from tennis practice. She was a sweaty mess. It was around 7:00 p.m. when she returned. By then Jay had analyzed my day to death. He was such a perv and everything always revolved around who wanted to sleep with whom. He believed it was the sole motivation in individuals over the age of thirteen. Clearly his opinions were the same regarding my job situation.

My mind was nearly spent by the time Emma was done with her shower and I got dinner on the table. Since I was the only one with significant time on my hands I had become the house cook. Emma was always occupied with tennis when she was not in class or at the bars. When Jay was not in class he was at work, watching his soaps or at the bars with Emma until she picked up the flavor of the evening.

This particular night was a rare occasion that we were all three home at once. For dinner I had made what my grandfather always referred to as "white trash chicken pot pie". It consisted of a can of chicken, "real chicken" in a can similar to Chicken of the Sea, but actual chicken, mixed with a can of cream of chicken soup and a can of mixed vegetables. After you stir all of that together in a casserole dish, you place sliced American cheese on the top and bake it until it is hot and the cheese has melted. This meal did not take any skill or effort and that was evident in the taste. It was never horrible, but it was nothing impressive. Regardless of how it tasted or what it was called, Emma and Jay always gobbled up whatever I made and tonight was no different.

Over dinner, Jay proceeded to recount his version of my day to Emma. I corrected him on a few points as he was grossly exaggerating what had gone on. To hear him tell it, Mr. Hewitt, henceforth referred to among us as, not Gabe, but Gabriel, was two heartbeats away from taking me in the parking lot which was so completely far-fetched that it was laughable.

"I don't buy it," Emma said. Emma was always the more level headed of the three of us. She was also the most experienced and successful with boys. Jay thought he was more experienced. Being gay and a boy and all, he thought that put him ahead, but he was sorely mistaken. I had seen Emma in action on a number of occasions and I knew that if she wanted to she could pick up the Pope at mass. She knew it too. If we were models, she would be Victoria's Secret and I would at best be J. Crew or Land's End or if there was a store called Plain Jane, I would have been their ideal model.

In her perfect British accent, Emma burst my bubble. "If he wanted her, he would have called by now," she said to Jay before turning to me. "I don't mean to hurt your feelings, Millie, but that's just how guys are. It is that simple."

Emma went on, "You don't have to work dear, so I don't know why you are worrying with all of this rubbish anyway. What's the big deal if you don't get a job at all? And on top of that, the two of you are stewing over a guy and this is like Jay, but not like you, Millie."

Even while I went to school in North Georgia and commuted last year, they were here, we visited enough that Emma knew me and she was right. I was not this way over guys. How had this turned from being about a job to being about a man? Earlier today it was about a job, but now...

"I like to work," I finally said. "I need something to do and to occupy my time. I can't just sit around here reading art history texts and waiting to prepare y'all's next meal. It just isn't me."

Jay piped up with a typical snap to lighten the mood, "Sounds to me like you don't need something to do; you need someone to do." He let out a little laugh.

"Millie, just hang in there and call tomorrow and then you will know. All of this analyzing is going to drive you crazy. If you get the job, great! If you get the job and the guy, if that is what you want, even better! You know you are in over your head with this one." What did she mean?

"In over my head?" I asked.

Jay interrupted and answered for her, "You said he is thirty and amazing. I am summarizing of course, but the point is; he ain't in the league with the one guy you dated that grew up around the corner from you and now works at the chalk mine."

"Ah," I sighed. "Point taken."

It was Emma who then had the last word on the subject, "Then I could be wrong. You may have met your match. You said he was an ass." Then we all erupted in laughter.

We cleaned up the kitchen together after dinner and then we all sat down and watched "Beverly Hills 90210" at 8:00 p.m. We all agreed that we would not talk about the job or Gabriel again until after I called the next day to find out if I had gotten the job.

Classes started early for me at 8:00 a.m. the following morning, but I was finished with all three by 1:00 p.m. The day seemed to drag on until I made the call at 2:00 p.m. as I had been instructed.

Mrs. Joan promptly answered on the second ring, "Port Honor Golf and Country Club, this is Joan. How may I help you?"

"Hi, Mrs. Joan, this is Millie Anderson. I was there yesterday afternoon for an interview for the server position," I reminded her.

"Right, Millie, lovely to hear from you," said Mrs. Joan.

"I hope I am not bothering you, but Gabr...Mr. Hewitt told me to call today and you would let me know if I had the job," I said sheepishly, bracing myself for the answer.

"Oh bless your heart. I am so sorry," Mrs. Joan started explaining to me. Of course when she apologized I jumped to the conclusion that I had not gotten the job. My heart sank. I thought surely I had turned the interview around yesterday and had the job.

Mrs. Joan continued, "I have not seen Gabe since yesterday and I had no idea that he told you to call. I tell you what, you call back here tomorrow afternoon and I will have an answer for you." What a relief, she was only apologizing because Gabriel had not given her an answer for me.

"Yes, ma'am. Tomorrow," I said before making my goodbyes and hanging up.

Is no news, good news?

Friday classes came and went. I was done by 11:00 am. The day drug on until I made the call.

I dialed and waited the two rings again before the sound of her voice, "Port Honor Golf and Country Club, this is Joan. How may I help you?"

"Hi! It's Millie Anderson from Wednesday calling about..." she cut me off before I could finish and my heart sank again.

"Oh, Millie, right, I was supposed to ask Gabe about the job. He was in and out so fast that it totally slipped my mind. I am so sorry honey. I tell you what; I will call you on Monday."

The weekend came and went and Monday came and went and no call. I nearly stayed home from class to make sure I did not miss her call. I stalked the answering machine all day and threatened anyone who got on the phone for more than a minute while I was home. They knew I was waiting on an important call.

Tuesday arrived and I was nearly over it. I was truly preparing myself to take the hint which is what Emma said I should have done on Friday. I was home for lunch when the phone rang. It was not Mrs. Joan, but it did prompt me to call her one last time.

I dialed the numbers and waited the two rings. Like clockwork she answered.

"Mrs. Joan, it's Millie. Millie Anderson." I could sense the desperation in my own voice. I sounded kind of pitiful. "I'm calling to find out about the job."

"Right, Millie. Sorry about yesterday. I had totally forgotten that we are closed on Mondays. I did talk to Gabe and he still has not made up his mind."

"REALLY?!" I exclaimed before I even knew the words were out of my mouth and the attitude displayed with them.

"Millie, did you know my husband is the General Manager of Port Honor?"

"No, ma'am."

"He is and do you know what that means?"

"No, ma'am."

"Millie, it means that he is Gabe's boss and if you want the job, I will get it for you, BUT, you will have to agree to do something for me in return."

"Anything!!!" I exclaimed without knowing what I would have to do. I am sure Mrs. Joan was not the devil so my soul was likely safe.

"I will give you more details later, but here is the gest: One of my sons is getting married next April and I want you to play the piano at the wedding. It is that simple. Still want the job?" she

28

asked. She paused for a moment before clarifying her question, "Both jobs?"

"Yes, ma'am, of course. Thank you so much!" I responded with glee in my voice. I just could not believe it.

"Alright, be here at the club on Wednesday at 4:00 p.m. That's tomorrow at 4:00. Wear a khaki skirt, white button down collared shirt and a tie. I will take care of the rest. Don't be late and remember the cows cross around 2:00 p.m." She was by far the sweetest lady in the world and she really did sound like one of the church ladies from back home.

"Thank you so much! Thank you! Thank you!" I professed before getting off of the phone.

When I hung up the phone, I squealed with such excitement that I scared Jay and he came running to see what was wrong with me. Jay and I danced and jumped around the room until the crazy cat lady in the apartment below started banging her ceiling with the broom and screaming for us to stop or she was calling the landlord. We did not care. We just kept jumping and dancing and laughing.

CHAPTER 2

"Millie, you are so cute that if my son was not already getting married, I would introduce the two of you," Mrs. Joan said as I entered the doors of Port Honor fifteen minutes prior to 4:00 p.m. "How was your drive out here today?"

"It was fine. No cattle crossing," I responded. I was actually early and since there had not been a cow crossing my hair and make-up had survived the trip.

Again I had hot rolled my hair and despite its length, which needed to be trimmed, it held the curl. It was fluffy and still hung in spirals and ringlet curls to about the middle of my back just below my bra clasp. I had pulled it from my face and pinned it back loosely at the top of my head in the back with a barrette. In the sunlight it sparkled with streaks of gold. I was one of the few girls my age that I knew who had never colored or permed their hair. Everything was natural except the curls which I had achieved with two sets of hot rollers. I had so much hair that it took the small rollers from two sets to get the look I had achieved.

My make-up was understated; again, less is more. I despised eyeliner, especially colored eyeliner, and even more so, colored mascara and matching eyeliner. I might have loved Cyndi Lauper's music, but that did not mean I wanted to look like her.

"Mrs. Joan, are you sure about this?"

"About what, dear? And call me Joan."

"Are you sure about hiring me? Are you sure Gab...Mr. Hewitt did not hire someone else?" I am sure I came off totally insecure, not at all like the girl that left there last Wednesday.

"Millie, leave Gabe to me," she said.

"I love your tie!" Mrs. Joan said as she got up from her desk and took a closer look at it. I still had not tied it and it just hung around my shoulders with my top two buttons open.

The night before Jay and I had ventured over to the mall in Macon and spent a small fortune at Macy's buying me what would be my uniform. I picked up several ties. This one was lavender with tiny white and yellow daisies. It reminded me of the floral

30

arrangement that had been on the piano the last time I was at Port Honor. Jay hated the tie and said there was a reason why it was on the clearance rack. According to him, no self-respecting gay or straight man would be caught wearing it. I suppose it was a good thing I was neither.

When we were quite done swooning over one another, Mrs. Joan led me downstairs to the bar where we found Gabriel behind the bar chatting with two older gentlemen seated at the end of the bar nearest to the door. Gabriel was quite befuddled to see me. It was written all over his face that he had no idea that Joan had gone over his head and hired me. He did not appear pleased, but he did appear every bit as pleasing on the eyes as I had remembered him.

"Would you excuse us for a moment, Amelia?" Eek, he said my full name again!

Mrs. Joan turned to me and instructed that I wait there as they went through the door at the end of the liquor cabinet. Again the door nearly swung off of its hinges until Gabriel reached back and stopped it.

As they walked away, I could not refrain from getting a good look at Gabriel from behind. This particular day he was wearing dark khaki pants that hung just off of his hips and fit his behind snug enough to reveal the fact that he had a great ass. He had coordinated the khakis with a white button down shirt with the sleeves rolled up to three-quarter length. There was nothing particularly spectacular about the outfit beyond what it was concealing. Some of my college girlfriends, who had more experience than I did, had the opinion that the male form was never a work of beauty like that of the female. I was in complete disagreement as I knew they had not seen the right one. I did not just suspect; I knew that if I ever completely saw him, I would know I was right. I was certain he was beautiful and the thought made me tingle from stem to stern.

I could hear them bicker behind the door. Gabriel started to give it to her good about interfering with his responsibilities, but Mrs. Joan gave as good as she got.

Mrs. Joan really got on to him, "Your responsibilities? You told her to call me at a certain time on a certain day for an answer and yet you left no answer. She called three days in a row to find out your answer and at no point did you mention her to me at all. I even called and left messages for you to let me know what to tell her. Is this how you handle your responsibilities by stringing folks along?"

"Joan, you don't know what you are doing!" he insisted.

"Really, Gabe, I don't know what I am doing? She is the pick of the litter of all of the ones you had troll through here over the last two weeks. She is smart, talented, determined and well just look at her. If she isn't eye candy for this place, I don't know what is."

She called me eye candy! Who knew?

"Joan, I do not dispute any of those things, but I am just not sure she is right for Port Honor," he argued. He thinks I am eye candy, too. Wow, the room was suddenly hot.

Joan shut him down, "Gabe, you need to trust me on this. She is going to be a breath of fresh air around here..."

At that moment one of what would be my co-workers entered the bar area from the dining room. He was reporting to work for the afternoon as well. With the noise from his entrance I could no longer hear Joan and Gabriel. I was horribly disappointed that the kibosh was put on my eavesdropping.

He was a sandy blonde-haired guy who was not as young as I am, but was not as old as Gabriel. Clearly, he was the bartender for the night. White shirt, khaki pants, apron and tie plus the fact that he so casually moved around behind the bar and started to make a drink. That's what gave it away.

I just stood there waiting and trying to hear Joan and Gabriel by the end of the bar opposite from the gentlemen and nearest to the swinging door. As I stood there, waiting, he spoke to me, "Hey, you must be the FNG."

It was in his voice that he had the epitome of cocky attitudes. I may have pretended to be cocky at my interview with my "I'm where it's at!" after my exhibition on the piano, but that was just an act. This guy was the real deal.

"FNG?" I asked.

The two older men at the other end of the bar snickered a little. Apparently I was the only one who did not know what that meant. The bartender laughed with them and rolled his eyes and shook his head at me.

Still not knowing what that meant, but guessing it was not something flattering, I decided to join in the fun. The older gentlemen were still looking on when I added to my initial response, "Since you seem to know I am the FNG, does that mean you are the PAB?"

A confused look came across his face especially when one of the gentlemen said, "Andy, I think you may have met your match in this one."

"PAB" was a term that the guys on the soccer team at my former college had made up to taunt one another. It stood for Punk-Ass-Bitch and I was fully prepared to explain myself, discretely, had anyone asked. Oh, what a first impression I would have made calling him that in front of guests. Thank goodness no one asked.

He had a name and it was Andy and Andy was clearly not one to be outdone. He had already taken down another one of the liquor bottles from the cabinet behind the bar and was steadily making a Dewar's and water for the gentleman sitting nearest to me. Andy had finished topping off the drink with water from the beverage gun when the comment about meeting his match was made. He placed the full rocks sized glass on the counter down near where I was standing and with one swift move he slid it down the bar. It stopped precisely right in front of the man who made the crack. Had I tried such a move, it would have surely tipped over or at worst slung all over the man, but not Andy. That was remarkably smooth and the fact that he knew it was reflected in him looking dead at me as he let go of the glass, not even paying attention to where the glass wound up, but instead staring me down and saying, "Watch out FNG, don't mess with the master."

Andy was about six foot three and broad shouldered. He had hazel eyes. His top lip was thin and his bottom lip full, but the most noticeable thing about his mouth was his teeth. He had pretty, white, straight teeth. He had likely spent a great deal of his teen years in braces and his parents likely spent an equally proportionate fortune on orthodontist bills. He was very good looking. He probably knew that too, which was always a turn-off to me. Although not enamored by his looks as I was by Gabriel's, I was definitely intimidated, but I would do my best to never let him know that.

About the time Andy finished with his mess with the master remark, Gabriel and Joan returned from behind the swinging door. Gabriel still looked a little irritated, but Joan flashed a smile and winked at me and told me, "Have fun and don't let me down." She gave me a pat of encouragement on the shoulder as she passed by me and proceeded to speak to the two gentlemen at the other end of the bar. She spoke to them for just a moment before taking her leave and returning upstairs.

Gabriel also moved from around the bar and again spoke to the gentlemen at the end of the bar. Everyone seemed to know everyone else. This was also evidenced by the fact that Andy had not asked the men what they wanted to drink, he just made the drinks and gave them to them. Gabriel called the men by name, "Mr. Baker, Mr. Lockerby, have you all met our..."

Andy cut him off, "met our FNG?" Gabriel cut his eyes at Andy with a speaking look of disapproval. I was right, FNG was not good.

Mr. Baker was the recipient of the drink that slid down the bar just before Gabriel had returned.

Mr. Lockerby had not spoken until that moment, "We have not been officially introduced," he said.

Gabriel responded as I continued to stand there, "This is our new girl, Amelia Anderson."

"Ah, the one that plays the piano?" asked Mr. Lockerby.

"One and the same," Gabriel responded and the proud look seemed to be creeping back across his face.

Mr. Lockerby continued, "Seems you are already famous among the ladies around here. My wife's friends with Joan."

Mr. Baker then chimed in, "My wife was changing in the ladies' locker room during your performance. She missed seeing you and had to get the scoop from Gabe after you left. She was so disappointed." He turned and looked at Mr. Lockerby, "You know how Rhonda likes to be in the know." While he was talking, he got up and strolled to the end of the bar to retrieve the bowl of pretzels which were near where I was standing.

"Looks like she was spot on with her description," Mr. Baker said to me as he crossed into my personal space. That was a little uncomfortable especially since had I been asked I would have kindly passed the pretzels and he smelled as if that was his fifth or sixth Dewar's. Mr. Baker appeared to be old enough to be my father and he also looked like he took his golfing fashion tips from Payne Stewart, nickers with high socks.

I was a bit uncomfortable with his proximity to me so I stepped back and closer to Gabriel. Gabriel took notice. Perhaps Mr. Baker noticed as well leading him to return to his seat at the far end of the bar with the pretzels.

"Andy, have you seen Praise this afternoon?" asked Gabriel.

"Nope, but she is probably in the laundry room," Andy answered as he polished glasses behind the bar.

"Alright, I will look for her there, but if you see her, send her down," he said before turning to me. "Come with me, Amelia, and we will get started."

I followed Gabriel as he led me behind the swinging door and through the enormous commercial kitchen where a couple of young men were already preparing for the evening. One of the guys was behind the prep line and the other was in the dish pit. The one on the dishes was younger and had more of a dark chocolate complexion. The other was taller and older by a few years. I found it a little rude that we passed by them without Gabriel introducing me.

"We are going to go out of the back door and down toward the cart barn to the laundry room. We need to do something about your uniform."

"Really? I bought exactly what Joan told me to," I said in defense of my attire.

"I'm sure you did, but this is not what I would have told you to buy so we will have to do what we can with what you have. Trust me on this and I will help you make a little more money," he said as he continued to lead me.

Out of the back door and down the long stretch of the loading dock I followed Gabriel. Mixed with the feeling of how I might follow him anywhere were doubtful feelings that I might be the lamb being led to slaughter. At the end of the loading dock we went down about five steps to where I could see the lower parking lot where the men were still zipping by from the course to their cars. This area adjoined the parking lot which also yielded access to the cart barn below the clubhouse.

Gabriel noticed me taking everything in as we headed down the steps. "That's the tee box for the first hole over there," he said as he pointed over to the left and past the clubhouse. From where we were standing, I could see the pads of shorter cut grass, some with gold tees, some with red and some with blue. Beyond them was a fairway that rolled gently uphill. It was lined with trees; pines, cypress, oaks, all of which appeared to be natural, but deliberately placed at the same time. Again, the grass beckoned for my bare feet. I am sure I looked wide-eyed over all of my surroundings and I was sure this facial expression might be permanent.

Gabriel continued to lead, making a turn at the bottom of the loading dock steps and heading down a steep concrete staircase into what appeared to be the bowels of the clubhouse. The farther we went down, the darker it became until we were deposited into the cart barn at the base of the stairs. It was dimly lit and consisted of aisle after aisle of dark green golf carts with the words "Port Honor" written in white with the logo underneath. Immediately to the right of the door we entered the cart barn was a small room brightly lit with florescent tube bulbs in the ceiling. That room turned out to be the laundry room.

Folding towels at one of the two washer/dryer sets was a scruffy country woman of not quite five feet tall. Compared to her, I was quite tall at 5'5". She had fried, bleached and teased blond hair and if the style for which she was trying was that of freshly electrocuted, she had succeeded admirably. She was wearing a hot pink Port Honor logo shirt, white shorts and sneakers in addition to ear phones from which Def Leopard blared. She was jamming hard and the music could be heard well beyond the distance that earphones should project.

Assuming this woman was actually named Praise, Gabriel called her and tried to get her attention four times with no effect. She heard nothing beyond the blaring of "Pour Some Sugar on Me" and the hum of the dryer. That all changed when Gabriel touched her shoulder. The poor woman had no idea anyone was down there. She jumped clear on top of the dryer and screamed bloody murder.

Once she got a hold of herself, she promptly chastised Gabriel, "Gabe, don't you ever sneak up on me like that again. You just took ten years off of my life!" Praise was definitely a hard living looking woman probably aged beyond her years, but even so, if ten years were literally off of her life, she might not be with us much longer.

Gabriel and I initially laughed, but ultimately he apologized to her and promised to refrain from sneaking up. When her nerves were calm enough to hear him, Gabriel introduced us, "Praise, this is Amelia. She is our new server and I need a little help with her uniform."

"Sure, Gabe. What do you have in mind?" she asked. Praise wore glasses and perhaps that was why she squinted at him. Perhaps it was her eyesight or perhaps they had worked together long enough that she did not pant over his looks as I did. Perhaps this draw to him would wear off for me as time progressed.

"Do you have a sewing kit down here somewhere?" Gabriel looked around to see if he could help spot one as she started to look around as well.

Suddenly, as if a light came on in her head, she scurried over to a tote filled with cleaning products sitting on the floor across the room. She bent over and came up squinting and adjusting her glasses to make sure of what she had in a little pouch. In the pouch was a needle, thread and the saddest little pair of scissors imaginable.

"That will do," said Gabriel as he dropped down on one knee before me and Praise returned to his side. As he knelt on the floor, I took a guarded step back. He placed one hand on my bare knee to steady himself and stop me from moving. I stopped and stood still as the hand on my knee had instructed. He then lifted the hem of the front of my skirt and flipped it under reducing the length by about four inches.

"Praise, can you hem the skirt up to about here?" as he leaned back for her to see. Then, he looked back at me and continued, "The higher the skirt, the higher the tips." He smiled and winked at me.

I stood there almost frozen, shocked that neither of them thought this was inappropriate. My new boss, on his knees in front of me lifting my skirt and instructing a woman I only just met to hem my skirt to a length that should I bend over my arse would surely shine someone. Regardless of the propriety of the situation, they carried on as if I was not there at all, but I was so there.

This was the most erotic thing I had ever experienced. Everything about me was standing on end. The hives were flamed across my chest and headed up my neck. As he held the hem of my skirt up so high, I could feel his hand brush up against my right inner thigh ever so slightly.

Praise answered, "Sure. It will only take me about fifteen minutes, but I can do it faster if she ain't wearing it while I do it."

"Alright, Amelia, lose the skirt," Gabriel said as he released the hem and got up off of his knee.

Thank heavens he moved and I was free of his touch, but "Lose my skirt?" I kind of gasped.

"Are you not wearing underwear?" My face went fire engine red over his question and the audacity he had in all of this. His face was stone cold serious.

"None of your business!" I responded as Praise adjusted her glasses while laughing at us.

"I'm just messing with you, Amelia. I am going to leave you two ladies, but when you are done, come on back up and find me." He then left the room at which time I did shimmy out of my skirt and handed it over for Praise to hem.

"Ms. Praise, you can call me Millie. Do you think it is necessary to hem the skirt that high? I know what he said about the higher the skirt, the higher the tips, but I am just not sure I need to make quite this much money." I questioned as I tugged at my button down shirt to hide my black lace underwear.

"Honey, I may have been born at night, but it wasn't last night. It's not like you and I both don't know you are dying to show him your cracker-jack. If I were you, I would have hemmed it at least that high before I left home in it." Although Praise was straightforward in her speech, she did not seem mean spirited toward me.

"I don't know what is going on with me. I cannot seem to help myself around him." That just sort of came out. "Did I say that out loud?"

"Don't worry about it. The same thing is going on with you that goes on with every woman who meets him. Not to worry. He never notices."

Before I knew it she was finished with my skirt and had tossed it back to me. "Ms. Praise, I appreciate you doing this for me and would also appreciate you keeping my crush between us."

"Millie, call me Praise. I can tell you are a sweet girl and you better believe I will keep this under my hat. I would not dare have his girlfriend find out about you."

"Girlfriend?" I shrieked. He has a girlfriend, of course he does.

"She's a real piece of work and you'd do best to steer clear of her." Praise was full of warning. "Anyway, you better get back upstairs before he comes looking for you. Not to get your hopes up, but he would come looking for you. He's never had me hem anyone else's skirt. Just keep in mind: rich bitch girlfriend and steer clear!"

"What about him? Is he nice? What's the deal?" I asked her as I slipped my skirt on and tucked my shirt.

"He's the sweetest, kindest boss I have ever had. He's so generous and super smart. The funny thing about him is he seems to have no idea just how good looking he is and what effect he has on women. Have you met Andy yet? He is the opposite of Andy."

"Yeah, I met Andy. You are so right about him." I paused for a moment, "Praise, I am so glad I met you today."

"Thanks," she said as she adjusted her glasses once more and looked away as if embarrassed. "I'm glad they finally hired another woman and I'm glad it was you. You be careful with those boys."

"Thanks! I will and I'll see you around." I told her and I ran back up the stairs to the kitchen.

I found Gabriel in his office on the phone. He noticed my return and gave me the hold- on a minute one finger wave. As I waited for him, Andy came back and commented on my skirt. "Nice," he said as he looked me up and down so blatantly checking out my legs while passing to the dry storage area next to Gabriel's office. Andy passed back by me after retrieving a jar of olives and cocktail onions and headed back to the bar. He looked at me up and down as he passed by again and nodded with approval.

Across from me in the stove and prep line area of the kitchen, one of the two guys busied himself by preparing a pork loin stuffed with apples and crusted with pecans. He was tall and very handsome, lighter skin than the guy in the dish pit. He whistled as he worked and seemed to really enjoy what he was doing. He did not notice me watching at all or if he did, he did not let on. He was completely engrossed in what he was doing.

When Gabriel got off of the phone and emerged from his office, he noticed that I was watching the man on the prep line. "Come on," he said as he passed by and led me over to introduce me. "Alvin, this is Amelia. She's the new server. Amelia, this is Alvin. Alvin is the best sue-chef on Lake Oconee."

"Please call me Millie," I insisted. "That looks like it is going to be wonderful! When you are ready for the quality control check, you just yell."

"Thanks! I will," he responded as he smiled a smile of wattage that could light the entire room.

Next we went around to the dishwashing area where we interrupted the teenager that was singing and dancing and loading the industrial-sized dishwasher with the rhythm of his giant boom box. "Hey...Hey, Rudy!" Gabriel yelled over the boom box. "This is Amelia!"

Rudy, the dishwasher, looked over at me and nodded his head in acknowledgement before going back to loading the dishes.

Gabriel turned back to me and we started to walk again while he spoke, "He's a good kid. If you need anything, you just ask him and he will do anything, just be prepared to help him out occasionally too." Gabriel rubbed his first two fingers with his thumb signaling money. "He likes money as much as the next person and he is saving for college so he needs all the help he can get."

There were two doors that led between the kitchen and the dining room. As we passed by the first one, Gabriel said, "This one you enter the kitchen by. They swing and you would be served well to always swing this one in. If it swings the other way you or someone else gets hurt. Capishe?"

We continued on around a wall that divided the first door from the second. Gabriel led out of the second door into the dining room. There was an air vent in the ceiling before the door and as Gabriel went through it, it swung back before I could go through. When the door swung back the wind from it blew past the air vent as I was standing under it. The wind dislodged about fifty roaches of varying sizes which all dropped down on my head!

"OH HOLY FUCK!!!!" I screamed and jumped around as the roaches went all over me. My tie was still undone and hanging around my neck and the top two buttons of my shirt were undone. It seemed like ten of the roaches were in my shirt, twenty on my head and in my hair. They were running up and down my legs and arms. I flailed and jumped and screamed and did it all again.

Gabriel came running. Alvin came running and the kid from the dishwasher came running. Andy from the bar was the only one that did not show up for the spectacle.

"GET THIS SHIT OFF OF ME!!!" I screamed as I started to strip out of my shirt and knocking them out of my hair at the same time, all the while forgetting I was wearing a freakishly short skirt. This was absolutely the most disgusting thing I had ever experienced, but it all happened so fast.

Initially the guys were a little shocked and they did their best to hold off laughing until it was all over. Gabriel stepped forward and grabbed my hands. He looked me in the eyes as he stilled my hands and with the calmest voice he said, "Just be still. It is going to be okay. Trust me. It is going to be okay."

I could feel tears start to swell in my eyes a little. As Alvin and Rudy brushed every last cockroach off of me, Gabriel was still holding my hands and continued to look me in the eye. The tears faded before they fell and everything went calm as I just stood there looking back at him. I could hardly feel Alvin and Rudy brushing the roaches off of me. All shame was also gone since I did not notice my shirt was half open and my bra and cleavage were out for anyone to see that dared.

"I think we got all of them," Alvin assured me.

"Yes, ma'am. I think that's the last of them." Rudy said as he stomped some of them as they scurried across the floor.

I would not have heard them had Gabriel not broke our eye contact and released my hands. I still stood there a bit shocked before a shiver of disgust ran over me.

"Thanks, fellas. I think we've got it from here." Gabriel waved the guys off and turned me away from them as I realized my shirt was still open.

I started buttoning my shirt back and I suppose had they not come to help me I would have taken the thing completely off. I was still buttoning when Gabriel leaned over to me and gently asked, "Are you okay?"

"I think I just lost all dignity, not to mention I just flashed my new boss and co-workers, but, other than that, I am stellar." I shook my head in embarrassment.

"And to think you would not lose your skirt for me earlier, but you couldn't get your shirt off fast enough," Gabriel joked.

"Oh, ha ha! Mr. Hewitt."

"Seriously, I will call the exterminator and get him out here tomorrow and I almost forgot, call me Gabe." Gabriel went on to explain that the club had just been purchased out of bankruptcy and while in bankruptcy the owners had let the exterminator go. Things were getting better and the new owners were making improvements in preparation for the '96 Olympics.

"As long as you call me Amelia, I will agree to call you either Mr. Hewitt or Gabriel," I responded.

Once my shirt was fully buttoned, I pulled my tie from around my neck and I leaned over and flipped my hair upside down in an attempt to make sure all of the roaches were definitely out of it. When I straightened back up, my hair was full and bouncy again and Gabriel just stood there looking at me. He shook his head as if trying to shake a thought out before turning and again going out of the swinging door into the dining room. That time I ran right behind him so that when the wind hit that air vent I was not under it.

I followed Gabriel and the tour continued out in the dining room. I had not taken very much notice of the dining room beyond passing through it on my way to the bar each time. I had noticed the wall of windows, but at this time of day, the approaching dusk beyond them was quite remarkable.

The view consisted of a downhill roll of the land from the clubhouse, down to the putting green and bunkers of the eighteenth hole, down more to a dock at the head of the cove and out through the cove into the open water of the main thoroughfare of the lake. What appeared to be either a new or a freshly stained seawall separated the water of the cove and land that butted up against it. As the cove opened up to the open water, on the left was the fairway of the eighteenth green and villas that overlooked it. On the right, were magnificent yards and mostly large, but modest homes, with one or two that were a tad over the top. The yards of the homes more so than the fairway were clustered with mature trees that were just beginning to hint at Fall's arrival. The slight yellows and oranges were beaming in the setting sun.

The carpet in the dining room was the same as that in the loft and the bar, but was showing more wear and tear than the other areas. There were three large round tables with seating for six. Two were placed at far corners of the room and the third was just to the right of the exit door from the kitchen and along the wall of the staircase. There were twelve other square tables scattered through the room, each of which would seat four individuals.

The most commanding presence in the room beside the wall of windows was the stacked stone fireplace in the middle of the room on the opposite side of the windows. This fireplace backed up to the fireplace in the loft area. It had a large hearth of stacked stone and a massive mantle made of a sleek hand carved beam of wood about the size of a railroad tie. Propped against the mantle was a painting of a fairway and pin at a hole in the distance. The painting itself was great; very abstract with its textured globs of paint giving the illusion of the image with color and light. It was not just a copy of a photograph reproduced with paint. The size of the painting and the frame were proportionate with the mantle of the fireplace. Although

42

the subject of the painting suited the clubhouse, the frame did not suit the painting and was out of place for the entire room. It appeared to have come from a yard sale at the chateau of Louis the XVI. It was thick and ornate and gaudy gold. The best that could be said about the frame is that it matched the color of the rope design in the carpet.

Across the room from the staircase was what my grandmother would have called a "Florida room". The Florida room overlooked a nice size pool. I wondered if I would be allowed to use the pool some in the summer. Access to the pool would be a nice perk, since I had not had access to a pool since leaving my apartment at Young Harris.

Along the same wall as the fireplace, closer to the kitchen door from which we had entered the dining room were two separate doorways. The doorways led to a hallway that led from the entrance door to the kitchen, past a storage closet, the bathrooms, and to an exit door at the far end of the building. Gabriel stepped from where we were in the dining room through one of the doors and pulled out a cart with everything needed for setting the tables for dinner; charges, dinner plates, salad places, bread plates, glasses, silverware and napkins.

"Do you know how to set a table for fine dining?" he asked as he approached one of the tables and I followed.

"No, I don't think so," I replied.

He turned and looked at me while taking one of the chargers from the cart. "Your mother did not bring out the fine china for Christmas dinner or anything and you never helped set the table?"

"I was lucky if Mother made it to Christmas and dinner amounted to a covered dish pot-luck at Aunt Dot's house," I explained.

He looked confused, but proceeded to demonstrate the proper way to set a table; placement of the dinner fork versus the salad fork and dessert fork. He explained why the knife faced blade in and showed me the proper way to place plates in front of guests and how he wanted me to ask, without interrupting with the use of words, if I may remove their plates. Gabriel explained that the signal for someone being finished with their meal was for them to cross their silverware on top of their plates.

Together we set all the tables in the room and learning from him was fun. The way he moved was, well, something I tried to watch without getting caught. I believe I succeeded in not letting

43

him know I was watching him as much as I was watching what he was doing. I would have set a thousand tables with him.

Just when I thought we were done and headed back into the kitchen, he stopped in the corridor right before the kitchen door and turned back to me, "Amelia, what did you mean 'I was lucky if Mother made it to Christmas?'"

"Long story," I said as I hung my head a little. This was not something I especially wanted to get into with my new boss or my heart's desire.

"Wednesday nights are usually slow, so we have time." It was a tight place there in the hall near the door and we were all alone. He seemed genuinely interested and I could feel the hives waiting to spring up on my chest. I could smell his cologne. It was an assortment of subtle hints, but cedar was the dominate smell. It reminded me of how Granddaddy smelled on the mornings that he returned from the woods with the Christmas tree that he found and chopped down. My knees were weak and I did not want to talk about my mother or my screwy upbringing with him and I did not particularly want to think about my grandfather either.

"She didn't always come to Christmas," I responded as I tried to go around him into the kitchen, but he moved to block me.

"You mean you weren't with her?"

"No." He had put up an arm to block me there in the hallway so I ducked and went under and through the kitchen door.

He was not giving up and he followed me into the kitchen. "Why not?" he asked.

Alvin was still prepping the dinner specials in the kitchen and I really did not want to have a discussion about my mother in front of strangers. I then turned and headed back out of the door leading into the dining room.

"Seriously, Amelia, what's the big deal?"

"The short answer is because my Mom remarried an asshole who tried to put his hands on me," I tried to just spit it out with the least amount of embarrassment as possible. I did my best to rip the Band-Aid off.

Gabriel had put his hand to his mouth as if he were in shock. "How old were you?" he asked while still covering his mouth.

"I was eight. Do we really have to talk about this?" I did not walk away, but stood there and faced him.

"Did he...?"

"God, no!" I exclaimed. "He tried and I ran and hid from him. As he searched the house for me, he screamed and screamed that if I told my mother she would not believe me. She came home before he found me and he was probably right about her not believing me, so I told my grandfather. He did believe me, and took me away from them. She did not come around much after that."

"She didn't leave him?" Gabriel asked.

"No. Her sole ambition in life was to be married to a doctor. It's why she went to nursing school, to get a job where doctors were. She snagged my dad and then when he got killed, she found a replacement." I paused for a moment as I noticed that he looked distant like he was not with me anymore, but thinking about something else.

"Look," I continued, "This is something that I have only ever told two people in my life. It is not something I talk about, ever. So, please," I said as I reached and took his hands and the current ran through me from his touch, "Please, do not tell anyone about this and do not mention it to me again."

"If that's how you want it to be, then it is our secret."

Just as Gabriel finished his assurances, Andy walked through into the dining room, "Gabe, there's someone in the bar to see you."

"Amelia, go into the kitchen and have Alvin explain the menu to you and tonight's specials," Gabriel told me before heading up front to the bar with Andy. I did as I was asked and went to find Alvin.

Back in the kitchen I found Alvin taking the pork tenderloin out of the oven. It smelled divine. The aroma of the meat and apples combined was just mouthwatering.

"Hi!" I said as I approached Alvin. "Gabriel asked me to have you go over the menu and specials for the evening with me. Do you mind?"

"Not at all," he responded graciously.

On the prep line, Alvin placed three of the china dinner plates. On one plate chicken marsala was served over pasta with a side of asparagus. The second plate had four beef tenderloin medallions topped with gorgonzola cheese sauce with sides of rosemary roasted new potatoes and asparagus again. On the third plate, Alvin placed two thick slices of the pork. The meat spiraled with the apples in the middle and the pecans crusted across the top, then he drizzled just a touch of a brown sugar glaze across it and added a helping of the rosemary roasted new potatoes and steamed green beans. He explained each dish as he went including all of their ingredients and how they were prepared. When he was finished he took a white towel and carefully wiped the rim of each plate. By the time he was done, each plate looked a lot like a still life one might be expected to draw in art class.

"Millie, run up front and get Gabe and Andy and tell them dinner is served. Get yourself something to drink while you are up there," Alvin instructed.

When I returned with Gabriel and Andy the three plates were on the side of the prep line where I had been standing. Alvin had put out silverware for all of us by the plates.

As he turned the corner and saw the food, Andy let out a statement of glee, "Awesome; my favorite time of day, dinner time!"

"Amelia, what do you think? Looks good?" Gabriel asked me as he picked up a set of the silverware and handed them to me. "We usually share these so we can all know what everything tastes like and how to sell it to the guests. Which would you like to try first?"

"I have been dying to try the pork tenderloin since I first saw Alvin with it this afternoon," I answered and Gabriel obliged by passing the plate.

The beef tenderloin was sitting on the line in front of Gabriel, but only until Andy reached over and switched it with the chicken marsala that had been in front of him. Gabriel paid little attention as he waited for me to cut and take the first bite before leaning over in my space and cutting and taking the second bite. I know we were supposed to share, but I suppose I assumed I would have been able to pass the plate back to him. Instead, there was that familiarity boundary that he broke again. Two can play, so I leaned across him and cut a piece of the chicken.

"Millie, have you ever had beef tenderloin before?" Andy asked while he chewed.

"Yes..."

"Good, then you know what this tastes like and won't mind if I kill it." And with those words from Andy, Gabriel snatched the plate from in front of him and gave him the chicken marsala back. Andy rolled his eyes at me as Gabriel gave me the plate with the steak.

I took a bite. "Wow! This is good! Alvin, do you cook like this every night? If so, I am going to love working here!"

Alvin chimed in, "Actually, Gabriel usually cooks, but Wednesday nights are all mine."

"To Wednesday nights then!" I grabbed my styrofoam cup of Coke and held it up to toast him. Alvin reached between the stainless steel shelves that separated my side of the line from his and clinked his bottled water to my cup.

***

The rest of the night went relatively quickly. There were ten couples that came in and I waited on eight sets of them. Andy helped out with the other two. Gabriel said this was the busiest they have been on a Wednesday night in he did not know when.

I was quite proud of myself. I made seventy-five dollars in tips. That's more than I had made at any of the other restaurants I worked at during the week. As it turns out, the members are obligated to spend a certain amount in the clubhouse per month and an automatic fifteen percent was added to their bill for gratuity. The majority of them never paid any attention to the automatic charge so they left an additional fifteen to twenty percent.

The night had wound down and I had completed the side work I had been assigned. I was milling around in the kitchen getting ready to head out for the night when Gabriel emerged from his office again, "Amelia, didn't you park in the top parking lot?"

"Yes," I answered as I loosened my tie and unbuttoned my top two buttons.

Gabriel's face suddenly went a little red and he looked away.

"What?" I asked shyly remembering that he had seen me unbutton my shirt earlier and nearly come completely out of it during the roach attack.

"Nothing. Come on, I will walk you out so I can lock the door up there."

Alvin heard as he wiped up the stove and prep area. I saw him cut his eyes at me as I grabbed my keys and headed into the dining room with Gabriel.

As we moved through the dining room, a thought crossed my mind. Andy was gone for the night and all of the guests were gone. We were in the dining room alone and I could see the landscape lights outside providing just enough light to be able to see the green of the eighteenth hole and the moonlight provided the rest with its reflection across the water. Directly across from the base of the staircase were glass double doors leading onto the deck and then out to the green.

"Do you have any place to be?" I asked Gabriel as I headed toward the double doors instead of the stairs.

"What are you doing?" he questioned as he stopped behind me.

I turned back and grabbed his hand and pulled him with me. It was me that crossed the familiarity barrier that time with the hand holding. I opened the door and continued out. "Come with me. I have to do this."

"Do what?"

"You will see, just trust me and come on." I did not let go of his hand until we were just about to the green. I only released it to bend down and untie my shoes with one hand and guard my skirt over my behind with the other. "I promised myself that if I got the job, I would run barefoot over the green. I have been dying to know what it would feel like," I explained as I slipped off my shoes and proceeded to step on to the grass of the green with my bare feet. "Gabriel, take your shoes off and come on!"

Gabriel shook his head at me signaling "no" as he stood there and waited. "I'm not coming back until you join me!" I yelled back followed by, "Seriously, you have seen me nearly come out of my clothes tonight with the roach incident. You can't come out of your shoes and join me?"

"Fair point, Miss Anderson." He kind of laughed as he squatted and removed his shoes and rolled up his pants just to his ankles. "You know we could be in real trouble if we get caught out here," he said as he took a few steps onto the green. There was a hint of glee that shined in his eyes as he took step after step feeling the

48

tickly blades of grass beneath his feet. He smiled at me and he was the stuff sweet dreams were made of, just a sexy delight to gaze upon in the moonlight.

"Well, I won't tell my new boss if you won't." I giggled and I wiggled my toes in the grass feeling the coolness of the dew that was already beginning to fall.

"Amelia, how old are you?" Gabriel asked as he took a few steps toward me. The mood seemed to be taking a bit of a serious turn. My heart raced a little at the question.

I had stopped and was staring out at the cove with my back to him. I could feel my face getting hotter as I thought about my answer. I looked back over my shoulder toward him and answered, "My date of birth was on my application, but why do you ask?" I turned back toward the cove.

Gabriel moved in closer and I remained still, just watching the moonlight on the water. I was not sure what was about to happen, but I waited and I could feel him standing behind me. He was taller than me by a fair amount and I could feel his breath behind me in the cool night air. His face brushed through the top of my hair and I could feel it when he took in a deep breath.

"You smell like strawberries," he whispered as he barely touched my hair to move it from my neck. Butterflies flipped in my stomach like acrobats and I wished he were mine. If he had turned me around and kissed me, that would have been the highlight of my year.

I leaned back into him and I could smell him, the cologne of lavender, jasmine and cedar. The hint of dew in cool night air along with his cologne was surely the smell of heaven. Little had changed in the scenery, but an outdoor light flickered on and off at a house on the right side of the cove. The flickering of the light caught his eye as well and I could feel him turn his head and with it he had returned to his senses. The mood was broken. Had I missed my moment to say something? Had I missed my opportunity to flirt, to give encouragement for whatever, a kiss? Damn that flickering porch light!

"Let's go Amelia," he turned and walked back toward the clubhouse only stopping to grab our shoes.

I stood there for a minute before running along behind him. Gabriel stopped when he got to the steps and handed me my shoes. I slipped them on and we went inside with him leading and me having to nearly break a stride to keep up. I was not sure what had happened, but the moment was gone. I could not help but feel disappointed somehow. At the same time I was fully aware that all of this was inappropriate. Inappropriate, but extremely fun!

"Just so you know. I plan on walking barefoot out there at every opportunity," I said in an attempt to lighten the mood back to what it had been when we were first on the green.

"I would not advise that, Amelia." He sounded stern and we continued up the stairs in silence.

When we reached the outer doors at the top of the stairs he advised me to park at the lot down the hill near the loading dock from then on. He also told me to be back on Saturday morning at 9:30 a.m. He then held the door for me and closed it behind me. I was not sure if he waited to make sure I got to my car safely. My last moments with him that night were as if I were dealing with a completely different person, dealing with the same ass I had to impress at the interview.

By the time I got home Jay and Emma were downtown at Cameron's or The Opera House so there was no one with whom to rehash my first day of work. It was nearly 11:00 p.m. so I showered and went on to bed. I read the history of the Acropolis until I fell asleep sometime after midnight.

Thursday came and went with my usual class schedule. The same went for Friday, but everything was a haze of daydreams of Gabriel. It was Friday afternoon before I saw Jay to give him the play by play on how Wednesday night had gone. Despite our analyzing, neither of us could make heads or tails of Gabriel shutting down on the course. We did agree that I was likely playing with fire and should probably try to squelch all inclination toward Gabriel if I wanted to have a pleasant working environment at Port Honor.

CHAPTER 3

Saturday arrived and at around 8:30 a.m. I started the journey back to Port Honor for my second day of work. Despite the way Wednesday night had ended, I could hardly wait to see Gabriel. It was 9:15 when I rolled through the gate and waved to Officer Ed.

Even though the lower lot was nearly full, I found a space at the far end near the driving range. I had barely shut the engine off when a young man of about sixteen came barreling down the aisle of the parking lot on one of the golf carts and parked right behind me. He looked like someone straight off of the Junior PGA tour.

As I got out of the car he quickly asked, "Ma'am, may I help you with your bag?" while he waited by the trunk of the Corvette. He had clearly mistaken me for one of the golfers. And, he knew nothing about Corvettes. There was no way the trunk of my car could have held a set of clubs.

"Actually, I am here for work. I am the new server in the clubhouse," I responded while walking around to the rear of the car. This boy was gorgeous; sandy blonde hair, green eyes, a magnificent tan, pretty white teeth and taller than average. If this cart attendant thing did not work out, he could surely find work modeling for Nautica or some like brand. I almost felt like a pervert looking at him even though I was only four years his senior.

"Oh, in that case, may I offer you a ride to the clubhouse?" he offered.

"Sure. Thanks!" I took him up on the offer and we hopped onto the golf cart. "I'm Millie."

"Right, I should've recognized you from what-all my mother's said." The conversation progressed as we drove the short distance to the clubhouse. "My name's Jason and I'm Joan's other son. I work in the cart barn as an attendant. Mom says you play the piano like nobody's business. She's been going on and on." He was quite chatty.

"Like nobody's business, huh? Rats, I was going for like a house on fire!" I joked while faking disappointment.

"I can see why Mom likes you. You better watch out though, Mom's a perpetual matchmaker." And with that, the conversation wound down as we were at the steps to the loading dock.

"Bye, Jason, thanks for the ride."

"No problem, anytime!" Then Jason was on his way to see about the next set of golfers who had pulled up in the parking lot.

Up the steps and along the loading dock I went. Through the back door of the kitchen I found Alvin busy preparing sandwiches at the back prep line just inside the back door. He was singing along with the boom box that was playing from the dishwashing station until he caught a glimpse of me from the corner of his eye.

"Good morning, Millie!" he greeted me.

"Hey! How are you doing this morning?" I asked.

"Great. And you?" Alvin sure was chipper for so early in the morning.

"Fine, just awake too early for a Saturday."

"You might have to get used to this. I hear you may be the new beer babe." Alvin laughed.

"Beer babe?"

"Gabriel left word for Matt to get you set up on the beverage cart... the ragged out, dump truck looking cart that you just passed by the loading dock steps."

"And Matt is???"

"The other bartender. Andy and Matt are the bartenders. Come on, he's up front. I will introduce you." Alvin stopped with the sandwiches and went to wash his hands before coming back to escort me up front to meet Matt.

I followed Alvin up front where we found Matt counting out the register and chatting with Mr. Baker and another gentleman.

Alvin excused himself and interrupted, "Matt, this is Millie. She's the one that Gabriel wanted you to get started on the beverage cart."

Mr. Baker overheard and contributed to the conversation: "Hot dog, Millie's the new beer babe!" It sounded kind of cute when

Alvin said it earlier, but Mr. Baker just made it sound kind of dirty, like he was going to be watching me work a pole or something.

"Millie, just give me a minute to finish up here and I will be right with you," Matt said as he paused from counting the money. Of the guys I had met so far, Matt was the least attractive, but that was not to say he was unattractive. He looked to be a couple of years older than I was. He was taller than I was, but not nearly as tall as Andy and not even as tall as Gabriel. He had brown hair, but also not as dark as Andy's. He had blue eyes and fair skin, like tanning might be a challenge for him where it wasn't for most of the other guys that I had met here so far. Matt was wearing a white golf shirt with the Port Honor logo on it and khaki shorts with Nike tennis shoes. He was a slight bit heavier, more filled out looking than Andy or Gabriel. The word my grandfather would have used to describe him would have been "stocky". To put it in sports terms, Andy was shaped like a quarterback, Gabriel a wide receiver and Matt was shaped like a catcher for a baseball team.

"Alright, take your time." I looked back to Alvin as he was turning to leave and asked him if there was anything I could do to help out while I waited for Matt.

"Sure, come on," said Alvin. He went back to making sandwiches, but proceeded to tell me what to expect while working the beverage cart and which of the members to watch out for and not to let them get too close to me. Apparently some of the gentlemen weren't so gentlemanly while out on the course. Alvin was so sweet and seemed like he was genuinely concerned.

"Are Andy and Gabriel coming in today?" I tried to ask without seeming like I really cared which was not difficult since I did not care if Andy was coming in or not.

"I think they are both working tonight."

In an effort to glaze over my question, I followed by asking him if there was anything I could go ahead and start doing in preparation for the beverage cart. Alvin was happy to assist. He gave me a large basket and told me which items to put in there, potato chips, crackers, candy bars and what not, and he told me where to find everything. I was just finishing loading the basket when Matt appeared from up front.

Matt took over assisting me with loading the drinks on the cart. First we went outside and put the cooler in the bed of the dump truck looking golf cart. That cart had seen better days. The cooler used to be white, but like most everything else there it appeared to have been let go a little during the bankruptcy. It had two sections to it and they opened opposite each other, one to the left and one to the right. It appeared very much like a tool box one would put on the back of a truck. In one side of the cooler we loaded a variety of beers. On the other side of the cart we loaded Cokes, Diet Cokes, Sprites, a couple of Dr. Peppers and a couple of Gatorades. Matt seemed to know just how many of each to load based on what typically sold on the course during the day.

"We've got a tournament of college boys starting at 10 a.m. so I am going to put another cooler up here in the floorboard filled with nothing but bottled waters. Charge them a dollar per bottle," Matt told me as he handed me a fee sheet. "See, it's on the sheet. Also, you will need to hang on to the cooler when you take turns or it will fly out." He picked up the cooler and put it on the cart.

"You seem to know a lot about the beverage cart. Did you used to be the beer babe?" I joked as I put the basket of dry items in the passenger's seat.

"You have jokes, huh? You know how to drive one of these things, right?" Matt asked as he shook the pole to the roof of the cart. I nodded my head yes, to which he responded, "I doubt you have ever driven anything like this one. It's a real POS."

"You don't say," I said in a smarty-pants voice. It went without saying that that thing was almost pitiful.

Matt gave me a couple of instructions on how to operate it and what to do on the course "If you see anyone teeing off or hitting, stop the cart. This thing is loud and noise pisses off the golfers when they are trying to hit. Pissed off golfers means less tips for you; happy golfers equals more tips for you. Got it?"

"Yes," I answered. I would learn later that the real joke was on me as he failed to mention that the brakes were all but shot on the POS.

"Wait until they are finished before you say anything or offer them anything. Also, and this is very important, drive in the opposite direction of the golfers."

"Why?"

"So that if some idiot can't hit and accidentally aims for you; you can see it coming. You know what 'Fore' means?"

"Look out?" I responded with a question as I was not sure of the exact meaning.

"It means I can't hit so get out of the way! If you hear that, get off of the cart and get down behind it as quick as you can. The windshield will not necessarily stop the ball. I am telling you all of this because the last beer babe drove with the flow of traffic and got hit in the back of the head with the ball. She was smokin' hot, but dumb as a box of rocks! She quit the same day."

"Wow! That sort of sucked for her."

"Have you ever been hit by a golf ball?"

"No."

"I have and it hurts so just trust me and do like I have told you and you will be fine," Matt cautioned. Matt was kind of bossy and who knew beer babe was such a dangerous job?

Everything was loaded so I proceeded to get on the cart. "One last thing," said Matt. "Just follow the cart path. Start at the ninth hole and work backward." Then he pointed over by the driving range and I could see the path start up by the side of the driving range and head off toward the woods along a fairway.

"Alright. I suppose I will see you in a little while." And with those words, I fired up the cart and headed off across the parking lot in the direction of the cart path near the ninth green. Matt turned to walk inside, but before either of us got very far, I stopped the cart and yelled back, "Hey, Matt," he turned to see what I needed, "Thanks for helping me this morning," I yelled to him.

"No problem. See you at the turn," he yelled back. More golf lingo, the turn being the halfway mark of the eighteen holes and the location of the clubhouse.

***

I putted along on the shake-mobile. Every rock or crack that I hit on the cart path reverberated through the entire cart rattling it to the point that it sounded as if all of the screws were going to spring loose. I fully expected the roof or the bed area on the back to dislodge and fall off in the middle of the path at any moment.

The sun was shining and the sky was completely void of clouds. It was still a little chilly so not that many golfers were out yet. The fairways and greens were empty. I drove along in virtual silence with only the trembling bolts of the cart to keep me company. It allowed me time to take in the sights of the woods, fairways with their bunkers and some with water features as well as the sights of the houses along the course. Everything was spectacular and I knew in that moment that this was the place for me.

In the first three holes that I passed I saw eight houses. Some of the houses were modest and others were quite extravagant. Some were set close to the course and others sat farther back. I could only see the rear of the homes from the fairways. Some I could see clearly and some I could scarcely see because of the trees or the proximity to the course.

There was one that was cedar and of a modern, split level style. It looked like my aunt Dot's house, but a little more maintained and the landscaping looked like a professional took care of it which was a far cry better than what Uncle Jim did for their yard. This particular yard had specifically placed plants that were manicured to look like woodsy art as opposed to a hodge-podge of things they found in the woods at our lake place and relocated to their yard.

My favorite house was somewhat over the top. It had a pool with a slide and a double decker back porch on it. The lower level of the house looked as if it were a basement that let out into the pool area by way of red brick arches that supported the deck above and gave cover to a large patio. There was also a dual sided fireplace built of the same red brick with two arches on each side of it. Although this house did not sit right up on the course and despite the yard having a fair amount of trees: a few oaks, a couple of dogwoods, a few palms around the pool, but mostly pines throughout the yard, I could see everything clearly.

I could see the oversized black wicker chairs with cushions, probably of a floral pattern with the color red being the dominant color. I could see a matching love seat and all of this was arranged around the fireplace on the outside. I could not see what sort of furniture might be beyond the arches although I stopped the cart to get a better look.

On the deck above the patio there were enormous ferns hanging in baskets above the porch that were centered to the arches below. That was about all I could see of that level but I imagined if the house were mine, I would have a large farm house dining room table on that porch where I would eat dinner as often as possible.

The rest of the house consisted of painted white siding. Although I could not see the front of the house, I could not imagine it having anything other than black shutters accenting the windows and a front door that was painted red.

The yard was just as stunning as the house and everything seemed to fit perfectly and complement one another. The red specks I could see in the cushions of the patio furniture matched perfectly to the giant pots holding proportionate palm trees around the pool.

I could imagine that the view from this house was exceptional as it sat directly across from the water feature on the seventh fairway. The water feature amounted to a small pond with water the color of emeralds bordered by a stacked stone retaining wall on the opposite side from the house. The pond was also fed by a small stream that led down from the fairway and had several tiny waterfalls along the way.

This house was truly a sight right out of Southern Living magazine and I was in awe. I could only hope that the family that lived there cherished what they had. I also hoped they did not come out at any moment and catch me gawking at their house. With that thought, I put the shake mobile in motion and started back along the cart path.

It was nearly 10:45 a.m. when I came across my first group of golfers at the sixth hole. Four elderly gentlemen and if any of them were a day under eighty, well they had clearly done some hard living. Three were walking back to their carts and one was still putting the pin back when I pulled up. Alvin was right about men not being gentlemen on the course. These fellas were old as dirt and they still looked at me like I was something to eat, salivating through their dentures. I sold them each a beer and one even bought a candy bar. The beers were three dollars each and the candy bar was one dollar so their total bill was thirteen dollars. The gentleman that paid me gave me a twenty and told me to keep the change. Another yelled back for me to make sure I came around with sandwiches for them around noon. Not bad, I was seven dollars richer.

At the red tee box for the sixth hole I came to another foursome, three elderly ladies, one thirty year old and no salivating. They heard me coming all shaking and rattling and the one that was taking a turn in the box, the thirty year old, waited for me to stop next to their carts. I thought she was being nice waiting so she would be less likely to hit me, but as it turned out she just wanted to be free of the distraction of the noise before she teed up and hit. Matt had been right about the noise pissing them off.

"Good Lord, honey," she said as she squared her shoulders and took a practice swing before officially entering the box, "That thing sounds like a death trap! Couldn't they find you something less offensive to my ears?"

"Don't mind Kimmie," said one of the others who was still sitting on her cart, tallying her score card and glancing back at me. "She's just bitter. I am whippin' her ass this morning, dear."

The other ladies were dressed conservatively; pastel colored golf shirts, matching shorts of nearly knee length, and then there was Kimmie. Kimmie was dressed like a Frederick's of Hollywood model who had just taken up golf. Anyone watching could tell her obviously store bought boobs got in the way of her swing. Guess you just can't have it all.

I don't believe Kimmie heard the lady on the cart, but the other two heard just fine and they laughed to themselves. I smiled back at her and waited quietly for Kimmie to swing. Practice swing after practice swing, it felt like an eternity as I waited for all four of them to hit. Finally they were done.

"Could I get you ladies anything this morning?" I asked with a big smile and continued by rattling off all of the items I had on the cart.

"Did the boys in front buy anything from you?" Kimmie asked as she raised an eye brow and looked down her nose at me. Ah, and there was the country club attitude to which I was accustomed.

"Yes, ma'am," I answered and Kimmie rolled her eyes.

At that point the lady who was whippin' Kimmie's ass interrupted. "I'll take a bottle of water, please."

"Great. That will be one dollar." I said as I moved around the cart to get the water from the cooler. I handed her the water and she handed me two dollars and told me to keep the change. The other ladies said they would catch me on the next round and then I was on my way.

By the turn, I had sold out of bottled water and was running low on beer and crackers. Not to mention, I had made twenty six dollars in tips. The course had been packed since the sixth hole. As to not upset the members, the tee times were alternated: members then college boys then members again and so forth. There were some good looking college boys and some pervy members and they had really distracted me from thinking about Gabriel or being disappointed that I was probably not going to see him today.

It was around 11:30 when I made it to the clubhouse and I replenished the cart. Matt was busy inside the bar serving lunch and Alvin was busy preparing the lunches so I had to reload the cart by myself. I made sure I grabbed some of the sandwiches that Alvin had been preparing earlier when I had first arrived. Alvin also gave me one to eat for my lunch as well.

I headed out on the back nine after leaving the clubhouse. The first group I ran across was the four old guys from the sixth hole. I found them at the fourteenth green. I waited for them to finish putting before getting off the cart and yelled to them, "Who wants sandwiches and more beer? I have turkey and ham and Miller Lite, Bud and Heineken!"

"Excellent!" One of the gentlemen exclaimed as he approached my cart. He picked over the items in the basket and took a sandwich and chips. "I'll have a beer as well." His bill was ten bucks and he gave me fifteen. The same thing happened with two of the others, but the last one went all out.

"I will have the same as them plus a hug," I was so excited about the fifteen dollar tip from the other three gentlemen that I almost forgot Alvin's warning. Huggie-man came in for a hug and luckily I came to my senses and managed to turn enough to give him the side arm job. I did it in a giggly friendly manner so as to throw off the thought in my head of "dirty old man".

"What's your name sweetie?" Huggie-man asked.

"Millie," I responded as he handed me a twenty and waived me off when I tried to give him change.

"Thanks, Millie. I'm Marvin," and then he pointed to the other gentlemen waiting on him. "That's Bill and Richard on the front cart and Don there is my chauffer on the other cart." I smiled and waved to them.

I thought I was done and was just about seated back on the cart when Huggie-man came back to the cart, "Hey, Millie, wait a minute. Let me go ahead and take care of the girls." He handed me a fifty and told me to let the ladies behind them have anything they wanted and to let him know when I came back around if I needed more money.

When I came to the ladies I once again found them at the tee box waiting for Kimmie to crank it and shank it. After I brought the cart to a stop, I turned it off and watched the calamity that was Kimmie's swing. She nearly lost a boob and threw her back out with the follow-through. We all watched as the ball went flying and then SMACK! It hit a goose that was crossing near the water feature. The goose let out a yelp and then fell over. The three older ladies and I could hardly contain our laughter. The one that was whippin'

59

Kimmie earlier let out a squeal of sheer delight. My laughing was promptly squelched when Kimmie cut her eyes at me and I am not one to read minds, but I understood what hers were saying quite clearly.

I quit laughing and said begrudgingly to them, "One of the gentlemen in the foursome in front of y'all paid me in advance for you to pick whatever you like. So help yourselves ladies."

Kimmie was the farthest one away from the cart, but literally skipped to the cart while cutting off the others and bragging that it was probably her husband, Marvin, that treated them. Of course Kimmie was married to Huggie-man. How fitting.

I continued along the back nine serving all of the golfers and taking in the sights. The houses on the back nine had been equally impressive as those on the front nine. There were also some on the back that were equally unimpressive as some on the front. The least impressive were the golf villas along the eighteenth green that faced the side of the cove, perpendicular to the clubhouse. They were painted in plain pastel colors with white trim; a yellow, a light grey, a baby blue one. They looked like older duplexes, yuck.

As for the houses I liked there were two in particular along the back nine, but none so much so as the house on the seventh fairway. These houses were of about the same size and their yards were pristinely landscaped, but the house at number seven was still my favorite.

By the time I made it back to the turn, I had made sixty dollars in tips. I reloaded the cart and it was about 1:15 p.m. when I started out again on the front nine.

I was not paying attention as I rounded the turn between the tee box for the sixth green and the putting green on the fifth. I had not slowed down early enough and when I tried I got quite the surprise. I pressed the brake and it went to the floorboard and nothing happened as far as slowing down. When I took the curve, I was too distracted with the failure of the brakes to remember to hold on to the water cooler in the floor board. I had been driving with one hand, fluffing my hair with the other and looking out across the lake as I went into the curve, but when the brakes failed, I grabbed the steering wheel with both hands.

There were four college boys walking from the fairway to the putting green when I slung the water cooler from the floor board of the cart. The cooler did not tip or anything. It just slid perfectly for about thirty feet out across the green, stopping just before it hit the pin.

I was mortified, but what could I do? I threw up my hand and waived to the boys and smiled. I held my head high as if I had slung the cooler out there on purpose. They all clapped as I jumped from the cart and ran around it toward the cooler. As they clapped, I stopped just beyond the cart and curtseyed to them.

I made it to the cooler about the same time as they made it onto the green. "Could I get you boys some water?" I beamed and bent over to get the waters. I probably flashed them my Joe Boxer smiley face underpants when I bent over, but wasn't that just par for the course? "If you all don't mention this cooler incident at the club, you can have whatever you want off of the cart?"

The best looking one in the bunch promptly said, "What I want from the cart is already off of the cart."

I blushed and responded coyly, "Alright, just bottled water it is, but you can have a candy bar too or some crackers." The other boys all just laughed at the banter and I handed them each a bottle of water. Eventually they all accepted a candy bar in addition to the water. Despite the fact that I had just shot him down, the good looking one picked up the cooler and carried it back to the cart for me.

"Which school are you guys from?" I asked him as we walked to the cart.

"Georgia College in Milledgeville." I felt somewhat foolish as he responded since all of their shirts were golf shirts with the Georgia College name and logo printed on them.

"Really?" I said with a touch of disbelief in my voice.

"Yes, and you? Do you go to school around here?" he asked me.

"Yes...Go Colonials," the Colonials were the mascot of Georgia College.

"Do you live in one of the dorms?"

"No, one of the Hillman House apartment buildings."

"Which one?"

"I live in Hillman House number eleven." Just as I finished speaking I noticed that the other guys were waiting on him to return to putt. "They are waiting on you."

"Ah, yes, I better get back. Maybe I will see you around campus." He was almost to the green before he shouted back to me over the noise of the cart which I had just started up, "I didn't get your name."

"Millie!" I shouted in return.

Again, another nice distraction from my thoughts of Gabriel which had been few and far between thanks to my being busy on the course. I was all the way to the third green and still thinking about the Colonial from the fifth green when I realized I had not asked his name.

***

It was about 2:30 when I made it back to the clubhouse again. My sales had not slacked off so I went inside to reload again. While inside I decided to consolidate some of my money. I went to the front of bar and found Matt. The bar was filling up with groups coming in from the course. Mr. Marvin and Kimmie were inside with the other gentlemen from his group. The other ladies had gone home already, but Kimmie remained, arm candy for Mr. Marvin while he played cards with the fellas. When Mr. Marvin was not looking, Kimmie flirted shamelessly with Matt, but Matt did not seem to notice.

"Excuse me," I said as Kimmie was trying to get Matt's attention with her far too unbuttoned shirt and boobs resting on the bar. "Matt, can I give you some of these ones and get back some larger bills?"

Matt never noticed Kimme, but turned to me and responded as he made a drink for one of the other gentlemen at the far end of the bar, "Sure, Millie. Give me just a second."

Matt finished the drink and slid it down the bar to the gentleman. He then turned to help me with converting the money and Kimmie rolled her eyes at me. I stared right back at her and looked her up and down with a look on my face as if to convey that something smelled. I suppose I thought I was letting her know there was a new "B" in town and if she got Matt's attention it was because I was giving it: "Matt, I believe Mr. Marvin's wife needs something. I am fine to wait if you want to take care of her."

That did not particularly work out the way I had intended since Matt acted as if I had not spoken. Kimmie took note and promptly threw her nose in the air and returned to Mr. Marvin's side empty handed. Matt then turned around and handed me the money. She was out of for Kimmie to hear so he proceeded to give me the dirt on her, "I think I am the only guy around here that hasn't had a turn with her. I like the old man and I don't want anything to do with the likes of her. You seem like a nice girl Millie, so you might do well to steer clear of her too."

Matt ended up leaving the bar and helping me load the cart again for one more round on the course. I tried to make small talk with him while he helped me.

"I thought I would see Mr. Baker on the course today, but I never did." I told Matt as we loaded the beverage cart.

"He stopped playing a few years ago. He still loves to talk about the game and shoot the breeze in the clubhouse."

"So how long have you been working here?" I asked him.

"About three months," he responded as he lifted the cooler with the bottled waters back onto the front of the cart for me. Although he did not appear in as good of shape as the other guys at the club, he did not break a sweat or seem to strain any time when he lifted the coolers during the day and he did not let me help him even though I offered every time.

"Did you have to do a little performance to get the job as well?" I kind of laughed as I asked. By now I was certain that everyone had heard about the piano concert I gave.

"No, you were not the first one to be late to the interview." Matt replied. "I was so broke before I got the job that I could not afford to buy a new alarm clock and mine had broken the week before. I nearly stayed up all night for fear of over sleeping. When I did fall asleep I over slept a little. Unlike you, I was only late by about five minutes."

"Nothing says 'I don't care' like being late to the interview, right?"

"I know, but here we both are," Matt laughed.

We were finished loading the cart so I headed back out on the course. I met up with the college boys from the fifth green again at the tenth tee box. I gave them free water again and found out their names.

Alex was the good looking one. He was a junior majoring in accounting and he planned to go to law school at Mercer. He was about the same height as Gabriel. He had dark brown hair, tan skin and green eyes. He was filled out more than the other guys, but not like the guys at the club. His teammates were JR, Chris and the second Jason I had met that day. Who knew what they were majoring in because Alex did not let them talk, but I suppose he was not all that interested because he did not get my number.

I made it back to the clubhouse and my sales had dropped off to such an extent that Matt said I could come in for the day. It was around 3:30 when I started unloading the beverage cart. By 4pm I was finished. I was at the bar turning in the money to Matt when Alex and the other Georgia College boys walked in carrying their trophy.

Mr. Marvin and his group were still playing cards and Kimmie was sitting on the arm of Mr. Marvin's chair, but that did not stop her from checking out the college boys as they entered. Her eyes got wide and she turned a little pea green when Alex approached me at the bar.

"Millie! I am glad I caught you," said Alex as he walked up to the bar. "We won second place in the tournament. We are planning on going out to celebrate. Would you like to join us?" He was beaming from ear to ear and he had a great smile.

"Congratulations!" and I leaned across the bar and high-fived him as I left Matt just standing there with the money. "I don't know if I can make it. I am not done here yet and I would have to go back home and change and everything."

"That's no problem, we have to do the same," he returned.

"I suppose I could meet up with you all later on to celebrate. What time and where?"

Alex put his hands in his pockets and kind of bounced a little on his knees which were bent slightly. He thought for a moment before speaking, "How about The Brick at 7:30?"

"Great! Would you mind if I bring one of my roommates?" I asked.

"Are you kidding me?" he asked and continued, "Do you see my teammates over there? They would love it if you brought one of your roommates, they would probably love it if you brought three roommates if you have them."

Just then Matt interrupted and sounded a bit pissed, "Millie, are you cashing out or what?"

"I'll let you get back to work. See you at 7:30." At that point Alex excused himself and returned to his teammates. They ended up leaving shortly thereafter.

All the while Alex and I had been talking, Kimmie did her best to eavesdrop. She could not take her eyes off of Alex. The brilliant thing was that he had not noticed her at all.

I finished with Matt and then returned to the kitchen to clock out. Apparently Gabriel had been in at some point during the day as a new schedule was up. I was scheduled to work the coming Wednesday night in the dining room followed by Saturday and Sunday on the beverage cart. There was also a note for me pinned to the schedule indicating I was to be back the next morning at 9:30 again for another turn as the beer babe.

As I was standing there with the schedule, Alvin called me over, "Hey, Millie, come try this."

I walked over to where he was working on the prep line nearest the stove. "Prime rib; quality check time! I am supposed to have this done by the time Gabriel gets here at 5 so let's have a taste and see if it's ready," he said as he cut a small piece off for me to try. He passed it over for me to take straight off of the knife, "What do you think?"

"I think it's wonderful! I did not realize I was starving until just now." I had only been able to eat about a third of the sandwich Alvin had given me at lunchtime.

"Stay right there, I will make a plate for you." Alvin turned to take a plate down from the stack under the warmer.

"No, no. I can't. I have to go," I tried to stop him. "I think I have a date tonight."

"A date?" Alvin's eyes got big as if he was a little shocked.

"Well, not really, maybe," I knew I sounded confused.

Alvin looked at me as puzzled as I felt, "Either it is or it isn't. So, which is it?"

"I suppose it isn't. We are meeting there and I don't know his last name. It's a group outing...I'm sorry. I am not good with boys, no good at these things, Alvin."

I had spent almost two weeks thinking of Gabriel and daydreaming about him at every opportunity, but now here I was exasperated about something that I really did not care about. It was something to do, but nothing beyond that.

"Maybe that's why God sent you to me, to help you figure these things out," Alvin grinned.

"Maybe," I smiled back.

"Here, I am going to make a to-go box for you...since it isn't a date." Then Alvin took down one of the to-go boxes and added so much food to it that the box would hardly close. There was a king sized slice of prime rib, a cup of au jus, roasted potatoes, grilled roma tomatoes topped with melted parmesan cheese and a large helping of sautéed spinach. The aroma was mouthwatering and I knew I would have to smell it the entire way back to Milledgeville.

I had thanked Alvin with a big hug as this would be the best meal I had had in months whether I ate it that evening or the following day and then I headed out the back door to the parking lot with the to-go box in hand.

I was just down the steps and into the parking lot when Andy and another girl were headed in. Still I had not seen Gabriel, but my need for a fix on him was gradually tapering off.

As I passed Andy I spoke, "Hey, how's it going?"

"Fine and you are no longer the FNG," he said with his usual attitude that called to mind the word "pig". "This is Cara and she's the FNG now. FNG, this is Millie."

Cara rolled her eyes at Andy as she reached out a hand to me to shake, "I have a feeling you and I are going to be fast friends, Millie. Gabe said nothing but good things about you in my interview."

"Really?" I was skeptical.

"I hope I make as good of an impression as you did," she said. With those words, Andy rolled his eyes and walked away heading on toward the loading dock.

"I'm sure you'll be great!" I told her.

Cara seemed extremely nice and I was quickly becoming convinced that she was right. We were going to be fast friends and probably allies against the guys around here. A petty thought crossed my mind just behind thinking what good friends we were going to be; she was dressed just like me except her skirt was

66

longer. Gabriel was supposed to be in at 5:00 and I wondered what he would think of her skirt. Would he think of her skirt at all? Even if he did think of it, there was likely nothing he could do about it because Praise was not working.

Cara was pretty in the same kind of way that Kimmie was pretty. They both put a great deal of effort into the way they looked. Cara not so much effort as Kimmie, but that probably had more to do with financial circumstances than intention. Kimmie had a sugar daddy and Cara probably did not at this stage of her life. I was confident from my experience on the beverage cart that day that if Cara wanted a sugar daddy this might be the right place to get one. In fact, the last portion of our conversation in the parking lot was her quizzing me about the guys; Andy, Matt and Gabriel.

"I'm not so curious about Gabe," she said and in my head I wondered if something was wrong with her that she was not curious about Gabe.

Cara continued, "Andy's HOT!"

"But he knows it," I interrupted her.

"You're exactly right," she laughed. "And, Matt is not as attractive..."

I interrupted her again, "But he seems really sweet."

"Right!" she agreed as if she were actually contemplating what to do with him right there in front of me.

"So, why aren't you curious about Gabriel?" I asked while trying to appear indifferent, but I had slipped and referred to him as Gabriel instead of Gabe. Maybe she would not notice.

"Like you don't know!" she gasped and noticed the look on my face. "Oh, you don't know. How can you not know?"

"Know what?"

"He's yours," she enlightened me.

"He's not mine! He's got a girlfriend and it's not me."

"Seriously, a girlfriend? We will see how long that lasts now. Trust me on this," she said, "No guy talks about a girl the way he talked about you and carries on with another woman unless his moral compass is flat broken.

Cara paused for a moment and glanced at her watch, "I better get inside before Andy starts screaming for the FNG. By the way, what is that?"

I rolled my eyes as I answered. "It means Fucking New Girl. He thinks he's being clever, but he's not."

"How did you know that?"

"I caught one of the members headed toward the restroom the day he first introduced me as FNG. I batted my lashes and twirled my hair a little at the old guy and he was all too eager to give up their inside joke."

Cara giggled. "I knew I was going to like you. Are you working the brunch shift tomorrow?" she asked.

"Not exactly, I am on the beverage cart again tomorrow."

"Good! We will still see each other and we will talk more then. Now I better get in there before Andy comes back." At that point Cara made off toward the loading dock while the to-go box and I carried on toward my car.

***

I made it back to Milledgeville in record time. It was about 5pm when I walked in to an unusually quiet apartment. I found a note from Jay stuck to the refrigerator saying that he was going to his Aunt's house for the night. Emma was the only one home and she was in her room with the door shut. I proceeded to the kitchen where I opened the to-go box and took a few bites of prime rib. Almost an hour old and it was still just as good as it had been when Alvin first offered it to me. I could have easily eaten the entire plate, but I held off and thought of meeting Alex and his friends at the bar.

The Brick was a traditional pizza and wing bar. The inside was set up a little like a Waffle House; a large counter and bar seating that were open to the kitchen. The kitchen and counter ran parallel and almost the length of the building, just one long stretch. In the kitchen/bar area there was a Jagermeister machine that chilled that toxic poison to almost freezing temperatures. According to Jay, the Jager machine was responsible for more date rapes than Rohypnol, GHB and Ketamine combined.

Behind the counter seating was a partitian that separated it from the row of booths along the opposite wall from the kitchen. The wall by the booths was painted white with blobs of pinkish-red sponge paint over the top in a dreadful late 8o's kind of way. On top of the sponge paint were a ton of neon beer signs: Miller Light, Bud Light, and Coors Light, but nothing too classy or anything imported.

Their primary business at The Brick was serving the college kids like us. I did not typically frequent the bars, but since I had moved here I had frequented this bar for dinner about once per week at least. Most of the time Jay and I would have an all carb feast of a double order of breadsticks, Coke for me and beer for him and only spend a grand total of seven dollars.

They had the best wings I had ever had and our apartment was within walking distance. Our apartment was actually walking distance from the entire downtown area of Milledgeville including all of the bars and the college.

When I finished chewing the few bites of the prime rib, I shut the box and placed it in the refrigerator and then went to get a shower. Although the uniform was not entirely uncomfortable, I had taken the tie off and loosened my top two buttons as soon as I clocked out and started to the parking lot at Port Honor. Now, getting out of the barely there skirt and the button down were overdue.

By the time I finished my shower Emma had emerged from her room. I was in a towel and she in her practice gear from tennis when we ran into one another in the hall outside of the bathroom door.

"I'm glad you are out of there," she said to me. "I came straight in from practice and took a nap. I have not showered yet and I probably smell."

"I was hoping you would be home. What are you doing for dinner?" I asked as she started around me and into the bathroom.

"I don't know. Why?"

"I met a boy at the club today and he has invited me to join him and his friends for dinner at The Brick and I was hoping you would come with me."

Emma looked at me sort of skeptical, but without asking any questions beyond what time, she agreed to come along.

"Great. Thanks so much!" and at that point I went to my room to get dressed and Emma continued on into the bathroom for her shower.

By 7:20 Emma and I were dressed and ready to walk to The Brick. Emma was stunning and appeared to be ready for a photo shoot for Vogue. She had pale white skin and jet black hair that hung in loose natural curls around her face and down her back. Even though she was English, there had to be some Greek in her heritage somewhere. There was little to say regarding her make-up as the bright red lipstick said it all. Emma was wearing a blue floral top that was nearly see-through with a tank-top under it and no bra. In the right climate, there would be nothing left to one's imagination. In addition, she wore a white skirt that flowed as much as one could when it's length was only two inches past her butt cheeks. To complete this outfit, she wore matching blue stilettos. I, on the other hand, was dressed a tad more conservatively.

I had chosen a white tank top with a bra. With the help of the padding from the bra and the length down my chest the neckline of the tank top fell, I gave the slightest appearance of cleavage, but nothing shocking. I wore my favorite jeans, ripped here and there, but not so bad that they should be thrown out. I also wore my black biker boots, and a matching, over-sized black belt. I accented the outfit with about ten sterling silver bracelets and no necklace. My ears were not pierced so no ginormous hoop earrings for me. From my ears to the neckline of the tank top, my neck and chest were bare as I had dried my hair straight which made it straighter than it would normally be and twisted it into a loose bun. I left some wisps hanging around my face. My make-up was understated as always in efforts to give the impression that I was not wearing any. Unlike Emma it was not my style to have my lipstick scream, "These are Millie's lips and this is Millie!"

All dressed to impress in our own ways, we headed out of the apartment and toward the bar. Finally an explanation for her look of skepticism earlier was explained. "I'm guessing we are not meeting up with Gabriel tonight for dinner." Emma said as we walked to The Brick.

"No. We are meeting up with the men's golf team."

"What happened with Gabriel?" Emma asked.

"Nothing happened with Gabriel. I didn't even see him today." I am sure Emma could sense the disappointment in my voice.

"He wasn't at work so you met the entire golf team? I did not think you had it in you, Millie."

"It's not like that," I shook my head at her.

"So still hung up on Gabriel and this is just a diversion? That's still progress, Millie." Emma encouraged me and I think she meant well.

"That about sums it up," and at that point we high fived, but it was not with the gusto that she had intended with her first attempt.

It was not a long walk from the apartment to The Brick and I made it in relative comfort, but not Emma. By the time we arrived she was nearly hobbled by the stilettos. It was a bit of a relief when she took them off and walked the last block barefooted while carrying them. It gave me a small amount of time when I did not look like a child walking next to her. She was already a substantial number of inches taller, but add on the extra five inches of the stilettos, and I definitely appeared as a child would next to an individual of average height. Just steps from the door to The Brick Emma dropped her shoes on the sidewalk and put them back on before entering the bar.

I noticed the guys from the Georgia College golf team were already inside when Emma and I opened the door to enter The Brick. Alex waived to me, motioning for us to come over and join them. As he waived the other guys took notice of Emma and their mouths fell open. They looked like Ralphy when he opened the Red Rider BB gun on Christmas morning. In fact, every guy in the place took notice of her, but none other than the guys from the golf team had the thrill of her attention during dinner. As we approached their table all three scrambled to pull out a chair for her as I went unnoticed by everyone but Alex. The rest of the night Emma was waited on hand and foot. Drink after drink plus the dainty dinner of just a few chicken wings and salad were purchased for her. JR, Chris and Jason argued among themselves as to which was going to lay down their cash next. If they thought this impressed her, they were wrong as this was how guys always behaved around Emma. Rarely did she have to open her own wallet at a restaurant or a bar.

Alex paid for my dinner and although guilt-ridden for doing so, I allowed him. Alex seemed really nice and he was attentive, but I knew that if Gabriel walked in Alex would not exist to me any longer. I felt ashamed of myself for knowing that. I knew that was unfair to Alex, but the spark that I felt when just standing next to Gabriel was not remotely there with Alex. I suppose the feeling I had felt when near Gabriel was the feeling a drug addict got on their first fix. Would I always be trying to get the next fix or could I get past this?

The evening rocked on and as Emma ruled her mini-kingdom, I got to know Alex a little better. He was the youngest of three children. His parents had married right out of high school and divorced fairly quickly after having him and his sister. He and his sister were only fifteen months apart in age. His mother remarried and he lived at home with his mother and step-father and commuted to school. By all account his step-father was the only real father he had ever known and basically considered his biological father nothing more than a sperm donor. His step-father came with baggage like his mother and Alex had a step-brother, but they all behaved like blood siblings instead of step.

Ashley, his sister, was a senior at Savannah College of Art and Design and lived in Savannah. The way he talked about her let me know that he missed her and they were very close. I envied him having what I would consider a normal family. We did not talk much about my family as every time the subject turned to me I diverted him and changed the subject. He did not seem to notice and enjoyed talking about himself.

I also found out that Alex was a junior here at Georgia College and about the same age I was. He was attending on a golf scholarship thanks to his brother.

"You may know my brother," he said as we ate our chicken wings in virtual anonymity from the rest of our group.

"I really do not know hardly anyone yet so I doubt it." I replied.

"I'm certain you know Andy. He works at Port Honor as one of the bartenders." True to form the look on my face gave it away when I realized that I did in fact know Andy.

"Of course," I said trying to hide the slight distaste I had for Andy as the word "pig" again came to mind. "I cannot believe y'all are brothers."

"We are and it's because of him that I have the golf scholarship," Alex said with blatant admiration in his voice.

"How so?" I asked.

"Andy's been working at Port Honor in some capacity since he was sixteen. So, he's been there ten years. You may not have been there long enough to know all of the perks of working there. One of them is golfing privileges. On Tuesdays through Thursdays the employees are allowed to play for free if they are not working that day and if the course is not booked for a tournament."

"I guess that's pretty great if you like to golf."

"It is," he continued. "Andy only lived with us for a little while, but he always did his best to spend time with Ashley and me. I was ten when he started working there and from the time I was eleven until I graduated high school, he picked me up from school on Tuesday afternoons and took me to Port Honor where we played golf. Occasionally we played on Thursdays as well, if he did not have to work. He was always friends with whichever golf pro was on staff at the time so I got free golf lessons."

"That's pretty awesome!" Although free golf really did nothing for me, I could understand how a young boy or most any man could be thrilled.

"It worked out really well for me since my sister was going to SCAD. Anyway, it would have been a real struggle for my parents to pay for college for both of us, let alone while one went to a private school. My mother absolutely worships Andy for helping get this for me, and the family as a whole, the lessons that led to the scholarship."

I was starting to see Andy in a whole new light. He was still a pig, maybe a pig with a good heart deep down somewhere. I also knew that no matter how nice Alex was or even if I could shake the lingering thoughts of Gabriel, I would not date Alex as long as I worked with Andy. If Alex could handle just being friends, then we would likely continue to see one another.

After about an hour and a half, dinner wound down and Emma and I decided to head home despite the begging of what could have easily become her entourage for the remainder of the night. Both Emma and I congratulated the guys again on their win that day and thanked everyone for the fun time we had as well as for dinner and then we made our way to the door.

Just a few steps beyond the door and out on the sidewalk of Hancock Street, Emma stooped down and removed her shoes again for the walk back home. We were not that far when Emma made her first assessment of our evening, "They were nice guys, but, wow, were they dull."

"I'm sorry you did not have a good time," I said very apologetically.

"I had a lovely time, Millie. I just could not take much more of hearing about golf and how I would enjoy it and which one of them would give me the better lessons. It's nothing against them, I just don't like golf."

"Truthfully, Emma, neither do I!" I laughed.

"So you learned your lesson from Brewers and did not tell them at your interview that you did not like golf." Emma commented and we laughed hysterically.

"My feet hurt, Millie." Emma said among the laughter.

"I'm sure they do. If you weren't so much taller than me and I was sure no one would see us, I'd offer you a piggy back ride," I could barely get the words out through my laughing. "As it is, you are just going to have to lean on me a little and hobble the rest of the way."

Despite our laughter, I could tell her feet genuinely did hurt and I felt sorry for her. My face hurt from laughing, but I knew better than to complain as Emma limped the rest of the way home. At one point I offered to go and get my car and come back for her, but she would not hear of it. I am sure that felt like the longest two and a half blocks of her life.

CHAPTER 4

It was only 9:00 p.m. when we arrived upstairs in our apartment. Emma headed off to her room to lie down, but it was still Saturday night and unlikely that she intended to stay in for the rest of the night. As she went one direction into her room, I went the other toward the kitchen-living room area.

Our apartment was more like two and a half bedrooms, but took up the entire top floor of one of the Hillman Houses. It was one of many of Milledgeville's large historic homes that had been purchased and converted into apartments primarily for rental by college students. Ours was one of a dozen owned by one particular gentleman who was retired and making a second career as landlord and handyman.

Once in the kitchen I found the message light on our answering machine blinking. We had a message. I pressed play and found the message was actually for me and had been left just five minutes before we got home.

The message was as follows:

"Hey, Millie, it's Cara from Port Honor. We met earlier today. All of us at the Port are going to Cameron's tonight and I do mean all of us. I just wanted to invite you to meet us there. We should be there around 11:00." She had emphasized the word "all" and she had already let me know her suspicions about me and Gabriel.

Before thinking too much into it, I grabbed a bag of ice from the refrigerator and ran to Emma's room where I found her sitting on her bed with her feet propped up. "Here, ice your feet and be ready to go again by 11:00," I said as I tossed her the bag of ice and ran out of her room to check my make-up.

"What has gotten into you?!!!" screamed Emma.

I yelled back from the bathroom, "Gabriel is going to be at Cameron's tonight!"

"Oh God, Millie! Two guys in one night!" Emma continued to scream.

Again, I yelled back, "Ice your feet and be quiet!"

***

Eleven o'clock arrived and we were ready to go again. I was dressed exactly the same except for the addition of my favorite perfume. My white tank top had survived dinner and I had not seen fit to change from that or my ripped jeans and black leather biker boots. My hair had also held up from dinner. Emma had completely changed into an outfit that was more modest and would accommodate flats; regardless though, she was still Emma.

We were nearly out of the apartment door when Emma stopped me and said, "I cannot let you go out like this again."

"What?" I shrieked, panicked that something was wrong with me.

Emma reached forward and took my hair down from the bun. "Now shake out your hair," she instructed.

I flipped my head upside down and shook my hair out and flipped it back again.

"Excellent! You look perfect!" Emma praised. Just for good measure, I ran back to check the mirror. I was pleased with what I found in the mirror and even though we had different styles, I trusted Emma with my looks.

We left the apartment for the walk to Cameron's. Cameron's was a typical bar without the restaurant fair of The Brick and without the dance club vibe of The Opera House. It was directly across the street from The Brick. It was made up of one large room with a big square bar in the middle. There were bar stools around the bar and a few booths along the walls. On the far back wall was a stage area and in front of that was a small area where guests stood and watched the bands.

During our walk there I asked Emma, "How are your feet?"

"I will not be dancing tonight, but they are not too bad. Nothing a few drinks cannot handle," she answered.

"Thanks for coming with me, Emma. I really appreciate this."

"No problem and I am going to stick with you until you give me the sign. You can give me the sign that you want to go home and we will go home, or if you find Gabriel and things go well then you can give me a sign to bugger off as well. Alright?"

76

"Are you sure?" I asked. I did not want it to be like I totally used her. She assured me that this was standard practice with her and Jay and that it was perfectly fine.

We arrived at Cameron's at ten minutes after 11:00 and the place was already packed.

"Do you see anyone you know?" asked Emma.

"No. Do you?" I knew this was hers and Jay's go to bar of choice so I expected the answer to be yes.

"What do you think?" she smirked.

Emma had a fake I.D. and she got a beer at the bar and we went to watch the band while we waited for the group from Port Honor to show up. We inched up close to the stage. Playing that night was a Jimmy Buffett cover band. Despite being considerably younger than Buffett, they sounded a lot like him. Although I had never seen him in concert, when I closed my eyes I could imagine it was him. They were quite good.

We were dancing and singing along with the band and the crowd to "The Southern Cross", actually a Crosby, Stills and Nash song, but Buffett did it better, when someone grabbed me from behind. It startled me and I turned to see who it was. It was Cara and that meant the Port Honor gang had arrived.

I did my best to introduce Emma and Cara through the noise of the singing crowd. We were so near the stage and the source of all of the sound from the band that I had to scream in order for them to even slightly hear me. Both Emma and Cara nodded with acknowledgement that they understood me.

"Stay here! I will bring the guys out here!" Cara screamed then left and returned with Matt and Andy, but no Gabriel. I could see through the crowd just enough to see that Gabriel was sitting at the bar.

"Emma!" I had to scream to get her attention. "Come with me! It's time for you to have another drink." I wanted her to see him so she could tell me once and for all that there was nothing going on and I could just forget all of this nonsense.

Emma and I made our way to the bar and squeezed in down from where Gabriel was seated. Emma was actually closer to him than I was at the bar. Gabriel appeared to be unaccompanied.

"That's him, five down from you in the light blue Polo shirt," I did my best to whisper to Emma.

"Holy shit, Millie, he's hot!" Emma did not whisper when she turned back to me from getting a look at him.

At that point the bartender approached us. "I'll have a Pink Panty Dropper," Emma said and I did not hear the rest as I looked back toward the band, which was now playing "Margaritaville" and the crowd was going wild. What I did not hear was her instructing the bartender to deliver the drink to Gabriel. About the time the drink was delivered, Emma tapped me on my shoulder and as I turned to see what she wanted she ducked down leaving Gabriel looking to me as the one who sent the drink. I looked down at Emma as she just squatted there and smiled up at me. I gave her a little kick with my foot and she yelped like she was truly injured before standing up.

Emma stood up and said, "I'm going back out to hear the band. Good luck!" And, then she slipped off into the crowd.

While Emma was taking her leave, Gabriel was making his way down to where I was. Initially Emma and I had just squeezed in at the bar, but just before Gabriel made it to me a stool next to me came open and I took it.

"Seriously, you ordered me a Pink Panty Dropper, Miss Anderson?" questioned Gabriel as he moved into my personal space so I could hear him. "Now, I love vodka and lemonade as much as the next guy, but is this really what you think of me? Or, were you trying to tell me something about yourself?"

"My roommate ordered the drink," I blushed.

"Roommate? I don't see anyone here, but you, Miss Anderson." The way he kept calling me Miss Anderson was a definite turn on and he looked smokin' hot tonight and he was definitely in my space. It was loud in there and on one hand we had to be close so we could hear one another without screaming, but on the other I was not sure it was necessary for us to be as close as we were. He had slipped in between my stool and the stool of the guy to my right. He was almost standing over me.

Gabriel was wearing a baby blue golf shirt, dark jeans and flip flops. His shirt was the perfect fit to showcase his broad shoulders and pecks. The top button was unbuttoned and no chest hair peeked through. He must have showered after work and before making the drive to Milledgeville. He looked so clean and masculine all at the same time. His hair even appeared to be just a slight bit

78

damp still and the color was darkened ever so slightly by the remaining water. Over all of the smoke and liquor smells that filled the bar, I could smell his cologne and it suited him.

I did my best to stop drooling over him by pointing out my lovely roommate, "See through the crowd to the Greek Goddess staring back at us? That's my roommate, Emma."

"She's tall," commented Gabriel. That's not the usual observation that guys give when they first see Emma, but I was totally fine with it.

"Yes, she is," I laughed.

"So what brings you to Cameron's this evening, Miss Anderson?" Gabriel asked.

I could not very well answer him truthfully. I could not tell him that Cara had called and told me to come out because he was going to be there. I also could never elaborate on why I did what she told me to. Of course I punked-out and told him, "I'm Emma's wing man, I mean wing woman."

"Yet she has bought me a drink in efforts to pawn you off on me?"

"Who's to say she did not buy you the drink in hopes that you would follow her to the stage?" I was doing my best to volley everything he tossed my way, but I missed with that one.

"Oh, was that her intention? Well then, Miss Anderson, please excuse me. There's a Greek Goddess that I must attend to." He then turned from me and started to walk away. He barely made a step before I reached out and gently grabbed his hand. With the touch of his hand the spark was there and that drug of a current ran through me. With that move, I was sure I had crossed the familiarity line again and given myself away.

Gabriel turned back to me immediately with the touch of our hands. He had the look of a cat that ate the canary on his face. All the while maintaining eye contact with me and still holding my hand, he ran his other hand through his hair. His hair appeared thick, but tame. How I longed to find out for myself. While I was thinking about running my hands through his hair, Gabriel appeared to think for just a split second about something as well. He slid his hand down from his hair and he slipped it into the back pocket of his jeans. He pulled out his wallet and taking his hand from mine he tapped the guy on the stool to my right on the shoulder. When the guy turned around Gabriel leaned over to him and said, "Do you think I could buy your seat from you?"

The guy just looked at Gabriel like he was crazy until Gabriel took a twenty dollar bill from his wallet and held it up lengthwise with his index and middle finger in the face of the well- on-his-way-to-being-quite-drunk-college-guy. The guy's facial expression changed to hint at glee. The guy took the twenty, hopped down from the stool and staggered off into the crowd. As obvious as it was that the guy who took the money was a lush, it was equally obvious that Gabriel was smooth, very smooth.

"I cannot believe you just did that," I said as Gabriel put away his wallet and took a seat on his freshly purchased stool beside me.

"What's not to believe? I needed a seat." He again smiled that smile, very Cheshire cat like and oh so sexy.

"I'm sure you could've gotten the seat for less."

"So you think I've been cheated? Should I go and get my money back?"

Before he could act like he was leaving I pointed down the bar, "You might as well stay. I think the money has been spent."

At the far end of the bar was the former owner of the seat. He had acquired another spot at the bar, ordered a pitcher of beer and was drinking straight from the pitcher. Gabriel turned back to me, "I think you are right, Amelia."

"Why do you call me Amelia?" I asked as he turned back to me.

"Why do you call me Gabriel?" he asked in return.

"You know why."

"Would you really like for me to call you Millie?"

I broke eye contact, looked down and shook my head no. He reached over and lifted my head back up gently by my chin. We just smiled at each other for a moment and I could feel the hives rising on my chest. The low cut, white tank top, oh no.

"Amelia, would you like a drink?" Gabriel offered as he lifted a hand to flag down the bartender.

"I'll have a Coke," I replied as Gabriel raised an eyebrow at me.

"Right, underage," he nodded in the affirmative as he spoke.

The bartender arrived and Gabriel ordered a Coke and said, "I will have another... Amelia, what's the name of this drink you bought for me?"

My face turned red and with full embarrassment, I rolled my eyes and just said it. "He'll have another Pink Panty Dropper."

The drinks arrived quickly and Gabriel raised his to toast. "To you, Amelia," he said.

"To you, Gabriel." I returned and we clinked our cups together and drank.

"Would you like to try this?" he offered.

"Okay." He handed me his drink. I lifted up the cup and took a sip. It tasted like pink lemonade, with a burn. I tried not to let on that it nearly took my breath. For whatever reason, I wanted him to think I was brave or adventurous enough to drink it or comfortable enough with him to drink after him.

As I was swallowing, Gabriel said, "So, I heard you had a date tonight. It could not have gone well since you are here with your roommate." Was he fishing?

I was honest with my answer and told him it was not a date. "It was just dinner with some new friends."

"So you won't be going out with Andy's brother again?" Gabriel asked as a smile crept across his face.

"I might have dinner with him again sometime, but I will not be going out with him as you put it." Gabriel seemed pleased, but I could not help, but ask, "How did you know who I was out with?"

"Alvin told me you were going out and Matt mentioned it was with Andy's brother," he answered as if it did not matter. "Why aren't you going out with him again?"

"If you must know, I didn't exactly go out with him. He was really nice, but he's Andy's little brother."

"You think it's inappropriate to date the brother of someone you work with?"

"I did not say that." I certainly did not want to seem the hypocrite, as it suited me fine to date my boss. I mean, talk about inappropriate.

"What are you saying?"

"I suppose I'm saying I don't want Andy knowing my business and the one sure fire way to avoid that is not to date his brother. Anyway, when should we expect your girlfriend to make her next appearance at the club?"

"Girlfriend? What makes you think I have a girlfriend?" he asked as if he had been smacked.

"Come on, you know folks like to talk," I shot back.

"I've not had a girlfriend in quite some time, Amelia," he said in a very stern voice. "I have a woman that I go out with from time to time, but that's of no concern to you."

"What is the name of the woman you go out with from time to time and does she know she's not your girlfriend?"

"What she knows is what she knows and I am not going to tell you what she may or may not know or think because it is not what I know or think," again with the stern voice. Like everything else about him that was hot as well.

Luckily, at that point, a ridiculously drunk girl fell into Gabriel and the conversation about my dinner and his girlfriend was cut off. I was somewhat relieved, except the girl was pretty and all over Gabriel. Literally, she fell face to crotch almost; her face to his crotch. Had that happened to me in either direction I would have been mortified, but it did not happen to me so instead the emotion that overtook me was pissed off that she was touching him.

"Hey, oh, excuse me," she said as she felt almost everything he had while straightening herself up and regaining her footing. Gabriel appeared the perfect gentleman and not put off at all by this girl.

The girl stood there apologizing and coming on to him as if I was not there. She actually stepped in front of me into the tight spot between our stools as if I had not just been talking to him. I realized we were not exactly together, but jeez. I could not stand for this.

"Oh, my God, Becky, is that you?" I tapped her on the shoulder and asked in a voice loud enough for both of them to hear me.

The spot she was standing in was so tight that she had to back up a bit when she turned around to see who was tapping her. When she saw it was me, her look went from not just drunk to drunk and annoyed. I did not care and I was well aware that her name was most likely not Becky, but it got her attention.

Despite her look, I was not scared and I continued, "Oh, I'm so sorry. You looked like Becky. Gabe, you remember Becky? She's the one that could not hold her liquor and smelled of puke. Sorry. You can see how I would be confused," I said to her as she just stood there looking drunk, confused and with a touch of insult added in.

Gabriel gave me this shocked look like he did not know what was about to happen. That was also the only time I had called him Gabe and I am glad he did not call me on it. I only called him that because I did not want the drunk girl saying his name at all let alone the name I called him.

Not so under her breath, not-Becky mumbled, "Bitch!" before she staggered away.

"I can't believe you just did that?" Gabriel gawked.

"Did what?" I acted all innocent. "Got rid of the smelly girl? If that's what you are into, I can go get her back."

I hopped down from my bar stool and hardly made a step before Gabriel grabbed my hand and pulled me back. "Miss Anderson, you are bad."

After all of that banter, the real conversation got started. It was like Gabriel and I were alone in a sea of people. The night rocked on and we talked like I did not even know was possible to talk with a guy that was not Jay. I would have never expected to talk to a guy that I was interested in as if he were one of my best friends. I was so comfortable with him.

"Yes, I am originally from Georgia and for the majority of my life I lived on my grandfather's farm about an hour from here in a town called Avera, and you?" I answered when asked about my Southern accent.

"From all over." Gabriel answered before elaborating. "My parents died when I was young and I sort of got passed from one relative to the next."

"I am so sorry about your parents, but kind of envious that you did not grow up in the same exact spot for your entire life."

"Don't be envious. Being passed from one relative to the next is not the ideal childhood or knowing that you're one extra mouth to feed...Don't look at me like that. I'm fine now," he said to me as he stroked the back of my hand with his thumb. He was still holding my hand from when I threatened to go and get the drunk girl to come back.

I sat silent for a moment before he asked me what happened to my dad. "I told you the other day that my mom's sole ambition was to marry a doctor. Well, my dad had just passed his Boards and was doing an internship at the Medical College of Georgia in Augusta when they met. My mother was a very attractive woman and from what I have been told, she bewitched him immediately and was pregnant with me before they married." I paused for a moment, thinking about what I was saying. "I suppose this is the long version. Sorry."

"It's okay. Go on."

"Well, they got pregnant and then got married; compounding one problem with another. He was not ready to get married and that's all she wanted. Anyway, from what I have been told they fought like cats and dogs. One night after a huge fight and both had had a few drinks, he got in his car and sped off down the road they lived on. The road dead-ended into Highway 1 between Wrens and Augusta. They say he never knew what hit him."

"So, I have two questions: Did that happen before you were born? And, so you would never marry someone or expect someone to marry you because you got pregnant?" Gabriel asked.

"No, to both," I answered.

"Really?"

I could tell he was thinking, but could not tell which question and answer he was hung up on. Most guys would be thrilled to hear that if by the off chance they got a girl pregnant that she would not have that expectation, but a thrilled look was not what was on his face at that moment. He seemed pensive. If he was feeling sorry for me, he shouldn't.

I felt I needed to elaborate. "I did not know him. The accident happened when I was about six months old. Sometimes I am sad about that, but I have had a lot of other good things in my life thanks to him. It was his dad that took me from her and, you know. And, his family, my family, they have been absolutely wonderful to me and I really do not know much else. My aunt Gayle is like a mother to me and she never had any children so we both

84

filled a need for one another. She taught me how to play the piano and tons of other things that I would have missed out on if things had been different. My grandmother died when I was six and my grandfather had almost lost the will to live until he took me in. My mom has the life she wanted and I am fine. It also helps that my father had the good sense to take out one hell of an insurance policy on himself and left me as beneficiary with my grandfather as trustee until I came of age. "

"How old were you when you went to live with your grandfather?" Gabriel seemed genuinely interested.

"I lived with him off and on all along, I suppose. My mom would send me to live with them when she was trying to catch a new man and then when she just about had him she would dust me off the shelf and sit me out for show you might say. She learned her lesson and did not send for me until she got the ring from the last one. I was seven and so excited to be going to live with her, but then...So when I was eight I was back with my grandfather for good. All in all she made it pretty easy for him to get custody of me regardless of what her husband tried."

Gabriel got this stunned look, "So you were eight when that bastard tried to molest you?" He was pissed.

"Right, but let's not dwell on that."

"Your grandfather did not press charges?"

"Oh, he threatened it and everyone knew the accusation was enough to destroy Charles's career."

"Your step-father's name is Charles?"

"Yes, Dr. Charles Cannon. Again, let's talk about something else."

"You're amazing, Amelia, just amazing," said Gabriel as his big blue eyes stared into mine and he took my other hand in his.

"I suppose we are both orphans in our own way, Gabriel, but seriously let's not dwell on that shall we? Let's talk about fun stuff. What would you like to talk about?" I did not want any more sad stories because I definitely did not want to cry in front of him. No one knew, but occasionally I did dwell on the fact that my mother did not want me. I did not ever want to think about that around him. I especially did not want to cry in front of him tonight and have him see me in all the ruined make-up when I had worked hard to look as pretty as I possibly could that night.

"What time is it?" he asked as he glanced down at his watch. "Amelia, it's almost 1:30 a.m. and you have got to be at work at 9:30 a.m. We better get you home."

"Right, boss," I agreed while holding back the disappointment in my voice that the night with him would soon be over.

"Do you have a way home?" he asked.

"Our apartment is right around the corner and I can walk home."

"Your roommate left about twenty minutes ago, remember? I can't let you walk home alone." He was right. I had given Emma the sign quite some time before that it was fine to leave me.

Gabriel stood from his stool and he let go of my hands and pushed his bar stool in before offering a hand back to me to help me down from mine. We never did establish exactly where he was from and although I did not think he was from the south, he did have a southern gentleman like way about him.

I held his hand and stepped down from my bar stool and he pushed it in behind me. The rest of the Port Honor crowd was still on the floor near the stage so I asked Gabriel to wait there while I told Cara I was leaving.

I nearly ran to find her in the crowd and when I did I gave her a huge hug, "I know we are going to be the best of friends and I can't wait to see you tomorrow. You have a way home, right?"

"Yes, I can get home fine. Are you leaving with Gabriel?" she asked.

"Yes and no. He is just walking me home." I responded. "I will see you tomorrow."

I returned to find Gabriel waiting by the door. He looked as good to me then as he had when I first laid eyes on him earlier. Again, the girls I knew who did not think the male form was beautiful had clearly not seen him.

Gabriel held out his hand as I approached and I took it. I wondered could he feel the tingle, the shock or whatever one would call it, that I felt each time we touched. I thought back for a moment about him potentially having a girlfriend as I took his hand. I wondered for just a second if she felt the tingle as well or was this

86

mine? A twinge of insane jealousy ran through me at the thought of someone else feeling any of this but me. I squelched the feeling and just felt grateful to be in the moment with him. He seemed to be mine at that moment and I would settle with that, for now.

When we approached the door Gabriel dropped back enough that I could get in front of him and he could still hold the door for me. He let go of my hand only to place his on the small of my back and guide me through the door.

Outside he stopped and looked at me from head to toe under the bright lights of the street. The street was busy from bar patrons starting to make their way home for the night. Cars passed by every few seconds with the changing of the red light on the corner, but all in all it was a relatively cool, quiet evening out on Hancock Street in front of Cameron's.
"It was so dark in there I have not been able to get a real look at you all night. Turn around and let me get a good look." Gabriel motioned with his hand for me to turn around.

I obliged and turned around slowly.

Gabriel gave me a smack on the behind and laughed as I jumped from the smacking. "Wow!" he said. "If only we could make this the uniform at the club, you would no longer need me directing you on the length of your skirts." He then laughed and took my hand again. We started to walk once more and I am sure I was smiling from ear to ear although the whack on my behind stung. This was definitely the happiest I had been in who knows when. I had nearly been devastated by the death of my grandfather and it had been taking a bit of work to get past it.

We were about a block into the trek to my apartment when Gabriel asked, "Are you cold? You must be in just the tank top." He pulled me close and put his arm around me before I could answer.

We walked the remainder of the distance to the front door of my apartment with his arm around my shoulders. When we arrived, I knew there was no way I was letting him in. I suddenly realized I was ashamed of the place. Seriously, my bedroom was not a real bedroom, but more of a passageway or large hallway between Emma and Jay's rooms. There was no privacy and although I was completely smitten with him, there was no way anything serious was going to happen. It was too soon and I was not that kind of girl. I did realize in that moment that if this were to go anywhere at all with him, I would have to somehow rectify my living conditions.

Once at the door to the house that held my crap-hole apartment, I was full of anticipation. Would he kiss me? He walked me all the way to the door so surely that was a sign.

Most of the way to the apartment we had walked hand in hand. Gabriel dropped back as we approached the door and he had let go of my hand at the steps. There on the stoop I turned, "Goodnight and thanks for walking me home. I had a great time tonight."

I tried to act like I did not care if he kissed me or that our evening was ending, but I am sure all emotion was written on my chest, my neck and my face. I could feel the heat rising off of me. I wanted to kiss him more than anything. The porch light was dim and perhaps he could not see that I was on the verge of coming undone.

I stood there with my back against the door and Gabriel stepped toward me, but he did not come for the kiss. Instead he leaned down a bit and hugged me. I reciprocated. My arms were around his neck and his around me with his hands on the small of my back. The hug started off innocent enough, but turned into quite possibly the most erotic hug in history. Most definitely the most erotic hug in my history.

Gabriel slowly moved one of his hands from around the small of my back and up into my hair. My knees were already starting to go weak when he started to whisper, "I'm not going to kiss you."

My heart did not have time to break over his words as he ran his hand up through the length of my hair and took hold of it near the base of my skull gently pulling my head back. As my head tilted back and my face lifted up toward his, I was not convinced he wasn't going to kiss me. He said it again as he dropped his face and ran his nose gently against my neck, "I'm not going to kiss you tonight because if we start, I won't stop."

I leaned into him and he did not budge except for inching his nose to the far tip of my left shoulder and then across and up my neck to my ear. As he slipped his nose across my skin he whispered, "I would kiss you here and here and here and here."

I panted and my blood rushed to every inch of the surface of my skin. I was becoming wet with the torture; sweet exquisite torture which he continued.

"I'm not going to kiss you tonight, but if I did..." He paused for a moment and the hand that was left alone at the small of my back started to move. He made circles with his fingers in that very spot and continued to whisper, "I would not stop with this spot either."

I could hardly stand and he pulled me closer still. My hands gripped around him and I am sure I was digging my fingers into his back. I could feel every bit of him against me and he continued. The muscles of his chest were firm against me and he was warm. He inched his hand that had been making the circles on the small of my back around my waist to my side and down my hip to one of the rips in my jeans. The rip was just below the crease where the bottom of the left cheek of my behind and my thigh met. He ran his finger across my bare skin through the rip. I had not thought my pants indecent until that moment, but I was well beyond caring that they were. I was actually quite pleased they were indecent in this manner. As he touched my skin, almost instinctively I slowly raised my left leg up his.

He continued to whisper while he touched me, "and here" as he slipped his fingers back and forth over my skin through the rip. "So I am not going to kiss you tonight. Do you understand?"

"Yes," I panted breathlessly. I wanted him and did not care what the apartment looked like anymore. Nothing mattered. I could think of nothing, but kissing him and more.

"If we ever kiss, I will ask your permission first, Amelia." He was still holding me, but he released my hair and moved that hand around the back of my neck. I resisted the urge to grant the permission right then and beg him to kiss me.

I nuzzled my face into his neck and ran a hand up the back of his neck just barely into his hairline. I took a deep breath, breathing him in. Most men or guys or anyone who had just left Cameron's after that length of time would smell like the ashtray of a 1970's Mustang II, but not Gabriel. Before I caught myself I whispered, "You smell like heaven." My lips touched his neck ever so slightly as the words were released.

Gabriel laughed ever so quietly, "You still smell like strawberries."

I was on fire for him and he must surely know it, but he tortured me anyway. Gabriel whispered again, "I'm not going to kiss you tonight and we are not going to talk about this at work. We are not going to talk about this at all. Do you understand?"

I could hardly speak. My heart was beating at a deafening rate. My chest was heaving and he asked again in a more stern voice, "Do you understand?"

"Yes," I whispered back.

"I'm going to release you now," Gabriel said as if warning me to get my bearings so I could stand. He released his hold around me and took my hands. I was light headed, flushed and horribly turned on.

I was half out of my mind with the delirium of the experience and there he was still standing in front of me. Our eyes were locked and his were still so intense and a blue that nearly gave off their own light in the darkness of the porch.

He broke the momentary silence, "Amelia, you know this is wildly inappropriate and that's why we can't do this."

I think my heart did break in that moment. I tried to be brave and nonchalant and said, "All we did was hug."

"We are going to pretend this did not happen," he said with a stern voice.

"If you insist," I responded as I let go of his hands. I was sort of mad that he was ruining everything. I fumbled to get my keys out of my pocket, even though I did not need a key at that point.

"I do insist. Now, goodnight, Amelia, and I will see you at work."

"Goodnight, Gabriel. Thanks for walking me home," I said, before turning to walk inside.

I could feel Gabriel still standing there watching me walk in when all of a sudden he stepped forward and smacked my rear again. I jumped from the impact and yelped. I jerked around to look at him and there he was with a devilish smile. "Don't let me catch you in public with those jeans on again, young lady," he said in a big daddy to little girl voice.

"Goodnight, Gabriel," I said in a stern voice back. I turned to walk inside again, but glanced over my shoulder to catch his eye and see if he was still there. I wanted one last look at him and to make sure he was not going to smack me for the third time that night. As I looked back, we made eye contact and I ran my own fingers across the rip in the jeans. "And, I like my jeans and I might just wear them all the time now." With those words, I quickly jerked around and backed through the door.

My senses were starting to return, but if I were a guy I would have still had the worst case of blue balls imaginable. I am not sure if there was such a term for girls as I had never needed the term before, but if there was a phrase for it, it surely applied to me now. Regardless, this was still the most amazing night of my life.

***

The next morning I woke to the clock radio alarm clock blaring out Melissa Etheridge's "I'm the Only One" at 8:00 a.m. I suppose that would be my anthem for the day. I definitely wanted to be the only one and I had almost drowned in my own desire the night before.

I popped out of bed with a bound, excited at what the day would hold for me at work. What Gabriel said was one thing, but what he did was a complete other. I was anxious to find out if his words or his actions would hold true. Would we not speak of last night? Could that even be possible?

Even though I had showered when I got in, I chose to shower again that morning. I just could not shake the hint of cigarette smoke from the bar. It seemed to be stuck in my hair. When Gabriel said I smelled like strawberries; it was actually my shampoo that he smelled. I wanted him to keep smelling the strawberries and not nasty ashtray hair. The down side of showering again was that I did not have time to roll my hair. I would have to wear it straight again and only had time to blow dry it half way. Thank goodness it was a sunny morning and not too cool so I could dry it with the windows down on the way to Port Honor. I took the T-tops off to aid in the hair drying process.

Matt had told me it would be alright to wear khaki shorts instead of the skirt and he had given me a white polo shirt with the logo on it to wear as my uniform for the beverage cart. I had the uniform on, which included the shortest khaki shorts I owned. My make-up was pristine, hair good enough for now, T-tops securely inside the house and I was just about out the door at 8:40 when the phone rang. I contemplated letting the machine get it, but resisted the urge and ran back.

I picked up the phone and it was Cara. She sounded hung over and wanted to catch a ride. She quickly gave me directions to her apartment. Luckily she did not live far and it was on the way. I pulled up in front of her apartment, another historic house conversion. This one was a giant white house at the corner of North Columbia Street. If you were coming back from Walmart, it was the house at the intersection where you turned to head back toward the college and downtown. You could not miss it.

I blew the horn and out came Cara, dark sunglasses and uniform all disheveled. She jumped in the car and we were on our way. Out North Columbia we went and on toward Eatonton across the Lake Sinclair bridge and past the freaky power plant with the looming smokestack towers. Steam was rising from the waters of the lake, a sign that water from the power plant was being recycled into the lake. I had heard that the water was perfectly safe, but if you swam in it on mornings like this it felt like a hot tub.

I halfway thought Cara was asleep when we came to the caution light about a mile after the bridge and she yelled, "Turn here! It's a shortcut."

I slammed the brakes and we skidded past the turn. Luckily, there was no one behind me and the other bright spot was that Cara was fully awake now.

"Are you going to tell me how last night went or what?" She asked as she reached over to fiddle with the radio.

I just looked at her with a huge smile.

"Well?" she demanded.

"He's our boss..." I replied with anxiety in my voice.

"So," she said as if it was no consequence. "I know he went home with you."

"He walked me home and that was it," I insisted.

"That's it? Who do you think you are kidding?" She seemed pissed that I was not giving her all of the juicy details.

"Honestly, nothing happened. He hugged me when we got to my door and that was it." I promised her.

"If you say so," she finally relented.

"So what about your night?" I asked her.

"It was relatively uneventful until I got home. I was up all night. I swear my apartment is haunted." During the rest of the drive to the Port, Cara told me about the many things that went bump in the night.

Cara had arrived home alone around 2 am and everything was fine until she got in her bed around 2:30. First, she said she thought she heard one of her roommates arrive home, but she knew both of them were supposed to be out of town until late Sunday night. Despite that, she just assumed it was one of them. She called out and no one answered. She convinced herself that it was definitely one of them and that they had just gone on to bed, until she heard the water in the kitchen turn on and she called out again. No one answered.

Cara claimed that was the most scared she had ever been and she just laid there in her bed too terrified to move. She thought about calling the police, but the phone was out in the living room and she would have to go through the kitchen to get to it. The rest of the night she laid there terrified and every thirty minutes the water would come on, then it would go off and whoever or whatever it was would walk back to one of her roommates' bedrooms. As soon as daylight arrived she got up, got the phone and searched the house. Her roommates' beds were still made and had not been slept in. The only thing out of place was a glass that had not been next to the sink in the kitchen before she went to bed.

"Who knew ghosts got thirsty during the night?" I said to try to lighten the mood.

"Thirsty my behind, he was dehydrated!" she laughed. "I may be laughing now, but it is only because I am so tired."

"I would tell you to just sleep the rest of the way there, if I knew the shortcut and did not need you to give me directions."

We were waved through the gate at Port Honor by another guard that morning right at 9:25. I still had five minutes before I officially had to be there. Cara was actually an hour early, but she had not wanted to drive because she feared she would fall asleep at the wheel. I actually left her to nap in the car before her shift.

***

Alvin was already working in the kitchen when I arrived, but there was no sign of Gabriel. I had not expected to see him so early anyway.

"Good morning, Alvin!" I greeted him as I walked past to get to the time clock.

"Good morning. How was your date, not date?" he inquired.

"It wasn't a date and it was fine," I responded.

"Did he pay?" Alvin shot back. "If he paid, it was a date. At least he thought it was a date, if he paid."

93

"Well, crap, Alvin! It's not going to happen again so what does it matter now anyway? It wasn't a date to me and I tried to pay my own way, but he insisted so it's his own stinking fault if he took it to be more than it was. Sorry." I really regretted snapping like that. I think he was just picking on me.

"Millie, I'm just messing with you."

"I know. I'm sorry. What are you making there anyway? It smells sweet and heavenly." I tried to change the subject.

"Gabriel called and asked me to make something with strawberries. He said he had been wanting strawberries for a few days so I am making a strawberry cheesecake for the brunch buffet. What you smell are the cheesecakes baking in the oven."

I am sure the school girl grin came across my face because inside my head I was screaming, "He's thinking about me!" accompanied by squeals of delight. That was a fabulous way to start off the shift; unfortunately, when one starts on that much of a high there is only one way to go from there and that is down.

***

The day was rocking along pretty well on the beverage cart. I had made about three passes around the course and some pretty good tips, until I came across one of the men that had been with Mr. Martin from the day before. I could not remember his name, but he was with another elderly man, not one of the gentlemen from the day before. They were on the third green when I first saw them. I eased up and rolled to a stop by their golf cart as they were finishing up their putts. While they were walking back to their cart I got off of the shake mobile and stood near the coolers at the back. I wanted to be ready to get them a drink if they wanted. This had become my practice so as to make things run more efficiently and get the golfers back to golfing, not waiting on me to get their items. Within about ten feet of me I could already smell them. Even though alcohol was not sold on the course on Sundays, these guys were tanked. I tried to pretend I did not notice.

"Hi! Would you all like something from the cart? A Coke or something?" I said as I turned to open the cooler on the back of the cart.

"Hey, Millie," said the one from the day before as he approached me. He was dressed in green slacks and a white Port Honor logo shirt like the one I had on. I had turned my back and was facing the cooler still when he walked up next to me, patted me on my behind and asked me, "What are you selling today, honey?"

My first thought was I was definitely not selling my backside so I took two steps back only to feel the other man behind me.

"Come on," said the other. "Why make us wait for the back nine?" He grabbed my shoulders and I could smell the liquor on his breath and the heat from it against the back of my neck.

The man from the day before was also stepping closer to me and I was almost sandwiched between them. I was beginning to panic a little, but then I realized I was holding one of the Cokes from the cooler in my right hand. I waited for the one coming at me in front to put his hands on me and I swiftly kneed him in the nuts. As he went down, the other gentleman got a tighter grip of my shoulders, but I swung back with the hand holding the can of Coke and hit him square in the balls as well. I had not noticed in the moment, but I had busted one of my knuckles on impact with his groin. I guess he should be glad as I had intended to hit him with the can, but somehow my hand got in between.

They were rolling around on the ground screaming about having me fired when I sped off in the beverage cart. I went straight to the clubhouse, passing by the golfers on the first and second fairways. I went through the kitchen and straight to the bar where I found Matt. The kitchen door was still slamming back and forth and just as I started to explain to him what had gone on, Gabriel walked in from the dining room and overheard.

"What did you say?" he demanded as he came closer to where I was standing at the end of the bar near the kitchen door. I feared he was mad with me. I was not being loud, but anyone could tell I was irate at what had happened.

"You might want to send someone out to the third green to get two elderly men up from holding their nuts!" I barked back.

"Why?" he asked.

When I started telling him what had happened I lifted my injured hand to push my hair out of my face. He noticed my hand, "What happened to your hand?"

"I will get some ice," Matt noticed as well and he turned and went to the back leaving me and Gabriel at the bar.

"Here hold your hand up before you get blood everywhere." Gabriel took my hand and held it up. I suppose I was operating on adrenaline as it did not hurt and I had hardly noticed that it was bleeding, but there was a trail of blood all down my arm. I guess I drove back with my left hand and had still been holding the Coke can all the way. Who knows what I had done with the Coke at that point.

Matt was back with a bag of ice and Alvin had come up front to see what had happened to me. Everyone was so sweet and concerned about me. I could see Cara coming from the dining room too.

"I'm fine. Someone needs to go see about them," I said as I began to remember their threats and screams as I left them out there.

"Matt, take Alvin and you guys go get them. Do not let them leave, bring them in here to me." Gabriel fumed. He was red faced and livid.

I was not hurt, except my hand and that really was nothing at the moment, but I could feel tears starting to swell in my eyes. Cara could see my face and Gabriel had turned from me and was pacing. Cara grabbed my hand and held the ice on it and tried to hug me from the side at the same time. I struggled to get the question out and choking back the tears I managed, "Gabriel, are you going to fire me?"

"What?!!" Gabriel turned back to me as one tear escaped my right eye and down my cheek it went. With what seemed like one move, he was in front of me and had pulled me to his chest and was holding me. Cara and I were both caught off guard and we fell into him, as Cara tried to keep the ice on my hand while it had gone instinctively around his back. I am sure had anyone been in the bar looking at us they would have thought this was some sort of group hug.

"No, Amelia. I am not going to fire you," Gabriel said gently as he brushed my hair back from my face and wiped the tear from my cheek.

That's when the tears of relief came. Cara had regained her footing and was no longer in the group hug, but now standing behind Gabriel holding the ice to my hand as I held on to him and cried.

"Amelia, I need you to stop crying. It is very important that you stop. Cara, take Amelia to the back and do your best to make her look the way she did when she first arrived this morning. Then the both of you get back up here as quickly as possible. Amelia, it is very important that you look unaffected when you return. Now, go quickly," Gabriel instructed.

Cara grabbed my left hand and pulled me to the back as instructed. Luckily, Cara had brought her make-up case and to the ladies room we went. Within a couple of minutes we had washed my face and began to reapply my make-up. Looking at myself in the mirror I looked almost back to normal, except my eyes. My eyes always gave me away when I cried. Their usual blue-green color turned to a bright, almost turquoise color and there was no hiding it.

"What's the point in this?" I asked Cara as she brushed the powder across my foundation.

"I'm not sure, but I think Gabriel intends for you to confront the bastards when Matt and Alvin get back with them and he does not want them thinking they got the better of you," she responded.

"You know the only reason I started to cry was at the thought of getting fired," I said as she added a little blush.

"I know."

When Cara and I were finished with my face we returned to the bar. Just as we came in from the kitchen Matt and Alvin were bringing the two men in from the course. The two men were still staggering and one was even holding himself.

"That's her!" said the guy in the green slacks.

"Yeah," said the other. "She's the one that attacked us!"

"Attacked you?!" Alvin laughed at the absurdity of the accusation.

The look on Gabriel's face was full rage, but he sounded very controlled when he spoke. "Amelia, are these the two men you left on the course?"

"Yes, sir," I answered.

"Matt, Alvin, did you find these two where Amelia said they would be?" Before Gabriel could finish asking both Matt and Alvin responded in the affirmative.

"So, gentleman, look around. All that you see right now is mine. This clubhouse, mine! These girls, mine! The two guys standing behind you, mine! This is my house!" Gabriel emphasized the word "mine" at each use of it. He was seething. The veins in his head were even popping out a little.

Gabriel was not done. "How dare you come to my house and act like this! You men are in your eighties and you tried to rape a twenty year old girl on a golf course? You likely have granddaughters older than she is. Not to mention she is a fraction of your size. I should call the cops!"

"Wait! Wait!" said the guy that suffered the blow from the Coke can. "Surely we can work something out."

Mr. Green Pants stood silent.

Gabriel continued, "You come in my house. You touch what's mine and you try to make a deal with me? Where was your deal making spirit when you two had the nerve to threaten to fire my employee after she defended herself? Hell, she kicked your asses!" Again with the emphasis on "my" and "mine" and when he paused Gabriel looked at me and gave a raised eyebrow at me and a slight nod of approval for my fight.

"Please" begged the one and Mr. Green Slacks still stood silent.

"Don, Al, I know both of you and I know your wives. As of Tuesday morning your privileges at Port Honor are revoked. Tell your wives whatever you want, make-up something. I don't care, but know this, if you ever show your faces at my club again, I will have this girl and those two boys beat the cold living shit out of you and she will tell your wives why. Also, if I get one sniff of a rumor going around about her, my club or any of this, I will beat the cold living shit out of you myself. Do I make myself clear?"

Don, formerly referred to as Mr. Green Slacks, finally spoke, "I suppose you want us to apologize to the tramp as well?"

Gabriel did not say anything he just nodded his head at Matt who was standing behind the idiot who clearly did not know with whom he was getting smart. Matt almost bear hugged the old man, locking his arms around the man's elbows. Once Matt had him secure, Gabriel said, "Amelia, take your best shot."

"No." Before I could explain my refusal Cara walked past me and slapped the elderly man across the face. You could hear the sting reverberate through the room. She really rung his jaw.

It was so quick, but when she was done Cara stepped back to my side. "Who's to say they would not have done the same if it had been me out there? It could have ended much worse, Millie." she whispered to me.

Matt released the man in the green and the other man hung his head and apologized.

"Get out of my club!" Gabriel demanded.

Don and his near partner in crime exited the bar through the doors that Alvin and Matt had brought them through. Everyone stood still and silent waiting for the two men to drive off on their cart before anything else was said or anyone moved beyond looking to make sure they were out of sight.

Gabriel did not speak, but moved from by my side and walked around behind the bar. He took out a rocks glass and sat it on the bar. He turned and reached up on a shelf of the liquor cabinet and took down the bottle of Jack Daniels. He poured himself a shot and sat the bottle on the bar. He drank the first shot, poured another and drank it as well. He was still red and visibly angry.

Alvin was the first one to break the silence. "Millie, I am not sure what you did to them, but they were still on the ground holding themselves when we found them."

At that point everyone busted out with laughter.

Through his laughter Matt said, "It took us a few minutes to get them to their feet and on to the carts."

"That's awesome!" said Cara. "I've got to get back to the brunch folks before they come looking for me, but way to go, Millie!"

In the midst of all the drama, everyone forgot about the people in the dining room that were there for the brunch buffet. Luckily, there weren't very many still left at that time.

"I know as a guy I'm not supposed to laugh at other guys getting popped in the nads, but seeing two obese old men rolling around holding their balls and knowing she did it to them...that's just priceless," Matt continued.

Alvin added, "I agree. Millie, you are all of what, five foot four and a buck-ten soaking wet? I suppose we are all kind of giants compared to you, but you really kicked their asses!"

Alvin and Matt kept laughing and I was even starting to laugh a little with them when Gabriel put the kibosh on everything, "You all realize she could have been raped out there?!! And look at her hand! You probably need to have that seen about!" He was not happy and we all stopped laughing.

"I'm fine," I insisted even though my hand was starting to swell a little despite the ice.

Matt moved behind the bar while saying, "I will get more ice for that," meaning my hand.

Alvin went back to the kitchen leaving Gabriel and I alone in the bar. "I need to get back out on the course," I said as the kitchen door was still swinging from Alvin's exit and I started to follow him.

"No, Matt will go out on the course for the rest of the afternoon," Gabriel barked.

"But..." I started and he cut me off.

"No, buts, Miss Anderson! You can't manage the cart with that hand." Matt returned with the ice just as Gabriel was assigning him to the beverage cart.

Matt agreed with Gabriel, "Yeah, Millie, you can't handle that POS with your hand like that, plus we need to make sure those guys are off the property before sending you back out."

"Exactly! Now that settles it. Amelia, you will stay in here and help out at the bar and the rest of brunch." Gabriel went on.

I planned to do as Gabriel was asking and handed over the cart money to Matt. Matt then left through the kitchen door nearly swinging it off of its hinges again. Gabriel and I both moved to quiet the door at the same time.

"Come with me. No one will miss us for just a minute." I did as he asked and followed him. He led me through the glass door at the far end of the bar opposite the dining room.

This was my first time going through that door and into that area of the clubhouse. It was a dimly lit area and I don't think I had seen anyone use the door in the time I had been there, but here we were using it.

Just beyond the door were two sets of stairs. One set was only a few steps down and it was straight in front of the door. As we turned away from those, Gabriel said they led to the pro-shop.

Gabriel proceeded up the second set of stairs and I continued to follow. This was a much larger staircase and obviously led to the top floor of the clubhouse, but on the far end of the building from where the loft was.

There was a landing and a turn back about half way up the stairs. At the landing Gabriel reached back and took my uninjured hand. We continued up the second half of the stairs and through a long hallway. In the hallway there were doors marked, "men's locker room", "ladies' locker room" and others marked for various offices.

Gabriel knocked on the door of the ladies' locker room. When no one answered, he pushed the door open and called out just to make sure no one was in there. Then, he pulled me inside. It was a beautiful room, not at all like the locker room assigned to the girls' basketball team I was on in high school. It was like the bathroom at the Radisson Hotel on Riverwalk in Augusta where one of my friends from high school had had her sweet sixteen party.

First of all, the room we entered was like a foyer for the actual locker room. The room smelled of fresh roses and there was a large arrangement of them on a table in the middle of the foyer.

The foyer led into a bigger room with actual lockers on one wall. These lockers were not your standard issue. They were actually made of ornate dark mahogany woodworked cabinets. On the wall parallel to the lockers was a countertop of tan and black granite that ran the length of the wall. There were three sinks flush mounted within the countertop and antique bronze faucet fixtures. There was about three feet of blank countertop space between each sink. Above the countertop and sinks was a mirror spanning the entire countertop. Everything about the room seemed to have been recently updated.

Gabriel led me over to one of the sinks. "Hop up here," he said as he pointed next to the sink. "Let's have a look at your hand."

I hopped up on the counter and held out my hand. Matt had tied the bag of ice to it with a white bar towel. Gabriel gently untied the towel and took the bag of ice off and sat it in the sink.

He held my hand and looked at it. "I'm going to run it under the water to get the rest of the blood off and get a better look."

"Sure." I did not care what he did with it as long as he was holding it.

"Good grief, Amelia." The stern voice returned and he looked as if he were becoming angry again. "What happened out there? What did they do to you? I can nearly see the bone at your knuckle here. This is probably broken." He said as he ran his index finger across the cut and the now swollen portion of the knuckle leading from my hand into my middle finger.

"It's not broken and I assure you this is not from what they did to me, but what I did to them." I kind of laughed at the thought of what I had done.

"I'm glad you find this funny because it scared the hell out of me! Do you know what could have happened?!!" He was pissed and could hardly look me in the face.

I reached out to him with both hands, the good and the bad, and grabbed fists full of his shirt. I took hold and pulled him toward me.

"I do know what could have happened, but it didn't," I whispered to him as I slipped my legs apart so I could pull him closer to where I was sitting on the counter. I scooted to the edge of the counter and letting go of his shirt I put my arms around his neck. This time it was me that hugged him and me that did the whispering. "I'm fine and in no time I will be playing the piano for you again."

Gabriel had almost resisted the hug, but quickly relented. His arms were around me and he pulled me even closer than we already were. There it was, my fix for the day. It was so tempting to lock my legs around him, but I refrained. I did press my luck and tell him, "You still smell like heaven."

"Amelia, I would have killed them," Gabriel said as he continued to hold me and I could feel him tense with the words.

I leaned back and looked him in the eyes, "I may be icing my hand, but they are likely icing something else so they probably wish you had just killed them. Don't worry about me." I laughed and this time he laughed with me.

"How did this happen to your hand?"

I explained to him about the Coke can, "Have you ever heard of putting a roll of quarters in your hand if you were going to a fight? Well, I did not have a roll of quarters, but I did have a full can of Coke in my hand when the second one put his hands on me."

"You punched an eighty year old man in the groin with a full can of Coke?"

"Sort of. When I swung it was in a blind rage so I did not connect the Coke can to him. My hand got sandwiched in between; thus, the busted knuckle."

"If there was enough force behind the can to do this to you, I can only imagine what it did to him. No wonder he was still limping when they brought him in the clubhouse."

"Yeah, I suppose the other one made out well since I only kneed him." I smiled at him and hopped down from the counter. "We gotta get back downstairs before you are missed. Plus, I've been wanting strawberry cheesecake all day. Come on."

"Just in case, I am going to ask that you go out first and go down the front stairs. I will go down the back." We were almost to the door when Gabriel grabbed my left hand, stopping me. "Amelia, I told you I would ask permission first."

I turned around in shock. Was this the big moment? In the ladies locker room?

CHAPTER 5

"No, of course he didn't!" I answered Jay with audible disappointment in my voice. "He took my hand and kissed my flippin' knuckle! Then he told me that I probably needed to go to the emergency room and have it looked at, if the swelling did not go down soon. The usual knee weakening, lightning strikes within me were there, but that's it."

The rest of the day at work had been uneventful, but the drive home was challenging. Not only did I have to drive with my left hand; I so desperately wanted to air my frustrations about Gabriel with Cara. I knew I could not do that, as such new friends, we just were not there yet. It did not matter whether I wanted to tell her or not anyway since she slept all the way back to her apartment.

Although I had not been up all night frightened of one of Milledgeville's many ghosts, I was exhausted all the same. My exhaustion stemmed from the events of the day. I could barely put one foot in front of the other to make it up the stairs to our apartment around 5 p.m.. Despite my exhaustion and frustrations over Gabriel, I was glad to see Jay was home when I opened the door to the apartment.

"What happened to you?" Jay screamed as he saw my right hand and my shoes in my left. He was already in his pajamas and appeared as if he had been that way all day long.

I had taken my shoes off in the car and walked up barefoot. At the door I had struggled to turn the knob with my right hand while I held my shoes. It seemed as though Gabriel might have been right, perhaps something was broken.

"I may have broken a bone in my hand, but I definitely busted a knuckle. I think you would have been proud of me." I sat my shoes down and asked, "Do you mind terribly if I change clothes before I give you the play by play of my weekend?"

I left Jay heading toward the living room while I turned and went in the other direction toward my room all the while stripping off my logo shirt and my shorts. I quickly returned to the living room wearing one of my old Young Harris t-shirts and a pair of Umbros. I was now comfortable in my clothes and had my hair pulled up in a bun on my head. Then, I headed to pour my cares out to Jay.

I started giving him the play by play of Saturday as I went to the refrigerator and pulled out the to-go box still filled with the prime rib.

"I know everything is inappropriate. He is my boss," I told Jay as I opened the microwave and put the prime rib inside. "I don't care and sometimes he seems like he does not care and then he pulls back. I feel like I am some sort of yo-yo for him. I cannot figure out whether he is toying with me or genuinely interested or what."

I shared the plate of food with Jay and told him about the hug on the front porch at the end of which, Jay asked, "I know there's no point in asking why you didn't just kiss him. I know you."

"I came close to doing just that, but I resisted. I knew Gabriel was right, if we started then it would not have stopped," I sighed at the thought.

I looked around the room: the sad painted-over wood paneling for walls, the black light still in the kitchen pantry where the last tenants were growing weed, and the three roaches that were lurking under the television stand waiting on us to drop a morsel of food. I also thought about the space Jay and Emma cut out for me to use as a bedroom and how it had been their study lounge where their desk was before I came to live with them. As Jay and I were curled up there on the couch sharing the food and the worries over my lack of love life, I seized the time to mention to him, "Jay, either we all have to move or I have to move."

I opened up the box with the slice of strawberry cheesecake that Alvin had sent home with me and offered Jay the first bite. Jay and I alternated bites of cheesecake as we talked.

"What? Where's this coming from?" he shrieked.

"No, no. Think about it. We both know I am not the type of girl that would have let him in last night, but what if I wanted to bring him in someday? You know I cannot have him see my room. For goodness sake, it's not a real bedroom. I appreciate you taking me in and all, but..."

"I see. What do you have in mind?" Jay asked as he shoveled in another bite of the cheesecake.

I slid the box toward me so I could cut off my bite as I said, "I think we should start looking for another apartment."

"I can barely afford this place and Emma is in about the same situation as I am," said Jay.

"Rent here is three hundred dollars per month, and we are splitting it three ways. I just made almost three hundred dollars at the club in the last few days. If you all agree to move with me and we keep the rent to five hundred a month or under, I could pay the entire thing if you and Emma could pay the utilities. I could do this with all of the money I make at Port Honor and still not have to touch any of the other money."

"You do not have to do that for us." Jay was a bit shocked by my suggestion.

"I know I don't have to just like you did not have to take me in," I reminded him.

"Do you ever miss going to Young Harris?" Jay asked.

"I try not to think about it. Of course I miss some of my friends and I loved the landscape up there. The mountains are beautiful this time of year, but I am glad I am here with you. It's definitely been an adventure so far." I hoped I had not hurt his feelings by mentioning the need to move. So far I liked it there, but I could not go on living like this.

Jay just listened as I continued, "Naturally, I wish I had transferred here under different circumstances. It was my decision to move home to help Aunt Gayle with Granddaddy. It's just that none of us expected him to go so quickly and commuting back and forth from home every day last year was dreadful, but I would do it again. Aunt Gayle knew someone who, fortunately, knew someone and was able to get me in then. She was pretty hell bent that I was not quitting school altogether. You know how she can be."

Jay immediately described her, "Single-minded, like someone else we know."

"Yes and speaking of single minded, let's start looking for a new place," I said as I finished off the last bite of cheesecake.

"If you insist, but we have to find something within walking distance from the school because Emma does not have a car." Jay was beginning to have a little light in his eyes over the possibility of us moving.

"Of course," I agreed with him, plus I did not want to be bothered with driving to class and having to find parking. "We will have to tell Emma about the plan when she gets in from tennis practice and start asking around and looking tomorrow. Right now I am going to get a shower and then start reading some of my chapters for the week."

Classes began for me bright and early at 8:00 a.m. on Monday mornings. This Monday was no exception. My hand still hurt from the day before, but I took some Ibuprofen and shrugged it off. Jay had helped me wrap it the night before and we were a little skeptical that it was broken, but I was too stubborn to go to the emergency room.

I had Astronomy first thing that morning, followed by Art History 201 at 9:00 a.m. and World History 410 at 11:15 a.m.. I had these same classes on Wednesdays and Fridays as well. On Tuesdays and Thursdays, I had Principles of Drawing III at 10:00 a.m. and badminton at 1:00 p.m.   Badminton was my favorite class and it was going to be challenging this week due to my hand.

When I arrived home around 12:45 p.m., I found a note from Jay. The note read:

"Meet me at 3:00 p.m. at the corner of North Jefferson and Montgomery Street. Walk up to Hancock Street and turn toward Cameron's. Continue to North Jefferson and make a left, keep walking until you come to the red brick building with the double decker front porches. I will see you out in front at 3:00 p.m. Love, Jay."

I did not have anything else to do other than study and no way to contact Jay, so I left on foot at 2:40 p.m. to meet him as instructed by 3:00 p.m. I crossed over Hancock Street and proceeded past Cameron's and in doing so I could not help but reflect on Saturday night. My heart fluttered at the thought when I passed by the door and remembered Gabriel holding it open for me as we left. I even turned around and walked backward for a moment as I spied the spot on the sidewalk where he had me turn around so he could get a better look at me under the street lights. He may not have kissed me and it may not have been anything more than flirting, but I would not trade my memories of that night for anything in the world.

It did not take me quite the entire twenty minutes to make the walk so I arrived at the two story brick apartment building before 3:00 p.m. Jay was not there yet, but this had to be the building; red brick and one porch on top of another. The building was comprised mostly of red brick and appeared to be divided into four sections based on the design of the two separate sets of double decker porches across the front. There was a downstairs porch and an upstairs porch on the left side and a mirror image on the right, four porches in all across the front. The porches were supported by red brick columns, but were mostly made of white painted wood trim and railings.

I took a seat on the steps of the stoop between the two sets of porches and waited until I saw Jay. Beyond thinking that the building appeared empty and perhaps Jay had found us a new place already, I had not given the place much thought.

"Hey!" Jay greeted me. "I see you must have found my note."

"Yeah. Do you think you have found us a new apartment already?" I asked.

"Maybe more than that," Jay was being a little cryptic.

"What do you mean?"

"I want you to keep an open mind. The owner will be here any minute. Come on let's walk around the building and get a better look at it." Jay took me by the hand and we walked to the right of the front porch and down a small driveway leading along the side of the house.

"The windows look in good condition and there are the air conditioning units. They look relatively new," Jay pointed out.

"I suppose," I agreed as I glanced over at the units. I also noticed the driveway, which was not a solid slab like most driveways, but it was two strips of concrete pavement just big enough for tire tracks. The building was fairly deep and the driveway passed along the entire length and made a turn at the corner and proceeded to the back of the building. We followed the tracks of the driveway.

At the back of the building we found a detached carport big enough for four cars. It was more like a shed than anything else. No garage doors were on it, just an opening to drive the cars in.

"One of those spots could be yours for the Vette." I smiled at the thought and Jay added, "In fact, they could all be yours, if you want."

"Why would I get all four spaces?" I inquired as a mid-1980's model, red Ford F-150 truck pulled around the back of the building. The brakes squealed and it rolled to a stop near us.

Jay took a tighter hold of my hand and he turned and looked me in the eye, "This is the owner and, again, I want you to remember to keep an open mind. Also, let me do all of the talking and play along."

"Okay." I agreed. Although I did not know what Jay was up to, I trusted him. He was probably only trying to get us cheap rent.

The older gentleman slowly slid out of his truck. Jay squared his shoulders, his gesture for when he was about to play it straight. He really did not need to do that though because most folks would not notice that he was gay unless they saw him dance. Regardless, as Jay approached the truck, he stood a little taller and readied himself for playing a part.

The gentleman was wearing overalls and a John Deer cap. He appeared to be in his late sixties or early seventies, with white hair and a bit on the portly side. He approached Jay and they shook hands.

Jay turned and introduced me, "This is Millie. I appreciate you agreeing to meet us today and show us the building."

It struck me odd that Jay said the building and not the apartment, but there was no time to dwell on that as he continued with the introduction. "Millie, this is Mr. Braswell. Mr. Braswell's friends with Uncle Lloyd from the Masonic Lodge."

"Well, would you kids like to go around through the front of the building or do you want to go through the back or would you like to start here in the yard?" Mr. Braswell offered as he took his keys from his pocket. His key ring made me think of my grandfather, who once won a door prize at a church function for having the key ring with the most keys on it. Mr. Braswell would likely have given my grandfather a run for the prize with the number of keys on his key ring.

"If you wouldn't mind, we'd like to start at the front door," Jay answered as he reached back and took my left hand to pull me along with them, still being careful not to touch my right and risk a reminder of the injury from the day before. Mr. Braswell started around the side of the house by way of the driveway taking the same path we had when we arrived.

"Do y'all like pecans? If so, and you aren't afraid of a little work, those trees produce about six Piggly Wiggly grocery sacks full of pecans each year. That's enough to make more pies than you could eat in ten years." Mr. Braswell pointed to the trees that ran along what was likely the property line next to the driveway.

"How old are the air conditioning units?" Jay questioned as we passed by them.

"About three years old now. There's seven years left on the warranty. I have the paperwork." The conversations seemed odd, but it still did not occur to me what was actually going on. My mind was wandering and thinking about pecan pies.

We continued to follow him as we made the turn to the front of the building, around the porch on the right side and onto the stoop we went. There was barely a step up onto the stoop and everything about it was overshadowed by the porches on either side. There was no way to access the porches from the stoop as it was blocked by the railings which encased them.

The front door on the stoop was oak and appeared to be old and solid. It was divided in two parts with the top half being made of stained glass and the bottom of solid wood. There were two locks on the door, one in the door knob and the other a dead bold that was much higher up.

Once Mr. Braswell had unlocked the doors we went inside to a little foyer area that held three other doors. There was a door to each side of the front door and then a door straight ahead.

"We will start with this one," Mr. Braswell said as he chose another key from his massive key ring and opened up the door that was to the right.

We all went inside what appeared to be the living room area of an empty apartment. Mr. Braswell began the tour. "This here's a two bedroom unit and it mirrors the one on the left side of the building. Everything you see here you would find on the other side. Of course, this is the living room."

Within the living room there was a door made of twelve white trimmed window panes and it led to the front porch. There was also a pair of windows next to the door on the front wall. The wall parallel to the driveway was without windows and blank.

Mr. Braswell had waited just a minute in the living room before moving toward the back. "You can see through to the kitchen from in here." He headed down the hall toward the kitchen as he spoke. "All of the appliances are the same brand and about five years old in this unit. Across the hall the appliances are all about two years old."

"And the appliances come with it, right?" Jay asked as I looked around at everything. The cabinets in the kitchen were stained oak like the front door and all of the walls had been freshly painted white. There were hardwood floors in both the living room and the kitchen and although they were worn, they had been freshly varnished and were not in bad shape. The floors were of a honey pine color and were quite pretty.

"Right." Mr. Braswell answered Jay.

The tour continued with Mr. Braswell, "You'll notice the kitchen is big enough to be considered an eat-in so there's no separate dining area." He then turned to the two doors across from the kitchen area. He opened the first door and explained, "This is the laundry closet. It'll hold those new stackable types, but not the old side by side sets. The washer-dryer that was in this unit died recently, but the other two units still have the washer and dryer." Both Jay and I stuck our heads in to get a look once Mr. Braswell stepped back to open the next door which was just a few feet farther down the hall barely beyond the kitchen.

"This is the bathroom. There's only one in this unit. Pretty basic." Mr. Braswell had explained after he opened the door. Again, Jay and I stuck our heads in to have a look. It was a good size bathroom with the same stained cabinets that were in the kitchen. It had a sink with a fair amount of countertop space, but nothing extraordinary, a toilet and a tub-shower combo with shower doors. The floor was predominately white tile with a piece of black tile stuck in every now and then just barely breaking the monotony of the white. The bathroom smelled of fresh cleaning products, in fact the entire place smelled strongly of Windex and Pine-sol with just a hint of Lemon Pledge.

Across from the bathroom was another door. It led to the first of the bedrooms. It was a good size bedroom. The hardwood floors had continued from the kitchen down the hall and into the bedroom as well. You could tell in the floor where someone had scratched it with what looked like the legs of a bed, but despite that they were again in pretty good condition. Mr. Braswell had gone over and opened the closet door for us to have a look. Jay went over and took a peep at it, but I just waited by the door to the room.

"Nice size closet," Jay commented.

"Yeah, all of the closets are roughly the same size throughout the building," Mr. Braswell added as he started out of the room.

The door at the end of the hall was open and we followed Mr. Braswell inside to the second bedroom. "You probably don't notice, but this bedroom is just slightly bigger than the last. It is so slight that I cannot imagine one preferring it over the other based on size alone."

This room had two windows along the back wall of the building, but no windows on the wall parallel to the driveway. It also had hardwood floors, the same size closet.

"I'll let y'all have a look at the other unit before you leave, but let's go upstairs next," Mr. Braswell said as he led us back through the apartment to the front door.

"What do you think?" Jay whispered to me as we followed back to the front door.

"I'm not sure why we are looking at two bedrooms, is Emma not moving with us?"

"Despite that, what did you think of the apartment? Did you see anything wrong with it, damage or anything?"

"No. It's fine. Way nicer than where we live now." I answered him, but it was hard to consider living there without knowing what was to become of Emma. We were not the absolute best of friends, but I did not want to put her out.

Back in the foyer area, Mr. Braswell took his keys out again and unlocked the door that was straight across from the front door of the building. Upon opening the door there was another landing and a large set of varnished stairs leading to the second floor.

"It takes me a minute to get up these, so you two go on up and I'll be there in just a minute," Mr. Braswell said as he appeared to gather his nerve to attempt to climb the stairs.

"If you don't mind us being up there alone, we'll just look around and come back with any questions," Jay asked as he patted the old fella on the back.

"Thank you, son, and I don't mind at all. In fact, I will unlock the door to the other apartment and then I'll just have a seat on the front steps and wait for y'all." Mr. Braswell stepped back from the stairs and let Jay and I pass.

"Thanks so much and we will be right back," Jay said as we started up the stairs.

"Take your time. I'm in no hurry." Mr. Braswell replied.

Jay then picked up speed climbing the stairs as he pulled me by the hand with him. He was excited. "Millie, you're going to like what you see up here," he said as we nearly ran up the stairs.

Apparently Jay had been here before because he led the tour. At the top of the stairs we entered a large open room, kind of like a great room. "This is the living room, over there's the galley kitchen, and back there the dining room," he said as he pointed in each direction.

The living room was in the center of the apartment and it was huge. The kitchen was to the right side of the building and had a bar that opened to the living room. It appeared to have space for about four bar stools. Behind the kitchen along the back of the house was where Jay had pointed for the dining room area. There were two double windows in that area and a door tucked to the side and hidden by the back wall of the living room area.

The entire place smelled of fresh paint and Pine-sol. It was all clean to the point of appearing new, but I knew this was not possible especially since I had noticed the finger paint type numbers in the concrete of the porch indicating 1933 as when the concrete had been laid for the porch. The building was forty years older than I was.

Jay went over and tried to open the door, but it was locked. "This is the back door and there's another staircase in here. You might have noticed a stoop and back door when we were outside before. This is where that stoop and door lead."

"Ok," I responded.

Jay came back into the living room area; there were four open doors leading to rooms off of the living room. Jay approached the first door to the back of the living room. "Come on, Millie," he instructed as he went in.

"This would be mine or Emma's room." This was a bedroom on the back side of the house. It had a set of double windows along the back wall like those in the dining room. He went across the room and pointed, "This is where I would put my bed, if it were my room. I don't mind drawing straws with her."

Then as quickly as we had entered, Jay left the room and went back into the living room and on to the next door. "This is the bathroom. There are two bathrooms in this unit and this one alone is bigger than the one all three of us share right now."

113

Jay was right, the bathroom was big compared to our current bathroom and all of the cabinetry matched in this apartment as it did in the downstairs apartment. There was also another tub-shower combo with shower doors and the same white and black tile on the floor and even more counter space.

I could hardly take it all in before Jay moved on to the next room. This time he went clear across the living room to the room on the front right side of the house. "This is the room Emma and I would have to draw straws over."

It was a big bedroom and appeared to be about the same size as the living room in the apartment below. Instead of the sets of double windows that the living room below had, it had two sets of French doors leading to the upstairs porch on that side. It also had an extra closet or pass through that led to the bedroom on the left side of the building. I stuck my head in that area, but Jay pulled my arm, "No, no," he said. "You have to see it from the main entrance to the room."

We then left that room and went back into the living room, around the stairs and into the only door we had not been through. The door led into a third bedroom. This bedroom was almost identical to the one that we had just been in. The only difference between the rooms was that this one had its own bathroom and the bathroom was roughly the same size as the one shared by the occupants of the other two bedrooms.

"This would be your room, Millie." Jay twirled around the room, "Picture your bed here. Not the bed you have right now, but the one we will go shopping for." He stood against the far left wall of the room and spread out his arms to indicate the space the bed would take up. "A queen size bed, right here, Millie! Can you picture it?"

I could feel the smile sprout across my face. "Yes, I can picture it, but why a queen size?"

"Because you can't have Gabriel in a twin or day bed or really anything less than a queen. And, because I say so." He had me at Gabriel.

"Jay, what's the catch? How much does he want to rent this place to us and why is the entire building empty?"

"Do you love it, Millie? Look at the French doors and think about studying in a swing out there on that porch. That's what I think about."

114

"Again, what's the catch?" I asked.

Jay walked back into the living room. "We could put the couch here and a TV over there, if you buy the place." He tried to just slide that in on me.

"What?!!"

"Millie, you have the money. He has not listed it with a realtor yet and he only wants fifty grand for it." Jay took out a folded up sheet of paper from his back pocket and handed it to me. "The only reason the units aren't rented right now is because he wants to sell it and he is only selling it because he is officially retiring and moving to live with his daughter in Florida. Look, I have done the math."

As I unfolded the paper and started looking over it, Jay went on explaining how I could afford this and how it would make money for me. "I have spelled it all out on the paper. You pay cash for it and you may be able to get it for less. You can rent out the two downstairs units for three hundred each and then Emma and I would give you what we are paying now so you would have eight hundred per month coming in. In our unit we would divide the utilities by three like we are already doing. If you pay cash for the place and pay yourself back five hundred per month from rental then you have also made the money to pay taxes and insurance on it plus your part of the rent and utilities. Also, when you graduate, you can sell the building for more than what you are paying or you can keep it and continue to rent it out."

"I could go on explaining to you how you are getting a deal and persuading you to do this, because you can do this and do it with little or no effort. Plus, you have Emma and me to help you. Your grandfather always invested for you, but he's not here anymore so you have to do it. You always saved well, now it is time to spend well, Millie." While he had given me the verbal play by play, I read over his notes. Of course this was all logical. Jay was majoring in finance and minoring in English so the numbers and the wording all worked out on paper. It was all very impressive and he had really taken the time to work it all out on paper to prove that it could be done and how.

Jay was one of the smartest people I knew and I conceded that, "Jay, I understand what you're saying and you're right. I do have to have a place to live, but this is a big step. It's especially a big step considering all of this came about on the off chance that I might want to bring a guy home. I can't just buy an apartment building in hopes that one day..."

He cut me off, "First of all, you need to stop doubting everything. You will bring him home at some point and I wouldn't have taken you down this road if I thought this was just about some guy. Millie, if I had the money you have, I would do this without hesitation."

"What if I loan you the money to do this?" I quipped.

"No, that's not the point." Jay snapped. "And I am being serious about all of this. Do you even like the place?"

"I love it!" I said with a hint of excitement. "I can picture us living here and being happy and not ashamed."

"Then what is the hold up?" I did not know the answer and I shrugged my shoulders in response to Jay.

"Millie, trust me. I want you to give him $500 earnest money. We will have to go back to the apartment to get your checkbook, I know. You are going to give him the money under the condition that the building passes an inspection. I'll call Uncle Lloyd and have him get someone out to do the inspection. The other condition is that we'll get the building appraised. If it appraises for seventy-five thousand or more and passes the inspection, then you will buy the place. If either of these things don't happen, then you will place a stop payment on the earnest money check and I will give you the stop payment fee that the bank will charge you."

"You are twisting my arm, but I think that sounds fair. You really think it will appraise that high?" I asked as I was completely clueless about these things.

"If it does not appraise near one hundred grand, I'll mow the yard for a year." Jay was confident. "Let's go back downstairs and glance at the other unit. I also have a couple more questions for Mr. Braswell, but they're nothing an inspector couldn't answer."

"Wait," I said as I ran back to the room that would be mine, "I just want to get another look at my room."

"That's the ticket, Millie. It's about time you got excited about something and got back to being yourself." Jay said as he clapped with excitement.

"I think if I do buy this place then you get to pick which room you want since you found it," I yelled back to him as I went into my bathroom for another look.

"Then I pick the front room!" I could hear him scream back as he ran into that room.

I loved the French doors to the upstairs porch. I loved the size of the room and that it was an actual room. I loved the size of the entire apartment. I loved the thought of shopping for new furniture and bedding. I was suddenly overwhelmed with the possibilities. I was starting to allow myself to hope and get past being scared about the money. All in all, fifty grand was really just a drop in the bucket for me and for a faint second I thought about my grandfather and how he would be proud if this worked out for me.

"Alright, let's go wheel and deal," I said to Jay as we both met back at the door to the stairs.

"Remember, when we get back downstairs, let me do the talking, good ol' boy system, you know," Jay insisted. He seemed to know more about this sort of thing than I did so I agreed that I would stay quiet again.

When back downstairs, we took a quick peek at the apartment on the left. It was in good condition and an exact copy of the one we had first seen on the right side of the building. The apartment on the left had also been freshly painted and smelled to high heaven of the same cleaning products as the others. Everything appeared in order and well maintained throughout the entire building and this unit was no different.

We found Mr. Braswell sitting on the steps outside as he said we would. Jay asked several questions about the building: age of the roof, age of the hot water tanks, made sure there were individual tanks for each unit, the last time the trim was painted, the age of the windows and things of that nature. Lastly, Jay said, "It's my understanding that you want fifty thousand for it. Is that your bottom line?"

Mr. Braswell took off his cap and ran his fingers through his thinning white hair, "I would take forty-seven if it was in cash and we closed within two weeks."

"We can do forty-five cash, but we need a building inspection and an appraisal and a termite inspection. If we can get all those accomplished and if they come back clean, then I don't see why we can't get it done in two weeks." Jay sure sounded like he knew what he was doing.

"You'll also want a title search," Mr. Braswell added. "I can call the attorney that I know in town and line that up and we'll need him to draw up a deed as well."

"Right," Jay continued to try to act like he had done this before. "I suppose you will need earnest money. We are prepared to give you five hundred dollars earnest money based on the conditions of the building passing inspection, the termite inspection and appraising for the amount that you are asking."

"I would like a thousand in earnest money, but I know your people so I guess five hundred will do." Mr. Braswell then stuck out his hand to shake Jay's. I just stood there as they spent my money and it occurred to me that this would be the last time that happened. If it were my money being spent, then from now on folks would deal with me and I would have some say, but for now Jay was doing a fine job. I kept quiet and kept my thoughts to myself.

Little other discussion was had. Then Jay persuaded Mr. Braswell to give us a ride back to our apartment so we could give him the earnest money check.

***

I found out later on that night that Jay had overheard his Uncle Lloyd talking with one of his other Mason friends on the phone while he was out there on Saturday night. He heard the details of the building and that it was about to be for sale. Jay understood from what Uncle Lloyd was saying that the seller was asking way under what the building was worth so Uncle Lloyd's friend was going to snatch it up as soon as he could secure funds. Jay knew the building as he had been to a party there his freshman year and loved the apartment on the second floor. Once I said something about moving, Jay seized the opportunity and got the information on the owner from his Aunt June and essentially swiped the building from one of his Uncle Lloyd's friends. As it turned out Jay was a sneaky wheeler and dealer.

***

It was around 9:00 p.m. when the phone rang and Jay answered it in the living room. "Amelia," Jay called in a mocking tone without covering the phone and not calling me Millie as he usually did.

I was in my room reading my history text so I picked up on the cordless in there, "Hello?" I answered.

"How's your hand? Beat up on any eighty year olds today, Miss Anderson?" I recognized the voice without him having to identify himself. I got chill bumps all the way down both of my legs at him calling me Miss Anderson.

"My hand is fine. Thank you for asking," I replied as my insides were jumping.

Jay entered the room and signaled a reminder that I had no privacy here and affirmed my decision to hand over the earnest money to Mr. Braswell that afternoon. As Jay flopped down on the bed, I got up and took my call to the bathroom, but Emma was in there.

"Am I interrupting you?" Gabriel asked as I believed he heard me moving.

"No, I am just going out on the porch so I may hear myself think and talk to you," I said as I walked down the stairs and out the front door.

"Really, onto the porch? Do you like the porch, Miss Anderson?"

"Do you like the porch, Mr. Hewitt?" I returned the question.

"I liked the porch on Saturday night, but I think you know that. Anyway, I just wanted to check on you and see how your hand was. Did you go to the emergency room?"

"My hand is a little sore, but nothing I can't shake off."

"So, you did not do as I told you and have it checked out. I should put you over my knee, Miss Anderson."

"Mr. Hewitt, are you threatening me?" How freaking hot was the thought of him trying to put me over his knee? Extremely! I reminded him, "You are fully aware of what happened to the last gentlemen that threatened me."

"Seriously, Amelia, you should have had that looked at. In what other ways are you defying me? Are you wearing the indecent jeans in public again?"

"Wouldn't you like to know," I did my best to taunt him, but I always felt out of my league.

"Do I need to drive up there at this time of night to check your wardrobe?" I wished he would drive up here, but what would I have done with him if he had?

"Who am I to tell you where you can and cannot go at this time of the night?"

"Right." He sounded as if I had let the wind out of his sails. With one word from him, it was as if the conversation had taken a turn.

"Gabriel, are you working on Wednesday night?" I tried to get back to the light hearted conversation.

"No," he replied.

"But, you might stop by?" I did not so much ask as I implied that he would stop by.

"I might," he returned.

"Good, I think it is time to walk barefoot on the green again."

"Goodnight, Amelia." He did not agree to stop by, but he did not say no either.

"Goodnight, Gabriel, and thank you for calling to check on me."

"Always, Amelia." Two words and with that he was gone. Two words I would replay in my mind for days and days.

***

Wednesday came and went and Gabriel did not stop by the club and he did not call anymore.

***

For the next two weeks, things were dreadfully uneventful at the club and classes were equally uneventful. I was making good money for someone my age and I was getting good grades. I rarely saw Gabriel during those two weeks. It was beginning to appear that I was purposely scheduled for times when he would not be there. My mind was so preoccupied with the purchase of the building that it did not bother me as much as it would have had I not been focused elsewhere.

I had dinner twice with Alex during the two weeks. I made sure that there was an understanding between us that we were just friends. I did not tell him about the building.

Jay and I took Emma to see the building and Jay informed her that we were moving and she was getting the room on the back of the house. Initially, she was fine until she saw my room and Jay's room and the French doors and the porches. Jay informed her that she would get over it and then showed her how much bigger the

120

bathroom was than at our current apartment. She quickly got over it.

The termite inspection came back clean. No termites. There were no termites in any of the trim and there was no wood to earth contact anywhere. The first of the obstacles in buying the building had been overcome.

On one hand, Uncle Lloyd was a little annoyed at how Jay eavesdropped on his conversation and then stole the building from one of his friends, but on the other hand, Uncle Lloyd was a little proud that Jay had the ambition to snatch up the property. All of that being considered, Uncle Lloyd referred us to a building inspector and was present with us when the inspection took place. Both Jay and Uncle Lloyd held my hands through the entire process.

The building inspection came back with no major problems. The electrical system was not up to code, but according to Uncle Lloyd it could be brought up to code with the installation of another breaker box. The roof was in good condition as well as the plumbing system. There were no cracks that could be found in the foundation. The inspector showed us where the hot water tanks for each unit were as well as the filters for the air conditioners and how to maintain all of them. He recommended that we install new thermostats for the heating and air to help save on electric bills. All in all, the major systems were fine and most everything had been updated in the last ten years from what the inspector said. There was nothing that would be a deal breaker. According to the inspector, the building was in great shape considering its age.

Lastly, the appraisal came back. Needless to say, Jay would not be mowing the yard unless he wanted to and certainly not because he lost a bet. The building appraised for one hundred ten thousand dollars so we were getting it for a steal at forty-five grand. Jay and I were giddy at the news. In one day, I would more than double my money.

Again, I thought of my grandfather and how he would be proud. All along I had kept my aunt Gayle informed of what I was up to, but she had not been down to see the building. Until I was twenty-one, which was in November, she had control of my inheritance. She was the one that issued my allowance check each month now that Granddaddy was gone. I think she knew better than to fight me on giving me the money to buy the building out right because she knew I had saved every dime of the monthly allowance from the day I started college. I had been depositing the thousand dollars in a savings account each month and living off of the money I made working. I had a total of twenty-five thousand in savings from the allowance alone. Aunt Gayle was a smart woman and she knew if I wanted the building all I had to do was put my twenty-five thousand down and any bank would finance the remainder based on the value of the building. I did not know that until Jay explained it to me. I also think it helped that she trusted me to do the right thing and not buy beans and plant a bean stalk.

***

The day of the closing finally arrived. I was so nervous that I almost skipped class that Monday morning, but my jitters would have only gotten worse if I sat home doing nothing. I went to class and it kept my mind off of things until the time I was due at the attorney's office. Jay met me at our apartment and we were both too excited to eat lunch. Jay set his VCR for the afternoon and then at 1:45 we started out on foot for our walk to the law office. The closing was scheduled to take place at 2:00 p.m. The attorney that Mr. Braswell had chosen to do the closing was located on McIntosh, one street over from the apartment building at the corner on Jefferson and Montgomery. It would take us about ten minutes to make the walk.

Once at the law firm, I was presented with only a few documents to review and sign.

"I think you are the youngest person I have ever sold an apartment building to and especially the youngest to have ever paid cash for something like this," the attorney remarked. I just smiled politely in response.

I read over everything and I made very few changes. Aside from changing the documents to reflect my legal name, Amelia Jane Anderson, instead of Millie J. Anderson as it was initially listed on the Warranty Deed, the other change that was important to me was in the legal description of the property. The building did not have a name and I thought it should have one. The majority of the other historic homes in Milledgeville had names so I insisted the name of the building be added to the legal description. The building was now to be known as The Jefferson. It was on Jefferson Street and I was from Jefferson County, Georgia so The Jefferson made sense to me. Jay approved of the name.

As soon as Mr. Braswell signed the Warranty Deed, he stood and shook Jay's hand and thanked him. Literally, the deed was done for him at that time. I stood as well and extended my hand for the shake. After all, I was the one actually purchasing the place. "Good luck, young lady," Mr. Braswell said as he shook my hand and then

122

handed me the keys to the building. "You can feel free to call me if you have any questions."

"Thank you so much and I just might call you if we get stuck and cannot figure something out. I have really enjoyed doing business with you," I told him as I took the keys. There were three keys for each unit; two keys for the tenants and one for me to keep as the landlord.

After we left the attorney's office, Jay and I walked straight around to The Jefferson and let ourselves in through the front door. We ran dancing through the building with excitement!

"I can't believe this is all mine! I can't believe I just did this!" Oh, no, buyer's remorse was about to take hold.

"Let's go celebrate! And then let's go pack and sleep here tonight! Even if we just have to bring covers and sleeping bags to put on the floor and enough supplies to get us started tomorrow morning, let's sleep here." Jay always knew what to say to get me back on track.

"Yes, let's, but before we go, there's something I have to do," I yelled back to Jay as I sprinted up the stairs to our unit. I ran through my room and out onto the upstairs porch I went where I yelled out to the neighborhood, "This is my first house! Mine! Mine! Mine!"

Then I turned and ran back downstairs to find Jay laughing hysterically. I grabbed him by the hand and pulled him with me, "Come on, I have not eaten hardly at all today and I could use some wings." We headed to The Brick where the wings were awesome, as always.

It was almost 5:00 p.m. when we arrived back at the Hillman House apartment. Emma was back from tennis practice so we all started packing feverishly. We rocked out to the Rolling Stones and Stone Temple Pilots and more as we packed. I picked "Paint It Black," of course, and we blared the music and jumped around with the joy of getting out of that place to the point that the angry cat lady from downstairs banged on the ceiling and threatened to call the landlord on us again. As usual, we did not care, but that day of all days, we really did not care.

In our minds we were not disrespectful to the cat lady that lived below us, we were just giving back a little of what we got while we had lived in the building with her. Miss Doolittle lived with her ten cats in the apartment directly below ours and she was certifiably, bat crap crazy. We believed she was on the furlough program at

Central State Mental Institute, the other institute in Milledgeville and the one that put Milledgeville on the map. Our dancing and jumping around was just payback for her Saturday morning performances. She liked to run outside naked on Saturday mornings at the break of dawn and sang "The Star-Spangled Banner" at the top of her lungs.

***

Drawing class went fine and I was home for lunch when I decided to call Cara about switching shifts at the club. I dialed the numbers and it rang three times before anyone picked up.

"Cara, it's Millie," I said as I recognized her voice on the other end of the line.

"Hey, Millie!" she responded very much with a smile in her voice.

"I hate to bother you..." I barely got out of my mouth before she cut me off.

"You are no bother, what's up?"

"I need a favor. Would you mind trading shifts with me this weekend? Can I take your Friday night and give you my Saturday on the beverage cart? My roommates and I are moving and I need Saturday off to move. I am so sorry for the short notice." I begged her and I truly did feel bad about asking.

"No problem. I'll be glad to trade with you. I've been wanting to do the beverage cart." Cara was so gracious about trading.

While on the phone I remembered the ride to work with Cara the Sunday that I hurt my hand. I figured I had two apartments that I needed to rent out so what would it hurt to ask her if she might like one of them. "How are you doing with your ghost situation?"

"It is driving me crazy! I can't stand to be alone in this place and my roommate is almost always at her boyfriend's apartment." Cara sounded somewhat terrified even when talking about it. "Seriously, I feel as if someone is watching me all the time when I am here."

This was sad for Cara, but perhaps a blessing for me. I tried to pretend that that was not almost exactly what I had hoped she would say when I responded to her since I certainly did not want her to hear that in my voice.

"Have you thought about moving?" Of course, I could not help but ask.

"I would move in a heartbeat except that everything within walking distance of campus is taken. I have looked." She sounded exasperated.

"I know of a two bedroom that's two blocks from the Biology building and I believe it to be ghost free," I confided.

"OMG!" Cara screamed!

"It's on North Jefferson, about two blocks from the college, and it is vacant right now," I went on.

"Do you have the number to the landlord?" Cara squealed over the phone with nothing containing her excitement.

"I can do better than that. I can meet you there and show you the place this afternoon if you like," I tried to contain my own excitement and glaze over the question about the landlord for now.

"Really? Well, I can't be there until 4:30 p.m. I'll have to bring my roommate and she does not get in from class until 4:00." Cara must have been desperate to get out of the haunted house because she did not even ask how much the rent was.

"Alright. I will see you at 4:30 in front of the red brick apartment building with the four porches across the front." I gave her the address one more time just in case she did not get it the first time. I am not sure she heard it the first time over her squealing.

After I hung up I screamed with joy! I was so excited that I had accomplished two things: switched shifts as I had initially intended and booked a prospective tenant for one of the downstairs units. I then said a little prayer that she would take the apartment.

I still had an hour before I had to be at badminton class so I used my time to create and print fliers to post around campus advertising the apartment for rent. After all, even if Cara and her roommate took one of them, I still had to do something with the other.

I quickly made the fliers and then headed off to my badminton class. On the way to class, I posted fliers on the bulletin boards in the student union, cafeteria and on the one by the front door of the gym.

By the time I returned from class around 3:15, I had three messages from people calling about the apartment. One of the callers forgot to leave her number, one sounded high and the other was one of the guys from badminton class. Although I did not recognize the guy as one of the ones I had just been matched with in class, he sounded promising especially since he left his number and did not sound like he had just drunk-dialed me.

The message was quite sensible and went as follows: "Hi, Millie! This is Travis from badminton. I hope you don't mind I got your number from Marty. I overheard you telling him about the apartment for rent. I would love to find out more about the place if you would not mind giving me a call. Thanks!" And he left his number for me to call back.

I had grabbed pen and paper and took down the number. I tried to remember which guy this was from class. I did sort of recognize the voice. Travis actually sounded like most of the guys from back home, thick Southern accent and as if he had a bit of chew in his mouth while talking.

I dialed the number and he picked up on the first ring. "May I speak with Travis?" I asked even though I already knew that was him.

"Millie, hi! Thanks for calling back so quickly. So, what's the deal with the apartment?" He got straight to the point.

"It's a two bedroom, one bath. The rent is $325 per month plus utilities and it is on the bottom floor of a brick building at the corner of North Jefferson over behind the Biology building." I tried to give enough information that he would want to see it.

"So are you subleasing it or something?"

I was not sure that I wanted anyone to know I was the landlord just yet so I responded, "Something like that. I will be there at 4:30 if you would like to swing by and have a look at the place." I felt I might as well kill two birds with one stone.

"Honestly," he said with a hint of hesitation, "it's a little out of our price range."

Oh yikes! I had only told him $325 because I was going to include one of the spots in the carport and make a little extra on it.

"How far out of the price range is it, if you don't mind me asking?" I figured it could not do any harm to find out what I was up against.

"We were hoping to stay at $300 or under." Even though he answered me, I could tell he wanted off the phone and was no longer interested.

"Why don't you come look at it and we can discuss the price further if you like it? What do you have to lose, but a little of your time?" I was confident most anyone would love the apartment because, not only was it completely roach free, everything appeared new and the rooms were huge compared to those of most of the other apartments this close to campus.

Travis agreed to come by to see it at 4:30 and said he would be bringing his girlfriend with him. Again, I was so excited that I was moved to dance around the apartment while I began packing.

Between the end of the phone call and 4:15 I managed to pack a few boxes to take over to The Jefferson. Instead of walking this time, I loaded the Corvette to the ceiling in the front seat and stuffed the tiny trunk to the point of barely being able to close it. That really was not saying much for the volume of packing I had accomplished.

I had parked around back in the carport, but carried two of the small boxes around through the front and up the stairs to my new home. I went ahead and unlocked the doors to the downstairs apartments before going up stairs.

I was emptying the contents of one of the boxes in my bathroom when I barely heard Cara yell up the stairs, "Hello, anyone here?"

I stopped what I was doing and ran for the top of the stairs. "Wait there, I'm coming," I yelled back.

I scurried down the stairs as quickly as I could to find Cara and her roommate waiting in the foyer area. Just as Cara was making the introductions between me and her roommate, I could see through the front door that Travis and someone I assumed was his girlfriend had arrived on the stoop.

"Excuse me just a minute," I stopped her and reached around them to open the door to Travis and the very attractive African American female that was with him.

"Hi, Millie, this is my fiancé, Stella." Travis said as she extended a hand to me.

"It's nice to meet you." I said before turning to make introductions between the rest of the occupants of the foyer. "This is

Cara and her roommate, Megan. I really appreciate you all agreeing to come and look at the place this afternoon."

I then turned and opened the door to the apartment on the right. "You all are welcome to look around," I offered as I backed out of the way for them to enter. "So you know, there are two apartments for rent. The one directly across the hall is a mirror image of this one and you are welcome to look in it as well."

Megan, Travis and Stella all entered the apartment one after the other, but Cara stayed behind with me. "I thought I might better ask you how much the rent is on the place since I did not think to ask you earlier," Cara asked as we stood in the foyer.

"It is $300 for the apartment. There's also a carport in the back with four spaces. If you want a space, then the rent is an additional $25 per space.

"Ok, I can go in now that I know it's not out of the price range. Also, I won't need a carport. Have you seen what I drive? I don't need anything special for Jiminy." Although I had first met Cara in the parking lot at Port Honor, I had not noticed her car. As it turned out, she drove a blue 1971 Plymouth Cricket that had seen better days.

"My daddy said it was a classic." She rolled her eyes as she finished describing her car.

I followed Cara into the living room of the apartment. Megan and Stella were in the kitchen and Travis had already made his way back to the bedrooms.

"This room is twice as large as the one at our current apartment!" Cara seemed to really be impressed, "and the floors are beautiful!"

"By the way, I will be living in the apartment upstairs with my two roommates. The extra bonus is that if you take the apartment, we can ride to work together occasionally if you like so you will save on gas money in the long run." I tried to sweeten the deal.

"Cara, you've got to see the size of the bedrooms," Megan called from the back of the apartment where she and Stella had joined Travis. Cara quickly went to find them.

When Cara left me, I went across and opened the door to the apartment on the left side of the building. While I was gone, apparently they all discussed among themselves that they wanted the apartment.

I was opening the front door to the porch of the left side apartment when Travis found me. "Millie, we want the apartment, but like I said, it is a little more than we want to pay."

"I can let you have the apartment for $300." I then explained about the carport. "There's a carport in the rear of the building and if you want a space in it then it would be an extra $25, but you don't have to take the carport."

"Excellent! Stella is going to be so happy! She loves the place."

We were still in the living room of the apartment on the left side so I asked him if he wanted to have a look at it while he was in there.

"Let me get Stella and I will let her pick which one she likes best," Travis then left the room to fetch Stella.

As Travis left the room, Cara and Megan entered. "Do you mind if we have a look at this one?" Megan asked.

"Not at all," I responded.

Megan left to have a look around, but again Cara stayed with me in the living room. "We want the apartment, but we have to give notice at our current apartment," Cara informed me.

"If you want the place and will sign a one year lease, I will waive the first month and you can move in now if you like." I told her and she looked at me with a curious face. I think it finally occurred to her that I was the landlord.

"Who should we be making our rent checks out to?" Cara asked.

"I will have to let you know about that. I'll have that sorted out by the time you have to write one." I did not deny that it should be made out to me, but I did not confirm it either.

"Millie, I think I need to trade back with you for my original work schedule because I need to move on Saturday too," Cara laughed. "You know, if you do own this place as I suspect, it will totally impress the guys at Port Honor. Does Gabriel know about this?"

"No and I don't want anyone to tell him. It is very important that you do not tell him."

"Why?" Cara was not going to make this easy.

"Because it is none of their business and I prefer to keep it that way for now."

***

By the end of the afternoon, I had rented out both apartments. Cara and Megan were taking the unit on the right and Travis and Stella were taking the unit on the left. I seemed to be getting the hang of being a landlord already.

CHAPTER 6

I arrived at work on Wednesday afternoon around 4:30 to find Alvin had called in sick and Gabriel was working in his place. Gabriel was busy preparing the specials for the evening on the prep line when I walked in and spotted him. I was not expecting him to be there and it seemed like forever since I last saw him. I had been so busy with the building purchase that I had not noticed until that moment that I missed him.

Gabriel was moving between the prep line and the stove preparing several items at once. He moved with such grace and command of the kitchen. I had never watched him work until then. I was usually in awe of him for some reason that was beyond me, his looks, that electric shock he gave me when we touched, the way the hair stood on the back of my neck when I was next to him. This time I was in awe just watching him work. I could have watched him forever.

Gabriel was wearing his usual work attire. He had on his white chef's coat with his name stitched over his left peck area and the sleeves rolled up to about three-quarter length and a white t-shirt underneath. He also had on his black and white checked pants and those God-awful black clogs. One day, I was going to work up the courage to ask him what the point of the clogs was. Notwithstanding the clogs, I was so pleased to see him that it really did not matter what he was wearing.

We were the only ones in the kitchen and I had been watching him from across the prep line for about five minutes before he noticed me. Evidently he thought he was alone and was just a little startled to see me as he dropped what was in his hand. I tried not to laugh, but the thought of me scaring him was a bit funny.

"Long time no see," I said as I stepped to a spot on my side of the prep line so he could have a better view of me.

"I have been meaning to call you, but I've been so busy," Gabriel made excuses for not calling me as if I might be upset with him or had my feelings hurt that he had not called. It had not dawned on me until that moment that maybe my feelings should have been hurt. I tried not to let it show that I was actually giving weight to having hurt feelings.

"My hand is fine. It really was nothing," I responded.

131

"Let me see it," he commanded as he motioned for me to come around the line for him to get a better look.

I walked around the side of the line nearest to the doors leading to the dining room. As I turned the corner and approached him I held out my hand toward him, but not within his reach.

"See its fine, no scar or anything," I said.

Gabriel stepped toward me and took my hand in his. My hands were small and delicate compared to his. He really appeared to examine it thoroughly. He ran his fingers across the spot where I had split the skin.

It's not that I had forgotten the effect he had on me, but it was always a surprise. At this point it was definitely not something I expected to happen each time I was near him or each time we touched. I still could not help but wonder if he had this sort of effect on everyone. I decided as I thought of these things that I would make a mental note to find a way to ask Cara if she ever experienced this with him.

My brief thought pattern was broken after a few seconds when Gabriel asked, "Have you played since this happened?"

I was not thinking straight, which was a common side effect of being near him. "Played what?" I said with wonder.

He had been looking down at my hand when he asked his question, but looked up at me somewhat puzzled by my answer. "The piano of course. What else would I be talking about?"

"Well, I do have badminton class on Tuesdays and Thursdays at 2:00 p.m., but no, I have not played the piano since I played for you the day of my interview."

"Oh," he said and again looked kind of confused. Even with a confused look on his face he was breathtakingly beautiful.

"I don't have access to a piano these days," I said as I slid my hand back from his. I could have stood there forever, but that was not productive for either of us. "I should probably go and see if we have any reservations on the book for tonight and make sure the dining room is set."

"You are probably right," he said as I left and headed for the door leading into the dining room.

I found the reservation book at the hostess stand and we had four reservations for the evening. There was a party of two for 6:30, two parties of four for 7:00 and a party of eight for 7:30. If there were four parties on the book, then we could usually count on two or three additional parties to show up.

I looked over the dining room and most everything was still in place from Sunday. I had to replace a couple of the chargers and aligned a few chairs, but other than that the room was ready for diner. After I finished the dining room, I returned to the kitchen where I found Gabriel working at the stove. Again, we were the only ones in the kitchen.

I moved to my side of the line as Gabriel was taking a pan of sauce off of the stove when I told him how many reservations we had.

"Total of eighteen people so far! That's pretty good for a Wednesday night." It really was not that many people, but Gabriel seemed pleased. "There were nights not too long ago when we had no one on Wednesdays."

"What are you making?" I asked him and I indicated to the sauce.

"This is gorgonzola cream sauce to go over the beef tenderloin that is still in the oven. In about five minutes I will give you a taste." Gabriel smiled at me and I could feel myself blushing just from him smiling at me.

"I'm going to go and get something to drink. Would you like for me to get anything for you?" I offered.

"You don't mind?" He asked as if he were shocked that I would offer to get something for him.

"Why would I mind? I am going that way and it is the polite thing to do," I shrugged my shoulders as I did not understand why he would think I would mind. "So, what would you like? As I recall you are fond of Pink Panty Droppers."

"Ha ha, Miss Anderson! I will have a Seven and Seven if you don't mind."

"I don't mind, Mr. Hewitt, and I will be right back with your Seven and Seven."

I left Gabriel in the kitchen and found Matt manning the bar for the evening. At that time, Matt was busy entertaining Mr. Baker and Mr. Lockerby who were perched on their usual Wednesday afternoon stools. I spoke to everyone, but quickly returned to the kitchen with Gabriel's drink and a Coke for myself.

When I returned I found that we were no longer alone in the kitchen. Rudy had arrived for work and was busy getting started on the dishes already in the dish pit. I gave Gabriel his drink and he was very thankful. I had not drank out of the Coke yet, so I offered it to Rudy.

"Thanks Millie!" he said.

"How's school going? Did I hear you are a senior this year?" I asked him.

Rudy seemed like a sweet young man and obviously shy. He hung his head and rarely made eye contact with me when we spoke. When he responded to my question, he did not vary his body language, "Yes, ma'am. I'm a senior this year. School's good."

"Are you planning to go to college?" I continued with my questions.

"I would like to, but I just don't know." He hung his head and stared at his hands.

"Let me know if you need help filling out applications or anything and I will be glad to help you however I can." I told him. "I know the guys give you rides home sometimes, if you ever need to, you can ask me. I will make sure you get home safely, I don't mind."

Rudy was a small guy and a very hard worker. My grandfather would have probably rolled over in his grave at the thought of me driving around a young black boy, but times were different and I aimed to treat him as I would anyone else. Plus, something about him gave me the impression that he had led a very hard life and that made me sad to think about.

"Amelia, Rudy, come here. I want you to have a taste of this," Gabriel did not typically include Rudy in our taste testing of the specials, but this time he did.

Gabriel had made a plate for both of us and Matt. He sent Rudy to get Matt and while he was gone, Gabriel again summoned me behind the line.

"What?" I asked.

"Taste this," he responded as he cut a piece of the steak which had been drizzled with the gorgonzola cream sauce. Then Gabriel proceeded to feed me a fork full of it. While I chewed and he cut another bite, he gave me a brief account of Rudy's circumstances. "He lives with his grandmother and has to work to help support the family. He was up for a track scholarship, but had to quit track and get a job to help out. When he quit track he lost all hope of the scholarship and of college. He is here almost every time the doors are open."

Tears welled up in my eyes as I thought about how awful that was. I had been working since I was fifteen, but that was at my grandfather's insistence for character building, not because I had to help support our family. That was so sad and I truly felt sorry for Rudy. I could barely swallow the food then for fear that a tear would fall with any movement of my face.

"Amelia, you have got to suck it up and not let him see you feel sorry for him or that you know. Plus, I can't stand to see you cry. Now stop it." Gabriel had put on an apron over his pants and he lifted the corner of his apron and wiped the tear. "Here, have another bite." And he shoved another fork full in my mouth. "What do you think?"

"I think I am going to full on cry. Stop being so nice to me!" Through no fault of my own, I lead a very privileged life and was feeling guilty about that right then. My life had been different with the lack of parents, but it had not been hard by any means. I was trying to shake the urge to cry, but nothing was working and I was getting frustrated. "And don't even think about hugging me, unless you want the waterworks! Just give me a minute and don't feed me."

I could hear Rudy and Matt coming back from the bar area so I scooted out the door to the dining room and down the corridor toward the exit near the pool. I fanned myself and I did my best to regain my composure. I waited until the tears had been squelched and my face was no longer red before I returned to the kitchen. I knew I could help Rudy, but now was not the time to think about that.

The night went by quickly. There were good parts and awful parts. We ended up having more people show up without reservations than we had expected. There were so many guests that Matt came out from the bar area and helped wait on tables. Among the guests that showed up without reservations and that I had to wait on were Kimmie and Mr. Martin. Another couple of the same approximate age as Mr. Martin joined them. Mr. Martin was his usual charming self and waiting on Kimmie was as thrilling as ever. If she did not have such a nasty attitude, I would have probably felt sorry for her since she was clearly the third wheel among any of their friend groups. Her cause would have been helped if she did not always dress like a high end hooker, but perhaps that's the way Mr. Martin liked her.

I also had to wait on Mr. and Mrs. Arthur, a very stuffy couple in their seventies, who arrived on their pontoon with their collie, Sir Lancelot. They tied the pontoon to the dock at the head of the cove in front of the clubhouse and tied Sir Lancelot to the front deck outside of the door next to the hostess stand. Sir Lancelot was a beautiful dog, regal even, with his white and sable fur. The dog was better behaved than most children that I had seen at the club thus far. He just sat there and waited for them to return. I also thought it was amusing that the Arthurs had a dog named Sir Lancelot. It made me wonder if Mrs. Arthur had to address Mr. Arthur as "King" in private.

The Arthurs were nice enough, but were not the type that expected their server to provide the night's entertainment. They were very polite, but waiting on them was strictly business. Their lack of eye contact with me suggested that there was no need trying to converse with them. I was to take their order, get their food, check on them once and be gone until it was time to take their plates away and get the bill.

Mr. Arthur barely ate his beef tenderloin and asked for a to-go box. I promptly took their plates to the kitchen where I intended to box up the left overs.

The night was winding down at this point and Rudy was picking up various dirty dishes from around the kitchen when I placed Mr. Arthur's plate on my side of the prep line. When I turned away to get the to-go box, Rudy took the plate and dumped its contents in the trash. I had waited on Mr. Arthur each Wednesday night that I had worked and knew he could be unpleasant, so I did not want to return to the dining room with a story of how his expensive steak had gotten thrown out. I remembered that last week Mr. Arthur gave his left overs to Sir Lancelot before they boarded the pontoon. I prayed he would do the same as I retrieved the steak from the trash and put it in the to-go box. Gabriel was at the bar, so I went behind the prep line to the stove and added fresh potatoes and asparagus to the box. By the time I was done, it appeared to be a completely new plate of food.

Throughout the night I thought more about whether or not my feelings should have been hurt by Gabriel not calling me. The more I thought about it the more I started to wallow in self-pity. The way he apologized for not calling implied that he should have called, but for whatever reason chose not to call. Why hadn't he called me? By the time the last guests were leaving, I had made up my mind that my feelings were hurt.

It was down to the four of us: Matt, Rudy, Gabriel and me, left in the building. Rudy had asked Matt to give him a ride home and they were headed to the back door when I returned to the kitchen from putting the finishing touches on the dining room. At that point Gabriel and I were the only ones left in the kitchen. Gabriel was coming out of his office there in the kitchen as I clocked-out.

"Amelia, let's go. It's time to play," Gabriel said as he took me by my right hand and twirled me around to come with him.

I noticed that Gabriel had taken off his chef's coat and was just in his white t-shirt, pants and he had even changed from the awful clogs into Nike tennis shoes. The t-shirt was a definite improvement, tight fitting and left nothing of his muscular chest to my imagination. The sight left me bewildered and without any recollection of my hurt feelings. As always my guard was down and I went willingly. Gabriel led me through the kitchen, into the dining room and up the stairs to the piano.

The only lights that were on in the clubhouse were the ones in the kitchen and the ones on dimmers that shown above each of the fireplaces. The upstairs lighting situation was no different. In fact, the light on the fireplace provided so little light that it magnified the quiet and stillness of the clubhouse at that time of the night with only Gabriel and I left inside.

"What would you like to hear?" I asked as I untied my tie and rolled up my sleeves and prepared to take my seat at the piano bench. Gabriel started to pull over one of the chairs from in front of the fire place, but I stopped him. "Oh, no you don't. If I am playing for you then you are going to sit here on the bench with me. You are not about to sit in that comfy chair over there in the dark and be lulled off to sleep."

"Go to sleep? I would never." He replied with the fake sense of having been offended in his voice.

Gabriel left the chair where it was and came to help me move the latest giant floral arrangement from the top of the piano. He took the arrangement away and put it on the coffee table while I lifted the lid to the piano. I know that I did not have to open the lid, but it was just something I preferred. Once finished with the adjustments to the piano, I pulled the bench to where one end of it was directly at the center and I took a seat at that end.

I motioned for Gabriel to join me by patting the seat next to me. "If you want me to play, come sit with me and tell me what you want to hear."

"What all can you play?" he asked as he approached the bench.

"You name it and I can probably play it." I responded while scooting over to make room for him.

"How is that possible?" He asked as he took the seat next to me. He was so close I could smell his cologne, the usual scent of heaven. Even though I had not struck a chord, I was beginning to perspire just at the nervousness of being alone there with him, plus the proximity. We were so close on the piano bench that our legs brushed one another, my bare leg to his in the checkered pants.

"I don't know. It's a memory thing I suppose. If I play something once, it just sticks." I shrugged my shoulders as I did not have a better explanation than that.

I opened the keyboard. I placed my hands on the keys and waited. Gabriel seemed to be thinking, perhaps trying to decide what to ask me to play. He finally spoke, "Can you play 'Endless Love'?"

I suppose most girls would have read something into his request, but not me. I almost laughed as I would have never taken him for a guy that even knew about that song. I tried to squelch the urge to laugh, but did not succeed very well when I replied, "Can I play 'Endless Love'? Any child of the eighties who took piano can play that song. I find it amusing that you know that song."

"My first crush was Brooke Shields." Gabriel smiled and I cut my eyes at him with a laugh as I began to play.

I played the song to the very end and Gabriel watched my hands the entire time. I worked the black keys and white keys as the music called and as I pressed the pedal at intervals, my leg rubbed against his. Gabriel seemed fascinated just listening and watching as I played.

"My turn to choose. Have you ever heard this? It's called 'Unbreakable Heart'." It was a song that I loved when it was sung by Carlene Carter. I knew all of the words by heart and I could have sang along as I played. It would not have been the first time, but I refrained and only sang them in my head.

138

I glanced at Gabriel as I played and his eyes were closed. He seemed to be wrapped up in the music and completely at peace. As always, he was something to behold and for now, in some simple way, he was mine.

When I finished playing, I looked at him and he opened his eyes. "Can you play something fast?"

"'Jailhouse Rock' or 'Crocodile Rock'?" I can do either."

Gabriel's face lit up, "'Jailhouse Rock', please."

I squirmed on the piano bench and bumped him with my hip, "You'll want to scoot down a little for this one."

Then I fired up the piano and gave it a workout all the while moving with the music. Gabriel really got into it as well. I followed Jailhouse with "Crocodile Rock" and that's when I really burned up the keys.

"If you don't mind I am going to play something slow now," I said as I was visibly winded. The piano was not the only one getting a workout with those songs.

I went on playing for about an hour total before Gabriel stopped me. "It's getting late and you still have to get on the road home."

"I'm going to play one more if you don't mind. Are you a Patsy Cline fan?" I asked as I started to play "Crazy".

"I don't know if I am familiar with her," Gabriel replied.

"Seriously, you don't know who Patsy Cline is?" I shook my head in disbelief. Who does not know Patsy Cline or the song "Crazy"? "Perhaps you will recognize it once I start. This was my grandfather's favorite thing for me to play."

Gabriel had scooted back closer to me and we were again touching hip to knee. It was probably for the best that he was not familiar with the song. I may not have read anything into his choice of "Endless Love", but I was completely open to him reading anything he might like into my choice of "Crazy" and maybe that was not the wisest thing. I was crazy for him in every sense of the word and the song fit perfectly, but letting any guy know that in this form might spook them.

I started to play and again Gabriel closed his eyes and serenity returned to his face. I was about mid-way through the song when I felt him place his left hand on my thigh. I was wearing the skirt that he had had Praise hem so high that while seated it rose up to a point about six inches above my knee. Needless to say his hand was on my bare thigh. It was distracting to say the least and I could hardly contain myself, but I continued to the end of the song before I acknowledged it.

When I finished playing I placed my hand on top of his. We sat in silence for a moment before he asked, "Amelia, when do you turn twenty-one?"

The question seemed out of the blue, but his voice gave the hint that it was something he had been thinking about for a while. He could have just looked at my application, but I liked that he asked.

"November 6," I answered. I wanted to know why he would ask, but I figured he would tell me if he wanted to. I also seized the opportunity to ask him how old he was.

"Old enough," he answered coyly.

"Seriously, you can look at my application and find out most anything about me, but I know very little about you. I figure it is only fair. Tell me how old you are," I politely demanded.

"Twenty-eight." Whew, he was just a bit younger than I had suspected. I would never tell I had thought he was thirty. I mainly thought he was older due to his position.

"So, twenty-one on November 6? We are going out that night." It wasn't a question, but a statement that Gabriel made. My stomach flipped and almost felt faint. Did he mean it? Was that his way of asking me out on a date? It did not matter if he was. My heart sank as I instantly remembered that I already had plans for that day.

I leaned my head over on his shoulder and squeezed his hand that I still held in mine on my thigh. Softly I said, "I can't. I already have plans that day. I am so sorry."

"That's well over a month away and you have plans already?" Gabriel was clearly disappointed that I had turned him down.

I tried to soften the blow by explaining, "I have to go back home to attend the final disbursement of my grandfather's will that day. I do not know what I am in for or how long it will take. I am so sorry." I apologized again. It never occurred to me to ask him to come with me.

Gabriel took his hand from my thigh and seemed to have been brought back to his senses. "It's late and you need to get on the road, Amelia. I am glad your hand is fine."

Gabriel stood from the bench and took down the prop that held the piano lid up. He closed the piano as gently as I would have. I stood from the bench as well. I straightened my skirt and was shaking out my hair when he turned back to me. He held out his hand to me, "Come on, Amelia, time to go home."

I took his hand and he walked me all the way to my car. "One of these days you are going to have to give me a ride in this car," Gabriel said as he leaned down to hug me good- night. His arms went around my back and he pulled me up onto my toes in his embrace.

"We could go now if you like?" I whispered as I wrapped my arms around his neck and fell into him.

Gabriel buried his face in my hair and took a deep breath. He whispered back, "Strawberries. Ummm." He paused for just a moment before he whispered again, "November 7th, no other plans."

I was almost unable to respond. I was just reveling in the thought. "Okay. No other plans." I forced out from my lips in a breathless whisper. As always when we were close like this, I was dying to be kissed, but it appeared I might have a month to wait for that relief.

***

After classes on Friday, I went home to Avera to pick up some items for the new apartment. Aunt Gayle was there and over lunch I told her all about Gabriel. Her advice was to be careful because he was not a college boy and even though he was only about eight years older, those eight years probably made a world of difference when it came to life experience. Aunt Gayle was the epitome of Southern ladies so it was shocking when she cautioned regarding sex and Gabriel, "If a man that age isn't getting it from you, he's getting it somewhere. Don't get your heart broken, Millie."

Aunt Gayle was wise and although she never married, it was not like she had not had offers. She dated occasionally while I was growing up, but few were serious. For the most part she had devoted herself to raising someone else's child, me.

The truth about Aunt Gayle was that she was suffering from a twenty-five year old broken heart. The one boy she ever loved had

141

died in front of her when they were in high school. They were swimming with some friends at the rock quarry near Sparta when he dove in water that was too shallow. Some people would look at her life as a waste, but not me; especially since I was a product of that life.

Aunt Gayle was beautiful and we looked enough alike that we were often mistaken for mother and daughter, but for whatever reason she always corrected people on the matter. I have never known why. I never minded the mistake and I would have never corrected anyone. I could understand the mistake, we had the same facial structure, hair and eye color and she was the right age to be my mother. The only major difference in our looks was that she was considerably taller than I was. She was a good seven inches taller than I was making her about five foot ten inches tall.

Since I was taking Cara's shift at the club, I could not stay as long as I would have liked to have. Aunt Gayle understood and she was having company over for dinner anyway so I did not feel so bad about leaving her.

"Would you mind terribly if I left the Corvette here and took Granddaddy's truck back with me?" I asked before we started loading the car.

"That depends on which one you want to take," Aunt Gayle responded as she walked to the spot in the kitchen where the keys were hung by the back door.

"I did not know I had a choice. I was never allowed to drive the C10," my eyes lit up with the thought of finally getting to drive it.

"Well, it is yours now so if you want to drive it you can, but if you wreck it I will kill you! Do I make myself clear?" She was stern.

"Back up. What do you mean, 'it is yours now'?" I asked.

"It is not officially yours until your birthday. It belongs to the estate right now, but I don't see the harm in you having it now...as long as you are careful with it!"

"If I get the C10, then what are you getting?" I did not know all the details of the Will and I certainly did not know what all there was to it. I only knew that most everything had been divided between Aunt Gayle and me. I suspected that I knew what she was getting and although I loved the C10, I was a touch envious.

Not only did Granddaddy buy a new Chevy truck almost every three years, he also bought and restored antique cars as a hobby. He bought, restored and sold a great many of them before he died. The Corvette was not one of them, but there were plenty of others. Granddaddy kept a few of them over the years. He kept the blue and white 1968 C10 Chevy Truck, which I was getting, and he also kept a 1955 white Ford Thunderbird.

I had driven the most recent of his newer trucks, but like the C10, I had never driven the Thunderbird. Granddaddy had had plenty of offers over the years, but that was his pride and off limits for anyone to drive, but him. It had red interior and he had painstakingly restored every detail of it to its original condition. It was in pristine condition as if it had just rolled off of the showroom floor in 1955.

"You got the Thunderbird? Oh, I am happy for you and I hate you all at the same time!" I told Aunt Gayle as I gave her a big hug and she handed me the keys to the C10. Like Granddaddy, I loved classic cars. It was in my blood. The same way Aunt Gayle had educated me on musical instruments, Granddaddy had done his best to educate me on restoring and maintaining cars.

"Millie, I would rather give you the Thunderbird and have Dad back any day of the week," Aunt Gayle said.

"I know, I would give anything to have him here too," I agreed.

After I had the keys to the truck, I went and pulled it around to the front of the house and then moved my car into its place in the barn. Aunt Gayle and I then proceeded to pack the truck with more of my personal belongings that I had not had room to take with me when I first made the move to Milledgeville.

As I was tying down some things in the bed of the truck with bungee straps, Aunt Gayle came out of the house carrying my fiddle case. "I think you should take this with you," she said as she went around the truck and opened the passenger's side door. "If Gabriel thinks you are good at the piano, just wait until he hears you play this."

I rolled my eyes at her as she placed the fiddle inside the cab of the truck. "Not everyone can play the fiddle you know and no one I know can play it as well as you," she continued. "You are a talented girl, Millie. I have never understood why you refuse to really use your talents."

"I know, I know, I won't be able to get by on my looks forever," I said as I made a silly face.

"Don't be a smarty pants!" she corrected me. She knew I was joking as I had never been confident about my looks. In all seriousness, I was a poor man's version of her. My mother had watered down the gene pool.

It was not long after that before I was on my way. There was no time to go back to Milledgeville to unload the truck so I had to drive straight to Port Honor. Aunt Gayle had cautioned me once more before I left about not harming the truck. I know she was concerned for my safety as well, but she took for granted that I knew that and mainly focused on the safety of the truck.

It was about an hour and fifteen minute drive from home to Port Honor, part of which was interstate. Regardless of the age of the C10, this was likely the first time it had been on the interstate. I-20 was somewhere Granddaddy would have never dared to drive any of his antique cars.

Once on the interstate, I floored the throttle and attained what appeared to be maximum speed at the speed limit of sixty-five miles per hour. Newer cars were passing me one after the other, but never during the drive did I pass any of them. It might not have been fast, but it was a smooth ride and a looker. Several of the cars that passed me slowed down to get a look at who was driving it. I loved the look of surprise on their faces to see a girl my age driving it. They clearly expected a driver of a much older age.

I arrived at work wearing my nearly knee length khaki Duckhead shorts, a Georgia Tech sweatshirt and Nikes. I was fully aware that I was out of uniform when I walked in, but I was carrying what I intended to wear as my uniform for the night. With all of the chaos of the move, I had not had a chance to wash the usual skirt so I brought my favorite khaki pants, a fresh button down shirt, and the blue tie that was identical to my lavender one. I planned to wear the same tennis shoes that I had on.

I came through the back door unnoticed and preceded to the downstairs ladies' restroom to change. I put on the fresh uniform, touched up my make-up, pulled my hair back from my face and pinned it in a barrette. I left the back hanging long down my back, but I brought a rubber band for pulling it back in a pony-tail, if anyone said anything. I had worn my hair in a braid for most of the day so it hung down my back fluffy and wavy from having been in the braid.

I checked my appearance in the full length mirror before emerging from the restroom. These were my favorite pants for a reason. They were low cut and I had added my thick black belt even though I did not need it to hold them up. The pants were just snug enough to accent the shape of my rear. Conservative, but attractive.

I left the restroom and headed back to the kitchen. It was 4:00 p.m. and I suspected I needed to get started setting up the salad cart and the dining room. This was my first Friday night shift and, according to Cara, Friday and Saturday nights were a great deal busier than Wednesdays. When I arrived back in the dining room, I could see Andy taking over for the evening from Matt. Just as I was checking the reservation book, one of the servers that I had not met came in from the kitchen.

A man clearly in his thirties approached me at the hostess stand, "Hi, and you are?" he asked.

"Hi! I'm Millie. I'm working for Cara tonight," I said as I offered him my hand to shake.

"It's nice to meet you, Millie. I should have recognized you from what all I have heard," he said as we shook hands. "I'm Daniel. Jerry will be here in just a few minutes."

Daniel was right. It was only a moment before another gentleman in a similar uniform to ours entered the dining room from the corridor that led from the bathrooms and the door by the pool. When Jerry entered it dawned on me that two of them were lovers. Daniel was a short well-built man in his early thirties with dark hair and a mustache. Daniel was the less obvious of the two.

Jerry was a gentleman of about ten to fifteen years older than Daniel and if there was such a thing as more gay, Jerry was more gay than Daniel. Any number of things could have given him away and unlike Jay, I doubted there was any bone in his body that could play it straight under any circumstances. From the way he walked, to the make-up, foundation and blush, Jerry was almost a big old woman.

As Jerry approached us, Daniel made introductions. I shook Jerry's hand and tried not to let it show that I was a bit put off by the fact that his handshake was more feminine than mine. It was feminine to the point that I wondered should I just kiss the top of his hand and watch him curtsy. Of course, this was not my first exposure to homosexual men, but none that I knew were like Jerry.

For whatever reason, I felt the same way about Daniel as I did Cara when I first met her. I knew straight away that Daniel and I were going to be the best of friends.

Just as we were finishing up reviewing the reservation book, the kitchen door burst open and Gabriel walked into the dining room. His face turned red and he got that look like he did with the gentlemen the Sunday I hurt my hand. It was clear that he had not expected to see me and he was not pleased as I had hoped he would be.

I did not understand at the time, but Daniel pointed at a name in the reservation book and cut his eyes at Jerry. They did not say anything out loud, but they were clearly having a conversation and it had something to do with Gabriel's mood and him seeing me there.

"Amelia," he said in his stern, unhappy voice. "I did not realize you were on the schedule for tonight."

"I hope you don't mind, but I traded with Cara. She is going to work the beverage cart tomorrow," I said in my sweetest, please don't be mad with me voice as I approached him leaving Daniel and Jerry at the hostess stand watching us.

"You should let me know these things." He was not budging. He was clearly put out. "And what are you wearing?"

"I really have to tell you something," I bit my lip and was about to confess to my purchase of the building, the move, and about the truck and everything, but the moment was shattered.

The bar door opened and Gabriel's face changed to mask whatever it was going on with me. It changed to almost glad to see someone, someone other than me.

Daniel ran to me and grabbed my hand. "Come with me, Millie. Let's go start on the salad cart." Daniel said as he pulled me away.

Jerry headed off the woman coming from the bar and Gabriel just stood there. There was a definite confusion that came over me when Daniel pulled me to the kitchen. I looked back to see Jerry talking to a tall, rake thin, platinum blond who appeared to be dripping with wealth. She was fresh off the course and I could hear her say to Gabriel that she would be back at 8:00 for dinner.

"Who was that?" I asked when the kitchen door shut behind us.

"From what I have heard about you, you probably don't want to know, Millie." While he spoke, Daniel tried to get my focus on

146

starting the salad cart by rolling the cart out from under the cabinet where the coffee maker sat.

"Oh my God!" I gasped. "He does have a girlfriend!"

Daniel handed me a stack of plates and continued to try to distract me. "Baby girl, you don't need to worry about her. Just keep being yourself and you will be fine."

Initially I thought I was going to cry, but then the notion that I did not care came over me. This woman was so clearly the opposite of me that I could not imagine Gabriel with her. I could not imagine them having the spark. I would not go so far as to say I was not shaken and that I did not feel at all insecure, I was just strangely, almost unaffected. The thing that did affect me was Gabriel's reaction. He knew he was about to be caught. Was he two-timing her or me or both? Whatever he was doing, it clearly was affected by the potential of the two of us meeting. Perhaps he had two worlds colliding and if he did, well, shame on him.

Daniel could see the wheels turning in my head. "Focus, Millie," Daniel said while taking out a table cloth and handing it to me to put over the cart.

I could not help, but ask, "What exactly have you heard about me?"

"Everything," Daniel responded with a raised eyebrow. I followed as he rolled the cart to the walk-in refrigerator.

"Everything like what?" I demanded as he handed me items and I put them on the cart.

"I'm not going to break a confidence beyond saying that someone has now been educated about Patsy Cline songs." Daniel looked me right in the eye and did not release the bag of lemons he was handing me until I looked at him and gave back the unspoken understanding.

Just at that moment Rudy arrived for work. "Whaz-up?" he said to us as he stuck his head in the open door of the walk-in refrigerator.

Daniel seized the moment to change the subject, "He is just the nicest kid, don't you think?"

"He is!" I agreed and Daniel and I finished in the cooler and rolled the cart back to the prep line.

147

We arrived at the prep line just as Jerry was coming into the kitchen.

"My Gawd, that skinny bitch has the worst case of the gone-ass I have ever seen!" Jerry said with exaggerated exasperation throwing a palm out hand across his forehead for dramatic effect.

The three of us busted out laughing. Gabriel returned to the kitchen as we were having our side splitting laughs. Daniel elbowed me to make sure I knew that Gabriel had seen us. I decided I would not tell Gabriel anything about anything for now. I would keep my big fat secrets to myself, just like he seemed to be doing with his skinny bitch secrets.

We finished with all of our prep work and setting the dining room. We had our taste testing of some of the items on the buffet and still Gabriel said nothing directly to me. I could have easily had my feelings hurt or wore my insecurities for everyone to see, but I chose to heed Daniel's words and just shake it all off. Que sera, sera.

The reservation book had indicated we were going to have a rather busy night. It was seafood buffet night; forty items in forty feet was the slogan. It was sort of like Bubba's list from *Forest Gump*; boiled shrimp, fried shrimp, bar-b-q shrimp, shrimp cocktail...Plus, prime rib, crab legs, fried fish, salad, and so much more, but no frog legs like the seafood buffets in the restaurants near where I grew up.

Eight o'clock arrived and so did Miss Moneybags. Yes, I thought that about her when I very well knew some might think the same of me. The difference was that I did not wear it for all the world to see. Daniel, Jerry and I had been taking turns at the hostess stand as people arrived.

"Table for three," she said as she looked down her nose at me not only because she was a giant compared to me, but because of her attitude. I would not describe her so much as good looking as well maintained and it obviously took a lot of money to make her that way. She was wearing a blue pencil skirt with matching blue leopard print sleeveless top, black sky high heels, and perhaps every piece of jewelry she owned. I could not quite tell if her boobs were her own, but I was guessing they were as store bought as her nose, nails and hair color. Miss Moneybags could give Kimmie a run any day of the week.

It was my turn to greet and seat so I did and knowing full well that Jerry was not a fan of her, I sat her in his section. I wasn't about to sit her in my section and wait on her or her and Gabriel and whomever. Not going to happen!

I could see Jerry roll his eyes at me from across the room. I just smiled back at him and I could see Daniel trying not to laugh as he saw what had transpired. After seating her, I walked over and wished Jerry luck.

"With all of her sophistication, you would think she would know animal prints aren't for white women!" Jerry said with distain. I could not help but laugh. His bitterness coupled with his body language, the swishing and hand gestures were hilarious.

All of the people who I had waited on that night were nice to me and I had made a great deal in tips. Despite how things had started, the evening had been okay for the most part and I had definitely found distraction with Daniel and Jerry. They had managed to keep me laughing all night.

Jerry and Daniel spent the majority of the night speaking to me in what they called my own language, "Southern." Whenever they spoke to me, instead of using my name, they referred to me as "honey-child". I was asked several times, "How's ya mama 'n dem?" and once if I had "chainch" for a dollar?

It turned into a game and we each presented words that our grandparents used and dared one another to use them with our guests while waiting the tables. We all threw in ten dollars. To win the pot, you would have to say to someone at one of your tables something that included the phrase "rurnt your britches". My grandmother used to say this and it had several possible meanings that were all essentially the same: ruined your pants, messed their pants, shit your pants or passed gas.

Things were winding down and Gabriel had joined Miss Moneybags and an older gentleman who appeared to be her father. There were still about four tables of guests left in the dining room and Rudy had come out from the kitchen to help bus them. That I was aware of, this was not required of him or part of his job duties, but something he did of his own initiative. Rudy was two tables away and I was nearly across the room refilling drinks for one of my tables when Miss Moneybags started snapping her fingers at him and calling, "Boy, Boy, come here."

Jerry was in the kitchen so he was not there to attend his guest. I stopped what I was doing and looked at her. Rudy stood still. This day and age, anyone with any sense at all knew better than to refer to any male of his race as "Boy". It was disrespectful and everyone knew it. Gabriel sat quiet and did not bother to stop her. This was not the Gabriel I knew.

"Excuse me for a moment," I said to the guests at the table where I had been refilling the drinks.

Rudy had started toward her, but I picked up my pace, cut him off and beat him to the table. With a firm tone, I asked Miss Moneybags, "Is there something I could get for you ma'am?"

Rudy grabbed the bus tub and returned to the kitchen. Gabriel might not have been paying attention to me before, but he certainly was now. He had a look of a deer caught in the headlights. Daniel had also stopped what he was doing and Jerry just returned from the kitchen and they tuned in.

"Yes, take these plates," she said with no "please" or "thank you" or "kiss my foot".

"Sure," I replied and proceeded to take up all of the plates. I managed to balance all of them up one arm. Before I left I asked her, "Will that be all?"

"Actually, no, that will not be all. Gabe tells me you play the piano. I would like for you to play for me." The tone of her voice indicated that she was not necessarily asking.

I glared at Gabriel wondering what he had told her about me. I could feel my face getting hot, but she would not notice as she did not bother to look at me at all. I could see why Praise gave me the warning to steer clear and why Jerry was the way he was about her earlier. I put the ix-nay on the steam coming off of me, gave Gabriel one last look of disgust and responded to her, "Sure, ma'am. Just give me one moment."

Seeing my face, Gabriel stood from his chair, "Millie, you really don't have to..."

I cut him off, "Oh, no, I don't mind." I smiled at him, an eat shit smile, but a smile all the same. "I will be right back."

I left the dining room with the plates and made for the kitchen, Daniel and Jerry were behind me.

"Ready your tables for a performance and check on mine as well. Tell them they are welcome to sing along." I instructed them before I headed out the back door of the kitchen to the parking lot. I went to the C10 and grabbed the fiddle from the front passenger's seat. I also grabbed my cowboy boots which I had placed in the floor board of the truck. If she wanted me to play something for her, I had just the thing for her and him.

150

I returned with the fiddle case in hand and in passing by Rudy I told him, "You will want to come to the dining room for this. Give me about two minutes and discretely come out there."

I continued on to the front prep line on the server side. I laid the fiddle case down and changed into the cowboy boots. I removed the fiddle and bow from the case and carried it with me. Before returning to the dining room I went through the bar and invited Andy and all of the patrons in the bar to join us in the dining room.

"Feel free to sing along if you like!" I told them as a few slipped from their bar stools and followed me into the dining room.

Miss Moneybags and her party were seated across the dining room at a table just before the entrance to the room overlooking the pool where we set up the buffet. Gabriel spotted me across the room when I came through the bar door. His eyes were wide with wonder as to what I was about to do and until that moment he knew little of my talents. He only knew about the piano and that was just the tip of the iceberg.

Andy and a couple of patrons from the bar were behind me. I held my head high as I walked across the room with fiddle in one hand and bow in the other. I was just about to the table when Gabriel stood. I ignored him and spoke, "I'm sorry ma'am, I didn't catch your name."

"You can call me Miss Reed," she said while finally making eye contact with me.

"And you can call me Millie." I returned. "And Miss Reed, here's a little something for you." I laid the fiddle across the table at the empty chair where a fourth person would have been seated while I unclipped my barrette, flipped my head upside down shaking my hair out and then back up pulling it into a bun and tying it back with the ponytail tie that I had been wearing around my right wrist.

I could see Rudy inching in discretely as I had instructed him, carrying the bus tub as if he were out there to continue his work. I glanced back and gave a nod to Daniel and Jerry. The rest of the patrons were watching as I raised the fiddle to my chin. With the striking of the first few strings everyone in the room knew what I was playing, "The Devil Went Down to Georgia" and it wasn't long before I had a back-up band of patrons tapping their feet and beating their tables in place of drums.

Daniel was probably the closest to me and I could hear him singing along. Daniel knew all of the words and kept time with the fiddle really well.

151

Johnny wasn't the only one that was playing it hot. I was getting into it; I stomped my feet for the beat and moved with the rhythm as I worked the bow and the strings. I knew I was putting on quite the show. All the while, I could hear more and more people singing along.

I could not see anyone's face or reactions because I had closed my eyes for concentration and feeling the music. I did not need to concentrate on this. I could have played it in my sleep since this was nothing that I had not done at every opportunity. This was another of my grandfather's favorites and he had loved for me to play it. I must admit that when playing it for him, I had not gotten into it as much as I was at this point; not nearly with this kind of satisfaction. That could have been because I typically played it for pleasure not to let someone know they were the devil and everyone knew it.

I continued on with the song. I was coming to the part where Johnny tells the devil that he's the best and I stopped threw my arms out perpendicular to my chest, the fiddle straight out in one hand and the bow in the other. I threw my head back as everyone in the room, but those at Miss Reed's table screamed, "I done told you once you son of a bitch, I'm the best that's ever been!"

I opened my eyes just for a split second to see Miss Reed's face and she was pissed, begging Gabriel to put a stop to this. There was nothing he could do without making a bigger scene and he likely knew it.

As soon as the screaming stopped, I played the fiddle hot again! I finished the song hitting the last note when everyone erupted in clapping. I opened my eyes and Miss Reed knew she'd been had. I did not bow and I just tipped my head to her and gave her a smirkish smile and rolled my eyes. She may have thought she was better than everyone else in the room before, but at that moment she knew I thought I was better than her. Her face was beat red. I believed I had embarrassed her. I suppose if she were my competition, I wanted her to know I was hers and I was bringing my A game.

I did turn and bow to the rest of the room. I rose from the bow and started for the kitchen, my head held high, never looking back.

At some point during the performance, Jerry had taken a stand next to Miss Reed's table. I did not look back, but I could hear Jerry say, "Why, Miss Reed, you look like you might have rurnt your britches."

I heard Jerry and thought, "Damn, he won the bet!"

Approaching Rudy, I put the bow in my hand with the fiddle and high-fived him when I passed by. Rudy and Daniel followed me to the kitchen heaping praise on me. I don't think any of us cared enough to realize that Gabriel was hot on our heels.

"Amelia, out back now!" Gabriel demanded as he grabbed me by the arm just above my elbow. Daniel reached out and took the fiddle while Gabriel pulled me to the back door. I looked back at Daniel with my eyes wide as I was pulled. I knew I was in trouble and in this moment I was fully aware of Gabriel's size compared to mine. He had pulled me with little effort and up on my toes we went like a parent with an unruly child.

When the door shut behind us, he really lit into me, "What was that about? I have half a mind to fire you!"

"As if you don't know!" I barked back.

"Were you trying to embarrass her? If so, you succeeded admirably! If you were trying to embarrass me, you succeeded admirably!"

"Good!" I snapped.

"Good? Do you know who she is?"

"The woman you go out with occasionally who does not know she isn't your girlfriend!"

"Is that what this is about? You are jealous?!!" He was pissed at me and it was obvious.

"No, this is about her being a rude bitch to all of us tonight and you allowing it. Snapping her fingers and all that, 'Boy! Boy!' business to Rudy. Don't you need to get back in there to her before she starts snapping her fingers for you?"

"Ugh!" Gabriel grunted.

Before Gabriel could say anything else, the back door popped open and Daniel stuck his head out, "The natives are getting restless and demanding an encore."

"I am not done with you!" said Gabriel, but Daniel grabbed my hand and pulled me back toward the door.

"Well, I think I'm done with you!" I shot back as I was being pulled along yet again.

153

Daniel glanced back at Gabriel and with a calm, stern voice he responded, "You are done for now."

As soon as we were out of earshot of Gabriel, I let loose to Daniel, "I am so mad! What's the deal with them and what's the deal with him?"

"Oh, I'm so relieved. I was afraid you might be crying out there or worse that you might quit. By the way, I sure hope you know another song." Daniel said as we headed through the kitchen to grab my fiddle.

I laughed until I confessed, "What have I done? I think I have really screwed up any chance I had with Gabriel."

"Don't you dare breakdown on me and don't you back down!" Daniel said as he handed me the fiddle. "You are going to have to trust me on this; I don't think you have lost him. You may have forced him to open his eyes to her and it may take him a while to come back around because of that, but you are going to have to be patient with him. Plus, if she's what he wants then you sure don't want him."

"What's she to him?" I asked, but was not sure I really wanted to know.

"It really isn't my story to tell, but she is his back-up plan and she is just waiting him out," Daniel summed up.

"Back-up plan?" What did that mean?

"If the real thing does not come along or if he can't make it on his own, then he will settle with her. They have known each other since early college and she got him the job here. He thinks he owes her something, but he doesn't owe her what she thinks he does."

"What does she think he owes her?" Again, I asked a question I was not entirely sure I wanted answered.

Daniel thought for a moment before he responded, "She wants from him what he seems to be fighting to keep from feeling for you. He is struggling. He's had a hard life, Millie, and she's always represented security for him, but it's never been the kind of security he wanted. And, you have thrown a wild card in there."

I shook my head and squelched the tears. "You seem to know him really well. I think he's lucky to have you."

"Go back in and offer an encore and play something that doesn't cause everyone in the room to call Beth a devil, even though we all know she is." Daniel paused for a moment before continuing, "Don't think for one moment that you didn't give him something to think about because you done told the son of a bitch twice that you're the best that's ever been!"

We both laughed hard and loud for a few minutes.

Miss Moneybags has a first name and it was Beth. I had always liked that name, but it had truly been sullied now. Beth, Beth Reed...yuck!

I gave Daniel a big hug and told him, "I think you might be the best there's ever been!"

Daniel and I laughed again and I took his word and went back in. We had taken our time getting back to the dining room and had taken the path through the bar again. Gabriel had actually beat us back in and clearly had cut through the kitchen door and was seated back by Beth's side.

"Would you all like an encore?" I asked the room as I entered. Most everyone in the room cheered in response, not Beth or Miss Reed or whatever she liked to be called.

Perhaps the majority of the guests did not realize what had actually gone on with the previous song so for me to return and play something else really was not a big deal. Beth got a look of skepticism on her face, perhaps she was afraid I was going to play "Devil with the Blue Dress On." It was tempting, but I refrained.

This time I performed from the center of the room and did not play directly to any one person or one table. The room was silent and dim and the few patrons that were left waited patiently as I decided what to play. I chose something sweet and non-confrontational.

I chose "Try Not To Look So Pretty" by Dwight Yoakam, one of my favorite songs. As soon as I started to play and knew there was no stopping, I became afraid that Gabriel would take her hand. Just in case, I closed my eyes and knowing the words, I sang along in my head. No one else knew the words so the room stayed quiet with only the sound of the fiddle floating on the air. Midway through I relaxed and allowed myself to feel the music again as I played. I just swayed with the whining sound of the fiddle.

When I finished playing, there was a moment of silence before everyone began to clap including Beth and Gabriel. I bowed before asking, "Would you all like another?"

The room was still as full as when I first started playing "The Devil Went Down to Georgia" and they all gave a roaring, "Yes!" back in response to my question.

I fired up the fiddle and gave it another go with John Denver's "Thank God I'm a Country Boy." Again, I moved with the music and gave the fiddle a good workout and the remaining guests in the dining room sang along.

By the time I hit the last string, I was nearly exhausted and we still had to finish cleaning up the dining room, kitchen and some of us still had to make the drive back to Milledgeville.

I gathered my thoughts. I did not want to play anymore. I just wanted to go home.

"Thank you all for coming out tonight," I said as I addressed the room. "I hope you enjoyed the dinner and the show. Please have a safe trip home. Thank you again!"

CHAPTER 7

While I was at work, Jay and Emma finished moving all of our belongings from The Hillman House to The Jefferson. There was still a great deal of unpacking to do: boxes and laundry baskets full of our daily lives were strewn and stacked everywhere throughout the apartment. They had actually been making their last trip over with Jay's Uncle Lloyd's truck when I arrived home from work.

Before turning in to my pallet on the floor for the night, and since the move was complete, we decided to go shopping the next day for new everything for my room. Jay and I had agreed to throw out the daybed that I had been sleeping on since I was a child and not allow it to make the move. Jay wanted no excuse to keep me from buying the bed as he had suggested. It was going to be a day of retail therapy to overcome the night I had just had.

When I finally awoke from the sun beating through the French doors in my room, I realized I was going to have to make a list for my shopping trip and on that list would definitely be new blinds and curtains for those doors. Although the light in the room was beautiful against the hardwood floors and really made them shine, this was entirely too early to be awake considering the emotional roller coaster I had been on the night before.

I staggered from my room around 7:15 a.m. and started unpacking the boxes related to the common areas of the apartment. Jay emerged from his room a little after nine and Emma was not far behind him in coming out of hers. Jay had indeed forced Emma into taking the room on the back of the house.

Emma and Jay had their coffee as they helped me finish unpacking. Jay worked on putting all of our books on the bookshelf and straightened up the dining room, pushing the mismatched chairs around the table and what not. Emma distributed the remaining boxes of personal items to each of our rooms from the living room and I finished the kitchen. I think each of us had inherited a partial set of dishes. The dishes and glasses were sort of like our dining room chairs in that each of us had one.

"Are you all partial to these mismatched dishes? If not, would you mind if we threw them out and I bought us a matching set while we are out today? Same goes for glasses?"

They answered collectively, "I don't care."

157

Emma added, "New dishes that match would be nice, but you really don't have to, Millie."

"It's okay. I want to," I replied. "Is there anything else that we need to add to my shopping list for the day? I need retail therapy and I am fully prepared to go wild today."

"Rough night?" Jay inquired. I had not told them about it when I got home last night. I had pretty much thanked them for finishing the move without me, mentioned shopping and then I went straight to my bed, currently known as the pallet on the floor.

"I will tell you on the way to Macon," I responded. Emma and Jay glanced at each other with raised eyebrows and shrugged shoulders.

"Does it have anything to do with Gabriel?" Emma asked.

I was about to say, "What do you think?" when Jay took the words from my mouth. He continued with, "You know, I still have not met this guy."

"I have," said Emma, "and everything Millie said about him before is true. He is HOT!"

I left the room to get ready while Emma went on and on about seeing him at the bar and how he had acted with me. It was a bit more than I wanted to hear right then considering all hopes might have been dashed by my behavior toward Miss Reed.

"We have a lot to do today so can you all be ready in about fifteen minutes?" I yelled to them from my room.

"Yes, mother!" they yelled back.

It was not long before we were on our way in the C10. Since I was driving, we made Jay sit in the middle. I chose to take the road through Gray because a large section was four lanes and it was usually the quicker route even though the other way was shorter. While I drove, I told them about my Friday night.

"I think your new friend Daniel is right. You just need to hang in there and keep being yourself," said Emma. "That's if you want to be bothered with all of this. You know there are other guys, other fish in the sea as they say."

"I agree," added Jay, "but how did you leave things with Gabriel?"

"Oh, that's the best part. He walked her out and before he did she insisted on saying 'goodnight' to me." I told them as I rolled my eyes. "Right there in front of him, after she made all nicey-nicey to me for his benefit, she leaned in while giving me a hug and whispered, 'You might have won the battle, sweetie, but I will win the war...'"

"What did you do?!!" Jay interrupted.

"I whispered back, 'Only if I let you!'"

This time Emma interrupted, "What did she do then?"

"She kissed him right in front of me. I thought I was going to vomit in my mouth. I played it cool though."

"How so?" asked Jay.

"I told them to get a room!" I replied.

"And what did Gabriel do? Did he kiss her back?" Emma asked. "If he did then you are definitely done with him."

"I think he was surprised by her kiss and he was embarrassed that it was in front of me. He totally pushed her off when I told them to get a room."

Just then as we were headed into the town of Gray, I noticed a yard sale. Among the items spread across the yard of a white antebellum house, was an antique iron bed frame. I started to slow down.

"It's too small, keep driving," said Jay.

I ignored him and parallel parked along the street in front of the house. "You can come with me or wait here," I told them as I jumped out of the truck. Emma followed me and we perused the items while Jay waited in the truck.

As it turned out, the bed frame was a queen size and I got it for a total of twenty-five dollars. It was fairly plain, nothing ornate, just painted white. It was perfect for me and the price could not be beat.

I also bought an old Fender acoustic guitar and a banjo at the yard sale. I knew a lot of famous musicians played Fender guitars: Merle Haggard for one and Richie Sambora for another. Although I could play the guitar, I could not play the banjo. That did not mean I could not or would not learn to play

159

it. Learning the banjo and focusing on that might be just the diversion I needed from Gabriel.

The instruments looked like they were in good condition, but the main reason I bought them was to use them as wall decorations in my room. I thought instead of hanging artwork or something above the headboard, I would hang the instruments, on their sides and one above the other. Plus, the Fender guitar would make a great addition to my collection and just because I hung it on the wall did not mean I could not take it down and play it. I bought both pieces for $75.

Once we loaded the bedframe and instruments in the back of the truck, we continued on to Macon. At the mall we bought a new duvet cover for my new bed. It was beautiful. The main color was red with a large blue and cream colored floral pattern. I bought everything in the store to recreate the model bed: blue striped sheets, eyelet bed skirt, red curtains, shams and throw pillows. I might have gone a little overboard when I picked up another set of sheets so it would all still match when I had to wash one set and put on the spare.

I had never had throw pillows or sheets that matched my duvet. In fact, I had never had a duvet before, only bedspreads. My family had always been practical if nothing else. This would not have been seen as practical.

I admit I spent a small fortune on the bedding, but I had really saved on the bedframe so I did not feel guilty. Jay and Emma just looked on as the clerk and I picked out everything. In fact, the Macy's lady was so helpful in picking everything out and making sure everything matched and coordinated perfectly that one would have thought she worked on commission. I could hardly wait to get back home and make the bed, but I still had to buy a mattress set.

When we left the mall, we headed to Pier One where I spent another fortune on new kitchen wares and accent pieces including an accent chair for my room. Our most daunting task was finding the right mattress. We were like the three bears in our tastes in mattresses: my bed's too hard, mine's too soft and so on. I finally found one that was perfect for me and best of all, we were able to take it home with us right then.

Lastly, we had a late lunch at The Bear's Den near the Mercer campus. By the time we left Macon, we had the entire back of the truck completely loaded down.

We arrived home to five messages on the machine. Two of the messages were for me, one was for all of us, one for Jay and one where the caller said nothing and just hung up. It had been a banner day for the answering machine.

The first message was from Daniel: "Millie, it was great meeting you last night and I just wanted to call and check on you today. Keep your chin up and here is my number if you want to call me. I will be home until I head to work at 4:00. See you later."

The second message was from Cara, "Hey, tart! You better be home when I get home. I hear you were quite the spectacle last night. Everyone is talking. Anyway, gotta get back to work. See you tonight and also Alvin says 'hi' and he is sending home some dinner for you so don't eat anything."

The third message was from Jay's Aunt June. "Haa-aay! It's Aint Ju-une and y'all better be home around six because I am fixin' dinner and bringin' it over with some house warming gifts. My best fried chicken, chocolate cake and what not. Plus, I am dying to see the new place!"

The fourth message was the person calling and hanging up once the machine picked up.

The last message was from Jay's mother. We all rolled our eyes when we heard her voice. She was more Southern sounding than Aunt June, one might think that impossible, but a translator was nearly needed for her message and the translation was this: "Daddy and I are driving down to see your new place tomorrow. We are going to swing by and get Jolene and bring her with us. We should be over around noon. I will call again to make sure you got this message. Jesus loves you, baby, and I'm gonna pray for you."

Jay's mother was a spectacle. Mrs. McDonald was all of about four foot ten inches tall and made me look tall, which few people did. She had a ton of ailments and loved going to the doctor about as much as she loved the Lord. She once told us a story over dinner that involved the Lord having spoken to her and having shown her the most beautiful colors. They had just appeared to her. She described it as the most amazing shades of pink and purple and yellow that just swirled around her room like a floating, spiraling rainbow. She also claimed it was the closest to God she had ever felt.

I did not say anything as she was telling the story, but I was wondering in my head if the experience was so close to God because she might be OD-ing on her pain meds. I could also hear "Lucy In The Sky With Diamonds" playing in my head while she went on and on about the experience.

We all recognized that his mother was clearly having a drug induced experience. Clearly, she was high. Unlike myself, Emma was not one to hold her tongue and before she knew it she burst out with, "Sounds like what happened to me the first time I smoked pot."

In Jay's mother's mind she was not high, had never been high and had no idea what Emma was implying, but she was appalled and shocked that Emma smoked pot. The rest of us knew, including Jay's dad who laughed at the situation, but Jay was horribly embarrassed.

Despite all of her quirky ways, Mrs. McDonald was one of the nicest, kindest ladies I had ever met. Since the day Jay and I met at piano lessons when we were little, she had treated me like one of her own. I came and went from their lives when I was yo-yoed back and forth between my mother and my grandfather, but as soon as I was back for good, I was about as much a McDonald as I was an Anderson. The family secret that was not really a secret was that Jay's parents hoped the "gay thing" was just a phase and that Jay and I would one day get married and have a few grandchildren for them. For the longest time before he came out he let them assume I was his girlfriend. I think until I marry someone else they will always hold out hope. They never understood that Jay and I were often more like brother and sister than he and Jolene were.

It was a shame I would have to miss Sunday with the McDonalds.

**

It was well after 4:00 p.m. when we arrived back home so there was no calling Daniel back. I knew he was close with Gabriel so I was anxious to find out why he called, but I would have to wait and hope that he was working Sunday brunch and talk to him then. The bright spot was that Cara would be home soon and it sounded like she had news.

**

Jay and Emma helped me bring in everything from the truck. We were also lucky that Travis and Stella were home when it came time for us to get the mattress up the stairs. Travis was glad to help us and Stella was anxious to get a look at what was upstairs. They were both impressed with our apartment even though it wasn't nearly finished. I ended up inviting them back for dinner on Tuesday night. I figured this would be a new age of traditions and Tuesday night would be family dinner night at The Jefferson.

Travis and Stella stayed for a little while and Travis helped Jay hang the curtains in my room. Emma put away the new items we bought for the kitchen. Stella helped me put the bedframe together, but as soon as we were done and Travis and Jay were finished with the curtains Stella and Travis left. They always acted as if they were afraid they were going to out stay their welcome, which could never happen.

It was not very long before I had the entire room complete. The bed was made with the new covers. It looked amazing, all fluffy and comfy. I could not wait to sleep in it. The bedframe combined with the height of the mattress set and the fluffiness of the bed covers made the bed look really high off of the floor. I loved it!

I also loved the accent chair which I had picked up at Pier One. There was red everywhere and the room was so much more grown up and womanly than any I had had in the past. A knock on the door came as I stood there admiring my new space.

The only drawback to our new apartment was that we had to go down the stairs to answer the door. We were expecting Aunt June at 6:00 p.m. and it was getting to be about that time. Jay thought it might be her so he went down the stairs to greet her and found Cara at the door. Jay let her in and Cara came running up the stairs.

I came out into the living room when I heard her yell for me as she ran up the stairs. "Millie!" Cara yelled a couple of times as she bounded up the stairs.

"Hey!" I greeted her.

"Oh, my God, what went on at the club last night?" she demanded with glee in her voice.

"I sort of put on a little concert..." I answered as she cut me off.

"A little concert?" Cara laughed. "Andy and Daniel went on and on about you. I think Andy has a little crush on you now. Several of the guests that were in last night came back today looking for Gabe so they could go on and on about you. I finally take a Friday night off and the place actually gets interesting!"

"What did Daniel tell you?" I asked.

Just as Cara and I were really getting started, another knock at the door came. This time it was Aunt June and I did not want to be rude, but I did not want to give up my conversation with

Cara either. I told Jay to give Aunt June the tour and I would be out in a few minutes. I then took Cara to my room.

As soon as we were in the door, Cara screamed, "I love this room!" and she ran and flopped on my bed. "This bed is amazing!"

"Come on, you know I am dying! Am I still employed?" I asked with a touch of panic in my voice.

"First of all, Gabe could not fire you now even if he wanted to. Second, from what I heard it sounds like you sent the wicked witch of the South packing. According to Daniel, this is the first time Beth has been in town since you were hired. Normally when she comes to town, Gabe leaves the club early and Andy locks up."

The wheels of my mind started to turn, "But Gabriel locked up last night and Beth left long before we were all finished cleaning up."

"Right. Apparently, Gabe had a talk with Beth about how she treated his staff and then put her in her car and sent her home alone."

"Re-ally?" I said with drawn out emphasis.

"Yep! Daniel said Gabe was ticked with you at first, but you held your own. He also said that everyone was impressed with you and the fiddle including Gabe. I have to ask, Millie, did you really have the entire room call her the devil?"

"It wasn't quite like that," I started to explain. "She was already being mean to Rudy when she said to me, 'so Gabriel tells me you can play.' She said it in such a superior, 'I'm better than you' tone. Plus, she implied that she wanted me to play the piano, but did not say it specifically. Anyway, I figured I would just let her know there was a new bitch in town you might say. Well, I picked the 'Devil Went Down to Georgia', as you probably heard, and everyone was singing along so when it came to the part about, 'I've told you once you son of a bitch, I'm the best that's ever been!' I stopped playing and the entire room screamed the words. That's everyone in the room, but her and Gabriel."

"You really were directing everything at Gabe and not her, weren't you?" Cara gasped

"Bingo!"

"Do you have any idea if he got it?"

"I don't know because when he drug me out back he just yelled at me for being mean to her and having embarrassed them so I don't think he got it."

"Millie, you may not have to tell him. From what I gather from Daniel, he may already know it."

"Cara, have you ever touched Gabriel?" I asked with caution.

"What do you mean?" she returned. "And I think it's cute that you call him Gabriel instead of Gabe."

"When you first met him did you shake hands? And did you feel anything?" Again, I asked with caution. I seemed to have a knack for asking questions to which I was not sure I wanted the answer.

"Yeah, so?" Cara replied.

"So, there was nothing unusual?"

"What are you getting at?" Cara was growing impatient, which I was fine with because she was oblivious to what I was asking and that meant the answer was that there was not anything unusual.

I decided to go ahead and explain it to her just so I could be clear. "Cara, this stays between us. Promise?"

"I promise." Cara assured me she would not breathe a word of what I was about to tell her.

"When he touches me or I touch him it is like an electric current runs through me. When he stands near me, I get flushed. He hugged me one night and my knees went completely weak. I have never had anyone have this kind of effect on me. Ever! I have been curious all this time if he has this effect on everyone. You know, like sparks?"

"Oh. No, I don't get that at all." Cara shook her head adamantly, very quickly back and forth in the negative.

"Alright, so you have helped me out with that. Let me ask you one more question. What are the odds that he feels the same charge or spark, for lack of better wording?" I figured I had asked her everything else, I might as well ask her the big one.

"Seriously, Millie, everyone saw you guys at Cameron's that night and they could tell there was something going on."

At that very moment, Jay knocked on the door and wanted to show Aunt June my room. I let them in and introduced Cara to

165

Aunt June. I was barely finished with the introductions when Cara excused herself. She insisted that we would talk again later while Aunt June became distracted with my new bedding.

"This is so lovely, Millie," I had Aunt June's approval. "I love what you all are doing with the place."

Aunt June was so sweet. She was the sister of Jay's mother and she lived just outside of Milledgeville with Uncle Lloyd. They had been a Godsend in all of the help they had given me since I had started college there. When we were not having dinner at The Brick, we were fixtures at her table. Tonight was an exception; she had brought dinner to us.

Aunt June brought fried chicken, fresh green beans, homemade macaroni and cheese, creamed corn and mashed potatoes as well as yeast rolls and a chocolate cake. She said she did not have anything better to do that day and she figured we needed a good meal after moving. She had no idea that the move was done and we had been shopping all day.

Aunt June also brought us something to put the meal on; she brought us her old kitchen table. It was one of those retro aluminum frame tables with the laminate top and vinyl cushions in the chairs. The top of the table was white and the trim around the edge was silver and red. The chairs had white cushions with red piping and matching aluminum frames and there were six chairs. This was probably not the dining set that I would have picked out myself, but it was free and it sure beat the tiny round mismatched table and three chairs that we currently had.

Dinner was wonderful and Aunt June stayed until nearly 9:00 p.m. just shooting the breeze with us. As soon as she was gone, Jay and Emma dressed in their finest and reverted to their true bar-hopping selves. In all honesty, they were beginning to have withdrawals and needed their night out. I, on the other hand, had a long day of beverage cart duty in store for me the following day and I could not wait to try out my new bed. As soon as Aunt June was gone, I showered, put on my PJs and headed off to sleep.

The bed was wonderful; the sheets were soft, the comforter was fluffy and the mattress was just firm enough. All in all, I had the best night's sleep I had had in as long as I could remember.

***

The most eventful thing about work on Sunday was that Daniel and Cara were both there. They worked the brunch shift in the dining room while I manned the beverage cart. Gabriel was a no show for work and Alvin filled in for him. I tried to shrug everything off, but I had not seen him since Friday night and I just wanted to know that everything was alright with him. I wanted to feel the spark if nothing else.

I had only a brief moment to chat with Daniel as he helped me load the beverage cart on one of my many refills of the day. Daniel reiterated what he had told me on Friday night, "Just hang in there Millie and be yourself. If things are meant to be, then they will be."

Clearly that was not the reassurance that I was looking for, but Daniel added one more thing that made me realize that I had to take his first advice. "You impress everyone with your kindness every time they see you." Daniel emphasized the word "everyone" in his statement. Again, he was not breaking a confidence, but giving me the hint.

***

October came and went. We had our family dinners on Tuesday nights at The Jefferson. I was doing well in school. I was on track to make the Dean's List. I continued to work at the club on Wednesday nights, Saturdays and Sundays during the day. I rarely saw Gabriel during those weeks. When I did see him he spoke and was cordial, but nothing more. He did not make eye contact and we were never close enough for me to physically touch him and feel the spark, but it was definitely there. I came close to swapping a shift with Cara so it would force him to notice me, but decided against it. It seemed he wanted distance so I went with it. It was not that I was trying to forget him. It was just that I was trying to have faith. The real bright spot of all of those weeks was that by all accounts Beth had not been back to the club. If she had, Cara would have told me.

With the potential to make The Dean's List, to buying The Jefferson, to making so many great new friends and learning to play the banjo from the yard sale, I had already accomplished more than I thought I would especially for only having been there for so little time. I was an overachiever, so what if I did not have a boyfriend. It was not like I had had much in the way of boyfriends in the past so why should this time in my life be any different?

***

I was already scheduled to work on Wednesday, November 1, but on Halloween I arrived home after class to a message on the machine.

167

"Hey, Millie, this is Praise from Port Honor, Gabe wanted me to call you and ask you to be at work tomorrow a little early. He wants you here at 2:00 p.m. Please call me back to let me know you got the message. Thanks!"

I thought about it for a moment before picking up the phone and dialing the number for the club to call her back. What in the world could be going on that I need to be there so early on a Wednesday?

I dialed the numbers on the cordless phone and headed to my room as the phone rang. Mrs. Joan answered on the second ring, "Port Honor, this is Joan. May I help you?"

"Hi, Mrs. Joan, this is Millie..."

"Happy Halloween, Millie, it's good to hear from you," she still sounded just as Southern as pecan pie.

"Happy Halloween to you as well. It has been a while, hasn't it?" I played along with the small talk as I flopped down on my bed and took my shoes off.

"I heard about you and the fiddle performance. I hear you really got Miss Beth's goat," Joan had a hint of laughter in her voice as she spoke of me getting to Beth.

"I don't know if I got her goat or not," I responded sounding like the wind were out of my sails since the goat was clearly Gabriel.

"Well, someone needs to bring her down a notch and if you are the girl to do it then I will buy you a steak dinner, Millie." It sounded like Mrs. Joan knew the name of the goat as well.

Mrs. Joan continued and we were back to business, "So, Millie, what can I do for you today?"

I responded with my purpose for calling as I fell back onto my bed, "I'm returning a call to Praise. I need to let her know I got her message."

"Hold on, I will try to find her for you," Joan said before placing me on hold.

Within about twenty seconds, Praise was on the line, "Millie, you got my message?"

"Yes, ma'am. Any idea why so early?" I asked.

"No idea. Gabe just told me to make the call so I made the call," Praise replied.

"You can tell him I'll be there. Thanks for calling me, Praise. I hope you are doing well."

"I'm well, thank you for asking. You are always such a darling, Millie. I'll see you soon. Bye." For as Southern and sweet as Joan sounded, Praise sounded gruff and like she had a two pack a day habit, but they were both as nice as they could be to me.

***

The next day I arrived at work at 2:00 p.m. as I had been asked. I was not sure what I was going to be doing, so I wore jeans and a GC sweat shirt. Praise was waiting on me in the kitchen when I arrived.

"Gabriel said to give you this," and Praise handed me a large black garment bag. "He said put it on and he'll pick you up at 2:30 so hurry up."

"What's going on? And what's in the bag?" I asked as I took it from her.

"All I know is you are supposed to be changed and ready. He tells me nothing," an exasperated Praise said. "Go get changed while I have a smoke. I'll be back to check on you in five minutes. You can use the ladies room down here or the locker room upstairs. No one's in the locker room as far as I know."

"I'll be in the ladies room down here." I felt there was no need to go trekking up stairs when I had no idea what was in the bag anyway and we weren't really supposed to use the locker room.

Once in the restroom I opened the garment bag to find a long black dress and silver strappy high heels. There was a note taped to the dress. The note read, "Amelia, get dressed and be ready by 2:30. I will explain everything when I pick you up." He signed the note with his whole name, "Gabriel".

I did as the note instructed. The dress was black satin. It gathered around my neck and tied in the back. It gathered again and tied behind my back at my waist, but with regard to having an actual back, it did not. There was no wearing a bra with the dress and that was something I was completely unaccustomed to unless I was sleeping.

The skirt portion of the dress was floor length and flowing, but had a slit up my thigh almost all the way to my hip. Without the heels it would have drug the ground, but once I put them on I realized the dress was actually the perfect length. The entire dress fit perfectly with the exception of the foreign feeling of being without a bra.

For a moment I admired myself in the floor length mirror in the ladies room. I was shocked at the transformation from girl to woman that I was witnessing.

Praise was coming through the door into the dining room as I was about to head into the kitchen to find her.

"Wow! Talk about long cool woman in a black dress!" Praise commented. "And I would kill for your hair."

Luckily I had curled my hair earlier that morning. I had pulled it back with a hair band into a bun, but that would not have done with the dress so I had removed the hair band and fortunately the curl had held and it fell into ringlet curls. My hair fell down my back by more than half way and was more than enough to cover the indention in my back that the bra strap had left.

"I completely agree, Praise," Gabriel said from the landing midway down the staircase. "Come around here so I can get a better look at you." Gabriel added as he descended the stairs all the while never taking his eyes off of me.

I did as he asked and Praise followed me. I did my best to hold my head high and walk with confidence even though I felt naked without my bra.

As long as he was on the staircase, Gabriel was cast in a shadow. That changed as soon as he hit the bottom of the stairs in front of the bar door. The afternoon sun was beating down through the wall of windows in the dining room and he was lit up as if there were a halo all around him. As always, Gabriel was not so bad looking himself. He had to be a Calvin Klein model in his spare time.

For most people it was their clothes that made them look good, but with Gabriel it always seemed to be the opposite. He could probably make an orange jumpsuit look attractive but what he had on was no orange jumpsuit. It was a black suit that appeared to have been tailored just for him. His white shirt was open at the neck by two buttons and he was carrying a silver tie in his right hand. The tie had a touch of texture giving the illusion that it had a checked pattern to it, but it was all one solid color. I suppose he had coordinated the suit with the dress since the shoes for the dress were silver as well.

His hair was combed back and had more gel in it than what he typically applied. He had a touch of stubble to his face which I had never seen on him before. One might think he had not shaved in two days, but it was perfectly manicured and nothing unkempt about it. The most noticeable thing about Gabriel was the way his eyes blistered blue in the sunlight and were the only real touch of color on him.

I had been so irritated with him for ignoring me this last month and now just the sight of him and I was slipping, bewitched as always. That was also irritating. I gritted my teeth as I approached him and tried to hang on to my free will of being mad with him.

"Looks like it fits," he added as we approached one another.

"I suppose it does," I said with skepticism boiling in my voice. "If I'm the hostess tonight, I have clothes I could've worn. No one had to buy me a dress, let alone something that bordered on being a ball gown."

"Look Amelia, I am sorry I didn't give you more notice, but quite frankly I just found out about this yesterday morning." Gabriel mustered an apology. He really had some nerve.

Praise interrupted, "If y'all don't need me anymore, I have some dish towels in the washer downstairs that need to be switched to the dryer."

"Amelia, do you need the dress taken in or up or anything, if so, you need to tell Praise and let her take care of it. I don't know how traffic is going to be and we probably need to get going."

"The dress is fine, except I could use...never mind about that. Anyway, I haven't agreed to go anywhere with you." Praise took her leave as soon as I said the dress was fine. I was still put out by him taking me for granted and I meant to show it.

Gabriel stepped even closer to me and I took a step back, "We both know that if you weren't coming, you would have never put on the dress."

"I don't think I like you very much right now and I don't believe I'm going anywhere with you until I get a few more details."

"We are going to Atlanta to the Georgian Terrace Hotel..."

I cut him off as he clearly had lost his mind and the part where he mentioned a function slipped mine as well. "I'm not going to a hotel with you and I am certainly not doing it on fifteen minutes notice!"

I am not sure what was funny about what I had said, but Gabriel burst into laughter. "What exactly is it that you think we are going to do?" he laughed. When he regained control of his speech he added, "Amelia, we are joining Dick and Joan for dinner with the owners of the club to talk about the Olympics. We are having dinner at the apartment where the owners are staying, that's all."

Well, didn't I feel like a fool. "Oh," is all I could get out. I think I had already said enough. Surely my face was beat red from embarrassment.

"Rest assured, if I am ever going to fuck you, Amelia, this is probably not the way I would go about it unless that is what you would like." As if I were not embarrassed enough, Gabriel's latest statement really cemented the feeling. And, wow, was he crass about it. I could have just died. Normally, I would have been all hot and bothered at the thought of having sex with him or just standing next to him, but this was an entirely different feeling. No sparks, just sheer mortified embarrassment.

"Are you coming or not?" he demanded.

"Fine!" I snapped back at him. "I need to call Jay and let him know where I am and that I might be later than usual."

"Fine! Go call him at the bar phone and then meet me at the back door of the kitchen in five minutes."

I went to the bar and called Jay. I got the machine so I left a message then met Gabriel at the back door. Gabriel held the door for me as we headed out onto the loading dock. As I walked ahead of him I could feel him looking at me. I dropped my head and looked back over my shoulder to catch him. I felt the urge to chastise him and he must have felt it coming and spoke before I could.

"What? You are a mighty fine woman, Miss Anderson. Who wouldn't look?"

"UGH!!!" I grunted, but did not look back at him anymore remembering the last time we were on the loading dock together.

"What?" he demanded as he walked faster and around me on the loading dock. Gabriel made it to the steps just barely ahead of me and held out his hand to help me down them.

"You are infuriating!" I said as I reluctantly took his hand. Oh, the sparks were there, but I was doing my best to ignore them and focus on not tripping on the hem of the dress or twisting an ankle in the five inch tall heels.

"And you are frustrating, so aren't we a pair?"

"I have nothing else to say to you." And I took my hand back as soon as I hit the bottom step.

"Well I still have something to say to you." I am not sure what I thought he was going to say, but I did think it would be more than, "That's my car over there," and he pointed to a black Acura Legend that was backed into the parking spot nearest the dock. He seemed to be enjoying the banter, but I screamed inside and outwardly rolled my eyes at him.

Despite our back and forth, he was still a gentleman and opened the door for me. I then did my best to gracefully sit in the car without flashing him my underpants due to the dramatic slit in the dress, which by some good fortune I had actually worn black underwear that day.

As he put the car in gear he mentioned, "We are going to run by Joan's house for just a moment. She is expecting us and has a couple of things to help complete your outfit. I can't have you going to dinner carrying your keys as your only jewelry around your middle finger." I looked down at my hands in my lap to notice he was right that was the only accessory I had on and it wasn't a real accessory.

Joan lived just around the corner from the clubhouse back toward the entrance gate of Port Honor. We arrived at Joan's house and she was waiting on me at the front door. She was dressed to the nines as well. She had on a red jacket and skirt made of a raw silk looking material and red lipstick and nail polish to match. She looked beautiful for a woman of her age that had had two children, but she almost had on too much red.

"Oh, Millie, you look so pretty. I am so glad you are joining us tonight. Promise me you will be sweet to Gabe tonight. He's had a rough couple of weeks." Joan told me as she handed me a silver clutch and some bangle type silver bracelets.

"Thank you so much for loaning me these, but what is the deal with him?" I asked her while slipping the bracelets on.

"I will fill you in at dinner while the boys talk business. Just hang in there and don't be too hard on him. Now go. Dick and I will be right behind you all," Joan said before turning to go back inside.

173

We drove a fair portion of the way down I-20 toward Atlanta in silence, no music, no nothing. He gripped the steering wheel at ten with his left hand and rested his hand on the gear shift in the center console area. He stared at the road most of the way there and I stared out the passenger's side window. We were nearly to 285 before Gabriel spoke.

"Do you know why they are staying at the Georgian Terrace?" he asked.

"No, why?" I said with little to no enthusiasm in my voice, as if I cared.

"They are from Germany and one of the guy's wives loves *Gone With the Wind*. Have you seen it?"

"Only small bits and pieces. Have you?" I asked and my interest was beginning to be peaked.

"Can't say that I have, but the trivia is that when it premiered in Atlanta at Loew's Grand Theater, Clark Gable and Vivian Leigh, who played Rhett and Scarlett..."

"I know who they are, I am from the South after all," I insisted.

"Well, they stayed at the Georgian Terrace while they were in town for the premier. Therefore, the owner's wife wanted to stay at the Georgian Terrace where Rhett and Scarlett stayed. It isn't a hotel anymore, it's luxury apartments so they rented an apartment there for when they come to town."

"That's actually pretty interesting. I might feel more nostalgic about being there if I had seen more of the movie," I was still annoyed with him, but I thought I would heed Joan's request.

"So what is going on that they want to talk about the Olympics with you all?" I asked.

"The owners are sponsoring the German Equestrian Team and they want the team to be housed at The Honor Inn while they are here competing at the Olympics."

"Aren't you just full of interesting information today?" I was doing my best to let go.

Gabriel finally took his eyes off of the road and looked at me. He reached over with his right hand and took mine from my lap. I tensed, but I did not resist.

"I want to clear the air with you, Amelia, not just before we get to dinner, but in general," he began. "I don't want to fight with you. I don't want you being mad with me. I want to go back to that night when we ran barefoot on the green."

He paused and I did not know what to say. Whenever I daydreamed, I dreamed of that moment, but I did not want to tell him that.

"Please understand that for so long, Beth was the only person who I felt really knew me and really cared about me. To me, our relationship was multileveled, but to her it went in one direction. The thing that I came to realize not too long ago was that Beth cares about Beth and she cares about her pets. She has a show pony and a dog and she had herself a football player turned Navy Officer for a while. I realized I was the same as the damn pony. She just kept me at a different stable. I have never thought she was a bad person and she was always good to me, but I don't want to be anyone's pet. She told me how to dress, where to be, how to speak, I could go on. Some might think she educated me on how the other half lives and I should be grateful. I am grateful, but I outgrew that relationship quite some time ago."

"You dressed me for tonight," I could not help but point out.

"Actually, Joan went to Athens and found that this morning," he corrected me.

"Who paid for it?"

"I did, but..."

"Right."

"Amelia, I know you could never be anyone's pet," he added sternly before returning to the subject of Beth. "I have avoided you because I had to really finish things with Beth and despite what others think she does not deserve to be hurt." By the word "others" I think he was just being polite in not using the word "you".

He went on to say, "I do care about her and I hope to remain friends with her."

I looked over at him. On one hand my heart broke to think that he once loved her. On the other, I was ecstatic that she was in the past. I was uneasy about him remaining friends with her especially since to her this was just a battle and despite what he thought of her, the fact that she was not a nice person oozed from her. I had only met her that one time and I knew that. Daniel knew it and most everyone except Gabriel seemed to know it.

"Ok, so enough about that," I said because I did not want to spend time with him talking about her.

"So we are okay?" he asked.

"We are as okay as you want us to be," I responded and the light that had been missing returned to his eyes and a weight seemed to have been lifted.

Gabriel was still holding my hand and he pulled it up and kissed it.

"Are you ready to have a good time tonight, Miss Anderson?"

"I think so, Mr. Hewitt!"

"I think so, too. Now hand me that CD case that's there at your feet, please. I think you need a theme song for the evening. There's a CD in there by The Hollies. Take it out and hand it to me."

Gabriel let go of my hand and I retrieved the CD from the case in the floorboard and handed it to him. We were taking the turn onto the I-75/85 connector when he slipped the CD into the player, punched up a song and it started to play. I had not recognized the artist's name, but I recognized the opening, the licks of the guitar and the thump, thump of the drum; "Long Cool Woman in a Black Dress."

"Oh, no," I said and I knew I was blushing.

"Oh, yeah!" he said as he smiled a thousand watt smile and started to move his head with the music and sing along. He also put his foot down on the accelerator and there was something thrilling about going fast through the city and listening to that song.

I chair danced along with the music as well, but I also plundered through his CD case and took out what was to be the next song. As The Hollies were finishing and we were just about to turn onto North Avenue, I slipped in the song I had picked.

176

"What's this?" Gabriel asked during the pause between songs.

"Your theme song for the night," and as soon as I finished speaking LL Cool J started.

"My theme song is 'Mama Said Knock You Out'?"

"Yeah," I said in a manner as if to challenge him to ask me why. He didn't have time to challenge before the music really got going and I was in full concert mouthing the words and dancing in the seat. Before I knew it we were both singing along and dancing in our seats as we sped long toward the Georgian Terrace. We pulled into the designated valet parking in front of the building on Peachtree Street, directly across the street from the Fox Theater, just as the song was finishing up.

Gabriel put the car in park and started putting his tie on.

"Don't. Just leave it. I like you just the way you look right now." I said as the valet ran out and opened my door.

"I can't," he responded.

"Leave it," I said again, looking Gabriel in the eye as I took the valet's hand for him to help me from the car. I moved my right leg to get out of the car. Purposefully, I moved letting the slit in the dress work its magic, the material falling so that my entire left leg was bare to my hip.

"Careful, Miss Anderson," Gabriel warned, but he put the tie back on the console and got out of the car. He tossed the valet the keys as I waited.

Gabriel picked up his stride coming around the car to fetch me as the valet ogled me. Gabriel gave him a speaking look as if to say, "Put your eyes back in your head, dude."

The valet immediately looked away and I turned to head in just as Gabriel made it to my side. He put his hand on the small of my bare back and led me up the steps of the hotel. "You are bad Miss Anderson," he whispered referring to the slit of the dress action as we climbed the steps.

Gabriel's hand on my back was distracting and I found it hard to ignore the tingle that ran down my spine. I cut my eyes at him and did my best to flirt without saying a word. Every dream I ever had was in the flesh right next to me as we took the steps to the Georgian Terrace together. For the night, he was mine. I relished the thought. Perhaps he read my mind since he responded with a glance, a smile and a wink of his left eye at me.

I really did not know anything of the old hotel, but looking at it as we made our way to the entrance that faced Peachtree Street I knew it was a piece of Southern history. The majority of the building was butter colored brick, accented on this side by a terrace of marble columns and floor to ceiling, two story windows. There were several groups of folks having drinks at tables on the terrace. It was a cool night and I would have been completely satisfied to sit among them for hours, gazing over at the Fox Theater and watching the traffic whiz past.

Frank Sinatra was playing on the sound system as we entered the grand lobby. The smell of lilies floated in the air. Gabriel stopped at the concierge and asked that the Von Bremens be made aware of our arrival. We were then directed to the elevators and to the tenth floor.

"If we are just going to their apartment, why are we so dressed up?" I asked as the elevator doors closed behind us.

"Wait until you see them and the apartment," Gabriel replied.

On the tenth floor we were met in the foyer just outside of the elevator by a woman with a heavy German accent. She introduced herself as Genevieve Von Bremen, but she preferred to be called "Viv".

Apparently, she and Gabriel had never met before since he introduced himself as well, "Good evening, Mrs. Von Bremen, I am Gabe Hewitt, the clubhouse manager from Port Honor, and this is Miss Amelia Anderson."

I was certainly glad he did not elaborate on a title or my position at the club. I was already feeling out of place enough without letting on that the serving girl would not be sitting in the kitchen for dinner tonight. She would be sitting at the main dining room with all of the important folk.

Mrs. Von Bremen looked like she could have been Gabriel's mother, same hair color and eyes, but a rounder face with high cheek bones. I anticipated her to be about fifty years old. She was wearing a deep green colored velvet jacket over a shell and a matching velvet floor length skirt. Her suit was trimmed with tassels of a lighter green color. Although I had not seen much of Gone With the Wind, I had seen and heard enough to know that one of the key scenes was when Scarlett had Mammy make her a dress using the green velvet

178

curtains. I instantly knew that this was the particular owner's wife who was fond of the movie.

Mrs. Von Bremen escorted us through the apartment, through the initial hallway, past the kitchen and through the sitting room. As we followed Mrs. Von Bremen, I clung to Gabriel, clutching his hand and doing my best to shake the feeling of being some place I did not belong. At one point I whispered to him, "I live in an apartment and this is no apartment. This is a palace in the sky." Gabriel cut his eyes at me and smiled trying not to laugh or even snicker. For all I really knew of him, he may have felt as out of place as I did, but he never let it show.

From the time we stepped foot off of the elevator we had touched nothing beneath our feet, but the finest looking Italian marble. There was gold trim, not brass, gold, on everything, door knobs, hinges and so forth. The ceiling was at least another six to seven feet above my head. It was made of tin-types with a fleur de lis design hammered into them and they were painted enamel white which shined every bit as much as the marble floor. Down the hallway the walls were divided three-quarters of the way from the floor by an ornate type of molding with white judges paneling below and wallpaper featuring scenes of a French countryside above. Midway down the hall was a chandelier of teardrop crystals which were blindingly reflective from the light itself and the reflection from the ceiling and the floor.

When we passed through the sitting room, I could not help but notice that it was quite the opposite from the hallway. It was dark with the exception of three dimly lit lamps. The lamps struggled to cast light in the room dominated by rich mahogany wood, book cases, coffee table, end tables, and accent chairs. The room also contained two dark brown, hobnail leather couches reminiscent of those near the piano at Port Honor. The marble tile had stopped at the entrance to the room and the floor was rich hardwood with a thick beige carpet covering most of the room. The carpet was fluffy, almost fur-like shag. I nearly tripped on it as the thin heels of my sandals seemed to get tangled in the strands of the carpet as I walked.

Through the sitting room, Mrs. Von Bremen showed us to the balcony where the men who had already arrived were smoking cigars. When we stepped out, they were all speaking German and looking out over what could be seen of the Atlanta skyline.

"Mr. Hewitt and Miss Anderson," Mrs. Von Bremen presented.

A rather rotund gentleman stepped forward and extended his hand to Gabriel, "Nice to see you are still with us, Gabe."

Releasing my hand, but placing his other around my back, Gabriel extended his right hand, "I'm sorry about all of that, Mr. Von Bremen," Gabriel said as they shook hands.

"And this is *the* Miss Anderson?" Mr. Von Bremen asked as he took his hand back and gazed at me. His emphasis of the word "the" and my name made me a bit more nervous than I already was.

"Amelia, this is Mr. Von Bremen. Mr. Von Bremen is the president of the board comprised of the owners of Port Honor. The remaining gentlemen are the other owners and board members," Gabriel stated.

"Nice to meet you all and thank you so much for having us tonight," I stated. I tried to hide my Southern accent with the use of the words "you all" instead of my typical "y'all". All eyes were on me and my first thought was of my lacking bra.

One of the other gentlemen stepped forward and extended his hand to me. I held out mine thinking he was going to shake it, instead he lifted it, inspected the top of my hand and kissed it. A very uneasy feeling was coming over me when he spoke, "I see your knuckle has healed quite nicely. No scarring. We are very relieved." His German accent was as thick, if not thicker, than my Southern.

I looked to Gabriel with so many unspoken questions. I was also beginning to notice that I was the only woman, aside from Mrs. Von Bremen, who was still waiting at the door to the balcony behind us. Mrs. Von Bremen stepped forward, "Amelia, if you would please come with me, I will introduce you to the other ladies."

I really did not want to leave Gabriel, but what was I to do. I still wanted to know how the owners of the club knew about the beverage cart girl's hand and everything that went with it. Clearly, this was not the time or place for that and perhaps this is what Joan was going to tell me about over dinner. Before I left, Gabriel gave me a kiss on the forehead and whispered, "Everything's alright. Go."

I followed Mrs. Von Bremen back through the sitting room and again my heels got tangled. Thank goodness she did not notice.

We were nearly to the hall when the doorbell rang. I waited in the hall while she answered the door. It was Dick and Joan. I was so happy to see another recognizable face. It was as if a weight had been lifted.

"The men are on the balcony, if you would like to join them, Richard," Mrs. Von Bremen said after making the usual pleasantries in the entrance way. "Joan, I am taking Amelia to introduce her to the other wives. Will you join us?"

"Of course, Viv, it is so lovely to see you again," replied Joan.

Mrs. Von Bremen led us back past the kitchen where I noticed a room full of caterers. The aroma coming from the kitchen was extraordinary. It smelled like prime rib which I hoped was as good as Alvin's. I had skipped lunch and the aroma reminded me of that detail. Suddenly, I was starving.

Beyond the kitchen and dining room was a Victorian music room where the other wives were congregated. There were six of them. The men had appeared to range in age from late fifties to early seventies. The women were comparable in age except for one who was scarcely older than me. They had all been speaking German until we entered the room, but very graciously stopped and spoke English the remaining time that Joan and I were present.

After about twenty minutes, Joan asked if I would accompany her to the ladies room. Needless to say she did not have to ask twice. I figured this was my opportunity to find out just what she meant about Gabriel and the last few weeks and how and why the owners knew about my hand.

The bathroom was on par with the rest of the Von Bremen palace in the sky, but I scarcely noticed. As soon as the door shut behind us Joan swore me to secrecy and went off about how Gabriel had really broken it off with Beth Reed. Joan proceeded into the water closet, leaving the door cracked so I could hear her as she explained that they had not been an item in quite some time, but Beth had held out hope that ultimately she and Gabriel would marry and they had just been on a break for him to sew some wild oats.

Joan went on and I just waited in the corner listening. "Gabe had no intentions of reconciling with her in the manner in which she wanted. In fact, Gabe had no idea until the night that you met her at the club that she still had any intentions toward him. She made a play for him after your Devil Went Down to Georgia performance and he shut her down politely. He explained that he did not want to lose her friendship and that he just did not have those sorts of feelings for her."

I did not say anything or ask any questions, but I had tons. Joan flushed the toilet and came out straightening her skirt while she continued, "Millie, he did not factor you into any of his explaining to her when he did not give in to her advances. Unfortunately, he had already told her all about you several weeks prior, thinking that he was confiding in his friend. He told her about you getting attacked on the course and him kicking the two men out of the club and everything."

"By Thursday morning, Dick had a call from Mr. Von Bremen all the way from Germany about the situation. He knew a version of the events, the wrong version, and he was out for Gabe's job and yours. No one said that it was Beth, but she is a spin doctor for WATL, a local news station, so she has connections, and we all know it was her. Gabe has yet to accept that it was her, but I swear it was her. Her nature, the timing, it was her. I have known her for years and she was always a spiteful girl."

My only response then was, "Walks like a duck, quacks like a duck..."

"Right and we have spent the last few weeks getting the story straight and doing damage control with Von Bremen and the board. The version of events that they had heard was that you went nuts and attacked two elderly gentlemen on the course and that Gabe covered for you since you were dating."

At that point I interrupted again, "We've not been dating! He's been avoiding me! And, I did not attack anyone!"

"I know, Millie. No one cared if you all were dating. After all, who is Richard to judge? I used to work for him and I still do. Despite that, we have statements from all of the employees at Port Honor attesting that you had not been dating. We also had Matt and Alvin attest to how the gentlemen were when they found them on the course and how you were. The thing Beth did not count on was that we rallied behind Gabe and we also found three other girls at the other resorts around the lake that had been attacked by those two jackasses. One did not get away and now charges are being filed. The owners were initially concerned about the reputation of the club because of Gabe kicking out members and what if that got out. Now, they are more concerned about you suing for getting attacked and that ruining the club's reputation."

"So what's going to happen now?" I asked.

"Well, that's the thing. I insisted that he bring you," Joan said. "I believe they are convinced that neither you nor Gabe did anything wrong and that you were the victim of the situation, but I wanted them to meet you."

"And?" I was totally out of my element there.

"Just be yourself." Joan said as she glanced at me through the mirror while reapplying her more than red lipstick. Everyone sure had a lot of faith in me just being myself these days.

Joan then changed the subject, "I see the dress fits. Do you like it?"

"I do like it," I confided. "Thank you so much for getting it for me. I hope it wasn't any trouble. If he had just told me what was up, then you would not have been put out like this."

Done with the mirror she turned to me. "It was no trouble at all. I love shopping and I never had a daughter so I got to pretend for a little while," Joan smiled a wide toothy smile as she gave me sort of a side arm hug. "We should probably get back out to the ladies before they think we fell in or something."

I was rarely in the same room as Gabriel during the evening. The men talked business in the sitting room and the ladies stayed in the music room. I was virtually on my own with the exception of having Joan. I did get to sit by Gabriel at dinner. He was on one side and Mrs. Von Bremen was on the other.

To shake my nerves, I did what I knew how to do best, I played the piano in the music room. I pandered to Mrs. Von Bremen's love of Gone With the Wind and I played Dixie. It worked and she was my best friend the rest of the evening. I now have a place to stay if I ever want to visit Germany. I invited her to let me know next time she was at Port Honor and I would give her a tour of Milledgeville and Madison and show her the sites that Sherman did not burn. She was thrilled and by the end of the night I had a genuine feeling that I would be hearing from her.

Mrs. Von Bremen was clearly the leader of their pack so once I was in with her the rest of them followed. Mrs. Lehmann questioned me about my German heritage. She said she could tell by the bone structure of my face. I explained to her that my great grandfather was German and he arrived in the states around the time of the First World War as best anyone knew. I explained that we knew little of him other than that he had a heavy accent and that he came to town as a railroad worker from Chicago.

Of course, the only one that seemed to be resistant to me was Mrs. Fischer. As it turned out, she was only three years older than me and had only been married about a year. She was a trophy wife. She reminded me of Kimmie from the club, but her husband was not nearly as old as Kimmie's. Mrs. Fischer was not mean to me or anything; the worst she did was point out that I was the only unmarried woman in the room.

It was just after 10:00 p.m. when we left the Von Bremen's apartment. By the time we started to leave I was exhausted and my feet hurt. They hurt so badly that I slipped off my shoes as soon as the elevator doors closed behind us. All evening I had thought about being alone with Gabriel in the elevator again. Unfortunately, by the time we left I was nearly dead on my feet.

"Did you have a good time, Miss Anderson?" Gabriel asked as we descended.

"I did and you, Mr. Hewitt?" I returned.

"As much fun as one can have while entertaining their bosses," he smiled at me. "It is going to be chilly outside so here take my jacket." Gabriel then removed his jacket and wrapped it around my shoulders. He then put his arm around me and pulled me close.

It occurred to me while we were standing in the cool night air waiting on the valet to bring the car around that it was going to be 1:00 a.m. before I made it home. The thought was daunting.

***

The next morning I awoke in a strange bed, wearing a man's white undershirt that smelled of Gabriel and not remembering how I ended up in either. My last thought was of getting into the car with Gabriel and heading home. It wasn't my first time going to Atlanta, but it was my first time paying attention and being wonderstruck by the lights of the city at night. I remembered us having a conversation about the lights, but that's really all I remembered.

Before getting up I noticed that my dress was laid over a chair in the corner of the room. My clothes from the day before, which I had forgotten and left in the ladies room in the clubhouse, were folded neatly and laying across the seat of the same chair where the dress was. It started to dawn on me that I had to be at Gabriel's house, but where was he? Was this his bed and had I slept next to him? How disappointing would it be if I had slept next to him and not been able to remember?

According to the alarm clock on the nightstand next to the bed, it was ten after eight when I woke up. A world of thoughts raced through my head as I got out of the bed and made my way across the room to my clothes. The thoughts mainly consisted of questions: was Jay worried out of his mind that I had not come home last night? Had he even noticed that I did not come home? Has he called the police or even worse, had he called Aunt Gayle? Where were my shoes?

There were so many questions that panic was starting to set in a little, especially over the biggest questions: How had I gotten out of my dress and into this t-shirt and where in the world was Gabriel? Had he slept in this bed with me and, although I could not remember much beyond the downtown connector, surely I would have remembered had I given away the ultimate trophy.

I was midway through changing my clothes, pants were on and luckily I was bared-backed to the door and not the other way around when Gabriel knocked and came right in. It was clear from the embarrassment on his face that he had no idea that I was up, let alone that I was changing clothes.

"Sorry," he shrieked and immediately backed out of the room, closing the door behind him. I am not sure why he was embarrassed at this point. I had a suspicion that he may have helped me from my dress and into the t-shirt so he had seen most everything by then.

I finished slipping on my bra and shirt before finding him waiting in the hall. He was dressed in black pajama pants with tiny white skull and cross bones on them. Although he only had on a white undershirt like the one I had been wearing and the pirate pajama pants, I was not sure if this wasn't the sexiest he had ever looked. The suit had been magnificent the night before and I had dreamed of him in it during the night. I had dreamed of getting him out of it; surely that had been a dream.

"Good morning, Miss Anderson," he said with a shy grin. "I made breakfast, pancakes; if you would like some or if you have time. I know you have class this morning."

I tried to look at him, but aside from Gabriel being painstakingly attractive with his bedhead look still going on and the way the pajamas hung on his hips, I was clueless as to how I had ended up staying there. I kind of wanted to scream at him, "What happened last night?" but I held my tongue with the exception of answering, "Breakfast would be nice, but I have to borrow your phone if I may?"

"Of course. You can use the one in the kitchen while I finish up the bacon," Gabriel said as he led me down the hallway.

His house was a ranch style and we passed by two other bedrooms on the way to the kitchen. The other bedrooms had the doors open and I barely got a look inside. One appeared to be the master and the bed was mussed as if it had been slept in. I was starting to feel a little more at ease about still having the trophy. My virginity was intact.

Once in the kitchen Gabriel handed me the phone and I dialed home. I was almost shocked when Jay picked up. He had noticed I was not at home mainly because Gabriel had left a message for him while he was at The Juniper Street Pub in Macon last night.

"Yeah, I got in about 12:30 and there was a message from Gabriel saying you fell asleep on the ride home and he was letting you sleep at his place. I only missed his call by about ten minutes so I called back and insisted he wake you up for me to make sure you were alright."

"We spoke last night?" I asked because I did not remember speaking with him at all.

"You don't remember? I am not surprised. You sounded out of it. I even questioned him as to how much you had had to drink. You managed to tell me that he gave you a shirt to sleep in and you were sleeping in his guest room." Jay seemed to know more about the ending of my night than I did. I was so glad he did, since that prevented me from having to ask Gabriel.

"I don't remember talking to you, but this explains a great deal. I have to go and I will see you after class." I was so relieved. It answered the question about the ultimate trophy. What a relief! If I ever had sex for the first time, especially with Gabriel, I damn sure wanted to remember it.

When I was safely off the phone with Jay, I found Gabriel heating up the pancakes and taking the bacon from the stove.

"I hate to dine and dash, but I have class at 10:00 a.m. so as soon as we eat will you please give me a ride to the clubhouse to get my car?" I asked as I took a seat on a stool at the kitchen island.

"I would except that I walked there last night and drove it back here," he said as he plated up my breakfast and handed it to me.

"First of all, you walked to the clubhouse after midnight last night and, secondly, you drove my car?" I questioned him while I cut my pancakes. I was a touch shocked at both.

"I could not sleep. Yes, I drove your car. Are you okay with that?" He seemed genuinely concerned that he may have crossed some line by driving the car and he went on to explain, "I did not want it sitting at the club all night and something happen to it. I also did not want Dick and Joan seeing it still there when they arrived at work this morning."

"Right. That's fine. I understand. You may find it interesting to know that you are only the third person, not counting anyone associated with Chevrolet, to have driven it." I bragged as I ate one of the slices of bacon.

"You mean to tell me that a twenty-one year old car has only been driven by three people?"

"Yes."

"Really? How do you know?" he quizzed me.

"The story is that my father ordered the car as a present to himself for graduating medical school and for landing his first job as a doctor. He never drove the car because it did not arrive until two weeks after he was killed. My grandfather tucked it away in the back of the barn and held on to it for me. He took it out and drove it occasionally to keep the engine running. He washed and waxed it until I came to live with him and Aunt Gayle, then I was responsible for washing and waxing it. Not too much longer after that, I was responsible for driving it to keep the engine up, driving it with him in the car with me until I was fifteen of course."

"You can't be serious! You learned to drive on a classic Corvette?" he was astonished by the story.

"I did not say I learned to drive on it. I learned to drive on a Ford tractor," I corrected him.

"You never cease to amaze me! Just for my own curiosity, how many miles did the car have on it when you started driving it?"

"One hundred twelve," I responded after thinking about it for a moment and gathering my memories.

"And how many miles does it have on it now?" he continued with his questions.

"I don't know. For all I know you drove it to Augusta and back while I was asleep. Which reminds me, why couldn't you sleep?"

"I did not drive it to Augusta and back," he laughed. "And you don't need to concern yourself with why I could not sleep. Eat your pancakes."

I did eat the pancakes and they were wonderful and the bacon was just right, not too crisp and not too limp. He had taken a seat next to me at the kitchen island and I could not help but watch

187

him as we ate. The stubble beard from the night before was a little more filled out and he definitely had not bothered with his hair, yet he was still perfect. I could have spent my entire day just looking at him.

"I had a great time last night," I mentioned as I stared at him.

Gabriel put down his fork and turned and looked at me. "I had a great time too and thank you for coming with me. I know it started off rocky, but you were a real hit with the owners wives and the evening ended well."

I thought about it for a moment, but my insecurities got the better of me and I had to ask. "How exactly did it end? I remember us talking about the city lights and then I woke up here this morning. I am so sorry."

"Sorry for making me drive home virtually alone or sorry for having to be carried to bed?" He sounded so serious.

I was mortified. "You carried me to bed?"

"Yes, and dear Lord you are deceivingly heavy!" He cracked and started to laugh.

"You should be ashamed of yourself!" I smacked him on the arm.

"Me, ashamed? You are the one that slept over and are doing the walk of shame in yesterday's clothes." He continued to laugh.

"Oh, ha ha!"

"Seriously, Amelia, nothing happened," Gabriel said with the absence of laughter. "I did carry you inside last night, but once inside you woke up enough to take the undershirt from me and dress yourself and then you were out again."

Once finished with breakfast it was nearly 8:45. I tried to help him with the dishes, but he insisted that I could do them next time. I liked the sound of that, "next time." Gabriel walked me to the car and I made it to my apartment in record time. I did not have time to get a shower, but I changed clothes and was only five minutes late to class.

I arrived home from class and there was a message from Joan on the machine. "Hey, Millie, you were great last night! You were so great that the ladies are coming to stay at The Honor Inn this weekend. I need you to call me."

There was also a message from Gabriel on the machine: "Just wanted to thank you again for last night and make sure you got in alright this morning. Call me at the club after 1:00 p.m."

I called Joan back and found out my new schedule for the weekend as tour guide and then I called Gabriel back before going to badminton class, but I had to leave a message.

I did not hear from Gabriel again until I had almost given up on him. I was just about asleep around 10:00 p.m. when the phone rang. I grabbed it on the second ring.

"Hello?" I answered.

It was Gabriel. He proceeded to explain that at the request of Mrs. Von Bremen, my schedule for the weekend had been changed. Mrs. Von Bremen wanted to see the Antebellum Trail and I was to be her official tour guide of the tri-county area.

I was not going to be at the club at all and would not see Gabriel. I did my best not to worry as this seemed par for the course for us, one step forward, two steps back.

CHAPTER 8

November 6, 1995, finally arrived. I turned twenty-one that day.

The appointment was set for 10:00 a.m. at the one law firm in my hometown. I was ten minutes early, because there was no traffic on the way from Milledgeville. This was the day that I would find out all of the details of my inheritance. I always knew the inheritance existed, but I really had no idea the extent of it and that's why we were there. We were there to have Attorney Lawson Bell explain every last detail to me.

Aunt Gayle arrived about five minutes after I did and was a vision of a fifty's movie star when she pulled up in the T-bird. She had on a wide-brimmed sun hat, tied securely around her chin to keep it from blowing off while she drove with the top down. She had on extra-large sunglasses over taking almost her entire face. As she pulled into the parking spot along Main Street in front of the law office, at least three chalk trucks passed and honked at her. One truck driver even leaned out of the window of his cab and cat called at her. Aunt Gayle took no notice at all as we went inside.

Aunt Gayle had agreed to go with me to the meeting and sort of hold my hand through it. The meeting lasted two hours and afterward Aunt Gayle and I went to lunch at Peggy's.

"I recommend you do not share the details of this with anyone," Aunt Gayle cautioned over her vegetable plate of butter beans, stewed yellow squash and sliced fresh tomatoes.

"I'm not sure I fully comprehend everything to be able to share it if I wanted," I responded. There was so much more and it was way more complicated than I would have ever imagined.

"What is it that you do not understand?" she asked.

"I don't understand how all of it is possible? How did it all come about?" I was baffled even though Granddaddy's lawyer tried very hard to explain it all and even gave me a ledger with lists of everything.

"Millie, just take your time and read the ledger and you can call Mr. Bell about anything you don't understand," Aunt Gayle advised.

"I know this is going to sound strange," I hesitated before continuing, "but I feel sort of depressed at knowing all of this is there and there's not much for me to strive for in life. I'm not ungrateful or anything. I just can't seem to shake this feeling of dread."

"Aww, honey," Aunt Gayle reached over and patted my head. "They loved you very much and your dad and granddad would have never wanted you to feel this way. It's just money, Millie, and it does not define you or limit what you can be in life."

Aunt Gayle and I continued to talk everything over and she cautioned me again and again not to tell anyone the details and if I did decide to tell anyone, then I was not to share all of the details. She felt if people knew how much I was worth they would never see past that and I would never be able to tell who my real friends were from then on out. I decided to follow her advice, but there was no way I could keep this completely to myself. I would likely be forced to tell Jay as he knew what was supposed to go on today and would be waiting with questions when I arrived home.

I was right. When I arrived home around 3:00 p.m., Jay was waiting with questions. I first made him swear on his grandfather's grave that he would never tell a soul one thing that I divulged. Then I gave him a summary of what I had learned.

"So, ballpark; how rich are you?" Jay asked after I finished speaking.

"Very," I answered as I did not have a definite number myself at that point.

"Like get nekkid and roll around in it, rich?" Jay asked with a wicked smile.

"Yeah, like get nekkid and roll around in it every day," I responded.

It was fun to talk to Jay about it because he could get me back to myself and help shake off that little pang of depression. In talking to Jay, I realized how ridiculous I was being. So many people would have killed to have what I have been given, the least I could do was not see it as some sort of burden.

"I hope you don't mind, we moved family dinner to tonight. Surprise and happy birthday! Everyone should be here at seven so you need to work on making yourself presentable. I hate to tell you, but you are looking old. Sorry."

"Who all's coming?" I asked.

191

Jay snapped back, "Don't you worry about that, just look your best. I've laid out an outfit on your bed for you. Also, don't come out of your room until I tell you. Watch TV in there or something, but don't come out."

I did as I was told and throughout the remainder of the afternoon, I could hear Jay and Emma banging around in the living room and the kitchen. I also heard Cara and Stella come and go a time or two. I really could not hear much of their conversations.

The outfit that Jay laid out for me was apparently my birthday present. It was a little red cocktail dress. It was made of satin and had an empire waist. I suppose it was of the baby doll style, low cut and short with cap sleeves. When I picked up the dress, I found a homemade card under it. It was a sappy poem he wrote about how he loved me just the way I was. I read about half of it before I felt tears, so I quickly put the card in my photo album with all of my other little treasures like that.

I could not take it anymore. I had a nap, a shower, curled and pinned my hair up and had been dressed and ready since 6:00 p.m. I stuck my head out from my door, "Jay, come here! Do I have to stay in here until 7:00? Seriously?"

Jay came over and my head was quickly shoved back in my room and the door pulled shut behind him. "Turn around," Jay stated as he motioned with his index finger.

I turned and he sized me up, "You look great. I know you're probably insecure about the length…"

I interrupted him, "You mean the lack thereof."

"Whatever. The dress fits you perfectly and your hair is amazing. I could not have done it better myself." He paused for a moment before he let out a sigh, "If ever anyone could change my religion, it would be you. You look like sex on legs, Millie." I blushed at Jay's comments.

Jay then turned and opened the door to exit while I managed to get a glimpse of the living room and there was twinkling lights hanging all across the dining room ceiling and the table and chairs were missing, "Where's the dining room table?" I yelled.

"No peeking!" was yelled back by Cara.

Seven finally arrived and I was allowed out of my room. Everyone I knew was now in our apartment. Jay had managed to track down Alex and his golf team buddies. Emma

192

invited some of my acquaintances from my classes. Travis had invited some of the guys from badminton class and Cara had invited everyone from Port Honor. Almost all of the Port Honor gang was there: Andy, Matt, Alvin, Jerry and Daniel. Although they had invited him and he was ecstatic to have been invited to his first college party, Rudy could not make it because of it being a school night and he still lived with his grandmother. Gabriel was missing as well, but I would not let that keep me from having a good time. Who was I kidding? I would likely be crushed if he did not come. They had to have invited him.

A collective "Happy Birthday, Millie," was cheered as I entered the living room.

Aside of Jay and Emma, of course, Daniel was one of the first to greet me, "Hey, birthday girl! I have a present for you," Daniel said, "but I am going to give it to you later."

"You shouldn't have," I replied.

"Wait until you see what it is before you try to turn it down," Daniel winked at me.

Jay walked up and forced me to introduce him to Daniel. If Daniel weren't already taken by Jerry, I would have totally fixed the two of them up. Jay flirted shamelessly and Jerry took notice and quickly claimed Daniel sending Jay on his way.

A lot of effort had clearly been put into the party by everyone. Jay, Cara and Stella made appetizers and Emma made what was now known as my signature drink, Pink Panty Droppers. Naturally, that brought back memories, but again, I refused to let that get me down. The music was rocking and there was no nasty cat lady to threaten to call the landlord on us while we were jumping around dancing.

This was the first night I had ever had any more than a shot of whiskey for a cough or a taste of something alcoholic. By 8:00 p.m. I had had three glasses of my signature drink when a knock at the door came.

"I'll get it!" I screamed over the music as I darted down the stairs. I was feeling the vodka and missed the last three steps on the staircase. I completely busted my rear in my heels and swanky red dress. The rest of the party-goers ran to the top of the stairs to get a look and make sure I was alright. I jumped to my feet as quickly as possible and pushed down my dress. Without asking who was there I threw open the door. Everyone except Daniel disbanded from the top of the stairs as I was left there facing Gabriel.

193

I was stunned. I glanced back up the stairs and Daniel winked at me again. "Happy Birthday! I hope you like your present," Daniel said before he moved from the top of the staircase.

Gabriel's eyes lit up when he saw me as did mine when I saw him. There he stood in a white fitted Port Honor logo shirt, dark-colored blue jeans, a white Nike baseball cap and flip flops. As was per the trip to Cameron's that night, this shirt fit him exactly the same. Nothing was left to my imagination as far as his physique.

Gabriel stood in the doorway holding a present. It was a small box with hot pink and white polka dot wrapping paper and a large hot pink bow on top that was as large as the top of the box itself. The present appeared to have been professionally wrapped. Gabriel looked like he always did, too good to be true, and although it was the liquor that loosened my tongue, it was the sound of the words that escaped my mouth that sobered me up. I was not talking about the present when I said, "Happy Birthday to me!"

"Yes, happy birthday to you, Miss Anderson." Gabriel said as he handed me the present. "Are you going to invite me in?"

Invite him in? My cloudy judgment right then would have given him the green light if he asked. I almost called him young Paul Newman to his face, but I pulled my thoughts together and answered like a normal, somewhat sober person. "Thank you and of course, come in."

I held the present in one hand and the other I held out to him. Without hesitation, Gabriel took my hand and it was so sweet to feel his touch again. His hands were soft and firm all at the same time. This really was shaping up to be the best birthday ever.

As we went up the stairs, Gabriel commented, "I see you moved."

"Yes, a little over a month ago." Little did he know, I had not just moved. I had bought the place.

At the top of the stairs the party raged on and the living room, kitchen and dining room were packed with guests. No one but Cara noticed us. She waved as I offered to give Gabriel the tour. "This is the living room. That over there where all of the lights are, that's usually where our dining room table goes, but right now it is our dance floor. That's the kitchen of course."

I continued to hold his hand and lead him through the apartment. We found the dining room table in Emma's room. The table was upside down on her bed and the chairs were stacked all around the room. Next I showed him Jay's room and the bathroom. Gabriel was amused by the poster of Alec Baldwin on the wall in Jay's room. I saved my room for last and thank goodness I had made my bed that afternoon after my nap.

"This is my room," I told Gabriel as I opened the door. The room was just as I had hoped it would look if he ever saw it. The bed was made and absolutely everything was in its place. I had just gotten around to hanging the guitar and banjo above the headboard last week. Jay had also taken black and white photographs of me while I was asleep and framed them for me. There was a series of three hanging vertically along the right side of the French doors.

I pulled Gabriel by the hand and he followed me across the room toward the doors, "Come on, there's something else I have to show you."

"Well, well, well, Miss Anderson, you have a fine room and a very comfy looking bed," Gabriel said as he stopped and seemed to take a good look at the photos of me sleeping.

"Jay took them," I said as I let go of his hand just long enough to open both of the doors and then I took it back. Never once did he resist allowing me to take his hand.

In the last week I had purchased a swing and Travis and Jay hung it on the porch outside my room for me. The swing was long enough for me to lie on if I wanted. It was huge. I had painted the swing white and rubbed it down with sand paper to give it a weathered, shabby look. I even bought another comforter and sheet set and made a cushion and throw pillows for the swing that matched my bedroom set. On one side of the porch was the swing and on the other an over-sized white wicker rocking chair and ottoman with matching cushions.

"I think I may like this porch better than the last, Miss Anderson, but I am just not sure yet," Gabriel said as he released my hand and approached the rail to have a look at the view. The view was of Jefferson Street below, cars parallel parked along it, antebellum and Victorian style houses across the street and trees that lined the street making it difficult to see the night's sky.

I moved to the rail and stood next to him as we looked out across the street. Gabriel then turned to me, "I thought you had plans tonight and couldn't get together with me. Did you not want me at your party?"

"First of all, my plans were earlier today and I was not sure how long they were going to take or what frame of mind I was going to be in. Secondly, you never mentioned it again so I had no idea that you would still want to get together," I paused to read his face. How could he have thought I would not want him at my party? "Plus, the party was a surprise to me until late this afternoon."

Gabriel had a look of hesitation before he spoke again, like he was carefully choosing his words or was unsure of something, "May I ask you what sort of appointment you would have on your twenty-first birthday that you thought might take all day?"

"The disbursement of my inheritance was today," I responded and made up my mind that I would try not to elaborate much beyond that.

"Tell me what you meant by disbursement of your inheritance? You have an inheritance?" Gabriel questioned and for a split second I realized what Aunt Gayle was warning me about. If I told Gabriel, and he suddenly came around, how would I ever know it was because of me and not because of the money?

Gabriel then took my hand and pulled me to the swing. "Can we sit and talk or do you need to get back to your guests?"

"It would be rude of me to stay too long. We can talk for a few minutes, but I want to talk about you. You know all about me and..." I was not completely finished when Gabriel cut me off and pulled me almost into his lap on the swing.

"What do you want to know?"

"Let's start with where you went to college or did you go to college?"

"I did go to college. I went to the Naval Academy."

"Did you serve in the Navy?"

"Of course, it's a condition of attending the Naval academy and I served six years after college."

"So, you haven't been out long. What did you do in the Navy and did you take part in any extra-curricular activities at the Naval Academy?"

"Let me just give you the bio, alright?" Gabriel said.

"Would you like for me to get you something to drink before you continue? That will allow me to make an appearance and stave off them missing me for a while," I offered as I got up from the swing.

"Sure. I will have whatever you have been having," Gabriel responded as he stood for me to exit.

"I will be right back," I assured him before I left and returned with a glass of my signature drink.

I handed him the glass. I made a move to retake my seat on the swing, but Gabriel stopped me. "Wait. I want to get a better look at you." I smiled and stopped in front of him. He motioned for me to turn around and I did as instructed. I turned around, careful not to spin and flair up the dress. As I turned back facing him, Gabriel held out his hand and pulled me back toward the swing.

It was a cool night and I had a little chill, but I loved the dress and I was not about to cover it up with a sweater or anything.

"You look amazing, Amelia. I think I may like this one better than the black dress," Gabriel said as he reached down and pulled my legs up across his lap. He also reached around my back and pulled me closer to him. Once he had my legs in place across his, he just laid his hands across my knees as if he was holding on to them before he continued. His touch was very distracting and I soon forgot about the chill in the air.

"So," he continued, "I joined the Navy just after high school and they found out about my football record. I was then offered a scholarship to the Naval Academy. I took the scholarship and after college I served as an officer on an aircraft carrier that was stationed off the coast of Osaka, Japan. I left the Navy last year just before coming to work at Port Honor."

"When did you meet Beth?" I asked.

"I have dreaded you asking me about her." Gabriel paused for a moment and took a deep breath. "I met her while I was in college. We were traveling to an away game and we were at the airport in Atlanta. She was sitting at the bar waiting on her father and I was lost. At that time, I was so small town and she was so big city. She noticed I was lost and she was friendly among other things. I suppose I was star-struck that a girl that looked like her would have anything to do with a guy like me."

"When you say 'a guy like you', what do you mean?" I asked attentively.

"I told you at Cameron's that night, Millie. It's not something I am proud of, but I was raised on the good graces of various relatives until their good graces ran out and I was passed to the next family member. I know I should consider myself lucky that I stayed out of foster care, but there were times when I wondered if I would have been better off." Gabriel just stared down at the floor as he told me this.

"So, you and Beth?" I wanted to urge him away from the bad memories.

"She gave me directions around the airport and her number. We dated for a long time during college. She loved to show off her prized football player from Annapolis to her dad who was former Navy. She made me out to be quite the prize."

"You said the other night that you had to tidy things up with her. How long have you all just been friends?"

Gabriel chose his words carefully, "*Friends* for some time now, but certain aspects about the friendship have been done for over two months now."

"She still wants more?" I asked, but I had already heard a version of things from Joan.

"Yes," Gabriel admitted.

"And you?" I asked and as usual I was not sure I really wanted the answer.

"No, not from her. That's been over for a long time." He assured me and I was relieved.

"What caused the two of you to stop dating?" I was curious.

"I broke it off because of my commitments with the Navy and being stationed so far away; at least that's what I told her at the time," Gabriel started to stroke my legs as he spoke and he continued to stare down at my knees. "I told you on Wednesday night, I got tired of being a show pony."

"How'd she take it, you breaking up with her?" I was curious as Beth clearly did not seem like she was taking no for an answer.

"I thought she took it well. We remained friends and because I had nowhere else to go while I was home on leaves, she would always invite me to stay with her family. At first it was innocent enough, but when my tour was up she expected things to

198

pick up where they left off and they kind of did. I suppose I was naive and did not realize..."

"You did not realize you were leading her on?"

"I don't think I realized she was even capable of being lead on. I always felt that she was the one leading me," he continued.

"And she got you the job at Port Honor?"

"Yes. Her father knows someone who knows someone and they are members at one of the neighboring clubs on the lake."

"Ah, so you feel like you owe her?"

"I guess I did at first, but..."

I cut Gabriel off and tried to finish his sentence, "Someone else may have gotten your foot in the door, but you have been doing the job for the last however long. If you said 'Thank you' to begin with then that should have been enough."

"Amelia, I don't want you thinking she is a villain. She has been good to me and it's not like I have not benefitted."

I listened and I thought of my words carefully before adding, "I don't necessarily think she's a villain. I only met her once and perhaps she was just having an off night. I just know I didn't care for what I saw of her that night."

"Beth said something to you when she hugged you that night; what was it?" Gabriel surprised me with his question.

I responded honestly, "She whispered to me that I might have won the battle, but she would win the war."

"And you responded how?" he asked.

I was embarrassed to tell him how I answered so I remained silent. Gabriel lifted his head and looked at me. He could tell I was blushing, "What did you say?" he asked again.

"I told her 'Only if I let you!' I did not know what to say and that just came out. Honestly, she is your business, not mine, and all of that nonsense is between the two of you. I just didn't like the way she spoke to me or Rudy or much of anyone else that night so if I got under her skin..."

"You definitely got under her skin," he muttered.

"You know, I really should get back inside. It's my birthday and I really don't want to talk about your former girlfriend all night. I mean, we could talk until the sun comes up, but maybe not tonight," I said as I started to pull my legs back to put them on the floor. I wanted to get off of the subject of Beth before I threw a hissy fit over what all Joan had told me while we were at the Von Bremen's. In Joan's mind, it was Beth who had stirred up trouble to try to get Gabriel fired from the club. Of course, I was curious as to his opinion on the subject, but that was not a topic for my birthday party.

"You're probably right, but would you like to open your present before we go back in?" Gabriel reached around me and handed me the gift from where it was sitting on the swing next to me.

"Thank you and you really shouldn't have," I said as I took the gift.

"You haven't opened it yet," he responded.

I looked down at the present and opened it gently only popping the tape and not tearing the pink polka dotted paper.

"Are you planning to rewrap something in this paper?" Gabriel laughed. "Come on Amelia, tear into it!"

"Alright!" and I tore into the paper and opened the box to find a strand of white pearls. I lifted them from the box and noticed the clasp had an engraving on it. It was my name, not Millie, which everyone else called me, but Amelia which only he called me. My insides were jumping with glee. I loved them, but...

"They are cold to the touch and that means they are...I can't accept these." They were real pearls and that was just too much. "These must have cost an arm and a leg!"

"Amelia, I want you to have them. They were my mother's and what am I going to do with them?" Gabriel said while he put up his hands in refusal to take them back as I was trying to hand the box back to him.

"You may have a daughter one day and want to give them to her," I tried to reason with him.

"I might and we will revisit that if it happens, but for now, they are yours and that's the end of it. I put your name on them so you couldn't give them back so say 'Thank you', Amelia, and let me help you put them on. Then, we are going to go inside and you are going to introduce me to all of your friends." I really liked it when he was bossy and I really liked the idea of introducing him to all of my friends.

"Thank you," I beamed as I handed him the box and turned around. My hair was already up so my neck had been completely bare until he put the pearls on me.

As soon as Gabriel put them on, I raised from the swing and before he could stand, I moved between his legs and stood. I leaned down and while hugging him, I kissed him on the cheek and then whispered, "Thank you for the necklace and I would also thank you to stop avoiding me at work."

I stood back upright and offered Gabriel my hand. Gabriel smiled at me and then got up from the swing. "I am starting to really like this porch, Amelia. In fact, I will agree to stop avoiding you at work, if you will agree to invite me back to sit in the swing again sometime."

"Gabriel, would you like to know something about me?" I asked as I held out my hand to him.

"I would like to know most everything about you, Amelia," he replied as he took my hand and we started back through the door of my room.

"I did not just move here, I bought the building," I confided.

"You did what?" I think he was shocked.

"I bought the building. I now own an apartment building. There are two more apartments downstairs and Cara and her roommate rented one of them. One of the guys from my badminton class and his girlfriend rented the other." I loved telling him. I do not think I was bragging, but just telling him a little more about myself.

"Why?"

"Why did I buy it? Because it was a good investment." I think I wanted him to be impressed with me. "I could tell you all of the details if you like. I am pretty proud of it."

"You bought this over a month ago and you are just now telling me?" he almost seemed offended.

"You scheduled me in a manner in which I really haven't seen you in a month. I thought you were avoiding me..."

"I was avoiding you, but I promise I'm not anymore."

The conversation had been quick as we passed through the room. I think I had given him something to think about with my capacity to buy the building. His head was probably spinning a little thinking back to the talk about my appointment of earlier in the day. He confirmed my suspicions as we reached the door from my room into the living room.

"Amelia, wait a minute," Gabriel said as he pulled me by the hand back into my room. "You play two instruments. You bought an apartment building as an investment. You received an inheritance today. What else have you not told me?"

"I play more than two instruments. I play the guitar and I am working on learning the banjo." I paused to take in the expression on his face. I could tell that's not exactly the disclosure he had in mind.

I continued, "Seriously, I would love to tell you about everything, but if you don't mind, I would like to save that for another day. Honestly, I would like to better understand it all myself before I try to explain it to anyone and get it wrong." I also wanted to be careful like Aunt Gayle had warned me, but at the same time it seemed like there was some sort of compulsion rising in me to just tell him everything. Could I trust him? Every time I thought I was getting close to him, he seemed to disappear. He was here now, but why should this time be any different?

Gabriel nodded in the affirmative accepting my answer, "Later, you'll tell me everything." If he stuck around, I would.

"One more question," he said.

"Okay."

"Who is Jay and why did he take the pictures of you sleeping," he asked as he pointed to the photos by the doors to the porch.

"My roommate, Jay, took those two weeks ago. I hate them, but he framed them and went to the trouble and all, so I felt obligated to put them up. They are weird right?"

"Why was your roommate with you while you were sleeping?"

"Because he has no sense of boundaries and he is like my gay adopted brother. I don't really know. I had not thought much of it?"

A look of relief flashed across Gabriel's face, but he asked anyway, "Really, gay brother? So, you aren't *special* roommates?"

I started to laugh, "You mean like you and Beth were special friends? GOD NO! That's repulsive! Seriously, like a brother, a really gay brother."

Gabriel started to laugh too. He was jealous.

"Come on, it's time for you to meet everyone."

I pulled his hand and we went out the door and through the living room. The music was thumping all through the apartment to "It Takes Two" by Rob Base. I stepped to the beat as I pulled Gabriel's right hand over my shoulder and led him toward the kitchen where I could see Jay making himself a drink. The path to the kitchen was crowded with dancing partygoers and I could feel Gabriel close behind me with his left hand on my waist as we passed through the make-shift dance floor. It was so tempting to stop and dance with him.

When Jay saw me, he approached and gave me a big hug, "Birthday girl! I was about to come find you," he said as he lifted me off of my feet forcing me to let go of Gabriel's hand. Jay glared at Gabriel over my shoulder.

Jay set me back on my feet and I proceeded to introduce them. "Jay, this is Gabriel." Gabriel rolled his eyes as I referred to him as my boss at Port Honor. "Gabriel, this is Jay. Short of some folks that I am related to, I have known Jay longer than anyone else in my life."

Jay extended his hand to Gabriel and they shook. Jay refrained from verbally threatening to kill Gabriel if he hurt me, but the look he gave him spoke volumes. Gabriel gave a nod of understanding.

"Well, I'm sure you two would like to dance so I won't keep you. Gabriel, it was nice to meet you." Jay was good and a bit manipulative, but that was alright since it scored me a dance with Gabriel.

"Yes, Amelia, let's dance," said Gabriel as he retook my hand and led me back to our dance floor.

Rob Base and DJ EZ Rock were just finishing and "Push It" by Salt and Pepa was starting as we hit the dance floor. Matt and Cara were dancing together along with Travis and Stella, and some of the other guests had paired off as well. I followed Gabriel as he pulled me to the middle of the group bouncing with the beat as I went. Gabriel turned to me and put his hands on my waist and pulled me in close as he bent his knees and stooped just a little. I lost my balance a little as he pulled me in and my hands went instinctively up to his shoulders to steady myself. I do not think he even noticed that I nearly fell as it was his intention to hold me close as we moved to the music.

We were nearly body on body and the room was hot with people, but it was like we were alone. In that moment, he was mine and I was his. I wanted to be all his. As the music pumped on, I lowered my hands down his arms and to his sides. I could scarcely keep my hands off of him. Moving my hips to the beat, my hands went to his hips. I started to turn, dancing and still moving with the rhythm and looking him in the eye. I ran my left hand across his chest as I turned and with my right hand I pulled the pins out that were holding my hair up. I slung my hair loose with the music. I worked my shoulders, back and hips, all with the beat and backed up against him. One of his hands went through my hair and the other around my waist pulling me closer into him. He was behind me, but my hands still had free reign of touching him as we danced. I also did one of those moves where I slid down him squatting just a bit between his legs and then back up.

I turned back to face him and I straddled one of his legs and we continued to move. Our hands mostly stayed in PG rated places, but at least once he slid each of his hands across my behind and I did not protest at all. If anything, I gave into his every touch as he did to mine. This was the most all over anyone I had ever been while I danced. It was probably the most I had ever been all over anyone period. My heart was pounding in my ears as much as the music was. The bumping and the grinding; I could feel every inch of him as we moved. It was absolutely exhilarating. I wanted him and I was fully aware that he wanted me as well even though no words had been spoken.

The music wound down and Andy approached us. "May I have a dance with the birthday girl?" he asked.

What was Gabriel to say? He stepped back and essentially offered me to Andy. House of Pain started to play "Jump Around." I am so glad Cara and her roommate, Megan, were at the party because all of the jumping would have been directly above one of their bedrooms. As Andy and I jumped to the music, he tried to ask me out. I thought he must be kidding. Either he had poor timing or perhaps he was just that full of himself. Had he not just witnessed my dance with Gabriel? I was not like that with just anyone and any idiot could have seen us. And, if that was not enough, he had to know that his brother, who was in attendance just a few feet over from us, had a thing for me. Despite the fact that I was repulsed by him at that point, I politely declined his offer.

When the song was over and I was quite winded from jumping around. I hardly had time to turn from Andy when Gabriel leaned into my ear and whispered, "No more dancing with anyone else, Miss Anderson."

He really had no need to worry that I would go back for seconds with Andy.

Just then Jay moved to the sound system and stopped the music. "Attention, everyone!" Jay yelled. It took him just a couple of yells and one ear piercing whistle from Cara before he had everyone's full attention.

Jay finally continued and the room parted so everyone could see me, "I would like to thank everyone for coming out to celebrate my best friend's birthday. I would also like to thank all of you who helped out with this party. So, without further ado, Happy Birthday, Millie! I love you and that dress looks better on you than it did on me! I hate you, you gorgeous tart!"

The room erupted in laughter and clapping and I could not help my reaction. I could feel my face turn red. I usually did not get this sort of attention unless I had just finished playing something.

Gabriel had been standing directly behind me during Jay's speech. I could feel his breath in my hair and his body against my back. I could feel Gabriel laughing with everyone else when Jay called me a 'gorgeous tart'.

"My turn," shouted Emma from the kitchen as she came running out. "Millie, Millie, Millie, welcome to the twenty-one club! Happy Birthday and Jay is right, you do look stunning in that dress. I love and hate you as well!" Again the room erupted in laughter.

Emma stepped aside and Cara stepped up. "I have not known Millie all that long, but she is the sweetest person I think I have ever met. I am so glad that Gabriel hired her and I am super glad that she thought of me when she bought this building. I really appreciate everything you have done for me, Mille, and I won't ever forget it."

When Cara said I bought the building several of the parties goers turned and looked at me as if they were a little stunned. I did not make eye contact, as that was not something I wanted everyone to know. Gabriel clearly noticed my shift in posture and my head drop. He immediately put his hands on my shoulders.

"Alright, I am next." Gabriel raised his voice to command the attention of the room. He remained standing behind me as he spoke and he did not let me turn to him. "Like Cara, I am extremely glad that Amelia harassed my secretary until I had no choice, but to hire her. I look forward to every day that I get a chance to see her at work. I don't know if each of you have had the good fortune to be exposed to any of Amelia's many talents. If you have not, then you are truly missing out. She plays the fiddle like the house is on fire and when she plays the piano the Earth stands still. I actually have to apologize to her right now because I think I hurt her feelings recently."

I turned around to Gabriel and I whispered, "You don't have to..." but he kept going.

Gabriel looked me directly in the eyes as he spoke and even though he was speaking to the room it was again as if we were alone. "I will not go into the details, except to say, I was wrong and I am sorry and I won't do it again. Happy Birthday! You never cease to amaze me."

I know I looked at him adoringly as he spoke and I made no attempt to hide it. As soon as he finished his speech, he kissed me on the forehead. Everyone clapped and cheered, "Happy Birthday, Millie!"

I took Gabriel's hand and turned to everyone, "Thank you all for coming and celebrating with me. I am very fortunate to have each of you in my life and I appreciate you more than you know." I squeezed Gabriel's hand as I made key points.

I continued, "I would like to thank those of you who played a part in planning and hosting the party. Jay, Emma, you are the best roommates I could ever hope for. Cara, Stella, I know you all had a hand in this and I love you both dearly. Gabriel thanks for driving all the way up here from Greensboro to celebrate with all of us. Same goes to Daniel and Jerry, thank you for making the drive. You all are the best! Thank you all for coming and let's get back to dancing!"

Before Jay fired up the sound system again, he cautioned as to what he was about to play, "Now, I am going to apologize as some may find this offensive to their ears, but it is Millie's party so we are going to have to play a couple of her favorite songs. Brace yourselves for some old country stuff." When finished speaking, Jay put on Patsy Cline's "Crazy".

Jay approached with the clear intention of asking me to dance and the look I gave him was speaking. "Are you insane? Go away!" Plus, I had already been warned that I was dancing with no one else the rest of the night.

Jay took the hint. I was thankful that he did not go away entirely and instead he grabbed Emma for his partner. Matt and Cara remained, but other than that the number of dancers dwindled.

The music floated through the apartment like a sweet scent in the wind. The sound of the piano, the pinging of the keys in the opening bade Gabriel to pull back and look at me, "Seems like I should know this song," he said.

"You should, not just because the last time I played the piano for you I played this, but because it is a classic" I responded. "This is the first time I have ever danced to it so be quiet and enjoy."

We swayed as Patsy Cline bellowed. I held Gabriel close and one would have thought this would be utter heaven for me, but by midway through the song I was nearly in tears. Gabriel noticed at some point and leaned even closer and whispered in my ear, "Are you alright?"

"Oh, yes, happy memories and sad memories all at once," I assured him and I reached to blot the tears back.

"Let's go back to the porch," he whispered.

"At the end of the song," I agreed.

The song ended and he turned to lead me back toward the front porch, but I stopped. "Go on without me. I just want to let Jay know where I am going and that I will be back."

"I'm going to grab us something to drink and meet you there," Gabriel said.

"No more alcohol for me, please," I responded as he strutted off for the kitchen.

I found Jay and Emma and thanked them profusely for the party. I made sure they understood that I was coming back, but that I was going to the porch with Gabriel for a little while and anyone was welcome to come out there if they wanted. I did not want them to think I was just abandoning all of the other guests for Gabriel; although, if anyone would have understood me doing that, it would have been them. I hugged them both.

As I went through my room I kicked off my shoes and headed onto the porch. I found Gabriel with his back to me. He was leaning on the railing looking out over the street. I was quiet and he did not hear me coming so he was just a touch startled as I leaned up next to him. He handed me the glass of water he had gotten for me.

"Thanks!" I said before nearly downing the entire glass of water.

"So, you wanna tell me what the tears were about?" he asked as he took my glass from me and sat it on the railing.

"Do you really want to know?"

"If you want to tell me, then I want to know."

"Fair enough. I think I told you before that I used to play that song for my grandfather. The whole story is that "Crazy" was the first song Aunt Gayle made sure I knew how to play that was outside of the realm of Bach and Beethoven. Having me learn to play this, and play it well, was our gift to my grandfather at his sixty-fifth birthday. I had practiced for weeks and weeks. I was ten and she threw him a huge birthday party. I played and she sang. She is a way better singer than I am. It brought tears to his eyes in front of all of his friends as he was so proud of both of us."

"You sing too?" Gabriel inquired.

"Focus, that's not the point of the story, but the answer is yes, just not as well as others."

"How am I supposed to focus? Now you are telling me you sing too," Gabriel sounded a bit exasperated, but not in a bad way. "Will you sing for me sometime?"

"Probably not," I replied almost before he could finish asking.

"Why?"

"Do you like to cook bad food?" I asked and he got this curious look on his face as if to say 'of course not'.

I continued to explain my reluctance to sing, "Right. You cook very well so why would you want to cook poorly. I do other things well so why would I want to do something that I am only mediocre at?"

208

Gabriel started to laugh, "Good point, but by all accounts what you do well is actually extraordinary so your version of mediocre is probably quite good when compared to a normal person."

"Anyway, the point of the story and not to be Debbie Downer, but this is my first birthday since my grandfather died and the song made me think of him. It's okay though because now I will have new memories of the song."

"New memories?"

I playfully bumped my hip to his and said, "Yeah, new memories of the best birthday party I've ever had. This has been a great night! Thanks again for coming!"

Gabriel put his arm around me and we leaned on the railing together looking out over the street. "I'm really glad I came, Amelia."

I leaned my head on his shoulder and we just stood there together in the quiet of the night for quite a while before Cara came out.

"Hey, Millie, I just wanted to say goodnight and wish you happy birthday again before I went downstairs," Cara said as she came forward to hug me.

"Thanks so much for everything," I said as I hugged her back. "I loved the party!"

"You are welcome!" Cara then turned her attention to Gabriel. "I hope to see you at family dinner soon."

"What's family dinner?" he asked.

"Millie will tell you," Cara replied before hugging him and taking her leave.

We watched Cara leave before I turned back to Gabriel, "On Tuesday nights at 6:30 everyone that lives in the building gets together in our dining room and we all have dinner together. We call it family dinner."

"I don't live here, but I could get an invite?" he asked.

"If you like. Living here is not a requirement. Cara has brought Matt the last two weeks, Megan's boyfriend joins us every week and Emma usually brings the flavor of the week and I don't mean ice cream." I explained.

"Are you having family dinner tomorrow since it is Tuesday?"

"Jay said this week was an exception and we were having the party tonight instead of family dinner."

"Well, count me in for next week." I am not sure if he could tell by the look on my face, but that pleased me to no end.

About that time, I heard Travis and Stella at the door of my room. They did not just come on through like Cara had. "Millie, we are going. We hope you had a great birthday!" yelled Stella from the doorway.

"Come on," I said to Gabriel, "I need to get back in there and tell everyone goodnight."

"Right and I should be going as well." Gabriel said as he took my hand to go with me.

It was not long and I had bid all of my guests goodnight and it was down to my roommates, Gabriel and me. Even though Jay and Emma told him he did not have to, Gabriel insisted on helping clean up. It also gave him a tiny opportunity to get to know Jay and Emma and for them to get to know him. Jay had the music almost blaring and we all danced around as they picked up the apartment and tried to put it back in order. Stella and Cara had both helped before they left so there really was not all that much to be done and the three that were left refused to let me lift a finger to help with anything.

Once finished, Gabriel said, "I really need to get going before I wear out my welcome."

"I will walk you out," I said as was becoming the usual. Gabriel held out his hand for me. We had hardly moved throughout the evening that we were not holding hands. It was simple, but I loved it.

We reached the bottom of the stairs and were in the foyer between all of the doors when Gabriel stopped. "I am not going to have you walk me all the way to my car. I'm the gentleman here, not you. That being said, Amelia, I also told you once that I would ask permission first and now I am asking. You asked why I couldn't sleep on Wednesday night. I could not sleep because I wanted to ask then, but you passed out on me. I am asking now."

Oh my God! My thoughts raced. The answer was most definitely yes, but I had never been asked before. The answer had

210

been yes, since before the night he said he would ask first; perhaps it had even been yes as far back as the first time I laid eyes on him. I had been kissed before, but no one had ever asked permission first, so how was I to answer without sounding as if I had been waiting for this moment all of my life?

I looked up at him. I know I was slightly biting my lower lip with anticipation, but as sweetly and gently as possible, I simply said, "Please."

It was not like the night on the porch at The Hillman House. He bent down to me all the while looking me in the eye. He slid his right hand around the small of my back and pulled me to him while his left hand went across my cheek. Everything seemed to be instinct on my part. I leaned into his touch on my face and closed my eyes, but his hand kept moving. I opened my eyes as his hand went around my neck and into my hair at the base of my skull. My hands had gone up his chest and found their way around his neck as he moved closer to me. It all felt like slow motion.

With his hand in my hair and his nose pressed against mine Gabriel whispered, "I have thought about this moment every day since I met you."

Gabriel pressed his lips to mine and I got an education on kissing. This was the most sensual moment of my entire life and if it never ended that would have been perfectly fine. He was magnificent and everything about me was on fire for him. During all of the interaction of our mouths, his hand that had been at the small of my back, left there and traveled up to join the other hand in my hair and then back again. Directing me with just the slide of his hand and a little pressure, I stepped backward to where my back was against our apartment door. I was on my toes stretching up to him. My chest was heaving and I wanted him. Everything was controlled and deliberate on both of our parts, but he was definitely leading and I would have followed most anywhere.

Gabriel moved back from kissing my mouth, but he wasn't finished. His hand in my hair gave just a gentle tug causing a ripple effect: my head to tilt, my neck to stretch and my back to arch as his tongue traveled down my neck. His right hand slipped around from my back and to my hip. I raised my left knee, sliding it up his leg giving in to the touch at my hip that kept coming, stopping only momentarily to run his index finger across my bare leg along the hem of my skirt before continuing on to meet my rising knee. He slipped his hand gently behind my knee, lifted so slightly and pressed his pelvis into me. I thought my heart would burst and I moaned with desire as he continued to kiss my neck, around the string of pearls his tongue went. I held him tighter and pressed my chest to his.

I leaned back as much as I could in that position and denied him further access to my neck only slowing him in an attempt to give him the same treat he had just given me. I moved one of my hands to the front of his throat, pushing gently, urging him to lean his head back. He did as I had bid giving me access to kiss his adam's apple. I slipped my hand back behind his neck giving a little pull for him to bend down for my reach. All the while I made a trail from his adam's apple with my tongue to his ear lobe. I nibbled just so slightly, but apparently that was too much. Again, he lifted my knee and pressed his pelvis into me and I could feel his erection.

Abruptly, Gabriel moved back. We returned to kissing mouth on mouth for just a moment more before he slowed things down to the point of stopping. He buried his head in my hair and my face in his chest. I could hear him whisper to me, "I warned you it would be impossible to stop."

"And you were right," I returned in whisper. We continued to hold one another for what seemed like an eternity. I think we both needed a chance to calm down.

Gabriel finally began to release me. "Would you mind if I called you tomorrow?" Gabriel asked as he stood there holding my hands.

"I would not mind. I would like that very much." I blushed.

"Good. Now, get back upstairs and get some rest. I know today has been a big day for you." Gabriel then reached around me and opened the door behind me to the apartment.

"Goodnight, Gabriel. Thanks for helping to make tonight wonderful." I said as I pulled my hair around my neck to hide the hives. While pulling my hair around, I brushed against the string of pearls and felt compelled to thank him again. "I love the pearls and you really shouldn't have and I want to reiterate, I am only accepting them on loan."

"You are welcome and they are yours for as long as you want them. Now, goodnight, Amelia." Gabriel gave me one last peck on the forehead before he smiled and took his leave.

***

My bed was so comfortable and I felt as if I was just rolling over good when I was abruptly awakened at 7:30 by the ringing

212

phone. I grabbed the phone from my bedside table as quickly as possible in an attempt to avoid waking the entire house. Tuesday and Thursdays were my days to sleep in since my first class did not start until 10:00 a.m. Jay and Emma were not the early birds that I was so they never scheduled a class earlier than 10:00.

I narrowly managed to answer it before the second ring. "Hello?" I greeted in little more than a whisper.

"Good morning, Miss Anderson. Did you sleep well?" It was Gabriel. He asked if he could call and he was calling already. I did not expect him to call so soon. In fact, I did not really expect anything as every single time things went well with him, they stalled immediately thereafter. So, it was quite the surprise to hear him on the other end of the line that soon and that early in the morning.

"I slept very well and you, Mr. Hewitt? I assume you made it home alright." I replied.

"Dodged a couple of deer in the road, but other than that I made it home just fine and had sweet dreams of someone wearing a red dress and sliding her leg up mine." What a way to wake up, being flirted with by Gabriel, my kind of alarm clock.

I rolled over from my back and kicked my feet with excitement, but withstood the urge to squeal like a delighted child. I flirted back, "You can tell that bitch to keep her legs off of you."

Gabriel laughed, "Jealous much?"

I rolled over in bed onto my back and giggled. "I like it when you laugh."

"Are you still in bed, Miss Anderson?"

"Aren't you, Mr. Hewitt?"

"No," Gabriel responded.

"And why not?" I asked him.

"I have already been out and ran the cart path on the course. And you?"

"Still snuggly in my bed." I was rolling around in my big comfy bed talking to him. "Did you just say you ran the cart path?"

"I like to run it at dawn. You should try it sometime. So, no class today?"

"I don't have class until 10:00 a.m."

"After your 10:00 a.m. class, what?"

"1:00 p.m. badminton."

"After badminton?"

"So do you have a roommate or anything? And I just have a little studying maybe, but nothing pressing." I was beginning to wonder where this was going.

"No roommate. Do you have plans for dinner?" Gabriel asked.

"I don't know, do I?" I replied.

"Yes. Is 4:00 too early?"

"A bit early for dinner."

"For sitting in the swing on your porch and then going to dinner anywhere you want."

It was good he was not there to see the cheesy grin that became plastered across my face. I was ecstatic at the thought of seeing him again. I did not want to jinx myself, but I could not help but ask, "You want to sit on the porch and swing?"

"I would like to sit on the porch, in the swing, with you. You can lay your head in my lap and study or you can sit next to me and play the fiddle or the banjo or whatever you like as long as you are sitting in the swing with me. And, then, around 6:00 I am going to take you out to dinner. I am picking the swing and you can pick dinner, deal?"

"Deal." I tried to hide my excitement with the tone of my voice, but I am not sure I succeeded. I think I came off more muffled than nonchalant.

"Good. I will see you at 4:00." Gabriel added before hanging up, "One more thing, and I would not be a man if I did not ask, what are you wearing?"

"Pajamas," I responded coyly.

Gabriel's tone was a little more firm when he asked, "Right, but what sort of pajamas? Tell me. You have seen mine, now the least you can do is tell me about yours."

"Red plaid pajama shorts and a red tank-top," I was a little insecure about my answer, but I was honest. Surely Gabriel having to imagine this paled in comparison to actually seeing me in his undershirt last Wednesday night.

Immediately, I was relieved at my honesty since the way he replied with the word "nice" was as if it was code for "hot".

"Ok, I am going to go now and catch a little nap before getting up for class. And you, get ready for work or something."

"Bye, Amelia."

"Bye, Gabriel."

***

Between classes I baked chocolate chip cookies. Jay said it was unnecessary since Gabriel was coming over again so soon. Jay figured I already had him so why bother with the effort. I made the cookies anyway. I made some with pecans and some without. I saved one pan's worth to bake right before Gabriel was to arrive so the apartment would still smell like the cookies. I also walked to the Golden Pantry and bought a fresh half gallon of milk, just in case he liked milk with his cookies.

I managed to shower, re-apply my make-up and roll my hair between arriving home from class, baking the remaining cookie dough and Gabriel arriving. I slipped on the forbidden jeans, a tank top and a light weight, but tight fitting navy blue cable knit sweater over it all right before 4:00.

I heard the knock at the downstairs door to our apartment right at 4:00 p.m. I ran to get the door and it was Gabriel. He always looked as if he had just stepped out of the shower and this time was no different. He could not have been in the doorway more than a moment, but the scent of his cologne flooded my senses immediately upon opening the door. It was the smell of hope; the smell of Gabriel.

Would I ever get used to seeing him and feeling the tingling in my knees on sight? It had been over two months since I first saw him and every time since he had the same effect on me. In all honesty, I never wanted the effect to wear off. It made me feel more alive than anything ever had.

"Hey, come on in," I insisted as I held the door open to him.

"Are those *the* jeans?" Gabriel asked as he raised an eyebrow.

I turned to walk up the stairs ahead of him and answered over my shoulder, "They are indeed."

Just then came a swift slap on my rear end and I nearly slipped on the stairs.

"Mr. Hewitt, that smarts!" I exclaimed as I rubbed my behind cheek.

"I know you are not wearing those out in public still," he said.

As my foot hit the top step, I responded with a bite in my voice, "Actually, I am wearing them in the comfort of my own home. Do you not like them?"

"Oh, I like them alright." And then he grabbed me and spun me around and tossed me over his shoulder in the fireman's carry. "Are we home alone?" he asked.

"Emma is in her room. Put me down!" I laughed and failed without any protest. It was in moments like this and like when he was kissing me against the door last night that made me fully aware of how much larger he was compared to me.

"How tall are you?" I asked as he carried me through my room to the front porch.

"Six foot one? Why do you ask?"

"Same reason you asked about my pajamas," I replied.

"Oh. Well, I am six feet, one inch tall and weigh about 180. And you?"

"Holy crap, you are seventy pounds heavier than I am! I am only five three and one ten."

Gabriel sat me down on my feet in front of the swing. "There's probably something we should get out of the way." He said as he took a seat on the swing.

"Really, what's that?" What did we need to get out of the way? I wondered.

Gabriel pulled me toward him and into his lap. "This," he said as he pulled me closer and kissed me. He tasted like grape

216

bubble gum. It was not a long kiss like the one from the night before. However, it was sweet and tender and head spinning all the same. All the while he kissed me, he had one hand in my hair at the back of my head and the other was tracing the rip in my jeans that gave just the slightest access to the crease where my leg and butt cheek met. My arms were around his neck and if he had touched them he would have felt chill bumps from shoulder to wrist. Kissing Gabriel was heaven on earth.

When he finally pulled back, Gabriel looked at me as if he were taking in every freckle on my face. "I have been thinking about doing that since we stopped doing it last night."

I could not help but smile, probably from ear to ear. "I have something for you," I said. "Stay here. I will be right back."

I jumped up and went to the kitchen and returned with the plate of cookies and glass of milk. "With pecans or without?" I asked.

"What's this?"

"I baked cookies. Would you like one with pecans or without?"

"With." Gabriel responded as I passed him the plate of cookies and handed him the glass of milk.

"Choose from this side," I pointed to indicate which side of the plate had the pecan infused cookies.

"You made these?" Gabriel questioned.

"Yes, from scratch, my grandmother's recipe," I replied as I took a seat next to him on the swing holding the plate of cookies.

"These are quite good!"

"Thanks! I hoped you would like them."

When he finished chewing the first cookie, Gabriel leaned over and kissed me again before taking two more cookies.

"No one has ever baked for me before," he said and he looked away.

"How long were you with Beth and she never cooked for you?" I inquired.

"Beth does not cook and we were together my last three years of college and..."

"Would you mind if we did not go out for dinner?" I asked. It had made me sad to think that he was twenty-eight years old and no woman had seen fit to cook for him.

"I would mind. I believe we had a deal," he said.

"I just thought I would cook for you."

"Amelia, you don't have too."

"I want to." I reached an arm around him to assure him I was alright with my decision.

"You are welcome to cook for me any other night, but tonight we are going out. You are changing those jeans first, but we are going out none the less. Remember the gentleman speech from last night?" Gabriel was adamant in his decision about dinner.

Gabriel finished off the last of the cookies that he had taken and I placed the plate of cookies over on the ottoman of the wicker rocking chair.

"Do you like the swing?" I asked Gabriel as I retook my seat next to him.

"I love the swing," he replied immediately.

"Would you like to love the swing more?" I asked.

"Ok?" Gabriel answered with skepticism.

"Lie on your back and place your head in my lap. The swing is long enough to support you if you will just prop your feet up on the arm between the chains. Trust me."

Gabriel followed my instructions and did as I had asked. Once his head was in my lap, I began to run my fingers through his hair and massage his head, neck and shoulders. "Oh my God, Millie, I am going to fall asleep if you keep this up."

"I suppose that would be payback for me falling asleep on the way home the other night," I kind of laughed recalling how I had conked out on the ride home from Atlanta.

"I suppose that would be payback," he agreed. "So what makes you such the expert at massages?"

"Years of practice. Aunt Gayle gets migraines and I spent hours rubbing her head," I said as I ran my fingers through his hair.

"You are very good at it, but you sound kind of like you were put out," Gabriel commented.

"Oh no, rubbing her head was the least I could do." I instantly felt ashamed that I had given that impression. "She raised me as her own. I'd gladly do anything for her. Absolutely anything!"

Gabriel lifted his hands and stopped me. He proceeded to sit up in the swing and face me pulling one knee up to sit almost half Indian style, mirroring me. There was a definite look of concern on his face when he spoke, "Let's get something straight. You don't owe me anything, Amelia. I don't want you doing anything with me that you don't want to do and I don't want you doing anything for me that you don't want to do."

Apparently I hit some nerve. Immediately I remembered the synopsis he gave me of his raising; being passed from one relative to the next and only being taken care of out of obligation. I hate that he had misunderstood my feelings toward Aunt Gayle. I felt terrible and I had to redeem the situation.

I took his hands and scooted in closer to him. I pushed his knee down from the swing to where his feet were both back on the floor. Once he was facing forward, I eased over and straddled him, taking my seat across his lap and facing him. I was balancing on my knees, looking him right in the eyes when I took his face in my hands. I just smiled and he looked at me with wonder. I eased my hands from his face around and down his back as I leaned in and eased down, releasing my weight onto him.

I whispered, "I would do just about anything for you and with you because I want too. I don't think you are ever going to have a reason to doubt that." Perhaps it was too much too soon, but I said it. I held back short of telling him that I absolutely adored him.

Gabriel's hands had been on me since I first moved on top of him. They were steadying me at my hips as I rested on my knees when looking at him, but now they were moving lower to grip my ass. I felt no urge to brush his hands away or stop him.

The light returned to his eyes and although his tone sounded serious, it was a different type of serious tone. The tone was a sexy, warning tone in the words, "Be careful, Miss Anderson."

Gabriel was moving toward kissing me again, a kiss that was guaranteed to be as hot as the night before by the way he was holding on to me. The kiss did not come to fruition as Jay arrived back home and came to find me. Without knocking on my door or anything, Jay came through my room and straight through the door onto the porch. We heard the footsteps coming through the doorway into my room and Gabriel and I scurried to look as if we were not up to anything.

"Oh, hi, Gabriel," said Jay looking startled to see him there.

"Good to see you again, Jay. By the way, you can call me Gabe." Gabriel stood and stuck out his hand to Jay. Jay reciprocated and they shook.

Jay cut his eyes at me, "I hope I am not interrupting anything."

Gabriel answered, "I was just defiling your roommate, that's all."

I gasped and Jay responded, "I've thought for a while that she needed a good defiling!"

Without thought I punched Jay on the arm. "Aww, that hurt, Millie!" Jay shrieked as he rubbed his arm.

"I'm going to grab another glass of milk so you two can talk for a moment," Gabriel said as he picked up his glass and started for the door.

"You don't have to leave Gabriel. I just wanted to tell Millie about my day and it's nothing you can't hear. Please stay. Plus, I don't want to interrupt the defiling so if anyone leaves, it should be me." Jay was so cordial to Gabriel. I could not have been prouder of him. I really wanted them to get along.

I stood and eased the glass from Gabriel's hand, "Jay, have a seat and I'll get the milk for Gabriel. Jay, would you like a glass of milk? You can help yourself to the cookies over there."

"Sure, I'll take a glass, if you don't mind," Jay answered as Gabriel got up and passed him the plate of cookies.

When I returned, Gabriel and Jay were laughing. Jay had been explaining a little of the background on his family tree so that Gabriel would understand better the story he was about to tell. Jay had explained to him that his Aunt June and Uncle Lloyd, who's actual name was John Lloyd Welton, had two boys, John, Jr., also known as Johnny, and Jack.

Johnny was the most useless thing around, and of the two of them, Jack was the one that was on track. On track being that he actually had a job and moved out of Aunt June's house. He worked part-time picking up bodies for one of the local funeral homes. He made a hundred dollars per body. Jack was the only person I had ever heard cheer out loud when someone died. Jay said each time he did it was unnerving.

Jack was about two years older than Jay and they grew up like brothers. I had met Jack on several occasions over the years, the last of which was when he came with Jay to my grandfather's funeral and brought his new wife, a pregnant seventeen year old girl named Stacy.

"So I went to Jack and Stacy's today. They live in a POS trailer out near Gray. She's about eight months pregnant now and looks like she is going to bust. Anyway, I took Stacy to the Piggly Wiggly for grocery shopping. While there we got nostalgic for Jiffy Pop. You know, the little frying pan popcorn, so I bought some."

I looked at Gabriel, "Have you ever had Jiffy Pop?"

"One of my aunts used to make it occasionally," he replied.

Jay continued, "We were watching our soaps when Stacy remembered the Jiffy Pop. She offered to get up and make it, but she looks like a whale so I thought I would be a gentleman and make it. I went into the joke of a kitchen, got it out and put it on the stove. I turned on the eye and gave it a little shake. All of a sudden, this loud boom came from the eye, a blue flame went around the room and a jolt went through my core."

Both Gabriel and I gasped.

Jay continued, "I thought, 'fluke', so I cut the eye off, waited a second and then turned the knob back to the on position. I gave the Jiffy Pop a little shake and then 'Whapow!!' the boom again, the blue flame around the room, the jolt and damn if my balls weren't tingling."

Both Gabriel and I were nearly on the floor laughing at that point.

Jay continued again, "Yeah, and Stacy leans back in the recliner so she can see me through the kitchen door and she says, 'Watch out, that right eye'll get-cha.' To which I responded, 'You don't say, my fucking pubes are probably gray now!'"

We were dying laughing. Tears were coming out of my eyes. Gabriel laughed through his words, "That right eye'll get-cha!! Oh my God! Dude, you got electrocuted twice!"

"No shit!" Exclaimed Jay and mocking Stacy once more. "I wonder how many times that fool has electrocuted herself and she couldn't think to warn me? 'That right eye'll get-cha.' Between her being electrocuted while pregnant and Jack being Jack, that baby does not stand a chance. It might as well stay in there because this is as good as it is going to get for that kid."

"And you are related to these people?" Gabriel asked Jay.

"Yes." Jay hung his head.

"Don't be ashamed, man, that's the funniest thing I have heard in months. Are you and Amelia related?" Gabriel continued to question.

I responded, "No, but we both wish we could trade some of our relations for one another."

Jay continued to hang out with us for a while before he left us and went in to study.

As soon as Jay was safely out of earshot, Gabriel turned to me and said, "That right eye'll getcha! My God, Amelia, he's lucky that didn't kill him!"

Gabriel and I laughed hysterically again, "I know and we shouldn't laugh." Of course, we continued laughing until our faces hurt.

Finally, our laughing wound down and Gabriel repositioned himself on the swing, laying his head back in my lap. "Miss Anderson, would you kindly rub my head again?"

"Gladly, Mr. Hewitt," I responded.

Time passed for a little while in silence as I massaged his head and the swing moved to and fro. I thought Gabriel was asleep when he broke the silence, "I envy your life right now, Amelia."

"How so?" I was curious.

"I think you're living the ideal college life," he replied as he continued to lay there with his eyes closed and me running my fingers through his hair.

"And yours wasn't ideal? You were on full scholarship from what I recall," I reminded him as I moved my hands down behind his neck.

"I know we mentioned that we weren't going to talk about her, but when I wasn't in class, at practice or playing football, I was being flown to Atlanta or wherever else...let's just say to this day, I know more about Atlanta than Annapolis. You just seem free, Amelia, and I envy that."

I leaned down and kissed him, soft, slow and upside down. I followed the kiss by saying, "I suppose I'm living the dream right now. Now, get up and let's go have some dinner. I'm starving."

Gabriel leaned up from the swing, "I believe you said you were going to change."

"I did and I will. Would you like to come in and make sure what I choose is suitable?" I inquired as I eased out of the swing.

"Watch out, Miss Anderson. Mess with the bull, you'll get the horns," he warned with a wink and another smack on my behind as I turned to walk inside.

Once I was properly dressed, we headed out on foot, hand in hand. We walked up Jefferson Street, crossing over at the light at Hancock, making a right and continuing west on Hancock to The Brick for dinner.

Dinner was amazing. We talked about any and everything and nothing all at once. It was lighthearted and did not have anything to do with our upbringings, lack thereof or Beth. We talked about our favorite restaurants. Mine was The Downtown Grill in Macon and his was Mary Mac's in Atlanta; apparently it was a landmark, but I had never heard of it. He was shocked and promised to take me there one day. According to Gabriel, it was the best of the best of Southern cooking and you got free pot liquor. I might have been Southern, but pot liquor was still swill to me. I cringed at the thought.

We also talked about the farthest we had ever been away from home. Gabriel had been in the Navy so he had been up and down and around the world. I had only been as far north as the Biltmore House and as far west as Aunt Dot's house when she lived in Birmingham and I had been as far south as Disney World.

After dinner, we headed back home on foot, hand in hand again, along the streets of Milledgeville. There under the street lights at the corner of Jefferson Street and Hancock and next to the

Historical Marker for Sacred Heart Catholic Church, Gabriel stopped and put his arms around me. "May I?" he asked.

"Please, and you never have to ask."

And just when I thought I had had an education, I realized my education was only just beginning, right there on the street corner for God and everyone to see.

CHAPTER 9

Work on Wednesday night was uneventful. The usual crew was on staff: Alvin, Rudy, Matt and myself. The usual members came in for dinner: Kimmie and Mr. Martin, the owners of Lancelot the Collie and a few others. There was nothing out of the ordinary.

I passed the time by reflecting on the conversation I had had with Jay after Gabriel left last night. Gabriel did not stay long after we walked back from dinner and as soon as I was back upstairs from walking him out, Jay came to find me.

I had barely changed into my pajamas when Jay knocked at my door. This was a first, Jay knocking.

"Come in," I answered. "What's with you knocking?"

"I suppose I better start. Never know when you might be getting defiled," he laughed.

I threw a pillow at him from the bed in response before asking him, "Here help me throw back the covers while I get the cushions off of the porch."

Our conversation continued as I headed through the doors and onto the porch.

"So what do you think of him? I know you have been dying to discuss him since you first met him last night," I yelled as I grabbed the cushion from the swing.

As I made my way back through the French doors into my room, Jay was taking a seat on my bed that he had just unmade for me. I took a seat across from him crossing my legs and settling in for what I anticipated would be a long conversation.

"You were not lying or over exaggerating when you said he was good looking. I think his eyes are the prettiest I have ever seen on a man. Good grief, Millie, he's the stuff dreams really are made of; well, at least my dreams, and I suspect yours now as well," Jay replied as he got comfortable on the bed.

"Thanks, I suppose," I replied with a pensive, fake concerned look as if I were worried about Jay having a crush on Gabriel.

"The way he looks at you, oh my God," Jay paused. "I hope he never stops, Millie. You have been through so much. You deserve this."

"Deserve what?" I was befuddled. I was not even sure if what Gabriel and I were doing was even dating. If there was such a thing as a human yo-yo game, that might be a better description of whatever was going on with us.

Jay took my hands in his and looked at me with such seriousness. "The way he looks at you when he thinks you are not looking, any idiot could tell how he feels. He loves you. I don't know why he has done this push and pull, back and forth stuff with you, but I would be willing to bet good money that that is over."

"What if it's not? I'm in so far over my head," I sighed and took my hands back to rub them over my face. I was getting tired and I had hardly slept the night before.

"I could be wrong. I mean, I only met him just last night and again today, but I like him and I would kill for someone to look at me like that. Don't think I didn't notice the way you look at him too." Jay had always been observant.

"I feel like every time I am near him, I completely lose myself. Do you know that all I had wished for on my birthday was for him to finally kiss me? That's all I wanted. After the night in Atlanta and waking up at his house, I really thought I was going to die if I did not finally get that."

"Well, I have a feeling that you have gotten it a few times by now," Jay smiled. "I also have a feeling that you're well on your way to getting something more if you want it. Heck, I want it for you."

My mind spun at the thought of more. I am sure I looked foolish to those around me throughout the evening, smiling randomly for no apparent reason.

***

Another reflection I had while working was of a conversation I had had that afternoon with Alex when he popped by the apartment just before I left for work. It was not the first time he had popped by uninvited, but it was not something that he did regularly. Even though I had decided all the while we were talking that I would never entertain his warning, the thoughts he planted just kept creeping in.

Jay had made a run to Aunt June's house and Emma was at tennis practice and I had been getting ready for work when I heard the knock at the door and Alex yell, "Millie, it's me. Come let me in."

I knew who "me" was so I ran downstairs to let Alex in.

"Awesome, I was scared I would not catch you before you left for work," he said with exasperation as I opened the door. "Do you have a few minutes?"

"Yes, as long as you don't mind me doing my make-up while we talk," I said as I turned to go up the stairs and he followed.

Once upstairs, I left Alex in the living room, "There are some cookies on the kitchen table that I made the other day if you would like any, help yourself," I offered him before I left to grab my make-up case from the bathroom.

I returned to find Alex with the entire plate of cookies in his lap and seated on the couch.

"Millie, it's no secret that I like you so I don't want you to think I am telling you this for selfish reasons," Alex started as I took a seat on the far end of the couch and opened my make-up.

"Telling me what?" I said as I started to apply my moisturizer.

"Andy and I could not help but notice at your birthday party that you appear to be involved with your boss from the club." Alex paused to chew and swallow his cookie. "These cookies are really good. You made them?"

"I did. What's this all about?" I asked as I began applying foundation and wondering exactly where this conversation was going.

"Here's the thing. He's not the right guy for you, Millie," he paused again to swallow.

"Really, Alex, and what makes you say that?" I asked with a bit of sarcasm in my voice.

"Andy says he has been with half of the married women at the club and that he just uses women," Alex seemed sincere, but the fact that he got his information from his brother the "Jump Around" king was priceless.

"Andy told you this? Did he know you have your own intentions toward me?" I asked again with bite, but not wanting to hurt his feelings. I applied powder over my foundation with gusto that was coming from getting annoyed at the nerve of them, Andy for telling Alex and Alex for telling me. Who were they to judge?

"Yeah, I have told him a great deal about you."

Immediately, I was irritated at Andy. I did not like him that much to begin with, but looking back on our dance at my party, my opinion of him that night was exactly right. He knew how his brother felt, but he made a play for me anyway. I should have thanked Alex for his warning and sent him on his way; instead, I did not use my better judgment and I lashed out.

"Really, did he tell you that he hit on me while we danced at my party and that I declined him? And as for any inappropriate behavior, I guess that would make him the authority since you say he knew how you felt about me." As soon as the words escaped my mouth, I regretted them. I knew how much Andy meant to Alex and I should have just let it go, but shame on me I didn't.

Alex immediately looked hurt. I tried to apologize, but it was of no use. I hoped maybe he did not believe me about Andy because even though I would have willingly hurt Andy right then, I never meant to hurt Alex. The look that had come across his face was as if he was an eight year old and I had told him there was no Santa. Alex had idolized Andy and I might have ruined that for him. He thanked me for the cookies and was on his way. I felt terrible.

***

I replayed the conversation in my head a dozen times throughout the evening, "getting something more" and "he's been with half the married women in the club". I had never had anything more than a few kisses and this concerned me. It was not like I had not been propositioned before. It's just that I had never been exposed to anyone from whom I wanted more and yet Alex's words haunted me. I had made a point in my life to avoid those who only wanted one thing and now here I was. Would I be able to refuse Gabriel and was I just another conquest?

***

It was about 9:00 p.m. when we finished up and were walking out. Alvin was walking me to my car when I noticed Gabriel leaning up against the Corvette waiting on me.

"I've got it from here, Alvin. Thanks!" said Gabriel.

"Okay. I'll see you tomorrow," Alvin replied to Gabriel before bidding me goodnight.

I continued the walk toward Gabriel. "What are you doing here and where's your car? Did you walk up here?"

"I did walk here and I came to kiss you goodnight," he held out his hands and stepped toward me as I was within reaching distance of him.

"You walked all the way here to kiss me goodnight?" My eyes widened with delight as I asked.

"Yes," Gabriel responded with seriousness in his voice and before I could ask any more questions, Gabriel pulled me in for the kiss. In that moment, I knew this would never get old. He twirled me around and it was I who was now leaning against my car.

Suddenly, Alex's warning rang in my ears and I brought the kissing to a halt. "May I ask you something?"

"You just did," he smirked.

"Seriously, someone told me this afternoon that you've been with half of the married women of the club." I paused, hoping he would answer without me having to actually ask.

Gabriel let go of me and backed up as if he were wounded. "Is there a question you would like to ask, Amelia? If so, you may want to think about whether you really want to know the answer."

I was hesitant to ask because he was right. Was I sure I wanted to know the answer? I would like to know who I am dealing with so, yes, I suppose I would like to know the answer. Before I could ask, Gabriel answered.

"I've been with one person since I met you and that was a colossal mistake. I have explained to you that things are over with Beth. As for married women, there was one, Kim..."

I cut him off before he could finish her name, "WHAT?" I raised my voice. I am sure my face went red with anger. I was mad about Beth, but I was spit nails, pissed about Kimmie. I slinked around him and opened my car door. I just wanted away from him at that point. That woman repulsed me and he was instantly not far from joining her in that category.

Gabriel grabbed my wrist, "Amelia, all of that was in the past. It means nothing. Don't you have a past?"

"No, I don't!" I felt betrayed even though I knew I was being unreasonable. He did not know me when he was with her so it's not like he cheated on me. I jerked my arm into the pressure point at his thumb. His grip on me gave and broke free.

"Excuse me? What do you mean?" he demanded while grabbing my car door to keep me from shutting it. Quickly, I was in and had already cranked the car.

"I have no past, you idiot! There's no one that's going to pop up and rear their ugly head for you to see all the time," I screamed at him and started to ease up on the clutch causing the car to roll.

"Amelia! Stop the car!" Gabriel screamed while still holding on to the car door. I revved the engine, letting up only a little on the clutch and the car rolled a bit more.

I was looking back to make sure I did not hit anything behind me when I rolled over something with one of the front tires. Gabriel had let go of the car door and when I looked forward he was on his knees. I wanted to give the car the gas and speed off, but I could faintly hear him screaming as he fell to the pavement, grabbing at his foot and ankle, "Amelia! Please stop the car! My foot! Shit! Shit!"

I had run over his foot and he was writhing on the ground holding it. I stopped the car, jumped out and ran to him. "I am so, so sorry, Gabriel!" I said as I ran to him and was already starting to cry. "I would never hurt you on purpose! I am so sorry! What can I do? I am so sorry!" I sobbed.

"Amelia, it's alright. No, it HURTS, but I know you did not mean to, just like I have not meant to hurt you." Even in all of this he was capable of putting things in perspective for me.

"I am so sorry," I continued to cry as I knelt there on the pavement in the parking lot next to him.

"I think my foot is broken so you are going to have to take me to the emergency room," he started trying to get up and I did my best to help him.

"Of course, of course!" I said as I tried to bear his weight. He was so much bigger than I was that all I was able to do was steady him.

230

"Amelia, you are going to have to run back inside and get me the bottle of whiskey to try to take the edge off until we can get to the emergency room and a bag of ice. I'm sorry, but this hurts, so go!"

"Ok, anything you want," I said as he tossed me the keys to the clubhouse. I secured him in the passenger's seat and ran as fast as I could and came back with the whole bottle of Jack Daniels, a to-go cup and a bag filled with ice to try to keep down any swelling. Normally, I would have been scared to be in the darkness of the clubhouse alone at night, but that thought never entered my head.

I got in the car and handed him the bottle and the cup. Gabriel threw the to-go cup out of the window and took about four shots worth straight from the bottle while I started the car. When we reached the gate of Port Honor, I made a right and headed back toward Milledgeville. I am not sure if there was a hospital in Greensboro or Eatonton that might have been closer, but I knew where the one in Milledgeville was so I just headed there and Gabriel did not direct me otherwise. In fact, I think the liquor was working its magic.

We were almost half way there when Gabriel spoke, "Amelia, I am so sorry if my past hurt you, but it is all in the past and you have nothing to worry about. Kim will never say anything to you because she is terrified enough already that I will tell her husband. It was a one-time thing and she knows that I would have never...you know, if I had known she was married."

"So your moral compass isn't broken?" I said with a sigh of relief.

"It was probably broken at one time, but I hope I have someone now that is helping me mend it," he replied as he reached out his hand to take mine.

"I am so sorry, Gabriel. I suppose we all have our secrets. I hope you are not disappointed in mine," I said as tears started down my face again and I pulled his hand up and kissed it.

"Amelia, look at me for a moment," he said as he tugged my hand. I took my eyes off of the road for just a second and looked at him. He continued once my eyes met his, "You are perfect the way you are and I am sorry that I'm not the same for you. Please don't cry. I just cannot stand to see you cry."

***

It was nearly midnight when Gabriel was released from the emergency room. X-rays showed that his ankle was broken in one spot and his foot was broken in two spots. Apparently, when the tire went over his foot he twisted and snapped his ankle in the process of trying to get free.

By the time we left, he was casted from just below the knee all the way to his toes, on crutches and well on his way to being looped up on pain medication and the whiskey. We were told that he would likely have to see an orthopedic for follow-up and possible surgery to repair his ankle.

I was not a night owl like my roommates so saying I was exhausted and emotionally drained was putting it lightly. There was no way I would survive taking him all the way back to his place and then driving all the way back to the apartment. I also knew that I could not just dump him off at his place with no way of making sure he would be all right. I felt I would either have to stay with him or he would have to stay with me. Taking care of him seemed like the least I could do considering my childishness was to blame for everything.

I knew that getting him up the stairs to my apartment was going to be challenging so I prayed someone, Jay or Travis or even Cara or Megan would be home to help me. Luckily, Travis was home and was able to help me get Gabriel up the stairs and to my bed. I was initially nervous to ask anyone to help me get my nearly passed out boyfriend upstairs. Ideally, Jay would have been home. He would be the last person to judge me. In the end, I comforted myself by remembering that Travis lived with his girlfriend so who was he to judge? I thanked Travis profusely and apologized for disturbing them.

Gabriel was about passed out by the time I got him in bed. I got the scissors and cut his pants leg so I could get his pants over the cast. This left him in his boxers. I also removed his polo shirt, but left his t-shirt on. This was the least clothed I had seen him and I admit I took a few moments just to admire him lying there in my bed. I came really close to taking a picture, but this time I used my better judgment unlike when I put the car in gear and ran over his foot.

While I tended to him, propping his foot up on pillows to try to keep the swelling down, I thought about sleeping on the couch. I was not entirely sure what the right thing to do would be. I would rather the first time I slept next to him be something he would remember and enjoy, even if all we did do was sleep, but I did not want to leave him alone. I did not want him waking up in pain or wondering how he got there. Plus, it's not like I had not been dreaming of just sleeping next to him and this was likely to be the safest opportunity for that.

I slipped on my pajamas, a red tank top and flannel shorts, and slid into bed next to Gabriel. Jay was right about the size of the bed. Once in it I could not imagine being in anything smaller with Gabriel and having any room at all. I thought about snuggling up to him with my head on his chest, but I did not want to take advantage of the situation so I rolled over on my side and backed up to Gabriel. He was lying on his back with his eyes closed and I thought he was fast asleep, but as soon as I touched him he rolled over toward me as best he could with his foot still propped on the pillows.

We were in the spooning position and he whispered, "I want to be the first to make love to you, Amelia."

Although I knew those words would ring in my ears for eternity, I really figured that was the pain meds talking. Despite that, I rolled over facing him and kissed his cheek. "Soon," I said before rolling back over opposite him. I pulled his arm around me and fell asleep shortly thereafter.

Neither of us moved through the night as we slept. Perhaps we did not move because I was thoroughly exhausted and he was equally sedated or perhaps this was the most natural way to sleep that either of us had ever experienced. When I started to wake, I found Gabriel's arm around my waist and mine over his. I could feel his pelvis against my rear and his bare legs against mine. I could feel the cast still propped on the pillows under the covers and it leaning on my feet. I could feel his chest through the t-shirt against my bare back around the straps of my tank top. I could feel his face buried in my hair and the locks of my hair moving with each breath he took.

I had not bothered to set the alarm clock the night before, but my bladder awoke me at 8:00 a.m. anyway. I did not want to wake him so I tried to ease out from under his arm, but it was of no use. I tried lifting his arm, but he just held tighter.

"Gabriel," I whispered as I wiggled just a little under him, "I have to go to the bathroom. Please let me up."

Gabriel let out one long breath and stretched just a bit. Then, it was as if his senses came to him and he jumped up in bed. I jumped as well and cleared the bed. It was apparent he did not know where he was. The awkwardness of the cast kept him from really getting up. Wild- eyed, he looked around the room. He was still a little asleep and dazed.

"Gabriel!" I said with a touch more volume than the whisper before. "Gabriel, you are at my house."

He whipped his head around toward me and rubbed his eyes, "Amelia, right, right."

"I'm going to go to the bathroom and I'll be right back," I said as I walked around the bed and attempted to kiss him on the forehead. I leaned toward him and he grabbed me and pulled me across his lap and kissed me.

"Good morning, Miss Anderson. Now you may go to the bathroom," Gabriel said as he released me.

"Good morning, Mr. Hewitt," I said sheepishly as I knew he had to be remembering the night before and that I ran over his foot.

I regained my footing and turned to start to the bathroom when the swift smack on my behind came nearly lifting me from the floor, "Ouch!" I whipped around to Gabriel.

"You are going to owe me big time over this one, Miss Anderson!" he smiled. He remembered and did not appear to be mad with me. I was so relieved.

When I returned, I found Gabriel had made his way onto the crutches. He headed in as I came out.

"I'm going to go and make us some breakfast. Just get back in bed and put your foot up. I'll be back in a little bit," I instructed him as we passed.

I started breakfast and then returned with orange juice. I found him back in my bed with his foot propped back up. My heart fluttered at the sight. He was in my bed, but this was not the way I had dreamed things would go. I shook off the thoughts of disappointment and handed him the orange juice and issued him two pain pills.

When I had finished making breakfast, I served it to him in bed. We made a plan for the day as we ate. Gabriel was adamant that I did not skip class although I offered. The plan was that he would call Joan and tell her what had happened and that he would not be in for the lunch shift, but he would do his best to make it in for dinner. He then called Alvin and had Alvin cover the lunch shift. I explained to him that our instructor for badminton did not care if we attended class or not as long as we were there more often than not. Reluctantly, he agreed that skipping badminton just this once was acceptable. We agreed that when I returned from my 10:00 a.m. class that I would take him home; until then he would stay put.

I also warned Jay and Emma when they awoke that Gabriel was here. They were amused when I explained the events of the last evening and that it did not include my having been "defiled" as everyone was now putting it.

The day was going according to plan. Jay helped me get Gabriel down the stairs and we were on our way to his house by noon. On the way there was ample time for me to apologize time and again, which I did, but he would have none of it.

When we arrived in the driveway at his house, I took notice of it this time. The last time I was there I had paid little attention. The house had a semicircular driveway in front of the main entrance and an off-shoot to the garage. I pulled up in front of the front door and parked.

The house was one of the more conservative houses in the neighborhood. It had white siding, black shutters and roof, and a red door. The yard was perfectly manicured. There were Leland Cypress trees at every corner and various sized boxwoods in between. In front of the boxwoods and within the pine straw were patches of yellow pansies. Edging the pine straw and separating the flower beds from the yard was a tiny wall of stacked stone, the same stacked stone that made up the bottom portion of the columns supporting the stoop over the front porch and made up the steps and base of the porch.

Once having parked the car, Gabriel insisted that I come in. I had anticipated having to help him to the door, but he was quite capable on the crutches. I was afraid that he would just want me to leave so he could get some peace and quiet, relax and put his foot up. That was not the case.

Gabriel had me follow him down the hallway to his bedroom, the master in the house. I stopped at the doorway and he continued in toward the bed. He propped the crutches against the night stand and took a seat on his bed and kicked off his one shoe. I felt a little unsure about entering the lion's den so I stood there waiting by the door.

"Amelia, I'm going to take a shower and then I'm going to lie down and probably take a nap. Would you care to wait for me to get out of the shower and then join me for a nap?" He continued, "I think you need to indulge me since you ran over my foot."

"Ha ha, Mr. Hewitt," I replied as I slipped my tennis shoes off by the door.

I tried to hide my shock when Gabriel removed his shirt and undershirt as if they were one and immediately followed with his jeans. I felt flushed, but there was no time to gawk at him or admire the view. My focus was on helping him and trying to make up for breaking his foot so when he stood, I dashed toward him and held out a hand to steady him, but he did not take it. He did all of this while balancing on one foot. I am not sure whether I was more impressed that he was nearly naked in front of me or that he got naked while balancing on one foot.

"Miss Anderson, are you blushing? It's not like you haven't seen me in my underpants before," he grinned.

"It is the first time I have seen you in nothing but your underpants," I said as I offered him the crutches so he might make his way toward the shower with a little more ease than the hopping on one foot that it appeared he was about to do.

Taking the crutches, he reminded me, "And the cast. Don't forget the cast."

"I don't think you are going to let me forget the cast," I said shaking my head.

I was sitting on his bed watching television when Gabriel returned from the shower. I could smell him as soon as I saw him and he smelled like Coast soap. I could have just inhaled him all afternoon. That was the main soap that my grandfather kept in the house while I was growing up. It was the defining smell of clean.

Standing in the doorway of the bathroom, Gabriel was bare-chested and wearing only his pirate pajama pants. The pants were tied with a drawstring, but hung low showing the "V", the muscles near his hips and below his abs, which were noticeably amazing. Gabriel was virtually hairless across his chest, but from his navel, and due to the low rise of the pants, I could see his happy trail.

There was no need for television at that point as I could have been entertained just by looking at him for hours on end. His eyes were as blue as ever and his hair was still damp. It looked as if he had only tried to towel dry it before running a comb through it and the lines from the comb were still visible.

"You know, I just don't think this is fair," he said as he looked at me there on his bed.

236

"What isn't fair?" I asked. Was he finally about to school me about my temper and running over his foot?

"You have seen me in my underpants twice and I still have to use my imagination when it comes to you," Gabriel said with a mischievous look on his face.

"Mr. Hewitt, may I remind you that just last week I slept in your guest room and I am quite certain you saw me in little more than one of your undershirts?"

Gabriel continued to stand there in the doorway, taunting me, "Miss Anderson, I was a complete gentleman that night and did not see you in any such thing. The most I saw of you was your bare back while you were fully clothed in your dress and then again the following morning, by mistake, when I saw your back again."

Did he seriously mean for me to undress and give him a show? My heart was starting to pound. No one and I mean, no one, not even my roommates or Aunt Gayle, had ever seen me in my underwear or less since I was ten years old. Insecurities raced through my head. Suddenly I was no longer concerned about his body and more worried about my own.

Gabriel then put the crutches in motion and made his way to the bed. He made using the crutches look easy. Again he placed the crutches against the bedside table and rested his casted leg on the bed.

"So, nap time. Below covers or on top?" he asked.

"Whichever you like," I replied.

"Below covers means you in your underwear and on top of covers means fully clothed. Your choice," he suggested.

I gathered my nerve and before I could answer, he added, "Amelia, I am not going to try much of anything as long as my foot is in this cast."

I stood from the bed and unbuttoned my jeans and slid then down my legs to step out of them. Gabriel stood, balanced on his one good foot and while watching me, threw back the covers and repositioned the pillows.

I turned my back to him as I eased my shirt over my head while thinking, "Thank goodness I was wearing matching bra and panties if by way of nothing more than both were black." Matching undergarments was not something with which I typically concerned myself, so for it to happen on this particular day was a stroke of luck.

Before I got into the bed, I don't know what possessed me, but I asked, "Have you and anyone..." I paused and looked at him and looked down at the bed and back to him hoping he would understand what I was asking without making me complete the sentence.

"No, not in this bed," he answered and I climbed in and so did he.

Gabriel extended his right arm, inviting me to lay my head on his chest. I did this eagerly. I lay on my side against him and propped my chest against his torso and rested my right hand against his chest next to my face. I also draped one of my bare legs across his which was still clothed in the pirate pants.

We laid there in silence for so long that I was nearly asleep when he whispered, "I am so sorry about any pain my past indiscretions may have caused you, Amelia. I know I would have felt the same way that you did last night, but I want you to trust me."

Gabriel had pulled his left arm around me and stroked my hair with his hand as he spoke. By the time he finished speaking, I could feel a tear run down my cheek and fall onto his chest. Gabriel began to speak again, "I cannot promise that I won't hurt you, but you must promise that you will not run away, Amelia. If you feel you have been wronged, then you must stand and fight. You must talk to me. Promise?"

I raised my head from his chest and looked at him and responded, "I promise."

I inched up toward him and I could feel the pull of his hand in my hair, pulling me closer as I inched up dragging my chest against his until my face reached his and I kissed him. This kiss was the most titillating of all. I could feel myself craving him.

I was balanced on one of my elbows which was driven into the mattress between his right arm and his chest. My other hand cupped his face at his jaw. The kiss went on, mouth on mouth, for some time before I tilted his head and moved to his neck and then to his ear. I circled his ear with my tongue and nibbled at his ear lobe. I could feel chill bumps descend his neck and across his right arm.

Gabriel's hands explored my back, up and down. He ran a finger between my bra strap and my skin and the chills were then

238

mine. He lowered his hands to my backside and after palming each cheek, he traced the line of my panties just under the hem around the openings for my legs. He was discrete, only slipping his index fingers under and followed the line from the front of my hips to my inner butt cheeks. It was all I could do not to allow him further access. I remembered what he had said as he drifted off to sleep last night and I wanted that as well.

To describe our kissing as making out or passionate was an understatement. I knew I had to wind things down. As I was making the decision to back off, Gabriel whispered while leaving a trail of soft kisses from the tip of my left shoulder, up my neck to my ear, "Tell me you are mine."

I responded without hesitation. Breathless, I whispered in his ear, "Gabriel, I am yours."

"All mine?" he continued.

"Yes, all yours." I wanted to ask him the same, but I held my tongue.

It felt as if he tried to roll me over, but was reminded of his broken foot and the cast. Things cooled and we fell asleep intertwined in each other.

It was nearly 3:30 when we woke. We had slept for about two hours and again it was my bladder that woke me. I slipped from the covers and he noticed. All insecurities had faded and I walked openly in my bra and panties to his bathroom with him watching. I returned the same way and as I approached his bed he rolled over onto his side, carefully and strategically moving the cast as he never took his eyes off of me while throwing back the covers for me.

I re-entered the bed and positioned myself like a mirror image of him. I was on my side, arm up and bent at the elbow with my head propped on my hand.

"You are so much more beautiful than I had imagined, Amelia," Gabriel said as he lay there looking at me.

Immediately I felt red overtake my face and I fell over on my stomach hiding my face in the pillow. I was embarrassed and how was I to respond? Short of a bathing suit, this was the most naked I had ever been in front of anyone. From the pillow, I said a muffled, "Thank you."

"Are you okay?" he asked as he tapped me on my shoulder.

"Yes, ...no ....yes. Yes, I am fine. Thank you." I gathered my nerve and rolled back over mirroring him again. "First time anyone has seen this much of me, sorry. I was fine until you said what you said."

"Ah," he paused and thought about it. "So no one has ever seen you..."

"No, not since I was ten and had the chicken pox," I said.

"Just be quiet and come here and kiss me!" Gabriel laughed. "Seriously, get over here or I am going to throw back the covers and stare at you some more."

I rolled right over and did exactly as told. We carried on for a moment. It occurred to me that perhaps it was too soon to ask, but here I was in only my bra and panties in his bed so perhaps the phrase too soon might have been past its prime. I decided to ask; what was the worst he could say, "no"?

I pulled back from him and asked, "What are you doing for Thanksgiving?" I bit my lower lip in anticipation of his answer.

"Working, like yourself," he replied as he pulled me back and continued to kiss my neck.

I pulled back from him, "Working on Thanksgiving?" I had never worked on Thanksgiving before.

"Lunch buffet at the club, we already have reservations for thirty people and it is growing. It's going to be our busiest day of the year." He seemed proud and I am sure I seemed devastated. I had never missed Thanksgiving before. It was my favorite holiday next to Christmas, of course. I am sure he could tell by the look on my face that I was disappointed.

"Not to worry," he said, "We are all done with the club by 2:00 p.m., so what did you have in mind?"

"You can say no, but I would like it if you would come with me to my aunt Dot's for Thanksgiving. They usually eat at noon, but everyone hangs out and they all eat again around 5:30. You can say no," I reiterated.

"Why would I say no?" he asked as he again inched me closer to him.

"Because I am essentially asking you to meet my family...all of them at one time," I spelled that out nicely. "It's too soon. I understand."

"Wait a minute. I have not said no yet," he said. "Have you ever taken anyone home to meet family before?"

"No."

"Why?"

"The only boy I ever dated grew up next door and everyone already knew him," I explained.

"Seriously, you dated the boy next door?"

"Yes."

"How long did you date and what happened to him?" Gabriel continued with the inquisition.

"We dated three years and I would not give it up in the bed of his truck the day he got his driver's license, so he found someone who would. I was sixteen," I laughed.

"And you were broken-hearted?" he asked.

"Not really. It just confirmed what I had always suspected. I wanted more from life than being the queen of the double wide trailer and that was where that was headed."

"His loss! Plus, anyone with a lick of sense knows that anything worth having is worth waiting for. Have there been any other boyfriends?" he continued with the questions.

"None worth mentioning."

"Why?"

"I was a perpetual victim of the three date rule," I said.

"Are you kidding?" he laughed. "What is the three date rule?"

"I can't believe you are a guy and don't know what the three date rule is. Get Andy to explain it to you. I am certain he knows what it is." I am sure Andy practiced the two date rule.

241

"Anyway," I continued, "There was no one worth my effort." Translation, effort means allowing someone in my pants. I don't think he got the translation which was for the best.

"And me?" Gabriel said and for once it appeared as though he were the one afraid of the answer. After my earlier admissions, he still needed reassuring? Perhaps he had his own insecurities. He wanted to know if he was worth my effort.

I snuggled up to him and said it. I did not whisper this time, "I am yours, only yours and all yours."

Gabriel slipped over to his back and my head fell to his chest. He stroked my hair and we just laid there in the still afternoon light that shown through the windows of his room. I could definitely get used to this.

Although I did not want the afternoon to end, it was ten after four and for whatever reason I had to ask, "Are you planning to go to work this evening?"

"I need to try," he replied.

"Then we probably need to get up and get going," and I rolled over and got up out of bed.

We got dressed and I dropped him at the club. I offered to come in and help him in the kitchen, but he would not hear of it. He also explained that he would get a ride home from Daniel and Jerry who were working that night.

The drive back to Milledgeville was such a haze of daydreaming about the afternoon that I missed the turn for the shortcut and did not even realize it until I found myself at the red light in downtown Eatonton. Past the red light and onto Highway 441, the daydreaming continued. Just the thought and I could taste the hint of soap on my tongue from his neck. Just the slow blink of my eyes as I watched the road ahead and I could see him standing half naked in the doorway of his bathroom. I squirmed in the seat of my car at the thought of his touch, his fingers running just under the lace of my panties and along my skin. My heart quickened.

Before I knew it, I was crossing over the Lake Sinclair bridge at the Power Plant. Typically, when I crossed the bridge, I could not help but look at the looming, massive smoke stacks and worry about what if. They made me paranoid to the tenth degree, but this time I hardly noticed them. I was lost in my own head. The images played on like a show for which only I had a ticket.

It wasn't a silent movie in my head. There were the words, "Tell me you're mine." And my response, "Gabriel, I'm yours, all yours." They played over and over like a soundtrack with a skip in the record. The entire day would ring in my head for the foreseeable future, but the words were what might linger in my ears forever. "I am yours," that's as close to telling a boy I loved him as I had ever come.

I had entered the city limits of Milledgeville. It was a cool night and I had driven back with the windows down. The night air was cool and refreshing on my face. The wheels of the Corvette rolled on and I cleared every light between the Walmart and The Jefferson, including the left turn arrow at Columbia Street. Time had changed the weekend before so it was darker earlier this time of year. It was not quite 6:00 p.m. and the street lights were on and they flickered through the T-tops as the flashbacks kept coming.

The last stretch of my route, down Columbia Street and over to Montgomery Street, I thought back to the night at the Georgian Terrace. When he was not holding my hand, he was leading me with just the gentle touch of his hand on the small of my back. Throughout the evening, if we were in the same room, he had a hand on me. I did not know a lot about boys and I did not pretend to know what went on in their minds, but if ever I knew anything, I knew he did not have to tell me with words that he was mine. Without the words, just with his touch, I knew he was mine. I felt it to my core every time he touched me.

I pulled into the driveway and around to the carport. I parked the Corvette next to Jay's car and although I loved my daydreaming, I was tired and glad to be home. It had been a very busy few days, a busy few days that I had enjoyed to the hilt.

I could get used to all of this. More than that, I wanted to get used to it.

***

Once inside the apartment, I spoke to Jay. Emma was not home. She was at tennis practice as usual. I had a little dinner of ramen noodles and canned chicken that Jay had made, poor man's chicken and dumplings. We rehash my last seventy-two hours and the last twenty-four in complete, no holds barred detail. It was not a conversation in which I was requesting his advice. It was just a conversation of me sharing my life with him. He was genuinely thrilled for me.

Jay did give one piece of advice, but not because I asked for it. Jay insisted that I introduce Gabriel to Aunt Gayle before

243

Thanksgiving. His reasoning was that she was the closest thing to a parent that I had and it would be unfair to her to introduce them at Thanksgiving as if she were just another member of the family. Jay was usually spot on with his advice, so I heeded it. I decided I would call sometime during the week and invite her to join me for dinner the following Friday night.

The thought of Aunt Gayle meeting Gabriel and vice-versa was the perfect mix of nervousness and excitement. From the moment I made the decision to follow Jay's advice until the moment they finally met, I would fret over concerns of whether they would like one another or not.

I excused myself from Jay around 8:00 p.m. and turned in for the night. I spent some time reading and getting ready for the week's classes and showered. I had hoped Gabriel would call, but by the time I was dozing off around 9:30, I resolved myself to it being alright if he did not. Just as I was about gone, the phone rang.

I snatched it up on the first ring anxious to find out how work went for Gabriel considering he was in a cast and the majority of the time he spent at work, he was on his feet. It was not Gabriel; it was actually Aunt Gayle calling to check on me.

"Hey, sweetheart," she greeted me after recognizing my voice. "I hope I am not calling too late."

"No, it's never too late. You can call anytime, you know that," I replied trying to hide the disappointment in my voice that it was not Gabriel.

"Well, I just wanted to call and find out how you were doing. How was your birthday party and are you feeling any better about the inheritance? I have been concerned about you." I had managed to cover the sound of disappointment in my voice much better than she hid the worry in hers.

"You shouldn't worry about me. I am fine. My birthday party was wonderful. Jay, Emma, Cara and Stella really outdid themselves. I could spend an hour telling you all about it. They invited everyone I know and everyone came." I really could have gone on and on, but she interrupted me with her contributions to the conversation.

"That's so wonderful, Amelia. It really is a testament to how much everyone loves you." Aunt Gayle was always going overboard telling me how much everyone loved me. She was sort of a broken record in that department. I know she meant well. She was protective of me and spent a great deal of time trying to compensate

244

for any lingering self-esteem issues I might have because of my mother. I knew as well as anyone that if my mother had loved me as a mother should, she would have never let me go, not for anyone.

"Or a testament to them finding out there was going to be free liquor," I replied in my usual deflective manner.

"Oh, Amelia, you sell yourself short."

"I am actually glad you called. There's something I want to ask you," I started and as I did I could hear the call waiting tone go off on the line. What timing! I had to click over because it might be Gabriel. "Aunt Gayle, someone is beeping in. Would you mind? I will click right back over."

"No, that's fine."

After she released me, I clicked over and it was just a call from one of Emma's guys to make sure she was going to be at Cameron's that night. I assured him she was as she was getting ready right then.

I clicked back over to Aunt Gayle. "I'm back. I want to invite you to come spend next Friday afternoon with me and then let me take you to dinner at Port Honor. You can even spend the night here if you like. I want you to meet everyone."

"That sounds like fun and I would love to come see you. I am not sure if I can stay over or not. May I let you know about that later in the week?"

"Sure," I replied as my mind wandered back to whether she would like Gabriel or not. "There's no rush. If you can't stay over that's fine, but I do want us to go to dinner and you have not seen The Jefferson yet."

"The Jefferson?" she asked.

"That's what I named my building. It's at the corner of Jefferson Street and all of the other old houses have names around here, so I figured it should have a name too." I had even had it put in the legal description of the deed so it would forever have a name, the name I gave it. In the weeks since I had bought it I had had a sign put up out front in the yard. The sign was cased in red brick, the closest red brick I could find to match the brick of the building; it was a touch off, but nothing obvious. Within the brick casing was a sheet of plywood which was painted white. On the wood were the words "The Jefferson" plus the year of establishment written in black. I had to get permission from the city before putting up the sign, but that was not as hard as I thought it would be.

"You always did name everything. We had to keep you away from the cows because it made it harder to send them to the slaughter house when we knew their names," she reminded me.

"I know, I know. It made them hard to eat too," I added and again the call waiting tone beeped. "I hate to do this, but the call waiting is going off again. Do you mind if I call you back later and we will finalize the details of Friday then?"

"No, I understand. I need to go let Tanner out to potty anyway. He's over here crossing his legs. He misses you a lot and so do I. I will talk to you later. Sleep well," Aunt Gayle said as she started to hang up.

"Goodnight and give Tanner an extra treat from me tonight. I miss you both as well." It made me sad to think of them missing me and being in the big house all alone. Tanner was Aunt Gayle's yellow lab, the sweetest dog ever. We figured he would more likely lick an intruder to death than he would bite them.

"Hello?" I said as I clicked over wondering if the caller had given up.

He was still there and thank goodness he could not see me. I had the kind of ear to ear smile over him that no girl wanted her new beau to see that early on in any relationship. "Good evening, Miss Anderson. I hope I have not awakened you."

"No, I was still up," I said still trying to stifle my joy in hearing his voice. "How was your night?"

"Good and bad," Gabriel responded as he went on to tell me that it had been the busiest Thursday night they had in months; perhaps even since he had started there.

"That's awesome!" I cheered.

"It is, except..." I thought he was going to say something about his foot hurting, so I cut him off.

"Except that I ran over your foot and you were miserable the whole time. I am so sorry!" I could not say it or think it enough. I truly was sorry and I still felt terrible.

"That's not what I was going to say. I was going to say, except that I wanted to get out of there so I could call you," Gabriel

246

said correcting me. "Amelia, this is not the first broken bone I have had and it's not likely to be the last."

"How many broken bones have you had?" I asked since it sounded as if he had had quite a few.

"Perhaps I will tell you all about that one day, but not tonight. Let's just say I have had enough to know how to get most anything done in spite of any cast or set of crutches." I shuttered to think of him being hurt enough to sound as if he was bragging about his abilities to have mastered getting on with life as he had said. It also started me wondering why he would not talk about his injuries right then if there weren't more to it than just the boys will be boys type of accidents or football injuries.

Gabriel had just settled into his bed when he phoned me. I had planned to get to bed early and I did, I just did not get to sleep early. We went on to talk for an hour. We playfully discussed what one another was wearing at first. Then, he gave me the play by play of the evening: who all worked and who did what plus what members came in and who ordered what.

The call wound down by Gabriel saying, "I wish you were here."

He said it and I had been thinking it. I did not care if we were at my place or his, but I wanted to sleep next to him again and again. Waking up next to him whether from a whole night's sleep or just a nap was what I imagined waking up in heaven might be like.

Gabriel continued, "I would like to kiss you goodnight."

My heart leapt in my chest and I subdued my response and replied with restraint, "I would like that."

What he did not know is that I was cuddling with the pillow he had slept on in my bed the night before. It still smelled like him and I sniffed it as he spoke. As he said he had wanted to kiss me goodnight, I hugged the pillow to my chest and inhaled. I closed my eyes and imagined him there with me.

"Amelia, say it for me again," he asked.

"Say what?" I was not sure, but I had an idea of what he wanted.

"You know," and with that I was certain.

"I am yours, Gabriel."

CHAPTER 10

"What are you doing?" the voice on the line asked as chills over took me. It was Gabriel. I had tried not to think about him all day other than hoping he would call. What else was there to do? I knew he worked on Friday nights and I did not.

"Studying," I replied with lame honesty. I had a history project that was due next week that I had to get started on.

"Are you serious? You are home on a Friday night studying?" Gabriel asked in shock. "I thought only social pariahs stayed home studying on a Friday night."

"Would you prefer I were getting ready to go trolling the bars with my roommates?" I questioned with the implication that I would do that if he wanted.

"No, and good point, Miss Anderson, well made."

"Yes, and thank you, Mr. Hewitt. Now shouldn't you be working?" It was only 9:00 p.m. when he called. Dinner did not usually wind down on Friday nights until about 9:30 and they usually did not get out of there until almost 10:30, sometimes it was as late as 11:00.

"Things are starting to slow down and I thought I would give you a call and ask what your plans were for the remainder of the evening." Excitement raced through me since it seemed to be implied that he wanted to get together.

"I had planned to continue doing what I am doing unless I get a better offer." I did not want to sound too available, but who was I kidding? I was available. I probably could not stop myself from being available to him.

"Would you mind if I caught a ride with Cara and came over?"

"Just remember I cannot stay up late since I have to be at work tomorrow morning and my boss is a bit of a stickler when it comes to me being late." It did not occur to me in that moment to wonder how he was getting home.

"Alright, we should be done here in about thirty minutes and on our way shortly after," Gabriel continued to say good-bye and something else, but I really did not hear much else before I spaced out and got off the phone with him. All I could think about was what a mess the apartment was in.

The place was in shambles and I had roughly and hour to put it back together and put myself back together as well. There were dirty dishes in the sink, laundry piled in the floor waiting for its turn in the washer. My bed was unmade and the sheets were in one of the piles of laundry.

I felt as if I was running around like a chicken with my head cut off. I managed to shove all of the dishes in the dishwasher and all of the laundry in the laundry closet. I also remade my bed with fresh sheets in a mad hot hurry. I managed to have everything mostly in order within about forty minutes. Then I took a shower, blow-dried my hair, reapply a slight bit of make-up and put on a fresh pair of jeans and a sweater.

I knew how long it took to get from Port Honor to The Jefferson. I also knew how long it would take them to finish up at the Club. Despite that knowledge, the entire time I was in the shower and while drying my hair I was afraid I would miss the knock at the door. Of course I did not miss the knock. I made it out with plenty of time and went back to studying.

I flopped down on the bed with my history text and the next thing I knew it was 1:00 a.m. and there was a fierce whaling on the door taking place down stairs. I jumped up all groggy and went for the door. It was Gabriel.

"Well, hey there, sleeping beauty," he said standing there on the crutches and holding a small overnight bag in his left hand. He was still in his chef's uniform from the Club sans clogs and wearing one tennis shoe instead.

"I am so sorry. How long have you been knocking?" I asked as I rubbed my eyes and held the door open for him. "Come on in. Can you get up the stairs?"

"I can make it up the stairs, but first come here and let me give you a proper 'Hello'," Gabriel said as he stepped into the doorway at the bottom of the stairs. He let the crutches fall against the wall and braced himself on his good foot. He dropped his bag and opened his arms to me.

This time as I approached him, Gabriel took my hands and before I knew it they were pinned behind my back. Suddenly, I was

249

awake and against the wall just inside my doorway at the bottom of the stairs. Gabriel kicked the door shut behind him with the cast.

Gabriel leaned in and a fair amount of his weight was on me. "Out of strawberries?" he said as he noticed the change in the smell of my hair.

"I changed shampoo," I replied.

He nudged my head back, but my hair was still around my neck when he ran his nose through it and started kissing my neck. "Is this peach?"

"Apricot," I whispered as I twisted in his grip. I wanted to touch him. I ran my leg up his and it was enough to distract him so that he loosened his grip.

"Whoa there, Miss Anderson," he whispered.

"What?" I replied all innocent like as I threw my arms around his neck and kissed him directly on his lips. I used all of my new knowledge.

Everything was going smoothly until Gabriel lost his balance and we took a tumble onto the steps. It was quick and I nearly ended up beneath him, but he rolled me on top of him on the way down to keep from crushing me on the stairs. It was laughable, very laughable and we laid there on the steps for a couple of minutes.

I peeled myself off of him, "Come on, Gabriel, let's go upstairs. You must be tired and apparently I need to rewash my hair in the strawberry shampoo."

"No need to rewash it. I love the strawberry, but I can cope with the apricot for now," he responded while holding out his hand for me to help him up.

Once he was on his foot, I handed him his crutches and I backed up to give him room to get by and I took his bag from him. He made it up about three steps before he spoke again, "I am sorry I was later than I had hoped to be."

It took him a little while and quite the effort to make it up the stairs. I stayed behind him as if I could actually help him if he started to fall back. Thank goodness he did not fall since the only good I would have done was soften his landing or break his fall. We would have ended up on the stairs again and this time it would not have been so funny.

Finally, at the top of the stairs, Gabriel appeared nearly exhausted. He went ahead and took a left and headed into my room. The room was softly lit by a small bedside lamp and the rebroadcast of the 11:00 p.m. news playing on the television.

"Do you mind if I get a shower?" Gabriel asked leaning the crutches against the wall next to my bathroom door.

"Not at all," I scooted past him into the bathroom and sat his bag down on the counter by the sink. "Just let me lay out a towel and wash cloth for you."

When I turned back, Gabriel had started getting undressed. He was shirtless and holding on to the door frame. I know my eyes lit up at the sight of him. I tried to keep from staring at him, but that was nearly impossible.

"Just yell if you need anything." I ducked my head and looked at my feet while I made my exit.

I went ahead and slipped into my pajamas. It was cool, but we had turned on the heat so I put on shorts and a tank top. I picked my spot in the bed and waited beneath the covers. It wasn't long before Gabriel emerged from the shower wearing only his pajama pants.

"How is your foot doing?" I asked him as he bounced to the bed on his uninjured foot.

"I hardly notice it," he assured me. "I see you are under the covers..."

"Yes, but I have on pajamas."

"Damn shame!" Gabriel announced as he threw back the covers and turned around to take a seat on the bed.

I don't know what came over me, but I heard myself say it and could not believe the words had come from my own mouth. "It's not like you aren't wearing pajamas."

As soon as the words escaped my lips, my hands shot to my mouth like I could stuff them back in. It was no use.

Gabriel was almost touching the bed when he stood back up, turned and with one hand grabbed the drawstring of his pirate pants, "This can all be rectified, Miss Anderson."

"Stop! Wait! Not yet." I had thoroughly embarrassed myself.

Gabriel smiled a sly smile at me. "Amelia, I told you nothing was going to happen as long as I was in this cast, but it does not mean I don't want it to."

I smiled back and leaned over and patted the bed gesturing for him to get in. "You like messing with me, don't you, Mr. Hewitt?"

"That I do. Now get over here and put your head where it belongs here on my chest," Gabriel demanded.

***

It was around 2:00 a.m. when I woke up to Gabriel calling my name, "Amelia! Amelia, wake up!"

I sat straight up in bed in a panic. I had closed the curtains on the French doors before I got in bed around nine. The curtains worked well at blocking out the street lights and any moonlight. The room was pitch black and I could not see a thing. Though I could not see him, I could feel Gabriel sit up with me. His arms were around me. My heart was racing and my breathing was more like panting. I had had the nightmare.

"Shhh, shhhh," Gabriel said as he tilted my head into his chest. "It's alright. I am here. I am not going to let anything happen to you."

Apparently, I had screamed in my sleep and Jay heard. Not knowing Gabriel was there Jay threw open the door to my room and barged right in. Light from the living room broke the darkness in my room.

"What's going on in here?!!" Jay demanded as soon as he laid eyes on Gabriel.

"I think she had a nightmare," Gabriel responded. "She called for her mother and then screamed."

"Ah, that's what I thought," Jay said. "Just give her a minute and she will be alright. I will get her some water."

Gabriel and I sat in silence with him stroking my hair as I tried to regulate my breathing and calm down. Jay returned pretty quickly with a glass of water for me. He handed me the water and took a seat on the edge of the bed at my feet.

"Did she scare the life out of you, Gabe?" Jay asked.

Before Gabriel could answer, I started apologizing, "I am so sorry I woke you both."

"You did not wake me," Jay replied, "I was just coming up the stairs when I heard you screaming like a banshee. I didn't know whether to think you were having a bad night or a particularly good one. And, I am sure Gabe has heard a woman or two scream before."

Jay tried to lighten the mood and he succeeded. Gabriel shot a warning look at him, but I could not help but laugh.

"You scared the crap out of me, Amelia!" Gabriel playfully nudged me.

"I am so sorry." I apologized again. "I suppose I should have warned you about that. I just..."

"She has not had one in about two months. We thought maybe they had finally gone away," Jay said and shook his head in disgust.

"You have these regularly?" Gabriel asked.

"I have the same one definitely more often than I would like, but it has never been every night," I explained.

"I swear if I ever meet her stepfather, I am going to kick that bastard square in the balls for doing this to her," Jay threatened. "Yeah, I know it's not cool for a dude to kick another dude in the balls, but I don't care."

Gabriel looked at Jay and asked as if I were not in the room, "What exactly did he do to her?"

Jay looked at me, "Do you want to tell him or shall I?"

Gabriel looked at me. The expression on his face was concern mixed with terror.

"It's not what you think. I told you once he did not do that," I started. "When I was eight I lived in Florida with my mother and Allen. She had sent for me not long after they had gotten married. Dr. Charles liked to hunt and one weekend he went hunting with some of his friends in the Okefenokee Swamp. They caught a wild boar. He brought it home and built a tiny cage for the animal. He put it in the backyard of the house where we were living. He said he was going to fatten it up and we were going to eat it for Christmas that year.

The cage was so small that the thing could hardly turn around. It was inhumane to say the least, but the worst thing was he made me feed it. I had to carry a bowl of food out and slip it in the cage at night, then I had to drag the water hose out and give it fresh water. I had to do all of this in the dark right before I went to bed. He would not turn on a light for me so I could not see what I was doing. The closer I got to it, the more the thing would rock its cage. I could hear the wild boar snorting at me, hissing and rocking the cage. I thought it was going to get out. It terrified me."

Gabriel covered his mouth in disbelief and I continued, "Sometimes it would terrify me so bad that I would not make it all the way to the cage, I would just throw the food toward it and run screaming for my mother. She never came to see about me. When Allen found out I did not properly feed his pet, I was not properly fed. That happened five times and the last time he made me go four days without food, it was a holiday weekend so I could not even get lunch at school. My mother never even tried to stop him from making me feed the boar or stop him from starving me. She would tell me, 'Don't ruin this for me, Millie. Do what he asks.' It went on for three months until she sent me back to my grandfather so she could try to get pregnant by him."

"If it had gotten out, it could have killed you!" Gabriel shuttered.

"It would have killed her!" Jay corrected.

"Anyway, I have had pretty regular nightmares ever since. They are always the same; I am eight years old all over again and on the mission to feed the boar when it gets out and chases me. The majority of the dream is me running, running, running and screaming for my mother to help me. I always manage to wake up just as it is about to get me and she is never anywhere to be found. To this day, I hate boars, hogs, pigs, any variation! The only good pig is a bar-be-qued pig."

"That's awful! I can't believe she never tried to stop him! I am so sorry, Amelia," Gabriel said as he shook his head in disbelief and reached his arm around me and squeezed.

"Don't feel sorry for me." I wanted him to understand I was serious about this point, so I turned to face him. "I am okay that she did not fight to keep me because Lord knows she freed me up to have a better life with Granddaddy and Aunt Gayle. I would not trade my

254

life to be with her on any day of the week. As far as I am concerned, she did me a favor by letting me go."

I continued to explain, "Most everyone wants to feel sorry for me that my mother gave me up so easily or that she did not want me. They really shouldn't. From this story alone and I have many others that are just about as bad, you can tell that my life would have been miserable had she wanted to keep me. He might have killed me or gotten me killed."

"Did she ever get pregnant by him?" Gabriel asked. I suppose he was as curious about that as Jay and I had always been.

Jay responded, "We don't know. She had not gotten pregnant by the time Millie last lived with them when she was ten."

"In all honesty, I really don't know where she is or if they are still together or anything. Her parents, my grandparents lived on the way to Thomson. They came to see me a couple of times after I went to live with Granddaddy permanently. Granny would go on and on about how great my mother was doing and made excuses as to why she did not visit them. The last time they came, Granny was going on and on about how Dr. Charles had taken Betsy to Hawaii and what a great time they had. I remember asking if I could go play outside. I went outside and climbed up one of the magnolia trees and waited for them to leave. It was summer and the windows to the house were up, so I heard everything from my perch in the tree.

"I am not sure who you all are trying to fool, yourselves or that girl," my grandfather said to them. "You might as well stop, because Millie knows exactly what your daughter is and I assure you no one in this house is buying the load of bull you are selling. If you can't do any better by Millie than this, then you might was well not come back either!' And they didn't come back after that."

"You never told me that," Jay said. "I know when we went to the prom that time we went by their house because you wanted to show them your dress. I thought you had kept in touch with them. I can't believe we never talked about this."

Gabriel added, "You two went to prom together."

Jay and I collectively answered, "Yes, as friends."

"I have always been his 'beard' when it came to his family, so yes, I was his date to prom," I admitted.

"It was a beautiful night. It's true what they say about proms and virginity," Jay toyed with Gabriel and Gabriel cut his eyes at me. Jay chuckled, knowing that he had gotten to Gabriel a little. "Don't be silly. Not to Millie, to the high school basketball coach."

Jay looked at his watch, "It's nearly 3:00 a.m. I should go and let you two get back to sleep."

"Yeah, we could talk about this crap 'til dawn, but it won't change anything," I added as Jay stood up from his seat at my feet toward the end of the bed.

We all said 'goodnight' and Jay left closing the door behind him taking all of the light from the living room with him. Gabriel leaned over to the bedside table and cut on the lamp before getting up and going to the bathroom. I laid back down on my side and was facing the bathroom door anticipating his return. I just wanted to look at him in the dim light of my room. Perhaps a look would prompt dreams of him for the remainder of the night.

When he came back he said, "Did you know it's not supposed to get out of the fifties tomorrow?"

"No," I responded as I wondered where he was going with the weather report while he climbed back into the bed ever careful of the cast and his foot.

"There won't be a handful of players on the course so why don't we sleep in and you come in to work tomorrow evening?" He said as he got comfortable on his side mirroring me.

"Ok," I said with restraint. I was thrilled since that might mean I get to spend the day with him.

"What do you say to bringing your fiddle and playing it and the piano during dinner? You won't have to wait tables, just play some. I will make sure you get paid." Gabriel was nearly insistent in his request.

"I don't know. I have never played for money before and when I play it's always been more like something I was giving with no pressure," I replied while losing the initial thrill of not working the cart tomorrow.

"But the day you interviewed with me you played for money; you played to get the job," he reminded me.

He had me there, but I was not giving up so easily, "Good point, but that's different!"

256

"How about we compromise?" he asked as he inched over toward me in the bed. "How about you come be the hostess and then play for me once everyone is gone?"

"Now that sounds like a plan!"

"One last thing, before I kiss you goodnight again. Perhaps you could think about getting a lock for that door. I know Jay means well, but..." I knew where Gabriel was going with that so there was no need for him to continue.

"Right. About that, it has a lock. I just need to start using it and perhaps there is no time like the present," I said as I eased from the bed and locked the door.

I typically waited for Gabriel to make the moves, but this time when I returned from locking the door, I threw back the covers and climbed over him. I straddled him and reveled in the shocked look on his face. "This time, Mr. Hewitt, I am going to kiss you goodnight."

Gabriel attempted to touch me, bringing his hands to my hips and when he did I took his hands and pinned them above his head with my own. I held him by his wrists and I know it was not really my strength holding him down, but him allowing me. As I leaned down while gripping his wrists, my hair fell down draping around his face. It was long enough that I was still not directly in his face and I could see him. For a moment, I paused just to look at him.

There were a couple of freckles across the bridge of his nose and his eyes were glistening in the light of the lamp. They were as pale blue as the stripes in the sheets. His hair was a little longer on top than the sides and it had always been so soft to the touch. It fell back against the pillow on top and appeared as if it were standing up just a little. I suppose he had bed head and it was from being in my bed. I still could not believe he was there with me and that whatever the magnetism was with us, I just could not believe that either.

"I am sorry about the nightmare and if I scared you," I said as I continued to study his face.

He looked up at me and smiled the sweetest most sincere smile. "You don't have to apologize. I am just sorry that that happened to you. I can't imagine anyone putting a child through that. I would be shocked if you didn't have nightmares."

Gabriel always said exactly the right things at the right time. I leaned down and kissed him. Soon I released his hands sliding mine down his arms and up his shoulders until I had his face in my hands. I leaned back from him as he moved his hands back to my hips. From nearly flat on his back he lifted me up and eased me back to where I was sitting on the top of his thighs.

It was all so quick, but he was then sitting up and we were face to face. His arms were around me and we were chest to chest. "Say it again," Gabriel requested. "I don't think I will ever get tired of hearing you say it."

"I am yours?" I questioned. "Is that what you want to hear?"

"Yes," Gabriel said breathlessly as he lifted me again and ignoring the cast he flipped me over. Still holding me around my back with one hand and balancing on his other, he flipped me in what appeared to be one swift move.

I was suddenly on my back with Gabriel hovering above me, "Why won't you ask me?"

"Ask what?"

"Ask me the same question that I keep asking you." He said as he bent down and kissed my neck and started down just a little. "Why haven't you asked?"

"I trust you will tell me..."

"I am yours, Amelia. As long as you want, I am yours and I will never let anyone hurt you again."

***

The next morning, I awoke entangled with Gabriel. It was 10:00 a.m., but little light was coming through curtains over the French doors. I laid there and watched him sleep. We had been in the spoon position with his arm around mine and mine over his when I first woke up. I managed to roll over onto my side facing him. The covers were pulled under his arm exposing his shoulders and just a bit of his chest. He was so beautiful and peaceful and mine.

I was tempted to stroke his cheek with my hand, but I refrained and settled with just watching him. It was not long before he awoke to find me staring.

"How long have you been awake?" he asked.

"Just long enough to enjoy the view," I replied as I leaned over and planted a gentle kiss on his lips. "Good morning, Mr. Hewitt."

"Good morning, yourself, Miss Anderson. Are you hungry?" Gabriel asked as he rolled me over on top of him. I propped myself up over his chest to look him in the face as he spoke again, "Let's get up and go to breakfast and then come here and do nothing all day."

"Sounds good to me."

***

It was chilly outside, but we decided to walk to the Huddle House on Hancock Street for breakfast. During the walk back to The Jefferson, Gabriel changed his mind about hanging out at my place all day and wanted to go back to his house.

As soon as we were back up the stairs to my apartment, Gabriel put his overnight bag back together and I started gathering a change of clothes for work as the hostess that evening. Once he was done, he had a seat on the bed while I picked out several outfits and let him choose which he liked.

Of the three outfits, Gabriel chose my navy blue suit. The jacket was solid navy and the skirt was pleated and had thin, vertical stripes of navy blue and white. The skirt was also short, very short. I am not sure if he chose it due to the length of the skirt or that it really was better than the other outfits that I had presented.

I thought I was done and ready to go when he asked, "Aren't you going to pack a bag and stay the night with me?"

"I did not realize I was supposed to," I responded.

"Excuse me?" he asked with a bit of a curious, hurt look on his face. "Do you not want to stay over?"

"You have not invited me," I replied as it was that simple.

"Oh, in that case, would you like to sleep over at my house tonight?"

"Okay." I gave a subdued response although I really wanted to scream, "Yes!" My favorite thing in the world right then was falling asleep next to him and waking up with him, that's aside from being kissed by him, of course. I still wanted to hold my cards a little close so as to not spook him.

I finished packing a bag and then mentioned to Jay that I would be spending the night at Gabriel's. While Gabriel made his way down the stairs, I pulled the C-10 around to the front of The Jefferson and parallel parked right at the front door. It was nearly noon and there was still a nip in the air. It was shaping up to be one of those Novembers where one day was cold and the next was hot, like the Lord could not make up his mind whether He was going to freeze us or burn us up.

There on Jefferson Street, the blue C-10 stuck out like a healed thumb as opposed to a sore one as the saying went. There wasn't a new car or one that had been freshly washed or waxed in the last three months among any parked along the street as far as the eye could see. Even if there had been; it would not have taken away from the beauty of the truck.

I had forgotten that I did not tell Gabriel I was not bringing around the Corvette so he just stood there on the stoop watching and waiting for me. He did not notice me in the C-10 although I was right in front of him.

I put the truck in park and leaned across the cab and rolled down the window.

"Hey, are you coming or not?" I yelled across the tiny yard to Gabriel. He noticed me at once and put the crutches in motion toward the truck.

"Where's the Corvette and what's with this?" Gabriel asked as he opened the truck, placing the crutches in before getting in himself.

"The Corvette is in the carport out back. I thought you, the crutches and the cast might fit in this better than in the car," I said as I pointed out the huge cab and bench seat.

"Good thinking, but will this thing make it to Port Honor?" he asked.

"Hey now, don't insult it, and it has made it there in the past. In fact, not to bring up old wounds, but you would know that if you had not been so wrapped up in Miss Reed the night I drove it there." I felt a little wary of reminding him of the night I met her, but it was the truth.

"Touché," said Gabriel as he closed the door and I put the truck in gear.

Gabriel stared out the window for a good portion of the drive. We were just over the Lake Sinclair bridge and making the turn for the shortcut toward the club when Gabriel finally spoke. "Is this truck a part of your inheritance?"

"Yes, do you like it?"

"Who wouldn't like it?" Gabriel asked as he turned to look at me. "Can I ask you something?"

"Sure." He could have asked me anything now whether I would want to give an answer or be afraid of his reaction to the answer that was another matter.

"You can tell me it's none of my business," he prefaced, "but, I am curious about the inheritance. Why don't you talk about it?"

"I don't talk about it because I have resolved myself to pretend that it does not exist for the most part. It kind of scares me," I confided.

"It scares you?"

"It's bigger than I ever imagined it would be," I kept my eyes on the road as I thought about how to put it without sounding ungrateful.

During my pause and moment to gather my words, Gabriel asked, "So what does that matter?"

"Here's the thing, I have had to work all my life. My first job was when I was fifteen, mucking stalls and teaching rich kids how to ride. I used to think of how they did not have to work for anything and therefore, they would likely amount to nothing," I paused again.

"When everything was laid out in writing for me, all I could think was now there was nothing to achieve in life. There was nothing to work for because now I had everything that most people would spend their lives working and slaving to attain."

"Amelia, that's ridiculous!" I took my eyes off the road and looked at him. "There's more to life than money."

"I know. There's also Aunt Gayle's warning of not letting anyone know about it or then I would not be able to tell who really loved me for me and not my money."

"Is that why you have not told me about it? Have you told Jay?" I knew what he was ultimately after. Had I trusted Jay and not him? Did I trust him at all?

"Jay does not know any more than you do. The only difference in your knowledge and his is that he knew where I was going that morning and he asked me about it immediately when I got home that afternoon. He asked how much. His exact words were something akin to 'Roll around in it or roll around naked in it?' He is so funny. He really helped me get past the way I was feeling about everything."

"Amelia, if you never want to give me the details of it, that's up to you. But, if you want to hurt me, give the details to someone else and let me find out about it. I can't tell you who you can tell and can't, but understand this is about trust. If we do not trust one another, then what's the point here? You can't live your life not trusting whether people are using you for your money or not no matter what your aunt says." Gabriel had reached over, past the crutches and took my right hand from the gear shift and held it as he spoke.

It was tempting to tell him all I knew then, but I held my tongue. The subject was dropped and we did not speak of it again that afternoon.

Once at Gabriel's house we had a lunch of microwaved popcorn while we watched *Gone With the Wind* from start to the point where Prissy didn't "know nothin' 'bout birthin' babies" then we had to get ready for work.

We had gotten dressed in his bathroom together. We were brushing our teeth in the dual vanity at the same time. I was the first to spit and rinse when it occurred to me, "Are we becoming too domestic?"

"Would you prefer we were feral?" Gabriel responded as he quickly drew back and aimed to smack me on the behind with his hand towel. I saw the towel coming and dodged it. He drew again and I ran squealing and giggling from the bathroom into his bedroom.

Gabriel hopped on one foot after me. "Don't run away Amelia. As hard as it is, I will chase you and I will catch you!"

He managed to tag me once on the rear with the towel and I screamed from the sting. I jumped up on his bed and ran across it.

262

"That's not funny, Mr. Hewitt!" I laughed as I rubbed the sting and bounced across his bed to the other side to where his crutches were. I grabbed the crutches and darted out of the bedroom door. Gabriel chased after me down the hall still in his boxer shorts from changing to get ready for work and still hopping on his one good foot.

I was through the living room and had the front door open when Gabriel entered the room from the hallway. I was holding the crutches out the door dangling them as if I would throw them out.

"You wouldn't!" Gabriel challenged.

"I would!" I said with a raised eyebrow. "Unless, you put down your towel."

Gabriel used his toes from the cast and his good foot and he charged me. I threw the crutches out the door and slammed it shut behind me and barred the door with my back leaving the crutches out in the middle of the driveway.

"Oh, Miss Anderson, you should not have done that," Gabriel's look was serious, but his tone was light. I giggled at the thought of the crutches and I did not move from the door.

Gabriel pinned me to the door much like he had done days before against the wall in the stairwell to my apartment, but this time he grabbed me around my thighs just below my behind and lifted me up as opposed to bending down to kiss me. For balance sake, I knew my legs had to go around his waist and they did. As soon as my legs were around him, he leaned into me pressing me firmer against the door and releasing my weight from his legs. He let go of my ass and took my hands lifting them above my head and holding them as he kissed me.

It was warm and the heat was on in his house when we arrived, so I had taken off my sweater and was left only in the tank top I had been wearing under it. He continued to hold my hands, but moved them into his left hand and let go with his right. He lowered his right to my shoulder and eased the strap on my tank top down so that it fell over my shoulder. I gasped just a little as the strap fell, but did not dare stop him. Down my neck and shoulder the kisses trailed. As Gabriel kissed me, he moved gently beneath me, rocking with his hips, a preview of what was to come.

"I want you, Amelia," Gabriel whispered.

I think he forgot himself for a moment. He let go of his hold on my hands and returned them to the place below my ass at the bottom of my thighs. It was as if he meant to carry me, but when he turned he was reminded of the cast and we fell. Down we went onto the floor with a thud. We just missed the end table by the arm of the couch.

"Are you alright?" I asked him.

"Nothing that a cold shower won't fix. And you?"

"I am stellar! You are quite the talented kisser, Mr. Hewitt," I praised him.

"It helps to have an inspiration," he said as he leaned down and kissed me once more. This time it was sweet and gentle. "And for your information, there's no one else I have ever wanted to be domestic with. Now, would you kindly get my crutches from the front yard while I take a quick shower?"

Gabriel managed to get to his knees just fine as I got up completely. I offered him my arm to help get him up the rest of the way. Once he was up he started for the back of the house toward his bedroom and bathroom and I hurried out to get the crutches. It was a quarter 'til four and we needed to get into our work clothes and be at the club by 4:00 p.m.

We dressed quickly. Gabriel was in his chef's jacket, black checked pants and the awful clog and me in my suit and we were just about out of the door when I just could not take the clog any more.

"One more thing before we go," I stopped just shy of leading us outside. "There's something I have wanted to tell you since the very moment I first saw you."

If he thought I was going to tell him right then that I loved him, he was to be sorely disappointed.

"Yes?"

"The clogs are awful." I pointed down to it and shook my head slightly no, no.

"That's what you've been wanting to tell me?" Clearly, he thought I was going to say something else.

"I don't mean to hurt your feelings. Please tell me they are super comfortable," I begged.

Gabriel kicked off the clog, but replied as he did so, "They are surprisingly comfy. I cannot believe you don't like them. Would you prefer tennis shoes for me?"

"You don't have to change. They are your feet and you should be comfortable," I tried to dig out of the whole of shame that I had clearly dug for myself.

"I could give a shit. They were a gift from Beth. Apparently they were all the rage with the chefs in Atlanta." And with those words, Gabriel threw the shoe in the trash. "I will throw the other one out when we get home tonight.

I was speechless. Gabriel threw the shoe away just because I did not like it. He then found his tennis shoes and put the one on.

***

One of the couples that were there the night of "The Devil Went Down to Georgia" performance was back in for dinner that night. As I seated them, Mrs. Durham begged me play it again for them. I had not brought my fiddle, but I had made up my mind that I would likely give it a go on the piano that night if for nothing else than because Gabriel had asked. After all, he had thrown away the clogs, the least I could do was tickle the ivories a little for him.

The dining room was busy that night. I seated members and guests left and right, but as I did, I made a playlist that would be the soundtrack of the night. I also helped out with keeping tea and water refilled as well as fetched drinks from the bar and gave other random assistance to Daniel, Jerry and Cara as they waited on the tables.

I sat the last party around ten after nine. Even though the Durhams had arrived at 7:15 p.m. and their dinner was well done by 8:15, they stuck around. Three times Mrs. Durham called me over to ask if I was going to play something. Apparently, she had heard that I played the piano as well.

At 9:30 p.m., all of the tables had their food and there were no more reservations on the books. I mentioned to Daniel where I was going so no one would think I just disappeared, although they would have known where I was once I laid hands on the piano keys.

Per usual, I removed the floral arrangement from the top of the piano and sat it on the coffee table upstairs. I opened the lid of the piano and adjusted the stool, since it had been moved from its spot at the center of the keys. I slipped my heels off. They were not as conducive to working the pedals as being in flats or barefooted. I sat them on the far side of the piano stool nearest the balcony so no one would fall over them if they came to sit on the bench with me.

My first number was something courtesy of Elton John, one of his lesser known songs at the time, "Tiny Dancer." Though lesser known it was nonetheless poignant than any of his more famous songs. It was a great song for a piano solo. It was also a great warm up song, not too slow and not too fast, but something that would get a body swaying and moving with the music. No one was upstairs with me when I started playing and I was certain the piano would drown me out so I sang along quietly.

I had just started my next song when Mrs. Durham and Mrs. Lockerby came up the stairs. They came straight to the piano. Mrs. Lockerby closed the piano lid so they could lean on it as I played. Closed or open it really did not make a difference with the sound. Having it open was just my personal preference as to how the piano looked.

I was playing "Let It Be" by the Beetles. Since I had an audience, I did not sing along, but they did. They knew all of the words.

Gabriel and Daniel arrived up the stairs about mid-way through the song. It appeared Daniel had told him what I was up to and they both came up to listen. They kept their distance from the ladies and stood behind the leather couch that was the closest to the staircase and to Joan's desk by the front door.

I looked up from the keys to see Gabriel and our eyes met. I smiled at him with every bit of me telling him that I was happy to see him. He smiled back a prideful smile. He knew I was playing for him. Regardless of that, I was winding down on that song and about to ask for requests.

Mrs. Durham asked if I could play "Crocodile Rock" and I obliged. It nearly wore me out. Mrs. Lockerby asked if I knew "Passionate Kisses" by Mary Chapin Carpenter. I glanced at Gabriel and my face went fire engine red when he winked at me. Daniel laughed out loud and Gabriel punched him on the arm.

"What do you know about passionate kisses?" Mrs. Durham teased her friend.

"More than you, Darcy Durham!" Mrs. Lockerby smarted back.

"I apologize. I do not know that song, but if you will agree to come back in next Friday night I will agree to learn it this week and play it for you then," I bargained with Mrs. Lockerby.

"I guess I will see you on Friday night then. Gabe, you've got quite the saleswoman in this one!" she said.

"I sure hope so," Gabriel replied.

I then called to Daniel, "Would you like to make a request?"

"'Can't Help Falling In Love' by Elvis?" Daniel asked. I nodded my head yes.

As I started to play Daniel walked over and asked Mrs. Durham to dance. Gabriel followed and asked Mrs. Lockerby to join him. Who knew Daniel could sing. He was no Elvis, but he was not bad and he knew the words. Knowing the words is half the battle. I am sure Daniel's charms worked some magic for Mr. and Mrs. Durham that night since she went downstairs and grabbed her husband to go home as soon as the song was over.

Mrs. Lockerby stayed behind and she and Daniel each took a seat on the couches across from one another. She kicked off her shoes and put her feet up on the coffee table. Jerry came up and joined Daniel. Gabriel came over and took a seat on the piano bench while I played the last song of the night. Poor Cara was the only one left downstairs attending the tables.

"This one's for you," I told him as he sat down next to me. Gabriel just smiled that gorgeous smile at me again.

I played Aunt Gayle's favorite song, "I.O.U." by Lee Greenwood, an oldie, but goodie. As it turned out, it was one of Mrs. Lockerby's favorites as well since she sang along starting just a couple of bars into it. Softly, I played and she sang. She was not the best singer, but she wasn't afraid to try to belt it out either.

Gabriel's hand was on my thigh and his eyes were closed as he listened. We swayed against one another as I played and Mrs. Lockerby sang. At the end of the song, Gabriel whispered to me, "This is another one I am going to have to ask Daniel about isn't it. Like Patsy Cline?"

"Probably," I kind of laughed. "I still can't believe you don't know any of these songs."

"Let's go home, Miss Anderson," Gabriel said as he stood from the piano bench and extended his hand to me.

"Yes, let's!"

We left everyone else at the Club still thanking me for playing, staff, club members and all. As we pulled into his driveway, Gabriel teased me, "Miss Anderson, you should consider yourself lucky that I have this cast or I might just carry you to my bed and defile you tonight."

CHAPTER 11

All night and all morning I had thought about what Gabriel said about living in fear of the inheritance and trusting people. I knew Aunt Gayle had a point, but so did he.

Gabriel had to go into work for Sunday brunch at the club, but it was cold again so he let me off the hook for the beverage cart. I dropped him off for work since he could not drive as long as he had the cast on. Between his house and the club, he mentioned that he had scheduled an appointment with the orthopedist for Tuesday afternoon. Before he could tell me of his travel arrangements or ask, I insisted on taking him to the appointment and he insisted that I not miss any more classes, not even badminton.

By the time we made it to the club, we had come to an understanding and had a plan on how to get him to the appointment. His appointment was at 3:30 p.m. in Milledgeville so I would pick him up after my 10:00 a.m. class. He would come back to my apartment where I would feed him lunch and he would wait there while I went to my 2:00 p.m. class. My schedule was such that I would be home around ten after three and then we would go straight to the doctor's office.

Like a dutiful student, I spent all day Sunday and Monday night studying and preparing for my history project. The project was to write a three thousand word work of historical fiction based on the name we drew out of the hat. The name I drew was John F. Kennedy. I chose to write a paper about his involvement in the Bay of Pigs told through the point of view of Marilyn Monroe's maid, Lena Pepitone. Pepitone is the maid that actually found the body of Marilyn Monroe at her death in 1962. She had been with Monroe from 1957 and stayed on with her after her divorce from Arthur Miller. The premise of my paper is that Kennedy and Monroe were indeed having an affair during that time, including April, 1961, when the Bay of Pigs took place. During the affair, Kennedy confided in Monroe of his concerns of the events and Monroe confided in Pepitone as she was not only Marilyn Monroe's maid, but likely her closest, truest friend.

Like a dutiful boyfriend, Gabriel called each night and we spoke of everything under the sun. On Sunday night, we talked for two hours. We would likely have talked longer had Jay's mom not called Cara to walk upstairs and find out why our phone wasn't working. It wasn't that it was out of order. It was that I was ignoring the call waiting beeping since I knew who it was and Jay was not home. She had already left four messages for him. I begged forgiveness from Gabriel, hung up with him and called Jay's mom and told her he was not home and no matter how many times she called, it did not change the fact that he was not home and I did not know when he would be home. After I read her the riot act for calling so much, she made me have prayer with her over the phone. Mrs. McDonald then proceeded to pray to the Lord to help me understand that she was just concerned about her son. I was surely going to burn in Hell for rolling my eyes during prayer.

On Monday night, among other things, we went over our plans for the following day. He agreed that he would be ready for me to pick him up at noon. We also talked about my history paper. Gabriel was amused at the angle I chose for writing about JFK.

***

I pulled up in the semicircular driveway of Gabriel's house at precisely 12:00 p.m. I am sure I could have just honked the horn, but Aunt Gayle said that was always so tacky and if any boy ever tried to pick me up for a date by pulling up and honking, I was not allowed out of the house. That only happened once. I lived by most of her rules and although I was not a boy, I felt it best to heed that rule about going to the door. It was just good form.

I rang the doorbell and waited. I could hear Gabriel gimping along on the crutches to answer the door. When the door opened, my stomach did flips. I had not seen him since Sunday morning and could not believe how I had missed everything, laying eyes on him, his smell, and his touch. I missed it all and I wondered if he could tell. Did the look on my face give me away?

"Come in, I have something for you," Gabriel said as he balanced on the crutches and held the door open for me.

"Ok," I smiled and slipped past him in the doorway.

Gabriel closed the door behind me and the next thing I knew I was against the door again. "Sunday was so nice, I thought we should try it twice," he rhymed with mischief in his voice.

The same technique: he lifted me and propped my back against the door, pressed into me and my legs went around his waist. My arms went around his neck and sweet Lord, I had never been so hot and bothered for anyone. My talents might have been musical instruments, but Gabriel's was definitely kissing and what

270

Jay would later define for me as dry humping. Sparks! Sparks! Sparks!

We carried on for at least fifteen minutes before I reminded him that we were on a bit of a schedule and that we needed to get back to The Jefferson.

"My God, I missed you," Gabriel said as he buried his head in my hair and allowed my legs to slide down and my feet back to the floor. My knees were weak and my legs were Jell-O. Luckily he was still bearing his weight against me since that is all that kept me from falling down against the door.

"Really? I could not tell." I replied as if I just did not have a clue what he was talking about.

Gabriel raised his head from my hair and looked me in the face as if I had lost my mind.

Changing my tone as his eyes met mine, I looked at him as seriously as I could and said, "I have missed you as well."

"Say it," he smiled at me.

"I am yours." It was always a pleasure to say it for him and it seemed he could never get enough of hearing me say it.

**

We were halfway back to Milledgeville when our conversation took a turn. Gabriel brought up the piano playing on Saturday night and the ladies of the club. "Amelia, you know you helped get Mr. Durham and Mr. Lockerby laid on Saturday night?"

"What?!!" I shrieked.

"Both of the men made special trips by the club on Sunday to let me know that their wives had not been like that in twenty years."

"Oh my God! I cannot believe you are telling me this." Despite our use of the door at his house, I was still easily embarrassed by such talk with him. I shielded my face by turning toward the driver's side window and rubbing my face with my right hand while I held on to the steering wheel with my left.

"Well, I kind of have to tell you so I can explain giving you this…" I turned back and saw Gabriel reach in his pocket and pull out two bills, a hundred dollar bill and a fifty dollar bill.

"They said to give this to you. The hundred is from Mr. Durham and the fifty is from Mr. Lockerby," he said as he handed me the money.

"You have got to be kidding me! I can't take this! Seriously, I just got paid for sex?" I started laughing.

Gabriel began to laugh as well, "Kind of. I suppose you did."

I laughed until tears came down my cheeks, "That just seems wrong," I continued to laugh.

Before he realized what he was saying, Gabriel laughed, "What would your mother think, young lady?"

As soon as the words were out of his mouth he realized, but I did not let that kill the mood and responded, "My mother would respond, 'You go Millie, now give me my forty percent!"

"You are not right, you know that!" Gabriel laughed.

"Give the money to Rudy to go toward his college," I instructed Gabriel.

"It's your money, you don't have to do that, Amelia," Gabriel said.

"When we get to my apartment I am going to show you something and after that we will revisit what to do with the one hundred and fifty dollars, okay?" I had decided well before that moment that I was going to trust him enough to tell him about the inheritance.

"Ok?" Gabriel was skeptical. I don't think he had any idea what I was up to.

***

When we arrived at The Jefferson, I parked out front and let Gabriel out. He waited for me on the front porch as I parked the truck under the carport and came around the building. It was our fourth cold day in a row and the wind was biting, so I picked up speed and nearly ran from the truck.

Despite the crutches, Gabriel always managed to hold the door for me and this time was no exception. Up the stairs we went and I left him in the living room.

"Help yourself to the remote," I said to Gabriel as I knocked on Jay's door.

"I'm back. Would you come out to the living room, please?" I yelled through Jay's door after knocking.

After calling for Jay, I went to my room. I grabbed my history paper and the ledger book Attorney Bell had given me. It detailed the terms, conditions and contents of my inheritance. I returned to the living room with the two items finding Gabriel and Jay chatting. Gabriel was seated on one end of the couch and Jay was in the armchair perpendicular to the other end of the couch.

I handed Jay the history paper, "Read it and mark it up for content and grammar. When you are done, give it to Gabriel to read and do the same."

I handed Gabriel the ledger book, "Read it and give it to Jay when you are done. I am going to trust both of you with this. Discuss it among yourselves if you like. I would love to talk to both of you about it, but I ask that you do not tell anyone else that you have seen it or the contents or anything about it."

"What is it?" Gabriel asked as he started to open it and several papers fell out.

I leaned over to pick up the pages that had fallen and as I handed them back to him I explained, "This is the ledger book detailing my inheritance and these are deeds. Make sure they stay with the book."

I went in the kitchen and started making sandwiches for lunch. I yelled back from the kitchen as I checked on the roast that I had in the crockpot, "Gabriel, I should have asked, but I just assumed you would be staying for family dinner tonight. Are you okay with staying?"

"I would love to stay. Thanks for the invite," he yelled back without taking his eyes from the ledger.

I proceeded with the sandwich making for the three of us. I was almost finished adding chips to the plates when I faintly heard Gabriel ask, "Jay have you seen this?"

"No," Jay answered.

"You are not going to believe what's in here," Gabriel said with amazement in his voice.

I came back in the living room carrying the plates of sandwiches all at once. I sat a plate in front of each of them on the coffee table.

"Jay what do you think of the paper?" I asked.

"I am about halfway through it and I like the direction you took. Content is good so far and I have only found a couple of typos," Jay replied.

"Gabriel are you okay?" I asked. Jay peeped up from the paper to gage Gabriel's expression.

"Amelia, do you know what all is in here?" Gabriel asked as he barely looked up. "Do you understand this?"

"Not entirely and that's partly why I am letting you guys look at it. I am hoping that by the time I return from class, we could all discuss it and I could understand it better. And, before either of you ask, no, I did not know the extent of it and I probably still don't, that's why I want to talk to you about it."

I finished my lunch and headed off to class, leaving them there still reading. I arrived home to find them just where I had left them. I heard them discussing what was in the ledger as I came up the steps.

"I never had a clue," said Jay.

"I would have never imagined," added Gabriel.

They put the kibosh on the conversation when I entered. There was a notebook in front of Jay with his writing. It appeared to be notes regarding the ledger. To the side, in front of Gabriel was my marked-up paper on John F. Kennedy.

"Jay, check the roast while we are gone. Gabriel, are you ready to go?" I addressed each of them as I went into my room to change.

I left the door to my room open and I could hear them start to talk quietly among themselves again. While I changed clothes from what I had worn to badminton into something more presentable for the doctor's office, I could not make out all of what they were saying, but it sounded like they were both dumbstruck over the inheritance.

***

On the way to the orthopedist, I asked Gabriel about the history paper. "What did you think?"

"It was remarkably interesting," he answered.

"Do you think it is an A paper?" I asked.

"I don't see why not. I liked the way you told the story in the context of them having an affair. You portrayed Marilyn not as an airhead, but as a sounding board for Kennedy's qualms about the invasion into Cuba."

"Good. I wasn't intending to prove or disprove or speculate even to her level of intelligence, but I did intend for her to be seen as a sounding board for him, so I am glad that you picked up on that."

"As far as I am concerned, you succeeded in that and I am not just saying that to spare your feelings," he added.

"Is there anything you think I could have done better or differently?"

"Nothing other than some wording issues, but I marked those on the paper. I think I marked the same stuff that Jay may have marked."

The doctor's office had not been terribly far from my apartment, so it did not take long to get there. I was pleased with that. I was not sure why, but I wanted to talk to them together about the inheritance, so limited time on the ride helped.

***

Gabriel received great news at the doctor's office. He had insisted that I accompany him in to see the doctor and did not allow me to just sit in the waiting room. I heard everything the doctor had to say.

The doctor removed the cast and took new X-rays. The X-rays showed that bones in his foot and ankle were healing remarkably well and he would not require surgery. I do not know which of us was more relieved, Gabriel or myself.

The X-rays also showed an old fracture of his tibia and fibula just below the knee in the same leg. When the doctor mentioned it, Gabriel immediately switched the conversation back to his ankle and foot. No further mention was made of the prior injury. I made a mental note to follow up on this with Gabriel later.

Before we left, another cast was installed and a walking boot was put over it so he could do just what the name implied. Gabriel could walk in this contraption, even drive if he saw fit. He was also provided a cane. The doctor told him he should be right as rain in about another six weeks, eight at the max.

On the way out of the office, Gabriel commented on his new accessories, "Oh, this is sexy!" Gabriel's words reeked of sarcasm as he rolled his eyes at the boot and cane.

"I don't know what you are talking about, you could pick your nose and still be hot," I whispered to him as I put my arm around him and we left the doctor's office. "Not everyone can pull that off you know."

"Amelia, you are a silly girl."

We were making our way to the C10 when I asked him, "Would you like to drive?"

"Alright, but had I known you would offer I would have insisted we bring the Corvette."

I tossed him the keys, "Mr. Hewitt, there will be plenty of time for that later."

Gabriel opened the driver's side door of the truck to be reminded that it was a stick shift and had a clutch.

"Amelia, perhaps we did not think this through," he said as he backed away from the door.

"What's wrong?"

"I appreciate your confidence in me, but I am not so sure I can drive a stick shift with a cast, you know, the clutch..." he pointed out.

"Ah...sorry about that. I'll drive." I then slid across the bench seat to the driver's seat and Gabriel walked around and got in on the passenger's side.

We were making the turn from North Cobb Street from the direction of the hospital and medical office complex when Gabriel asked, "I don't remember, but is the Corvette a stick as well?"

"What do you think?" I kind of smirked knowing he was not going to like the answer.

"Jesus!" Gabriel exclaimed.

"Another six weeks in the cast and then you can play with my toys," I consoled him with a hint of laughter.

***

276

We were just about home when Gabriel could not take it anymore and asked about the contents of the ledger. "Jay and I were wondering: did you have any idea the extent of what is listed in that ledger? Jay said you had no idea."

"No, I didn't. I think I might have told you before that I knew there was something, but I just had no idea about all of this," I shook my head still in disbelief.

We got stopped by the light at the corner waiting to turn onto Jefferson, right next to the apartment. While we waited I could tell from the look on his face that Gabriel had at least a dozen more questions regarding the inheritance.

Before the light changed and traffic cleared I interrupted his thoughts and asked, "Would you like for me to drop you at the front door or can you make it around from the carport?"

Gabriel answered just as the light changed, "The carport is fine."

Down the driveway and around to the back of The Jefferson, I drove to the carport and parked the truck in its spot next to the Corvette.

"Are you having a hard time coming to grips with everything you have learned this afternoon?" I asked him as I cut the truck off.

"I can see why you told me on your birthday that you did not understand it all and that you did not want to tell something and get it wrong. Have you looked at it anymore and do you understand what all is there now?" he asked with a great deal of concern in his voice.

Gabriel paused before making one more statement, "I see why your aunt would caution you on telling too many people about this now that I have had a look at it."

"Are you saying I should not have told you?" I asked hesitantly. My hands were still resting on the steering wheel from having parked the truck and I let my head drop against them wondering had I screwed up in sharing the details with him.

"That's not what I am saying," Gabriel reached over and took my hand. "I am so thrilled that you trusted me enough to show me and not just tell me. Honestly, I would have never believed you if you had just told me."

"You would not have believed me?" I questioned.

"Let's go inside and we will include Jay in this conversation. I know he has the same questions I have and this will save you having to tell it twice. Plus, it's cold out here." With those words, we got out of the truck and headed inside.

As soon as we opened the door at the bottom of the stairwell we could smell the roast cooking in the crockpot.

"Whatever that is smells awesome, Amelia," Gabriel praised after taking in a great big sniff of the aroma.

"It is an eye of round with carrots that are slow cooking in the crockpot. I plan to slice it and put it in gravy and let it simmer until dinner time," I explained as we climbed the stairs.

Once upstairs, we found Jay waiting in the living room. He had the ledger and the deeds unfolded and laid out beside them on the coffee table.

"Hey," Jay said as we came in, "I thought we would talk about this stuff before everyone arrived for family dinner."

"Is Emma home?" I asked while closing the door behind Gabriel and myself. Gabriel proceeded to take a seat on the couch and started looking over the deeds.

"No, she's at tennis practice," Jay replied.

"Good. I am thinking the less people that know, the more comfortable I will be," I said as I took a seat on the couch next to Gabriel.

I picked up one of the deeds and as I started to read it, Jay started to speak, "Alright, so there are numerous accounts."

"Right, according to the FDIC you cannot have more than one hundred thousand dollars in a single account for it to be insured," Gabriel explained. "Anything over that amount could be lost if the bank went under."

In all likelihood, he noticed us looking a little amazed by his knowledge, "What? I went to college and took a few finance courses," Gabriel added.

"Alright. So there are twelve different accounts spread among four banks, as far as I can tell." I said.

"That's 1.2 million dollars," said Jay.

"Right, that's just the cash that you could put your hands on if you needed to, but this is the really interesting thing..." Gabriel said as he handed me something that resembled the deeds.

I took it and started reading it. The heading was a One Hundred Year Land Lease. Gabriel then handed me one of the deeds and started to explain again, "The land lease goes with this deed and this contract. Under the terms of the lease or the contract, the holder of the lease and owner of the land is to receive a royalty payment every year for the duration of the lease in exchange for the mining of the minerals from the land by the leasee, i.e., the kaolin company. There are three deeds and three leases. There's seventy years left on the lease. So, based on what is here regarding past years payments it looks like you could expect around seventy thousand dollars per year for the foreseeable future. The bad thing is that if they stopped mining the money would dry up."

Jay then picked up where Gabriel left off, "There's more, but what I want to know is how your grandfather acquired all of this."

Gabriel concurred, "Where did it come from?"

"Aunt Gayle said that my grandparents inherited what was farmland from their parents. They did not need it so when the big wigs from the chalk mine came calling, they agreed to lease the land. He then purchased one of the farms next to the one owned by Granny's parents' and leased it to the chalk mine too. I think that's where the three deeds come in."

Jay reached over to the coffee table and picked up another stack of deeds, "What are these?"

"They are deeds for timber tracts. The timber is four years shy of maturity," I explained. "Toward the back of the book there are directions indicating who I am supposed to contact in four years to harvest the timber and how much I should expect to get."

Jay picked up the ledger book and flipped through until he came to the page and his mouth fell open. "That will add another fourth to what you have in cash."

"I won't receive all of that because I have to pay to replant so that in another fifteen years I will be able to harvest again."

Gabriel interjected, "So every fifteen years you will get another four hundred thousand?"

"Not quite," I corrected him. "I don't know how much it is off the top of my head, but there is a cost for replanting that comes out of that figure. You all can tell I have studied this stuff and I understand the timber way more than I do the mining."

Jay put the ledger back down on the coffee table, "This is just the inheritance from your grandfather, right?"

"In the ledger, yes," I replied.

"And that does not count what you got from your dad?" Jay again questioned.

"There's more?" Gabriel asked.

"Yes. My dad had a million dollar life insurance policy of which I was the beneficiary and my grandfather was the trustee. That's kind of a funny story actually," I began to tell them as I kicked back on the couch and put my feet up on the coffee table.

I continued, "Granddaddy found out that computers were the wave of the future so he invested seven hundred and fifty thousand of the million in Radio Shack, Apple and Commodore when they were penny stock. According to Aunt Gayle, by the end of 1984, he had turned it into a little over five million. That's still wrapped up in various stocks: Coke, GE, ones that are less risky stocks than penny stocks."

"So if you got all of this, what did your Aunt Gayle get?" Jay inquired.

"She got the mill and the business that goes with it, the rental properties and the same amount in accounts. She also got all of the land that did not have the chalk mines attached to it, Granddaddy's house and the farm and her house, of course, because it sits on that land."

"I would have never suspected that you all were that rich," Jay aired his observation.

"Me neither! I mean, you all can see why this has been so mind-blowing to me. Like I told Aunt Gayle, this is what people spend their lives trying to acquire and it was just handed to me. Kind of makes me wonder what to do with myself? Perhaps that's why they never told me; they did not want me to be one of those kids that had no reason to get up in the morning. And, how ungrateful do I sound when I put it like that?"

"Now I know why you would not take the one hundred and fifty dollars earlier today and told me to give it to Rudy," Gabriel admitted.

"I kind of feel guilty knowing all of this is there for me and then knowing the predicament that Rudy is in. I am not saying I want to give it all away, I am just saying..." Jay cut me off and interrupted me.

"They made you work so that when you did get this you would appreciate it, but not let it define you and so that you would have compassion for people who have not been given everything," Jay said as he leaned forward and nudged me. "Now, let's stop with all of this. I still have to make the tea for dinner and I believe you have to finish the roast, Millie."

Jay and I got up and headed to the kitchen. Gabriel stood and asked if there was anything he could do. Jay and I answered him in unison, "Sit down and put your feet up."

***

It was around seven when everyone started to arrive. Travis and Stella brought macaroni and cheese which Stella had made in a crockpot from scratch. Cara brought mashed potatoes, green beans and Matt. Megan showed up sans boyfriend, but with a three layer chocolate cake. The last addition was Emma who came running in from tennis, showered and threw together a tossed salad.

Jay helped Travis carry up extra chairs from his and Stella's apartment. There were nine of us in all and we crowded around Jay's aunt's old dining room table. For the sake of room, we left the food in the kitchen and served ourselves buffet style. Once everyone was at the table, we all held hands and Travis led us in saying grace.

Dinner conversation was a free for all of everyone talking at once until Travis started telling about hitting a turkey on the way to Sandersville a few days before. Then it turned into a battle of who had the worst road kill story. It was totally inappropriate for table talk, but no one cared.

Initially, Travis was just telling Matt about the turkey incident, but he started the story over when he noticed that everyone was listening in. "So, I was headed to my mama 'n' dem's for dinner last Thursday. I was on the back road to Sandersville from here and this turkey comes out of nowhere and WHAM! It slammed right into the windshield of my truck. It scared the living shit out of me, pardon the language. There I am on the side of the road with a turkey butt stuck out of the windshield and his head on the inside of the windshield. The dang thing was hung by the neck through the windshield. Anyway, there I am walking around the front of the truck wondering what I am going to do because I can't drive the next twenty miles with a dead turkey staring at me when this trucker pulls

281

up. Dude gets out walks around and looks at the turkey. 'Hit a turkey huh?' Yeah, he was observant. He goes on to offer to trade me a roll of duck tape for the dead turkey. I didn't see the point in the trade, but told him he could have the turkey. So he returns to his rig, comes back, climbs up on the hood of my truck and snatches the turkey out of the windshield by the feet. The head snaps off inside my truck. He then duck tapes my windshield together so I can drive."

At that point, everyone at the table was dying laughing, but Travis continued. "Right. Despite the turkey blood, the spider web like cracks, the duct tape and the general appearance that the windshield is screwed to hell and back, I could still drive. Lastly, the guy reached in the cab of my truck grabbed the turkey head and threw it in the woods before thanking me for the turkey and driving off. Yeah, I drove the rest of the way home with a duck taped windshield."

Laughing through his words, Matt said, "If that ain't redneck, I don't know what is!"

We were all still laughing when Cara says, "I have a road kill story."

"Do tell," said Emma as tears were still running down her face from laughing at Travis' story.

"Ok, before I worked at Port Honor, I worked at the Piggly Wiggly here in Milledgeville. One Sunday afternoon, I was scheduled to work at 4:00. I had been to visit some friends in Augusta and was on my way back to work. I was driving behind one of the chalk trucks on the by-pass around Sandersville. We were doing about seventy miles per hour and up ahead was this old house. I could see this little dog running toward the road. He was far enough back that I figured we would pass by before he made it to the road. What I did not see, because there was a hedge, was the big German Shepherd type dog that the little dog was chasing."

Stella gasped and we all had an idea of where this story was going.

Cara continued, "The German Shepherd ran out in front of the chalk truck and by God I have never known a dog could bust like that. It rained dog guts all over my windshield and I had to cut the wipers on just to see."

The guys were laughing at the thought of raining dog guts, but Stella and Emma were gagging. It took a lot to gross me out and this was coming close.

Cara continued on, "When I cut the windshield wipers on there were intestines stuck around the wipers blades flopping back and forth. I had to pull over and vomit. Then when I got to Milledgeville, I had to pull over and wash the car. When I got to work, late of course, I told the manager this story and he accused me of lying. As if I could make that up!" Cara finished with exasperation.

"Amelia, do you have a road kill story?" Matt asked.

"No, not really. I hit a squirrel once. It spun out across the road like blades on a helicopter,"

"Yeah, you should have just stuck with 'no'," Matt said all disappointed.

"Gabriel, what about you?" Jay said trying to make sure Gabriel felt included in the conversation.

"I don't think I can compete with the turkey," Gabriel admitted as he rubbed his forehead in thought. "I have something, but it's not a road kill story per se, but I on the way to Macon about a month ago, I got behind three of the biggest, fattest rednecks you ever saw. They were letting the low side drag, as in the fattest ones were sitting on the same side, in the tiny, ragged out Chevy Cavalier that they were driving. Well, Bubba, Earl and Junior had been out hunting that morning. I could tell this by the fact that they were all still wearing their camo and the dead deer that was tied across the entire car. Picture this, the feet are tied to the corner of the front passenger's side bumper, the legs are across the hood, the body is stretched cattycornered across the windshield, cab, back window and trunk and the head was tied to the back driver's side bumper nearly dragging the ground. I followed those fools all the way to Gray. The deer was as big as the car."

"Ah, the things you see in Middle Georgia!" said Emma.

***

Dinner wound down and since Jay and Emma's only contributions were salad and tea, they were in charge of the majority of the clean-up. Gabriel and I excused ourselves since I had to drive him back home.

Gabriel begged me to stay at his house for the night. I was so temped to stay, but it was either drive back then or drive back early in the morning. Either way, the choice was not that great. Although my favorite past time was sleeping next to Gabriel and waking up next to him, second only to kissing him of course, ultimately we agreed that sleeping over during the week was not conducive to my class schedule at that time.

By the time I got back to Milledgeville, it was midnight and I was dreading my 8:00 a.m. class. Gabriel had insisted on me calling to let him know I arrived safely and I did as he had asked. Before we hung up, Gabriel thanked me again for trusting him with the knowledge of the inheritance. I went to bed that night feeling as if a weight had been lifted by just sharing the information with Gabriel and Jay.

***

Class came early the next morning, but I made it through the day. I spent the afternoon correcting the edits that Jay and Gabriel had made to my history paper on JFK. Before heading off to work, I called Aunt Gayle and reminded her about dinner on Friday night. She informed me that she would not be able to stay over, but would come down and meet me for lunch on Friday, hang out with me and then go to dinner with me at Port Honor.

After I hung up with Aunt Gayle, I headed out to work. Alvin out did himself with the evening specials. My favorite was the Bourbon Street New York Strip. I had never had that before and it was exceptional. Matt was working too and insisted that I try Pinot Noir with the steak. He also insisted that I try Cabernet. I was then given a lesson on the differences in the wines. I was not that fond of either, but if I had to choose, I liked the Pinot Noir the best. It was smoother with a touch of a pepper taste. The Cabernet was not offensive to my taste buds, it just left me wanting something else to wash it down. This had been my introduction to wine.

The usual Wednesday night group came in, plus some new members. The only thing eventful was that Gabriel called and asked that I stop by his house before I headed home. I agreed and after we were all finished at the club, I drove over.

When I pulled up Gabriel walked out to the truck. He was in a different pair of pajama pants. They were red plaid and hung so that I could see the V. It was warmer than it had been in a few days so the pants were all that he had on and his hair appeared damp as if he had just gotten out of the shower. He was as breathtaking as ever.

I opened the truck door to get out and he stopped me. "I am not going to keep you," Gabriel said. "I just wanted to kiss you goodnight."

I smiled at him and reveled in the thought that he was mine. The kiss was sweet, right there with me still sitting in the driver's seat and Gabriel standing in the doorway.

"I am not going to ask you in because I don't want to start something that we can't finish tonight," he said as he pulled away.

"I understand," I responded as I pulled him back for one last kiss.

"Friday night, Miss Anderson..." I cut him off.

"I will see you at the club at 8:00 p.m. for dinner," I informed him.

"You will?"

"Yes, I have a dinner date."

"You do? With whom?"

"My aunt will be joining me for dinner at Port Honor on Friday night. Plus, as you may recall I am supposed to know all about 'Passionate Kisses' for Mrs. Lockerby by then."

"Ah, yes, 'Passionate Kisses'. I think I can help you with that," and once more I was educated on Gabriel's art of kissing.

***

Everything, from the time I left Gabriel's driveway on Wednesday night, was a haze of anticipation until Aunt Gayle arrived at The Jefferson a little after noon on Friday. I was confident of my work and I turned in my history paper that morning, but beyond that my thoughts were elsewhere, looking ahead to introducing Aunt Gayle and Gabriel. What if she did not like him? What if he did not like her? So many what ifs...

It was another warm November day in Milledgeville, so I was waiting in the porch swing so I could see Aunt Gayle pull up. I had not been home from class and in the swing long before I heard the roar of the truck engine pulling up. Before she could open the truck door, I sprang from the swing and ran down to greet her. This was her first time seeing my apartment or the building in general and I was anxious to show it off.

I threw open the front door to find her standing there in front of the building assessing the place. Large black wide brimmed sun hat in hand along with her purse, oversized sunglasses, form

285

fitted black blouse, wide legged jeans and black high heel cowboy boots on, Aunt Gayle was every bit the sophisticated Southern lady. Not a hair on her head was out of place. She was so pretty and ever since I was a little girl I had wanted to be just like her.

As soon as she had heard the door, Aunt Gayle lowered her shades in my direction and her eyes lit at the sight of me.

"Hey!" I screamed as I ran to hug her. I was so happy she was there and I prayed she would be proud of me and not disappointed in the way I had spent the money on the building. She often thought like Granddaddy when it came to money and so pleasing her would be just as good as having pleased him.

"Millie!" she screamed as she held open her arms to me. "It looks good from here!"

"Do you really think so?" I squealed.

"Yes, now are you going to show me inside?" she asked.

We were like giddy girls in the school yard. I grabbed her free hand and pulled her inside quickly with excitement. I pointed to each door inside the foyer and explained the layout of each and who lived where. I apologized that I could not show them to her because no one was home. They were either still in class or at work.

We went straight upstairs where I gave her the full tour including Jay and Emma's rooms. I had spent every spare minute of the last two days scrubbing the place from top to bottom and it showed. The place smelled to high heaven of Pine-Sol and Pledge.

"Millie, the place is beautiful," she was saying even before I threw open the door to my room.

"Do you really like it?" I so wanted her to be proud of me.

"And this is your room?" she asked as she walked in.

"Yes, ma'am," I replied while moving around her and heading toward the open the doors to the porch.

"I love the bed and the covers. They are so pretty! You all have done a great job with every room, Millie."

"Just wait, you have not seen my favorite part," I said to her as I opened the French doors. I had swept off the porch and put out all of the cushions on the swing and the wicker rocking chair.

I stepped to the side and allowed Aunt Gayle to go onto the porch ahead of me. "I LOVE IT! I have never wanted to live in town, but I might could live here on this porch, Millie. It is absolutely lovely."

I was pure giddy inside. I had her approval and she even said the words, "Millie, I am so proud of you."

Aunt Gayle took a seat on one end of the porch swing and me on the other. We chatted for nearly an hour. I told her the details of the purchase of the building. I told her about my classes and how they were going. I told her the gossip on Jay and Emma's lives. I started to tell her about Gabriel. I had told her a little in the past, but held off so she could judge for herself when she met him at dinner.

We talked until we were both starving. We went to lunch at Café South in Hardwick. They had the best Southern food in town, actually, the best of any kind of food in town. Friday was chicken and dumpling day at Café South. After lunch we agreed that those were a close second to the chicken and dumplings that Granny used to make. It was kind of nostalgic since neither of us could make chicken and dumplings so we had not had any worth eating since Granny died when I was six years old.

I confessed, "I eat lunch here almost every Friday because it helps me remember Granny and I only buy Coast soap because it smells like Granddaddy and helps me remember him."

"Oh, Millie, that's so sweet, but don't let trying to remember them keep you living in the past. They would not want that for you," Aunt Gayle said as she reached across the table and patted my hand.

"I know and I don't. I just don't want to forget them and this helps."

After lunch, Aunt Gayle wanted to go shopping so we took a ride to the Macon mall. She treated me to a new outfit for dinner and to having my make-up done at the Estee Lauder counter at Macy's. We had a real girls' day out and all the while Aunt Gayle apologized profusely for not being able to stay over and spend more time with me. As always, I was reminded that she was the closest thing to a real mother I had ever had and I imagined that this was the type of day regular mothers and daughters had.

It was around 5:30 p.m. when we arrived back at the apartment from our trip to Macon. Jay was home and Aunt Gayle insisted on inviting him to join us for dinner at Port Honor. Jay politely declined since he knew I had planned on introducing Aunt

Gayle to Gabriel. Aunt Gayle persisted, but Jay remained firm in his refusal.

Just after seven, we were ready and on our way to the club. I rode with Aunt Gayle and told her that I could get a ride home from Cara and she could head back to the farm via I-20 without having to come back to Milledgeville to drop me off. Little did she know I had sent a bag with Cara in case I was invited to say over at Gabriel's, it was the weekend after all.

I had also grabbed my guitar to bring with me because as it turned out, the song 'Passionate Kisses' might have started out on the piano, but it was actually a song dominated by the guitar. Aunt Gayle questioned me bringing the guitar and I just told her she would have wait and see.

CHAPTER 12

It was dark by the time we made the turn onto Port Honor Parkway off of Highway 44. We had taken the shortcut around Eatonton so it was closer to 7:30 p.m. when we pulled up to the guard gate. A new officer was working the gate that night and I did not recognize him. Even if one of the regulars had been working, we would have had to stop anyway since we were in Aunt Gayle's truck and they would not have recognized it.

Aunt Gayle had experienced the luxury of attending the Masters once or twice in Augusta, so I fully expected her to be unimpressed with the club, but as we turned in she asked with a tone of disbelief, "You work here?"

"Yes, ma'am, well, I work at the clubhouse," I specified. I guess I was insecure about her making the comparison between it and Augusta National, so I started listing the statistics that I knew about the club. "Not everyone knows this, but Port Honor was the first resort built on Lake Oconee in 1986. Not long after it opened, it was ranked number two in the state, second only to Augusta National, home of the Masters."

"Millie, I know what Augusta National is," she informed me as we pulled up to the guard shack by the gate.

"Good evening, ladies," the new guard with name tag reading "James" greeted us as soon as Aunt Gayle lowered her window.

"Good evening," Aunt Gayle replied.

I leaned across the cab so that the guard could see me, "Good evening, we have reservations for dinner at the clubhouse in the name of Millie Anderson."

"Good evening, ma'am," James replied as he leaned down to see me. "I was left instructions to call down when you were on your way. I will get the gate. You all have a good- night."

James stepped back through the sliding doors of the guard shack and hit the button to raise the gate. Aunt Gayle put the truck in gear and James waved us through.

"Tell me again how you found this place, Millie," Aunt Gayle asked as we headed past the real estate office that sat to the right just inside the gate.

"The placement office at the college had a job listing for servers here," I answered.

"It is quite a drive out here," she commented.

"Yeah, but I don't mind. I really like it here," and soon she would find out just why I liked it here so much.

We made the turn toward the clubhouse and were passing by the Inn when Aunt Gayle asked, "What is that building?"

"It's The Honor Inn, the hotel." I answered and continued to explain, "If you ever want to come and stay over, I can get a night's stay there for $50. You should see the inside. There is a four sided, rock fireplace that stretches to the ceiling and sits in the center of the lobby. It is really pretty. What I would like to do is sit in the rocking chairs on the back porch and just rock while I look out over the croquet course. Look back over your shoulder and you can see what I am talking about with the porch and the croquet course."

Aunt Gayle looked back, "I see. You are right. It is quite pretty."

The back of the inn was just as lit up as the front. The rocking chairs on the second floor could be seen as clear as day and all of the lights were on over the three croquet courses.

It wasn't much farther to the club, just down the hill. I was sure the guard had called down to the club and Gabriel would likely be waiting. My stomach was churning and suddenly I was so nervous and excited.

We parked on the upper level with all of the other guests. I could tell Aunt Gayle was taking it all in.

"Come on," I said as I exited the truck. "I can hardly wait for you to meet everyone."

"Don't you want to bring your guitar in?" she reminded me.

"Right," we had only taken a couple of steps, so I went back to get it.

Once inside the front door, I went and placed the guitar on the piano bench. Aunt Gayle waited by the railing at the top of the stairs as I had asked her. When I returned, we started down the stairs together. The dining room was full of regular members and as expected Mr. and Mrs. Lockerby were in attendance with the Bakers.

Something about the dining room made it look different than usual to me. Initially, I thought it was just because it was a little more crowded than typical. That was not it. Finally, I noticed that the room was lit only by candles. There were candles on every table and there were large five branch floor candelabras made of iron standing in four spots around the room. The fireplace was also burning. In all the nights I had worked, the fireplace had never been on before.

Daniel was waiting at the hostess stand and noticed us when we reached the landing about halfway down the staircase.

"Millie!" I could hear the excitement in Daniel's voice at the sight of us. When we reached the bottom of the stairs, he gave me a huge hug, lifting me off of my feet. Aunt Gayle stood a little in shock.

When Daniel put me down, I introduced them. "Daniel, this is my aunt Gayle. Aunt Gayle, this is Daniel. He is one of my favorite people here at the club."

Daniel blushed, "At least I am someone's favorite since Millie is everyone else's favorite."

Just then Cara came through the bar door, "Hey Millie! I love the dress and your make-up! You look beautiful!" she said insinuating this was not my norm.

Cara was right. My usual less was more look had been murdered by the Estee Lauder girl at Macy's earlier. Tonight I looked like me, but in Technicolor.

My mind was wandering and my insecurities over my looks were starting to take hold while Cara continued to gush over me. Suddenly I heard Gabriel's voice come from behind me. "Good evening, may I show you ladies to your table?"

When I turned around, all insecurities were gone as I could tell he was pleased to see me. There he was, not in his usual white chef's coat and checked pants, but wearing a white button down shirt, khaki slacks and a tie. His sleeves were rolled up to three-quarter length. Of course, he was still in the walking cast and had the cane, but he had on a Bass buck shoe instead of those awful clogs or even tennis shoes. It appeared he was dressed to impress.

"Hi," I said to him and it was suddenly as if we were alone in front of everyone.

"Hi," he replied and there was a momentary pause between us while everyone just stood there. He looked me up and down as if he were seeing me for the first time in weeks even though I had just seen him last night. I could feel every breath more deeply than the one before as I wondered what he was thinking. Did he like what he was seeing? Was the make-up too much?

"Good evening," Aunt Gayle said breaking the silence.

"Aunt Gayle, this is Gabriel. Gabriel, this is my aunt Gayle," I introduced them.

"It is an honor to meet you, ma'am. No pun intended," Gabriel said as he took his eyes from me and turned his attention to Aunt Gayle.

Aunt Gayle had already been sizing Gabriel up. I had told her about him in the past, but had not mentioned much of him to her since things had taken off with him. This was kind of my night for rectifying that.

"It is lovely to meet you as well," Aunt Gayle said as she offered her hand.

As Gabriel and Aunt Gayle shook hands, Jerry approached the hostess stand where we were all still congregated. "Well, Miss Anderson, how nice of you to grace us with your presence on your night off," he said in his usual manor of sarcasm. It was always hard to tell if he was joking or put out. Jerry returned a couple of menus to the hostess stand and then continued into the bar.

"Who was that?" Aunt Gayle asked looking a little shocked by how Jerry had spoken to me.

"That's just Jerry. He's always like that," Gabriel said.

"Yeah, if he did not like you, he wouldn't speak at all," added Cara before she also exited the dining room into the bar.

"I suppose I should show you all to a table," Daniel chimed in.

"Thanks, Daniel, but I've got this one." Gabriel took the menus from Daniel, then reached back and returned them to the hostess stand.

"You won't need these tonight," he said to us with a smile. Gabriel then offered his hand to me and asked Aunt Gayle and I to follow him.

Gabriel led us across the room to a table set for three in front of the fireplace. It was virtually the only table left unoccupied in the room.

On our way to the table, Gabriel leaned down and whispered in my ear, "You look amazing tonight."

"Thank you," I replied. I wanted to tell him he did not look so bad himself, but I did not want to appear as if we were having some sort of secret conversation in front of Aunt Gayle. She always thought it was rude to whisper in front of others and I agreed. She said it made people think they were being talked about and if it wasn't worth saying aloud in front of someone, then it wasn't worth saying. She was wrong in this case. His whisper to me was definitely worth saying.

Once beside the table, Gabriel released my hand and pulled out a chair for me. As soon as I was seated, he moved to a chair to the side and pulled it out for Aunt Gayle. He was going the extra mile when it came to being a gentleman.

Although there was a place setting for him, Gabriel did not take a seat. Instead, he asked, "May I get you ladies something to drink? A glass of wine, Ms. Anderson?"

I almost laughed. Initially I thought he was speaking to me since we often referred to one another by our sir names in jest, but he was actually speaking to Aunt Gayle.

"Please call me Gayle and I will have a glass of Chardonnay, if you wouldn't mind," she answered.

"Right and call me Gabe, please. Only Amelia here insists on calling me Gabriel. Amelia, what would you like?" he asked.

"Sweet tea, please," I replied and Gabriel quickly excused himself and headed toward the bar to get our drinks.

As soon as he was out of earshot Aunt Gayle gave her first impression of Gabriel, "Millie, you did not tell me how good looking he is."

I am sure I blushed when I replied, "I really had not noticed."

293

"Young lady! Who do you think you are fooling?" she said slightly chastising me, but then she added, "Millie, he seems nice and the way he looks at you..."

At that time, Mrs. Lockerby approached our table. "Excuse me, Millie," she said. "I believe you promised me a song."

"Yes, ma'am. I have not forgotten. Would you mind if I get to that in a few minutes? This is my aunt Gayle and I am treating her to dinner tonight." I fully intended to play for her, but I had just sat down.

"Oh, that's fine. We are in no hurry. I mainly just wanted to remind you and let you know I had been looking forward to hearing you play all week. Mr. Lockerby has been looking forward to it as well," she added.

I know my face went red instantly as I recalled the money that Gabriel had tried to give me from Mr. Lockerby on Tuesday afternoon. I bet it wasn't exactly my playing that they were looking forward to.

As soon as Mrs. Lockerby left our table Aunt Gayle had barely had time to ask what that was about when Gabriel returned with our drinks. He sat the drinks down and then proceeded to take a seat in front of the other place setting. He also commented on having observed Mrs. Lockerby leaving our table. "So, is she after you to play already?" he asked.

"Yeah," I responded knowing there was a hint of a giggle in my voice.

Gabriel then enlightened Aunt Gayle with the G-rated version of the story, "Amelia has developed a group of fans among the members here at the club. I am beginning to suspect that she is the Pied Piper."

"Last week I played and Mrs. Lockerby, whom you just met, asked if I knew a particular song. I did not know it, but I agreed to learn it this week and play it for her tonight," I explained to Aunt Gayle in more detail than Gabriel had.

"And that is why you brought your guitar?" she inquired.

"Yes." I answered. "The song that she wants me to play starts off with a piano opening, but the radio version of the song is dominated more by the guitar, so I decided I would give it a go on the guitar."

Gabriel sat running his hand through his hair probably contemplating that I could play the guitar as well. The fire crackled and I could feel the warmth from it. I could also feel Gabriel reach for my hand under the table.

"Gayle, Amelia has not told me how she learned to play so many instruments. Would you mind enlightening me?" Gabriel asked.

"Well, she first started taking piano lessons and she did so well at it that I figured we would see what other instruments she might be able learn." Anyone could hear the pride in her voice when Aunt Gayle spoke of my accomplishments.

In reality, Aunt Gayle had read too many Jane Austen books and was training me on how to fetch a husband as if we were living in the Victorian era. Gabriel was impressed with my musical skill, so perhaps her plan was working. I sincerely doubted it and would not dare allow myself to think of such, the prospect of one day being Mrs. Gabriel Hewitt. No, I would not allow myself to even fantasize about the possibility.

"So, Gabriel, tell me more about you. Where were you born and raised?" Aunt Gayle asked Gabriel and for once he did not skirt the question.

"I was born in Dallas, Texas and grew up all over. I lived in Chiefland, Florida the longest, but also Hodges, South Carolina which is just outside of Greenwood; then Charleston, and I graduated high school in Nashville, Tennessee," Gabriel listed as I hung on his every word.

"Where did you live the longest?" she continued with the questions.

Gabriel thought a moment before he answered, "I lived in Dallas until I was six, so I suppose I lived there the longest."

"What did you think of Nashville? I have always wanted to go to the Grand Ole Opry." Aunt Gayle stated before she took a sip of her wine.

"I loved Nashville and I have always wanted to go to the Opry as well," he replied. "I did work at the Opryland Hotel one summer running room service orders up to guests. If you ever go to the Opry, you should make sure to stay there, but only if you spring for one of the rooms that open into the atrium. It has to be one of the most beautiful hotels I have ever seen."

"What is the difference in a room that opens into the atrium?" I asked.

"There are nine acres of indoor gardens including a couple of waterfalls and a river. There are rooms that have balconies that open into the atrium. Some of the rooms are right behind the waterfalls, so if you left the doors open to the balcony, you could hear the water flowing..." Gabriel was describing the Opryland Hotel when Aunt Gayle interrupted.

"Sounds like my kind of place," she commented. "Perhaps Millie and I will have to take a trip up there sometime."

As soon as Aunt Gayle finished speaking, Daniel rolled the salad cart over to us. Since both Gabriel and I were accustomed to the Caesar salad, we allowed Aunt Gayle to instruct Daniel on how she wanted it made. She was kind enough to hold the onions on my account.

"You don't like onions?" Gabriel observed.

"No, actually, I love them. It is Millie who does not like them," she said as she waived Daniel on adding more parmesan cheese.

"Really?" Gabriel cut his eyes at me. "I had no idea. What else can you tell me about Amelia?"

"Lots," Aunt Gayle said with wink toward me. "I have photos."

As Daniel placed the salads in front of each of us, Aunt Gayle dug through her purse and retrieved her wallet. She thanked Daniel for the salad and preceded to hand Gabriel my tenth grade school photo. School photos were taken on a Friday that year, so there I was in my cheerleading uniform. My hair was dreadful. I had talked Aunt Gayle into giving me a perm the Sunday afternoon before and I looked like a poodle that had stuck its paw in an electrical socket. I had attempted the claw bangs and wings on the side, but my hair was too fried and heavy to hold. There was not enough Aqua Net in the world for my hair to have held the style I was attempting.

Daniel had lingered at the table to get a look at the picture over Gabriel's shoulder. Gabriel gasped at the sight of it and Daniel burst out into laughter, "Hello, Ugly Duckling!"

"What were you thinking?" Gabriel asked me he cracked up.

"All of the band members of Flock of Seagulls at once?" Daniel continued to laugh.

"Alright, now." I cautioned. "Aunt Gayle, just remember I know where the photos of you in the bikini on the hood of the T-Bird are. Sure would hate to have to bring those out at Thanksgiving."

"Really, Gayle?" Daniel flirted.

"Yes, I will bring them in sometime," I promised. "She has quite the figure."

Aunt Gayle pulled another photo from her wallet. "No need to get the bikini photos out and scare folks, Millie," she said as she handed Gabriel another photo.

"This is more like it," Gabriel commented as he looked at the photo and then passed it to Daniel who was still standing over Gabriel's shoulder.

It was my senior photo, the standard black off the shoulder shot that all the girls had. I had finally decided to embrace the fact that I had straight hair. The braces were gone, but if they had seen my eight grade photo, they would have known that the braces were worth every red cent and the three years I had spent enduring them.

"Well, I must go and make fun of my other guests now," Daniel said excusing himself from our table.

We continued to talk in between bites of our salad and Aunt Gayle and Gabriel were getting along famously. I could not have been more pleased.

"Millie tells me you are going to be joining us for Thanksgiving," Aunt Gayle said to Gabriel as she finished her salad.

"Yes, ma'am, and I appreciate you all agreeing to have me," Gabriel responded and again he took my hand under the table.

"Of course," she returned before asking how much I had told him about some of our relatives.

"No, I have not told him about them," I said trying to put the kibosh on the conversation.

"What is there to tell?" Gabriel asked with curiosity written on his face.

"You know the phrase, 'Every family has one'?" I asked, and he nodded, yes.

Before I could finish, Aunt Gayle took the words from my mouth, "Well, our family has two."

I started explaining, "Granddaddy had two sisters, Aunt Dot and Aunt Ruth. Aunt Ruth had children late in life, so they are only a few years older than I am and Aunt Ruth's kids...well, they're just a little different."

"So that we do not seem unladylike, Gabriel, we will just let you find out on your own at Thanksgiving. You will know them when you see them," said Aunt Gayle.

Gabriel looked at me with wonder, but did not say anything else on the matter. He really did not have a chance to say anything because Jerry, Cara and Daniel arrived with our dinner.

Gabriel had instructed that everything be served family style. There was a platter of teriyaki marinated, grilled salmon, another platter of sliced beef tenderloin with port wine reduction sauce drizzled over it and topped with sautéed mushrooms, three large twice baked potatoes on a smaller platter, a plate of grilled Roma tomatoes with melted parmesan cheese on top and a dish of steamed broccoli. Everything looked wonderful.

"Please help yourself and let me know if I may pass anything to you," Gabriel offered to Aunt Gayle. He was so sweet and attentive to her. He was really doing his best to make a good impression, but without being fake.

The conversation continued through our meal.

"Gabriel, have I understood that you are the chef and the manager of the clubhouse?" Aunt Gayle asked as she took her first bite of the salmon.

"Yes, the goal is to rebuild the business here at the clubhouse and then hire another chef, but for now I am it. I have a great staff, so business is really taking off," Gabriel answered while cutting his tenderloin.

"I think business has already doubled in the time that I have been here," I added.

"The salmon is awesome and you made it?" she inquired.

"Yes, thank you, and I am glad you like it." Gabriel went on to explain to her that Alvin helped him and how lucky he had gotten when he found Alvin. He actually went on to explain how lucky he was to have found each one of us; looking at me while he spoke about me in particular.

"Amelia told me about her interview," Aunt Gayle started.

"Oh, we don't have to rehash that," I tried to stop her.

Aunt Gayle went on, "The guy she described from the interview does not seem like the same guy that we are having dinner with tonight."

Gabriel cut his eyes at me. I am sure he was wondering what else I had told her about him, like how he had been at the interview. "I must admit I was kind of an ass that day, but your niece held her own."

"That's my girl!" Aunt Gayle said with approval. "Gabriel, you will do well to remember that Millie has been raised to give as good as she gets."

"I'll keep that in mind," he replied.

Dinner carried on. Daniel checked on us a couple of times before taking our plates and returning with strawberry cheesecake for dessert. Before she took a bite of her cheesecake Aunt Gayle asked to be excused and left the table for the restroom.

As soon as she was a safe distance away and sure not to hear, Gabriel still whispered, "You are gorgeous tonight and I can't wait to kiss you."

I bit my lip and looked away shyly.

"Don't look away. Kiss me now," Gabriel demanded as he grabbed my hand and pulled slightly to command my attention.

"No, not in front of all of the members. I have to go and get my guitar from the piano bench upstairs. Come with me," I told him.

"Fine and by the way, you did not tell me your aunt was so young."

"What did you expect?" I leaned in and asked.

"I think I expected someone in her sixties or something. She can't be much older than I am." Gabriel aired his observations.

"She is twelve years older than you are," I clarified.

"You are lying. She's forty?" he gasped.

"Yes, forty."

"She is beautiful and you look a lot like her," he added.

"I hope I am as beautiful as she is when I am forty," I said and I knew he could sense the admiration I had for her and my admiration extended way beyond her looks.

"So what does she do for a living?"

"She is a vet, a good old fashioned country vet." I replied knowing I would have to explain my answer.

Aunt Gayle returned to the table just as I was about to clarify the term "country vet". Gabriel stood for her return as he had when she left the table.

As they took their seats, Gabriel asked the question of her, "Amelia tells me you are a country vet. Is that different from a regular vet somehow?"

"I don't just treat dogs and cats," she answered matter of fact-like.

I knew exactly the difference and there was more to it than that. "She has lost a watch or two over the years birthing calves. She has also been paid in chickens before."

Gabriel's mouth fell open, "Where exactly are you all from that chickens are considered currency?"

"I guess you will see when you come to Thanksgiving," Aunt Gayle joked.

"Would you all mind excusing me for a moment? I need to go and get my guitar from upstairs. I can see Mrs. Lockerby is getting restless over there." I stood from my seat and Gabriel stood as well.

"Would you mind, I would like to show Amelia something about the piano. I had it tuned this week and…"

Aunt Gayle cut him off. "Fine, just leave me here all alone," she said teasingly and with a wave of her hand dismissing us.

She was actually a good sport about us leaving her. To make sure she did not feel abandoned, when we passed by Daniel at the hostess stand, Gabriel instructed him to go and keep Aunt Gayle company while we were upstairs.

Gabriel took my hand at the bottom of the stairs and we ran up them as best as we could while wearing my floor length dress and cowboy boots and Gabriel in the walking boot still, but who knows what he did with the cane because I had not seen it in a while. I was nearly out of breath when we reached the top of the stairs. As soon as my foot hit the top floor of the clubhouse, Gabriel turned and twirled me into his arms.

"You are so beautiful. I have been dying to do this all evening," he said openly and leaned down and kissed me.

It was not a long kiss, just something to tide us over for the time being. Despite the length of the kiss, the butterflies in my stomach were in full force. When Gabriel pulled back and released me, I quickly ran and picked up the guitar case. As I hurried back, he held out his hand to take mine for heading back down the stairs.

"Wait," I stopped him while he was just one step down from the top and I was still on the top floor. "I love kissing you." I said to him as we stood eye to eye. I sat the case down, and with one finger hooked at the top opening of his shirt I pulled him toward me. There was a moment of eye contact and me biting my lower lip before I kissed Gabriel.

When I released him, Gabriel reached down and picked up the guitar case for me. He also allowed me to pass him. I had the skirt of my dress pulled up with one hand, my hand locked in his and then his other hand was carrying the guitar case as we headed back down the stairs to the dining room.

"Love the white dress and the boots," Gabriel said to me as we descended the stairs. "Very country girl looking, I like!"

"Thanks," I looked back at him and smiled. "I like that you and Aunt Gayle are getting on so well."

We returned to the table to find Aunt Gayle talking with another gentleman other than Daniel. In fact, Daniel was nowhere to be found.

"Good evening, Gabriel," the gentleman greeted.

"Mr. Graham, good to see you," Gabriel reached out a hand in addition to his reply.

"I am going to get this over with, if you all will excuse me," I said as I left them and headed over to Mr. and Mrs. Lockerby's table.

The Lockerbys were still seated with the Bakers and they noticed as I approached the table. "Good evening, Millie," Mrs. Lockerby said.

"I learned the song as I told you I would, but I am not going to play it on the piano. I hope you don't mind," I said as I gestured with the guitar.

Mrs. Lockerby seemed to be fine with my choice of instruments so I began to play "Passionate Kisses". The song went smoothly even though I did not know much about being in the mood until recently; I did know that this was not that type of song. Despite that, Mrs. Lockerby led the room in clapping for me as soon as I struck the last note.

After the clapping stopped, I offered them another song. They encouraged me to continue. This pleased me as the song I had in mind was a definite mood setter and a sure fire way to increase Rudy's college fund.

I motioned back to Aunt Gayle and she excused herself from Gabriel and Mr. Graham. She was just about to me when I asked if she would mind joining me.

Aunt Gayle might have thought I was calling her over to introduce her to more if my new friends, but when she took a stand at my side, I leaned back and whispered to her, "Would you sing along?"

We discussed it and she agreed to sing the song I suggested, "You Belong to Me", another Patsy Cline song that I knew how to play. We discussed that it further and agreed to change instruments. Aunt Gayle agreed to sing while I played the piano.

I explained to the Lockerbys and the Bakers that we were going to move to the piano. "You are welcome to join us upstairs, but you should be able to hear just fine from your table." I said before turning to ask Gabriel to come up with us.

Gabriel addressed him only by his last name when speaking, "Graham, you are welcome to come up with us if you like."

"I don't want to impose," replied Mr. Graham.

"It is no imposition at all," Aunt Gayle told him and apparently her asking carried more weight than Gabriel as he eagerly agreed to join us then.

I had not noticed when I first sat the guitar on the piano bench or when Gabriel and I had gone back upstairs to get it, but the floral arrangement had already been removed and the lid was open. The piano had also been polished and dusted, inside and out. The polish job was so good that I could see my reflection in the black shine of it as I approached. It appeared as though someone had gone to a great deal of effort to prepare the piano for me.

I took a seat on the piano bench and Aunt Gayle proceeded to take a position standing behind me near the railing overlooking the dining room. Mr. Graham and Gabriel had initially stopped to stand near the end of the fireplace closest to the piano, but they could not see us for the open lid of the piano.

"Would you mind if we closed this?" Mr. Graham asked.

I stood to help him close it, but before I really had a hand on it, Gabriel stopped me. "I have got it, Amelia," Gabriel insisted.

Once they closed the top of the piano, Gabriel and Mr. Graham took places standing around the piano as Mrs. Lockerby and Mrs. Durham had done the week before. Gabriel was closer to me and Mr. Graham was at the end, facing us.

I began to play and Aunt Gayle followed with singing. Mr. Graham could not take his eyes off of her. I always believed she had the voice of an angel, soft, but powerful at the same time. This song was meant for Aunt Gayle's voice and it floated sweetly from the balcony down into the dining room.

The patrons of the club cheered as well as Mr. Graham and Gabriel for more when Aunt Gayle's rendition of "You Belong to Me" ended.

Once they began to settle back down, Aunt Gayle asked, "Gabe, have you had the pleasure of hearing Millie sing?"

This was her way of coaxing me and aiding Gabriel in her attempt. I shook my head "no" insisting that I did not want to sing.

"I have only barely heard her sing along with the radio once, but that does not count. She was hardly loud enough to be heard," Gabriel replied with eagerness written all over his face.

"Millie, it's your turn," Aunt Gayle said as she patted me on the back. She then turned from us, leaned over the balcony and yelled to those waiting below. "Would you all like to hear Millie sing? She's actually quite good."

The loudest of them yelling back was Cara. I could hear her voice above all others screaming an exuberant "Yes!" She exuded enthusiasm and was backed by the rest of our audience.

I was on the spot. I just shook my head, but there really was no getting out of it.

"Okay, okay," I conceded. "Give me a minute to decide what I am going to sing."

"Can we make requests?" Mr. Graham chimed in breaking my thoughts.

I was going over the song in my head that I was intending to sing. It was as if he had interrupted my rehearsal and I quick to reply, "Not this time."

I figured it was now or never and I struck the first few notes from Sarah McLachlan's "Ice Cream." I played through the opening and began to sing. I had first tried to get Aunt Gayle to play while I sang, but she said she did not know the song.

I made my way through most of it with my eyes closed only looking up once or twice at Gabriel. He looked mesmerized. Would he think this song was just for him? It was. I had squelched all inhibitions and gave it my all to serenade him right in front of everyone.

When we finished, the whole room clapped and clapped. Gabriel walked over and in front of Mr. Graham and Aunt Gayle, he kissed me on my forehead, "I thought you said you did not sing well?" he shamed me. I just blushed and hung my head.

"Don't hang your head, Miss Anderson," he said as he lifted my chin. "That was very, very good. You have a beautiful voice."

While Gabriel was gushing over me, Mr. Graham gushed over Aunt Gayle. It appeared she had a new admirer.

Aunt Gayle and I went on to perform for another thirty minutes. By the time we finished, Jerry, Daniel and Cara had picked up the entire room, completed all of their side-work and were waiting on everyone to leave. Matt was still serving drinks, but all in all the night was over. Sales-wise, it had been a banner night at the club and a banner night for me.

It was around 10:00 p.m. when Aunt Gayle decided she had to get on the road before it got any later. Gabriel and I walked her out to the truck. As she hugged me goodnight before getting in her truck, she whispered to me, "I think he is a keeper and we will talk more about this later."

Aunt Gayle released me and turned her attention to Gabriel. She opened her arms to hug him and he accepted the invitation. She did not whisper to him, she said it openly, "I like you, but if you hurt her, I will kill you and her roommate, Jay, will help me dispose of the body."

Both Gabriel and I were taken aback by what Aunt Gayle said. Although she said it with a chuckle at the end, I doubted she was anything but serious. She smiled a sly, friendly smile, but I could tell when she was joking and she was not.

We watched Aunt Gayle drive away and as soon as her truck passed the Inn and we could no longer see it, Gabriel and I went back inside. It wasn't ten minutes until he was leading me by the hand toward the back door of the kitchen.

"Hold on," I said as I turned to go back, "I need to get the key to Cara's car and get my bag."

Gabriel held tight to my hand and pulled me back, "I already took care of that. It's in my car. Now, come on!"

Out the back door we went. In the dark, at the end of the loading dock, and even though he was the one with the broken foot, Gabriel carried my guitar case and held out a hand to help me down the steps. Aunt Gayle was gone and there was no one to see but me so he could have turned off the charm. He didn't; he was still the perfect gentleman and so utterly sexy in the light of the moon.

Within moments we pulled into the garage at Gabriel's house. He got out, grabbed my bag from the back seat and then opened the car door for me. He held out his hand to help me from the car.

As soon as we were inside, Gabriel led me to his bedroom. Gabriel put my bag down on the bed and started toward the bathroom door, "I am going to grab a quick shower, okay?"

I had taken a seat on his bed and was taking off my boots. I must have had a disappointed look on my face as he said he was going to take a shower because he immediately came back to me. He pulled me to my feet and held me close to him.

"I had a great time tonight," he said.

I leaned my head back to look up at his face. "Thank you so much for having dinner with us and meeting my aunt. I know she liked you."

I stood on my toes and kissed him, "Thank you so much!"

"Join me in the shower," and just as he asked the phone rang.

Gabriel released me and went for the phone. He looked at it, rolled his eyes and allowed it to keep ringing.

"Aren't you going to get that?" I asked.

"No," he replied and he continued to the bathroom and it appeared the moment had passed.

Gabriel went on into the shower and I went to the kitchen. I rummaged through his refrigerator and found a bottled water and some cheese cubes. I returned to the bedroom with my snack to find the bathroom door open. I could hear the shower running, but could not see him. I felt a little like I was spying, but surely that was not possible since he had just asked me to join him in the shower.

When Gabriel emerged from the shower and returned to the bedroom, he was wearing nothing but a towel. I was sitting on his bed still in my dress eating the cheese cubes and watching the 11:00 p.m. news on one of the Atlanta stations. Of course, my attention was drawn from the news of the local murders and hit and runs to Gabriel wearing only a towel. My face went red as I could not take my eyes off of him.

"Go ahead. Get a good look, Miss Anderson. Just remember I am going to want one in return," he said removing the towel with his back to me as he strolled back into the bathroom.

I was given a full shot of him naked only from the rear, but naked from head to toe, with the exception of the cast. He seemed taller naked. The muscles in his back were almost as amazing as the shape of his ass. He had the slightest tan line around his waist and again just a couple of inches down his legs. My heart raced at the sight of him and I immediately looked away just in case he looked back. I did not want him to catch me staring, which was something I could hardly help doing.

I could not see anything of the front of him, but seeing from the back was titillating enough. I could feel the heat coming off of my face. I tried to fan myself before he returned. I almost got caught, but slid my hand into my hair from fanning it in front of my face.

Gabriel returned wearing my favorite pirate pajama pants. I decided to repay the glimpse he gave me. As he sat down on the bed, I offered him the bottled water and he took it. I got up from the bed leaving him there sipping the water. I picked up my overnight bag and started from my side of the bed toward the bathroom. Once between Gabriel and the television, I pulled the string from around my neck and let my dress fall to the floor. It was a halter dress and I had on a white lace bra and matching panties under it. When it hit the floor, I stepped out of the pile the dress lay in on the floor. I looked over my shoulder at Gabriel and smiled. I continued into the bathroom with him watching.

I returned from the bathroom, freshly brushed teeth, fresh face without all the make-up, but still wearing only my underwear. Gabriel was sitting up on the bed, propped up by two pillows against the headboard. He had turned off the sound to the television, but it still provided the only light in the room.

"Come here," Gabriel said as he held out a hand to me.

I did as I was asked. Taking his hand, he pulled me toward him. I climbed on top, straddling across his lap. Gabriel's arms went around me and his hands roamed up my back past my bra strap and into my hair. I had placed my hands on each side of his face and I was leaning in for the kiss when he took hold of fistfuls of my hair and pulled my head back. He was in control and I did not mind at all, I dare say I liked it.

As my head tilted back Gabriel place soft kisses down my neck, trailing down to my chest. The bra I was wearing was strapless and little more than white lace and a little padding on the outer edges to push together what I had in the way of breasts. It did not leave much to the imagination. I had gained a little weight since I bought it so my breasts were stuffed in it to the point of nearly busting loose. Plus, the more aroused I became the more they heaved upward with every breath I took.

Gabriel continued his descent of kisses until his face came to rest between my breasts. I arched my back and gave into him. As I leaned back he released my hair and slid his hands down my back to my bra strap. Like he had done with my panties days before, he slipped the tips of his index fingers just below the top line of the material of my bra. He traced around from the clasp in the back to the center of my chest.

My God, I thought I was going to come undone just from his touch. Every time we were together, it was more intimate than the time before. While he felt his way around the top of my bra, I was certain he was going to slide it down and finally start to have his way with me. I came close to begging for him to do just that.

"Gabriel," I exhaled.

I could feel his erection under me. I remembered the way he moved back and forth beneath me when he kissed me while holding me against the door the last time I was at his house. It felt amazing and I had wanted him to move like that again.

I steadied myself on my legs and transferred my weight to my knees off of him all while my back was still arched and he planted the softest kisses between my cleavage. I lowered myself down against him. I did it again, hoping he would take the hint.

"Amelia, careful," Gabriel raised his head and looked at me. "Mess with the bull, you get the horns," he cautioned. That seemed to be a favorite phrase of his as it was not the first time he had used it to warn me to settle down.

"Really?" I said daringly and I lowered myself down to him again. I teased him doing almost a backbend, laying completely back on his legs, my hair likely landing near his feet and placing my entire body on display.

As I lay back, Gabriel reached out and touched me starting at my neck and running his fingers slowly down through the middle of my chest, down my stomach. He circled my belly button with his right index finger then continued running his hand down to my panties. With both hands he reached around and grabbed me by my butt cheeks. I raised up to face him using only my ab muscles and pushing up with my thighs. I threw my arms around him and we kissed so deeply, I felt as if I could feel it to my toes.

I pulled away from him and eased up onto my knees taking his face in my hands again. I tilted his face to the right to give me access to kiss his ear. I ran my tongue around the outside rim of his ear and then sucked on his earlobe. I released his face and ran my hands down his neck and across his shoulders. I left a trail with my tongue down to his Adam's apple where I placed deep sucking kisses, but careful not to leave any signs of affection. Gabriel gripped my ass as I proceeded down from his chest.

"Oh God, Amelia!" Gabriel moaned.

I straightened up and smiled at him. I reached around and took one of his hands from my behind and pulled it around to me. I raised it to my mouth and slid this index finger in my mouth. I twirled my tongue around and sucked. I was so young and inexperienced, I had no idea what I was emulating. I had just thought it was something fun to do in the moment.

I started with his second finger and Gabriel pulled his hand back, "Whoa, Amelia!" A shiver ran over him and I could tell he moved a little as if to shake it off.

"My God, you make it impossible to stop with you," Gabriel said breathlessly.

"I am yours," I said as I fell against him. He understood I was giving him the go ahead not to stop.

"Not tonight. Not with the cast. I want you so badly, more than anything, but when we do this I want to be one hundred percent," Gabriel whispered in my neck as he held me tightly to him.

"You torture me, you know that," I whispered back. "I want you too and I have never wanted anyone."

Gabriel kind of laughed at my statement about never wanting anyone, "I should feel special then, huh?"

"You are special," I said as I leaned back to look him in the eye and assure him.

"Don't," Gabriel said and he looked away. He tried to move from under me, but I held my spot.

"Gabriel, look at me," I said as I took his face and turned it back to me. His vulnerability was showing as he initially resisted, but gave into me. I looked him directly in the eye. "Gabriel, you are the most special thing to me. I know you feel it when we touch."

Gabriel's eyes widened. This was the first we had spoken of the spark. "You feel it too?"

"Since the very first day I met you," I said with a giant smile.

"I thought it was just me," he responded in kind. "I thought I was going crazy."

"I shrugged it off and assumed you had that effect on everyone," I said with complete honesty.

"I doubt that and no one has ever had this effect on me, not ever. I tried to fight it. You must know that."

"I do," I said as I eased from on top of him and got out of the bed.

"Where are you going?" Gabriel asked.

"To get something else to drink. Would you like anything?" I offered.

"I will just take a swallow of whatever you are having," he called to me as I headed down the hallway toward the kitchen.

I was in his kitchen, on my tippy toes and reaching for a glass when I felt him behind me.

"I love this look on you," Gabriel said as he wrapped an arm around me and with the other he moved my hair to one side, exposing one of my shoulders and my neck. He proceeded to kiss me on my shoulder. I could feel his bare chest on my back.

"You like the look of me in my underwear?" I asked.

"Yes and barefoot in my kitchen."

"Are you trying to start something again, Mr. Hewitt?" I asked with a grin.

"Just a little something," Gabriel replied as he turned me around, lifted me and sat me on the countertop.

CHAPTER 13

Saturday was another warm day. I was back on the beverage cart and the course was packed. Everyone was out and I made a killing in tips. I reloaded the cart so many times that I lost count. Typically sales tapered off around 3:00 p.m. and I was finished and off work by 4:00 p.m., but not that day. Sales did not wind down until later so I was stuck there until 5:00.

Gabriel's and my shifts overlapped by an hour. He insisted that I stay for dinner at the club. I was not comfortable with that; just hanging around waiting on him in front of everyone. He was easily convinced that I would be more comfortable hanging around waiting on him at home, his home, so he packed a to-go box of dinner for me.

I was glad to accept the carry-out box that Gabriel packed. Alvin had slow cooked baby back ribs. They were so tender that they fell off the bone when Gabriel was transferring them from the pan to the box. They also smelled like my favorite bar-b-que restaurant back home. The side items consisted of homemade potato chips with sour cream and chives to dip them in. I could hardly wait to dig in.

"I will do my best to be done by nine," Gabriel said as he kissed me goodbye on the back loading dock and handed me the box containing my dinner.

"Take your time. Just call me when you are done and I will come get you," I replied and he handed me the keys to his car, the Acura Legend. It was a pretty sweet ride and ultra-modern compared to my 1974 Corvette, but I still preferred the familiarity of my own car.

I went back to Gabriel's house, let myself in, took a long hot shower, sat on the back deck and had dinner while I read my history chapters for the week. I sat outside until I could bear the cold no more. I had not brought a jacket with me and there was a bit of a chill in the air that night.

I came in around 7:30 p.m. and perused Gabriel's movie library. I picked one and put it in. I saw the first five minutes and then woke up to the phone ringing around 9:15. The credits from the movie were playing on the television. I picked up the phone, thinking it was Gabriel calling for me to come get him, but there was no one on the other end of the line. I hung up and went to stop the VCR.

It had only been two minutes since the last call and the phone rang again. Again I answered and no one responded. I hung up again and went back to turn the VCR off and to finish putting away the movie.

Five minutes later the phone rang again.

"What?!" I answered with annoyance in my voice.

"Amelia?" This time it was Gabriel.

"Oh, sorry, someone has called twice and hung up," I apologized and explained to him. "I would not have answered except that I thought it might be you calling."

"That's okay. I am ready for you to come get me, so come on. I will wait for you upstairs. Just drive up to the front door."

It had been peaceful there at the house and I did not mind waiting on him, but the hang ups were giving me the heebie-jeebies and I was ready for him to be home. As soon as I got off of the phone with Gabriel, I picked up the keys and went straight on to get him.

***

Gabriel brought home dessert, chocolate cake with chocolate frosting which we had fun feeding to each other after he got a shower. Then we called it a night. Again, he insisted that I sleep in my underwear. I was not used to sleeping this way, but it was not something that I was opposed to especially since I had upgraded my undergarment wardrobe while shopping with Aunt Gayle at the Macon mall the day before. There had been a bit of explaining to do with her over my need for upgrades, but I chalked it up to being a big girl now and needing big girl panties and not the same old Hanes cotton briefs. Aunt Gayle may have known what was up, but she never let on.

I put up no resistance to turning in around 11:00 p.m. The highlight of my day was being able to lay my head on his chest and fall asleep in his arms. I was exhausted and I had been looking forward to falling asleep with him.

The next thing I knew it was a little after three in the morning.

"Gabriel! Gabriel! Wake up!" I whispered in urgency as I nudged him repeatedly trying to wake him. "Gabriel, there's someone in the house."

I was awakened by the sound of someone trying the front door knob. At first I thought it was a dream or my imagination. Those thoughts were shattered by the sound of someone trying the back door. I sat straight up in bed, frozen, listening, as whomever it was actually managed to open the back door. I snapped out of it in a panic when I heard the footsteps in the kitchen.

I left off nudging Gabriel and nearly shook him and again in a more panicked whisper I said, "Gabriel, wake up! Someone's in the house!"

At that point Gabriel nearly jumped from the bed. Like I had done, he froze, listening until he heard the footsteps. It sounded like they had made it to the far side of the kitchen and were about to head into the living room.

Quickly and quietly, Gabriel got out of bed and handed me the phone, "Call 911, then call the guard shack."

I did not move from the bed.

"Amelia, focus! Get up!" Gabriel demanded as he handed me a robe on his way to the window.

Gabriel opened the window as I pulled the robe on. "Go next door and wake up the Rosenthals and wait there with them until I come for you."

As soon as Gabriel was done opening the window, he went to his closet and grabbed a golf club. I believe it was a nine iron, but I was still unsure of all of the names of the clubs. Everything was all done so quietly and with such speed. The footsteps were now coming from the living room as I protested leaving him.

"Go!" Gabriel said again with demand in his voice. I just stood there and he came and put me out of the window and shut it behind me.

There I stood in the yard, in my finest black lace underwear with only a robe to cover me and I was barefoot. I watched Gabriel through the window and dialed 911. Before going through the bedroom door and into the hall, he looked back at me once more and commanded me to go with the motion of his hand and the expression on his face.

As I ran barefoot and near naked in the dark to the Rosenthals', I explained to the Green County 911 dispatcher that there was someone in the house.

"Ma'am, what's the house number?" the dispatcher asked.

"I don't know! I just know it is on Starboard Harbor Drive. It's a white, one story house on the left. Please send an officer! There's an intruder in the house! Please!" I begged as I ran through the hedges between the two yards. The robe got caught in the thicket and I had to pause to free it.

"Ma'am, can you get out of the house?" the dispatcher asked as I jerked the robe loose.

"I am out of the house, but my boyfriend is still inside. Please send someone!" I begged again.

"Ma'am, did you see the intruder? Do you know if they or your boyfriend are armed?" she asked more questions, but still had not said she was sending someone.

"I started to cry at the thought of Gabriel being inside with an armed intruder and I ran faster through the yard of Mr. and Mrs. Rosenthal with no regard for my bare feet. "I don't know if they are armed! Gabriel is not! I don't know!" I screamed through the sobs at the 911 operator.

I was at the Rosenthals' front door out of breath and banging away and screaming for them to come to the door, when the operator finally said that an officer was on his way. I was scared sick that Gabriel could be dead for all I knew by the time any officer arrived. My nerves were not soothed when the Rosenthals, both in their night clothes and in their eighties, opened the door. I knew they would be of no help either.

I could tell by the look on their faces that all of my commotion had scared them out of their wits. Mrs. Rosenthal was holding their cordless phone and she had already called the guard shack before opening the door to me. I hurriedly explained who I was and what was going on.

Mr. Rosenthal was holding a 12 gauge shot gun and offered to take it and go over and see about Gabriel. His offer was immediately followed by caution: "I don't know what good I would do him since I can't find my glasses and I am blind without them."

I declined his offer because if Gabriel had bested whoever was in the house, I did not want well intentioned, but blind Mr.

Rosenthal, going over and shooting him by mistake. As soon as we agreed that they would wait on their porch with me until Gabriel came for me, James from the guard shack drove up.

James squalled the tires as he made the turn into the driveway at the Rosenthal's. The little, white Ford Ranger pick-up that he was driving had hardly stopped and was barely in gear when he jumped out.

"Is everything alright?" James yelled to all of us as he darted toward the house in haste.

"Everything is fine here, but someone's broken in next door at Gabe's," Mr. Rosenthal replied while we all pointed toward Gabriel's house.

James was just about to Gabriel's front door with his gun drawn when we heard sirens screaming in our direction and two Green County sheriff's department patrol cars came speeding down Starboard Harbor Drive. Mrs. Rosenthal was still commenting on how she did not realize that the guys from the guard shack were allowed to carry guns when I ran from the porch to wave down the sheriff's deputies. Mr. and Mrs. Rosenthal ventured gingerly off of their porch, quite the opposite of my full sprint through the yard and toward the street.

The deputies saw me as I motioned them toward Gabriel's house. They also spotted James and they fishtailed their cars into the semicircular driveway at Gabriel's. James waited for them in the yard. Everything was so quick, but at the same time seemed like slow motion to me.

By the time the deputies were exiting their cars, the Rosenthals had made it to where I was standing at the edge of their yard. Mr. Rosenthal grabbed my hand as I started to leave their yard and venture back into Gabriel's, "Dear, you need to wait here. There's no telling what they might find."

If he was trying to comfort me or reassure me that everything was going to be alright, he was doing a poor job of it.

The officers were almost to the front door when it started to open. In that moment, I had never been so scared. I felt faint and sick all at the same time. What if whoever was in there had done something to hurt Gabriel?

I genuinely thought I was going to throw up until I laid eyes on Gabriel and saw that he was fine. The worries were nearly put to rest, except that Gabriel was escorting Beth Reed out of the house. My fears had been squashed by a feeling of relief that he was okay. I wanted to run to him and throw myself around him and stay that way forever. I was so thankful that he was unharmed, but at the same time, the sight of Beth made my blood boil.

The officers swarmed on Gabriel and Beth and he never looked over to me. The Rosenthals were relieved that Gabriel was safe as I was, but they had had their fill of excitement for the night. They quickly said their goodbyes and headed back inside their house. I suppose we had all had our fill of excitement for the night and it was getting on toward 4:00 a.m.

Clearly, Gabriel was not coming to get me and I was not even sure if he could if he wanted to because of the officers. I started walking across the yard and back to Gabriel's house and rage was beginning to take hold of me. It occurred to me that I hated the thought of her having any of his attention. Also, the question begged: what was Beth doing at Gabriel's at that time of night?

The closer I got to where everyone was congregated in the front yard, the more clearly I could hear the conversation.

"I am not an intruder! I have a key!" Beth snapped at the officers. Also, the closer I got to them the better I could see her.

The blue lights from the patrol cars were still flashing through the night air. The light bouncing across her face did her no service. It made her look like a blue Cruella Deville who had been on a three day bender. Her make-up was running down her face. Mascara streaked from her eyebrows nearly to her jaw line. Lipstick was smudged to near non-existent on her mouth and her blond hair, that had been styled in a sleek bob when I first met her, was teased to the point of fried looking. Although it was Gabriel and myself who had been scared out of our minds by her entry to his house in the middle of the night, it was Beth who looked the most frightened and frightening all in the same instance.

The deputies were giving her a good what for about showing up in the middle of the night at someone's house unannounced.

"Miss Reed, I don't care if you have a key to Fort Knox, at 3:00 a.m., you call ahead and let someone know you are coming," the older of the two officers chastised her.

"I have a key!" she nearly screamed at him while looking to Gabriel to corroborate her claims.

316

The deputy glanced toward Gabriel, as did I. Gabriel also noticed my approach making eye contact with me before he agreed with Beth.

"Yes, she has a key, which I gave to her months and months ago when she agreed to do me a favor and let the cable guy in while I was at work," Gabriel explained. He continued to look at me and I rolled my eyes at him.

The deputy bought Gabriel's story and acknowledged that Gabriel was not entirely happy with the situation. I decided to trust the deputy's instinct and trust that Gabriel was not just spinning a line to cover for Beth's B&E. I was relieved at the thought of Gabriel being put out with Beth and this time I got to witness it.

On my walk back, I had also noticed the car in the ditch at the house on the opposite side of Gabriel's from the Rosenthals. No one else had noticed and the irritation in me demanded satisfaction for Beth showing up like she had. I remembered how Beth had told me, "You may have won the battle, but I will win the war." I decided that since she thought this was war, then perhaps my satisfaction would come from winning another battle.

I stifled the urge to scream at her for everything from breaking and entering to driving drunk to just plain ruining my sleep. Instead, I politely asked, "Beth, if you will hand me your keys I will be glad to move your car out of the neighbor's ditch."

While Beth let out a giant sigh, rolled her eyes, and turned her back to me, all other eyes in the yard turned toward her BMW in the ditch next door. The deputies, Gabriel and James, the guard from the guard shack who was still hanging around, all laid eyes on the car at about the same time. Their eyes followed from the car backward to the grooves of the tire tracks in the muddy grass from the ditch through the yard, back into the ditch and to the skid marks where Beth had braked hard and slid before first entering the ditch. From the skid marks in the road, their eyes all returned to Beth.

"What?!!" Beth barked at them. She turned her glare from them to me, but I just smiled sweetly back at her. She had no idea what was about to happen to her, but I did. I had worked at Attorney Bell's office after school for the last half of my senior year. Attorney Bell had a great deal of DUI clients and I learned a lot.

"Give me your keys, please. I really don't mind moving the car. You can come inside and sleep it off in the guest room," I said as though butter would not melt in my mouth. Beth just rolled her black smudged mascara eyes at me. I knew full well my invitation

317

was vacant because she would be sleeping it off somewhere far less comfortable than just down the hall from Gabriel and I.

The younger of the two deputies interjected as Beth glared at me, "Ma'am, have you been driving that tonight?"

While he started questioning her, the older one returned to his squad car.

"Well how else do you think I got here?" Gabriel had tried to stop her, but she was belligerent in her answer. She just could not help herself and I had known that.

"And that's your white BMW?" the deputy continued as he gestured toward the car.

"Duh!" Beth was becoming the queen of eye rolling. I hoped this was the alcohol talking because it really would be a bad personality combination for her to be arrogant and stupid. I could see Gabriel grab her hand and squeeze trying to get her to take the hint. Instead, she jerked her hand away and complained that he was hurting her.

"Ma'am, how much have you had to drink tonight?" the deputy asked as the older one returned and handed him the breathalyzer.

"None of your God-damn business!" Beth raised her voice and sternly said right in the deputy's face while exaggerating each word.

I don't know if he was fed up with her or if he could tell how much she had had by the mouth full of her breath the poor guy inhaled. Either way, he skipped making her blow in the machine.

"Ma'am," he said with more authority in this voice and while attempting to take her hands, "you are under arrest for driving while under the influence of alcohol. If you would please place your hands behind your back..."

Obviously not knowing when to stop, Beth snatched away from the deputy, "I will do no such thing!"

Beth looked to Gabriel, but Gabriel had taken a step back as he knew better than to get any more involved. I seized the opportunity and I moved to get between Beth and Gabriel. I also casually let the collar of the robe drop a little bit so Beth would have a little something to think about later. Let her wonder what exactly Gabriel and I had been up to before she so rudely interrupted. Gabriel noticed the slip of the robe and reached around me and pulled it back up into place. I eased closer to him when he reached around to pull the robe up. I took his hand and held it, keeping his arm around me.

"Beth, just calm down. I will call her father. Don't worry." Gabriel said calling her attention to us.

Beth still had not gotten the picture and as the deputy put his hands on her again she twisted away once more.

"I am Beth Reed! My daddy owns a third of Fulton County. You will turn me loose or I will have your jobs!" Beth continued to struggle.

The older officer snickered, "I guess it's a good thing we are in Green County then and not Fulton."

I had to turn my head to keep Gabriel from seeing my amusement.

The younger deputy remained professional in his demeanor and sternly asked, "Ma'am, would you like to add resisting arrest to your list of charges?"

"List of charges?!!" Beth gasped as the older deputy began reading her the Miranda Rights.

When the older deputy finished reading her rights, the younger one listed the charges against her. The charges included DUI, reckless driving, destruction of federal property, she had run over the neighbor's mail box, unlawful entry, entering Gabriel's house without his permission regardless of her having a key, and trespassing as evidenced by her car still in the yard next door. Most of the charges were of little consequence and she could likely have them dropped with payment of a fine or if the property owners were not willing to press charges, but the DUI would likely be a bit more problematic for her. At the very least, it would be embarrassing since all of the local papers ran mug shot photos of the folks that were arrested on DUIs and what not.

The deputies cuffed her and started walking away with her. It wasn't until then that Beth Reed finally started to show a sign of having feelings. She looked back at Gabriel and there were tears building in her eyes.

"Wait!" Gabriel called to the officers and they turned to him. "If you don't give her a breathalyzer now, are you going to take her blood at the station?"

"Well, we will be taking her to the emergency room to have blood drawn there," the older officer said.

"But if she consents to the breath test, you won't do the blood test?" Gabriel asked. Beth was looking concerned.

"Right," the deputy responded hesitantly.

"Beth, you have to consent. You have to take the breath test." Gabriel begged her as I looked on. I am sure I had a concerned look on my face as well. What was he up to? Did he know it was a little less damning to have a poor score on the breathalyzer than bad results from drawn blood?

"Fine," Beth agreed in a defeated voice.

The deputies proceeded to administer the test. They did not say what she blew, but shook their heads and continued to the car with her. Beth glanced back over her shoulder at Gabriel pleading with her eyes for him to help her. Instead of interfering any further, Gabriel shook his head at her.

Gabriel did say to her one last time, "I will call your father for you."

As they put Beth in one of the patrol cars, Gabriel led me back inside. When the door closed, it was on! Against the door I went, with Gabriel's pressing. He was so strong and distracting. He did not kiss me immediately. Instead, he asked, "What was the meaning of the slip of the robe?"

"What was the meaning of making her take the breathalyzer test?" I returned while suspended against the front door with my legs and arms around Gabriel.

"Beth often likes to mix a little something with her drink," he said as he held me there eye to eye with him. "And an explanation for the robe?"

"Thought I would give her something to ponder while she was in the drunk tank. What did you mean, 'she likes to mix a little something'?"

"If they gave her a blood test they might find traces of coke or something? What was it you wanted her to ponder?"

"You are a big boy, figure it out!" And, I demonstrated by pulling my arms from around him and slouching my shoulders and letting the robe fall down my arms.

"You are bad, Miss Anderson!" Gabriel said as he dropped me suddenly. I managed to get my feet on the floor only to be snatched up over his shoulder and carried to the bedroom.

"We have got to get some sleep," he said as we went through the house still making fine use of the walking cast.

Before getting back in bed, Gabriel did try to call Beth's father. He had taken the phone into the bathroom so as to avoid making the call in front of me. He returned rather quickly.

"Did you get him? What did he say?" I asked as Gabriel sat the phone on the bedside table and climbed into bed.

"No, there was no answer. I got the machine," he replied.

"Did you leave a message? How odd would that be," I said before mocking the message that he could have left. "Hi, Mr. Reed, your daughter is in the Green County jail charged with DUI. Hope you get this message." I tried not to laugh, but of course I did not succeed.

Gabriel did not say anything. He did try not to laugh as well and he succeeded better than I.

Once we were lying in our usual spoon position to drift back off to sleep, Gabriel buried his head in my hair. "I am sorry about all of this tonight."

"Why did she come here tonight?" I asked.

"You don't want to know," he replied.

I rolled over still in his grasp and faced Gabriel. "When you motioned for me to leave the window, I thought I might never see you again," I whispered.

Tears began to run down my cheek as my mind revisited the situation and the thoughts of what could have happened.

"I am so sorry, Amelia. I know it won't make you feel any better, but I had the same fear. I was so scared that I had done the wrong thing by putting you outside. I feared someone else might have been waiting in the yard. In fact, I was turning around to come after you when I heard Beth and realized it was her."

Gabriel felt the wet tears from my face fall to his chest. "Are you crying? Please don't cry," he begged and held me tighter.

"I can't help it. She scared me so bad, Gabriel," I said, wiping the tears from my face with my hand. "I didn't like her to begin with and now I just plain can't stand her!"

"Amelia, I promise I had not heard from her in weeks. As I implied, she came here for something and she had never come here for that before. I don't want to upset you further, but..."

I interrupted and sort of finished his sentence, "She used to summon you for booty calls."

"Like a pet," he described. "Honestly, Amelia, you are the first and only person I have ever shared my bed with." Gabriel emphasized the word "my".

Gabriel went on, "You are the only person I have ever felt comfortable enough to sleep next to."

"You mean to tell me that after she summoned you and you did what you all did, she sent you on your way?" I inquired.

"Pretty much. Most of the time I was dismissed to a room down the hall from her, but I really don't want to talk about her anymore. We really need to get some sleep," Gabriel said as he stroked my hair.

I leaned up and kissed him one more time goodnight. It made me feel sorry for him and elated all at once to know that I was the only person he had ever slept with in the literal since of the activity. As per usual, we drifted off to sleep in each other's arms.

***

Morning arrived entirely too soon. I was scheduled for the beverage cart again so I had set the alarm clock for 8:00 a.m. Even though I had gone to bed a little after eleven, the hour and a half that I was awake between three and five due to Gabriel's crazy ex-girlfriend and her drama, was already affecting my level of enthusiasm for the day. I did not want to get out of bed. I just wanted to sleep.

I reached over and smacked the top of the alarm clock, stopping it from that "Bonk! Bonk! Bonk!" noise that it was making. I rolled over and snuggled up to Gabriel and drifted back off to sleep. The next thing I knew, I rolled over and realized that the alarm clock had not gone off again. I had meant to hit snooze and instead hit off.

"Gabriel! Get up!" I screamed as I sprang from the bed.

Gabriel jumped up, startled as if someone were in the house again. "What?!"

"I am late for work! It's 9:15. Get dressed, you have to take me to the clubhouse!"

"Lord, Amelia, you scared the life out of me!" he responded as he calmed down and headed for the bathroom.

I quickly dug my uniform from my overnight bag and started putting it on. I was sitting on the bed putting on my socks and shoes when Gabriel returned.

I have a couple of calls to make before I go in so just take my car and then swing by here and pick me up on the beverage cart when you are near the fifth green," Gabriel instructed as he strolled through the room and proceeded to get his keys for me.

Gabriel returned to find me brushing my teeth. "Here's my keys," he said as he handed them to me. "Here's some orange juice and I have a bagel in the toaster oven for you. It should be done in just a couple of minutes."

"Thanks and you shouldn't have. I could have picked up something at the club. Alvin always takes care of me," I said without thought.

"Well, I take care of you now," Gabriel insisted as I rinsed and he slid the orange juice toward me.

"Thank you, Mr. Hewitt, and yes, you do take care of me quite nicely and I appreciate that," I said picking up the orange juice. I then leaned over and kissed him on his cheek.

"Surely you know that is not a proper good morning kiss," Gabriel responded as he pulled me into his arms.

"I do realize that, but I am late. I do not have time to start anything with you this morning."

"Who said anything about starting something?" Gabriel said as he slid his hands down my back and across my behind.

I started to let him kiss me, but remembered the night on the porch at the Hillman House and his warning about not stopping. I was now the one that did not want to stop. I stood on my toes and leaned into him and whispered, "I am not going to kiss you because if I did, I would not want to stop."

I said all that as I slipped my nose down his neck. Then, I let go of him, slipped from his arms and darted out of the bathroom with my make-up case in hand. Gabriel chased after me into the kitchen.

"One kiss and I will stop," he promised.

"Fine," I said while faking reluctance.

The kiss was sweet and short, keeping to his word. When he pulled back there was an expression on his face as if he was curious about something.

"What?" I asked.

"Later," he replied wiping the curiosity from his face. "I will ask you later."

"If there's something you want to know, ask now."

"Why aren't you mad about last night?" he asked as the look returned to his face.

"Should I be mad?" My response caused a confused look on Gabriel's face. Apparently he had expected me to be mad.

"Gabriel, who should I be mad with? Did you know she was coming over? Did you know what her intentions were? Had she given you any indication that she would stop up here in the middle of the night? Have you lied to the sheriffs about why she had a key?" I asked him all of the questions that would have changed my feelings about the situation.

"No."

"I am new to all of this stuff; relationships and the drama, but I see no reason to be mad with you because you had no control over her actions. Now, if you want to know if I'm mad with her, well, aren't you?"

"Yeah," he relented.

"And you are mad with her because?"

"She broke into my house and scared us half to death?"

"Don't say it like you are asking me if that's the right answer. There's no right answer and although that is why I might be mad with her, you have every right to be angry with her for your own reasons."

324

"Amelia, I want to be completely honest with you. I am going to call until I get her father this morning so someone will go see about her," Gabriel braced himself suspecting this would anger me, but it didn't. I was not fond of his involvement, but I would have done the same thing if she were a friend of mine.

"I knew you were going to," I said with a light laugh.

"You did? And you are okay with that?"

"You said once if we don't trust one another..."

Gabriel cut me off, "That's twice you have used my words this morning," he said.

I replied coyly, "Then you know I am listening. Now, I have to go. It's nearly 10:00 a.m. and you are supposed to be at work by then."

I backed up toward the door with make-up bag, keys and bagel in hand.

"Ugh!" Gabriel grunted. "I will see you at 10:15."

And, out the door I went.

***

In the parking lot I applied my make-up, less than usual, just mascara, a little blush and some lip gloss. Once inside the clubhouse, I loaded the beverage cart in record time, adding only enough to make it around the front nine. By 10:15 I had not seen a single golfer, but I did find Gabriel walking with his back to me on the cart path next to the fifth green. I had planned to turn off and pick him up at his house, but just as I was about to make the turn, there he was.

I slowed down and rolled to a stop next to him. I am not sure how he did not hear the cart behind him. I mean, we call it the shake mobile for a reason, but it appeared he did not.

"Care for a beverage, sir?" I said in my most professional cart girl voice.

Gabriel nearly jumped out of his skin. "Don't sneak up on people!" he screamed at me.

"I'm sorry," I quickly apologized. "I thought you would have heard this thing coming a mile away.

325

"No, I am sorry. You are right, I should have heard it. My mind is a million miles away." Gabriel got on the cart and took my hand.

"You are thinking of Beth," I observed.

"Yes. She was really out of her head last night. I think it was more than the alcohol. I tried calling her parents' house this morning, but got the machine again. I am afraid they might be out of town." Gabriel appeared to be truly worried.

"You aren't thinking of bailing her out are you?" I asked, hoping the answer was no.

"I really hope it won't come to that," he replied as he shook his head back and forth, appearing as unhappy with his answer as I was.

We drove the rest of the way to the clubhouse in virtual silence with the exception of speaking to the golfers we found and sold snacks to starting on the third green.

Quite the opposite of the day before, the weather was cooler and the course was slow. In addition to not making any sales, I was freezing. Gabriel reluctantly let me go home around 1:00 p.m. Thank goodness I did not really need the money since I only made thirty dollars in tips, a far cry from the day before.

The downside of getting off early was that Cara had called in sick, so I had to call Jay to come and get me. Although he knew better, Jay begged me to let him drive the Corvette out to pick me up. Of course I said no. I did agree to let him drive the C-10. He wasn't as thrilled, but he did it anyway.

Gabriel insisted that I have lunch while I waited, so I helped myself to the brunch buffet. One of the four top tables was taken up by Mr. Martin and the fellas playing poker, but otherwise the bar was empty. I took a seat at the counter and Matt shot the breeze with me while I waited.

I had not been sitting there eating long when a man's voice said, "Millie, right?" as the barstool next to me was being pulled out.

I turned my head to see who was speaking to me before I responded, "Yes, sir."

It was Mr. Graham from Friday night and he was taking the seat.

"Good afternoon, sir. May I get you a glass of tea or a Coke or something?" Matt asked as Mr. Graham took a seat.

Mr. Graham glanced at my plate and my drink before answering, "I will have what she's having and put her's on my tab."

"Thank you, sir, but mine is already on the house," I responded as Matt turned to get a glass of sweet tea for Mr. Graham.

"Well, can't blame a guy for trying," he said as Matt placed the glass of tea in front of him and handed him a plate for the buffet.

I was not the greatest at guessing people's ages, but if I had to guess, I would probably guess that Mr. Graham was a man of about fifty-five years old. His hair was maintaining most of its dark brown color, but he was starting to gray from his temples toward and just above his ears. It gave him a distinguished look. He was about as tall as Gabriel and dressed as though he spared no expense on his wardrobe. If he had only had a British accent, he could have easily been a contender to play James Bond.

Mr. Graham continued, "Millie, may I ask you something?"

"Sure," I replied.

"I know this may be inappropriate, but, is your aunt married or seeing anyone?" Mr. Graham asked.

What to say? What to say? No one had ever asked me about Aunt Gayle like that before. What would she want me to say? I decided to go with the truth and if he asked for her number, well, I did not know what I would do.

"She's not married and she is not seeing anyone that I am aware of," I replied.

"Good. Do you think she would mind if I gave her a call?" he asked.

"I suppose not."

No sooner had I answered did he ask for her number. I decided to give it to him. What could it hurt?

As Mr. Graham was about to step down from his bar stool to head into the dining room and make himself a plate from the buffet, Mr. Lockerby and Mr. Baker walked into the bar.

"Millie, we got a late start today, but had hoped to see you on the course," Mr. Lockerby said as he took out his wallet and slid a hundred dollar bill next to my plate.

"Tell your Aunt we really appreciate the other night," Mr. Baker said and not to be out done this time, he empties his wallet of five twenties and slid them next to the bill that Mr. Lockerby had laid down. Mr. Graham stood there watching in wonder.

"Thanks again, Mille!" The two men said in unison before looking to Matt. Matt passed a cooler bag full of God knows what over the bar to Mr. Lockerby.

"What's the damage, Matt?" asked Mr. Lockerby.

"Twenty," Matt replied and Mr. Lockerby handed him two twenties and told him to keep the change. Even though we were not allowed to sell alcohol on Sunday, I was fairly confident that Matt had given them some sort of hook-up, hence the fat tip. I could be wrong since they had just given me two hundred dollars for...

Mr. Graham waited and watched until the two gentlemen were back outside and driving away on their golf cart and Matt was distracted with the four poker players before he asked, "Millie, may I ask why they just gave you two hundred dollars?"

"You are welcome to ask, but I'm afraid you are going to have to ask Gabriel." My face was beat red and I am sure I was giving the wrong impression. "I cannot tell you, but I am sure Gabriel will be fine with telling you."

Mr. Graham looked bewildered and left for the buffet. I continued to eat my lunch and wait for Jay. No sooner had Mr. Graham returned with his lunch did Gabriel emerge from the kitchen and take a spot standing behind the bar in front of us.

Naturally, Mr. Graham did not wait until I left to ask Gabriel about the money and Gabriel responded.

"They paid her for sex," Gabriel said with a deadpan, straight face.

I shrieked! I could not believe he just said that! If my face had not been red before, it surely was then. I was embarrassed beyond belief.

"Seriously, they gave her the money for playing the other night. It sort of loosens up their wives and helps them to have a really happy night."

Mr. Graham laughed, "I don't know whether to think you are overpaid for your performance, Millie, or that their wives are undervalued for their performances. Do their wives know?"

"God, I hope not," I muttered not so under my breath.

Just then, Jay caught my eye as he came down the stairs. Jay entered the bar and I introduced him to Mr. Graham. He already knew Gabriel and Matt.

"Jay, have you had lunch?" Gabriel asked.

"Yeah, thanks anyway," Jay responded politely.

"Well, at least grab some dessert for coming out to get Amelia. There's cheesecake, chocolate cake and peach cobbler out there," Gabriel then handed Jay one of the smaller to-go boxes from behind the bar. "Why don't you help yourself while Amelia gathers her things."

While they were talking I had gotten up from the bar stool and was picking up my plate and saying goodbye to Mr. Graham. I then headed to the kitchen to put my plate away. Gabriel followed shortly thereafter.

I am not sure where Rudy or Alvin had gone, but Gabriel and I were the only ones in the kitchen. He caught up to me near the dish pit.

"I wish you did not have to go home," Gabriel said as he took my plate for me and put it in the dish pit for me. Then he took my hands and pulled me toward him.

"I know. I don't really want to go." I always hated leaving him, but this time was worse. I really hated leaving since things were not resolved with Beth and who knew what he was going to do once I left. I knew I just had to trust him.

"I will call you tonight," Gabriel insisted and he pulled me to him and kissed me.

***

On the ride home, I explained my entire weekend to Jay. I gave him the complete play by play of Aunt Gayle meeting Gabriel as well as the details of the middle of the night visit from Beth Reed.

"She just showed up in the middle of the night and let herself in?" Jay asked with concern.

329

"Yeah, and you should have seen how she treated the sheriff's deputies and the look on her face when they arrested her! Oh my God, it was priceless!" I laughed and laughed.

"And, Gabriel told you that she had never done that before," Jay seemed to be stuck on her just showing up out of the blue.

"Actually, while I waited for Gabriel to call and let me know to come get him, two calls came and each time I answered whoever it was just hung up," I explained. I had told Gabriel about the hang ups, but we never revisited it. "I think it was her. I mean, it makes so much sense now."

"If it was her, did she just think you were there and then leaving? Would she have shown up if she knew you were there?" Jay asked.

"I don't know, but if it wasn't her, then who else?"

"I don't know either, Millie," Jay said, shrugging his shoulders. "Perhaps you should get Emma's opinion on all of this."

Once home, we proceeded to get Emma's opinion. Emma believed Gabriel about Beth being there for a booty call. Both Emma and Jay had questioned me on if Gabriel and I had had sex yet. I said no. They questioned me about the reasons for waiting considering we were sleeping over with one another at every opportunity. I did not have a really good reason according to them.

Emma's final opinion on the subject of Gabriel was a blunt, yet cautionary one. "Millie, I don't want you to get your heartbroken, but if he isn't getting it from you, he's getting it somewhere. A man his age is not going without."

I then left them in living room and went to my room. I had had my fill of talking about it. What if she were right and what if that wasn't really Beth's first time over like Gabriel had said?

Jay followed after me catching the door as I was shutting it behind me. "Don't listen to her," Jay said. "She's right most of the time Millie, but not this time. I have seen the way he looks at you and he's not getting it somewhere else. I am sure of it."

"How can you be so sure?" I asked as tears started to stream down my face. Jay and I both sat down on the edge of my bed.

"He's the one for you, Millie, the one. It is way too soon for you to know it, but he knows it. I know he knows it and I would be willing to bet all of your money and what little I have, that he's discussed this with your buddy Daniel from the club." My stomach stirred with butterflies over Jay's words and the thought of being "the one" and Gabriel knowing it. I had not allowed myself to think beyond the moment with him. I always felt so caught up in awe around him that I did not dare think of him in the future, because I was still so surprised to be in the here and now with him.

Jay continued to reassure me, "Don't let Emma get to you. You are going to just have to trust me on this and trust him." Jay was barely a month younger than me, but he was my big brother.

Jay then hugged me and I thought about all that he had said.

"I do trust you both, but it is hard sometimes," I said as I wiped the tears on his shirt.

Jay could always be counted on to lighten the mood, "Anything worth having is always hard. You don't know so you will have to trust me on that as well."

Jay and I continued to talk and I also told him about my time spent against the inside surface of Gabriel's front door. That's when I was educated on dry humping.

"Whatever it's called, wow!" I said with a sigh remembering the moment.

"Millie, are you nervous about what your first time will be like?" Jay asked.

I felt a little weird discussing such with him, but was more comfortable discussing it with him than I would be anyone else.

"A little," I responded. "One of the girls at Young Harris described her first time as like letting someone else pick her nose."

"For some people it is like that," Jay conceded. "I have a feeling that you are not going to have an experience like that."

"How do you know?" I asked.

"Gabriel is priming you for it. I am sure he is experienced and that really does count for something. I don't care what the folks at church say." Jay spoke with such authority; I figured I would take his word for it. What else could I do?

Finally, we agreed that I would go and take a shower and after I did that we would share the dessert that he had taken from the club.

***

Gabriel called that night as he said he would. It was around 8:00 p.m. when the phone rang. I let it ring twice before I picked up.

"Hello?" I answered. I had kept the cordless phone charging all day until just before he called and I took it to my room so I would be ready.

"Amelia?" Gabriel asked as I answered the phone.

"Hi." I was so glad to hear his voice. I was always glad to hear his voice.

"I miss you and I don't usually miss people," Gabriel confided.

"I am glad," I responded.

"You are glad?"

"I am glad you miss me and if you don't usually miss people and you miss me, then that means I am special. I like that." I explained to him.

"You are fine with me confessing that I am somewhat emotionally damaged as long as it makes you feel special?" he asked.

"I guess when you put it that way, it does make me sound a little damaged as well."

"It's okay, Amelia. I will take what I can get when it comes to letting you know that you are special to me," Gabriel admitted.

He paused for a moment before he continued, "What must you have thought about my admission of you being the only person I have felt comfortable sleeping next to."

"What can I say?" I sighed.

"What am I going to do with you?" he laughed.

"I love to hear you laugh," I told him as I pushed my history book to the side.

332

"I love to hear you laugh too and you are really going to laugh over this. Well, you may be a little upset at first, but then you are going to laugh at my stupidity. I called several times throughout the day trying to reach Beth's family. I only got their machine time and again and no one has called me back yet. To make matters worse, I figured I would go down and see about bailing her out. Oh, don't worry, I was going to make her give me the money to bail her out, but when I got down to the sheriff's department I was told that she was bailed out at 6:00 a.m."

"I knew you were going to go down there and see about her. You know you could have called and they would have told you whether she was there or not," I said.

"Well, the kicker is that I have no idea who would have bailed her out. If it were her family, surely one of them would have called me. I mean, at least returned my call." I could tell from the sound of his voice that he was disgusted with the entire situation.

"Gabriel, I am so sorry. I don't know what to tell you. I can tell this is eating at you, but I just don't know what to say." I felt sorry for him because I knew he tried to help her and this was the thanks he got.

"It's okay, Amelia. I am sure you are glad I am done with her. Not that I wasn't done before, but I mean I don't want her nonsense in our lives and this was all just nonsense."

"My grandfather always used to say, 'You can't be nice to some people,' and I have a feeling Beth might be one of those people," I told him, trying to make him feel better about the situation.

"I know you are right," he replied.

I felt terrible about him being alone and I missed him. I thought about it before I asked, "Are you doing anything tomorrow morning?"

"No, why?"

"I was just thinking, I have not had a proper goodnight kiss and I think I would like one," I baited him.

"So you want me to drive there just to kiss you?" he asked and I could tell that he liked the idea of that by the way his voice lightened.

"Well, I thought it was implied by my question as to your plans tomorrow morning that you would sleep over," I went on to specify.

"Your offer is tempting, but I really should stay here. I hate to deny you a proper good- night kiss, but I am planning on having the locks changed on the house tomorrow." He may have declined my offer, but I was fine with him staying home if it meant that Beth Reed would no longer have access to his home.

Gabriel and I continued to talk and by the time we hung up it was well after 10:00 p.m. I fell asleep shortly thereafter knowing that I hated being apart from him. I was addicted.

CHAPTER 14

Thanksgiving, 1995, was the day I learned the true meaning of "Home is where the heart is."

Gabriel had me come in earlier than most of the other staff to set up the dining room so that I would be able to leave first. All of my tables were finished and I did some clean-up work as I felt guilty about leaving early and certainly did not want anyone to think I was abusing my position as the boss's girlfriend. Shortly after 2:00 p.m., Cara approached me and told me to go and get changed. She and I had had an ongoing discussion all week about Gabriel meeting my entire family and how that was going to go.

I followed her instructions and changed in the ladies' locker room upstairs. When I was dressed, I left the locker room and found Gabriel changed and waiting on me at the top of the staircase. I would never get used to looking at him and being absolutely dumbstruck by the thought that he was mine even for a moment.

Gabriel looked as though he had showered. His hair was still damp and he had a glow about him. He had not shaved in a couple of days and looked very much the way he did the night we went to the Georgian Terrace, minus the suit. I had warned him that Thanksgiving in our family was a casual affair and advised him that he would be overdressed if he wore anything beyond a nice sweater and jeans. He had followed my instructions and wore just that, a navy blue sweater with a gingham collared shirt under it, light colored jeans and brown Timberland lace- up boots.

"You look amazing," I said to him. I squelched the urge to kiss him on sight.

"Thank you, but I believe I am supposed to say that to you, Miss Anderson," Gabriel said as he offered his hand to me. "I see you are wearing your pearls. I like that."

"They are your pearls. I am merely borrowing them and I thank you," I replied and I placed one hand on the pearls and accepted his hand by placing my other in his.

Gabriel had insisted on driving. He still could not drive a stick or we would have taken my car. Gabriel remained in the walking boot and cast and would be for another four or five weeks. His car also held all of the items I had made to take to Thanksgiving at Aunt Dot's house. I had made a red velvet cake, fudge, and green beans. They fit nicely in the trunk of the Legend with my suitcase.

Although he was reluctant to do so, I convinced Gabriel to pack a bag and stay over with me at Aunt Gayle's house. I think he resisted mostly because I warned him he would have to sleep in one room and I would have to sleep in another. Separate sleeping arrangements disappointed him. He agreed to stay one night as long as I agreed to stay with him at his house the remainder of the weekend. A compromise was met and his overnight bag was in the trunk next to my suitcase.

"So, tell me again where we are going today," Gabriel said as we headed for the gate at Port Honor.

"We are going to my aunt Dot's house. You will need to make a left and head toward I-20 when we get to the main road," I instructed.

"And Aunt Dot is???" Gabriel prodded.

"She is my grandfather's older sister. Her house is just down the road from the farm and she has been hosting our family's Thanksgivings as long as I can remember," I explained.

We stopped at the guard gate on our way out and Gabriel gave James three plates of food consisting of generous portions of everything that we had served on the buffet. James thanked Gabriel profusely and then we were on our way. Gabriel made the left onto Highway 44 as I had instructed and we headed toward Greensboro and I-20. We would get on I-20 about two miles before the actual town of Greensboro.

Once on Highway 44, I went ahead and gave Gabriel the next portion of the directions, "When we come to I-20, you will need to get on and go toward Augusta."

"Okay. So, how many people will be at Aunt Dot's today?" he continued with his questions.

"I am not sure," I paused for a moment to think about who all would be there based on how things usually went. "It just depends. Most everyone typically arrives between 10:00 and 11:00 a.m. They eat lunch at noon and then most everyone sticks around for dinner, but a few folks leave and go to in-laws' houses, some just go home. By the time we get there, I think there will be about twenty folks still there."

"Twenty people?" Gabriel sounded a little shocked.

"Yeah, give or take. Shall I list them or would you like to just be surprised with all of the introductions?" I asked.

Gabriel half-heartedly laughed, "Surprise me."

We rode in silence the remainder of the six miles from Port Honor to the interstate. As we approached the on ramp, I reminded Gabriel of the directions. "You need to go east toward Augusta."

"But we aren't going all the way to Augusta are we?" Gabriel asked while making the turn onto the ramp with a little hesitation in his voice

"No. The distance will be about the same as if we were going all the way to Augusta, but we are going to get off in about three exits. Be on the lookout for the 'Norwood/Washington' exit. You will need to take that exit and at the end of the off ramp, you will make a right and go toward Norwood." I was notorious in my family for failing to give directions until we were almost past the turn, so I was doing my best to give Gabriel the directions well in advance.

"You tell me to turn toward Norwood as if I know where Norwood is," Gabriel observed.

"No, I just trust that you will read the road signs," I smarted off to him.

Gabriel was already holding my hand as he drove and he gave it a little squeeze in reprimand, "Oh, Miss Anderson, no one likes a smarty pants."

"Speaking of smarty pants, you are very likely to meet my cousin Dixon today. He is not smart, but he does not realize that," I began to explain.

"What do you mean, not smart?"

I continued, "He was diagnosed with something as a child, but I don't know what it was. There's just something that's off. He's really the sweetest thing."

"He's not bright enough to know he's not bright?"

"That about sums it up." I could have stopped there with my warning, but I really wanted everyone to like Gabriel and I knew how

Dixon could get on folks nerves, so I went on. "I just wanted to warn you so you did not get frustrated with him and say something that could be perceived as mean. The most disappointed I ever made my grandfather was when I made fun of Dixon to his face one day and Granddaddy heard me. Needless to say, I got the beating of my life and was forced to apologize to him. He really is as sweet as can be, but just...you will see."

"Is there any chance that I will just be able to avoid him?" Gabriel asked, bringing my mind back to the topic of Dixon.

"Not a chance. I hate to break it to you, Mr. Hewitt, but you are likely going to be the bell of the ball."

"Why is that?" Gabriel asked.

"Because aside from the boy down the street, you are the only person I have ever brought home, let alone to Thanksgiving or any sort of family function." My answer made me wonder how many times had other girls taken him home to meet the family, so I asked.

"Short of the one you know about, this is it," he responded. I was relieved by his answer, but turned my head so he would not see the glee on my face.

The telephone poles and pines clicked by like boards on a fence as we sped along I-20 and before we knew it we were approaching the exit.

"You did say the Norwood/Washington exit right?" Gabriel asked.

"Yes. You need to start slowing down, the ramp has a pretty harsh curve and it has scared me a time or two when taking it too fast," I cautioned.

"Toward Norwood, right?"

"Right."

Within moments we were passing through the blip of a town called Norwood. All that was left of it was a caution light, a convenience store and a gas station. Like many dots on the map in this area, it was a relic of a bygone era.

We continued on through Norwood to Warrenton, which were only five miles apart. The stations from Atlanta faded on the radio just before Warrenton so with his permission, I tuned the radio to WSGA a country station out of Thomson, Georgia. For the longest time that was the only radio station we could pick up at home and every single Saturday of my youth, I endured the Old Radio Hour. The DJ was notorious for playing music that made Hank Williams, Sr.'s look modern. When he wasn't playing country music from the dawn of time, he was allowing most anyone over the age of ninety to call in and shrill their way through their favorite gospel song. My personal favorite was "Bringing in the Sheaves" sung by Mrs. Bessie Stevens on her one hundredth birthday. Although I would never do it in front of Gabriel, my imitation of Mrs. Bessie had gotten me a ton of laughs in the family and among my friends over the years. The Old Radio Hour might have been offensive to my young ears back then, but it was a staple of my childhood and I would give anything to be sitting back at the kitchen table listening politely with Granddaddy.

WSGA was already playing Christmas music this particular afternoon. Gabriel and I sang along to "Jingle Bell Rock" as we made the turn onto the Gibson Highway.

"What's your favorite Christmas song?" I asked him.

"'White Christmas' by Bing Crosby. What about you?"

"'O Holy Night' by my aunt Gayle and the church choir."

"Can you sing it too?" Gabriel asked.

"No. I cannot hit the high notes like she can and I hate it when anyone butchers that song, including me."

We continued to sing along with the Christmas carols and it wasn't long before we had made it from Warrenton almost to the city limits of Gibson.

"What is that?" Gabriel asked as he pointed off to the left hand side of the road. There was the foundation and shell of a house that had clearly been there for quite some time.

"That's what was going to be the sheriff's new house," I responded.

"What do you mean by 'was going to be'?" he questioned.

"The man that is the sheriff of Glascock County has been the sheriff for years and years. He has a farm and a nice big house over near where Jefferson, Warren and Glascock counties meet on the far side of the county. The story is that he decided that he was tired of driving all that way to work, so he bought the land over here and started building. When he finally brought his wife by to surprise her with the new house, with the construction well under way, she told him there was no way she was moving or living in the city. Construction stopped that very minute and that house has been that way for twenty years or more."

"Wow! All that money just wasted," Gabriel observed. "It looked like it was going to be a good sized house."

"Yep. Now, you are going to need to make a left onto East Main Street and head toward Avera," I instructed.

We were almost to Avera and I had given the last few directions, but there was a question eating at me. "I hope you don't mind me asking," I said trying to soften the coming question, "but, what was Thanksgiving like in your family and when is the last time you went home?"

"I have not been to what one would consider home since the day I entered the Navy," he responded and my heart sank. I could not imagine not going home for Thanksgiving or any major holiday for that matter.

Gabriel continued, "When I was little, holidays were great. My sister and I were the center of our parents' universe and my mother made a big deal of everything..." I cut him off. This was the first I had heard of him having a sister. How had I not heard of her before?

"You have a sister?" I gasped.

"I had a sister," he corrected.

"What happened to her?" I asked.

"Same as my parents," he responded hanging his head and looking away.

I decided not to press him. It was a strange answer and I was certain that there was a story there, but I would continue to wait for Gabriel to tell me in his own time and without my probing. I also did not want to spoil the day by having him relive whatever had happened to them.

"We are almost there."

"Good, because this conversation will keep until later," Gabriel said as he started to apply the brakes and slow the car for the turn. "I promise I will tell you everything sometime, but I don't want to put a damper on the day."

"Alright," I said and he turned back to me. "Whenever you are ready is fine."

It was a short distance from the last turn to the next one, so I again reminded him of the turn, "Now, you are going to need to take the second right onto Hadden Pond Road. It's not much farther."

I commented on the landscape as we made the turn, "You know since Thanksgiving is a day to be thankful, can I tell you how thankful that it is sunny today. You are probably noticing and have been noticing since we got off of the interstate that there is nothing but fields and pine trees down here. This time of year, what's left of the fall colors are beautiful when the sun is shining, but when it is overcast, and thanks to the volume of empty fields, it can look a lot like a barren wasteland down here. So, today, I am thankful that it is sunny and you hopefully get to see it the way I see it."

In all of my rambling about being thankful, I almost let him drive right past Aunt Dot's driveway. We were nearly next to the mailbox when I realized and screamed, "Dang it! That's the driveway right there."

"Are you kidding? You mean the one we just missed?" Gabriel asked as he brought the car to a stop. He checked behind us and then backed up and turned into the driveway.

"Sorry," I said.

Of course, several of the men folk were milling around in the yard and noticed what had just happened. By the time we were parked in the driveway, they were on us like a swarm of locusts. Uncle Jim was among those who approached the car.

We were getting out of the car when Uncle Jim greeted us. "Hey! Can we give you folks a hand with anything?"

Uncle Jim was Aunt Dot's husband and one of my favorite family members. He had all sorts of interesting stories from when he served in World War II. I could not help, but brag on him when I introduced him to Gabriel.

"Uncle Jim, this is Gabriel," I said as I finished giving Uncle Jim a hug. Uncle Jim extended a hand and Gabriel reciprocated.

I continued the introduction as they shook hands, "Gabriel, you are in for a treat. Uncle Jim here is a real live war hero from World War II. He stormed the beaches at Normandy. You will have to get him to tell you about it."

Next, I introduced Uncle Bud and Cousin Dixon and handed them each an item from the trunk to take inside. Cousin Dixon loved homemade candy as much as Jay's dad so I usually made a paper sack full just to take home with him.

"You can go ahead and put that in your truck so no one gets it if you like," I told Dixon as I handed him his bag of candy.

"Thanks," he said as he pulled me into a giant bear hug, squeezing until I screamed for him to let me go. His hugs tend to hurt a little.

Gabriel stepped toward us with a look of concern for me. "Hey, you all can call me Gabe," he said as he stuck out his hand to Dixon. Dixon had to release me in order to shake Gabriel's hand which is what Gabriel intended. Dixon hung his head, a little bashful of new people like Gabriel, as he stuck out his hand to shake.

On our way to the house, Gabriel took my hand, the free one that wasn't carrying the remaining contributions to the food table and pulled me back so the other men folk would not hear what he had to say.

"Amelia, you did not tell me he was like Lenny from Of Mice and Men and you were the bunny," Gabriel discretely chastised me.

"Really?" I whispered back. "I thought that was exactly what I was telling you, but without the literary reference."

We continued on toward the door under the carport following Uncle Jim, Uncle Bud and Dixon. Uncle Jim and Aunt Dot's house was a modest one by Port Honor standards, but almost over the top for rural Jefferson County. It was a 1960s red brick ranch with black doors and shutters and white trim most everywhere else. It had four bedrooms and two and a half bathrooms, a dining room separate from the kitchen and a den separate from the living room. Multiple bathrooms and living spaces were all a luxury when it was first built.

Aunt Dot and Uncle Jim were not the over the top type, but had gotten a good deal on the house and land when the prior owner died and his children from Atlanta wanted to unload it quickly. They had lived in Birmingham, Alabama for most of the seventies and Aunt Dot wanted to move to Florida to retire. Since that was out of the question, she settled on moving back to Jefferson County where she grew up. When Granddaddy told her that one of the many Mr. Haddens had died and that the property was for sale so cheap, she and Uncle Jim jumped on it.

Once inside the house, the whole room turned to get a look at us. The mouths of my female relatives fell open at the sight of Gabriel. I do not believe he noticed at all.

Gabriel was taller than most of the men in my family; Dixon being the closest to his height, but Gabriel had him by an inch or two. Gabriel was about the same age as my Cousin Bonnie's husband, Doug, but in way better shape. One would think that Doug would have been a little more fit, since he had three children under age five to chase after, but no. Doug's only muscle was table muscle.

Gabriel was amazed by how many people were there. It appeared that everyone who had been there at lunch time had stayed for dinner and more had arrived. In a quick scan around the living room, I counted twenty. I could hear more people in the rest of the house.

Being the proper hostess, Aunt Dot was quick to greet us first, "Millie, Gayle said you were bringing someone and isn't he handsome!"

Gabriel and I both blushed.

"Aunt Dot, this is Gabriel." I had barely gotten the words out of my mouth before she was hugging Gabriel. Aunt Dot was a hugger. It was how she greeted most everyone.

I could see her face as she hugged him and mouthed at me, "Oh my God, he's cute!"

"You can call me Aunt Dot," she said as she released him.

"Nice to meet you, Aunt Dot, I'm Gabe."

"You come on with me, Honey, and we will get you something to drink." Aunt Dot had yet to let go of Gabriel following the hug and now she was pulling him off in the direction of the kitchen.

"Wait a minute," I said catching them just before the kitchen door, "I need to introduce him to everyone."

Aunt Dot promptly solved that problem. She turned to everyone in the living room and announced, "This is Millie's beau, Gabriel, but you all can call him Gabe."

Again the whole room turned to look at us. It was the first time I had seen Gabriel's face turn red. Aunt Dot then started to lead

Gabriel from the room with her arm locked in his at the elbow, "Let's see what Aunt Dot can find for you, Sugar."

I followed them to the kitchen as best I could while being stopped by most everyone along the way. Hug after hug after hug, by the time I made it to the kitchen, the folk in there were having a good laugh about how Aunt Dot had offered Gabriel, "Coffee, tea or me." I observed the conversation as I put the items I had brought on the buffet in the kitchen. Aunt Dot was a harmless flirt.

"Of course she says it's for medicinal purposes, but she's also got some Jack Daniels in the cupboard if you would like a Jack and Coke," Ben added as he made fun of his mother. Ben was Aunt Gayle's cousin and Bonnie's father. He was the oldest of Aunt Dot's three children. His philosophy was the same as my grandfather's had been: if he wasn't picking on you then you would think he didn't like you. He really liked his mama and it appeared he was well on his way to liking Gabriel.

"It is for medicinal purposes. I take it for my nerves," Aunt Dot added as she grabbed a dishtowel and snapped Ben's thigh with it.

"Then you are on your last nerve nightly," Ben yipped as he rubbed his leg in the spot where the dishtowel stung him.

"I will pass on the Jack and Coke, but thank you all for the offer," Gabriel said. "I would take some sweet tea if you have any."

"Lord, Sugar, do we have sweet tea?" Aunt Dot feigned insult at Gabriel implying that she might not have sweet tea. "That's the Champagne of the South; of course we have it!"

"So sorry. I thought Mint Juleps were the preferred drink of the South," Gabriel teased back.

"Don't you know anything?" Aunt Dot kept up the banter, "we only drink those in the summer when we wear petticoats and hoop skirts to bar-b-ques at the Wilkes.'"

"Ah, a Gone With the Wind reference, you thought I would fall for that," Gabriel said trying not to let Aunt Dot get the best of him.

Bonnie chimed in, "You would think, but she is actually telling the truth. Anyone who's anyone in these parts goes to a 4th of July costume party at the neighbor's down the road who just happen to be named Wilkes."

"NO!" said Gabriel with amazement.

"Yes!" Bonnie and Ben said in unison as Bonnie reached over and pulled a picture of Aunt Dot and Uncle Jim from the refrigerator.

"This is Nanny and Papa at this year's party," Bonnie said as she handed Gabriel the Polaroid. Gabriel took the photo and tried not to laugh.

"I see you want to laugh," Aunt Dot said faking a stern voice. "What? Do I not look like a Southern Belle?"

Gabriel could no longer contain himself. I intervened at that point, "Come on, Gabriel, there's some more people for you to meet."

I took him by the hand and led him through the house introducing him to everyone including Cousin Dixie. He did not say anything, but I could tell by the look on his face that he did not quite know what to make of her. She was an unfortunate looking soul, took after her daddy's side of the family. Her eyes were so big that when she was first born the doctor thought she had Downs Syndrome. Uncle Bud was quite upset since he had the same bulb-like eyes. Needless to say they stopped seeing that particular pediatrician as he was deemed incompetent for thinking "Downs Syndrome" as opposed to "Aww, she looks like her daddy." Furthermore, she was not like Dixon at all. She was quite smart. She and I were the same age and she had the same knack for music that I did. She was fond of the cello which everyone joked was just a big, giant fiddle and that she was trying to out-do me.

It was nearly 5:00 p.m. by the time we finished making all of the rounds of introductions. Bonnie approached us carrying her six month old son in one arm and her two year old in the other.

"Gabe, you like kids?" Bonnie asked as she handed Gabriel the baby and the two year old to me.

"Sure," Gabriel responded as if he had a choice since the baby was already in his hands before Bonnie had finished her initial question.

"His name is Bryce and he just ate so don't jiggle him around," Bonnie cautioned and Gabriel's faced turned to concern as he looked over at me.

"What can I say?" I responded to his look as I bounced Bryce's sister, Becca.

345

"Baptism by fire?" he replied as he held Bryce to him and started to sway a little.

"You two will be fine. Just hang on to them while I help heat everything back up and get things on the table for dinner," Bonnie said before returning to the kitchen.

Bryce was a bald little fella with big blue eyes. In Gabriel's arms, they could have easily passed for father and son just due to the shared eye color. For just a brief moment, I allowed myself to imagine and just when I thought Gabriel could not have been any hotter, he was. That baby made him damn sexy. Who knew babies could do that?

I was brought back to reality when Gabriel asked: "Wanna trade?" and he tried to hand Bryce to me.

"Nope." I shook my head in the negative as I made funny faces at Becca and she squealed and laughed at the sight. "He suits you and he just ate."

At that moment Doug came chasing their oldest through the living room where we were holding his other two children.

"Come here, Brian!" Doug yelled. Brian, the five year old, paid no attention and ran figure eights between Gabriel and me as Doug continued the chase.

"Stop right now, young man!" Doug ordered in that booming voice that only dads can do, but all children still ignore.

Conversations in the room were starting to turn to the commotion. My family was a fun loving bunch, but they were quick to criticize each other for their parenting skills or lack thereof. Brian and Doug were on their third lap around us when Gabriel threw out a leg and tripped the tyke. I gasped at Gabriel tripping him, but Brian took just enough of a tumble that Doug was able to lay hands on him.

Gabriel responded to my gasp, "He's close to the ground. Trust me, it did not hurt him."

"Thanks, man," Doug said as he patted Gabriel on the back and drug Brian away under his other arm.

"You are not right!" I said with a snicker.

Gabriel leaned in and whispered, "I will tell you what's not right and that's your Cousin Dixie. That's a dude in a dress."

At that point my snickering turned into full blown, head thrown back laugher. Becca squirmed as I laughed and repeated, "Dixie ain't right."

I laughed harder, "Now, look what you have done. She's not a dude and she is sweet."

Aunt Gayle entered the room. We had last seen her in the dining room helping to sit out items for dinner. "What are you two laughing at?" she asked as she took a spot standing next to us.

Becca answered in her sweet little voice, "Dixie ain't right."

Aunt Gayle tried not to laugh and struggled to remain composed, "Amelia Jane Anderson, did you tell that child to say that?"

"She did!" said Gabriel and I shot him a look of 'you are in trouble'.

"Millie! Shame on you!" Again, Aunt Gayle tried not to laugh as she got on to me. She was not doing a good job of holding it together, so she quickly made an excuse to leave the room. We could hear her in the kitchen laughing and quietly trying to explain to Aunt Dot what she was laughing about.

Once Aunt Dot quit laughing, she called for everyone to come to the dining room. Gabriel and I followed the crowd still holding Bonnie's children. Gabriel was amazed by the food set out around the room. My family tended to over-do it when it came to most any family meal. Although there was not the volume that had been on the buffet at the club earlier, we made up for it in variety.

Chairs had been removed from the dining room table and scooted to the edge of the room. The entire table was covered with food: turkey and ham at one end, salads including pear salad, potato salad and congealed salad, followed by every side item you could imagine. The antique sideboard was covered with desserts. The card table held drinks and Cousin Ben's second wife, Martha, was still filling red solo cups with ice and her daughter, Marie, was pouring tea.

Uncle Jim stepped forward from the lot of us and spoke. "If you all would join hands, please. Dot and I would like to thank you all again for being here this year. I thought we would take a moment and go around the room and tell what we are thankful for this year before we say grace."

Aunt Dot was to Uncle Jim's right. "I will start," she said turning on her serious side. "I am thankful that most all of us have lived to see another Thanksgiving. And, for those of us who have moved on, I am thankful that their suffering has ended and they are at the table of our Lord today."

Bonnie was next and she chose to lighten the mood after Aunt Dot's seriousness. "I am thankful that Millie is not married and does not have kids of her own so that she could hold mine," Bonnie said with a laugh.

The thankfulness continued around the room. It finally came to Aunt Gayle. She hesitated a little before she began; "You all know how my year has been so I am thankful that we have had such a good turn out again this year and if the good Lord willin' and the Creek don't rise, we will all be here again next year."

I was next to her and since I was still holding Becca, and Gabriel was holding my free hand, Aunt Gayle placed her hand on my arm that was supporting Becca. She gave my arm a little squeeze when she spoke about everyone being here next year. I looked at her and smiled. Although she had told me as much on the phone last Sunday, this was the first time I had seen her in person since the night she met Gabriel, so again she was assuring me that she approved.

I was next to say what I was thankful for that year. It would have been the truth to say that I was thankful that I had found Gabriel and things were going better than I could have ever imagined. I felt then was not the time and this was not the appropriate audience for that speech.

I gathered my nerve and spoke, "I like to think that Granddaddy is smiling down from Heaven on all of us today. Although I am still sad that he is gone, I like to think that he is still with us and I am thankful for the time I had with him. I am also thankful that Aunt Ruth made my favorite mac and cheese!"

Gabriel was on the opposite side of me from Aunt Gayle and he was up after me.

"Let me start by saying that I too am thankful that Millie is not married with children, because that would make today really awkward for me," Gabriel said and the whole room erupted in laughter.

"I like that guy," I could hear Uncle Bud say to Aunt Ruth.

348

"Next, I am very thankful that Amelia invited me to join you all and participate in your family Thanksgiving. Thank you all for having me. I really appreciate being included." Gabriel looked at me as if to thank me personally as he spoke his last sentence.

I also heard Aunt Ruth comment to Uncle Bud about how Gabriel called me Amelia. "I don't think I have ever heard anyone refer to her by her given name, except when they called her across the stage at her high school graduation."

As the rest of the family members continued the speeches around the room, I looked at Gabriel and thought how I liked the sight of him here with my family. He seemed to really be fitting in and I was thankful for that.

Finally, the speeches came to an end and Uncle Jim said the blessing and finally Bonnie and Doug came and took their children from us.

As Gabriel and I got in line for dinner, I whispered to him, "Aunt Ruth makes the best macaroni and cheese that you will ever put in your mouth. God only knows what the recipe is because she refuses to give it out."

"Alright, but why?" Gabriel said kind of loud as we each took a plate from the line.

"Shhh," I whispered and pulled him down toward me so only he could hear, "Most of the women have a signature dish and hers is the macaroni and cheese. The story is she gave the recipe out once, to Bill's first wife, Connie, and Connie showed up with that for Thanksgiving and it turned into a feud. You just don't show up with someone else's signature dish. Seriously, faces were slapped in the yard before tires were squalled on the way out of the driveway. The rumor is that that was the beginning of the end for Bill and Connie."

Aunt Gayle was in front of me in line and heard me. "Millie!"

"Well?" I returned as if challenging her to tell me I was lying.

Gabriel just laughed at us. "Isn't she bad?" he commented.

"I know! I thought I raised her better," Aunt Gayle leaned around me and replied to him.

We continued through the line and then found a space to take a seat back in the living room on the hearth of the fireplace with

Aunt Gayle. The brick from the hearth matched that of the exterior of the house.

"You kind of have to sit where you can find a spot," I explained.

"This is perfect, Amelia, you need to stop worrying if I am having a good time because I am." Gabriel said while he sat down next to me.

It was a real working fireplace and they were burning hickory wood in it. It smelled like memories of my childhood and the wood burning stove that Granddaddy had at his old house. It was the smell of winter. The fireplace gave off just the right amount of heat so that the bricks were warm when we sat down, but not scalding.

"Who made the butter beans?" Gabriel asked.

I had no idea, so I looked to Aunt Gayle to respond, "Aunt Dot made them."

"They are great. Everything is good, but those might be my favorite," Gabriel commented as he took another bite.

"Have you tried the macaroni?" I asked him.

"You were right, it is to die for and I am not a real fan of pastas including mac and cheese." Gabriel's plate had been piled up, but he was well on his way to clearing it.

The three of us continued to plow through our dinner and Aunt Gayle even cautioned Gabriel that he needed to pace himself and save room for dessert. Gabriel all but ignored her and ate like I had never seen him eat before. He asked first if it would be alright, and then returned for seconds. When he came back to his seat, he also brought one of the tea pitchers. He proceeded to refill everyone's cups.

Aunt Gayle and I waited for Gabriel to finish his seconds and then we took him to the dessert table. There were about twenty different cakes, pies and homemade candies. My red velvet cake was nearly gone, but a slice of it was the first thing both Gabriel and Aunt Gayle approached.

"Millie makes an outstanding red velvet cake," Aunt Gayle praised as she put a slice on her plate.

"Really? And are you the one that taught her how to make it?" Gabriel asked while placing a slice on his plate.

We sort of glazed over his question and went on to explain minced meat pie to Gabriel. Although he was supposed to be the chef among us, he had never heard of the stuff.

"It is nasty!" I exclaimed.

"It is not meat. It's mystery fruit," Aunt Gayle added.

"Granddaddy really liked it and I suspect that Aunt Dot only made it this year on the off chance that his ghost would show up," I lamented.

Busted! Aunt Dot was behind us. "I heard that y'all! Gabriel, you come sit by me and leave these bad influences. Here, Sugar, let me help you with that plate," Aunt Dot said as she took Gabriel's plate and piled it with her picks from the dessert table.

"Watch out for the fruit cake!" I yelled as she led him away. It wasn't just each of the people in my family that had a story. Most of the food had a story too and the story with the fruit cake is that it had so much liquor and sugar in it that it actually made now deceased Uncle Albert go blind for a day after he ate too much of it. Of course, the real culprit was likely that he was eighty and a raging diabetic.

Aunt Dot took Gabriel to sit at the kitchen table with all of the grown up relatives. Aunt Gayle warned me that if Gabriel did not run screaming into the night after being grilled by all of them, then he was definitely a keeper. Her warning left me wondering if she had put Aunt Dot up to that, but Aunt Gayle wouldn't do that. Would she?

I checked on him a couple of times and he was holding his own. They were quizzing him on everything from where he was from to how we met, to the fact that he was my boss. I was a little afraid that he would let something slip about the inheritance even though I firmly believed that it was the farthest thing from his mind.

Granddaddy had always been very private about his financial affairs and no one knew just what all was there. It was not that he wanted to keep them guessing, he just figured it was better that way and no one else's business. There was a real competitive streak in our family and the less everyone knew the more the competitive streak would be kept at bay.

There was a phrase by most of the other family members, "Must be nice." It was often used in situations like when Bonnie got a new car her little sister Marie said, "Must be nice." It was a way of letting someone know that you did not think they deserved whatever it was they achieved or bought as in the case of Bonnie and her sister and the new car. It was just jealousy. Granddaddy loved everyone, but he always hated that aspect of our family. He said we should be happy for one another's achievements, but also taught us never to expect them to be happy for us. Anyway, the family finding out any detail of my inheritance would have put a kibosh on the fun of this Thanksgiving.

Dinner wound down and all of the women folk pitched in to help clean up. Gabriel could have joined the men folk in discussing politics or sports or even watching sports with them in the den, but instead he came to find me and Aunt Gayle. I was washing and rinsing and she was drying the dishes when he found us in the kitchen. Aunt Gayle had amassed a pile of dishes waiting to be put away.

Gabriel kindly took the towel from Aunt Gayle, "I will dry and you put them away. I would put them away, but I have no idea where anything goes."

Soon we were finished with the clean-up. I wanted a little time alone with Gabriel, so I asked Aunt Gayle if she would mind if we went on to her house. It used to be Granddaddy's house, but it was hers now. I knew I did not have to ask, but they did raise me to be polite and considerate. Aunt Gayle said she would be along behind us in just a little while.

We said our good-byes to everyone. Gabriel thanked everyone again for having him. Aunt Dot invited him back for Christmas, which I had been planning to do if Thanksgiving had gone well and it had. When they finally turned loose of us, Gabriel and I locked hands and headed to the car and virtually across the road to Aunt Gayle's house.

As soon as we were alone in the car, we started rehash the evening.

"I hope you had a good time and you don't have to feel pressure to come back for Christmas," I said as I buckled my seat belt and we started down the driveway.

"Are you going to be here for Christmas?" Gabriel asked.

"I plan on it," I said before directing him to Aunt Gayle's. "You will need to go back to the left and then take the first driveway to the right."

"You plan on being here for Christmas?" he asked again as if he was confirming what I had said.

"Yes," I replied.

Gabriel made the turns as I had instructed while explaining to me, "Amelia, I will be where you are for Christmas. If you want to be here, then we are here. If you want to be in Hawaii, then Hawaii it is. If you just want to stay at my house, then that's what we will do. I am yours remember."

"Here is fine and I take it you had a good time," I responded as I pulled his hand to my lips and kissed it.

"I had a great time."

We continued down the driveway until we came to the house. When the headlights lit up the entire front of the house I announced, "Welcome to Stillwater Plantation. I meant to point out the historic marker by the road, but forgot."

"This is where you grew up?" Gabriel asked. He seemed amazed at the sight.

"Not entirely," I replied as he turned the car off. "Granddaddy bought the land and house out here when I was twelve. Before that, we lived kind of between Wrens and Stapleton."

"Again you say that like I know where these places are," Gabriel observed.

"Doesn't everyone know where Stapleton, Georgia is?" I asked as if it were as widely known as Atlanta or Savannah. "Come on, let's go inside. I need to give you the tour and we only have a few minutes before Aunt Gayle arrives."

"So why did you all move?" Gabriel asked as we got out of the car.

As I walked around to the trunk to help with our bags, I explained to Gabriel, "Aunt Gayle had always loved this house. One of her childhood friends used to live here. She was going to buy it, but they could not decide with which one of them I would live, so he bought it before she could and we all moved. In case you have not guessed by now, Granddaddy sort of liked to be the one always in control."

It took me all the way to the front door to finish that story. Once inside the house, I started giving Gabriel the tour, but that soon fell by the wayside. The farthest we made it in the tour was me showing Gabriel the room I would be sleeping in. Gabriel left the door open so we could hear if Aunt Gayle came in. He dropped his overnight bag next to the door and then backed me toward the bed. I hardly had one good kiss, which I had been dying for all day, when we heard Aunt Gayle open the front door.

"Hang on to that thought for tomorrow. I have a surprise for you," I said as I slipped from under him and darted for the door.

***

Watching Gabriel with my family on Thanksgiving; how well he fit in, how everyone liked him, how he looked holding Cousin Bonnie's baby, hearing the words he said, it cemented a feeling I had had for him for quite some time. As I had watched him throughout the evening, a sense of peacefulness came over me that I had never felt before. Not only did I love him beyond words, but I knew he was home to me.

CHAPTER 15

When we came in Thanksgiving Day, I had just assumed I would be sleeping in my old room. I had placed my things in there and did end up sleeping there, but nothing about it was my old room. I had taken a lot of my things with me when I moved away to college the first time and even more when I moved away the second time, but I did not take everything. Little to no trace of what I had left behind was still there. Little to no trace of my having live there at all was left as there were only a couple of pictures of me on the night stand. It was even different from when I was there and picked up the truck. Some families build shrines to their children in their former rooms when they leave home, but clearly Aunt Gayle and I were not like those families.

Although the new mattress, in what was so obviously now a guestroom, was quite comfy, the place just seemed a bit too much, too soon. My room was not the only one that had undergone an extreme makeover. Aunt Gayle had been remodeling and redecorating the entire house in the months since Granddaddy died and I left for college again. Perhaps she was trying to shake the fact that he had died there in the house or perhaps she was just trying to make it her own since she had gotten it as a part of her share of the inheritance.

With the exception of feeling as if I were at a totally different house, the improvements Aunt Gayle had made were great. The kitchen had been completely renovated adding modern appliances, new cabinets and countertops and the old, fake wood looking linoleum floor had been replaced with real tile.

The dark wood paneling in the living room had been sealed and painted heather green with white trim. The old shag carpet was taken up and hardwood floors had been put down, but not just in the living room, but throughout the house, except for the kitchen and bathrooms. In the living room she covered the hardwoods with a large rectangular carpet. It was primarily brown with magnolias on it. The color of the leaves on the magnolias matched the walls. Aunt Gayle even added a new overstuffed couch and two matching chairs. The color of the couch and chairs were the same as the blooms of the magnolias in the carpet. The entire room looked as if she had hired a decorator.

The only things in the room that remained and gave a hint of my former home were Granddaddy's favorite leather chair and my piano. Even those things shown in a new light next to all of the new stuff; the leather chair was the perfect shade of brown to match the brown in the carpet and the piano had family photos topping it that were in white frames that matched the white trim on the walls and the white frames on the walls. Everything had its place in the new room, but me.

The rest of the house was just as immaculate as the living room and the kitchen. Aunt Gayle had given Gabriel the tour after she got home from Aunt Dot's. I joined in and it was as if the both of us were seeing the house for the first time. The sad thing was that I liked the way the house used to be. I am sure I would like the new stuff, in someone else's house.

Why couldn't she have just slapped a coat of paint on the outside and called it a day? Lord knows the columns could use a few coats and there was rotted wood on the trim above the front door. This was like a culture shock. She should have just started fixing what wasn't entirely broken on the outside and worked her way in.

I almost cried myself to sleep that night thinking about how the house I had loved was so different. As I laid there in bed, all I could think is that I felt a little homeless. I tried to make myself feel better by thinking about The Jefferson and my apartment there and reminding myself that that was my home now. I also tried to take comfort in thinking about how I felt when I was with Gabriel at his house. I thought about the changes I was making and somehow that started to lessen the blow that the changes Granddaddy's house had undergone. Just thinking about Gabriel and reminding myself of how I felt seeing him fit in with all of my family, helped in starting to make me feel better. I hung onto those thoughts as I drifted off to sleep. I also wondered what he had thought of everyone and everything.

***

I awoke the morning after Thanksgiving to Aunt Gayle poking me. "Millie," she whispered as she gave me another slight jab in my shoulder. "Millie," she repeated.

I rolled over to avoid another poke. It was just too early, way earlier than I had grown accustomed to getting up those days.

"Millie, I have to go down to the Wilkes'. They've got a heifer in labor," I rolled back over toward Aunt Gayle as she sat on the edge of the bed. She proceeded to explain, "I don't know how long it will

356

take, so I wanted to say goodbye before I left just in case you were gone when I got back. I left some breakfast in the kitchen for you all."

I rubbed my eyes and leaned up to hug her. "Thanks for having us and for making breakfast."

"Of course," she replied. "I am going to tell you now, but you are probably so asleep that you might not remember; I really like Gabriel and he seems to suit you. I am so happy for you."

I was suddenly awake. "You like him?" I shrieked and sat straight up in bed and hugged her.

"Yes, and so did everyone else! After you all left, that's all everyone talked about," Aunt Gayle said as she hugged me back. She released me and pulled back to look at me. "My baby is growing up."

Aunt Gayle has never called me her baby before. Tears started to come to my eyes.

"Now you just dry those up," she demanded. "It's only 5:00 a.m., so go back to sleep and then get up all rested and pretty and go show that man the town."

"Show him the town? Seriously?" I asked as I wiped the tears away. We both kind of laughed a little.

"Well, show him the countryside. Anyway, have a good time and if I'm not back by the time you all have to leave, I love you." Aunt Gayle hugged me again and then left for the Wilkes' to birth a calf.

I listened as Aunt Gayle went through the house. I could hear her every step on the new floors until she went out the back door. I also heard her crank the truck. I heard it rumble down the driveway and fade into the distance down the road. When I could not hear the truck anymore, I thought about getting up and going into Gabriel's room. I resisted the temptation and went back to sleep.

It was nearly nine when I woke up again with the light shining through the windows. In the hours since Aunt Gayle had left and I went back to sleep, I dreamed of Gabriel. I awoke with an anxiousness to see him. I went to the bathroom and brushed my teeth and washed the sleep out of my eyes before I went to find him.

I tiptoed down the hallway and found Gabriel in another of the guest rooms. He was in bed and appeared to still be asleep. He

357

was lying flat of his back and looked so peaceful that I was hesitant to disturb him. I was not so hesitant that I resisted though. Aunt Gayle still had not come back, so I eased into bed with Gabriel. There was definitely a taboo feeling about climbing into bed with him. No matter how many modifications Aunt Gayle might make, it would always be Granddaddy's house.

I cuddled up next to Gabriel, laying my head and torso against his chest. I draped an arm across him resting my hand on his shoulder, almost hugging him. His skin was so cool against my face. He did not flinch at my presence until I ran my leg up his stopping my knee just shy of his crotch. Just as I stopped, Gabriel began to stir. He reached over and ran his hand up my leg starting at the back of my knee and ending at the line of my panties. His hand had brushed against the shirt I was wearing which was now hiked up above my underwear.

"Your legs are so smooth," Gabriel admired as he started to wake up.

"I forgot my pajamas," I whispered while feeling his hand grab a fist full of the shirt I had on.

"What are you wearing?" Gabriel asked as he started to open his eyes.

"One of your t-shirts. I hope you don't mind, I got it from your bag while you were in the shower last night," I explained as I moved my arms back rolling a little and propping myself up on my elbows so I could see his face better.

"Do I mind? I actually like the idea of you sleeping in my shirt," he said before he let go of the shirt and returned his hand to my thigh.

"Good, because I think I am going to keep this one," I smiled at him.

"I am getting used to waking up next to you," he smiled back.

I hung my head to hide the excitement his words ignited in me. The spark was still there every time we touched and when he said things like that to me, I felt like my insides were going to explode. It was like something inside me wanted to jump out of my skin and do cartwheels or a victory dance. I wondered if that feeling was written all over my face. He was still more experienced with all of this than I was, so I was constantly unsure of how much to let him see.

Gabriel reached over and lifted my head by my chin. "Don't you like waking up next to me?" he asked.

I was not sure if I had completely shaken off the stupid grin that I knew had come over my face so I bit my lip. I thought for a moment before I answered. I had decided that I was going to risk telling him I loved him today, but this was not the time and not a part of the plan.

"Waking up next to you or even seeing you wake up is among my favorite activities these days. Sometimes I fear you are going to get bored with me since most of our time together is spent sleeping next to one another." As I had answered his question, a goofy grin came over Gabriel's face.

"I have been thinking the same thing, wondering if you were going to get bored with me and this." Gabriel rolled me onto my back and smoothly and suddenly he was on top of me. He had certainly become more proficient with the cast. Things were about to get hot and heavy, but I stopped him.

"I don't think I could ever get bored with you and I don't want you to get bored with me. I have actually planned something for today," I said all of this as Gabriel planted soft kisses along my neck.

"Please don't misunderstand," I said as I arched my hips up to him, "it's not that I don't want to do this with you, I just think I have a better place in mind. There's something I want to show you today. As I mentioned last night, I have a surprise for you."

"Then I suppose we should get up and get dressed," Gabriel sighed as he rolled off of me and onto the other side of the bed.

"Right," I said as I got up from the bed. With my back to him and with only one hand, I pulled his shirt over my head and threw it over my back to him. I looked over my shoulder to make sure he was watching and he definitely was. He sat up in bed to take in the view as I strutted from the room wearing nothing but my white lace boy shorts panties and my hair flowing down my back.

"Miss Anderson, you did not just do that!" Gabriel gasped. "I thought you said you were keeping the shirt."

"You don't have another one, plus I might take it back from you in a little while," I called back to him from down the hall.

"Now get up and get dressed!" I yelled.

I applied my make-up as quickly as possible, pulled on some jeans, cowboy boots, a button up shirt and braided my hair in a single pony tail which I pulled to one side. I met up with Gabriel in the kitchen. He was dressed almost as casual as I was with a Navy football sweat shirt, jeans, a tennis shoe and the walking boot over the cast. We ate the breakfast that Aunt Gayle had left us standing around the new kitchen island.

"When do I get my surprise?" Gabriel asked as he polished off his second country ham biscuit.

"It is not something you get. It something you..." I paused and considered it. It could be something he would get, one day. It was something that I hoped to get one day. I started again, "You are just going to have to wait and see and let me explain then."

I finished my biscuit and we killed off the orange juice. I sat the glass in the sink and turned back to Gabriel with my back against the sink. "I know you can't ride a horse in that cast," I said, as I let my eyes fall toward his cast, "but you think you can manage riding on a 4-wheeler with me?"

"I am not crippled, Amelia," Gabriel replied as he stood in front of me propped against the kitchen island.

"Ok, then let's go," I grabbed the canvas cooler from under the kitchen sink and slung the strap across my body. Then I took Gabriel's hand and led him out the back door of the house and to the barn.

As threw open the huge barn door, I explained to Gabriel about the 4-wheeler. "I was taught to save, but since I did not have to save for a car, when I turned sixteen I used a portion of my savings to buy this."

The door of the barn glided open with my all of weight behind it to reveal a shiny, red full sized 4-wheeler. "I got in some real trouble over this thing. One of my friends got her driver's license before me and was allowed to drive in Augusta. I had her take me to Augusta one afternoon to the Honda dealership and I bought this brand new. I bought it without Granddaddy or Aunt Gayle's permission, paid cash and had it delivered the next day. You should have seen the look on the sales guy's face. I will never forget it. He just about passed out when I opened the Piggly Wiggly paper sack full of cash and handed it to him. I had called a few days before and found out the exact amount to bring with me."

I laughed as I told Gabriel the story. "My God they were furious. It came while I was at school and the delivery guy had quite the showdown with Granddaddy about being the right house or not. When I got home that afternoon, well, needless to say I was not allowed to ride it for a solid month. They almost made me return it and Granddaddy probably would have returned it himself except that he was in between trucks at the time and the old Chevy was in the shop. He could not very well get it back to Augusta in the T-bird."

"It looks brand new," Gabriel observed as he ran his hand from the rear rack up the seat over the body and to the left side handlebars. He stepped back and took an admiring look at it.

As he stepped back I threw a leg over and climbed on. I sat the cooler between my legs and let it rest on the body of the 4-wheeler in front of the seat.

"Yeah, this barn has kept a lot of things looking brand new over the years," I said referring to my Corvette.

"I would have killed for one of these things when I was sixteen," Gabriel commented while he climbed on behind me and I cranked it up.

"Hold on tight," I told him. He grabbed hold of me around my waist and I put the 4-wheeler in reverse and backed it up out of the barn.

The driveway was an eighth of a mile in distance before it reached Hadden Pond Road, the primitively paved road. The driveway was little more than a tire track, red clay road with mature pine trees on both sides. I opened up the throttle on the 4-wheeler along the length of the driveway. I felt Gabriel squeeze and hold me tighter as I accelerated.

At the end of the driveway, I stopped to look for traffic before making the right turn on to the paved road. I also wanted to make sure that he was okay with the speed and my driving thus far. I asked and he responded, "The speed did not bother me until your hair hit me in the eye."

"Oh, God, I am so sorry. Are you alright?" I asked as I looked over my shoulder.

Gabriel had let go of me when we stopped and he was rubbing his right eye a little. "It just stings a little, but nothing that will keep me from my surprise."

"Good. We have to run an errand in town first and then the surprise. Okay?"

"It sounded like you just said we were running an errand in town first?" Despite the rumbling of the engine, I could hear the skepticism in Gabriel's voice.

"That's exactly what I said," I replied because taking the 4-wheeler to town was perfectly natural to me. Everyone around here did it.

"My Lord you are country," he shook his head in disbelief.

"Wearing it with pride, Mr. Hewitt," I replied as I hit the gas catching him off guard and causing him to nearly go off the back of the seat. He grabbed hold of me quick and tight and I could feel him shake against me as he laughed.

I did not make the left to go back to the main road that we had come in on yesterday. I stayed straight until I got to Main Street where I made a left. The elderly couple that lived caddie cornered to the old ball field was already out on their porch for the day and waived at us as we drove by. Gabriel released one of his arms from around my waist and we both waived back.

That was not the only elderly couple already out in their porch chairs. Every other house had spectators who watched cars, trucks, tractors, combines, 4-wheelers and golf carts pass by all day. These people had been manning their posts all my life and had watched me grow up. Gabriel and I waived to each one as we passed and they waived to us.

We reached the caution light at the main road and I stopped to check for traffic. Right across from where we were sitting was the heart of Avera.

As the engine idled and we waited for a truck and a tractor to pass, I could hear Gabriel say, "That has to be the oldest and smallest strip mall in America."

I laughed. For all I knew, he could have been right. It was definitely the smallest in these parts. It was definitely old, but whether it was the oldest around I did not know. What Gabriel had referred to as a strip mall was actually a series of four buildings with a shared parking lot. To the far right end, in the direction of Stapleton and Wrens, was the Avera Post Office. In the middle was a now defunct gas station with the antique Amoco sign still standing out by the road. It had closed down about three years ago when the owner, Mr. Jake, died. My grandfather had been good friends with him and bought gas there until the day Mr. Jake died.

The main part of the shopping center was an old brick building. The bricks were the color of Georgia clay, an abundant source for brick in these parts. The building had massive picture windows that along with a wooden porch running the length of the building, and leaning a little closer to the ground on the front end, made up the front of the building. The windows were gray from years of dust build up and you could hardly see in. I suppose it was the poor man's version of window tinting.

There were two shops that made up the old brick building, but only one of them was still in business. The other had been closed and used as a storage facility since before my time. The business that was still thriving was the Avera General Store. It was run by another of Granddaddy's friends and his wife. He was the butcher and she was the cashier. You could find anything in there from steaks to stakes, can goods to canning supplies and in the day where the can was king, you could still find a Coke in a glass bottle.

The road cleared, so I hit the throttle and across we went. I parked in one of the parking spaces right out in front of the grocery store. I shut the 4-wheeler off.

"Let's go," I told Gabriel.

I waited for him to get off and then I got off. I brought the little cooler with us. I offered Gabriel my hand and led him toward the front door. When we stepped up onto the porch the ancient wooden planks gave and dipped a little more toward the ground. The planks were about ten feet long and they ran perpendicular to the front wall of the building making a bit of an uphill walk to the door.

The bowing of the floor boards of the porch caused the roof to also dip and the tin to make a sound like rolling thunder. I was looking ahead to the door when, through our joined hands, I felt Gabriel pause. I looked back to see him checking the sky for clouds.

"Gabriel, it was the roof. Watch," I said as I jumped causing the whole porch to bounce and the tin roof boomed time and again like a summer storm.

"Don't do that! This thing might fall on our heads!" Gabriel clutched my hand and demanded.

"Come inside and let me get what we came for and be on our way scaredy-cat," I chuckled as I rolled my eyes at him.

I pushed the rickety door open and we went inside. The lighting was bad and the floors on the inside were not much better than those of the porch, but I looked beyond all of that. I was not sure if Gabriel could.

Mrs. Poole was perched behind the register when we entered. "Good gracious! Millie, I almost didn't recognize you!"

Like I believed that, I had been coming in that store since I was born. Mrs. Poole was a dark haired lady of about seventy with cat-eye shaped glasses that hung on a chain around her neck. They had been hanging like that ever since I had known her and I could not recall ever seeing them on her face. When I was little, Mrs. Poole was my favorite person because she had been letting me help myself to M&Ms from the candy cabinet since I was tall enough to reach inside. I had changed little since I had seen her last which was the day I picked up the Chevy truck, so for her not to recognize me, well that was just her way of making small talk.

"Who's your friend?" Mrs. Poole asked and I made the introductions.

"Mrs. Poole, do you happen to have a couple of empty and clean milk jugs?" I asked.

"Sure do," she answered as she moved from behind the register to fetch the jugs for me. I followed her and Gabriel followed me and we all went down the front aisle, across the store and down the aisle that ran the length of the wall on the left hand side of the store. Almost all the way to the meat case in the back where Mr. Gerald was standing, Mrs. Poole stopped and reached up on a shelf and pulled down two milk jugs. When she turned and handed me the milk jugs, she asked if we were going to the springs.

"Yes, ma'am," I replied as I accepted the jugs. I took them and undid the strap on the cooler. I ran the strap through the handle of the jugs and secured them to the cooler.

"What else could I get for you?" Mrs. Poole asked.

"I don't suppose you have any Brunswick stew ready yet?" I asked.

"I believe it should be ready," she said as she started back up front.

Gabriel and I followed and as we turned from the side aisle back to the one that ran along the front windows, I stopped at the big, red Coca-Cola chest cooler. I slid the top of the right side open and reached in and pulled out two ten ounce bottles of Coke.

I continued to hold the chest cooler open. "What would you like? There's Coke, Yoo-hoo, Sprite, Dr. Pepper, A&W, all in bottles. It's all better in real glass bottles."

Gabriel smiled, "Most people say that about beer, but I have never heard anyone say that about sodas before."

"You spent too much time at Annapolis, if you are calling it soda," I replied. "Surely you know that in the South, 'Coke' is universal for everything with carbonation."

"Miss Anderson, you are such a smarty pants," Gabriel sighed as he reached in the cooler and pulled out a Coke. I reached in and grabbed a second for him. I put the two I had pulled out for myself in my canvas cooler which I was still carrying strapped across me. I put the one for Gabriel in there as well and offered it to him to put the Coke he was holding in too.

"Would you like any snacks: M&Ms, peanuts, chips or anything?" I offered.

I reached in the candy cabinet and grabbed my usual, peanut M&Ms. Gabriel took a bag as well. I also grabbed two bags of Tostito chips for us and then headed toward the counter. Mrs. Poole was waiting.

"How much stew would you like?" Mrs. Poole asked.

"Two pints," I replied. "Rice on the bottom if you have it."

"Anything for you, Millie," Mrs. Poole smiled and turned to dip the stew from the pot on the hot plate on the counter behind her.

"We are also going to need a couple of spoons and if you could spare a bottle opener, I will take one of those as well," I asked.

Mrs. Poole reached below the counter where the register sat and pulled out all of the supplies I had asked for and started putting them in a small paper sack with the pints of stew. I took the paper bag, folded it over the top and squeezed it in the cooler with the four bottles of Coke.

I pulled out cash from my jeans pocket with the intent to pay for everything when Gabriel also pulled his wallet from his jeans. We argued for a moment as he protested me paying.

"This is my day to treat," I insisted.

Gabriel leaned in and tried to whisper, so that Mrs. Poole would not hear, "What will this lady think if I let you pay for all of this?"

Mrs. Poole was standing right there and she might have been late in life, but she was not deaf. "Mrs. Poole, so we are clear, Gabriel here is quite the gentleman. One of the best I have ever known. Short of me cooking at my house for him and some friends, this is the first time he has ever not paid." I then looked to Gabriel, "Are we good now?" I asked as I handed my money to Mrs. Poole.

"She's used to getting her way, so I would let her if I were you," Mrs. Poole said in observation to our back and forth over who was paying.

After I paid, I packed everything in the cooler and out to the 4-wheeler we went. Again, I got on first and secured everything, the cooler and the milk jugs were placed in the space in front of me. I suppose I could have strapped it all to the rack on the back, but I had to reserve that for Gabriel to sit as there was not quite enough room for both of us on the seat.

We headed back from downtown Avera the way we came, but instead of staying straight onto Hadden Pond Road and going back to Aunt Gayle's house, I did not cross over Southern Road. I turned to the left onto it. It was barely a few feet from the turn that the pavement ran out. We continued down the dirt road about a quarter of a mile before making a right onto yet another dirt road, Seven Springs Road.

All the while, I gave the 4-wheeler the gas and we sped along with dust, dirt and clay flying up behind us. The sides of the road were thick with woods on each side. There were a couple of abandoned logging roads that jutted out from time to time on each side, but this land had not been logged in many, many, years and the density of the woods reflected that. Like everywhere else down here, the woods were predominantly made up of pine trees and sprinkled with a mix of hardwoods: oaks, maples, and other random species like fur, cedar and dogwood. In many areas, branches hung generously over the road and shadows loomed.

I knew the area like the back of my hand so, not quite a half mile down the road, I let off of the throttle and slowed us as we came to the aluminum gate. On a light pole next to the gate was an enormous "No Trespassing" sign with all sorts of threating disclaimers. The gate was open and we rolled through.

Since the engine was not operating at full force, I could hear Gabriel ask about the "No Trespassing" sign.

I slowed the 4-wheeler a little more before I answered, "That sign does not apply to me since I am the one that put it up."

We rolled forward and came into view of the road's name sake, Seven Springs, the old hotel. The road turned into a driveway. Part of it branched off to the left toward a barn that had doubled in the past as a car shed. The main part of the driveway continued straight ahead, running parallel to the hotel and opening up into what was once a parking lot type area. I stopped the 4-wheeler and shut it off well before the space for parking.

"Surprise," I said to Gabriel.

Gabriel got off of the 4-wheeler. As I got off, I watched him standing there looking all around at everything. "Is this part of your land?"

"No, it's a part of Aunt Gayle's, but it is going to be mine." I responded. As I pointed left to the creek and followed it around while I spoke, "If you follow the creek, it will empty into the pond behind Aunt Gayle's house."

"What do you mean it will be yours?" Gabriel asked.

"Why don't you let me show you around and I will tell you as we go?"

Before we left the 4-wheeler, I took the Cokes out and handed two of them to Gabriel. I then took his free hand and we started down the hill to the left and toward the creek.

"The creek runs 62 degrees year round so we will put these in the creek to keep them cold," I said as I led Gabriel down to the edge of the creek.

At the spot where I intended to dunk the Cokes there was a railroad tie laid across the creek from one bank to the other. I shimmied out across the railroad tie to the middle, squatted and laid my two bottles in the water. I walked back and took Gabriel's then returned to the middle and laid them in the water next to mine. As I walked back I started to tell Gabriel the history of Seven Springs.

"First of all Aunt Gayle now owns acre after acre on each side of the dirt road there," and I pointed back to the gate, "all the way back to the dirt road we turned off of and all along the creek, the pond and to her house. It's a lot, but I just want the land from a little before the gate to about twenty acres circling the hotel. The hotel is the main thing I want. I would also like an easement for hunting rights on some of the rest of the property."

"That building?" Gabriel asked motioning toward the four story wooden building up the hill across from where we were standing.

"Surprise," I said before elaborating. "You are likely looking at my life's ambition. I would like to turn it back into a hotel. It was built at the turn of the century and people would get off of the train in Avera and then come out here to stay. They would get water from the springs and play in the creek. From what I have heard of the history of it, it was a magnificent place at one time."

The hotel was a four story wooden building that had long ago been painted white. Green shutters had been applied around each window. There were fairly new, black painted, screen doors, one on the front and one on the rear. The screen doors did not match the building at all. Those were the least of my concerns as to what the building would ultimately need in the way of repairs and updating.

I took Gabriel's hand again and we walked along the edge of the creek following it's flow. About fifteen yards down from the railroad tie where I had left the Cokes, the creek made a turn to the left and there was a tiny waterfall. After the turn, the creek made a semicircle around a meadow on the side where the hotel was.

We walked to the middle of the meadow and I released Gabriel's hand, "Stay here and imagine this," I said as I walked away from him toward the middle of the semicircle that the flow of the creek made.

As I approached the edge of the creek I said, "I would like to hold weddings out here. Picture a pagoda here with some sort of ivy or vine growing over it, like wisteria. The bride, groom and minister will stand under it and it will go here."

Gabriel watched while I went on. Walking back toward him, I explained that I would like rows of seating in the meadow with a center aisle for guests.

"I would like the bottom floor of the hotel to be a restaurant that eventually has a reputation on par with the Dillard House or The Blue Willow Inn," I continued until I reached him, "and the receptions for the weddings would be held in the restaurant or if they wanted it outside, then it could be under a tent back over there next to the creek where the railroad tie is." I pointed to the level area of land along the creek near the railroad tie.

I never lost Gabriel's attention in all of my rambling. Where I pointed he looked. Where I walked, he followed.

"I know this is just a dream right now, but I have dreamed of it since I was a child and they used to bring me here to play in the creek. Aunt Gayle wanted the house by the pond and I wanted the old hotel. Some dream, right?" I said as I continued to walk back to Gabriel.

"I admire that you have dreams, Amelia. What's holding you back?" he asked.

"Other than the fact that this entire place has been neglected for nearly fifty years?" I replied with my own question.

I took Gabriel's hand, "I'm not done."

"There's more?" he inquired while following me farther downstream along the creek.

We continued to walk along the bank of the creek until we were directly behind the hotel where we came to another railroad tie that crossed the creek. The railroad tie upstream where I had dropped the Cokes in was just for sitting on and dangling your feet in the water. On the other side of the creek at that point was just a huge hill. One could sit and dangle their feet in the water from this railroad tie, but its purpose was more of a bridge. A path could clearly be seen on the other side, a path that I had walked a hundred times. I stopped in front of the railroad tie.

I turned back to face Gabriel as I spoke to him. "If I thought you would not fall in, we would cross the creek here. I would show you the land over there, but we probably should not chance crossing so I will tell you."

"That's probably a wise decision," Gabriel agreed.

"Ok, so just a little ways down the path on the other side," I started to describe as I gestured across the creek, "is a clearing. I used to think that I wanted to build a house and live there. Then after I moved to college and had to carry my groceries in all by myself, I realized how far I would have to carry groceries to the house from where I parked and rethought having a house across the creek."

"Yeah, I suppose if you parked up there where the road ends then that could be a pain and balancing across a railroad tie every time you left home could be problematic," Gabriel said in jest. "So where do you plan on putting a house now?"

"I have not entirely decided, but I was thinking about putting it back up the road a little ways, maybe using one of the old logging roads as a driveway. I will have to take a better look at the land sometime," I went on.

"There looks like a clearing over behind that barn next to where we first came in. What about putting the house there?"

"I had not thought of that, but that could work. My one requirement is that the house is not seen from the hotel or the grounds of the hotel."

"Why's that?" Gabriel asked as he turned to look at the hotel building from where we were standing and then toward the barn.

"I want it to feel almost like stepping into another time back here and I don't want my house taking away from that," I explained.

Before Gabriel could say anything else, I said, "and, I almost forgot, I would like to build four guest cabins on the other side of the creek. I doubt people will be carrying groceries and I would replace the railroad tie with a small foot bridge."

"So you want it to be like a retreat," Gabriel said in observation of everything I had described.

"That I do," I replied. "What do you think of all of this?"

"I think it is a wonderful idea, but without even seeing the inside of the hotel, I worry that it is a money pit for you." Gabriel ran his hand through his hair and pondered his next statement. "The thing is, Amelia, I know you well enough to know you will not be deterred from this, but, again, just seeing the outside of it, you might fare better to tear it down and rebuild it altogether. I know that's not what you want to hear, but whatever you decide I will help you."

"You will help me?" I asked in amazement.

This was a long term project, likely my life's work. I did things to try to improve the possibilities that Gabriel would be in my future, but I never allowed myself to count on it. I still tried to keep my thoughts of planning a future with Gabriel not to extend more than a couple of weeks. It always came back to my own insecurities, but for him to help me that would mean that he was around for the long haul. Of course, I wanted him in my future, but only time would tell.

While I was milling over my insecurities, I hardly noticed that Gabriel was looking at me puzzled. "I am yours, Amelia, so of course I will help you," Gabriel responded.

I smiled at him, that infectious grin that I could not help hide whenever he said sweet things to me. I threw my arms around him, stood on my toes and pressed my lips to his.

"Are you ready for lunch?" I asked when I pulled back from the kiss. "Or look inside the building first?"

"Lunch. Breakfast was good, but it has not lasted long."

"Okay. I am going to go and get the cooler and the Cokes and I will meet you back over there." I pointed to where I had described building a pagoda. "I will be right back."

Once at the 4-wheeler, I grabbed the cooler with the milk jugs still strapped to it and a blanket that I kept in the storage compartment beneath the seat. Prior to going to retrieve the Cokes, I shut and locked the gate so that if anyone came down the road, we would notice them before they noticed us. When I turned around from the gate, I could see Gabriel out on the railroad tie, walking boot and all, stooping down fishing the bottles of Coke from the water.

Gabriel had taken off his sweatshirt and laid it on the bank. Up top, he was wearing only the undershirt that I had just slept in the night before. He was elbow deep in the water when I heard him scream, "Shit! That's cold!"

I picked up my pace walking toward him for fear he was going to fall in. When I reached him, he had just managed to scramble back to the edge of the bank. I made sure his footing was secure prior to speaking, "I told you the springs run sixty-two degrees year round; dead of winter and heat of summer, even on mild fall days like today."

"You weren't lying," he responded as he picked up his sweatshirt and used it to dry his arm.

We walked back to the spot in the meadow where I intended for us to have a picnic. I put the cooler down on the ground and then threw out the blanket.

Gabriel commented as he helped me straighten the blanket on the ground, "I did not notice you had brought a blanket."

"You wouldn't have," I replied. "I keep it in the storage compartment on the 4-wheeler all the time."

"Why?" And there was that puzzled look on his face again.

"I usually sunbathe in this very spot on this blanket. I lock the gate like I have done now so no one can sneak up on me. That happened once and now I can never show my face again at the Jet Food Store in Gibson." My face turned crimson as I told Gabriel. I had forgotten about that until that very moment.

Gabriel gasped, "Were you naked?!"

I turned my head in embarrassment. I had forgotten there was one person who had seen me naked as an adult.

"You were!" he gasped again.

I sat down on the blanket and started pulling out the stew, spoons and bottle opener from the cooler. Gabriel took a seat on the blanket next to me. I handed him the bottle opener.

"So who's this character that saw you naked?" Gabriel asked as he removed the caps from the bottles.

"He's just this guy that works as a cashier at the main convenience store in Gibson, the one right next to the courthouse. We passed it on our way here yesterday. Anyway, he came out here to get drinking water from the springs. I was lying on my stomach with head phones on and did not see or hear him when he drove up. He thought I was a dead body that someone had put out and he came to check it out before he went for help. He was almost all the way to me when I got the strange feeling that I was not alone. I lifted my head and looked over my shoulder. The fact of the matter is that I scared the poor guy as much or more than he scared me. When I jumped up, I jerked the blanket off the ground to cover myself and he jumped back as if I had shot him, but all the same I know he saw me, all of me. I also think he was as embarrassed as I was. He threw down his water jugs, ran for his car, didn't even put it in reverse, just threw it in gear and spun around and hightailed it out of here."

Gabriel threw his head back laughing while I was telling him about my most embarrassing moment.

"What's your most embarrassing moment? I told you mine. It's only fair."

"I really can't compete with that. I don't think anyone has ever accidentally seen me without my clothes," Gabriel continued to laugh.

"It's not a competition, now out with it," I said as handed him a pint of the stew and a spoon.

372

Gabriel took a bite of the stew before he started his story. He took a few moments to think and chew before he started. "In addition to football, I also played baseball in high school. We were playing the rival school which was located in one of the other suburbs just outside of Nashville. It was a bitter rivalry. We were the visiting team and we were getting the beating of the year. I was playing third base. There were two outs and no one on base, when a fly ball was hit beyond the foul line along third base. I ran for it like it would prevent the winning run from scoring. I mean, I gave it my all, sprinting for the ball, arm fully extended and glove out stretched. Then, 'BAMMMM!!!' I hit the fence. It knocked the wind out of me. There was an imprint of the chain link fence on my chest for nearly a week and I still have a scar from where it cut me."

I was eating my Brunswick stew and hurried to swallow so I could interrupt and ask Gabriel if he caught the ball.

"Of course not! My best friend at the time was also on the team and saw everything. I think he was the only person on or at the field that day that didn't laugh. He said I never stood a chance of catching the ball. My aunt attended the game that day and she later told me she could hear the impact all the way in the stands."

"Seriously, Amelia, I never saw the fence at all and I was at full sprint. Talk about keeping an eye on the ball; I only had eyes for the ball. A picture of me running for the ball right before I made contact with the fence made the school yearbook." Gabriel started to laugh at his own story.

We continued to eat and tell one another stories of our other top five most embarrassing moments. We agreed that the rest of mine paled in comparison with being caught sunbathing naked by the convenience store cashier.

After we finished eating, I collected everything and returned what was left to the cooler. Gabriel was impressed that the creek had kept the drinks cold as I had said they would. He was also impressed with Mrs. Poole's stew and insisted that I at least try to get the recipe from her. I agreed that I would do that next time I was in town.

While I had packed up the cooler, Gabriel laid back on the blanket. "Have you ever been out here at night and just watched the stars?"

"No, I am brave enough to come by myself during the day, but I have always been too chicken to come at night," I replied as I laid down next to him.

It was a beautiful sunny day, but there were a few clouds in the sky. Gabriel and I laid on our backs, staring up, watching them pass overhead and just talked for a while. He had stretched out his arm for me to use as a pillow and he used his folded up sweatshirt.

"Have you ever brought anyone else out here?" Gabriel asked.

"No."

"Does anyone else know about your plans for the place?"

"Aunt Gayle knows, but she does not really approve," I replied pensively.

"Why not?"

"My dad was a doctor, she's a vet and I am what? The most noteworthy thing about me is that I am gifted with music and now that's almost negated by my foolish idea of turning this giant shack, her words, not mine, into a working hotel again. More is expected of me."

"Like what?"

I sat up so I could see Gabriel. The conversation had turned serious and I could not have it while not looking at him and lying on my back. "She knows I am not stupid and that I do well in school. Even though I graduated and started college early, she also knows that I would never make it through anything more than an introductory biology class. I can't handle dead things. I can barely see road kill and not vomit. I could never touch anything dead; therefore, medical school or veterinary school for me is not an option."

"So what does she have in mind for you?" Gabriel asked as he propped himself up with his hands behind his head while still lying on his back.

"She will give me this place once I finish law school. She is so insistent that she has filled out the applications for Mercer, UGA and Georgia State and sent them in for me. All I had to do was take the LSAT and write the essays that went with the applications. She can't send them in yet since I have over a year left of undergrad. She has also agreed to pay for my law degree even though I have not asked her to do that. I have tried offering to buy this place from her. I have even tried negotiating with her recently offering her what a degree at Mercer, the most expensive, would cost plus whatever she wanted for the land."

"And she won't budge?"

"No."

"Would you ever want to be a lawyer?" Gabriel asked as I repositioned myself to lay on my stomach and prop my face in my hands while still looking at him.

"I am not entirely opposed to it, but it would be nice to get started on the work around here. I understand that she thinks I need something to fall back on if this place fails, but if you go into something thinking it will fail, then it is going fail."

"You know," Gabriel started, "it's not a bad idea to have a safety net and if she is paying for it, why not?"

"The last few months I have been excited about getting done with my undergrad. I have even rearranged some classes and changed my major so I could graduate early. I am afraid of what will happen if I sign on for three more years of school..." I caught myself and stopped any further elaboration. I wondered how long he would stay tied to someone who was always in school.

Our age difference was significant and the fact that I was in school only called attention to it in my mind. Jay and Emma had tried to assure me that I was crazy and that if it was meant to be, then none of this would matter. Emma just thought I was crazy because it was too soon to plan anything, something she never did.

My insecurities were creeping in again, so I changed the subject. "Show me the scar." I insisted.

"What scar?"

"The scar from the fence." I sat up.

"Oh." Gabriel paused and then he sat up and pulled the t-shirt over his head. He placed the shirt on the blanked next to him. Sitting up even more straight and tall, he pointed to a place about an inch above his left nipple and said, "Here."

Gabriel wasn't one of those men that was covered in chest hair. He was virtually smooth so had I looked closely I could have seen the scar a dozen times in the past, but it was so slight that I would have had to have been looking for it.

I could see the scar from where I was seated, but I moved in closer as if I were taking a better look. That was just a diversion. I hoped to avoid being obvious in my wanting to touch him. I looked at the scar for a moment before I kissed the tips of the first two fingers of my right hand and then touched them to the scar.

Gabriel took my hand from his chest and kissed the two fingers that had just touched him. He pulled me closer to him and I crawled onto his lap. He was sitting Indian style and I was now sitting on top of him with my legs around him. After steadying myself in position on his lap, he secured me by holding me around my back. I placed my hands on his arms and ran them up his shoulders.

I bit my lip in anticipation. I had thought about this moment for days. I gathered my nerve, slipping my arms over his neck. Pressing my chest to his, I could feel him breathe in my hair, the scent of my strawberry shampoo was present as he liked. I buried my face in his neck and whispered, "I love you."

I could feel Gabriel breathe as he held me tighter. I kissed his neck and said it again, "I love you and I cannot remember when I first knew."

Gabriel eased a hand up my back to grasp my neck with his hand. Still holding me steady with his other arm around my waist, he pulled my neck back so that I was denied any further kisses to his neck, but more importantly, we were now eye to eye. I was becoming nervous that I had said it.

Gabriel took a deep breath and sighed, "Say it again."

Tears started to creep into my eyes as mine connected with his. "I love you," I said without hesitation.

A tear slipped from my right eye and started to trickle down my cheek. Although I had told myself that I would be fine, I would survive him not saying it back, I desperately wanted to hear it from him.

My powers of telepathy actually worked in this situation and Gabriel bent to my will and reciprocated. He pulled me close again, holding me tight and burying his face in my hair.

Gabriel whispered, "I have loved you since I first laid eyes on you. I don't know why exactly. It is beyond your beauty, beyond your music or talents, beyond anything I can put into words. I just do. I tried to avoid you, to fight this."

This time it was me that pulled Gabriel back to look at him. I quieted him when I pressed my lips to his. I kissed him with all the skill that he had imparted to me in the last month. In every second of that kiss memories of moments with him flooded my mind and I kissed him for each. I held his face in my hands and his hands were in my hair as we kissed. This was another record breaker for being the best kiss yet. I wanted him right there, right then and nothing else mattered.

We continued mouth to mouth for some time before Gabriel leaned back. He spoke quietly, "Say it again."

"I love you, Gabriel. I am yours."

As I finished his request, I was not expecting Gabriel to fall back flat on the blanket. Had my arms been around his neck I likely would have gone down with him, but instead I stayed astride him and upright. Gabriel closed his eyes and let out a huge sigh.

"The gate is locked and no one can see us," I said as I started with the top button and began unbuttoning my shirt slowly. "I know you said you wanted to wait until the cast came off, but..."

"Are you sure?" Gabriel asked as he watched me.

"Never been more sure of anything," I responded.

Gabriel leaned back up to a sitting position just as I finished with my buttons. He slid his hands over my shoulders and eased my shirt down as he kissed my neck. I shimmied my arms free and Gabriel tossed the shirt to the edge of the blanket. My arms went around his neck and explored his back as I kissed his right ear. Things were really heating up and Gabriel was unhooking my bra and commenting that he longed to feel my skin against his when suddenly there was the roar of a truck engine and a honking horn at the gate.

We probably would have stayed silent except that followed by the honking, the engine shut off and a voice called from the gate. It was Aunt Gayle. Even if she were standing on the gate, she still could not have seen us in the meadow, but Gabriel and I scrambled to get our shirts on and get to our feet anyway especially since she was the only person aside from myself that had a key to the gate.

"We will continue this later," I said to Gabriel.

"Yes, we most definitely will," Gabriel responded as he quickly kissed me.

"Wait here and I will go see about Aunt Gayle." As I turned to walk toward the gate, Gabriel smacked my behind. Normally I probably would have protested, but this time I laughed. I liked his big signs of affection, but I liked the little ones too. I turned back and kissed him once more. "I love you, Gabriel Hewitt."

Apparently Gabriel was not the only one who had been changing locks lately. Not because I told her, but because she knew me that well, Aunt Gayle knew I was going to take Gabriel to Seven Springs. She knew this yet she forgot to mention to me that morning that she had changed the locks on the doors of the hotel. That's why she finished birthing the calf at the Wilkes' farm as soon as she could and came to find us. She explained all of this when I made it to her. Lucky for us, I had locked the gate since she decided to bring me the new key to the hotel.

While I was gone to meet Aunt Gayle and open the gate, Gabriel packed up the items from our picnic. I could not send her away and I am sure Gabriel knew that. Once Gabriel was up the hill with the cooler and empty milk jugs still attached to it, he met Aunt Gayle and I at the truck and we all walked to the front door of the hotel together.

"Millie has such dreams for this place. I am sure she told you all about them today," Aunt Gayle conveyed to Gabriel as she unlocked the front door.

The front door was actually on the second level of the building and it let into a large hallway that ran the length of that floor cutting it in two. Instead of explaining what the rooms were, I explained what I envisioned them being as I led both Gabriel and Aunt Gayle through the building.

"In all honesty, this is too small to be a full-fledge hotel so it will probably have to do as a bed and breakfast. This room will be the living room for the guests," I described everything I imagined would be in the first room to the right off of the hallway just inside the front door.

Across the hall from the living room, in the room to the left of the front door, I explained that this would be my office. Behind that room was the kitchen and across the hall was the dining room that would service the guests for the hotel. Between the living room and the dining room were the staircases to the basement and the second floor. The second and third floor I explained would be guest rooms. There were four on each floor and I planned to add bathrooms for each of the guest rooms. We went upstairs and I gave Gabriel a glimpse of the guestrooms, but there was little to see so that part of the tour did not take long. I did describe how I wanted one of them to look. I gave every detail right down to the rug on the floor.

Once back on the first floor, I explained that the most dramatic change I wanted to make to the building other than the addition of more bathrooms, was to add a porch across the front of the building and around the left side and around the back. I was thinking it would be made of wrought iron and painted black.

There was so much work to be done. The building would definitely have to be painted, perhaps even rebuilt all together. What did I know? I just had a dream at that point; a big, fat, money-pit dream. It was the same dream I had had since I was ten years old.

Lastly, we went to the basement. I had never really noticed until then that the ceilings were a little low. Gabriel was taller than both Aunt Gayle and I so it kind of magnified the low hung ceiling. I hardly let Aunt Gayle and Gabriel talk during the tour with all of my commentary, but in the basement I wanted Gabriel's input. Could a restaurant even be put down there?

Gabriel walked all around and looked everywhere. Aunt Gayle and I waited and watched. "This is what I would do if it were mine," Gabriel started. "I would accentuate the fact that it is a cellar and the décor and ambiance and everything would center around it being a wine cellar. So the hotel is named Seven Springs, I would name the restaurant The Cellar at Seven Springs. Everything would be dark oak wood, leather, stacked stone and dim lighting like a cellar."

"I love it!" I said as I threw my arms around him. I loved that he could imagine how things should be.

Aunt Gayle was not impressed. She did not want me hanging on to what she considered a pipe dream. She wanted me to go to law school and become a lawyer and that was that. For all she cared, the hotel could be torn down altogether. Gabriel saw the look on her face.

"So how long do you think it would take to get this place to resemble Amelia's dream?" Gabriel asked her.

"I don't know. It needs a lot of work. I don't even know if the building is salvageable. Plus, Millie has something she has to do before she gets this place," Aunt Gayle eluded to my attending law school.

"Do you think three years is a good estimate or would you say four?" Gabriel asked.

I stood there in awe. He was working on her for me. He was facilitating the compromise between me and Aunt Gayle. He continued, "Amelia, where would you like to go to law school?"

"Mercer in Macon," I replied.

"Do you think you can get in at Mercer?" he asked.

"I think so. I am waiting on a response to my application right now."

"She is smart as a whip, of course she can get in," Aunt Gayle insisted. I believe she was offended that he would ask.

"I think we can all agree that this place needs a lot of work," Gabriel said and my heart sank a little. "I think we can all agree that it will take a while to get this place in working condition. Law school is not what Amelia really wants to do, but she understands that it will make a nice back up plan in case this place does not work out."

I nodded my head in agreement.

Aunt Gayle started to see where this was going. "Gabriel, I don't see where all of this concerns you."

"It concerns me because it concerns Amelia and I want her to be happy. Anyone can see that she loves this place, so you can set a hundred hoops for her to jump through and she will do it or you can set a few and she can jump through them as she fixes this place up. What do either of you have to lose?"

"Gabriel," Aunt Gayle said with that familiar sternness to her voice that I knew so well, "Amelia knows what the terms are."

"I do know the terms, but I would like to add to the terms," I thought out loud. "I will go to law school and I will pay for it, but I want the hotel and twenty five acres around it sold to me at the end of law school, but for now I want you to rent it to me so that I may begin work on it."

"You think you can finish college, work at the club and remodel this place all at the same time? I know you are an overachiever, Millie, but that's just too much for anyone," Aunt Gayle lamented.

"Yes, it is too much for one person," I agreed, "but I have Gabriel, Jay and all of my new friends at school that will help me and for all of us it will be a breeze. Plus, it will be spread out over three and a half years."

"There's no talking you out of having this place is there?" Aunt Gayle asked as Gabriel and I began to realize that she might actually come around to my way of thinking.

"No."

"Let me think about it and I will give you an answer no later than Christmas," she said with skepticism.

Gabriel and I were ecstatic that Aunt Gayle was even considering my proposal. She added one more statement; I think she wanted to test the waters with Gabriel to see how serious he was about me.

"Gabriel, do know Amelia wants to build a house and live out here?"

"Yes, ma'am," he responded.

"Do you think you could ever live someplace like this?" Aunt Gayle asked. An instant fury ran through me. What was she doing, trying to scare him away?

Gabriel did not flinch at her question. He replied in what seemed to be genuine honesty, "Right now, I think I could live anywhere just to be near Amelia."

CHAPTER 16

The hour long drive back to Gabriel's house from Aunt Gayle's was full of anticipation. I just knew we were going to pick up where we left off in the meadow at Seven Springs, but no. That's not how the rest of the evening would transpire.

As we pulled up to the guard gate, we were waived through by Officer Ed. After all these months at the club, I still owed him a ride in my Corvette, but that was the least of my concerns at that particular moment. My thoughts were all of Gabriel. I had hardly taken my eyes off of him the entire drive back. It had been almost a whole hour of foreplay.

We did little more than hold hands until we were across the Glascock County line and into Warren County. I knew from the time in the swing that Gabriel liked massages so just outside of Warrenton, I climbed into the backseat of the Legend. I eased over behind him and proceeded to rub his neck and the back of his head. Massages were as good as chocolate for being a natural aphrodisiac.

I continued the massage until after we hit I-20. There were times when I could hear Gabriel moan with pleasure that the massage was yielding. I concentrated on his neck, but I eased my hands down his arms and took care of his shoulders and biceps as well. It also did not hurt that I leaned over and kissed his ears while my fingers worked the tissue of his neck.

We were crossing into Taliaferro County, the county along I-20 just before Green County, when Gabriel insisted I return to the front seat. "You are exceptionally talented at giving massages in case I have not told you that before, but I would like for you to come back up here."

As it turned out he did not necessarily want me back in my seat, but back up front. When I started to put my seatbelt back on, Gabriel reached across and put his hand across the receiver portion of the buckle.

"Not yet," he said. "Don't get the wrong idea, but would you mind laying your head in my lap?"

"Excuse me?" I said.

Gabriel slipped his sweatshirt over his head hardly taking his eyes from the road. He kind of wadded it up and put it in the space across the gear column. Then, he flipped the arm rest up.

"I have never done this before, but turn and face your window and then lay back," he instructed me. "Trust me."

"Ok," I replied before turning and doing as he asked. I shimmied around in my seat and then leaned back, resting my head on his left leg and the small of my back on the sweatshirt. I bent my knees and rested my legs and feet against the inside of the passenger door.

It was not the most comfortable position, but the lack of comfort was made up for by the thrill of it. Gabriel continued to drive with his left hand at the ten o'clock position on the steering wheel. Initially, he rested his right hand on my mid-drift and I placed my hands across his.

I am sure a couple of miles passed before he spoke again. He eased his right hand from under mine and asked, "Would you mind trying something else?"

Before I could answer Gabriel began to unbutton my shirt. I did not answer verbally and Gabriel glanced down, taking his eyes from the road only for a moment. Our eyes met and I suppose he could tell that I had no intention of stopping him, whatever he was going to do. I closed my eyes and enjoyed the excitement inside of me as he continued to unbutton my shirt using only his right hand.

Each time he succeeded in undoing a button, Gabriel flipped open my shirt a little more. I could feel his fingers across my skin and as always the hives were out in full force. I could feel the heat coming off of me as my insides were on fire for him. I could also feel my chest heave with each breath that I took.

Once my shirt was completely unbuttoned, Gabriel ran his index finger from the top of my jeans up between my breasts. I arched my back and leaned up into his touch. Gabriel continued to make a trail with his finger all the way to my mouth where I took his hand in mine and kissed each of his fingers.

"You always have the prettiest bras and panties of any college girl I have ever known," Gabriel gave a strange compliment followed by the question, "May I?"

Without knowing what exactly he was asking to do, I nodded my head in agreement. I did not care what he was wanting my permission to do since I would have granted him anything.

"How many college girls have you seen in their underwear?" I teased him.

Gabriel snickered a little with his response, "I'll never tell."

Gabriel then ran his hand down my cheek, down my neck, and across my shoulder to my bra strap. Gabriel slipped his fingers between my bra strap and my skin. The movement of his hand was slow and deliberate. He continued down until he came to the top edge of my bra. Again, I could not help myself but to give into his touch as he slid his fingers under the lace and across my bare breast.

"Oh my God, Gabriel," I sighed as he gave just a little squeeze before sliding his hand back out of the cup of my bra. He moved his hand across my sternum and to my left where he slipped his hand in. I sighed again, but not voluntarily. It just happened.

"Are you okay with this?" How could he ask?

"Ok? I am better than okay, much better!" I replied as I raised my hands above my head and untucked his shirt.

As best I could reach in that position and somewhat blocked by the steering wheel, once his shirt was untucked I eased my hand under. I ran my right hand up his chest. His skin was so smooth, yet hard with muscle under it. I could feel him flex his chest with my touch. He amazed me.

"It's all I can do not to pull the car over, Amelia. We are about fifteen minutes from home," Gabriel looked down at me and said as he eased his hand down to my stomach again. At first I thought he was going to keep going into my jeans. I tilted my hips in encouragement, but he stopped just shy of the button. It was as if I was losing my mind from the torture of wanting him.

The gate to Port Honor was about six minutes from the exit ramp of I-20, so despite how hot we were for each other, we cooled it in those six minutes so we could be presentable for passing through the gate. Gabriel's undershirt was tucked back in and his sweatshirt on and my shirt was buttoned. Gabriel's right hand was high up on my inner thigh, much farther up and he would have felt how excited I had been for him. He waived to Officer Ed by simply raising the fingers of his left hand from the steering wheel while still guiding it with his palm. We did our best to look as unaffected and normal as we could be, but that was not the case at all.

"Amelia, you are so beautiful and I cannot wait to feel your skin against mine," Gabriel said as he pulled my hand to his mouth and kissed the back of it.

We made the turn on to Starboard Harbor and I was already unbuckling my seatbelt again. I was leaning across to kiss him and my hand was climbing his thigh when he stopped me.

"Oh, shit!" Gabriel nearly shouted.

I jumped back thinking that I had done something wrong, but that was not it. Gabriel had noticed that Daniel's car was in the driveway and Daniel was sitting on the front steps as if he were waiting on Gabriel to get home.

"Amelia, you are going to have to get out of the car and greet him. I am going to need a moment," Gabriel said as he shifted in his seat.

"Can you get rid of him?" I asked.

"We can try," Gabriel said, "but first I would rather him not know that I have a raging har.."

I cut Gabriel off, "I got-cha. You get our bags and I will get Daniel. Gabriel, I want this too and I am not going anywhere. I guess what I am saying is that there's always tomorrow."

Gabriel just smiled back at me as I got out of the car and went to greet Daniel.

While Gabriel went ahead and parked the car in the garage, I greeted Daniel on the front steps. As it turned out, Daniel and Jerry had had a fight and Jerry had put him out. He said it was only a matter of time before he was allowed back in, but he needed a place to stay for the night. From the way he communicated it to me, this seemed to be part of their M.O. He did not even appear concerned about the situation.

Daniel and I sat on the front porch for a while talking before Gabriel came to the front door and let us in. Gabriel welcomed Daniel in without pause. As Daniel passed through the door in front of us and safely had his back to us, Gabriel mouthed the words "twice in one day" to me. I almost laughed out loud.

Daniel explained everything to Gabriel after they had both flopped down on the couch. I excused myself to the bathroom and gave them time to talk. When I returned to the room I heard Gabriel say, "At it again, huh?" as if he knew this was common practice.

"I suppose it seems that way," Daniel replied as he threw his head against the back of the couch and rubbed his forehead.

Apparently, Jerry had his fair share of insecurities like the rest of us. Daniel and Jerry had been together since Daniel was eighteen and they met at Backstreet, a drag club in Atlanta. Jerry had been a performer and Daniel was a valet. They had been together ever since, almost thirteen years. I sat with them and listened and Daniel brought me up to speed.

I felt honored to be included, but got stuck on the fact that they had been together for thirteen years. They used to fight over silly stuff just so they could make up. Now they fought about stuff like whose turn it was to do the laundry or the dishes or they fought because Jerry was bored or he thought Daniel was going to leave him for someone younger. I wondered if that's what Gabriel and I would be like after thirteen years.

"I am going to make some popcorn. Could I get you all something to drink while I am up?" I asked them.

"She is quite the hostess, Gabe. I think you should keep her," Daniel admired before asking for a Coke.

"Amelia, you do not have to wait on us," Gabriel said as he stood.

"It's no trouble. Please sit. I will be back with the popcorn, a Coke and a Seven and Seven for you, Gabriel?" I asked with a smile.

Daniel stood as well as I left the room. I could hear him as I crossed the threshold into the kitchen, "Gabe, she suits you."

I also heard Gabriel's response, "She told me she loves me."

I stopped inside the kitchen door, but out of sight and listened. "What did you say? Did you say it back?" Daniel asked Gabriel.

"I said it back," Gabriel replied as he stood from the couch. I thought he was coming toward the kitchen, but instead I could hear his footsteps turn toward the TV.

Daniel gasped, "Have you ever said that to anyone before?" He asked as if he knew the answer already, but Gabriel responded none the less.

"No." Gabriel's voice was calm and low and he sounded sad.

I continued to eavesdrop and Daniel continued with his questions: "You meant it, right?"

My heart initially sank at Gabriel's response, "It just sort of came out. It wasn't something I had thought about." He paused before he added. "I don't know that I have ever meant anything as much. I love her. She is so young and..."

I stopped listening at that point and finished doing what I went to the kitchen to do, make popcorn and get drinks. I did not want to ruin it by hearing any of his doubts if that's what he was about to share. When I re-entered the living room with the snacks, they had moved on to sports and who was playing in the college games the next day.

"I know Georgia and Georgia Tech are playing tomorrow, but beyond that I really don't care until the Army-Navy game next weekend," Gabriel said as he tossed a football that typically sat on the mantle to Daniel. Daniel was not the stereotype, not only did he talk sports, but he caught the ball as well.

I handed them their drinks and then asked to speak with Gabriel for a moment in the kitchen. We excused ourselves and Gabriel followed me to the kitchen.

"I think I am going to go home for the night and let you and Daniel have a guy's night," I pondered aloud. I did not want to leave him, but it seemed like the thing to do.

"You want to go home after the day we have had?" Gabriel asked in shock.

"No, I just think Daniel needs you and I'm a third wheel," I explained.

"I need you and you will never be a third wheel. He is the third wheel!" Gabriel exclaimed.

"Shhh. He will hear you," I said as I put my index finger to his lips. "Plus, absence makes the heart grow fonder."

"I don't want you to leave," Gabriel said as he backed me into the corner of the kitchen cabinets. "We started something twice earlier and I want to finish it."

"Yes, we started twice today and I think something is trying to tell us that today just isn't the day. Plus, there's always tomorrow," I added.

I gathered my belongings from Gabriel's bedroom and returned to say my goodbyes to Daniel. He apologized for running me off and begged me to stay. He even offered to leave, but I would have none of it. Gabriel then walked me out.

Gabriel opened the car door for me, but before I got in, he kissed me gently. "I can't help but think of the night on the porch of your old apartment," Gabriel confessed. "I feel if I kiss you anymore I won't stop."

"If you get a chance, you are welcome to call me tonight, but if you don't I will see you at work tomorrow." I started to back into the seat of the car and thought of one more thing I wanted to ask him. "Did you like your surprise today?"

Gabriel looked puzzled. "What exactly was the surprise today? The hotel and the land or you telling me that you love me? Or was it what else you intended to give me today?"

"Everything," I answered.

"I loved it all. The entire day has been the best adventure, Amelia, now go before I change my mind," Gabriel said as he kissed me once more.

***

The Jefferson was virtually empty with the exception of Cara and I. She heard me come in and came to check on me. She was shocked to see me home from Gabriel's, but glad to see me just the same. Cara and I ended up walking to the Brick and having dinner together.

Cara went on to tell me that Alvin had manned the kitchen during the day on Friday and she had been on the beverage cart while Gabriel and I were off. She thanked me for taking the day off because Huggie-Man was on the course and had tipped her fifty dollars.

"What sort of hugs are you giving?" I asked her. "Because I only get four bucks for my hugs."

"What sort of hugs are you giving?" Cara asked as if four dollars was not the norm for her hugs.

"I am giving the side arm type to that perv and you?" I replied in shock of what she was going to say her hugs were like.

"I have to pay for my own college so I am giving the full frontal," Cara said as she demonstrated by shaking her boobs at me.

"Oh my God, you are nuts!" I exclaimed.

***

That night Gabriel called as he said he would and as usual we talked about any and everything and nothing at all until the wee hours of the morning. The next day, I hardly saw him at work.

It was unseasonably warm again on Saturday, so we were busy, busy, busy on the course all day long. I refilled the beverage cart so many times I lost count. I also made a great deal of money and all I could think about was spending it on Christmas presents for Gabriel. If he had not been home for Thanksgiving in years, then he likely had not had a proper Christmas in years either.

I knew better than to think Gabriel was going to let me go home again Saturday night, so I did not even bother to mention it when we passed each other when he came in at 4:00 p.m. for the dinner shift. My sales on the course had just started to slow up when he came in so by the time I unloaded the cart and cashed out, the evening shift employees were there.

Gabriel included me in the nightly taste testing. My favorite of the night's specials was the Coq Au Vin. That was not something that someone from my neck of the woods had served to them just any old time. I dare say it was my first time having it and it was pretty good. Gabriel acknowledged my enthusiasm for the dish and packed a to-go plate for me to take back to his house for dinner. He already knew that I did not like the idea of him fussing over me at the club and I was not open to sitting at the bar and having my dinner.

Little did Gabriel know, as good as my to-go dinner was, I had no intention of eating it. All day long I focused on getting off work and then going to Athens to look for Christmas presents at the mall. I did just that. I found some things for him, but not the big gift. I had no idea what the big gift would be at the time, but I figured I would know it when I saw it.

While I was at the mall, I bought my first silk night gown as well as my second and third. I gave the Victoria's Secret girl a real workout and she gave the same to my purse. I bought a robe to match each of the night gowns and a few new bras and panties. I made it back to Gabriel's house with my loot well before he got home. In fact, I made it home in time to get some of my reading done for the coming week's classes, shower, slip into one of my new nightgowns and climb into Gabriel's bed.

It had been a long couple of days and I was in bed before eleven. The covers of Gabriel's bed were nearly as soft as those on

389

my own. I loved my own bed, but there was nothing quite like sleeping in his even when he wasn't in it because it smelled like him. It smelled like Gabriel Hewitt, sweet and masculine all at the same time. Between being tired and the bed being so comfortable I was asleep within minutes of climbing into bed.

Gabriel did not get home until after midnight. He showered and eased into bed next to me. I barely woke as he snuggled up to me. I could feel his chest against my bare back and his breath in my hair. He ran his hand up my leg and around my midsection as if checking to see what exactly I was wearing.

"I love you," he sighed as his hand came to rest around my waist.

"I am glad you are home. I missed you," I said before rolling to face him and giving him a long kiss goodnight. I then rolled back over and pulled his arm back around me.

"I love you to the moon and back," I whispered. I felt Gabriel squeeze me to him and that was the last I knew until the alarm was going off.

It was 9:00 a.m. and I had to be at work at ten. I hit the off button shutting it down before Gabriel woke up. I quickly dressed and started breakfast for us, my standard pancakes and bacon. Gabriel also had to be at work for the brunch shift, so I tried to wake him at 9:45 a.m.

"Gabriel, it's time to get up," I called to him from the kitchen.

Soon Gabriel found me in the kitchen. I was in my uniform for the beverage cart and taking bacon from the pan as it finished cooking. I had my back to the doorway and I did not hear him come in for the sound of the bacon sizzling and popping. Gabriel put one arm around me and moved my hair to one side exposing my neck before he ran his tongue along my neck from my collar to my ear lobe.

"Good morning, Miss Anderson," Gabriel said after leaving the trail of kisses along my neck and chills down my left leg.

"Good morning, Mr. Hewitt," I turned to him. He was still in his pajamas; shirtless, with my favorite pirate pants. As usual the pants hung low exposing the "V" and I could not help but think of what we had started on Friday and never finished. It was tempting to forget about being on time for work and pick up where we had left off especially since he was my boss. Before I could fully decide what to do, the smell of the last few strips of bacon burning caught my attention and I turned my focus back to the stove.

Gabriel stole a couple of slices of the bacon before leaving me to get dressed. He returned wearing his chef's coat, black slacks and a giant smile.

"I could get used to having you here," Gabriel said as he helped me take the plates to the table.

"Don't get too comfortable, I have to go back to my apartment tonight and back to the real world tomorrow," I replied as I took my seat at the bar.

Gabriel's face fell a little and I could not help but notice. "What's wrong?" I asked.

"Amelia, this is the real world for me. There's no differentiating, there's just when we are together and when we aren't and I hate to think that you think the real world is when you are going to class." I felt terrible that I had clearly hurt his feelings.

"I am so sorry. I did not mean it like that. Being here with you is more real and wonderful than anything I have ever experienced," I apologized profusely.

We continued to eat our breakfast in virtual silence. When we were finished, he insisted on cleaning up the dishes since I cooked. I went on to work and he followed about thirty minutes later.

The weather had taken a turn. It was now more like November in the rest of the country, cold and damp. The day drug on and on while I was on the cart. Thanks to the weather, little to no one was on the course that day.

I finally came in from the course around 1:15 p.m. I had had enough of the cold and doing nothing. I was determined to beg Gabriel to send me home or give me something to do in the clubhouse.

Daniel and Cara were working the brunch shift in the dining room. I saw Cara first when I came in and asked if she had seen Gabriel.

"He was in the dining room last I saw him," she replied as she carried dirty dishes to the dish pit.

As I started toward the door leading from the kitchen to the dining room, Daniel came into through the other door also carrying dirty dishes to the dish pit.

"Hey, Millie," Daniel said as he handed me half of the dishes he was carrying. "Here help me out. Take these. Thanks."

I was freezing, but I removed my hands from my pockets and took the dishes from Daniel as he asked. After we finished in the dish pit, Daniel asked me to fetch him a Coke from the bar. I did that and thought little of it until I returned with the Coke and he assigned me another chore. I did not mind helping him, but something was starting to seem a little off with him and I still had not found Gabriel.

"Have you unloaded the cart yet?" Daniel asked.

"No, I wanted to find Gabriel to ask if it was alright to come in. Have you seen him?" I asked Daniel who seemed preoccupied.

"Not in the last few minutes," Daniel replied, but I felt he was not telling the whole truth. "I am sure he won't mind if you come in. Just go ahead and start unloading it. I will come out and help you in just a minute."

There was something off and I wanted to find Gabriel to make sure everything was okay. I agreed to start unloading the cart and told Daniel I was going to get something to drink from the bar and then I would start unloading. I left Daniel in the kitchen and I went to the bar and kept going around to the dining room.

As soon as I stepped into the dining room, I realized why Daniel was trying to keep me from finding Gabriel. Beth Reed was back and there was Gabriel lounging at the table with her and Dick, Joan's husband, the general manager of Port Honor. I stopped at the hostess stand and took in the sight.

I had been freezing my ass off outside while they were having a good old laugh inside. More importantly there was Gabriel seemingly having a great time chatting it up with Beth and the last we had seen of her was when she was carted off to jail with a pending DUI. Just when I thought I could not hate her more, there she was and they were having a great time as if nothing had ever happened. Beth's hand was high on Gabriel's leg, holding on as she carried on about whatever it was they were talking about as if it was the most hilarious thing since Eddie Murphy.

"Oh Gabriel, stop!" Beth threw her head back and giggled as she patted the spot on his upper thigh. Were we anywhere else I probably would have screamed for her to take her hand off of him, but since we were at work and that was the big boss sitting with them there was nothing I could say or do.

I stood there only a moment before Gabriel noticed me. Our eyes met and I raised an eyebrow with a scowl, took in a deep breath, rolled my eyes at him and turned and went back through the door into the bar. Through the kitchen I went and Daniel saw me.

"I tried..." Daniel started as he saw my nostrils flare and the pace with which I was storming through the kitchen.

"Stop trying!" I growled at him.

I continued through the kitchen and out the back door to the cart. Daniel followed.

"Millie, don't let her get to you!" Daniel all but demanded.

"It's not her that gets to me, it's him!" I growled as we approached the cart.

I started slinging things off of the cart to carry inside as I continued with my tirade, "Oh, don't get me wrong, I hate her ass, but I hate the way he carries on with her as if nothing has happened!"

"What would you have him do? She came in with Dick and..." Daniel was just getting interrupted left and right and this time it was by the kitchen door being thrown open by Gabriel.

"I will leave you two," Daniel said as he picked up the basket of chips, cookies and crackers from the seat of the beverage cart. Daniel then started inside carrying the snack basket and passing Gabriel at the steps of the loading dock.

Gabriel did not even wait to make sure Daniel was out of range of hearing us before he asked, "Are you upset with me?"

I could not imagine that he actually looked puzzled when he asked and my response questioned just that. "Seriously," I snapped, "You have to ask?"

"You are upset," he exclaimed as if he were in shock or that I had no right to be angry. In all honesty, I was furious with Miss Moneybags for continuing to put her hands all over him, but I was almost as mad with him for continuing to allow it.

"What was it that gave it away, the rolling of my eyes or me storming off? I mean, you clearly do not seem to think you have done anything!" I huffed.

I continued unloading the drinks from the cooler in the bed of the beverage cart as we went back and forth. The more Gabriel failed to see what the problem was, the more I slammed around the drinks coming out of the cooler. I never raised my voice, but there was a definite and continuing elevation in the noise the cans made as I nearly threw them on the rolling cart that was parked on the loading dock next to where I had backed up the beverage cart.

"Amelia, seriously! What is your problem?" Gabriel demanded.

"Right, it would be my problem wouldn't it because it sure didn't look like your problem. Honestly, why would it be a problem for you having two women falling all over themselves over you? Forget that one is a self-centered ego maniac that is bat-shit crazy and the other is just…" My face was becoming hotter and hotter the madder I got until he cut me off.

"Is that what you think is going on with me?" Gabriel snapped back at me.

"I saw you! I saw her!" I steamed.

"Jesus, Amelia, you are being a child!"

"Really, I am being a child? I guess I am a child compared to the competition! Come on, how would you like it if you walked in and caught some guy with his hand almost all the way to Christmas on me? Especially if I were all smiles and giggles?" At the completion of my rant, I openly mocked him. I tossed back my head and let out the biggest fake laugh, "Oh, Beth, ha ha ha!" And then with a straight voice I continued, "Oh, yeah, it was real funny when I walked in and saw you all. Real funny!"

All the while during my diatribe, I finished unloading the beverage cart, up the steps I went and started toward the door with the rolling cart. Gabriel followed close behind and through the back door of the kitchen we went.

"Are you saying you don't trust me?" Gabriel questioned as he pulled me into the dry storage area just inside the kitchen door. He tried pinning my back against one of the shelving systems, but I ducked under his arms and scooted around him.

As I was fleeing I gave my reply, "What I don't trust is her hand so high on your thigh for all-the world to see."

"Amelia, come back here!" Gabriel ordered in a stern, but whispered tone trying to keep from openly airing our dirty laundry for everyone in the kitchen to hear.

I did not bend to him. I continued on to the bar to cash out. Gabriel broke from his hushed whisper and yelled after me, "We are not done!"

I ignored him and through the swinging door out of the kitchen and into the bar I went and there was Beth sitting there at the bar. The words "Double shit!" popped into my head at the sight of her. In the few times I had met her, she had never looked better. Her hair and make-up were pristine. The platinum blonde bob was back. She had it parted on the side and the cut was angled from the back to the front. Not a hair on her head was out of place.

Beth's make-up was more conservative than the first time I had seen her and not streaked all over her face like the second. It was rare that I had seen a woman of her fair skin tone pull off red lipstick the way she did that day. It was the color of the cherry red Alpha Romeo that I registered a hundred times to win from the Augusta Mall the year I turned sixteen. That color made most light skinned women look old and their teeth look more yellow than they would with a shade of pink, but not Beth. She looked glamorous.

She had on the most beautiful cream colored cable knit sweater I had ever seen. I had noticed that much while watching her grope Gabriel in the dining room before. Beth looked like a model, someone straight out of Vogue, and I looked like a pissed off popsicle. I had only started to thaw from being outside in the cold all day and that was only hastened by the spike in my blood pressure over my fury. I did not want her to see me rattled. I tried to ignore her and I headed straight to Andy to turn in the money from the beverage cart.

"Hi...oh gosh, you are going to have to tell me your name again," Beth leaned across the bar toward my direction and said.

I did not want to appear to be rude in front of the other guests in the bar so I replied, "My name is Millie."

I likely failed in my attempt not to seem rude since the look on my face spoke volumes and volume one was titled something that could not be printed on the outside of a book.

395

"Right... Millie. How could I forget that?" As always, the hint of superiority was in her voice and she just could not resist the urge to try to mess with me.

I turned back to Andy, "Do you need me for anything else? I have really got to get going."

"Gotta get home to study?" Beth interjected again.

"Something like that," I replied.

Beth raised an eyebrow at me, "Have you seen Gabriel? I totally forgot to tell him what a good time I had last night. Would you mind giving him the message if you see him on your way out?"

Beth knew exactly what she was doing and though I did not want to give her the satisfaction of knowing she was getting to me, she was. I did my best to stifle my rage in front of her, but I could feel the heat coming off of my face again.

"Alright, we are done here," Andy said to me.

"You are exactly right," I replied to Andy while looking directly at Beth, "We are done here."

I turned to walk away to leave and she just could not let me go. I had gotten so far as to place my hand on the kitchen door to push it open when she called out to me, "Don't forget to give Gabriel my message. Thanks!"

I turned around to her and if looks could kill she would have been so dead that we could have smelled the body. I walked back toward her. Andy took notice and moved to get in front of her. Perhaps he thought I was going to jerk her across the bar or perhaps he thought I was going to climb across after her, I am not sure.

I was confident that she had lied about being with Gabriel the night before. I figured one lie deserved another. With searing deliberation to hurt her I spoke. "You seem bent on having me know that you have been with Gabriel so let me just go ahead and clue you in. He has told me all about his time with you. He said it was like throwing a hotdog down a hallway."

That was not an original insult that I came up with. I actually quoted Jay. He coined the phrase when talking about his one and only sexual encounter with a female.

396

Beth leaned across the bar from her stool and started to speak, "Let me tell you ..."

Everything was fairly discrete to the rest of the room. I was doing my best not to make a full on scene, but when Beth started, I shoved past Andy, leaned across the bar and got in her face.

"Seriously, you've got a come back? A burn? Let me hear it?" I barely waited for her to answer. She seemed dumbstruck by my audacity. Perhaps she was catching on to the fact that she wasn't the only one in the world who could be mean.

I continued, "No, then let me tell you something. Next time you decide to dress up as Cruella Deville and go trick or treating in the middle of the night at Gabriel's house, rethink it or there will be another jail cell waiting with your name on it."

I successfully backed her down to her side of the bar. She was speechless and flopped against the back of her stool. Her ass was hardly back in the seat before she grabbed her purse from the bar top and started to storm out.

With cheer in my voice to again avoid raising any suspicion by other guests, I sent her off with one last snap. I called to her like she had called to me when my hands touched the kitchen door to leave. When Beth laid hands on the door to the dining room, I said, "By the way, just one more question. How many battles have I won now?"

As the words escaped my mouth, Gabriel appeared through the glass on the other side of the door leading from the bar to the dining room. Beth let out a huff at what I had said. She did not notice Gabriel on the other side of the door and shoved through nearly hitting him square in the face. He threw out his hand to stop the door from hitting him and that's what called Beth's attention to his presence.

"Hotdog down a hallway, huh? Well, you need to get your hotdog out of your new girl's purse!" Beth slapped Gabriel across the face, shoved past him and stormed up the stairs to leave through the front door.

I am sure Gabriel was stunned and as Beth slapped him, Andy whispered, "You are lucky she did not slap you a minute ago, but that was awesome, Millie."

"Thanks!" I said with a roll of my eyes. I did not stick around for anything else. I had cashed out and that meant my shift was over so I left. I felt bad about her slapping Gabriel over what I had said, but it really was like she needed to keep reminding him that she was psycho.

I was a third of the way to Milledgeville on the back roads when I noticed what appeared to be Gabriel's car catching up to me. At first I thought it was my imagination, but he was really closing in. When I came to the four way stop at the intersection of Old Phoenix Road and New Phoenix Road, I slowed down enough to get a good look and confirm my suspicions. It was definitely him.

In the months that I had been taking those roads I had only seen one sheriff's department car. I figured the likelihood of seeing one that Sunday afternoon was probably slim to none so I floored the gas pedal on the Corvette. Gabriel's Acura Legend was doing surprisingly well keeping up until one of the curves, then he backed off. I took the curve while only letting off the gas just a little. The Legend sat low to the ground, but not nearly as low as the Corvette so where I hugged the curves, he did not.

Although I was pissed with Gabriel, I had never been in a car chase before and this was quite exhilarating. The faster the car went, the more I liked it. I always did like showing off my car, but this was a new version of showing off. I also liked that he was the one chasing me.

The closest Gabriel came to catching up with me was at the turn from North Columbia Street onto Montgomery, but since no traffic was coming I blew through the red light. I was out of the car and in the front yard, headed toward the front door of The Jefferson when Gabriel parallel parked in the one vacant spot in front of the building in one swift move. He made no attempt to do the forward and reverse maneuvers to perfect his spot in the space before he jumped out and marched toward me.

"What do you think you are doing?!!" Gabriel demanded to know. His eyes were burning and his voice was nearly raised to the point of yelling at me. "Were you trying to kill yourself? You hit speeds in excess of ninety miles per hour!"

"Gabriel, go home," I said as I walked past him. Of course I did not want him to leave, but I did want to prove a point with him.

Gabriel grabbed me by my left arm just above my elbow, whirled me around causing me to lose my balance and into his arms I went. Even though I am sure that ended up as he planned, he had not counted on me losing my balance. He probably did not count on me struggling to get free of him either. Unfortunately, as I had lost my balance, I racked him. As I had struggled to get free, Gabriel had also doubled over from the blow to his groin allowing me to easily slip his grip. In getting free, I had not noticed what had actually happened and that Gabriel was actually well on his way to hitting his knees when I jerked away and again headed for the door.

"That's awesome, Amelia!" Gabriel nearly screamed at me. "You are running away and I am injured again as a result of your tantrum. Is this how it is going to be with us?"

"Injured?" I turned around quickly to see him holding himself. "Seriously?"

"I am sorry. I did not mean to hit you there," I added knowing that I had just lost all ground with him in the argument.

"You can forget about me going home. Now get over here and help me up," Gabriel demanded.

I did as he instructed and returned to help him. As I steadied him for getting back to his feet, including the one that was still in the walking boot from my last jealous fit, I apologized again.

"Amelia, what else do I have to do to get across to you that Beth is no threat to you? You called her the competition earlier, but you fail to realize that there's no competition. I only tolerated her today for the sake of Richard," Gabriel explained as he limped a little while we proceeded toward the door of The Jefferson.

Once on the front porch, I poured out what I was feeling about the situation. "I am confident that you are not cheating with her. I just hate that she has no boundaries with you and you seem to allow it. I think I was a good sport when it came to the break-in at your house, but today..." I paused before continuing. "Well, I am just tired of being a good sport. The bottom line is, I want her to keep her hands off of you. There was just no need in her touching you like that and it needs to stop."

"So the only person you want touching me..." Gabriel started his question, but I answered it before he finished.

"Is me." I was serious about my answer and I did not take my eyes from his.

"I think that request can be accommodated," Gabriel agreed, but he had a request of his own. "I want something in return. I want you to stop running when we have a disagreement. Not only do you not solve anything by running, but it seems to end in me getting injured so let's agree that I will not allow Beth to touch me beyond a handshake and you will not run when we disagree or argue."

"Agreed," I said as I held out my hand, "Shall we shake on it?"

"One more thing," Gabriel added to his request, "no more driving like a bat out of hell. No risking your life like that."

"Yes, Daddy," I smirked and held out my hand.

Gabriel took my hand only for pulling me to him. "Handshakes are only for business. Come here and kiss me."

After we came to an understanding, things blew over with Gabriel and me. Once inside my apartment and alone since Jay and Emma had not returned from their holiday yet, Gabriel wanted to pick up where we left off on Friday, but I was not up for that.

Not only was I having a hard time shaking the bone chilling cold I had endured from being out on the beverage cart all day, something else had arrived. Thank goodness Gabriel had gotten the picture with a few hints before I had to spell it out. Being vague about the issue was bad enough. I am fully aware that as he put it, "it's a natural part of life", but I still had never told anyone of the opposite sex about that time of the month. It may have been a natural part of life, but it would have been totally unnatural for me to have had to spit out the words.

Despite my predicament, Gabriel stayed and we hung out for a while before he took me to dinner. We went to Brewers, the coffee house where I had also interviewed prior to getting the job at Port Honor. During dinner, I thought about how different life would have been if I had not tanked that interview and actually gotten the job there. Gabriel and I had some laughs when I told him how the interview went. I also told him about the failed interview at Merry-Go-Round in the mall. We had even more laughs about that one.

After dinner Gabriel dropped me back at the apartment and we said our goodbyes. It was back to class for me the next day and, for him, it was back to whatever it was that he did on Mondays while the club was closed. I did not ask, but he assured me that he would call me when he got home and again on Monday night and Tuesday night too. He apologized again for causing me any grief with Beth earlier in the day. I apologized for my actions as well and our parting words were "thank you" for the best Thanksgiving weekend either of us had ever had and a mutual "I love you".

Gabriel kissed me slowly and gently, then got back in his car and drove away. I stood there on the front porch of The Jefferson and watched until his taillights were so far down Jefferson Street that I could no longer see them. While watching him fade into the distance I thought about how we had been nearly inseparable since last Tuesday when I arrived at his house to start preparing the food we were taking to Thanksgiving and now I would not see him for three days. I was convinced those three days would feel like an eternity and I was saddened by the thought. Standing there, I was headed toward a little depression until the wind blew through the trees lining the street and the night air snapped me out of it. It sent me running inside out of the cold.

When I opened the door at the top of the stairs I found Jay and Emma had made it home while we were at dinner. They were waiting on me and anxious to hear all of the details of my holiday and I theirs. Emma's was the most exciting, but mine came in a close second.

If it had truly been a competition, I would have won had Emma not given it up already and had a spectacular sex story with Mr. Bama. It would have been hard for anyone to beat a story involving sex on the fifty yard line of Bryant-Denny Stadium. Mr. Bama had an uncle on the coaching staff of the University of Alabama and when he got drunk at Thanksgiving, his keys were lifted. Needless to say, Emma got more than a tour of the locker room.

Emma had gone to Alabama to stay with a friend she had met at tennis camp during the summer. This time she met the friend's brother, and though we would have never thought it possible, it appeared as though she might have fallen in love.

Just when you thought Emma could not have been any more beautiful, she was happy and that really made her more beautiful than words could describe. Jay and I could already see a change in her and initially I thought it extended beyond her looks to her disposition, but that thought was premature. Being in love suited her and the differences I noticed in her made me wonder if people noticed those things about me since I had met Gabriel. Did he make me a better person like this new guy made Emma? She wasn't a bad person by any means before, she was just somehow better now.

We gave Jay a hard time because he did not have a story to tell at all and he returned the gesture by giving me a hard time about still not having given away the ultimate trophy.

Jay and I were lounging on the couch in the living room while Emma was in the shower.

"I just cannot imagine what Gabriel is waiting on! What is wrong with him?" Jay wondered aloud while I tried to concentrate on reading and listening to him.

"I don't think there's a thing at all wrong with him," I peeped over my textbook. I was a little wounded by Jay's words.

Emma heard as she exited the bathroom. While passing to her room in nothing but a towel on her hair and another around her, she contributed her two cents. "I am going to say it again, if he isn't getting it from you, he's getting it somewhere."

"He's not getting it anywhere else! Now shut-up about that once and for all!" If I were an animal, I would have been baring my teeth at her at that point. I was so sick of her saying that.

"Simmer down," cautioned Jay, "and Emma, you really are beating a dead dog with that one."

Emma and I backed off of one another and it seemed like hours that I spent catching up with her and Jay. Although I had enjoyed every minute of being with Gabriel for nearly a week, I soon realized I had missed them. As much as Gabriel was becoming home to me, I was not ready to let go of my home with Emma and Jay, but that did not mean I didn't jump and run for the phone as soon as it rang.

"I am sorry I did not call sooner," Gabriel apologized as soon as he recognized my voice on the line.

"Yes, you should be ashamed," I replied in a chipper tone. I was still giddy from all of the stories Jay was telling about the time with his family. He never failed to deliver the good stories when he returned from his visits home. His opinion was that every family has one, but his family has ten crazy people.

It was nearly midnight when I got off of the phone with Gabriel. As usual, we discussed any and everything and this time I even put him on speaker phone and played the violin for him over the phone.

"I wish I had stayed there tonight," Gabriel said just before he hung up.

"I wish you had stayed as well, but we are okay and nothing is going to change that," I assured him.

"I know we are okay, I just like being with you more than anything," Gabriel replied before making his request. "Tell me again."

"Tell you what?" I played dumb.

"You know."

"I love you, Gabriel, to the moon and back. I could spend the rest of my life kissing you and it would not be enough."

***

Gabriel typically called around 9:00 p.m. so one could imagine my anxiety when Emma was still not off the phone at ten. Emma had been camped out on the phone with Mr. Bama since the time her foot hit the threshold of the apartment upon her return from tennis practice around 6:15 p.m. From that moment on Emma had paraded from her room to the living room to the kitchen and beyond all the while still attached to the cordless phone. I believe she even took a bath while talking to him and, knowing Emma, I shudder to think how that portion of their conversation went.

Even though I waited and waited for her to get off the phone, Emma did not get off until after 11:00 p.m. I thought surely she would get off well before she did.

I was still up when she burst in my door. "Gabriel called, I think about five times, but I may have lost count and it could have been Jay's mom. You know how it is with call waiting."

"Seriously, Emma, five hours on the phone?" I said with a roll of my eyes.

"Yeah, well, Gabriel said he would just call you in the morning," Emma said as she left my room and slammed the door behind her.

Emma could be a bit abrasive, but she wasn't usually quite this inconsiderate. If Jay's mom had called as many times as she usually did, as in calling until she actually got Jay on the phone and all the while worrying about his safety, then she was likely about to have a stroke. It crossed my mind for a split second that I might need to put in my own line and then it occurred to me that the line we had in the apartment was already mine.

I jumped from my bed and stormed after her. I snatched open my bedroom door and into the living room I went. Emma was just about to close her door when I demanded her attention. "Emma, we are all happy for you, but if you are going to be on the phone that long, then maybe you should get your own line."

A roll of her eyes and flip of her hair was the only response I got from Emma as she proceeded into her room. Jay was sitting on the couch in the living room watching TV and heard everything. He could tell I was about to go after her and stopped me.

"Let it go for now," Jay said without taking his eyes from the television. "All of this will wear off with her. Just give it a couple of days."

I let out a similar huff and returned to my room.

***

The next morning I awoke not to an alarm clock, but to the ringing of the phone. I had been all snuggly in my bed with my head nearly buried under the covers. I shivered from the cold when I reached an arm out and banged around the nightstand to find the phone. It took three rings before I found it on the nightstand.

It was Gabriel. Our conversation consisted of me telling him all about Emma and Mr. Bama and their phone call. I apologized profusely for Emma and her lack of consideration for all of us and the use of the phone. Aside from being disappointed that he did not get to talk to me, he was fine. There was also more bargaining between Gabriel and myself. He agreed to come to family dinner that night, in exchange for me agreeing to work as the hostess on Friday night.

"Would you mind wearing the dress that I bought you to wear to dinner with the Von Bremens?" Gabriel requested.

"Ok, but won't I be a little over dressed for being the hostess?" I asked.

"Actually, we are holding the annual Delta Digital Christmas Party on Friday night, so it's a bit more of a big deal than just the regular Friday night dinner for members and guests," Gabriel explained.

"Do you have any other requests?" I teased.

"Maybe, but we can discuss those later," Gabriel returned in the same spirit.

CHAPTER 17

The week zipped by in a flash and before I knew it, it was Friday afternoon and I was getting ready for work. As I dressed, I reflected on the week; specifically, the times that I had managed to see Gabriel.

Family dinner had been fun on Tuesday night and everyone in the building was in attendance plus Gabriel, but less Matt. Although I had only gone one whole day without seeing Gabriel, I was thrilled when he arrived for dinner. Despite the fact that Gabriel had not brought clothes and my monthly friend was still visiting, I tried to convince him to stay over. I failed and Gabriel left around 9:30 p.m., but not before he reminded me to wear the dress from the Von Bremen dinner on Friday to work and to wear my hair up and off of my back.

Wednesday at work had been the very definition of blah until I found Gabriel waiting by my car when I was leaving. Beside the goodnight kiss he gave me, the real bright spot was him mentioning that he been back to the orthopedist about his foot that day. Things were healing so well that he only had another two weeks in the cast. He would be out of it before Christmas. I was thrilled for him.

Before opening the car door for me, a gesture which still left me awestruck, he handed me a CD. Gabriel smiled and leaned on the car door as he explained his gift. "Play this in the car on your way home. I think you will like it and find that my taste in music is expanding."

I had accepted his gift and then taken my seat as he spoke. I laid the CD on the passenger's seat with my purse.

"Expanding?" I asked as I inserted the keys into the ignition without taking my eyes from Gabriel's.

"It's something country and you know that's not been a big part of my musical repertoire until you came along, so yes, expanding," he replied.

I laughed at the thought of me educating Gabriel on anything. Usually, I was the one under his tutelage.

"You need to be getting home. I don't like you being on the roads between here and Milledgeville at night." Who knew Gabriel was a worrier.

"I will call you as soon as I get home," I assured him as he closed the car door for me.

Through the open window of the car window he told me, "If I do not hear from you by 10:15 p.m., then I am coming to find you and if I find you..." Gabriel's little lecture sounded very much like the ones Aunt Gayle and Granddaddy had given me each time I left for the drive to Young Harris last year.

"Okay," I agreed as I got in the car and Gabriel pushed the door shut for me.

I was barely out of the gate of Port Honor when I put the disc that Gabriel had given me in the CD player. The song was called "When You Say Nothing At All". I recognized the song as a remake of one previously sung by Keith Whitley and he was right up there with Lee Greenwood for Aunt Gayle, so I was quite familiar with the song. This version, however, was sung by the soft whisper-like voice of a woman with little more than the light strumming of a guitar accompanying her. I dare say I liked this version better than the one by Keith Whitley. In fact, considering Gabriel introduced me to it, I loved it and played it repeatedly all the way home.

Initially, I did not sing along, I just listened to the words. Was Gabriel trying to tell me something? How lucky was I if this is how he truly felt about me? As I drove along, my insides jumped up and down at the thought as if I was cheering for myself. Could he really love me that much? Every time I thought I was happy, Gabriel somehow made me happier. By the fourth time through the song, I found myself singing along. I must have sung the song ten times on the way home.

I arrived home with time to spare before the 10:15 p.m. deadline for calling Gabriel, but Emma was on the phone again with Mr. Bama. First I knocked on her door and begged to use the phone for just a moment and then I banged on her door and demanded to use my phone for just a minute. All of my attempts went unanswered. I was infuriated.

It was getting on toward my deadline when I walked downstairs. I knocked on Cara and Megan's door and they were home. I asked to borrow the phone and called Gabriel. I cut the conversation short with him, only letting him know that I had made it home safely. I also let him know that I loved the song and thanked him for giving it to me.

After hanging up with Gabriel and thanking Cara and Megan for the use of their phone, I went back upstairs and politely explained to Emma that if I was not allowed to use my own phone then I might as well have the thing cut off. I explained to her that I had come close to getting out the hedge clippers and cutting the line myself, but felt I would try once more to talk to her about the situation before going to that extreme. I cautioned her that I would have the phone cut off and purchase cell phones for Jay and myself if things kept going as they had been. I suppose she believed me since she apologized profusely and begged me not to cut the phone off. By the end of the night, we had made a compromise as to which nights she could stay on the phone for hours on end and those were the nights when I had to work. We also came to an agreement that if Jay or I asked to use the phone for a moment to let our families or other loved ones know that we arrived home safely, then she would gladly share the phone. We were best buds again before we turned in for the night.

Thinking back on that moment with Emma as I applied my mascara while getting ready for work, I was proud of myself for standing my ground. I had come a long way from the cheerleader in high school that let everyone run all over her. I had also come a long way from the same girl who rarely dated in high school.

I packed a bag and finished getting dressed for work. I put on the dress and I completed my look by pulling my hair up as Gabriel had asked. I called Jay in to have a look at me because his opinion was so much better than just using the full length mirror.

"Wow!" Jay began with the compliments. "I did not get a look at you the day he took you to Atlanta. I now see why you were concerned the next morning. I really don't know how he kept his hands off of you. You are stunning!"

I laughed and shook my head back and forth from side to side, saying no without actually verbalizing it. "Don't make fun of me. I feel weird enough in this thing without my bra so I don't need you picking on me."

"I know you are sometimes insecure about, well, everything, but you really needn't be. You are the prettiest woman I have ever seen," Jay said putting an arm around me and giving me a side arm hug as we stood there looking at ourselves in the mirror.

Jay was a little wary of me making it down the stairs in the high heel shoes, so he helped me and carried my overnight bag to the car. Similar to Gabriel, Jay opened doors for me including the car door. After ushering me into the car, Jay put my bag in the passenger's side seat and wished me a good weekend, since he knew I likely would not be back until Sunday evening.

Although I did not play my new favorite song repeatedly all the way to work, I did play it a time or two and I sang along. When I crossed the Lake Oconee Bridge on Highway 44 I was in full concert singing along with Allison Kraus to "When You Say Nothing At All". The song was not getting old for me. I was waived through the gate at Port Honor with a smile by Officer Ed at ten til five that afternoon and when I arrived in the parking lot of the club the cars of everyone on staff were already there.

On the way to the back door, I found Daniel taking a smoke break and sitting on the steps of the loading dock.

As I approached, Daniel stood and wiped his forehead as if to swoon and gave me a greeting that fit with the send-off that Jay had given me: "My, my, Miss Anderson, don't you look fine?! I believe you might be able to change my religion tonight."

I did not say anything, but hung my head and blushed as I passed by Daniel and continued to the kitchen door.

Once inside the kitchen, I found Alvin busy prepping hors d'oeuvres and Cara at the prep line polishing silver with a new girl. Cara introduced the new girl as Kelly. Kelly could not see Cara's face as Cara was introducing us, so she could not see Cara roll her eyes as she spoke.

The thing that struck me about Kelly was that she had huge green eyes and she was still wearing braces at her age. The more Cara spoke, the bigger Kelly's smile became and the wider her eyes became as well. Kelly was a freshman at Georgia College and lived in Bell Hall. She seemed like a sweet girl and I believe she would have told me her entire life story inside of five minutes if I had not excused myself and left for the dining room.

In the dining room, I found the room totally transformed from the way I was used to seeing it. All of the tables had been removed except for about four along the wall that ran the length of the staircase. A dance floor was set up in the dining room along the far wall next to the room that overlooked the pool. At the front end of the dance floor was the largest karaoke machine I had ever seen.

The room overlooking the pool was set up for the hors d'oeuvres buffet. At the right side of the room was a rolling bar with a Japanese man in a chef uniform standing behind it. Gabriel was also in his chef's attire and was standing in front of the bar with another Japanese man in a suit and tie. The three men appeared to be chatting it up and having a great time with one another. Gabriel looked very much in his element.

I stood there and watched them for a few moments and then Matt and Jerry came in from the direction of the bar.

"Hey, Millie," Matt called to me from across the room.

Gabriel heard Matt and turned from the gentlemen in the buffet room. His eyes lit up when he saw me. He smiled in my direction and gave me the thumbs up and then signaled that he would be just a moment more.

In the meantime, Matt and Jerry had made their way over to me. Jerry was carrying a tray of glasses and Matt was carrying a couple of cases of wine stacked on top of one another.

"I would ask you to get one of these for me, but in that get-up, looking like that, I am not sure you can manage." Normally, no matter how I was dressed, I would have offered to help Matt, but since my eyes were still on Gabriel I hardly noticed he had spoken.

"Millie!" Jerry snapped his fingers in my face and brought my attention back to them. "If you are here to work, then give us a hand. You can stand around and look pretty later."

I did as I was asked and grabbed the tray stand for Jerry to sit the tray of glasses on. They were setting up a wine station right there in the dining room to save guests the trip to the bar unless they wanted a beer or a mixed drink.

Gabriel seemed to be stuck with the gentlemen by the buffet and I was becoming more curious about the bar set up in there. It was clearly not drinks and was not being manned by one of our staff members. I finally asked Jerry and Matt if they knew what was going on in there.

"It's a sushi bar," Jerry began.

"You can go in there and the guy will let you try something. That's if you are brave enough to eat raw fish," Matt teased me.

"Where I am from we call that 'bait' and I assure you, I am as brave as Jerry is," I joked back. Matt laughed, but Jerry was clearly not amused. Everyone suspected, with good reason, that Jerry might be clever, witty and quick with an offense, but brave he likely was not.

I continued to follow Matt and Jerry around aiding them in what I could while dressed like I was going to a formal function. My feet were beginning to hurt and we still had another hour before the event was to start. Matt and Jerry had each gone their separate ways, Jerry on a smoke break and Matt getting a drink at the bar while I was left alone to finish polishing the wine glasses in the dining room. I figured while no one was around, what would it hurt if I got some relief from my shoes for a little while. I was bent over slipping off the heels when Gabriel finally came to greet me. I did not realize anyone else was around when he walked up behind me and ran his index finger down my bare spine. It would have scared the wits out of me if I had not recognized the black and white checked chef pants when I flinched at his touch and noticed his legs just behind me.

"Please stand and let me get a good look at you," Gabriel requested.

I did as he requested. I stood on tip toes to create the look as if I had on my shoes which were now sitting to the side of the credenza just outside of the door leading in from the kitchen. Gabriel appeared to be pleased with my look and he should have been since I had dressed and worn my hair exactly as he had asked.

As Gabriel stood there looking at me, I was reminded that he had a way of biting his lip that made my skin tingle at the sight. I reached to touch his lip to stop him, but he grabbed my hand and pulled me toward him. Before I could protest that someone might walk into the dining room at any moment or the chef at the sushi station might see us, in a move resembling a dance he twirled me into the corridor leading toward the downstairs restrooms. Before I knew what was really happening, he had leaned me against the wall behind the fireplace. I could feel the warmth of the fire through the wall on one side of me and the heat from Gabriel on the other.

"You look perfect," Gabriel whispered as he pressed his face into my hair and breathed in the familiar scent of my shampoo. "Ah, strawberries," he commented.

We were in the darkness of the corridor and I could feel every inch of him pressed against me. One hand bracing my neck and the other of Gabriel's hands was still on the small of my back from where he had guided me there. I could not speak. My thoughts were racing between how badly I wanted him, to how torturous all of this was. I tried to squelch everything by thinking of my make-up and how we should not ruin it before the night got going. We still had to work the party and I needed to look presentable. Perhaps he was thinking the same thing since he had not kissed me yet.

"I need a favor," Gabriel began. He had moved the hand that was on my back down and around. He clearly remembered the slit in the dress and made use of it. Delicately with his fingers, he inched the dress up and slipped his hand through the slit. He continued until he found the hem of my panties.

"Anything," I breathed as I pulled back to look him in the face.

"I would like you to sing tonight..." again I interrupted Gabriel, but I dared not move a muscle as he traced the inside of the hem around from my hip toward the back so very slowly. Short of his kiss, that was his best move for making me pant for him.

"What?" I smiled at him. I was thinking, keep doing that and you can have whatever you want. I did not say it out loud. That thing he did was always so knee weakeningly erotic.

"Did you listen to the song I gave you?"

"Yes," I replied in a sigh, trying to remain composed while he was so distracting.

"And you sang along with it?" Gabriel held me tight and leaned in to kiss my neck. He had turned me in such a manner that anyone coming through from the kitchen or dining room could not see where his hand was.

"Yes," I exhaled while distracted on multiple levels now.

"Sing it tonight. You know you can do it," Gabriel assured me as he continued to try to keep my focus from the task.

I grabbed fistfuls of his white chef's coat and tried to steady myself for reasoning with him as to why I could not do it.

Gabriel leaned back from me, "Here's the thing, there's a karaoke contest and first prize is $500, second prize is $350 and third prize is $100. They have agreed that it is open to anyone in the building tonight including the clubhouse staff. This was my first job with the club last year and the guy that won last year's first prize was a real jerk..."

I stopped him, "You want me to win? And seriously, you have me this worked up just to manipulate me into singing for you?"

"Kind of." Gabriel went on to explain his intentions.

411

I cut him off. "You are highly frustrating." I lowered my leg and squirmed a little to adjust my panties. "Do you know what you do to me Mr. Hewitt?"

"The guy that won second place should have won. He has a much better voice, sounds just like Elvis, but he's no showman; the type of guy that has the perfect face for radio, if you get my meaning. The guy that won is young and full of himself, but his voice isn't in the ballpark with the likes of the other guy. It was like watching Vanilla Ice beat Elvis, painful, very painful. Anyway, I just thought you could even the playing field a little."

"Gabriel, I have told you, I am not the best at singing," I said with caution.

"Amelia, looking like this," he said as he looked me up and down, "it almost won't matter what you sound like, but you will be great. I just know it,"

"So, let me get this straight, you don't want me to beat anyone, you actually want the guy that sounds like Elvis to win?" I asked.

"Right. And, I am sorry if you feel that I have manipulated you, but I did not believe you would do it just because I asked you." Gabriel slowly released me as if he was letting me go and waiting for my answer.

"I will do it for you, but I think you have too much faith in me."

"You forget I heard you sing with your Aunt the other night and I know you don't have enough faith in yourself."

"Fine," I said placing both of my hands on each side of his face and standing on my tip toes again, I kissed Gabriel. It was a sweet soft kiss thanking him for believing in me, but nothing that would have ruined my make-up; I could not say the same for my underpants. Then we left the corridor and returned to our tasks. Gabriel also went to change into a suit and out of the chef get up. He was leaving the rest of the real work in the kitchen that night to Alvin.

Between 7:00 and 7:30 p.m., the employees of Delta Digital trickled in and the party was in full roar just before 8:00. I am not sure how the word got out, but it had spread through the staff that I would be participating in the karaoke contest and this was setting my nerves on edge. The contest was set to start at 8:00. So things would not be so horribly obvious, Gabriel convinced Kelly to enter the contest as well. He failed to tell her that her entry was just a formality.

There were fifteen participants and we were divided into groups of five. As luck and Gabriel's wishes would have it, Kelly was among the first five to perform as was the winner from last year. Mr. Ross aka Elvis and I were in the last five.

Kelly chose to sing "Material Girl" by Madonna. As my grandfather would have put it, "She could not carry a tune in a bucket." She was absolutely terrible and Gabriel should have been ashamed of himself for putting her up to that. She could not keep the beat while trying to dance along. She missed words and could not keep up with reading and singing at the same time. It was pitiful and brought back memories of the Gong Show and surely she would have been gonged within fifteen seconds of her performance, but instead we all had to endure over three minutes of her attempt.

The guy that Gabriel had described as Vanilla Ice followed Kelly and compared to her, he was dang near awesome. He was a guy of about twenty-five and looked like he could have been a member of New Kids on the Block in his younger years, but now he was just a guy who sang karaoke at a company Christmas party. By some standards, he was a good looking guy, but he had nothing on any of the guys that worked at Port Honor, not even in the ballpark with Gabriel, Andy or Matt. He wore a decent suit and his date looked like she might still be in high school. His name was Robbie Gleason and he had on so much cologne that one might think he bathed in it.

When it was Robbie's turn at the mike, he did not face the karaoke machine, he faced the crowd. He did more gyrating than dancing and, for whatever reason, the women swooned, all while he sang "Hotel California", the Al B. Sure version, but the music on the karaoke machine was set to the tune of the Eagles version. Once he was finished, the crowd clapped and clapped and his date fanned her face and appeared flushed. Gabriel was right about him. I liked the Al B. Sure version and I liked the Eagles' version, but this was almost painful to watch. He was definitely more of a showman than a singer.

There were other contestants who tried and there were some who did not try at all. One woman sang "Look At Me, I'm Sandra Dee" from the Grease soundtrack and her husband sang "Beauty School Dropout". They were hysterical and everyone was amused. Not everyone was horrible, but by no means was everyone good.

Every so often as the night progressed, Gabriel would find me and give me a little pep talk. By the fourth pep talk, I asked him to stop. It was not helping at all. In fact, it was making me more nervous.

I tried to think of things to do to keep busy and to be helpful with the party. After all, I was there to work. I checked on the buffet several times and reported back to Alvin regarding what items needed to be refilled. I picked up stray glasses that people had discarded and took them to the dish pit.

Finally, it was my turn at the karaoke machine. Gabriel sent Cara and Kelly out to help me pick my song even though he had made that decision quite some time ago. The three of us scrolled through the list of songs until we came across "When You Say Nothing At All" and I picked it. Cara and Kelly both commented on how they had never heard it as the man operating the machine handed me the microphone and punched in my choice.

Initially, I faced the karaoke machine, but as the song opened I turned to find Gabriel in the crowd. He was wearing a dark blue suit and a white button down shirt with no tie. I was not the only one who looked like a version of themselves from the night we went to the Georgian Terrace. As always, he was the stuff of which dreams were made. My mind slipped to thoughts of how badly I wanted to kiss him and I would do just that as soon as I was done with the song.

I had seen Gabriel just as it was time for me to join my voice with the music. He smiled one last smile of encouragement as I closed my eyes and began. I could hear Allison Kraus' voice in my head and I had sung with her all week long. Her voice was light like a whisper and each time I did my best to mimic hers.

I was so nervous I could feel the hives spring to my chest. I pushed on. As I sang, I could feel that someone dimmed the lights in the dining room, but there still seemed to be a spotlight on me. I had insisted on having the microphone on the pole when I sang and initially I hung on to it for dear life with both hands, but by end of the first chorus, I was loosening up and letting go a little.

When I first started, I could hear the voices of people talking in the room, but by the middle of the song the room was silent. The room was spinning for me and the butterflies were ever present in my stomach. I tried to focus on the words, but it was as if I could feel Gabriel's gaze beating down on me. Though the room was full, without a doubt, I was singing to him.

Hands free of the microphone pole, but eyes still shut, I lost all inhibitions and gave into the music. I swayed with the beat and I could feel the material of the dress gently flow against my legs as I moved.

I knew this was likely the performance of my life. I could scarcely believe it was my voice that I was hearing. I had never sung alone in front of people like this before and I even though I did not want to win, I did not want to embarrass myself either. I prayed I did the song justice and I prayed I did not look like Stevie Wonder bobbing my head while singing with my eyes closed.

I opened my eyes briefly and sang the end, the final round of the chorus, as my eyes locked with Gabriel's. It was as if we were alone, but as soon as the song wound down the applause erupted and the room was suddenly filled with people again.

I could see Gabriel clapping feverishly with everyone else and smiling so proudly at me. He mouthed the words, "I knew you could do it," to me. It was at that point, that I took a bow. When I stood back up, I could see he was trying to make his way toward me, but Cara and Kelly made it to me first with their congratulations and compliments. They were followed by Daniel and Matt and several of the partygoers. I felt as though I was never going to get away from all of them and I could no longer see Gabriel and his was the only opinion that I really wanted.

I was finally able to make a break and excuse myself. I found Gabriel in the bar making a drink for himself and talking with the gentleman that I had seen him with when I first arrived at work that afternoon. Unlike earlier, this time when Gabriel noticed my presence, he took his leave from the gentleman at once.

There were few other people in the room other than those that were seated in the barstools at the bar, so Gabriel gestured for me to follow him over to the fireplace. Normally, he would have taken my hand or led me with his hand placed gently on the small of my back, but this time he did not lay a hand on me and did not even offer.

"You will forgive me, but I cannot touch you right now," Gabriel said as we stood side by side in front of the fire.

It was as if he had read my mind because at first I was concerned that he was disappointed in me, but then he continued, "You've never been more beautiful and I have never wanted you more than I do right now. Remember what I told you the night on the porch? If I start, I won't stop."

We stood there together warming our hands at the fire and I cut my eyes at him and smiled. "You liked the song?"

"Liked it? I loved it!" Gabriel replied and slid a step to the side, in the direction opposite of me. He put even more distance between us. We continued to stand there in silence for a few minutes. All I wanted to do was to grab him and test him, see if he really would forget the world for me. I refrained and stayed on my side of the fireplace.

I wanted to see Mr. Ross' performance, so I finally broke the silence and told Gabriel that I was going back to the dining room. He agreed that that was probably for the best.

I arrived back in the dining room just as Mr. Ross was taking his place at the microphone and the karaoke machine. I had spoken with him earlier before I sang and he introduced me to his wife. She looked like she could have been a cousin of Jay's mother; there was a slight resemblance. He looked like he had the man's version of the Dorothy Hamill haircut, very similar to the one I had when I was a little girl. Mrs. Ross was wearing black slacks and a Rudolph the Red Nosed Reindeer sweater, yes, his nose was glowing. Mr. Ross was dressed similarly with black jeans and an equally ridiculous Christmas sweater. They appeared to be about the same age and if I had to guess, I would guess they were probably in their early fifties. Again, Gabriel was right. They were not the most attractive people, but they seemed exceptionally nice.

While Mr. Ross was picking his song, Mrs. Ross had made her way to the edge of the dance floor. Mr. Ross picked "Always on My Mind" by Elvis Presley. Like Robbie Gleason and I, Mr. Ross did not need to face the karaoke machine for reading and singing along with the words. Mr. Ross knew all of the words and gave a fabulous performance directed specifically to his wife. I stood next to Mrs. Ross so I could see him as he sang, but most of the time my eyes were closed and he sounded so much like Elvis that that's who I saw in my head as the music played.

I glanced at Mrs. Ross a couple of times as her husband sang. Her eyes were glued to him and her hands were clasped over her heart. You could tell from the look on her face that she adored him and the way he sang to her, any fool could tell the feeling was mutual. I was fascinated to see a couple their age still so very much in love. My mind wandered a little toward the end of the song and I allowed myself to wonder if Gabriel and I would still look at each other like that when we were their age.

Mr. Ross received just as much applause as Robbie Gleason when he was finished singing. As everyone clapped for him, and some even cat-called, Mr. Ross' eyes were still on his wife until he took a bow. When the clapping started to wind down, Mr. Ross walked over to Mrs. Ross and kissed her.

Soon after Mr. Ross left the stage, the Japanese gentleman that was speaking with Gabriel when I first arrived at work took the microphone and started to speak. One could look at him and guess that he was not a native of rural middle Georgia, but when he spoke the accent definitely gave it away. His accent was thick and he was a little hard to understand, but from what I could tell he stated the following:

"On behalf of the other owners of Delta Digital and myself, thank you all for your hard work with the company. It has been another great year and it is all due to you. Thank you."

A short woman, who looked like the typical rural Georgia forty-something-year old woman, brown football helmet hair, Christmas sweater and black slacks and Santa earrings, handed him an envelope.

The gentleman opened the envelope and then cleared his throat before speaking. He smiled a huge toothy smile as he spoke, "This year we have a tie in our annual karaoke contest. The finalists are Robbie Gleason and Dean Ross of Delta Digital and Millie Anderson of Port Honor."

When the gentleman spoke my name, I was shocked. I immediately glanced around the room for Gabriel. I could hardly see him. He was standing near the door leading from the kitchen with everyone on staff, but Andy who was still manning the bar. They were all cheering and clapping vigorously for me. I smiled back bashfully. I was completely in shock that my name had been called as one of the finalists. I had not had Gabriel's faith that I would even come close to winning.

While the gentleman continued his speech about winners, I also noticed Mrs. Ross was hugging Mr. Ross and heaping tons of compliments on him.

"It is my suggestion that the finalists must sing again and if their first song was a slow song then their second song must be a more up tempo song. Now we will draw straws to see which of our contestants sings first."

The straws were drawn and, discounting the other contestants, the order of the three of us was unchanged. Robbie Gleason was to go first, I was in the middle and Mr. Ross was to close the show. Even though I was to perform second, Mr. Ross insisted that ladies got to choose first and Robbie reluctantly went along. He was not the gentleman that Mr. Ross was.

I quickly picked my song and then went to find Daniel while the other two picked their songs. I found Daniel easily enough, but avoiding Gabriel in doing so was another matter. I saw Gabriel coming, so I ducked through the crowd and went through the bar. I looked back to see that Gabriel had been pulled by the arm into a conversation with the gentleman throwing the party.

Once I had dodged Gabriel, I pulled Daniel into the kitchen by the door to the walk-in refrigerator. I asked Daniel hurriedly, "Please distract Gabriel while I run to my car."

"I don't know that there will be any distracting him. I think he wants to congratulate you and help pick your second song," Daniel responded.

"Just keep an eye on him and if you see him looking for me, grab him and I don't know, tell him you spoke with me and what I am going to sing is a surprise," I insisted as I started backing away from Daniel and heading toward the back door of the kitchen.

I only had about ten minutes before it would be my turn to sing. In those ten minutes, I managed to run to my car, grab my overnight bag and return to the ladies room to change. I had a plan which might not win the contest for me, but it was likely to rock Gabriel's world or I was likely to embarrass myself beyond belief.

Through the walls of the ladies room, I could hear Robbie doing a bump and grind version of "Little Sister". That ass was trying to beat Mr. Ross at his own game by usurping Elvis. As I pulled on my jeans, the jeans I was forbidden to wear in public, I thanked God that I was in the restroom as opposed to witnessing the butchering of what was previously a fine song. Sadly, I could just imagine from the muffled sound coming through the walls, how the murder was coming along. I grunted and rolled my eyes at the noise as I took my hair down and shook it out in the mirror.

I emerged from the restroom with little time to spare. I passed Gabriel on my way to the karaoke machine. His eyes lit up when he saw me.

"Come with me," I told him as I passed him, grabbing his hand and pulling him with me.

"What are you doing? What are you wearing?" Gabriel questioned as I pulled him along. What I was wearing was the same outfit I had on the night we met at Cameron's, ripped jeans, white tank top, but with my cowboy boots this time. My hair was longer now than the night at Cameron's and, not only had I curled it before pinning it up, it had held the curl and the twisting from being pulled up just made it that much more wavy, dang near pageant hair. I had also taken a moment to apply heavier eye make-up than was my norm. I looked to be quite the vamp.

Robbie was finished, the clapping was winding down and I was just about to the dance floor with Gabriel still in hand when I waived to the man operating the karaoke machine to let him know I was ready. I gestured with the circling index finger in the air for him to fire up my song and he started it. I also motioned for him to crank it up loud.

The man at the machine did as I had asked and the music started thumping just as my feet hit the dance floor and I let go of Gabriel's hand. I started moving to the beat as I walked farther toward the machine. The man tossed the microphone to me and I held it behind my back as I turned back and said to Gabriel, "Don't go anywhere."

My insides were quaking with nerves and I could not believe I was about to sing the Joan Jett song that nearly got all of us cheerleaders expelled from school when we did a dance routine to it my senior year of high school. We were tired of the football team getting all of the attention, so one of the girls suggested this song and I was the only one that voted against it. I still knew the routine and the words were a breeze to remember, but my knees were nearly shaking all the same.

It had taken so much for me to commit to singing the first song of the night that I could not believe I had selected this song, but I did not see any other fast songs with which I was familiar. I did my best to leave my inhibitions, which were extensive, on the other side of the ladies room door. This song was so out of character for me that everyone was likely to be shocked, but I was determined to give it my all. Mostly, I loved the look of pride Gabriel had had on his face after I had finished the first song. I loved the way he had looked at me and I wanted that again. I would sing anything, embarrass myself in any number of ways, just to have him look at me like that.

The whole crew from Port Honor had pushed their way to the edge of the dance floor to see me. They flanked Gabriel and I gathered my nerves.

I started to sing the words of Joan Jett. Most of her songs start out with similar beats, so I am not sure if anyone knew what I was about sing until I started.

419

"We've been here too long trying to get along, Pretending that you're oh so shy, I'm a natural ma'am doing all I can, My temperature is running high, Cry at night no one in sight and we've got so much to share, Talkin's fine, if you got the time, but I ain't got the time to spare, yeah," I belted out keeping to the beat as I circled the dance floor. I ran my hand across the chest of all of the men that were standing near the edge of the dance floor.

I had started with Daniel who was standing to the left of Gabriel. I kept going and until I worked my way back around and made it to Gabriel just in time for the chorus, "Do you wanna touch, Do you wanna touch me, Do you wanna touch me there? Where? There, yeah!"

Gabriel's face was a little red, but he was smiling like there was no tomorrow. Everyone was bouncing with the beat.

I continued on with the song and my dance, but focused more on Gabriel. Everyone was getting into it including Gabriel. In response to the question in the chorus, the whole room answered, "Yeah!"

"Every girl and boy needs a little joy. All you do is sit and stare. Beggin' on my knees, Baby won-cha please, run your fingers through my hair." With those lyrics I rolled my shoulders, swayed my hips, bent my knees and wiggled to a squatting position while keeping to the beat and running my hands through my own hair right in front of Gabriel.

"My, my, my, whiskey and rye, don't it make you feel so fine? Right or wrong, gonna turn you on..." the song continued on.

Again when it came to the chorus, the whole room answered and sang along: "Yeah! Oh, Yeah!" just like in the actual Joan Jett performance.

When the song stopped, the whole room erupted in clapping and cheering. I turned and tossed the microphone back to the man that was operating the karaoke machine. I did not wait to make sure he caught it before I turned back around and took a bow. I then strutted toward Gabriel. From his speech earlier, I knew better than to jump in his arms. I had been worried when I first came out with the forbidden jeans that he would not necessarily be pleased and on top of the wearing the jeans I had just performed Joan Jett's Do You Wanna Touch, but from the look on his face he was pleased. He was grinning from ear to ear and likely clapping harder than anyone else in the room. As I approached him, I threw up my hand and high-fived him and kept walking, head held high, all the way to the kitchen door. I totally faked it; I was about as nervous then as I had been when the song first started.

I put everything I had into singing and dancing. It was the first time I could recall doing both at the same time short of in the comfort of my own home. I was winded to say the least and still embarrassed that I had actually picked that song and then really went for it. Not to mention, most everyone I worked with had just witnessed my routine. I did my best to portray confidence and hide any embarrassment or shame.

Andy had avoided the crowd in the dining room, went through the bar and was the first one to find me catching my breath in the kitchen.

"Wow, Millie! I did not know you had it in you," Andy commented.

"Yeah, me neither," I sighed while knowing my face was red and the hives were out on my chest.

"Would you like a drink? I will get you whatever you want from the bar," Andy offered.

"I would love a Coke. Thanks!" I replied as everyone else started to trickle into the kitchen to find me.

Andy left to fetch me the drink just as the roar of the dining room seemed to take over the kitchen. I was leaning up against the stainless steel kitchen shelves on the front line when Daniel was the first to grab and hug me. He heaped praise on me.

"Not bad," Jerry added and from Jerry that was as good a compliment as he ever gave. He was always one to accept compliments, but rarely one to give them.

Cara was ecstatic and was all "Take that, greasy Robbie Gleason!"

Matt's words were, "Damn, that was hot, Millie!" to which we all laughed.

Alvin and Rudy had even come from the kitchen and witnessed everything as well. Their compliments began with a collective, "Wow!" and culminated with Rudy stating, "Dang, that was smokin'!"

"Are you all sure that wasn't too much? Please tell me I did not just embarrass myself in front of the whole room," I begged.

Daniel patted me on the back and in front of everyone explained, "Every woman in the room wanted to be you and every man in the room wanted to...touch you 'there'."

As we all started to laugh, I heard Gabriel's voice come from the other side of the prep line. "I could not have put it better, Daniel," Gabriel said.

"I told her to even the playing field you all. I did not tell her to win, but I think she may have," Gabriel explained to everyone with a big grin on his face.

I smiled so big at Gabriel that everyone probably thought my face was going to break. . Seriously, it was ear to ear and he just shook his head at me and smiled back. My smile at him was for what he said and for my thoughts of going home with him that night. I could hardly wait.

The moment was broken when Andy returned with my Coke.

"Thanks!" I said as he handed it to me. I started drinking it, but heard the music start to fire up for Mr. Ross' song. I put the glass down and we all ran back out into the dining room.

We were too late to get spots near the dance floor, so we all ran to the stairs so we could get a better view. I started to grab Gabriel's hand as we started up the stairs, but he gave me a reminder of the speech from the fireplace earlier. "Just wait," he whispered and I nearly giggled out loud at the thought of later.

Each of us took a place on a step starting at about the fifth step from the bottom. We barely made it to our spots before Mr. Ross started to sing. Despite the Gleason guy's attempt to steal Mr. Ross's market on Elvis songs, Mr. Ross still chose another one by Elvis. It was likely that the only songs Mr. Ross was comfortable with were those sung by Elvis since he sounded so much like him.

This time Mr. Ross sang Burning Love. We all leaned against the rail on the staircase watching and dancing along. When I closed my eyes I could see myself sitting on the floor in Granddaddy and Granny's living room as Granny listened to her Elvis records. This song was one of her favorites. Her record had a slight skip, but it was not so severe that we had to get up and move the needle of the record player.

"...Your kisses lift me higher, like the sweet song of a choir. You light my morning sky, Burning love..." Gabriel mouthed the words as Mr. Ross sang.

"...I feel my temperature rising. Help me I'm flaming..." I could almost hear Gabriel on one side of me and Daniel on the other singing along. "...It's hard to breathe; my chest is a heaving...A hunk-a hunk-a burning love..."

Mr. Ross gave quite the performance. He did his best to keep up with the other two of us. He shook his bum and used a chair as a prop. He wasn't all bump and grind like his co-worker had been and he wasn't as interactive with the audience as I had been, but he did his best and it worked for him. It helped that he did not try to be something he wasn't and that was sexy.

The one thing that Mr. Ross did do that seemed out of character was at the end of the song. He ran from the far corner of the dance floor toward the chair until he came to the chair and ran up on it tipping it over and riding it to the floor. It would have been devastating if he had fallen, but he didn't. It was pretty smooth move for a fifty year old man. That he even chanced it was amazing, I thought. As soon as his feet hit the ground safely, Mrs. Ross ran and jumped in his arms and we all squealed, jumped up and down and cheered for him.

Shortly after Mr. Ross' performance, the owner of Delta Digital took the microphone again. He announced the winners and Gabriel's plan had worked. Mr. Ross won first place, I won second and Robbie Gleason came in third. We all congratulated Mr. Ross. As it turned out, he had a son serving in the Army and he was stationed at a base in San Diego, California. If Mr. Ross won, they planned to use the money to pay for Mrs. Ross to go and visit him for Christmas. They could not afford for both of them to go. I ended up endorsing the check for my winnings and giving it to them, so that Mr. Ross might be able to go too. It took a great deal of persuasion, but they reluctantly and thankfully accepted it.

It had been near 10:00 p.m. when the winners were announced so it wasn't long before the party was winding down and Gabriel came to find me. I had changed back into my dress and pulled my hair back up. I had only done that because jeans were not allowed in the clubhouse and I had been horribly under dressed in the jeans and tank top. I was helping pick up glasses from around the dining room and taking them to the dish pit when I felt someone behind me.

"Miss Anderson, are you ready to go home?" Gabriel asked in a whisper over my shoulder.

I turned and smiled at him but before I could verbalize an answer, Gabriel spoke again. "Let's go," he said and he took the

423

glasses from my hands and put them back down on the table. "Someone else will get these."

Gabriel extended his hand to me and I took it. We stopped only to get my overnight bag before heading out; all the while we were hand in hand. It was undeniable, a thousand lightening- strikes under his hand on my bare back. I could hardly wait to be home, alone, with Gabriel.

I followed Gabriel home in my car. I had tried to convince him to let me ride with him, but he would not hear of me leaving the Corvette parked at the club. He argued with me that it was the most important thing to me and he would not want anything to happen to it.

Being the gentleman he was, he parked then came to open the car door for me. As soon as he opened the door, he offered his hand to help me get out. In that moment, I corrected him regarding what was most important to me. "It used to be the most important, but it pales in comparison to you."

Gabriel did not respond with words to what I said, but as I stood from my seat in the car, he pulled me into his arms and held me for a moment. It was cold outside and I was hardly dressed compared to him in his suit. Normally my arms would have found their way around his neck, but instead I snuggled into his chest and wrapped my arms through his jacket. The lining was cold and I shivered as Gabriel pulled the pins out that were holding up my hair. I held him tightly and tried to focus on the moment and not the fact that there were chill bumps down my back which only had my hair covering it. These were not the usual chill bumps from his touch, but actual chills from the cold.

Gabriel tilted my head and kissed me softly right there in the yard between the door and the cab of the car. All thoughts of being cold escaped my mind while Gabriel ran his right hand up my leg through the slit in the dress. His hand kept traveling up, up, up until he ran his hand around my left butt cheek. He traced the leg line of my lace panties and slid his finger under the hem again. I did not think I would ever get used to how that trick of his made me feel. I lifted my leg and propped my foot on the door frame of the Corvette as his fingers continued just under the hem line of my panties.

"What would you say to me taking these off of you right now?" Gabriel asked as he gave the panties a gentle tug.

"Here in the yard?" I stifled my gasp so as not to appear a prude. On one hand I was shocked, but on the other I was incredibly turned on and would have indulged him most anything.

"Here in the yard," he replied.

With little hesitation I gave my consent and using his hand that had been tracing the hem, he managed to slide my panties down my thighs until they fell loosely to the ground and I stepped out of them. Gabriel slid his hand down my leg while he bent over to retrieve my panties.

Gabriel only removed his hand from my leg long enough to stuff my panties in the pocket of his jacket. As he ran his hand back up my leg, he commented softly, "If it weren't so cold out I would have you right here against your car, Miss Anderson."

"Words like that make me eager for summer Mr. Hewitt."

Again, Gabriel's hand was on my backside. This time there were no panties, just bare behind. As his hands gripped my behind and pulled me so close to him that I could feel what was in store for me, his mouth was providing continued education on kissing. I was quite sure I was about to get an education on another subject matter and everything about me wanted to learn.

The activities in the yard continued for some time before Gabriel pulled away.

"You are freezing. Let's get you inside," Gabriel insisted before taking my bags from me. He opened car doors and carried my luggage.

Despite the fact that he had wrapped his jacket around me for the short walk from the driveway to the porch, goose bumps covered every inch of my arms and legs. Normally, in this weather, in this outfit, I would have been chilled to the bone, but instead I was cold on the outside and on fire on the inside. I huddled against his back while Gabriel unlocked the front door.

Once inside, I fully expected another turn against the front door. Perhaps I even expected more against the door since I was already without any trace of underwear. I dare say I had looked forward to it, but instead Gabriel stopped only long enough to free me from his jacket and lay it across the couch. He then proceeded to lead me down the hall toward his room in the back of the house.

When we arrived at the door to his room, Gabriel released my hand and moved across the room to sit my pink duffle bag in its usual spot in the armchair near the window. When he left me standing there next to the door to dispose of my things and cut on the lamp, it was as if I did not know what to do with myself. The gravity of the moment was starting to fill my thoughts and I fidgeted in my shoes from nervousness and the pain of the heels. Before my thoughts could completely run away with me, Gabriel returned to take my hands.

"May I?" I asked him as he had asked me in the past.

"Yes, of course," he replied with a slight hint of thrill for me to have asked.

Instead of kissing him, I eased my hands to the top button of his shirt and began. I worked my way down to the last button and slipped it loose. Gabriel had stood still, only running his fingers across my back as I went about the task with the buttons. I would have likely finished sooner had I not had to contend with the bewilderment of his touch up and down my spine.

Our eyes remained locked as I finished with the buttons and slid my hands up his chest parting the white dress shirt until I came to his shoulders. I ran my hands under the shirt and slowly pushed it away. It fell down his arms and he released me from his touch only long enough to let the shirt ease off and drop to the floor.

I fidgeted again on my feet trying to get relief from the sandals. This time Gabriel noticed.

"May I get those for you?" Gabriel began to squat, first positioning his hands on my hips while doing so. Then, the slit in the dress came in handy again. From my hips, he moved his hands to my left leg, one hand on the inside of my leg, so high that I felt him brush gently against what would have normally been covered by my panties, but they were now in the pocket of his jacket laying on the couch. The other hand was placed on the outside of my leg.

"Smooth," he commented as he proceeded to glide his hands down my leg until he came to the latch of my right shoe. He lifted my foot slightly and unbuckled it, eased it off and laid it to the side.

Despite the dress and the lack of a slit on the other side, Gabriel removed the right shoe following the same series of events as the left. Again, there was a gentle grazing past my labia and my insides quivered. I stood there on my toes wondering what was next.

"Would you like to shower?" Gabriel did not so much question as he offered.

"With you?" I asked in a hushed tone almost with the hint of shock or skepticism. What was I thinking? Of course with him. How could I have asked?

"If you like," he replied while pulling his undershirt over his head leaving him bare- chested. His slacks and a dress shoe were all that remained of that evening's wardrobe as he headed into the bathroom.

I think everything about me stood at attention when he said it. The words still rang in my ears and he was well out of the room. I was like a kid in a candy store when it came to looking at him. He never ceased to mesmerize me with his looks and with the things he said to me, but each time I thought I was going to fully experience him, things stalled. Could tonight really be the night?

In the bathroom, I found Gabriel's slacks across the counter by the sink. Gabriel was already in the shower. Steam was starting to build and had glazed over the shower door. I could scarcely see his outline, with the exception of the bright blue waterproof cast that he was still obligated to for another couple of weeks. Beyond that, the mystery of him remained.

I untied the strings around my neck that held the dress in place and likewise around my waist. I let the dress fall to the floor and there I stood, completely naked. I pulled my hair back up to keep it from getting wet and then I opened the shower door.

"I was beginning to wonder if you were coming in," Gabriel said as he turned toward me and offered his hand to help me step in.

Beads of water started to hit me, they were hot and the whole shower was warm. My chill from earlier was starting to fade. I had been impressed with the size of the shower in the past so the fact that both of us fit in there with plenty of room was no surprise. The real surprise was that all insecurities were wiped away and I could hardly think at all. I could hardly breathe. I was just me, plain old Millie from Avera, Georgia and that was not anything that I was insecure about, it was just the way it was, but Gabriel could have been Michelangelo's inspiration for David.

I felt tears start toward my eyes. Gabriel noticed the tears. He did not pull me toward him; he came to me and enveloped me in his arms.

"Are you alright?" Gabriel asked as he stroked my cheek.

"I am better than ever," I said as I looked up at him and a tear escaped my right eye. "If I've ever been happier, I cannot remember it."

Gabriel leaned down and kissed me. It was sweet and gentle, yet passionate and knee weakening. Within seconds, Gabriel pulled away from the kiss leaving me wanting more.

"Let's finish up in here, shall we?" Gabriel smiled before he took the washcloth and lathered it up. "Turn around and I will do your back."

I did as he requested and turned from him. Gabriel did not stop with my back. He continued from my back to my shoulders to my chest and stomach area and finished with my arms and legs. I melted against him as he ran the washcloth over me. He was careful not to wet my hair.

Gabriel stepped aside and allowed me to rinse.

"Shall I return the favor?" I asked him.

"Not this time," Gabriel replied. Gabriel then opened the shower door and began to step out. He turned back to me, "Take your time if you like."

I finished up in the shower quickly. I exited to find a new terrycloth robe laid across the counter by the sink where Gabriel's pants had been when I entered the shower. The robe was embroidered with "Mr. Hewitt" on it. Not only had he put the robe out for me, but he had put it in the dryer and it was still warm when I wrapped it around myself. I pulled it around me and up to my nose to smell. It was like breathing in Gabriel and the scent was intoxicating.

I found Gabriel in the bedroom pulling the drapes closed. I stood in the door and watched him for a moment before I spoke. He was wearing my favorite pirate pajama pants and that was it. When he turned back he was surprised to see me, but his look turned quickly from a look of surprise to a look of serenity.

"Would you say it?" he asked as he stood and stared at me. The robe was so big that tying it round me was not enough and I had forgotten that. I stood with my hands by my sides and the neck of the robe fell leaving one of my shoulders uncovered except for my hair that rested on them and flowed down my back.

"Say what?" I asked as if I were confused. I was completely toying with him, but I liked to hear him ask.

"You know."

He was right, I did know and I responded, "I am yours."

"And the other," Gabriel requested as he bit his bottom lip and awaited my response.

I secured the robe before strolling across the carpet to fulfill his second request. I stood on my toes and reached my hands up to hold both sides of his face. The slight stubble on his face was prickly against my fingers.

"I love you more than words can say," I assured him as I looked in his eyes.

Gabriel pulled me close and again I was on my toes. Instinctively, my arms went around his neck. One of his hands was in my hair, gripping me. I had never been held so tightly or kissed so deeply, with such passion. The kiss was so deep and intense that I was almost instantly wet.

Gabriel leaned back from me and whispered, "Are you certain about this, Amelia?"

I answered him with the slight nod of my head. I was breathless and weak kneed from the kiss and on fire for him all at once.

Gabriel returned with a second kiss and with the hand that was not in my hair and steadying my neck, he lifted me.

There was no music in the room, but Mazzie Star's "Fade Into You" played in my mind. I loved that song and it had meant nothing beyond pretty music to me until that moment. I had heard once that it was actually written about being in love with a heroin addict. Perhaps I was the addict. Perhaps it was me that never knew. I had never known I had the capacity to love someone that much until then and perhaps I had become addicted to that feeling.

Everything about the way Gabriel moved was slow, gentle and deliberate like the rhythm of the song. From laying me on the bed to planting kisses down my neck and beyond; a light in me was coming on slowly. The music in my head played on and I did not notice the loss of the robe.

Aunt Gayle had always cautioned, "Don't let anyone use you and remember it's most special with someone you love."

I doubted she knew what she was talking about since I had never known her to be with anyone. I still did not know how she knew, but she was right. I loved Gabriel to the moon and back, to Pluto and back a dozen times maybe more and I could not imagine anything having been more perfect. It really was as if we had faded into one another.

I have heard that some people are afraid their first time. All my life had been building toward this moment and now that it was here, I knew who I was supposed to be. I was the person meant for Gabriel Hewitt and my only fear was what if he did not know that too.

There was a split second when everything was finished that the song ended in my head and my mind was flooded with insecurities. I had enjoyed the night's lesson immensely, but what if Gabriel was disappointed. What if he realized he wanted someone that he did not have to constantly teach?

Gabriel had rolled onto his back and before my mind could get carried away any further he pulled me over on top of him. "We are going to rest for a little while and if you are up for it, we will try that again."

"I am up for it if you are," I said softly as not to seem overly eager, which I was.

"I love you Amelia and you are amazing." It was as if he could read my mind and knew exactly what to say to squash the demons of insecurity. I could feel him breathe as I laid my head on his chest.

CHAPTER 18

As was typical of Georgia that time of year, the weather had shifted drastically in the last few days. Friday had been in the forties, Saturday in the fifties and then today had been an Indian summer with temperatures in the mid-seventies. There was sunshine to spare and that meant tons of golfers on the course, me on the beverage cart and tips galore. It also meant I had not gotten off work until almost 5:00 p.m.

I had been so busy that I hardly had time to mentally savor my weekend until the drive home. Once I was on the road to Milledgeville, the memories of the weekend began to play in front of my eyes as if there was a silver screen on the windshield. I could almost feel Gabriel still on my skin and I got chill bumps from the thought. I had been so lost in thought that I missed the turn for the shortcut. It was not the first time I had done that, found myself essentially waking up in Milledgeville at the intersection of North Columbia and Montgomery Streets not one hundred percent sure of how I had gotten there. I made the entire drive, passing through Eatonton, crossing Lake Sinclair, the power plant and its ominous smoke stacks, all on autopilot.

Jay's Mazda, which he referred to as the "poor man's Porsche", was under the carport when I pulled in. This was a good indication that he was home and I was thrilled at the idea. Although I would have been content staying at Gabriel's indefinitely, we had a deal about weeknights and school, plus I could not wait to tell Jay everything, well almost everything.

Emma had gone to Alabama for the weekend and it was far too early for her to be home. In fact, she had warned us that she might not be back until Tuesday and that was fine. This meant I had Jay's undivided attention.

I grabbed my bag from the car and went in to find Jay sitting on the couch. The back of the couch faced the door and from where Jay was sitting all he had to do was tilt his head back to greet me.

"How was your weekend?" Jay asked.

"If you really want to know, you are going to have to cut the television off," I replied as dropped my bag just beyond the door as it shut behind me.

The words had scarcely escaped my lips when Jay snapped to, cut the TV off and turned around. He scooted to one end and pulled his legs up in the crisscross apple sauce style on the couch. He had also turned to face the space I flopped down in at the other end. I pulled up my legs and sat in the same fashion facing Jay.

"Oh my God," I squealed as I grabbed Jays hands.

Jay truly was my oldest and dearest, somewhat girlfriend. Jay knew immediately just by the look on my face and he squealed as well. "Finally! How was it? Tell me everything!"

"As I have told you before, one of the girls at Young Harris described her first time as like letting someone else pick her nose. Clearly the guy she was with had no idea what he was doing because that is not the way it was with Gabriel at all." As I described to Jay how things had gone, it was hard not to relive the experience as I had done in the car on the way home.

"What do you mean?" Jay was intrigued. "And to be clear, most folk's first times are awful."

"I mean, I hate Beth Reed to the ten thousandth degree, but I suppose I don't mind so terribly much that he had a test dummy until he met me." Just saying it felt like spitting out vinegar pepper sauce, but I continued. "You know how Emma seems to have the opinion that experience is a good thing? I think she might be a little right. Now don't misunderstand, on one hand, the thought of him being with or having been with anyone other than me, just disgusts me, but I think I may have benefitted from his experience."

Jay started to laugh, "So you think there's some validity in the phrase 'practice makes perfect.'"

"Now, now, I don't want to think he practiced a lot or anything," I corrected Jay. "I am telling you, he knows, and I emphasize, *knows*, what he is doing. I had no idea and he was patient with me and reassuring and...just the most amazing..."

Jay cut me off. "He made you orgasm during your first time?"

"Yeah, and by the way, Aunt Gayle did not explain that part of everything the day she explained sex by breaking Barbie's leg off and pointing to where the stuff under the Ken doll's plastic underwear was supposed to go. Naive me had no idea that was going to happen or was even supposed to happen. We didn't talk about those sorts of things at the Anderson house, you know."

432

"I'm sorry, I'm stuck on the whole image of Barbie's leg being broken off during sex," Jay gasped.

Jay and I laughed together for a little while before Jay asked in a serious tone, "So tell me how it first happened."

"You know how I was dressed for work on Friday. He had told me to dress that way and wear my hair that way, so I did. We had a big Christmas party at the club that night and they had a karaoke machine. There was a contest and Gabriel actually manipulated me into singing that night. I was okay with it and I actually did surprisingly well. I sang two songs and almost won the contest," I said shrugging my shoulders as if I still did not believe it.

"Anyway..." I continued and Jay hung on my every word. I told him about the kiss in the car door. "Once inside, he asked me if I wanted a shower and I asked 'with you' and he said 'if you like.' I showered with him and it was the first time I saw him completely naked."

I went on and Jay listened attentively. "We had a male model in drawing class for a while when I was a freshman. One of the girls in the class said that the naked male form was not as beautiful as that of a woman. I believe she was trying to compare them like works of art, but she was a fool. Clearly, she has not seen the right male form. Gabriel is the most beautiful thing I have ever seen. His chest, his arms, his legs, regardless of his penis as you know I have nothing to compare it to since his is the only one I have seen, but he's spectacular to look at."

"You know it's about more than his looks," Jay added.

"Yes, when he touches me, just a hand on my back, takes my breath away. The thought of his voice gives me chills. I love the way he looks after everyone that works for him. Right now, he's trying to figure out how to get the kid that washes dishes to college. His name's Rudy and he's in high school and has worked every time the doors are open at the club to help his grandmother raise his younger siblings. He was going to get a track scholarship, but had to quit track to get a job. A couple of weeks ago, Gabriel helped get him a car so he could get back and forth to work without having to depend on anyone to take him home or come get him. I so admire that about Gabriel."

"So, do you regret it?" Jay asked. "Most people have some regret."

"I don't regret the first time or the multiple times throughout the weekend that followed. I regret that I have to come home and

433

am not there with him right now," I sort of bragged. I had yet to believe that buying The Jefferson was a mistake even though it was no longer home. Home was wherever Gabriel was and that could have been in a dirt hut in Cambodia for all I cared, as long as we were together.

"I have hardly been away from him more than an hour and I already miss him. It is like this ache inside me," I explained. "It's strange, I feel like I have loved him all of my life."

"Please be careful, Millie. I understand how you feel and you probably can't help it, but he's the first and...just try not to get your heart broken."

"I don't know that it is possible not to get my heart broken. It breaks every time I think of losing him. We were lying in bed this morning after, you know, and he picks up my left hand and he traced my ring finger with his index finger, around and around, where a ring would go. I thought he was just playing with my hand as we cuddled and he broke the silence and said, 'One day.'

"Did he propose to you?" Jay shrieked. "It's so soon. I know what I told you about him on the porch that day. I know how he looks at you. I am certain how he feels, but guys don't say things like that this early on."

"I don't think that was a proposal. It was more like he was thinking out loud and once he said it he rolled over and kissed me and we went for it again." I was getting thirsty so I got up as I finished my sentence and headed for the kitchen.

***

That night Emma was not home to compete with me for the phone and Jay's mother called early. That meant I had the entire night to talk to Gabriel if I wanted and I did want that. He called right on schedule, 8:00 p.m. We talked until eleven and then I played the violin into the phone like a lullaby for Gabriel to fall asleep.

Monday was long and I missed Gabriel profoundly. The phone rang right at 8:00 p.m., but it was Emma's guy calling to make sure she got home safely. They remained on the phone until nearly 9:00 p.m. and as soon as they hung up, the phone rang and it was Gabriel.

"I was about to drive up there," was his greeting when I answered.

"I wish you would," I said in a smarty pants tone, but I was not joking. I would have given anything to see him. I changed my tone and added, "You have spoiled me and I hate sleeping without you."

"If you like, I can be there in about thirty minutes," Gabriel offered.

"I can't ask you to do that." It was so sweet of him to offer and, of course, I wanted him to come, but I did not want to put him out.

"Amelia, I am hanging up and I will see you in about thirty minutes." Gabriel hung up shortly thereafter, but not before I told him to be careful.

I had thirty minutes to freshen up and just like he said the knock came on the door at precisely 10:00 p.m. Jay and Emma were hanging out in the living room watching TV, so Jay let Gabriel in and he headed straight to my room. I met Gabriel just inside my room door.

I was wearing one of my new silk night gowns and Gabriel was in jeans and a white logo shirt from the club. His hair looked like it was still damp from a recent shower. He was probably overdue for a haircut, but I liked it. I liked the way it parted on the side and fell just below his right eyebrow. I could hardly keep my hands out of it.

This time, I thought it would be his turn against the door. I was careful when I pressed him against the door, keeping in mind that Emma and Jay were sitting just on the other side. As Gabriel stepped back, I slid my hands down and un-tucked his shirts, top shirt and under shirt. He allowed his leather duffel to fall to the floor as he gave into me and raised his arms. I proceeded to stand on my toes and reach as far as I could in removing his shirt. I was not tall enough to do the job by myself, so Gabriel pulled the shirts over his head all in one swift move.

I may not have been tall enough to get his shirt off by myself, but I was tall enough to plant soft kisses all along his chest. I could feel him sigh as I kissed him. I could feel and hear him sigh even harder when I unbuckled his belt. The best sigh was the one that included my name, "Amelia."

Before I could finish unbuttoning his jeans, Gabriel reached down and picked me up. I wrapped my legs around him as he carried me to my bed. This would be the first time we made love in my bed and I was truly glad that I had followed Jay's advice and purchased the queen size bed, but that was not what I was thinking about in that moment.

"I missed you," I breathed into him just prior to him laying me down.

He was so strong and it appeared I was light as a feather for him. With little effort he gently placed me on the bed as he came down over me. He beared none of his weight on me, yet I could feel him against me.

"I can't stop thinking about you. I cannot seem to help myself," Gabriel said as his lips met mine.

We had not tried many varying positions. I think he had been taking it easy on me and letting me get used to it. I was in awe of everything I had experienced with him thus far, but I did not want him to think missionary style was all I was up for or that I was fragile. I also wanted him to know that I wanted him as bad as he seemed to want me.

I took a chance and squirmed beneath him. There was no way I could roll him over without his consent, but he gave it and rolled to his back. I proceeded to slide his jeans down followed by his boxers. I then climbed on top of him, lifting my nightgown without revealing much as I straddled him.

"Oh my God, Amelia," Gabriel whispered, still cognizant that Emma and Jay might hear.

As we started to move I could feel the strap of my night gown fall down from my right shoulder. My breast was nearly exposed, but it did not matter. Slow and deliberate we continued with Gabriel's hands guiding me and mine placed against his chest for balance.

"You are so beautiful," he said as he let go of my hips and sat himself up right as we continued.

Though I was not completely naked, this was quite possibly the most titillating time yet. There was just something more exciting about moving against him, face to face and eye to eye. His hair, which was usually brushed back with gel, flopped against his forehead still parted to the side as we moved. His eyes were more piercing blue than I had ever noticed before and he tasted like apple Jolly Ranchers.

When we were finished, I fell down against him to rest, but I did not really feel like going to sleep yet. In fact, some of our best conversations had taken place afterward and this night was no different.

I worked up my courage and asked the burning question, "How many women have you been with?"

"You are welcome to ask me most anything else, but I will not answer that," Gabriel responded as he shifted up on his pillow so he could see my face better.

"Why?" I wondered out loud.

Gabriel reached down, brushed my hair from my face and tucked it behind my ear before he answered, "Because it does not matter and you will never be satisfied with the answer. It will only hurt your feelings and I won't do that. Anyway the answer is not a number; the answer is I have been with enough."

I sat up, what sort of answer was that: "Enough? What does that mean?"

"It means I don't want anyone but you, so I have been with enough," he answered as he leaned forward and kissed me softly.

Gabriel pulled back and smiled at me. "We know how many people you have been with, but how many guys have you kissed?"

"Enough," I replied with a smile.

"Good answer, Miss Anderson." Gabriel threw his head back and laughed.

It was a little over two weeks before Christmas and it suddenly popped in my head that I should ask him, "Are we still going to Aunt Gayle's and Aunt Dot's for Christmas?"

"If you are going, I am going," Gabriel answered.

"I was hoping you would say that," I grinned. I was delighted with his answer. "I hope you don't mind, but Aunt Dot called today and wanted to know if she should include you in the Christmas name drawing and I told her yes. You don't have to do anything. I will pick up a present for your person."

"You don't have to do that. I can get the present. Whose name did I get?" Gabriel inquired.

I had to use the bathroom so I got up from the bed while the conversation continued. "Seriously, I don't want you to feel obligated. I will take care of it," I continued to try to assure him.

437

"Amelia, either I am participating or I am not. Now, whose name did I get?" Gabriel said with a little more volume to his voice so I would hear him in the bathroom and probably so I would know that he was not backing down.

"She drew Dixon for you," I kind of yelled to him. "The limit on the gift is twenty dollars."

"Well, what should I get him?" Gabriel paused to think and continued with guesses of what to get Dixon, "A belt buckle the size of a hubcap or shot gun shells?"

"Mr. Hewitt, you are bad!" I chastised him in jest as I returned from the bathroom and started to climb back onto my side of the bed.

I was hardly on the bed before I could realize what was going on, Gabriel scooped me up and tossed me onto my back. "That's not what you said a few minutes ago, Miss Anderson!" he said as he proceeded to tickle me.

***

It was the week before Christmas and things were crazy. I had been studying for finals and taking them one right after the other. I had a full week working at the club with Christmas parties every night and we had a wedding coming up that Saturday. Christmas Eve was on Sunday and Christmas Day was on Monday. There wasn't much time and I still had to find the perfect present for Gabriel which was eluding me. More important than any of that, Gabriel was scheduled to have the cast removed Thursday morning and I could hardly wait.

"I know you have your history final, so don't worry about going with me to the doctor. I was going to go by myself, but Daniel has insisted on taking me." Gabriel assured me as we spooned before falling asleep on Tuesday night. "Daniel said it's payback for interrupting our Thanksgiving weekend. Perhaps you will be done with your test and we can all have lunch together."

"I am so sorry I can't be there for you. I just hate this, but I will make it up to you," I promised him.

"I look forward to it," Gabriel said as he nuzzled his face into my hair. He seemed to always fall asleep with his face planted securely in my hair. I am not sure how he could breathe, but he was comfortable there, so who was I to complain?

Two finals down and one to go; I had studied all I could. My feeling was that if I did not know it by now, I would never know it, when I headed out to class on Thursday morning.

The test was comprised of two essay questions and a series of twenty-five multiple choice questions. The test proved to be easier than I thought it would be, which was not necessarily a good sign. Typically, if I thought I did well then I bombed. What was done was done and I was out of there by 11:45 a.m.

After the test, I walked my usual route back to The Jefferson. From the Arts and Sciences building in the middle of the main campus, I crossed in front of Bell Hall and continued up McIntosh Street past the police station and on to North Jefferson Street. At the intersection of McIntosh and North Jefferson, I made a left and continued on toward The Jefferson. I was crossing over Wayne Street and I could see all the way down the sidewalk to where Gabriel was standing out in front of The Jefferson, cast free.

I was so excited and happy that he was finally out of the cast. To on lookers such as Daniel, Gabriel and I were probably like a couple of characters out of a cheesy eighty's miniseries when we ran to one another. We probably looked ridiculous, but that never entered my mind as I jumped into his arms and he spun me around right there on the sidewalk with cars zipping by.

"Get a room!" Daniel yelled at us.

"I am so happy you are out of that thing!" I said to Gabriel as he spun me.

"That makes two of us!" Gabriel laughed. "Now come on, I owe Daniel lunch. Where should we take him?"

"Café South, it's the place to eat lunch in Milledgeville during the week," I replied while Gabriel let me down slowly to regain my footing.

After we returned from lunch, Gabriel and Daniel left for the club. They had prep work to do in order to get ready for the Christmas party that night. We were hosting the annual Christmas party for the Green County Board of Education. I was not due to work until 5:00 p.m., so I stayed behind and decided to make a run to Macon to the mall, still on the hunt for a present for Gabriel.

I was halfway to Macon when I realized what the perfect present would be. I continued on to Macon and picked up a few things for Gabriel to wrap and put under the tree; three new ties, a new leather jacket and a few photo frames, but none of those would be his main present.

I arrived back with only minutes to get changed and get on the road to work. I was mid-undress when the phone rang. It was Aunt Gayle.

"Millie, dear, Aunt Dot says you are still bringing Gabriel to Christmas," I think she was asking a question, but it was worded more like a statement.

"I was planning to bring him if that's alright." I continued to get dressed as we spoke.

"That's fine, but I need to warn you about something." Aunt Gayle paused as if she was working up the courage to tell me something and I really did not have time to wait on her today.

"Aunt Gayle, what is it?" I was a little nervous. I had never heard her like this before, giddy and scared at the same time.

"I have been seeing someone," she spoke softly.

I was shocked. My response was not as soft, "Really?!! Who? Do I know him?"

"Do you remember Mr. Graham from the club the night we sang?" she asked.

"Of course and that's who you have been seeing?"

"Yes, and he is coming for Christmas and bringing his mother. They will be spending the night so we have a bit of a problem with the bedding situation. I know you are a big girl Millie and I suspect from the way that Gabriel looked at you at dinner that you all are doing more than just dating." I was not sure what else she was about to say, but I cut her off. I did not have time to dilly dally around and all of this was just weird and shocking coming from her.

"Did you just ask me if I am sleeping with Gabriel?!!" I slapped my forehead in disbelief. I could not believe this was my prudish, never dated while I was growing up, aunt.

"Millie, I am trying to discuss this with you like an adult," yet that phrase was her reprimanding me like the child she still saw me as.

"Right. What do you have in mind?" I really had to finish getting ready for work and with the cordless phone still in hand I tried to tie my shoes and cut to the chase with her.

"With all of the renovations and remodeling I have been having done around here, I went ahead and had an apartment built in the top of the barn for you in case you moved home after college. It has a bedroom, full bath, kitchen and living room. The decorator is finishing it up today. You and Gabriel will stay there over the holiday, but you are to tell no one in the family that I have condoned anything and you will mention nothing that goes on in my house. Am I clear?"

Oh, she was clear alright and Granddaddy was likely spinning in his grave to the point of combustion. Not only was she having a man sleep over in her house, she was essentially suggesting and allowing me to do the same. What was the world coming to? What else was I supposed to say other than, "Okay."?

"I have to finish getting ready for work, but I want to continue this conversation. I want to know all about you and Mr. Graham. Every detail, so I am going to call you back tonight. Also, there may not be anyone here regularly after today, so just in case you ever need to find me, let me give you Gabriel's number," I proceeded to give her the number to Gabriel's house and then we said our goodbyes.

I was the last of the three of us to finish finals. Emma had arranged to take all of her tests on Monday. She was going home to London for Christmas break, so her tennis coach spoke to her professors and arranged early finals due to her flight. Mr. Bama picked her up on Monday afternoon and they went to Atlanta for the night before she boarded the plane on Tuesday morning. It was unfortunate, but Jay and I both missed meeting him due to our class schedules. I was curious to meet him, but missing the opportunity did not devastate me the way it did Jay.

Jay's finals did not conclude until Wednesday afternoon and his holiday plans were likely the most lackluster of all of us. Although I had kind of led Aunt Gayle to believe that no one would be at The Jefferson much during the holidays, I had not exactly been truthful. Jay was probably going to be there most of the time. I did not want her to feel sorry for him. He was actually hosting Christmas at The Jefferson for his family. His parents had never really had the money to take a vacation so he had invited them to stay at The Jefferson while everyone was away and he was going to pretend that it was an actual vacation for them. He planned on taking them to all of the touristy sites Milledgeville had to offer, the tour of the Governor's Mansion, the museum at the college, the museum dedicated to Flannery O'Conner, the Hay House in Macon and if the weather permitted, he was going to take them to the Indian Mounds in Macon as well. It was not his parents' first trip to Milledgeville, but he intended to act as if it was and in doing so show them the best vacation ever.

***

Cara and Daniel were working the dining room with me for the Board of Education Christmas party. There was a lull while all of the teachers played the white elephant game. Each of the teachers had brought a gift to contribute to the game. When they arrived at the party, they placed their gifts under the twelve foot Christmas tree that was in the far corner of the room blocking the exit to the pool from the dining room.

The tree was a beautiful, real Douglas Fir, decorated with white lights, gold ribbon, red ornaments including a present and a teddy bear stuffed among the branches and a foot tall gold and white angel atop it. Joan had decorated it and it was the most elegant tree I had ever seen. It was unlike any of the trees that anyone put up in my family. Aunt Dot's tree was comprised of colored lights and every ornament she had ever bought or been given dating as far back as her childhood. The tree that Aunt Gayle put up was not nearly as tacky as Aunt Dot's, it was thin and tall and new. Aunt Ruth did not put up a tree because Cousin Dixon electrocuted the family cat in one when he was a child and it took her a year to get the smell of fried cat and cedar out of the house. She had been a little neurotic toward trees since and it had only been in the last year that she allowed them to decorate one of the trees in the yard.

The white elephant game went on and on. There were thirty-three teachers, eight board members and six administrators present from the school system and they had drawn numbers for the order in which they would pick their presents. Each time one picked a present, they could trade it for any present in the room that had already been opened and possessed by someone else. They were scarcely halfway through the game at 8:30 p.m. and the presents ranged from a dancing Santa to a silver teapot to a bag filled with chocolate bars, an ovulation kit and a pregnancy test. Everyone in the room howled with laughter including Cara, Daniel and I when the sixty year old male principal from the high school drew that present.

By 8:45 p.m. the three of us had lost interest in the game. The party goers had finished eating by 7:30 and we had long since picked up all of the dishes and were down to just waiting on them to leave so we could reset the dining room. There was little else for us to do, so we moved our own party to the bar.

Gabriel had let Matt leave already and there was no one left in the bar, but us. Just as we had taken our seats at the bar, Gabriel emerged from the kitchen and asked Daniel if he wanted to go home since he had been with him all day. Cara and I assured Daniel that we would be fine without him and we did not mind if he went on. Reluctantly, Daniel agreed and left through the kitchen door with Gabriel following behind still thanking him for taking him to have the cast removed earlier in the day.

No sooner had the kitchen door stopped swinging behind Gabriel and Daniel did Cara bust out in the most scandalous story.

"Alright, so I have been dying to tell you," Cara leaned across as if to whisper to me even though we were completely alone in the bar. The only sound we were to compete with was the crackling of the fire.

"Tell me what?" I leaned in to hear.

"One of my friends works at the resort that shall remain nameless," Cara referred to the larger more prestigious resort on the lake. We called it that because the members from that club often played at Port Honor and when they did, they acted as if we were all quite beneath them.

"Okay," I urged her on. I thought she was going to have a good story about one of the members, but boy was I wrong.

"So last Friday, my friend Ann was working the lunch shift when Joan approached one of the other diners. Ann only found out who Joan was after the spectacle."

"Spectacle?" I interrupted. I could hardly imagine prim and proper Joan, the picture of Southern ladies, making a scene.

"Yes, apparently she waltzed right in, up to this young woman and announced to her in front of the whole dining room over there that she knew the woman was having an affair with Dick. According to Ann, Joan greeted the woman by asking, 'When should I send for your things?' The young woman looked like a deer caught in the head lights, but Joan continued, 'I hear you are quite the item with my husband and I was just thinking that I could use some help around the house, raising his three children and washing his dirty drawers. So, whenever you are quite ready, I will have the guest room cleared out for you because if you think for one instance I am giving up my home and all that I have endured from that man for the likes of you, then you are sadly mistaken, but if you are going to continue screwing him under my nose, then you might as well take on the whole package. No hard feelings, you just let me know when I should expect your things. And, don't you worry your pretty little head; I will make sure Dick knows that you and I have come to an understanding."

"Oh my God!" I gasped. I did not know whether to laugh or applaud for Joan. Now that took spunk on her part. "Who was the other woman, any idea? What did the other woman do?"

"No, some blonde fresh off the tennis courts. That's all Ann said, except that the young woman was beat red in the face the entire time Joan was there and so were the three trust fund bunnies she was having lunch with," Cara answered.

"That's no help, but perhaps we will recognize her from the scarlet letter Joan labeled her with," I laughed. "That story is priceless!"

Cara suddenly turned serious. "Millie, would you mind not repeating this story to Gabriel?" Cara asked. "He has to see Joan all the time and we don't. It's a funny story, but Joan's so nice, I would never want it to get back to her that we were making fun of her or anything."

"I don't tend to keep things from Gabriel, but I can't see any point in telling him about this," I assured her before getting up from my barstool and going to check on the party.

***

There were more Christmas parties on Friday and Saturday night. Almost everyone on staff pulled doubles both days. I hardly had time to prepare the Christmas goodies that I intended to bake and give to everyone. Gabriel was shocked to find me working in his kitchen when he awoke Friday morning, but by the time he got up at 8:00 a.m., I had already finished the Kahlua balls and four batches of fudge. I had a whole list of items that I was going to make so that was just the tip of the iceberg.

Gabriel strode into the kitchen wearing nothing, but red plaid pajama pants. I had made coffee for him and I stopped what I was doing when he entered the room and poured a cup for him.

"Try this," I said as I handed him a Kahlua ball.

"My God, Amelia, it's a little early for that," Gabriel commented as he swallowed. I suppose the alcohol gave him a bit of a shock. "I thought it was a chocolate doughnut hole," he added.

"Didn't you get a surprise then?! It's actually a Kahlua ball: crushed Oreos, powdered sugar, Kahlua and a smidge of Karo syrup. The fudge is still warm, but you can try that as well if you like," I said gesturing to the remnants in the bowl by the sink. I had already put the pans filled with fudge in the refrigerator to chill.

Gabriel appeared to still be wiping sleep from his eyes as he reached over and ran a finger through the bowl I had used to mix the marshmallow cream, chopped pecans and chocolate morsels with the cooked sugary portion of the recipe. "That's quite good, Amelia, and I see you have put good use to one of my undershirts again."

Gabriel took a couple more swipes from the fudge bowl before he grabbed me from behind. I had finished putting away the leftover ingredients for the fudge and Kahlua balls and was taking out the ingredients for the chocolate covered pretzels that I intended to make next.

"You are not going to have time for that this morning," he said as he turned me around and lifted me onto the countertop. "I don't like waking up without you."

"Really? You missed me?" I asked as I draped my arms around his neck and pulled him closer to me by wrapping my legs around his waist. I could already feel what he had in store for me.

"You know I missed you and I believe you know how much I love waking up with you," Gabriel said as he lifted the under shirt above my head. "You are amazing and you smell like fudge."

"Do you think you will ever get tired of this?" I was curious as we had been together like this daily, sometimes multiple times in a day, for nearly two weeks. I did not think I could ever tire of him, but my insecurities crept in about his desires.

"I could never get tired of you or being with you," Gabriel tilted my head back so I would see the seriousness in his eyes. "Are you getting tired?"

"That's the thing; I don't think I will ever get tired of you. I have no experience with drugs, but I think you are likely my drug or my addiction. Maybe I should not tell you these things," I expressed while I nuzzled my face into his neck. Gabriel never had that greasy smell that my grandfather used to have in the mornings, but this morning he smelled even better than usual. He smelled like fabric softener from the sheets which he had washed the day before.

"Amelia, you can tell me anything and it will not change anything between us and I hope I can do the same."

"Of course. You can tell me anything, always," and I kissed him.

My education then continued with an amazing time on the kitchen countertop followed by the kitchen floor. One might think activities on the tile floor of the kitchen would hurt or at the very least be cold to the touch, but I did not notice at all.

As we finished, Gabriel asked, "Shall we christen every room in the house?"

I could not help but giggle almost with embarrassment since my answer was most definitely, "Yes."

"But maybe not today," Gabriel added as he lent a hand to help me up.

"Right," I replied. "I don't think my boss would like it if I were late for work."

Gabriel snickered and gave me a smack on the behind as I headed for the shower with him close behind me.

Every day seemed to be an adventure with Gabriel. Luckily, Gabriel's house was nestled among mostly weekend homes so there were no neighbors to hear us if we got a little loud or if we forgot to close the curtains. The one set of neighbors that were permanent residents, the ones I had scared nearly to death when Beth broke in in the middle of the night, had gone to Ohio to see their children for the holidays, so we did not have to worry about scaring them or giving them a show.

***

It's not like we weren't busy, but I suddenly had the urge to kiss Gabriel right in the middle of my first shift. I decided that despite the morning's activities, it was still an itch that needed scratching. The party that I was working was occupied eating and I had a little time before I needed to check on them again, so I went to the kitchen to find Gabriel.

"Gabriel, could you help me find the tea soap?" I asked and Gabriel happily followed me to the dry storage area.

On one of my first days at the club, Andy had sent me to find the tea soap. Andy said it was in the dry storage area and it would help get the stains out of the tea urns. I did not know it was a prank so I spent half the evening going back and forth between the dry storage area and Andy trying to find the tea soap. At one point, Gabriel had asked what I was doing and when I told him he had quite the belly laugh at my expense. Now Gabriel helping me find the tea soap, which did not exist at all, was code for let's make out in the dry storage area.

"Now, Amelia," Gabriel said as I pushed him up against the racks of canned goods. "I don't want the cocktail onions to think I am that kind of guy."

It was as if my giggle box turned over. I could not stop and through my laugher, I managed to get out the words, "Way to ruin the moment."

I turned to head back to the kitchen and Gabriel took a swipe at the back of my skirt flipping it up. I felt the draft of air against my back side and I suspected he caught a glimpse of my Joe Boxer smiley face underwear. I was correct in my suspicion.

"Amelia, I hope you asked Santa for some grown up underwear," Gabriel commented.

"You don't like my panties? Perhaps I should take them off," I suggested and I headed back past him into the dry storage again. Gabriel followed. Once safely out of sight of the kitchen, I bent slightly and slipped my panties down enough that they would fall on their own. Gabriel's face was priceless, a combination of shock and restrained lust.

"Amelia, you've got to put those back on."

"No, I don't," I said as I bent over, picked them up and then tossed them to him as I went past him on my way back to the kitchen.

Gabriel followed with my panties in his hand. Just outside of the passageway that led past Gabriel's office to the dry storage, Gabriel was detained by Alvin who had just arrived for the day. Alvin had questions as to what needed to be done to prepare for the evening party.

I had started toward the bar, it was a tight hallway with the walk in beer cooler on one side and liquor closets on the other. There was a window on the swinging door to the bar, but no one ever used it so there was no risk of anyone seeing me, plus,

447

everyone else was occupied with the Christmas party that they were working in the dining room.

Alvin's back was to me and I could see Gabriel's face. He had still been watching me as I started toward the bar. I stopped in the hallway and inched my skirt up my left leg. I did my best to portray come hither eyes at Gabriel. Alvin did not notice that he had lost Gabriel's attention and that I had it. I could see Gabriel bite his lower lip as he often did when he was turned on. He bit his lip and shook his head back and forth letting go of a heavy sigh.

Still looking past Alvin, Gabriel interrupted him and directed a comment toward me. "What am I going to do with you?" his voice raised so I could hear him from where he was.

Alvin immediately turned to see who Gabriel was talking to and I had not expected any of that, not Gabriel to draw attention to me or Alvin to whip his head around so fast. I was nearly exposing myself, but I immediately dropped my skirt and crossed my hands behind my back.

"What?!!" I responded all innocent like, all the while knowing I had nearly been caught.

I had not completely thought through my impulse to ditch my panties. The party that I was attending was a small party of ten men from the local Methodist Church's men's club. They were seated in the private dining room which was located upstairs above the door to the bar. It was also open to the dining room. It had not occurred to me that anyone below might be able to see my "cracker-jack", as Emma called it, if I stood too close to the railing. The rest of the shift I was paranoid that I would stand too close and with every move, I was visited by a draft in the air and the thought that I might flash someone.

I could not believe I had to finish off my shift sans panties. I had also counted on Gabriel coming to find me and insisting that I put my underpants back on. Instead, when I headed to my car to take a break from two until I had to return at four, I found them tucked under the driver's side windshield wiper with a note that said, "I started to wear these as a hat to teach you a lesson. Let this be a lesson to you, mess with the bull and you'll get the horns!"

I did not see Gabriel's car in the driveway when I drove up and I thought I had seen it still in the parking lot when I left the clubhouse. I assumed he was still at the club, not taking a break and working through preparing for the party that night. I put the key in the door only to discover that the door was already unlocked. Perhaps I had been wrong, perhaps his car was in the garage and he was home.

As soon as I stepped in to the living room I called out to Gabriel and no answer came. I noticed a present on the coffee table. I was more interested in finding Gabriel. I searched the entire house and not that I had ever seen him go onto the back deck, I checked there as well. I even looked in the garage for his car. Gabriel was nowhere to be found.

I started to get the heebie-jeebies about the door being unlocked. I did not believe that anyone was in the house, but there was a strange vibe coming from within it as if someone had been there. When I was returning from checking the garage for the car, the present on the coffee table in the living room caught my eye again. It also occurred to me that Gabriel and I had left the house at the same that time that morning and I started to wonder who put the present there.

I approached the present. It took up a large portion of the coffee table and was probably about the same size box as the twenty-six inch television was in that I got for Christmas last year from Aunt Gayle. It was wrapped in red foil paper, nothing like the candy cane paper my TV came in, and it had a huge green foil bow on top. It looked to have been professionally wrapped and when I saw my name on the card I just assumed Gabriel had had Joan do his wrapping for him again.

I was distracted by the present and the weird vibe of someone having been in the house was starting to fade. I went to the kitchen and called the club. I was curious to know when Gabriel had slipped out and brought the box home.

Matt answered the phone at the bar. "Hey, it's Millie. Is Gabriel around?"

"Sure. He's right here. Hold on." Matt returned.

Within a moment Gabriel picked up the phone. "Hey, what's up?"

"I am not sure what's in the package, but since it is from you, I am sure I will love it," I said with glee jumping through the phone.

"What are you talking about?"

"The present on the coffee table and, by the way, when you left it, you forgot to lock the door."

"What??!!!" Gabriel's voice boomed through the phone. "Get out of the house! I am on my way!"

I was stunned and dropped the phone and ran outside. From his voice, I could tell something had spooked Gabriel. I did not fully comprehend what was going on, but I did as I was told. Gabriel and Matt arrived at the house within a matter of a couple of minutes. Officer Ed was right behind them and the sheriff's department shortly thereafter.

Matt and Officer Ed waited with me in the yard while Gabriel and the sheriff's deputy went inside. I could see them discussing the present through the living room window. It appeared the deputy was trying to stop Gabriel, but Gabriel tore into the package. The look on his face changed from desperation to fury.

The deputy emerged from the house carrying what was left of the present. The wrapping paper ripped and torn and hanging from the bottom of the box and the lid open. I wanted to see what was in the box, but on my approach to the deputy, Gabriel ran from the house and snatched me from my feet to keep me from seeing. It felt as if I had been clotheslined. He nearly took the wind out of me.

"Good grief, Gabriel. It's not like there's a horse head in there is it?" I asked as I struggled to breathe.

Gabriel grabbed my face in his hands. "Look at me!" he demanded in a way I had never heard him speak to me before. "Let's go back to the club and let the deputy do what he needs to do. I need you to trust that I will tell you about this before the night is over, but you need to let me cool down now."

All I could muster to respond was, "Okay."

"Officer Ed needs to return to the gate. Matt, if you would please stay here with the deputy until he is done, I would really appreciate it. I will make sure you are paid for your time." Gabriel then turned his attention back to me as Officer Ed made his way back to the Port Honor security truck, the same Ford Ranger that had come to the house the last time. "Amelia, we are going to go back to the club as if nothing has happened. I will come back and get your things later this evening. Trust me; everything is going to be alright."

This was not the middle of the night. It was broad daylight, but I was starting to get a clue. Beth Reed had something to do with whatever had been in that box.

The night was never ending. It was 1:00 a.m. when the last guest left and we were all exhausted. Gabriel insisted on us riding back to The Jefferson together and he left his car at Dick and Joan's.

I was so tired, physically and mentally exhausted, but I drove. I think Gabriel knew we would not sleep that night until he told me what was in the box. He remained silent until we made the first turn off of Highway 44 to take the back roads to Milledgeville.

"There were photos of you in the box. One was of you walking to class, another was of you getting in your car at the club, another of you walking with Jay in downtown Milledgeville, and you appeared oblivious to the fact that anyone was following you or taking pictures. Even more strange was that they were all framed. I would have never thought her capable of this..." Gabriel trailed off as he laid his head against the head rest and stared out of the passenger side window into the night.

"You changed the locks, so how did she get in the house?"

"I don't know," Gabriel quietly responded. "I will call an alarm company tomorrow, but they probably won't be able to get anything installed until after the first of the year."

We drove in silence for so long that I had begun to think that Gabriel had fallen asleep. When he finally spoke again it startled me and I jerked the wheel of the car slightly.

"I don't want this to ruin our first Christmas together," Gabriel said when he broke the silence.

"I love you, Gabriel and as long as we are together, nothing is going to ruin Christmas," I lifted his hand to my lips and kissed it. "We can stay at my place tonight and then tomorrow we will stay at Aunt Gayle's."

"Ah, Aunt Gayle's and the separate rooms. You can imagine how I am looking forward to that. I will finally be free of your snoring," Gabriel's spirits were lifting and he attempted to make a joke.

"Right and I will be free of your roaming hands," I shot back all in jest.

"We should not be laughing. This afternoon scared me. The deputy said he would do what he could to investigate. He made a report and all, but I could tell he did not hold out any hope of really finding out who was behind this." Gabriel's tone was that of exasperation. "I think I know who is behind this. Beyond putting in an alarm, I don't know what else to do."

"Do you really think she would try to hurt me?" I asked and I am sure my face had a puzzled look. I just could not believe this was coming from someone he used to date and who he considered his friend until very recently.

Gabriel answered and his face was likely as puzzled looking as mine had been. "If you had asked me this a few months ago, of course I would have said no, but something has changed with her."

"If it will make you feel better, I will try to find someone to walk to class with. I have another 8:00 a.m. class this semester so it will be hard to find anyone for that one, but if things get weird, I will get Jay to get up early and walk with me."

"He would do anything for you, wouldn't he?"

"Probably."

To Gabriel this had been about more than some photos of me. He felt Beth was stalking me. She may not have been personally following me and taking the pictures herself. That made it all the worse to him because if it were her, then I would be more likely to notice than if it was someone I did not know. He was also afraid that stalking might be only the beginning.

"We will mention none of this to my aunt or anyone in my family," I insisted and Gabriel agreed.

It was almost 2:00 a.m. when we finally made it to my apartment. Jay was home, but his room door was closed and he was likely asleep. Normally he would have just been getting in from the bars and I would have told him everything right then, but with Emma gone, Jay had no wingman and he most likely stayed in for the evening. The events of my day would have to wait to be shared with Jay the next morning and that really was for the best since I was nearly dead on my feet.

I was certain Gabriel had hardly slept. He tossed and turned all night and even mumbled a little when he did sleep. Over the years, I had fallen down on saying bedtime prayers, but that night I prayed for Beth Reed to find something else to occupy her mind and to leave us alone. I also prayed that it would rain on Saturday so the club would be slow.

We were due back at work by 10:00 a.m. on Saturday morning and when I looked outside it was raining cats and dogs. One prayer had been answered.

The morning shift was slow as there were no golfers on the course. That worked out perfectly since we had the member Christmas party that night and it gave everyone time to prepare for that.

Sometime during the morning, Matt reported to Gabriel everything from his time at the house with the deputy the afternoon before. The deputy said that people got broken in on every day and we could not just abandon the house over this. We had to be cautious, but stand our ground. Matt said that the deputy agreed that they would do more patrolling through Port Honor in general, but for us not to be afraid to go home and that he believed whoever left the photos was just out to scare us and not actually hurt us.

Between shifts, Gabriel and I returned to his house. We did our best to shrug off the strange vibe and while Gabriel packed his bag, I continued with my baking. I only had a couple of hours before we had to be back at the clubhouse, so I was not able to make all the items I had planned. Luckily, I had already finished a number of items and taken part of those back to The Jefferson for Jay's dad. I divided the rest between what I was going to share with our co-workers and what I was going to take to Christmas with the family.

The last batch of mini pecan pies were in the oven, so I used that time to repack my suitcase for going to Aunt Gayle's. I wanted to take the pearls Gabriel gave me to wear on Christmas, but I could not find them anywhere.

I heard Gabriel coming back in from putting stuff in the car. I was reluctant to ask him because I did not want him to think I had lost something as precious as his mother's pearls, but I needed help. I called to him from the bedroom, "Gabriel, did you pick up the strand of pearls?"

I don't think he fully heard me and asked, "What?" as he entered the doorway of the bedroom.

I was bent over searching under the bed when I asked again, "Have you seen the pearls you gave me?"

"No, the last time I saw them they were on the nightstand on your side of the bed." Gabriel stood at the end of the bed behind where I was now standing back up on my knees in front of the night stand.

453

"I know I laid them there two nights ago. I was going to take them to wear on Christmas day, but I cannot find them anywhere. I don't want you to think I lost them. I would never misplace them." I was panicking that he would be mad with me for losing them.

"I know you wouldn't," he assured me as he came around me and opened the drawer of the nightstand and checked inside.

"Seriously, I put them right there," and I pointed to the top of the nightstand.

I think it occurred to us at the same time. We had been so preoccupied with the photos of me and the present that we had not checked the house to see if anything was missing.

I stood up from the floor and turned to look at Gabriel, "You don't think she stole the pearls, do you?"

"That's exactly what I am thinking," he replied.

"What else did she take and we have not realized it?"

"I don't know," Gabriel replied as he went to his chest of drawers and opened the case where he kept his cuff links and watches. I did not know what else was in that case, but apparently something was missing.

I looked on as Gabriel grabbed his head and his face turned red, I could see the veins in his forehead. "SHIT! SHIT! SHIT!" Gabriel shouted at a volume the neighbors likely heard. It was so loud that it scared me. I winced and moved back against the wall of the bedroom as if I were retreating.

I did not have to ask, Gabriel turned with the case in hand, showing me the contents. "My mother's wedding set is gone."

I was at a loss for words. Gabriel glanced around the room, but did not find whatever it was he was looking for. Taking the case with him, he left the room and I followed.

In the living room, Gabriel found the phone and dialed the sheriff's department. He explained who he was and referred to the events of Friday afternoon. Gabriel went on, "I need to amend the incident report."

I could not hear the voice on the other end of the line, but Gabriel responded, "There were items stolen."

Apparently he was then asked to list the items, "A ten inch strand of pearls and an antique wedding set with diamonds totaling two carats."

Gabriel paused, "No, I have not found anything else missing yet, but I will keep looking and call back if I find anything else. I really want you all to find who did this."

Once off of the phone with the sheriff's deputy, Gabriel immediately dialed another number. Again, I stood listening. It was clear no one answered and he had to leave a message.

"Beth, you know who this is and I know what you have done. If you do not return the items you took from my house yesterday and if you do not call off your bloodhound following Amelia, I will have you prosecuted to the fullest extent of the law. Do I make myself clear? Remember, mess with the bull and you'll get the God damn horns!"

Gabriel had used that phrase with me before, always in jest, but this time I believed he was not joking when he said it to Beth's answering machine. I shuttered to think what she might be on the receiving end of if he caught up with her because he was fuming like I had never seen him before.

It took a few minutes for him to calm down after he hung up with her machine, but he finally turned and asked, "Do you want to drive to your Aunt's after we get off work tonight or do you still want to go tomorrow morning as we planned?"

"It's totally up to you," I replied as I headed to the kitchen and Gabriel followed. I took the mini pecan pies from the oven. I thought I might better keep quiet regarding what all had just gone on, so I offered him one of the pecan pies. "Would you like to do the quality check on one of these?"

I put the pan down on the stove top and popped one of the mini pies out with a butter knife.

"It's hot, so blow," I cautioned. I am not sure why I bothered to caution him, I am sure he was more experienced with cooking and hot foods than I was.

"Would you mind terribly if we stayed here? I just feel that if you don't stay, you might never stay again." Although I did not like for Gabriel to be unhappy or worry about anything, it was a little nice to see that he had insecurities as well. It was especially nice that his insecurities were about me since it showed he cared. It also showed that he was trying to get his emotions about Beth and the missing items under control so as not to wreck the day any more than it already was.

Perhaps I was naive, but I really did feel as though nothing would happen to us as long as we were together. I tried to ease his concerns by responding as much: "If you want to stay here, then we stay. I am sure everything will be fine."

"Good and these pies are really good." Gabriel took another pie and on his way out of the room he turned back, "I am going to be wrapping a few presents, so stay up here until I come and get you. Okay?"

"That reminds me," I called to him as he started through the living room. He stopped and turned back to see what I wanted. "Would you like to exchange gifts here tomorrow morning before we head out? I plan on taking one or two presents to put under the tree at Aunt Gayle's for you for Christmas morning, but perhaps we should exchange any big gifts here. What do you think?"

"You are probably right. Now, seriously, stay here until I return."

CHAPTER 19

It was the morning of Christmas Eve 1995, and all was right with the world. We were going to take my car to Christmas with my family until Gabriel discovered after many attempts that the present he had gotten me would not fit in the trunk of the Corvette. It was only 10:00 a.m., but it had already been a busy morning.

That morning I awoke first due to the sunlight filling the room despite the blinds and curtains. I snuck out of bed and busied myself by quietly making breakfast for us. I had found a waffle maker in the kitchen days before when I was preparing my Christmas treats. I knew then what I would be making for breakfast for us the morning of Christmas Eve.

After I finished prepping the tray that I would present to Gabriel for breakfast in bed, a glass of orange juice plus three strips of bacon and Belgian waffles topped with strawberries and whipped cream, I added the final touch. I added the small wrapped Christmas present and then tiptoed back down the hallway toward the bedroom.

"Gabriel," I whispered as I entered the bedroom. "Wake up, it's Christmas."

Gabriel rolled over and snuggled back into the covers while reaching an arm out to find me. He stretched a little more after running his hand up and down the space that I typically occupied and not finding me there.

I whispered again, but just a bit louder, "Gabriel, wake up."

Gabriel rolled over on to his back and his eyes began to open. I sat the breakfast tray across his lap. Gabriel immediately perked up at the sight and the aroma of the bacon. He also noticed the present. It was not wrapped as pristinely as the freaky box of photos of me had been wrapped the day before. The paper was red and white and resembled a candy cane and I had wrapped it myself.

I noticed that the small box had caught Gabriel's eye as much as the waffle and bacon did. "Go ahead and open it and quickly before your breakfast gets cold," I said. I could hardly wait to see if he liked what was inside.

Gabriel picked up a piece of bacon and put it in his mouth. While chewing he reached for the Christmas present and swiftly tore into the paper. He opened the box and his eyes lit up.

"You shouldn't have," Gabriel gasped.

"I didn't really..." I paused to take in the sight of him removing it from the box. "It was my dad's."

"Amelia! I can't accept this. You should keep this forever and never give this to anyone!"

"You mean like you and your mother's pearls?"

"That's different. I am not going to wear a strand of pearls."

"Well, I am not going to wear a man's Rolex," I snapped back. It was not a nasty banter that we were having, just a little argument in which Gabriel's face never changed from the kid in a candy store smile.

"Why would you not wear it?" Gabriel asked as he held it closer for further inspection and noticing that it still worked. Gabriel also glanced at the alarm clock and found that it had the correct time.

"It is too big for my arm and I would never alter it to remove links," I explained. "I hope you will never need it, but I have the paper work for it. It's a 1972 Rolex Submariner Red 1690. You will notice the word 'Submariner' is printed in red, thus the name."

Gabriel slipped the stainless steel band over his hand and on to his wrist, still admiring it before he asked, "So what's the story behind the watch?"

"My dad was hired by Tallmadge hospital in 1972, and this was the welcome onboard gift they gave him. He had also been offered a job by a big hospital in Atlanta and they offered him a Mercedes, but he turned it all down to stay close to home," I explained as I reached to help Gabriel with the clasp. "I hope you don't mind, my father's initials are on the back. They are the same as mine. AJA."

"I don't think you have ever told me what his name was."

"Andrew James Anderson."

"While I am asking, what was your mother's?"

"It's Christmas, do I really have to..."

458

"I am only asking you to tell me her name, not exercise demons."

"Fine. Her real name was Rhonda Marie Thigpen, but when she went to college she reinvented herself and started going by the name Natalie." I rolled my eyes as I said the name. "And she never told anyone her last name."

"Where did the name Natalie come from?"

"Natalie Wood was her favorite actress."

"So it had nothing to do with anything, she just picked it for the sake of picking it?"

"Right." I reached across and took a bite of the waffles.

"Do you ever miss her?" Gabriel asked as he admired the watch.

"What's there to miss? Not being fed? Seeing your mother prance around like Cinderella on her way to the ball while you wore the same outfit three days in a row? Even a four year old knows something is not right about that. Or, am I supposed to miss longing for her to wake up and love me?" I shook my head, shaking off the thought of her so she could not ruin my day. "I thought we weren't exercising demons."

"You are right."

I looked at him and it occurred to me to ask more about his family. I suppose I had a curious look on my face as the wheels turned in my head.

Gabriel ate the last piece of bacon before noticing me staring at him. "What?"

"What are your parents' names?"

"You mean, what were your parents' names."

"Right, so what were they?"

"Samuel and Grace."

I took it a step farther, "You said once that you had a sister. What was her name?"

"Amelia, I don't want to do this today."

459

"Okay." I did not want to press him. Baby steps.

"I love the watch. I love it! It is the best Christmas present I have ever received," Gabriel had hardly taken his eyes off of it since he removed it from the box. Gabriel continued, "I feel guilty taking it."

"Why?" I really could not understand what the difference was between it and the pearls.

"Because your Dad earned it and it's just being given to me."

"It's kind of funny that you say that. I believe that's almost the same thing I said about the inheritance." The fact that he felt that way about the watch just made me know that I had done the right thing and had given it to the right person.

Once Gabriel finished his breakfast, he asked that I stay put. He then left the room and returned with a large wrapped tube with a big bow on top. He handed me the tube. "This is not your main present, but it is the one I want you to open before we get to your Aunt's house."

I ripped off the paper and bow and popped off the lid. I slid out the roll of papers.

"Here," Gabriel offered as he reached to help me, "lay them across the bed so you can see."

The papers were architectural plans. Across the top of the page in bold and underlined letters, were the words, "Seven Springs". There was a page for each floor and a couple of pages of the rendering of outside views of the building.

I looked over each page and Gabriel explained. "I had these drawn up based on what you said during the tour."

"How did you do this?"

"One of the members of Port Honor is an architect. He agreed to draw up the plans if I got the specs of the building for him. I looked up the number for the store in Avera and I asked Mrs. Poole if she could find out the measurements of the old hotel at Seven Springs. I offered to pay her, but she would hear none of it. She ended up calling your cousin Dixon to take the measurements and she had an answer for me within two hours of my initial call."

I continued to look over the plans, page by page. I was absolutely giddy over them. Not only had Gabriel listened while we were there that day, but this also showed that he cared about my dream. It really was the thought that counted.

Page after page, each floor was drawn just as I had described. "The basement is mine so you will see how my ideal commercial kitchen would be," Gabriel explained.

"Perhaps we will christen your kitchen there someday." I smiled.

"You better believe we will!" Gabriel laughed before he pushed the pages off of the bed and went on to tickle me.

I was pinned down and nearly breathless from being on the receiving end of the tickle monster. "I love you and hope this is the best Christmas you have had in a long time." I gasped between words.

"It already is the best!" Gabriel stopped and sprang from the bed. "I almost forgot. I have one more present for you that I would prefer that you open here. I'll be right back."

Again, Gabriel left the room. From the sound of his footsteps I believed he went to the kitchen. I was still seated Indian style on the bed when he returned with an envelope in hand.

"I did not pay for the first one so it does not really count. This is the real one, but it's for the both of us," Gabriel said as he handed me the envelope.

I looked at him filled with curiosity. He had really surprised and impressed me with the plans for Seven Springs. I could hardly wait to see what was in the envelope.

I tore it open to find a confirmation for two night's reservations at the Opryland Hotel for the last weekend in January. My eyes lit up on sight of the reservation.

"Isn't this where you said you worked in high school?" I asked.

"Yes, and I have wanted to go back for the longest time, so you and I are going. I hope you did not already have plans." Gabriel continued to talk while he ventured into the bathroom and left the door open. Talking was not the only thing I heard. Apparently we were becoming more and more domesticated as this was the first time I had heard him pee or that he had left the door open while he went to the bathroom. Well, the first time other than the night we first showered together.

461

Presents had been exchanged and despite his efforts to pack the Corvette, we were now in the Legend and well on our way to Aunt Gayle's house. It was raining and the day just looked miserable, but it was quite the opposite. Before we left home, we had briefly caught the weather report and this rain was expected to turn to snow and it was possible that Georgia was going to see a white Christmas as far south as Macon and as far east as Augusta.

"So what is on the agenda for the rest of the day?" Gabriel questioned while making the turn off of I-20 at the Norwood exit.

"Agenda? You mean 'tradition'. The tradition for Christmas Eve, well that was when we exchanged gifts with Granddaddy." It was not that I had forgotten him, but all that was going on with Gabriel had distracted me from the fact that this was my first Christmas without Granddaddy. In that moment, the devastating loss came rushing back to me. I took several deep breaths and came close to asking Gabriel to stop the car. I felt as if something or someone was sitting on my chest.

Gabriel responded to the sound of my breathing, "Amelia, are you alright?"

I did not respond straight away and continued to fight the onset of nausea. "I think I'm..." I gagged a little, and threw my hands across my mouth, but did not throw up.

I could feel the car slowing down abruptly, pulling off the shoulder of the road and coming to a stop.

"Amelia, look at me," Gabriel said as he unbuckled his seatbelt. He leaned over and unbuckled mine as well. I turned to look at him and he pulled me to him the best he could with the armrest down in between the seats. "Surely your grandfather would not want you to be like this, so let's think happy thoughts. No more tears. You need to be brave for the rest of your family. Everyone misses him and everyone knows you miss him the most. If you break down, everyone breaks down. You can cry with me in private, but you must get it together for your family, don't you agree?"

I squeaked out a "yes". Gabriel wiped my eyes and I sucked back the Hoover Dam's worth of tears.

"That's my girl. Are you okay for us to go now?" I nodded my head yes and sniffled in response to Gabriel's question.

It was right at lunch time when Gabriel and I arrived at Aunt Gayle's. Despite it being daylight out, the extent of the Christmas decorations on the property could still be seen.

Although the house sat nearly a quarter mile down the driveway and was shielded from the road by thick woods, Aunt Gayle always decorated it to the hilt for Christmas. This year was no exception and I dare say it was bigger and better than ever.

As soon as the woods opened to the yard and Gabriel could see everything, his mouth fell open.

"It's a bit much, huh?" My comment really was more of a question to him. I was always a little unsure as to whether Aunt Gayle had crossed the line from elegant excess to tacky. If she was not there this year, she was real close.

"This must cost a fortune and take a month to put up and another month to take down," Gabriel observed.

"It definitely helps the local economy with supplying jobs and all." Gabriel laughed at my response and shook his head as if he just could not believe the sight.

There were huge red ribbons spun around each of the four columns across the front porch. The ribbon ran their length, from where they touched the eves to the base on the porch. It was as if giant sticks of candy canes were supporting the roof.

No expense was spared when it came to lights either. There were lights that outlined the pitch of the roof, the windows, the garland around the front door, in the shrubs along the front and sides of the house, in all of the trees that were part of the landscaping in the yard and outlining the split rail fence that separated the yard from the woods. She even had the barn outlined. And, as always, on one side of the yard there was a life size Santa in a sleigh and all of his reindeer.

Once Gabriel parked the car and we got out, he stood and looked all round. "All that was missing was a snow blower and snow," he laughed.

I was just a touch embarrassed and began to explain to him the purpose behind all of this, "One might think it is a total waste of time and money since the decorations cannot be seen by passers-by, but that is not the case. In all of the years we lived here, Aunt Gayle has hosted a Christmas party that rivals that of the Wilkes' 4th of July Bar-B-Que. It started out as invitation only for family and friends, then it grew to word of mouth invitations from Aunt Gayle to almost everyone she came in contact with through her veterinary services. In the last few years, it grew again because she started publishing an invitation to the general public in The News and Farmer, the local newspaper."

I continued on with the story as Gabriel and I unloaded the car and took all of the presents, candy and our luggage inside. "Granddaddy had not liked the idea of inviting the public into the house. He said it was just begging to be robbed. As with many other subjects on which they disagreed, Aunt Gayle ignored him and did what she wanted to do.

"There were people from all walks of life and from as far away as Atlanta and Savannah that attended the party. You and I were invited, but this year's party was on the same night as the Delta Digital party at the club."

Gabriel held the door open for me. "That's awful. I would love to have gone."

"Maybe next year." I looked over my shoulder at him as I went inside.

The inside of the house was decorated almost to the same extent as the outside, just a bit more subtle. I had been a little afraid that since Granddaddy was not there to stop her or because she might try to cover her grief with ribbons and bows that the inside of the house might look like the Christmas Shop in Helen threw up. I was relieved that it looked tasteful and not too over the top.

We finished unloading the car and sitting the packages under the Christmas tree. The Christmas tree rivaled that of Port Honor, but the thing that caught Gabriel's eye were the snow globes.

"Do you think she has enough snow globes? I think I have counted fifty in this room alone."

The rumbling in my stomach forced me to change the subject. "I wonder where Aunt Gayle is. I am starving."

I wandered to the kitchen and found the note she left for us on the island. "Hey, Gabriel," I called back to him in the living room. "How do you feel about lunch at the store in Avera?"

"Love the idea," he called back. "I need to thank Mrs. Poole for her help with your gift."

As I walked back into the living room, I remembered we were not bunking in the house. "Before we go, we should probably take our things to the barn."

"What?"

"Aren't you up for a roll in the hay?"

"Always."

"Well, not now, but maybe later. Seriously, in all of her remodeling she had an apartment built for me in the top of the barn. She actually agreed for us to stay out there together." I grabbed my suitcase as Gabriel grabbed his. We headed to the barn.

At the top of the new staircase, I opened the door. The apartment was beautiful.

"Wow, this is like something straight out of Southern Living!" Gabriel gasped.

"And it's ours! Not too shabby for a hay loft!"

***

We caught up with Aunt Gayle at the store just as she was about to give up on us. There were three old kitchen tables in the back of the store and we were fortunate to get one of them. I had my usual pint of Brunswick stew and rice. Aunt Gayle had a bar-b-qued chicken sandwich and a bag of chips. Gabriel branched out and tried the pulled pork plate with Brunswick stew and potato salad. While there, the three of us chatted about anything and everything. At one point, Gabriel slipped away to use the restroom and I know while he was gone he thanked Mrs. Poole profusely for her help in getting the measurements for the hotel. Gabriel also took the time away from the table to pay for all of our meals.

We stepped out onto the steps of the store and the tin roof boomed like thunder as usual. I thought Aunt Gayle stopped to tell us she would see us back at the house, but that was not what she wanted.

"Would the two of you mind running to Wrens and picking up some things at IGA for me?" Aunt Gayle handed me a list before she even finished asking. "Gabriel, you don't mind taking a little ride with Millie do you? She can give you a tour around the county."

"Not at all, ma'am," Gabriel replied as he stepped off of the porch and the boom scared him. Both Aunt Gayle and I grabbed our breath and tried to stifle our laughter before it escaped.

"I see you, go ahead and laugh!" he said as he laughed at himself.

Aunt Gayle headed for her truck which was parked two cars over from Gabriel's. "Just be back by 5:00 p.m. I need those items for dinner."

"I'm sure we will be back well before 5:00," I directed toward her before turning to Gabriel. "Do you mind if I drive?"

Gabriel's answer was to toss me the keys and start around from the driver's side to the passenger's.

I turned on the radio as soon as I cranked the car. WSGA was playing Christmas songs again when we headed out of the parking lot of the general store in Avera. I made a left onto Highway 102 toward Stapleton. Once in Stapleton, I made a left next to the old Bank of Stapleton building onto Highway 296. It was a few miles outside of town and just after crossing the railroad tracks, I made a left onto Gene Howard road. The first place I took Gabriel was by the house we had lived in near Stapleton because it was the closest. Ultimately, we would make a circle and end up at the IGA in Wrens.

"See the house over there to the left? That's where we lived while Granny was still alive and before we moved." I kept my left hand on the wheel and pointed to the house across the field with my left.

"Did you like living there?" Gabriel asked.

"I loved living there. I love the house in Avera and I love where I live now, but all of my childhood memories are wrapped up in that house and at the lake. I know the house isn't much to look at like Aunt Gayle's Greek Rival, but life was wonderful there." I could have told him story after wonderful story of everything that went on there.

"I take it you did not want to move."

"Why would I have wanted to do that? Everything I had ever hoped for as a child was there...Let's go before I start to cry again." I had pulled over to the edge of the road so Gabriel could get a good look when the house first came into sight, so I put the car back in gear and away we went.

I continued down Gene Howard Road to its intersection with the Wrens-Warrenton Highway where I made a left. At the four-way stop, I made a right back onto Highway 296. Just before it intersected with the Thomson Highway, I turned on to Briar Creek Road.

Briar Creek Road went right past Briar Creek Baptist Church. "That's where all of my family on my father's side is buried." I said as I pointed, when we went by the church. It was an old wooden country church, painted white with stained glass windows that were pretty typical of churches in the area. It might have been typical, but it was still pretty and peaceful looking there. A dirt road circled around the church from the paved road. The church faced the dirt road and the cemetery was between the church and the paved road. Our family plot was closer to the paved road than the church and if I had slowed any at all, we could have seen their headstones.

"Is your father buried there?"

"Yes."

"And.."

"Yes." I focused my eyes on the road ahead and before long the church and graveyard were a fading picture in the rearview mirror.

Gabriel got the hint. He likely figured I would cry. He did not ask any more questions and we continued on.

At the end of Briar Creek Road, I made a left onto the Thomson Highway and just before the big chalk plant and just across the Warren County line, I turned back to the right and we headed down a dirt road. Christmas songs were still playing on the radio and Gabriel was singing along. I suppose I should have interrupted his singing and asked if I could take his car down a dirt road, but it did not occur to me until after I had already made the turn.

"See the trailer there?" I pointed to the pale blue singlewide in the trees about thirty yards off of the road. Gabriel nodded.

"That's where my mother grew up. Her parents still live there."

"So that man right there, coming out of the barn, that's your grandfather?" Gabriel twisted in his seat to get a better look as I did not slow up.

"I prefer to call them my mother's parents. I know what grandparents are and they are not it." We kept going. The place was becoming more and more run down as the years went on. Had I not been so bitter toward them and my mother, I likely would have felt sorry for anyone living in such conditions. I likely would have already bought them a new trailer or built them a house with my inheritance. Feeling like this about them certainly did not make me like myself, but I just was not ready to get over it and it was not like they had ever given me a reason to move on.

The road my mother's parents lived on came to a dead-end into Highway 221, and when it did, I made a left and headed toward Harlem, Georgia. We only went about a mile before I turned onto another dirt road. This road was primarily used as a cut through for the big trucks hauling chalk between the mines on one side and the plant off of the Thomson Highway. The road bordered Fort Gordon on the left and farm land, chalk mines, and a handful of houses on the right.

We were just about to Highway 1 when I pointed to another house on the right. "That's the house where my parents lived when I was born."

It sat up a hill and was less than a mile from Highway 1, the Augusta Highway. It was a small house that they rented and only meant to be a start for them. It was empty and looked as if it had not been lived in since the night my father died, but I knew that was not the case. I knew some kids in school that had lived there when we were growing up. When I was younger, it had been a light green house, but over the years it had turned a dark, slime green color from mildew. The place had been neglected for God only knows how long.

I slowed down and explained further, "I think I told you they fought that night after they had been drinking. My father got in the car and came out of the driveway and continued down the road as we are now, but much, much faster."

I slowed as we came to the intersection with Highway 1. "This is where my dad died. They say he never slowed up and he never saw it coming. My aunt Gayle has made some off- handed remarks about my mother over the years and said he never saw her coming either, but she spotted him like a buzzard spots road kill."

I don't think Gabriel knew what to say. I did not leave us there, parked at the stop sign for long before I turned back toward Wrens.

"Now I am going to show you some places with happy memories," and we continued to town.

I could tell Gabriel had so many questions, but I think he realized it would not take much to get me started and if I got started, that might ruin Christmas. We drove in silence for a couple of miles. He had his thoughts and I had mine. I had just shown him every landmark in the county that housed all of the demons of my childhood and he had continually refused to give me a glimmer of his. I did not want to ruin Christmas, but now he knew even more of me and I still knew so little of him.

My eyes were fixed on the road ahead when I verbalized my concerns, "Gabriel, you know everything about me and I know so little of you. I have also done as you asked and kept it together while giving you the tour. I don't want to ruin Christmas, but I think it is high time you let me in..."

From the corner of my eye, I could see Gabriel turn his face toward his window. Although he was not looking at me, he spoke, "You are so much braver that I am."

"I don't expect you to tell me now, but soon. Whatever it is, you can tell me."

"I know I can tell you, I just don't want to. I don't want things to change. I don't want you to look at me differently and I don't want you to feel sorry for me."

I reached over and took his hand from where it rested across his lap. I tugged just a little, "Gabriel, look at me."

He turned his head and his face was veiled in sadness.

"You have to trust me, trust that nothing you say and nothing that happened when you were a child could make me feel any differently about you." I smiled at him, a serious, but affirming smile. "Everything is going to be okay. You just have to trust me."

Gabriel just nodded and tried to smile a little back at me.

A mile or so more and we were coming around the curve at Pope Hill into Wrens. I pointed to the left as we came out of the curve. "Happy memories now: that's where I went to high school. I was a cheerleader. Can you just imagine?"

"I have never dated a cheerleader before. That's like a poor man's Bond Girl. I like it."

"I always have wanted to be a Bond Girl," I laughed and we were back to being ourselves.

"Let's get the items your aunt needed from the store and head back," Gabriel said.

"Sure, the IGA is just past the red light."

We were walking into the IGA when I saw one of the girls that graduated high school with me. She did not see us yet and without her noticing, I had the opportunity to point her out to Gabriel. "Her name is Angel Martin and she's the reason why many nice girls did not get dates in high school."

"Nice girls didn't get dates?" Gabriel questioned.

"Why buy the rest of us dinner when they could get dessert from her without wasting their money? I used to be disappointed about all of that, but I am not anymore."

"Do you want her to eat her heart out?"

"What do you have in mind?"

"How do you feel about PDA?"

"What's that?"

"Public displays of affection. You are so naïve, Amelia."

I giggled. "I will follow your lead, but remember everyone knows everyone in this town and whatever we do someone will call and tell my aunt. She will know before we even get to the parking lot if we do anything to embarrass her."

"Fair enough," Gabriel replied.

"Are you going to act like you are really super into me or something?" I was curious as to just what he had in mind.

"Oh, dear Amelia, don't you know by now? It's not an act."

***

By the time we got back to Aunt Gayle's, Mr. Graham and his mother were there. It was hardly five minutes before Aunt Gayle asked to see me in the kitchen, alone. I was right when I warned Gabriel about someone calling Aunt Gayle.

"Millie, I hear you and Gabriel had a little fun in the grocery store this afternoon," she said with a tone.

"It was just one kiss," I tried to explain.

"I hear that one kiss nearly fogged the windows of the entire store and that your arch nemesis from high school was also a witness. I know you don't care about people's opinions around here, but if you plan on running a business here, then you might want to reconsider alienating people." Aunt Gayle put the final touches on the appetizer tray as she cautioned me.

Aunt Gayle said she would let me know by Christmas if she was going to let me go forward with my plans for Seven Springs. Was this her way of letting me know her decision? Was she going to agree to Gabriel's suggestion for me to rent it and begin the work right away?

"Are you saying what I think you are saying?"

Aunt Gayle put the dip onto the tray and headed back toward the living room. I followed, waiting for her to answer. Once in the living room, Aunt Gayle passed the hors d'oeuvres and took her time about answering me.

I was so focused on Aunt Gayle that I hardly noticed that Mr. Graham was seated in Granddaddy's favorite chair. As far as I had known, no one had sat in that chair since Granddaddy. I am sure I would have found it more than peculiar had I not been dying to know Aunt Gayle's decision about the old hotel and the property.

"Aunt Gayle." I almost whined trying to get her to answer me.

"Are y'all ready to open a few presents?" she asked all of us, still not having answered me. It was starting to annoy me as I was desperate to know her decision and I had a feeling from her lecture in the kitchen that she had made one.

Aunt Gayle picked presents from under the tree. She handed a present to each of us beginning with Mr. Graham. We opened our gifts in the order in which she handed them out and I was last. She had gotten Mr. Graham a new dopp kit: leather case, gold plated razor, etc. I had a feeling that was not his main gift, but one that was suitable for opening in the midst of everyone including his mother.

To his mother, Aunt Gayle gave a set of regional cookbooks. They included the August Junior League's Tea Time at the Masters and one from the Blue Willow Inn in Social Circle. Some

471

might have been insulted that someone they had only just met gave them cookbooks even taken it as an insinuation that they could not cook, but apparently Mrs. Graham collected cookbooks so the gifts were perfect for her. Mrs. Graham gushed and gushed over them.

Aunt Gayle gave Gabriel some very nice cutting boards. "Gabriel, you will have to forgive me that I don't know you better and did not know exactly what to get you. All I really know about you, other than that you are fond of Millie and you call her Amelia, is that you lived in four states in your life. So, each of the cutting boards is the shape of a state that you have lived in: Tennessee, Florida, Georgia and the smallest is Maryland for when you were at the Naval Academy. I figured you could use that one for serving cheese. Anyway, one of my clients made them. I hope you like them and they aren't too redundant."

"I love them! I don't know if I will use them or just hang them up in my kitchen for décor." Gabriel looked at each one and ran his hand across them admiring how smooth they were. "You said one of your clients made them?"

"Yes, it's kind of a sad story," Aunt Gayle started to tell the story of the man who made the cutting boards. "He's a Vietnam Vet who lives off of disability and makes these cutting boards to help support himself. His dog ate something in the yard and got sick so when I treated the dog, he paid me in cutting boards. He told me any state I wanted and I thought of you."

"I'm so glad you did. Thank you so much! I really do love them." Gabriel passed Georgia to me so I could see how smooth it was. It was made of bamboo and they were sanded to the point of being almost slick. They were quite lovely in the way of cutting boards.

The last present Aunt Gayle handed out was mine. It was large and flat and from the feel of it, I could tell it was something framed. I tore into the wrapping paper as if I were still five years old. I was right. It was something framed. I looked closely at what was inside. I gasped and passed it to Gabriel for him to see.

"A deed. Is this to the hotel?" Gabriel asked me as Mr. Graham and his mother looked on at us.

Gabriel and I were seated on the hearth of the fireplace and Aunt Gayle had never left my side after she gave it to me. "You will notice it is post-dated to 2000. You cannot file it until after you graduate law school. I figured I would frame it and give you a little something extra to work toward. Also, I will lease it to you for the duration of your education, provided that before you do anything at

472

all you hire a general contractor to go over the place thoroughly. I want to be with you when he gives you a report on the building. Should he tell you that the place is not worth saving, I am going to tear it down. Merry Christmas, Millie, those are my terms."

I jumped up and hugged her. "Thank you! Thank you! Thank you! I love you so much and you will not be sorry!"

"I know I won't be sorry. You will be the best attorney in the county and everyone needs a hobby and this will be your hobby, Millie, not your livelihood." She was stern.

While Aunt Gayle and I had hugged and I had done my happy dance, Gabriel brought the rest of the room up to speed. I could hear Mr. Graham congratulate Gabriel on having such a pretty and ambitious young girlfriend. No one had ever referred to me as ambitious before, over achiever, yes, but not ambitious. I liked that description.

As soon as we were done hugging, Aunt Gayle invited everyone to the living room for dinner. "We will open more presents tomorrow morning."

This was my first time noticing that Aunt Gayle had remodeled the dining room as well. I was thrilled to see that she had kept my grandmother's dining room set. She had recovered the seats, but other than that, it was still the same Drexel Heritage set that I grew up aspiring to eat at with the adults one day.

As we took seats at the table, I was reminded again just how different this year was when Aunt Gayle took a seat at the head of the table. I wonder if it felt weird for her like she was sitting in the lap of Granddaddy's ghost. I would have felt that way if I sat in that seat. I suppose it was officially her house now, so she was the head of the household and she could sit at the head of the table if she liked.

I was really impressed at Mr. Graham not taking the spot at the opposite end of the table. Instead, he waited for Gabriel and me to take our seats and then he sat across the table from Gabriel. Mrs. Graham sat across from me and I sat to the right of Aunt Gayle. I think Mr. Graham sat in front of Gabriel in an effort to force his mother to get to know Aunt Gayle better over dinner.

After the blessing was said and after everyone had been served I mentioned one of our traditions from Granddaddy. "Granddaddy used to suggest a topic of discussion for all of us at dinner. Politics, religion and money were off limits, but anything else was fair game. He especially liked to do this when we had company. In my younger years, he felt this was a great way for me to learn about other people and our differences."

"That's a wonderful idea," Mrs. Graham said while she served herself a helping of pear salad. "I think we should all share our favorite Christmas stories. Amelia, I think you should go first."

I told the same story that I told at Granddaddy's funeral about how he built me the pirate ship. I did not want to depress everyone, but the story would not have been the same if I did not give the background. It was the first time the Grahams and Gabriel had heard it.

"It sounds like your grandfather was a wonderful man." Mrs. Graham wiped tears from her eyes.

Gabriel squeezed my hand under the table. I looked at him and his facial expression was that of someone heart broken. "I can't imagine what you went through and I am so sorry."

"I did not tell you all this to feel sorry for me. I feel very lucky and fortunate to have had someone that cared about me like Granddaddy did and like Aunt Gayle has too. If y'all are feeling sorry for me, then you missed the point." I did not dwell on the nonsense that my mother dished out and as far as I was concerned, she freed me up to have a better life than she ever thought about providing.

"I'll go next," said Mr. Graham and he proceeded to tell a lighthearted story about his mother. "I was five and I had asked Santa for silver pistol cap guns, a cowboy hat and a rocking horse. I wanted to be the Lone Ranger. We were not always as fortunate as we are now, but I had no idea. So that I would not be disappointed come Christmas morning, my mother baked banana bread every afternoon after she got off work for a month. When she got home every afternoon, she baked six loaves and while they were still hot she loaded me into my wagon and pulled me around the neighborhood, going door to door selling fresh baked banana bread for $2 per loaf. Come Christmas morning, I was a sight on my horse with my cowboy hat and pistols. Of course, I did not know for many years that that is what we were doing when we were selling the banana bread."

Mrs. Graham wiped her eyes again. "You all are determined to make me cry tonight."

"What is your favorite Christmas story?" Aunt Gayle asked Mrs. Graham.

"That's simple. The week before Christmas in 1968, we got the letter that David here had been accepted to Harvard." Mrs. Graham glanced at Aunt Gayle and then to me. "From what David has told me about you, I know you will understand this and, Millie, despite how your mother was, I suspect you will understand this one day as well. Your children are your greatest achievement. So, for a woman who sold banana bread just to buy plastic cap guns for her little boy's Christmas, to have that little boy grow up to be accepted into Harvard, that was my best Christmas."

"I agree," Aunt Gayle said as she reached across the table and took my hand that was not already being held under the table by Gabriel. "You are my life's work," she smiled, "and I would not change a thing."

"Me neither," I smiled back.

"Gabriel, what is your favorite Christmas story?" Mr. Graham asked.

"My childhood was similar to Amelia's, but I had my parents a little longer than she did. I was seven when they died and I won't go into those details, but if ever two people loved each other it was my parents and that love extended to my sister and me. I can't tell you all that I have one good Christmas story, I have three and those are the three Christmases I remember from age four to age seven. Everyday life with them was an adventure so you can just imagine how Christmas was and, like Millie's story, it wasn't about the gifts. It was about them teaching me how to love. Don't get me wrong, I loved my parents, but I did not fully realize that lesson until after they were gone." That was the most I had heard Gabriel say about his childhood or his parents up until that moment. This time it was me that was squeezing his hand under the table and my heart ached for his loss.

Again, Mrs. Graham tried to lighten the mood as she wiped her eyes. "You all really are going to make me cry and I am going to give each of you a big hug before I turn in for the night."

"Alright," said Aunt Gayle, "my favorite Christmas story is a little more lighthearted. Millie was five and we had her again for Christmas. My mother had actually insisted on getting her for the month of December and her mother agreed. This gave my mother the opportunity to enroll Millie in our church children's program. Mother bought Millie the frilliest little red dress, matching bow for her hair and black patent leather shoes. Mother was so proud that Millie had been chosen to sing a solo in the pageant and they had practiced and practiced singing 'Silent Night'. The day of the program, Mother spent all afternoon curling Millie's hair into

475

little ringlet curls. She was the prettiest little thing you ever saw and Mother had invited all of her friends from around the county to come and see her granddaughter in the Christmas pageant. There were four other songs to be sung before Millie's big number and while waiting, Millie became bored. She started to sway with the music. That wasn't such a big deal, but then she started to twirl. Then she started to twirl and pull her dress up. Then she started to twirl, pull her dress up and shake her little bottom to the audience all the while doing the dance that John Travolta was famous for in Saturday Night Fever."

Aunt Gayle stood and demonstrated the dance. Everyone at the table cracked up. Mrs. Graham was again wiping her eyes, but this time it was from laughing so hard she cried. Gabriel was hanging his head and holding his sides. One would have thought I would have been embarrassed, but I wasn't. My face hurt from laughing just as much as anyone else in our group. I did it, so what could I say?

Aunt Gayle continued, "You all can imagine my mother's face. She was mortified. Initially, she tried motioning for Millie to 'straighten up'. Millie was oblivious to Mother's attempts to get her back in line. The whole church was in stitches as Millie stole the show without even singing. The best was when that little satin dress went up over her head and my mother gasped, Amelia Jane Anderson! Millie then got this sweet, innocent look on her little face like 'Me?' You all can imagine how my mother never lived that down among the church ladies. There were jokes for years about how Millie was going to grow up to be a pole dancer."

Mr. Graham laughed through his words, "Millie, do you think you could sing Silent Night for us after dinner?"

"NO!" I faked embarrassment, but I could not help laughing with them.

After dinner, even though we told them they did not have to and Aunt Gayle nearly refused their insistence, everyone helped us clean up. Gabriel and I cleared the table and packed up the leftovers. Mr. Graham rolled up his sleeves and washed dishes and his mother dried while Aunt Gayle put the clean dishes in the cupboards.

Once the kitchen and dining room were back in their normal order, we returned to the living room. I played the piano and Aunt Gayle sang. After much persuasion and making a request of my own, I agreed to play 'Silent Night' after Aunt Gayle agreed to sing "O Holy Night", a cappella. If Mr. Graham was not already smitten with her

476

as I suspected he was, he definitely was after he heard her sing "O Holy Night". She hit the high notes flawlessly.

As soon as the song was finished, Mrs. Graham announced, "Present time! I have presents for everyone!" and as best a woman of her age could, she darted under the tree for a present for me.

What was with everyone and professionally wrapped presents these days? Did no one wrap their own presents anymore? It was gorgeous! Again, I was afraid to tear the paper because it was so pretty. It was more muted than some of the other presents I had received recently. The paper was of plain white and it had a strip of red velvet around it and on top, a red and white bow made of real candy cane. I had to ask, "Is this bow edible?"

"Yes, indeed it is," Mrs. Graham answered.

"Mother made it herself," Mr. Graham answered.

I snapped the tape holding the bow on and sat it to the side. I finally opened the box to find that the highlight of the whole thing was likely the candy bow. How could the inside of such a pretty box only contain knitted Santa socks? My thoughts were usually reflected by the looks on my face, so perhaps my face gave me away.

Mrs. Graham moved to see what was actually in the box. "Oh dear Lord, Millie, I am so sorry. I had two boxes wrapped exactly the same. Those are the socks that were for my hairdresser's ten year old daughter. I am so sorry. I guess I am going to be the talk of the salon since I got the ten year old a Victoria's Secret gift card."

"Mother!" Mr. Graham gasped.

"That's not the half, the card read, 'I hear you have a hot boyfriend. Call me. We'll go shopping. The annual sale is coming up and I will show you what to buy." Mrs. Graham was what Granddaddy would have called a card. I hardly knew her, but I loved her. She was hysterical and like none of the stuffy older ladies from these parts. It was quite foreign to see a woman over seventy with a sense of humor. I thought she was just awesome and reminded me a little of Aunt Dot.

"MOTHER!" Mr. Graham's face was so red, so very, very red and priceless.

Gabriel just hung his head and snickered to himself. He finally caught his breath from snickering enough to tell Mr. Graham,

"David, I had no idea you thought I was hot!" and he broke up and laughed openly.

***

"If Christmas Eve is this great with your family, Amelia, what will Christmas day be like?" Gabriel asked as I crawled into bed and laid my head across his chest.

"It will be the best ever because you are here," I tilted my head up to him.

"Oh, Miss Anderson, you say the cheesiest things!"

CHAPTER 20

"Sweet Jesus!" a strange man's voice screamed at the sight of me in the doorway of my own apartment. It was all such a flash; literally, that I really did not see too terribly much as he dropped behind the couch leaving Jay completely toppled over and exposed behind him.

"Dear Lord, Millie! I didn't expect you home before, well I don't know when I expected you home." Jay scrambled to get cover himself as did his conquest, the strange naked man now crawling behind the arm chair.

They were in the throes of passion when I opened the door and started into the living room. My eyes and the couch would never be the same.

"Pants! Pants!" I screamed as Jay stood up. Luggage still in hand, I whirled around on my heels, eyes closed tightly and felt for the door to my room.

I could still hear the two of them scrambling behind me. "Do you think she recognized me?" the voice said. Their bare feet slapped against the floor as they scurried to Jay's room.

"Yes," I yelled back. "I recognize you from the news on one of the stations out of Macon, but you are also the strange naked man in my living room!"

I could hear Jay giggle and the normally very stuffy news anchor respond back in a hushed voice, hoping only Jay would hear, "It's not funny! You said no one was home."

"There wasn't and now there is." I could hear them through the wall separating our bedrooms near the front of the house. I could tell by the tone of Jay's voice that he did not particularly care what this guy thought and he was not at all upset by my arrival. Jay was attractive and this was not the first forty-something year old man he had snared at the Juniper Street Pub in Macon and it likely was not going to be the last. It was not very long before the slapping of bare feet was replace by the stomping of a man's hard soled dress shoes, followed by the slamming of the door and the continued stomping down the stairs.

I stuck my head out of my bedroom door. I could not see Jay, but I could see light coming from his room indicating that the door was open. "You decent? Is it safe to come out?" I called.

"Safe as can be," Jay hollered back. "He's gone."

"I am sorry I ruined your afternoon," I apologized for my interruption. I walked around and found Jay in his room, fully clothed and folding his laundry.

"Oh, you did not ruin my afternoon. I had already gotten mine. You ruined his afternoon, but oh well. You can apologize when you see him tonight."

"See him tonight?"

"Yeah, I'll put the news on for you." Jay laughed.

"Seriously, how was your Christmas?" I asked him.

"It was okay," Jay began. "You know Mama, just in case the Lord came back or some natural disaster happened to prevent us from having Christmas, she gave us our presents in September so as usual there was nothing to open on Christmas morning short of what you left for me and daddy."

"Oh, that's terrible," I replied as I reached over to hug him.

"It's typical is what it is." Jay shirked the hug and walked over to his closet to hang up a few shirts. He was a lot like me in the fact that he did not like for people to feel sorry for him.

I took a seat on his bed and started matching his socks for him. He looked back over his shoulder at me, "You know what my favorite thing this Christmas was?"

"What?"

"Seeing my dad open that paper sack full of homemade treats that you gave him," Jay turned away from me and faced into the closet as he spoke. "It's not often that I see true joy on my father's face, but this Christmas he was over the moon at that bag of stuff. Millie, he ate until he about made himself sick. If one can be drunk on sugar, he was."

"I am so glad he liked it!"

"His favorite was the Kahlua balls."

"Did they like all of the tourist activities that you had them do around Milledgeville while they were here?"

"They liked it as much as they can like anything short of staying home, shut up in the house, day in and day out." Jay made his way back over to the bed to put more items on hangers. "Mama insisted on staying in your room. I thought she was going to fight Jolene for it. I hope you don't mind, but Jolene stayed over too. She stayed in Emma's room. This was the first time she had seen the apartment, which I still find ridiculous since she lives in town. It's not like I haven't invited her time and again."

"So they liked my room?"

"Jolene loved the entire apartment to the point of jealousy. You should be glad you do not have siblings. To feel like you are made to compete your entire life and then guilted over whatever small victory you might have. Oh, it's not a competition until I win. Ugh!" Jay sighed and threw up his hands as if he were fed up with the entire situation.

"I know and you can't worry about that."

"Enough of that. How was your Christmas and where is Gabriel?"

Jay's Christmas did not sound that wonderful, so for his sake I did not want to go on and on about mine, but at the same time, I wanted to tell him everything. "It was the best Christmas ever. Gabriel is working tonight and then he might come over after he gets off."

"That can't be all you have to say on the subject." Jay grabbed the laundry basket and started out of his room likely going to get more items out of the dryer.

I followed him. "It's most definitely not all I have to say, but I feel it is all I should say."

"Why don't you want to say more?"

"Because I don't want to hurt you further by going on about my Christmas."

"Millie, you are so sweet. I want you to tell me absolutely everything so I may live vicariously through you. I think you owe me all of the juicy details since you cock-blocked me earlier. I mean, it's the least you can do. If I can't get more of my own jollies, then you must tell me about yours."

"I am not telling you about getting my jollies!" I turned away to hide my embarrassment. "I will tell you about the new apartment that Aunt Gayle had built for me in the loft of the barn."

"Why would she build you an apartment?"

"I don't think it was specifically for me. I am not sure why she built it, but it sounded nice saying it was for me, made me feel special. Thanks for ruining it." I punched Jay in the shoulder.

"Ouch! That hurt."

"Good. So she built this nice one bedroom apartment in the loft of the barn. It was amazing. Decorated to the nines. You remember where the first horse stall was on the right when you first entered the barn? Well, she took it out and put in a staircase made of reclaimed barn wood from one of the other old barns on the property. At the top of the stairs was a door leading into the apartment. Beyond the door was the kitchen. Everything was all shiny and glistening, and the smell of the whole place was the epitome of newness. The kitchen had granite countertops with shades of browns, beiges and black with a matching speckled tile back splash all against cherry wood cabinets. The appliances were black and all of the faucets and door knobs were silver. It was the prettiest and tiniest kitchen ever.

"The kitchen had a breakfast bar that overlooked a small dining room with a barn wood table with four ladder back chairs and beyond the little dining room was a proportionate living room."

"Blah, blah, blah...get to the bedroom," Jay rolled his eyes. "No one cares about the fabric on the couch."

"Fine, the bedroom had a queen size bed in it. Four poster. It was tall and fluffy with flannel sheets, a down comforter and a pale blue ruched duvet cover, white eyelet bed skirt and matching pillow shams and throw pillows and a white velvet quilt folded over across the foot of the bed. The headboard was tufted, pale blue linen of the same material as the duvet and there was no footboard. Instead of a footboard there was Granny's cedar chest. There was also a side chair much like the one I have in my room here, but blue and white plaid."

"There you go with the material again. No one cares."

"Moving on. Gabriel and I were both impressed with the place and from the inside no one would have ever expected that it was in the top of a sixty year old barn. It was like a nice hotel until

482

we went to bed Christmas Eve and realized it really was too good to be true." I paused for dramatic effect.

"What was wrong?"

"The heat did not work, only the air conditioning," I pretended to shiver.

"It was thirty degrees that night," Jay gasped.

"How well I know. Imagine this; okay don't really imagine it, but anyway. We were too wrapped up in each other and the idea of a new place that we did not notice when we first walked in that it was cold. We went on to take a shower together in the tiny bathroom. The steam filled the room masking the fact that it was freakishly cold in there."

"We made good use of the steam and the bathroom countertop. We opened the door to leave the bathroom thinking that we were going to continue things in the pretty, pretty bed. Wrong! Thoughts of the bed were shatter as we opened the door to the frozen tundra that was the rest of the apartment. In a flash we were in our pajamas, in the bed and had the covers pulled up to our ears. We tried every position of cuddling in efforts to get warm."

As I recounted the story to Jay, I could feel the cold take over me as if I were back in the moment. I could hear Gabriel's words to me, "Fuck! It is cold in here!" I could almost feel him rubbing up against me trying to make friction to add more warmth. It did not help.

I went on detailing the night to Jay. "Nothing worked and all the while it felt like the temperature was dropping. We talked about going back inside, we talked about leaving, driving back to Gabriel's and then driving back in the morning, but we were too chicken to get out from under the covers. We pulled up the quilt at the end of the bed and huddled as close to one another as we could get."

"By 1:00 a.m., I could not feel my fingers and toes any more. When we left Gabriel's house we packed in one suitcase and it was on his side of the bed. Gabriel got the idea that we should put on our top clothes over our pajamas and see if we could get warm that way. He reached out from under the covers and slid over the suitcase. He drug out an item at a time and handed it to me. We proceeded to pull on our clothes without getting out of bed. Can I tell you we looked like hobos? We had on every article of clothing that we had with us by 2:00."

"Gabriel draped himself all around me and thanks to him, I had finally gotten warm enough to go to sleep and somehow he managed to fall asleep as well. We awoke at about the same time. It was about 6:00 a.m. and we could see our breath in the room. We got up and pared down our clothing. I kept on three pair of shocks, but headed to the big house where we put on coffee and then went back to sleep. Gabriel let me have the couch and he took the floor next to me. We felt completely stupid for not coming in to sleep in the living room when we first figured out that the heat was not working. I think the best sleep we got was that morning."

Jay appeared to be getting bored with my story, "So, you froze to death. Get on with it. I am dying to know what he got you for Christmas. Spill it already!"

"And I'm dying to know how you snared the TV news anchor," I popped back at him. "Was it a Merry Christmas at the Juniper Street Pub?"

"It was a Merry Christmas at the Juniper Street Pub, but that was three days ago. The morsel you met earlier was courtesy of my friend, Chad and his internship at the station."

"Chad? The one that called last week and left the message for you to turn on the television at 3:00 a.m. during the night on Wednesday?"

"The same." Jay replied as he wandered from his room to the kitchen. "I am hungry. You want anything?"

"No thanks. Stay focused. What was on at 3:00 a.m.?"

"His pecker."

"WHAT?!!"

Jay began to explain. "Chad works overnight and is in charge of taping the shows like 90210 when they are sent over from the satellite. Anyway, he got bored and figured who actually watched TV that closely in the middle of the night in the Macon area."

"And the natural thing to do to ease his boredom was to flash his privates on television?"

"Naturally." Jay fixed himself a glass of milk and gathered some cookies from the pantry as he replied so casually as if there was nothing out of the ordinary. "Did you watch? Did you see anything?" I leaned over the kitchen countertop to await the remainder of the story. I admit I was curious. Not curious to see

Chad's junk, but curious as what could be seen and as to whether Jay actually tuned in.

"It was so close up on the camera that it was blurry and you could not tell what it was."

"Well thank God! He could have gone to jail if someone turned him in." I was disgusted by the audacity of his friend Chad, but Jay seemed almost impressed as if he thought Chad was brave or something. I knew he knew better and would never do such a thing. He had some conquests, but he wasn't a complete deviant.

"Anyway, Chad had to work over Christmas break so he only went home to Millen for one day. He ended up coming to Christmas night here and he brought Ted with him. He thought he was going to score with Ted, but turns out Ted's not into the queens." Jay laughed as he called Chad a queen. I could not help but share in the laugh since Chad was very much the slang definition of the word.

As we stood there having our laughs in the kitchen, the phone suddenly rang. I ran to get the cordless which was lying on the couch. "Emma! How are you? Where are you?" I responded to the sound of her voice.

I motioned for Jay to pick up the other phone. Emma sounded like the wind had been let out of her. "I am in Jacksonville, at the airport."

"Why on earth are you in Jacksonville?" Jay demanded.

"Apparently there's a storm hanging over Atlanta, so they routed us to Jacksonville." There was no mistaking the exasperation in Emma's voice. "Wynn was supposed to come from Montgomery to bring me home, but he can't come all the way to Jacksonville, bring me home and make it back to Montgomery tomorrow morning." Mr. Bama had a first name and it was Wynn.

"Isn't the airline making arrangements for you?" I asked. It seemed like there was something missing.

"They are making arrangements, but they are aiming to send us by bus to Atlanta and then I have to get a ride from Atlanta to Milledgeville tomorrow. Wynn cannot come tomorrow because he already promised his mother he would take his step-sister to her mother's house in Birmingham. Are either of you in a position to come and get me tomorrow?"

"I can't," Jay said reluctantly.

"Millie?" Emma hesitated. I know she was expecting Jay to jump at the chance to do her a favor. Although I had kept my thoughts to myself, I had felt for a while the she tended to use Jay a bit more than she should.

I could see Jay looking at me. He was expecting me to jump in his place as I would to help him. Of course, I was going to get her.

"I can come get you. It's no problem. What time do you think you'll make it to Atlanta and where would I need to meet you?" I was not excited about to driving to Atlanta alone, but they would do it for me.

"Thank you so much, Millie! You are a dear!" Emma's accent had been reinforced by her time at home in London with her family over Christmas break.

Once everything was settled and I was off the phone with her, I suppose I felt a little like the naked man I had surprised when I arrived home earlier. I did not expect Emma back so soon and was sad that my alone time with Jay was being cut short.

Jay and I spent the rest of the afternoon swapping stories about Christmas. I finally told him about the keyboard that Gabriel had gotten me for Christmas. "It's a full size, electric piano and I need you to help me get it out of the car."

"You managed to get it in your car? How?" I guess Jay was having trouble imagining how we got a full size piano keyboard in the Corvette.

"I'm not sure how, but Gabriel managed to get it in the passenger's seat. He let it down and I really don't know what else, but it's in there and I need you to help me get it out and bring it up the stairs." I grabbed my keys and without verbalizing his agreement to help, Jay stood and followed me out to the car.

Jay and I managed to get the keyboard inside and set up. I played for nearly two hours straight, until Gabriel called.

"I am on my way," he said. I loved to hear his voice and loved his presence even more.

"Okay, but what are you doing tomorrow?" I asked him before allowing him to hang up.

"New Year's Eve, I am preparing for the member New Year's Eve party most of the day and then we are working it tomorrow night. I don't suppose I could persuade you to sing?" he responded. I could hear him moving around, walking while on the phone with me. I figured he was likely packing a bag for staying over.

"Dear Lord, I had completely forgotten about it being New Year's," I sighed.

"You forgot? And, you've made other plans?"

"I have to pick up Emma in Atlanta at the airport and I had planned to ask you to ride along with me. I was going to treat you to lunch somewhere in the city." My plans had been dashed, but I still had my obligation to Emma. "I guess I will be going it alone."

"You most certainly will not!" Gabriel did not typically talk to me like this. He seemed angry and ordering.

"Excuse me?" I was shocked and needed an explanation for his tone. It sounded as if he were forbidding me and that did not sit well. Perhaps I had misunderstood.

"Let me put this more clearly, you won't be going to Atlanta alone."

"WHAT?!!!" I immediately saw red.

"Amelia Anderson, do you not recall the incident at my house just before Christmas? The photos of you?" He had toned it down a little, but was still adamant in his position. I could also hear that he had stopped moving around and I did not think it was because he had suddenly finished packing. "We can talk about this more when I get there."

"We can talk about it now or you needn't bother coming," I matched my tone to his, calm, but stern.

"You don't mean that."

"I do mean it. I am not fond of being ordered around or forbidden to do things, not by anyone." I was now the one pacing around the room. I meant what I said, but that did not mean I was nonetheless nervous about it.

"The bottom line is this, I will not allow anything to happen to you. You're not thinking of your own safety and this angers me. I'm sure you can hear it in my voice and my words. You are not thinking," he repeated.

"I am not thinking?" I was livid at him. "I believe it is you who's not thinking. I've been taking care of myself all of my life and I am not going to be intimidated by anyone, certainly not someone cowardly enough to hide in the shadows and take photos of me. I will do what I want, when I want and how I want. I will not hide and I will not be chaperoned constantly. If you are so damn frightened for my safety, then have a clear word with the one that's always jerking your chain!"

"Please, Amelia, we'll talk about it when I get there." Gabriel begged and I could hear the tone changing, calming. He might as well calm down as he was getting nowhere otherwise.

"We can talk about it now or not at all. I have an obligation to my friend."

"I would like to think that you have an obligation to me," and as soon as the words escaped his mouth, he hung up the phone. I heard the click of the receiver and could not believe it.

"Gabriel? Gabriel?" There was no answer. I was stunned. In our arguments I had always gotten the upper hand in the past. Gabriel usually incurred my wrath, but this time I think it was I who was incurring his.

I waited a few minutes. I thought surely he would call me back. I managed to hold out three minutes before I broke and dialed his number. I did not know what I would do about Emma and I was certain that I could not give in to him. The more I was frightened of what his hanging up on me might mean, the more I started to bend toward seeing his point. I knew him well enough to know that he was not the domineering type. When he was domineering, it was in a completely different way, not the big daddy to little girl way that he had just been. I just hope he knew me well enough to know that I was the stubborn type, but not worth giving up on.

There was no answer when I tried calling him the first time. No answer the second or third time I called either. In fact, it was as if the phone had been taken off the hook because there was that old busy signal sound of "bonk-bonk-bonk" that just went on and on. No one had a busy signal anymore since call waiting came out. Had he taken his phone off the hook so I could not call back?

I was sitting on my bed doing my very best not to dial Gabriel again and not to cry when Jay walked in. "Hey, I have some Ben and Jerry's, chocolate fudgy brownie." Jay's giant smile with his offer quickly faded when he saw my face. "Millie, what's wrong?"

I was in the middle of spilling my guts detailing every aspect of the Beth Reed's stunts when the knock at the door came. I sprang from my bed and sprinted down the stairs toward the door. I snatched it open and threw myself into Gabriel's arms.

"Don't ever do that to me again!" I raised my voice to him and then I held him tightly, so relieved to see him.

"What?"

"You hung up on me! Don't ever do that!"

"I did no such thing. There was a horrible storm and the line went dead." It then started to really occur to him. "You thought I hung up on you. I would never. I told you I wanted to discuss the situation in person, but I would never just hang up on you."

Jay had followed me to the door, not with my speed, but all the same he was standing behind me about four steps from the bottom as I gave Gabriel the combination of a good scolding and hugs and kisses. In the middle of everything, Gabriel noticed Jay standing there. "Is there a reason you are not going with Amelia to get Emma?"

"We are on baby watch for my cousin's wife," Jay replied.

"Has she gone into labor?" Gabriel asked.

"No, but she dilated to one centimeter." Jay needed to give up. He could explain all he wanted, but Gabriel seemed to be set on Jay going with me.

"She could be at one for weeks. Plus, even if she went into labor tonight she likely would not have the baby until lunchtime tomorrow or later." Gabriel was not letting Jay off the hook.

"I will be fine going by myself. I am supposed to pick her up at noon and I will go straight there and straight back." I interjected mainly to prove that I was still there since both of them seemed to have forgotten that small detail.

"NO! You will not. Jay either goes with you or you don't go. You are not making a trip to Atlanta by yourself. You probably do not even know how to get to the airport. Seriously, I would go with you, but I have to work." Gabriel was becoming more frustrated with the situation. "Also, if we must continue this discussion could we do so with me actually inside the apartment and without all of us standing in the stairwell?"

Jay turned and went up the stairs and Gabriel and I followed. I moved to take a seat on the couch while Gabriel reached around the door and dropped his leather duffle bag inside the door of my room. Jay took a seat in the armchair and cut the television on.

"It's not that I don't want to go with her, but I have commitments to my family," Jay said.

I chimed in before Gabriel could, "Come on now, I will buy you lunch at the restaurant of your choice. You know you would rather come with me than wait around here on the off chance that Stacy goes into labor. Gabriel's not going to give up and we are all going to just end up mad at one another so you might as well."

"Way to cave, Millie." Jay rolled his eyes before he caved as well.

No sooner had Jay agreed to go with me was his attention pulled toward the television. It was a rerun of Friends, but it was one of his favorite shows. He turned in the chair and flopped his legs over the arm of the chair closest to the television and leaned back against the other arm.

Gabriel took a seat on the couch with me. He put his feet up on the cedar chest that we were using as a coffee table and I snuggled into his shoulder and chest. Gabriel draped his arm around me as I had hoped. All was right in my world and the three of us watched television together for the remainder of the evening.

Around 11:00 Gabriel and I turned in to my room. He had showered before he made the drive to The Jefferson that night, but decided to join me in mine anyway.

I had taken off my socks and jeans and was unbuttoning my shirt when Gabriel entered the bathroom. His attire was nearly the opposite of mine. He was only wearing his jeans at that point.

There are passages in the Bible that tell us that man was created in the image of God. I was not much for religion, I believed some things to be true and others farfetched, but when I looked at Gabriel, I was certain that he was created in the image of God. I still could not help but stare at him sometimes and just admire how beautiful he really was. Gabriel's jeans hung low and the V showed just below his abs. He was so tall that when I was flat, barefooted, the top of my head just came to the base of his neck. I don't even think I reached the bottom of his Adam's apple.

"Let me help you with that," Gabriel said as he replaced my hands with his to unbutton my shirt.

I traced my fingers around the waistband of his jeans as he unbuttoned my shirt. "I don't want you to worry about me. I will be fine. Jay will be with me and we will be back with Emma before you know it." I lifted my head and smiled at Gabriel.

Gabriel had just finished with my buttons when I completed my assurances. He pulled me into his chest and kissed the top of my head. "I still love the smell of your hair. I look forward to the scent filling my nostrils every time I came to see you."

Gabriel paused and slid my shirt down my shoulders dragging his hands over my arms as the sleeves descended. When the shirt fell to the floor, Gabriel began to speak again. "I daydream about every time we have been together and I don't just mean times like this. I dream of the first time we met and the first time you played the violin into the phone for me to fall sleep. I think of these times too. I count the hours until we are together again, so please understand how I hate that anything or anyone in my past could hurt you."

I had buried my head in his chest as he spoke, but before he finished he reached down and lifted my chin so that I might look him in the face. "I hate to think of it, but I would rather lose you and know that you are safe than be with you and have something happen to you. I am begging you Amelia, be safe tomorrow and always return to me. Promise me."

"I promise," I said in a voice barely above a whisper. He seemed so serious that it almost brought tears to my eyes. I reached my hands around his neck and ever so gently, I kissed him.

Gabriel held me tightly when we kissed, so tight that I could hardly breathe. When we released each other, I again attempted to assure him. "I could not imagine not returning to you. Nothing will happen to me. I swear."

It was suddenly as if a light bulb had gone off in Gabriel's head. "You are right," he said, "nothing will happen to you. You will take my car to get Emma and I will take yours. I know you are funny about people driving your car, but surely I am not 'people' these days and you did promise me after my foot healed that you would let me drive it."

I could not refuse him. "Fine. What's mine is yours."

"And likewise. What's mine is yours," he replied.

"One more thing," I blushed at the thought of what I was about to say.

"Anything."

"I don't want to make love in the shower tonight. I want you in my bed," again I blushed.

"Well, Miss Anderson, how forward of you."

I slipped out of my clothes and into the shower. Gabriel joined me. The water was warm and relaxing and for a few moments we just stood there holding one another with the water running over us. Gabriel stepped from the shower first and left me to finish bathing. I could hear him dry off and leave for the bedroom. It was not long before I left the warmth of the shower, threw on my robe and joined him.

The room was dimly lit. Once I turned off the bathroom light, the only light in the bedroom was that of the torch lamp that stood in the corner of the room opposite the bathroom door. Gabriel was lying on the bed on top of the covers. He had only mussed the bed by tossing a couple of the throw pillows on the floor. I was quiet on entrance, but made just enough noise that Gabriel turned to get a glimpse of me. He smiled slightly and held his hand out for me. I smiled sweetly back, but shook my head so gently in the negative, almost timid like in refusing him.

I made my way across the room to the piano. I asked Gabriel to join me on the bench at the new piano which Jay and I had sat in front of the french doors. We figured it was winter, so blocking access to the porch was of little consequence. Gabriel obliged and joined me on the piano bench. I could still feel the spark from him as his leg brushed against mine when he took a seat next to me.

The real beauty of an electric piano was that I could adjust the volume or I could switch the settings to operate as a real piano. I did adjust the volume to keep the noise of the piano from echoing through the apartment at that time of night. I began to play.

"Do you remember this?" I asked as I softly struck the keys.

"I do. It's 'Crazy' by Patsy Cline."

"Thank you for the piano," I said as I continued the song. "I appreciate it more than you know."

We swayed against each other to the music. I was nearing the second round of the chorus when I felt Gabriel's gentle touch as he eased my robe gently over my right shoulder. I was fully distracted, but I continued to play. Gabriel brushed my hair from where it hung across my shoulder and my back to lay across my left shoulder. The right side of my neck and shoulder were bare and my robe had fallen nearly to my elbow. Gabriel began at the base of my neck where it branched out to my shoulder and he placed kisses from there to the very tip of my shoulder.

I barely made it to the end of the song before turning to him. I wanted him so very badly. There had been spans in the last weeks where we had nearly consumed each other every single day and some days it was morning, noon and night. I wondered if he would ever tire of me and at the same time, I knew I would never tire of him.

I took my hands from the keyboard and when turning to Gabriel, I placed them on his chest. It was smooth, but I could feel the muscles underneath were firm. I noticed for the first time that he had three freckles that looked very much like the constellation known as Orion's Belt across his left peck and about three inches above his nipple. I was distracted by them and I ran my index finger over them before returning to my mission of kissing him.

As I inched down his neck with my kisses, Gabriel whispered, "Did you say something about your bed earlier?"

I glanced up at Gabriel, "Um-hum." I answered him and this time I nodded my head in the affirmative.

Gabriel stood from the bench and again offered his hand to me. I placed mine in his and he led me across the room to the bed. He threw back the covers and before I knew it, I was on my back. Foreplay was over.

Gabriel's hands were so warm as they slid between the cloth of the robe and my skin. He slipped the robe open without it touching more than with the backs of his hands. His palms and fingers brushed against me so lightly that it tickled and sent chill bumps down my legs. It always surprised me that as much heavier as he was than I was, I never felt his weight. It was not something that I typically noticed when he hovered over me and my pelvis raised to meet his, but this particular night, I could not help notice the muscles in his arms as he braced himself over me. It was as if he was doing push-ups and the muscles of his arms were as taunt as those of his chest. If he wasn't perfection, I would never know what was.

"Would you like to try something new?" Gabriel asked without breaking his rhythm, slow and methodical and I liked it. I loved it actually, just like this, but I was putty in his hands. I thought I would have done anything he wanted.

I answered as much as one could with a sigh, a barely audible, "Yes."

There had not been an inch of me that was off limits to Gabriel, but he slid down kissing from my mouth all the way down to my belly button. Suddenly the thrill was gone and it occurred to me where he was headed. I had not thought like this in forever, but I was struck by the question, "How many women had he gone down on?" I tried to shake the thought, but it was just stuck there at the forefront of my brain.

"Stop!" I jumped up and pulled the robe.

"What?" Gabriel was suddenly sitting up at the end of the bed and I had recoiled to the head.

"I know I'm being silly," I said, trying to avoid the real answer.

"What's wrong, Amelia?"

"I am so sorry. So sorry."

"For what?" Gabriel scooted up to sit closer to me.

I shook my head. I really did not want to tell him.

"Come on, what is it?"

I blurted it out, "How many women have you done that with?"

"WHAT?! Is that what this is about?"

"I am so sorry." I buried my head in his chest. "I didn't mean to offend you."

"No, it's fine. The answer will not wipe away..."

"I know I'm being ridiculous."

Gabriel scratched his head before he answered and when he did, he looked away as if he was embarrassed. "I sometimes forget how inexperienced you are."

Gabriel got up and found his boxers; pulled them on and started for the bathroom. I felt hopelessly ashamed that I had asked and in such a manner. My timing was so terrible, I suppose I did not deserve an answer. He had been so good to me and I repaid that with immaturity.

494

Gabriel stopped in the frame of the door and turned back. "The answer is one. I have only done that with one other person. It is not something that I go around doing on a whim to just everyone, if that's what you were wondering. If it makes you uncomfortable, then I won't do that to you and I certainly won't expect you to reciprocate."

Gabriel proceeded into the bathroom. I just sat there. I really did not know what to say and before I could have said anything, he had shut the door behind him. When Gabriel returned, he climbed back into his side of the bed. His side was the closest to the bathroom and he rolled over onto his side and faced the bathroom door.

For the first time in our little history, it was me that had caused the rift between us and not Beth Reed. I tried to make things right. I cuddled up next to him. "I am so sorry. If you would like to try again..."

"That ship's sailed. Go to sleep, Amelia." There was a bite in Gabriel's voice.

I matched the bite with tenderness in mine. "I don't want to go to sleep. I would very much like to finish what we started." I kissed the nape of his neck and slid my bare leg over his.

"Don't!"

"Why? There's only one way to solve the problem with my inexperience." I ran my hand down from where I had first placed it on his chest, sliding it all the way down to the waistband of his boxers.

Gabriel rolled over to me before I could continue my venture into his shorts. He grabbed my hands and pinned me to the bed above my head. This time I could feel his weight on top of me. I did not bother to struggle. For one, I did not want to get free of him and if I had struggled, it would have been pointless.

Gabriel's hair fell down over his face and his eyes were as blue as ever. Just prior to speaking he shook his head to try to toss his hair from his eyes. He was sexier when he was a little heated.

"I can't stay mad at you and I don't want that to change." Gabriel gritted his teeth. I think he was frustrated with himself for not being able to stay angry with me. "I don't mind that you are inexperienced. It's refreshing until it's pointed out how much I am not. So, please don't ever question me about where I have been again. Nothing good comes of those kinds of questions or their

495

answers. It only matters that I'm with you now and I'm not going anywhere."

"I'm sorry. I didn't mean to sound like I was judging you. I'm coming to understand that I benefit from your experience and I apologize if I have not communicated that, but with your experience comes the thought of you with other women. I just hate that."

"I know and I'm sorry too, but I can't change any of that. I'm asking you to stop worrying about what you can't change. Alright?"

"Alright."

Gabriel released me and rolled over onto his side, facing me. I rolled over to mirror him. He took my left hand, held it against his chest and began to do that thing he seemed to like to do, tracing his index finger around my ring finger.

"It's just you and me." He said as he stared at me.

I closed my hand over his and repeated back to him, "You and me."

***

The next morning I awoke in the same spot I had fell asleep, still holding Gabriel's hand. I was the first to awaken and I should have been thinking about getting on the road to get Emma, but instead all I could think about was how peaceful he looked.

I eased from under my covers. There was a nip in the air, so I quickly tiptoed to my chest of drawers and from the top drawer I took out my camera. The camera was already loaded with black and white film. I thought how wonderful it would be to have photos of Gabriel on my wall like the ones that Jay had taken of me. I would much rather have photos of Gabriel than myself. I quickly returned to my side of the bed and snapped a couple of pictures of Gabriel as he slept.

The snapping of the shutter in the manual Cannon camera gave me away and Gabriel began to wake. I had not intended to disturb him and I did not want him to know what I was up to. I eased the camera under the bed before he saw and I snuggled into bed and under the covers. I shivered at the touch of the sheets until I found the warm spot that I had recently vacated.

"Good morning," I whispered while reaching to pull him toward me.

"Good morning." Gabriel smiled at me.

"I would like to finish what we started last night if you're up for it," I asked cautiously.

Gabriel did not answer with words. With his hand in the small of my back, he pulled me even closer to him than we already were. I could feel every inch of him from the top of his chest to his pelvis and down his legs against mine. The hair on the back of my neck stood up as the hand that was on my back inched downward and cupped my behind.

I had slept in nothing but black lace panties and those were still in place. "You won't need these." Gabriel said as he eased a finger into the leg of the panties, hooked them and began to slip them down.

Just the way he spoke was erotic let alone the act that followed. Gently, Gabriel urged me onto my back. I gave in and was in a better position for him to finish the job removing my underpants. Of course, I aided in this and drew my legs up one at a time for him to slip them off. This also allowed for a full frontal view of me, all of me. I no longer noticed the chill in the air and no longer cared about anything else, but experiencing whatever it was that he was about to impart.

I had enjoyed every position with Gabriel so much thus far while only experiencing what I would assume was regular intercourse that I could not imagine anything being any better. There was a difference in what he was doing now and what we had been doing together.

Gabriel's tongue found its way to hit spots that I scarcely knew existed. I preferred not to think about practice makes perfect and instead opted to think of this as just another talent of his. He knew exactly what he was going; where to touch, how much pressure to use and how to combine the use of this tongue with the use of his fingers and where to put them.

Although I did not allow these thoughts to fill my head in the moment, I knew I would describe to Jay later that I felt intercourse with Gabriel and I had always been an expression of love, but this was different. This was not better. It was just different, like truck versus car, both got you down the road. This was totally for pleasure and not necessarily expression.

When climax came, I screamed his name, "GABRIEL!!!" It was the most intense yet. I drew my knees together and rolled over to hide my face in my pillow. I was not embarrassed, but almost giddy at the thrill of it.

Gabriel crawled back up and flopped down on his side of the bed. "Don't hide your face. Did you like it?"

I peeped from the pillow and cut my eyes toward Gabriel. "Did I like it?!! You have to ask?" I could hardly contain the smile on my face.

This was sex and although I enjoyed it immensely; toe curling, eye rolling, stomach clenching, the definition of mind blowing, it was still not my preference. This was an exceptional change, but I much preferred the giving and receiving exchange of making love with Gabriel.

***

Before we left, Gabriel and I exchanged vehicles as we had agreed the night before. Jay and I left in Gabriel's Legend and Gabriel left in my Corvette. We followed Gabriel as far as the caution light outside of Milledgeville where he made the turn to take the shortcut around Eatonton. Jay and I continued toward Eatonton. We would continue on Highway 441 until we came to I-20 just outside of Madison.

I would never give up my Corvette, but Gabriel's car did make me long for something more modern. The sound system that I had installed in my car made music sound like the love child of an eight track and songs that I had recorded on my boom box off of the Rick Dee's Top 40 Countdown as oppose to CDs that I had actually purchased. The Legend had a Bose system and it sounded as if the bands or musicians were in full concert just for us.

We found Emma at Hartsfield Airport with no trouble. The Legend had driven like a dream and it definitely had enough room for all of us. Emma looked as if she had not slept in days. Jay and I had planned on going somewhere in the city for lunch, but Emma looked dead on her feet. Once in the car, both Jay and I encouraged her to take a nap in the back seat as I drove us back. With all of her luggage in the trunk, she had plenty of room and heeded our instruction and fell quickly to sleep.

Jay and I continued our banter and before long we were at the gate of Port Honor. It was nearly three and we had not had lunch, so I insisted they come inside the clubhouse. I was sure Gabriel would feed all of us.

Jay held the door for Emma and me to enter the clubhouse. Just inside the door Joan, was manning her desk.

"I can't believe you are here on New Year's Eve," I said to Joan before introducing Jay and Emma. "They are my roommates."

"It's wonderful to meet y'all," Joan replied as she gave each of them a hug. Emma was not one for hugging, but Joan got her first and there was no avoiding it.

"So will you be at the members' party tonight?" I asked her.

"Probably, but I should get home to change." She started closing up her desk as she finished her sentence.

I began leading Jay and Emma toward the stairs, but told Joan I hoped to see her that night.

We were only about five steps down from the top when Joan came running to the top of the stairs, "Millie," she called to me. "You might beware, Beth Reed is in the bar. I just thought I would warn you."

"Thanks, Mrs. Joan," I replied.

Jay rubbed his hands together with glee when he spoke. "Oh goodie. I have been dying to know what Cruella Deville looked like in real life," said Jay. When I told him about the break in at Gabriel's house that night, I had described Beth as Cruella Deville and apparently Jay had remembered.

I was not thrilled at the thought of seeing her or at the thought of her seeing Gabriel. At least at this point I knew where she was and that she wasn't waiting in the bushes to jump out at me and do something crazy.

"Bloody hell, Millie, of all days I look like rubbish!" Emma said as she grabbed my hand. "I would rather meet the devil while looking my best."

I put on a brave face and the three of us giggled as we proceeded down the stairs. Alone in this situation, I probably would have been ready for battle, but with the two of them flanking me, I was cool as a cucumber.

At the bottom of the stairs, I turned to get the door to the bar, but Jay cut me off. Again, he opened the door for us. Such a gentleman he was.

Once in the bar, we found Cruella seated in one of the stools closest to the door. No one was behind the bar and there were no other patrons at that time. Apparently Joan had called down to Gabriel because when he came through the swinging door from the kitchen he seemed startled to see Beth at the end of the bar. Gabriel was looking at us as we entered behind Beth. Being as self-centered as she is, she naturally thought his smile was for her. Had she not gotten the message that he left the night he discovered the items stolen from his house?

The opening of the door from the dining room had not first caught her attention, but it did when Gabriel looked past her. Beth turned to look at us as we entered. We were a bit of a tornado of laughter as we passed her and all three of us gave her a good looking over with our noses turned up as if something smelled and it was her. Of course, I was not on speaking terms with her and both Jay and Emma knew where their bread was buttered. They followed my lead, rolled their eyes and looked away as opposed to really acknowledging her.

Beth immediately turned back to Gabriel who was now approaching one of the four top tables near the fireplace. She tried to get his attention. "Gabriel!" Beth called to him, but he ignored her and winked at me.

As if we did not know already, Beth could not take a hint. She called to him again, "Gabriel, I need to talk to you."

Initially my blood pressure started to rise at her persistence and then I thought about last night. Gabriel's words were in my ears again, "It's just you and me." And "I am not going anywhere." I was suddenly aware that she no longer fazed me.

It occurred to me that I did not care if Gabriel spoke to Beth because as soon as I entered the room, his eyes were glued to me. Jay led Emma and me to the table that Gabriel had picked out for us. Gabriel's eyes followed me as I made my way to the table where he had pulled out a chair for me. He was all smiles and it had to be obvious to Beth now that his smiles were not for her.

Jay pulled out a chair for Emma and we took our seats. Gabriel leaned down and kissed the top of my head while he remained standing behind me. As soon as our behinds touched the seats, Gabriel offered to make us lunch. We happily accepted his offer and he excused himself to the kitchen, but before he did he cautioned me that he was going to speak to Beth. She had remained seated at the bar and watching all of us the entire time. The look on her face indicated that she was less than amused.

"Perhaps if I just go ahead and see what she wants, all of the nonsense that's been going on might stop. I dare say I would love it if she were here to return the things she stole and if she doesn't then I will love calling the sheriff's department to come and get her." There was something in his voice that made me wonder if he even believed his words.

As soon as Gabriel was out of earshot, Jay and Emma both started with their analysis of Beth Reed. The seat that Gabriel chose for me was positioned with my back to the bar and Beth. The seats that Jay and Emma chose gave them full view of her.

"I think your use of the description of Cruella Deville was spot on," Emma observed. "I could totally see that tart torturing puppies."

"She's beautiful," Jay observed and Emma and I gasped before Jay finished his sentence, "but it's not without a great deal of effort. She's not in the ball park with you, Millie."

Emma added, "She looks miserable."

"Y'all are sweet," I said with a scowl. "I think she's gained some weight and I am not just saying that to be snide. I think she's put on about fifteen pounds since I first saw her. Her face is definitely fuller."

"I don't think you have anything to worry about when it comes to her," Jay said.

"I agree. I would not touch that skank with Jay's dick." Emma commented. I laughed and Jay shivered in disgust at the thought.

Our laughter was abruptly cut short by the boom of Gabriel's voice, "THAT'S NOT TRUE!!!"

My head whipped around to see what the commotion was all about. Gabriel's face was red and the veins were protruding. We had not heard what Beth had said to Gabriel, but we had a pretty good idea when the three of us saw her get to her feet from her stool. I shrieked at the sight of her. I had not noticed at all the Sunday I had last seen her. Evidently, I was not the only one who did not notice that day.

Beth responded to my shriek. She gritted her teeth and the words hissed through. "It is true!"

Tears were coming to my eyes and I desperately did not want that bitch to see me cry. She was pregnant and clearly she had told him it was his. I suddenly felt sick. I was going to vomit. I did the only thing I could do. I ran.

I ran past Beth. Jay and Emma were quick behind me. I could hear Gabriel despite the ruckus made by door from the three of us.

"What have you done?!!!" he screamed at her.

I took the stairs two steps at a time. Jay and Emma struggled to keep up and I faintly heard one of them trip behind me, but they were on their feet and running with me. Joan was gone from her desk when we topped the stairs. I was in the parking lot before I realized we had run as far as we could. Gabriel had the keys to my car and I still had his and even if I had had my keys there were three of us. There was no getting three of us back in my car.

I turned and threw myself into Jay and cried. Jay and Emma both held me. Gabriel had chased after us. He had likely been slowed by coming around the bar and it was also likely that Beth tried to stop him.

Jay released me to Emma as Gabriel approached. He stepped to block Gabriel from me. "I think she's had enough, don't you?"

"I didn't know! I'm so sorry."

"You spend your life apologizing to her and for what? Only to disappoint her again and again!" Jay was no match for Gabriel in size, but he wounded Gabriel with his words. Jay stood firm and Gabriel fell to his knees.

"Amelia, you must believe me. I had no idea. I am so sorry. This is the first I have heard of this."

"Sorry for what?" Jay screamed at him. "Sorry for fathering a child with someone else? Sorry for breaking her heart? Sorry for continually allowing that bitch to get at her? Exactly what is it that you are sorry about?"

"Stop it!" I let go of Emma and stepped away. I took Jay's hand to steady myself. My knees were weak, but I had to ask. "Could it be yours?"

Tears trickled down Gabriel's face. I could barely hear him when he answered, "It could be."

"Well, she said she would win the war!" I stifled back tears and wiped my eyes. I walked to Gabriel and held out my hand. "Give me the keys to my car."

"What?"

"The keys! Give them to me!" I held my hand flat and demanded with it.

"You're in no condition to drive," Gabriel begged.

"Give me my keys!" I shook my hand in demand again and gritted my teeth. I did not raise my voice. I loved him more than anything and I would never scream at him, but I had to get away from him. I just wanted to go home and there was no telling when the mother of his child was going to make another appearance to rub it in some more.

Gabriel stood and handed my keys to Jay. I turned and snatched them from Jay. I did not look back at him when I said, "They will bring your car back to you tomorrow."

Jay and Emma followed me and I tossed the keys to Gabriel's car to Emma. Neither of them bothered to warn me that I should not drive as Gabriel had. I am sure they were thinking it, but they knew there was no effort in it being voiced aloud.

"Please don't go. Don't leave me." My heart broke a thousand times at his words.

I turned back to him. Jay and Emma stopped and I went past them. I fell to my knees in front of Gabriel and took his hands. "If the child is yours we will never be free of her. You will never be allowed to be truly happy and I want you to be happy. I want that more than anything. Find what happiness you can in your child and protect it from the kind of mother that I had."

"I am begging you don't leave." Gabriel pulled me to him and kissed me.

"I am begging you to forget me and try to find happiness." I shrank from his embrace and again wiped tears from my eyes.

"There's no happiness without you."

CHAPTER 21

Jay and Emma did not waste any time and returned Gabriel's car on New Year's Eve. It was there in the parking lot waiting on him when he got off work in the wee hours of New Year's Day.

Jay told me later that Gabriel had started knocking on the door of our apartment at 1:45 a.m. First it was knocking, then it was knocking and begging me to come out, then it was banging and did not stop until Cara let him in her apartment. Cara said he sat on the couch all night and did not sleep a wink. The next morning, Gabriel sat in the cold on the front porch of The Jefferson and waited. He waited all New Year's day for me, but I never returned. On New Year's Eve, I went straight from Port Honor to Aunt Gayle's where I stayed until the very moment my classes started back.

While Gabriel sat in the cold, I poured my heart out to Aunt Gayle. I had arrived at her house a little after 4:00 p.m. and I went straight to bed, in my bed, in my old room. I cried until there were no tears left and I fell asleep. Before I fell asleep, Aunt Gayle checked on me a few times, but did not press me. While I slept, I dreamed of Gabriel. It was a beautiful dream in which he was mine and there was no competition and there was peace in our lives.

I slept until almost 10:00 a.m. on New Year's Day. When I finally woke up, I realized that that was the first night I had spent without him in two weeks. My heart shattered again and I wondered how would I ever get past this? It took me almost an hour before I could get out of bed and dry my eyes enough to see Aunt Gayle without her worrying any more than she likely already was.

Aunt Gayle was sitting with her feet up on the couch reading the Augusta Chronicle on New Year's morning as I staggered into the room. When she first laid eyes on me, Aunt Gayle declared, "You look as if you have cried a river. Is it really that bad?"

My eyes were on fire and I dared not look in the mirror before I came down. I was sure my face was puffy and my eyes were a flaming blue as that is what they turned when I cried for any length of time. Had my eyes been that color all the time, I suppose I would have been something to see. The best way to describe them would be to say they were the color of smurfs.

I flopped down in the puffy chair at the end of the couch and hung my pounding head in my hands as I answered. "It is worse than the worst has ever been."

I told Aunt Gayle everything there was to tell. Without hesitation, she listened like the good mother she had always been to me.

"Do you think you could carry on with Gabriel and accept the child?" Aunt Gayle asked as she laid the newspaper across the coffee table so as to give me her undivided attention.

"I don't know if I could raise someone else's child." As soon as the words escaped my lips, I realized how I might have offended her. I apologized immediately. "I didn't mean that. Please forgive me. I don't think I could help raise that child. I don't want Gabriel to live a life stuck between his child and me."

Aunt Gayle looked puzzled at my response. "Why do you think he would be stuck? You imply that he would have to choose."

"Remember my friend, Kay from middle school? Her parent's divorced when she was really small and her mother raised her to hate her father. It was not until high school that she realized that she had just been her mother's weapon against her father. It nearly broke her father. He remarried only to have that marriage break-up because he was always being jerked around by Kay's mother over seeing Kay. That's exactly what Beth would do to Gabriel. I don't want that for him. I want him to have a chance at happiness."

"You have only been with him mere months and you love him enough to sacrifice your own happiness for him?" Aunt Gayle seemed both astonished and proud of me all at the same time. She scooted to the end of the couch near me, leaned over and rubbed my head in an attempt to comfort me. "You are the sweetest girl I have ever known, Millie. There will be other loves for you."

"There won't."

"What do you mean there won't? Of course there will."

"I don't want anyone else."

I was lost in my thoughts and Aunt Gayle was just opening her mouth to formulate more of an argument for her point when the phone started to ring. Aunt Gayle looked to me as if to ask permission to get it. There was nothing more to be said on the subject as far as I was concerned, so I nodded my approval for her to answer it.

Aunt Gayle left me in the living room and went to take the call in the kitchen. I could not hear the entire call, but I could tell it was Mr. Graham. "I don't see the point in making the man suffer. Yes, you can tell him she is here. You may also tell him that if he thinks of showing up here he will be met with the business end of my shotgun. She's in no condition to see him."

I could not hear Mr. Graham's side of the conversation, but after her last line I leaned in to listen to what Aunt Gayle had to say next. "No, I don't think you understand. I have spent the better part of this girl's life making sure she was not broken by those who were supposed to love her. I will not have him undoing it. He needs to just back off for now."

In the beginning Gabriel called three and four, sometimes five times per day. He left messages on the machine when Jay and Emma were not home to take them personally. My heart broke again with every message. I returned none of his calls, yet he persisted. I finally asked Jay and Emma to stop giving them to me and they did. I think they even started working to catch and erase the messages on the machine. I was completely, emotionally, trapped between wanting him to give up and not wanting him to give up.

Everyone at the club had heard what had gone on and had called to check on me. Cara stopped by almost daily. As if I did not know it from the messages, Cara described Gabriel as being as heartsick as I was. She also told me that Beth was nearly a permanent fixture at the club since the first of the year. Cara assured me as did everyone else that called, especially Daniel that Gabriel was not the least bit interested in Beth.

Daniel called almost every day. He begged me to please talk to Gabriel. He said he had never seen Gabriel like this and he was worried about him. It hurt me to think of Gabriel in pain and I explained that to Daniel, but I could not give in.

Both Daniel and Cara relayed messages that the members were asking about me and they all missed me. Those who did not know that Gabriel and I were dating were connecting the dots: with Beth showing up in her condition and throwing herself at Gabriel and with me suddenly missing. Daniel said the members were not happy and that they all loved me and sent their condolences. Everyone was so sweet and everyone begged for me to come back, but that just was not in the cards.

It was three weeks into the semester and a little over three weeks since I had seen Gabriel. Per usual, I had an 8:00 a.m. class on Mondays, Wednesdays and Fridays. It was Monday morning and I was walking home from that class. I was passing in front of Bell Hall and there he was, sitting on the steps of the dorm. My heart fluttered at the sight of him and my knees went weak. I tried to walk on by, but I was so stunned by the sight of him, I tripped over my own feet. To the pavement I went. Gabriel was already starting to stand when I first noticed him and he did his best to catch me, but it was no use.

"My God, Amelia, are you alright?" Gabriel bent down to help me up, but I scrambled to my feet. What did he ever see in me? So clumsy.

"Why won't you talk to me?" Gabriel asked as I tried to pass him and he followed.

I did not respond and tried to keep walking, quickly, picking up the pace. I could hear the rustle of his jeans and the urgency of his footsteps as he followed behind me. I did not know what to say. I was so stunned to see him and so embarrassed for face planting on the sidewalk. It was taking everything I had not to jump into his arms and beg him to take me back or just plain run.

"I miss you." Gabriel reached out and touched my shoulder. The current was there like always. The tingle went all the way to my core; that certainly had not changed.

I could not look at him. What was I to say? I had always been honest with him in the past. If I turned and looked him in the face, I was done for. I remained with my back to him, but the words escaped my lips, "I miss you too."

"What are we doing?" he asked.

I could hardly speak. The tears were coming. "We are moving on," I mumbled.

"I am not moving on. I won't."

"You must." I started to walk again, still resisting the urge to run. I had made it to the far side of the dorm's parking lot with Gabriel still keeping up.

"I will follow you all the way home until you talk to me. I tried to stay away, but I just can't. I won't. I will follow you to and from class every day until you talk to me."

"Just give up!" I know I said that, but I had not given up. The highlight of my day was going to sleep and dreaming of him. Sometimes the dreams were so real that I could see, touch, taste and smell him. They were as vivid as if he were still in the bed right next to me, in his spot. I had lived the dream until the last day of December and since then I had been sleeping while awake and living while asleep.

Beyond the dreaming, I had saved all of the messages he had left on our answering machine that Jay and Emma had not wiped out and I listened to them over and over again in the last few weeks. I had a personal favorite that I played each night before going to bed. In that message Gabriel told me, "I love you. Sweet dreams and goodnight."

I was such a sap I had kept a picture of him under my pillow and I kissed it before saying a prayer for him every night and going to sleep. I prayed that Gabriel was safe and that he would find happiness. Occasionally, I said a selfish prayer and asked God for Him to let Gabriel find happiness with me.

"Amelia, I won't give up and I am certain that you don't really want me to." He was right and I did not want to fight with him. Maybe God was throwing me a bone and answering my selfish prayer. If so, the least I could do was pull my own weight a little.

I turned to Gabriel. His eyes were my undoing, so blue, the shade of the ocean in the gulf in October. Self-preservation beckoned from within me. I did not want to ask, but I had to. "How sure are you that the child Beth is carrying is yours?"

He had not had a haircut in a while and his hair flopped toward his face as he dropped his head. With hands in his pockets, Gabriel looked to the ground as he answered me. "I told you, I was with her once after your interview, so with her being five months along, the timing is right."

"First of all, what's done is done so we will have to deal with it together. No more looking at the ground and being ashamed. It's done, so hold your head up. As long as you are ashamed or embarrassed or are afraid that something might hurt me, then you are likely not to tell me everything and I think for things to work out between us, then we are going to have to tell one another everything.

"Secondly..."

With no restraint at all for public displays of affections and before I could finish my sentence, Gabriel snatched me up in a giant hug and whirled me around, "Are you saying you will give us another chance?"

"Yes, but secondly, I don't want to work at the club anymore. I don't want to sound selfish, but I have a lot riding on this semester and I would prefer to keep my life here in Milledgeville and untouched by Beth. The sight of her pregnant possibly with your child devastated me. The thought of it makes me physically ill. I cannot do anything about her coming to the club, but I can keep myself from being subjected to her as much as possible. That's my condition."

Gabriel conceded. "I completely understand and in the last weeks I have done my best to make peace with it myself. Please know that I am so sorry and this is not how I wanted things to go for us."

While we were apart, my life had been a scratched record of "It's My Party and I'll Cry If I Want To." The title portion of the song that made up the chorus had played on in repetition from the moment I drove away from Port Honor on December 31, 1995, until the day we made up in the parking lot of Bell Hall. I hated that song and I was glad it was over. No one should ever have to endure that as the theme song of their life as I had recently.

Gabriel and I continued our conversation as we walked back to The Jefferson. I suppose I would hold out hope that it was not his child until it was proven otherwise and I had no real way of making anyone prove that to me. He would have to be the one that did that, but I could not help but ask, "Do you have any reason to suspect that it's not your baby she's carrying?"

"I suppose it is always possible, but she never mentioned anyone else and you know how she has pursued me." With his hand that was not firmly gripped to mine, Gabriel scratched his head and smoothed back his hair as he answered.

"You mean how she's stalked me, stolen from you and tried to intimidate us? Anyway, have you asked her?"

"Yes and she has denied there being anyone else."

"And you believe her?"

"I don't know what to believe. I just know that I agree with your statement from the day we found out. If it is my child, I certainly do not want it growing up with only Beth as an influence."

"Regardless of what becomes of you and me, I hope it's not your child so you are not tied to her for the rest of your life." In the last three weeks, I had learned not to take having a future with Gabriel for granted.

We were in the middle of crossing the street, but Gabriel stopped and looked at me. "What does that mean, 'regardless of what becomes of you and me'?"

"Well, we've only been together for just over two months so..."

"As far as I am concerned, we have been together since the day I met you," Gabriel huffed.

"Really, if we were so together from the day we met, then surely we would not be in the quandary we are in with Beth in our lives."

"I see your point, so please let me explain. I know this comes across as an excuse, but it was one time and I was so drunk that I do not know how it happened."

"Excuse me? You don't know how it happened?" I could not just stand there in the middle of the street with cars honking and going around us, so I proceeded to walk again.

"Please don't walk away." Gabriel followed me. "I don't want to tell you the gory details, but I was at the club and Beth had come in the Friday night after I hired you. I was waiting for everyone to finish so I could lock up for the night. She hung out at the bar with me and waited. We talked about old times and I opened a bottle of wine and we had a few shots of tequila. I don't know how I got home, but I woke up naked in a bed at her father's villa with a note from Beth on the pillow."

"What did the note say?"

"It said, 'It was fun as always. −B.'"

"So you don't even know if you slept with her?"

"Unfortunately, I think I did. I was still drunk that morning, but how else would I have gotten there and naked?"

I just shook my head. I could not believe all of this was happening to us and it was probable that he did not even sleep with her. I suppose there was no arguing with him since he thought he did. I decided I would save that argument for another day. I had so many questions about everything with Beth that I don't think I had let myself start to be happy that he was back.

We made it to the steps of my building and although I just wanted to jump in his arms and kiss him until the cows came home, I could not resist wanting to know what the plan was and where things stood with Beth before letting go. Before letting him in, we sat on the porch and continued to talk.

"Beth has apologized for all of the stunts she pulled. She wanted me to relay that to you. Over the last few weeks, she has been nothing, but amicable. She says she wants me to be a part of the baby's life. She claimed that the night she broke into the house was the day she found out and that she panicked. She said she was going to tell me that night, but things just went horribly wrong. She had not expected to get pregnant and certainly not by a man who did not want her."

"Oh, boo-fucking-hoo!" I rolled my eyes. As if I would ever believe anything from her.

"Amelia." Just in the tone of him saying my name, I knew he was chastising me and I did not like it.

"What?!"

"I am still pissed with her about everything, but what can I do? I think keeping her calm might be our best strategy at this time."

"Fine." I did not want to fight with him because I had a feeling that was what all of this was about, just another tactic to get rid of me. This time her game was to kill me with kindness. Ugh!

"One more thing, did she give the pearls back or your mother's wedding set?"

"No." Ah, and there was his true feelings written across his face. He was disgusted at her.

By the time we finished the conversation, I had allowed Gabriel to convince me that everything was going to be alright. "Nothing and no one is going to come between us."

I got up from the step and held out my hand to Gabriel to help him up.

"It's cold out here. Let's go inside," I said as he took my hand.

When Gabriel stood, I did not back up. He came so close to me that we were virtually chest on chest. "May I kiss you?" he asked.

My heart pounded in my ears. I would have been happy just to have stood next to him forever, but the thought of kissing him again made my heart race. Distracted by desire for him, I could hardly mumble my response, "Please."

Gabriel enveloped me in his pea coat and I was warm against him. The smell of someone burning hickory in their fireplace nearby was overtaken by the scent of Gabriel's cologne. I looked up at him and was again in awe. There were freckles across the bridge of his nose that I had never noticed before and a slight scar in the top of his right eyebrow near his nose. Despite that, he was as perfect as ever.

Our eyes locked and remained that way for a moment. He leaned down and pushed the hair out of my face using only his nose as his arms stayed firmly in the coat wrapped around me. His nose was cold and it tickled a little which made me smile. I bit my lower lip in anticipation of the kiss while his face was buried in my hair.

I could feel him breathe in my hair before he sighed. "I can't be near strawberries without thinking of you. I can't be around anything without thinking of you."

Gabriel eased his face out of my hair and again looked me in the eye. The look was brief and then he gave me what I longed for, the continuation of my education in kissing. His lips were tender and his tongue searched for mine and found it with little effort. The butterflies spun in my stomach and I was immediately on fire for him.

My word, I had missed the taste of him. The feel of the stubble on his face from not shaving that morning was so familiar and even though it had sometimes left my face a little chafed, I had missed that as well. I missed everything about him.

As Gabriel kissed me, a tear began to fall and streak down my face. I held him so tightly and kissed him back as though the world were ending. He must have noticed since as we kissed, he gently stroked my face and wiped the tear away. I am not even sure why the tear sprang up, perhaps it was just the relief of having him back.

Gabriel leaned back for a moment, "Please don't leave me again. I am going to make everything alright and we will be fine as long as you trust me."

There were good times and there were bad times in the next couple of months. However, in the first few weeks, we picked up right where we had left off.

The good times included our trip to Nashville. We saw the Parthenon and stayed at the Opryland Hotel as he had planned as one of my Christmas gifts. We stayed in one of the rooms that had a balcony that opened into the atrium behind a waterfall. We made love that night with the doors of the balcony open and heard the rushing water all the while. It was quite possibly the most romantic night of my life, but Beth was constantly in the back of my mind.

Family night dinners picked back up at The Jefferson and we were toying with buying a larger dining room table because our group had grown. Not only was Gabriel a permanent fixture at the table now, but so were Jerry and Daniel and the rest of the residents from the building. Matt and Cara were on-again, off-again all the time, but they always seemed to be on come Tuesday night, so Matt was a regular at dinner. Jay was like a Baskin Robbins with his flavor of the week. It became a running joke to call his guest "Flavor". Aside from being a rude joke, remembering their name was pointless since we would never see them again.

Gabriel found out in February that the German Equestrian team would definitely be staying at The Honor Inn during the Olympics. He was thrilled. We had known that the trip to the Georgian Terrace was to promote the club to the board in preparation for the Olympics, but we had not known until mid-February that they were actually going to be staying at Port Honor. This meant hiring more staff and a few minor renovations to the Inn.

Gabriel was promoted to Food and Beverage Manager where initially he had been the chef whose duties included managing the restaurant. His new position allowed for him to hire another chef. Gabriel was disappointed that he was not allowed to promote Alvin to the position of chef, but the owners wanted an actual four star chef hired strictly for the Olympics. Alvin remained sue chef and Robert was hired. Robert came to Port Honor on a referral from Jerry. They had known one another from their days at Back Street. No one would have known it, but Robert put himself through culinary school by performing as a drag queen. His resume included stints at Hotel Nikko, the Swiss Hotel, the Ritz and most any other of the prominent hotels worth mentioning. It was quite the list and his food was divine. I knew that because Gabriel often brought me home dinner.

My letter arrived in late March from Mercer. I had been accepted to law school and would start there in August. Gabriel could not have been happier for me. He threw a party for me at his house and invited all of the family from Tuesday nights plus a few of my actual family members. Aunt Gayle and Aunt Dot made the trip out from Avera. Aunt Gayle and Mr. Graham were still an item, so he invited Mr. Graham and his mother. Everyone that was invited came.

Things were going great until the party. It was close to 9:00 p.m. and the party was going strong when the phone rang. Daniel answered it.

"Gabriel, its Cruella!" Everyone had taken to calling her that except Gabriel.

I did not hear any of the phone call, not even Gabriel's side of it. All I knew was that within moments, Gabriel was by my side with his coat on. "I hate to do this, but I have to leave. Beth is on her way to Northside Hospital with contractions."

The room buzzed around us, but it was as if we were alone. Had Aunt Gayle not been wrapped up with Mr. Graham and his mother, I am sure she would not have been pleased that Gabriel was leaving the party. Daniel was the only one who knew and that was only because he answered the phone and he was pissed.

"What? Hold on, I will get my things and come with you. Everyone will see themselves out. I will have Daniel lock up for us." I turned to go and get my coat, but Gabriel stopped me. He pulled me back to him.

"If things take a turn for the worse, I don't want you there. We both know how you feel about this pregnancy and if she loses it..."

"Gabriel, I had not even thought of that. I would never wish that on anyone, not even Beth if she truly wants the child. Oh, well, I suppose it's nice to know what you think of me."

"You know that is not what I think of you. It's just that her family is going to be there and I don't think..."

I cut him off again. "I would only be coming for moral support for you, but if you don't want me there..."

"You know I want you with me all the time, but I am trying to think of people other than just the two of us. Just stay here and I will be back as soon as I can."

"I hate that you are driving to Atlanta at this time of night."

Gabriel placed his hands around my face. "Nothing is going to happen to me. I love you and I will be back as soon as I can. In fact, you will probably wake up with me asleep next to you."

"I am going to hold you to that." I smirked at him.

Gabriel kissed me and I told him I loved him and then he was gone.

The party ended around midnight. Daniel offered to stay at the house with me so I would not be alone. Jay, Emma and Cara offered the same. I did not feel right about letting anyone stay. I did not want Gabriel coming home to others in his house. I especially did not want him arriving home to anyone waiting to pass judgment on him for leaving my party.

It was not long after everyone left that I dressed in one of my silk teddies and was in bed by 12:30 a.m. My plan was to remind him exactly what it was he was leaving behind as soon as he arrived home and crawled into bed. Unfortunately, my plan was a failure since I awoke the next morning without Gabriel having come home.

The light broke through the crack where the curtains did not quite meet and woke me around 9:30 a.m. I tried to squelch all insecurity, but that was nearly impossible. I tried to occupy my mind by keeping busy. I changed into more conservative pajamas and brushed my teeth. I made breakfast including enough for Gabriel in case he came home. All the while, my mind raced from one thing to another ranging from had Gabriel been in a wreck, had Beth miscarried, had she had the baby, was Gabriel just hanging out with her and her family? Where was he?

My questions were not answered until around 10:30 a.m. when the phone rang. I grabbed the cordless, which I had in the bed with me, on the first ring.

"Hello?!!" I answered frantically.

"Amelia." I recognized his voice. It was Gabriel.

"Gabriel, where are you?"

"At Beth's house in Atlanta. I am just about to leave here and head home. I figured you were worried, so I wanted to call you."

Gabriel was hardly finished with his sentence before I heard Beth in the background, "Gabe, get back in here. She's moving. You have got to feel this!"

"Sounds like you need to go. I will see you when I see you," I replied and hung up on him. If he could not feel the roll of my eyes through the phone, then he was a fool.

As soon as I hung up the phone, I called Jay. He was still asleep so it took him three rings to pick up.

"Gabriel just called," I told Jay. "I could hear Beth in the background."

I mocked her words to Jay and he laughed before becoming more serious. "So, they are having a girl?"

"Apparently so."

"What are you going to do, Millie?" Jay asked.

"I don't know, but I don't want to compete and I really feel like I will always be competing for Gabriel as long as Beth is in the picture, whether he realizes and admits it or not."

"I am not sure what to tell you. I know he loves you and this is going to be a struggle. I think maybe you just need to decide if he is worth the struggle." I could hear Jay rolling over in his bed and rustling his covers as he spoke. "Perhaps you need to tell him how you feel."

"Maybe you are right. Perhaps I just need to talk to him and perhaps I would if he ever came home." The longer I waited for him, the more insecure I was becoming.

It was nearly noon when Gabriel finally arrived home. I had packed my things and was in the yard loading my car when he drove up.

"Where are you going?" Gabriel asked as he got out of his car. He looked like he had not slept at all, other than that, he looked exactly the same as when he had left.

I hardly acknowledged him beyond answering, "I am going home."

"Now? Why?"

I stopped loading the trunk and turned to face him. "Because maybe Beth has won the war. Maybe I don't want to stick around and have it rubbed in my face."

"What are you talking about?" Gabriel asked while starting to take my suitcase back out of the trunk.

"I don't want to compete." I paused for a moment before picking up my suitcase again. "I can't compete with a baby and I won't try."

"There's no competition. I keep trying to tell you. There's only you." Gabriel grabbed the free part of the handle of the suitcase and kept me from loading it back into my trunk.

"You don't see it, but that's exactly what is going on. Just because the game has changed does not mean Beth has stopped playing, she just upped the ante that's all..."

"So my child is an ante now? Just a piece in a poker game?"

"That's my point exactly. You have started seeing it as your child and I have yet to stop hoping that it's not yours. There's no place for me in this." I shook my head in aggravation that he did not see it.

"So, you are going to run?"

"It's what I do."

"You said you would not leave."

"I don't want to leave, but I don't like what this is going to turn us into. We aren't married, so it's not like I am going to be a stepmother or anything to this child if it is yours. I am just out here waiting for the leftovers. I don't want leftovers. I want you. All of you and last night and this morning just proved that I won't ever be able to have that again."

"So, it's all or nothing?"

I had once wondered when the charms of Gabriel's looks would wear off. I thought this might be the day, but I was wrong. Before I knew it, he grabbed me and kissed me. The next thing I knew, we were in his room and the shirt I was wearing was now ruined from Gabriel ripping it open. Buttons from it were slung all over the room and they pinged and cracked as they hit the hardwood floor and rolled like marbles.

All thoughts of leaving were purged from my head. His hands locked in mine over my head and bore his weight. This was the most deliberate and forceful Gabriel had ever been with me. It was as if he were trying to reinforce that I was his and he was not letting me go.

Right in what I would consider the middle of passion, Gabriel stopped. He lifted off of me and just stared at me. I could still feel his legs against my inner thighs and I wanted to rise to meet him, but he was stronger and had me pinned.

"Say you are mine." Gabriel beseeched me.

It seemed so cruel for him to stop as I wanted him so badly. "You know I am yours."

"And we won't fight about this anymore. Nothing will come between us. Say it."

I would have said almost anything to have him again, for him to finish what he had started, but I would not lie. "Please, Gabriel."

"Amelia."

"I don't want to fight, unless this is the way we are going to make up." I voiced a compromise because who knew what the future held.

I had not expected this and I think the shock of it all added to the thrill and it was the absolute best sex we had ever had. It probably also helped that Gabriel got his point across, a point he was unable to make with his words while we were in the yard. As soon as I had submitted to Gabriel and agreed that we would not fight anymore, the context of the events changed from sex to love making.

I did not press the issue of Beth and the child anymore. I decided that there was no use worrying about something I could not change. I did my best to believe that things did not have to be all or nothing and convinced myself that I could live with whatever there was left, whatever time I had with him would have to be enough. In a week's time, that changed again.

It was afternoon on Friday and I had driven out to Gabriel's house for the weekend as I had been doing. I usually got there around one and Gabriel had lunch waiting on me. After lunch we did any number of things. One Friday, we went shopping at the mall in Athens, another we went antiquing in Greensboro at Pages and Moore, others we laid around the house, and then there was the one where we got ready for my acceptance to law school party. After our afternoon together, Gabriel would leave for work around 4:00 p.m. and not return until 9:30 or 10:00.

This particular afternoon, I arrived and everything went as usual. It was warm, so I put on a pair of shorts and ran the cart path. It was getting late in the afternoon so the course was empty and there were no golf carts to dodge. I managed to make it past all eighteen holes and back to the house in about forty-five minutes.

I could see the white BMW in the driveway as soon as I started around the curve on Starboard Harbor Drive toward the house. The closer I came, the more visible Beth became. She was seated on the front steps waiting. I came close to running back the other way, but that would mean running back to the club and she would likely go there too. Ultimately, I figured there was no time like the present to start taking it on the chin if I was going to stick around.

I did not stop running until I reached the mailbox at the end of the driveway. I did not speak until I was halfway up the driveway. I am sure I stated the obvious, "Gabriel's not home. Perhaps you would like to try him at the club."

"I know and I am not here to see him. I came to see you," she explained as she stood up.

The full length site of Beth made my stomach curdle. The baby was not due until the first week of July, but at six months along she was already huge. She could have been smuggling a beach ball from the looks of things. All of this was made more evident as she stepped aside so I could ascend the steps to the front door.

"You are here to see me? Why?" I just could not help myself, I know I had a screw-you tone to my voice as I walked past her. I unlocked the door and never looked back at her while I continued, "What could you possibly have to say to me?"

It is a good thing I did not expect an apology since that was certainly not why she was there.

"I thought we should go ahead and start setting some ground rules for your involvement with my child," Beth said as she followed me inside.

"I don't believe I invited you in," I said as I heard her cross the threshold of the front door behind me.

"Well, it's not your house is it?"

"You have a point and it's not like this is the first or second time you've been here uninvited. Also, I think the ground rules for your child are best left between you and the child's father, whomever that might be," I said as I headed back toward the door.

Beth stepped between me and the door, "Oh, the father of my child is Gabe and if you want to leave well it is high time you did. Seriously, I was beginning to wonder how big of an idiot you were."

"The fact that you are pregnant is the only thing that is keeping me from throwing your fat ass out of here so the next time you think of calling me an idiot, rethink it! Just so you know, I made a 170 on the LSAT, 1550 on the SAT, I speak three languages; Je joue quatre instruments and acabo de recibir aceptado en la escuela de derecho en Mercer, so I can do this in English, Français or Español, puta de mierda. I run an eight minute mile, and I weigh 105 pounds and nothing about me is fake. Shall I give you my measurements too?"

I did not mean for her to answer. I only paused just to catch my breath before I started again, "And by the way, I am obscenely, stinking, filthy rich. My money, so I don't have to hold my hand out to anyone. Now, would you like to list your accomplishments and we can see how you stack up once and for all?"

Beth stood silent. Her mouth dropped open. Her face was red causing her bleached hair to appear whiter than it actually was. Maybe the only thing that was keeping her from throwing my ass out was also the fact that she was pregnant. I am certain from the look on her face, she would have laid hands on me had she not considered her condition.

Before she could say anything, I started again. "Honestly, you act like you are so much better than I am and what do you really have going for yourself? You are taller than me, I will give you that, but you are also thicker and that's regardless of you having killed the rabbit. You went to college to get your Mrs. Degree and that didn't work out, so daddy scored you a job at WATL." I twirled my index finger in the air as if to signal 'big damn deal'.

I continued, "You have drug issues and at least one DUI. Your hair color is from a bottle and your roots are always showing. Your nails are fake, your teeth are fake, your boobs are fake, and so is the act you have been giving Gabriel. Nicey-nicey just isn't you. You are chasing a man who does not want you. You got knocked up by someone that has clearly left you high and dry and now you are passing it off on Gabriel. I have no proof, but I am certain of it. You are an unhappy, bitter woman who people hate to see coming. Does that sound about right?"

"It is Gabe's!" She growled.

"That's all you took out of that?" I was floored. Had anyone insulted me like that I would have either left or had a mouthful to say in return as evidenced by my prior bragging on myself. "And you said I am an idiot? Whoever the father is, I hope his DNA can water down whatever it is you have going on over there or I feel sorry for that child."

"You feel sorry for my child?!!" Beth raised her voice at me. She was still blocking the door.

This was getting nowhere. I was tired of being bothered by her. "Please just leave. Think of your child and go home. You don't need to be upset, so just leave. I don't want to fight with you all the time."

"You better get used to fighting because I will never give up on Gabe and I have only just begun to fight."

I just walked off and left her standing in the living room.

"Where are you going?" Beth demanded. "Don't you walk away from me!"

"Let yourself out," I said back to her without raising my voice. I continued down the hallway to the bedroom and shut and locked the door behind me.

I packed everything I owned within about fifteen minutes and returned with a duffle bag in hand. Beth was seated on the couch when I returned. I did not say anything to her and I went through the kitchen and left through the back door. Luckily, she had parked to the side of my car. I was backing out of the driveway when she appeared on the front porch. She waved to me as if she had won and I flipped her the bird.

I was still dressed in my running shorts and a long sleeved t-shirt and even though I knew that was not proper attire for the club, I stopped by there anyway. I went through the kitchen door off of the loading dock and found Gabriel on his usual side of the prep-line. It was about 6:00 p.m. and he was prepping plates for the first few guests of the night. I hated to interrupt him, but I could not leave without saying something to him.

Daniel was on the other side of the line when I walked up next to Gabriel. Gabriel did not notice me at first, but Daniel did.

"Hey stranger!" Daniel greeted me.

"Hi!" I replied. "I need a moment with Gabriel. Would you mind finishing this up for him? I will only be a minute."

Gabriel glanced up at me as I spoke to Daniel and he could tell something was off with me. "What's going on, Amelia?" Gabriel asked.

"Come with me," I said sweetly as I took his hand and led him back out onto the loading dock.

Once on the loading dock, I grabbed the top of straps of Gabriel's apron and pulled his face down to mine and I kissed him gently. Gabriel gave no protest. He was so beautiful and I loved him more than I thought I could love someone else.

When I pulled back from him, I held his gaze for a moment and did not speak. I just looked at him, the way the sun at dusk shown in his eyes, they were bluer than blue and the way he looked at me always spoke volumes. Just a look from him could send chills down my legs. I never wanted that to change, but if we continued on like this I knew all of it would end badly.

"I love you more than anything. I have told you that before..."

Gabriel interrupted me, "What is going on?"

I did not give him the play by play of Beth stopping by, but I did tell him she showed up and that she was still there when I left. "I don't want you to think I am running. I am not running, but I need a break." I told him.

Gabriel fell back against the wall of the building. "A break? What does that mean?"

"It means I would like for you to sort things out with Beth and your child. After you get that sorted out, if you still love me and want to be with me, come find me then. I have told you before that as long as Beth is in the picture, we will never be allowed to be happy and she said as much this afternoon. I don't want to get to where you and I fight all the time and we end up hating each other. I want you to be happy whether it is with me or without me."

"Wait," Gabriel ran his hand through his hair as if he were trying to figure out what was happening, what to say next.

"Wait, that's what I am telling you I will do. I don't want anyone else and I know there's no one else for me except you, but I want you to be free and right now you are not free. I also don't want to have to compete for you and that is exactly what I feel like I am continually having to do and that's through no fault of yours or mine. I am so sorry. I need you to get things sorted out with Beth and until you do," I paused to gather my nerve to finish, "I can't be with you. This is not good for you, for me or for Beth while she is pregnant. I just won't fight with a pregnant girl. I don't want to be that person."

In the past I had run because I was a young, inexperienced girl who did not know what else to do when we fought. I had never really fought with anyone that I cared about before that was not my family. Gabriel schooled me about standing my ground and fighting for us, that it was more acceptable to stand and make my point than it was to run away. I had grown up a lot since I had met him and I was definitely better for having known him, but I did not want to lose myself. I was his, but that could not come at the price of not liking myself and that afternoon when envisioning myself fighting with a pregnant girl, I did not like me. I was not someone who openly bragged on myself to make someone else feel small. And, if I did not like me, how was I to expect him to continue to like or love me?

I could tell Gabriel did not know what to say.

"You don't have to say anything, just let me go. If you don't come for me, then I will know that this was not meant to be." I did not start to tear up until the thought of us not being meant to be was verbalized.

"We are meant to be. I know we are. I will sort this out and I will come for you."

I buried my head in his chest and started to cry. I breathed him in and did my level best to make another mental image of his smell. I did not think I would ever forget that scent, but I wanted to make sure since I would have to rely on memory for the foreseeable future.

"I cannot imagine life without you," Gabriel whispered as he held me.

"What's the saying, 'if you love something set it free and if it returns then it is meant to be?' Please come back to me." I kissed Gabriel again and I turned to leave.

523

I suddenly felt the sting of the hard slap on my behind. I was shocked and whipped around to Gabriel, while rubbing my behind.

"Miss Anderson, this is only a break and I don't want you getting comfortable without me. I **will** come for you."

All sad thoughts left my mind and I threw my arms around him and kissed him. It was bitter sweet. "I love you and I trust you. I know this is not the end of us."

I smiled at him and then eased back, my hands still locked in his. Gabriel did not let go of my hand until our arms were completely outstretched and our fingers slipped apart. I turned back to look at him one last time as I took the first step at the end of the loading dock, another mental memory to be stored away.

CHAPTER 22

On May 4, 1996, I graduated college. Aunt Gayle was there and she brought Aunt Dot with her. They were regular traveling companions. Although Jay and Emma were not graduating, they were a year behind me, both were in the audience along with Jay's parents and his Aunt June. Everyone I knew and considered family was sitting together including Daniel who had been a permanent fixture in my life since the beginning of the hiatus from Gabriel.

The day was sunny and bright. Warm, but not hot and not humid. It was the perfect day and I know Granddaddy was smiling down on me. As I sat there waiting on my name to be called, for a moment I looked out into the crowd and I could have sworn I saw Granddaddy. He was wearing his Sunday best. He was as clear to me as anyone else that had come to see me get my diploma, but I knew it was an illusion. I knew that he and Gabriel were the only ones missing and I wished they could have been there.

Even though my name was among the first fifty called, I had to remain seated there for the entire three hour event. There were two hundred in my portion of the year's graduating class, the first half of the alphabet, and there were another two hundred graduating in a ceremony after us that afternoon. Our ceremony had started at 9:30 a.m., but I had to get there at 8:45 a.m. sharp. It was turning into a long day, but by 10:15, I was officially a college graduate.

After the ceremony, we all went to lunch at Choby's on Lake Sinclair and Aunt Gayle invited the whole group back to The Jefferson for cake after lunch. When I returned home, there were three dozen yellow roses waiting for me. Jay said they were delivered right after I left for commencement. He put them in the center of the dining room table and the fragrance from the roses filled the whole apartment. They were beautiful little blooms of sunshine and in a blue vase that looked to be of painted milk glass which reminded me of the sky.

Not very many people knew that yellow roses were my favorite, so I thought maybe Aunt Gayle had sent them. I tossed my cap on the end table next to the couch as I headed toward the dining room to check for a card.

I found the card stashed among the roses and pulled it free. I opened it and found that the roses were from Gabriel. It read,

"I am so proud of you and I would be there if I could. I am yours. Love always, Gabriel."

Aunt Gayle was not happy at the roses or the card. In the months since our break began Aunt Gayle had voiced hundreds of times that I should move on and gestures like these and the occasional phone call between Gabriel and I, well, she just considered him stringing me along. Needless to say, she did not like it and the more this went on, the less she cared for Gabriel and the less sympathetic she was to his predicament.

Our break this time was much different than the break up the three weeks back at the first of January. This time I went about the business of being me. I focused on school and honoring the deal I made with Aunt Gayle over Seven Springs. Also, if Gabriel called me, I talked to him. There were times when we spoke for hours, but the subject of Beth was always off limits. Not that either of us set those limits, it just seemed to be something that was understood. Before when we spoke on the phone as he said goodbye Gabriel would always tell me that he loved me, but during our first phone call he started to say it and caught himself.

"I am not going to pour salt in your wounds by telling you how I feel about you. Words mean nothing without actions and right now I know you are waiting for my actions," Gabriel signed off.

One particular night he insisted on seeing me. It was his birthday and I gave in. I gave in to a great many things that night and he did not bother to stop himself from telling me how much he loved me. For a moment, he really was all mine again and the cares of our worlds faded away, but after that night things returned to our new norm.

From then on, Gabriel ended most of the calls with the words, "You know how I feel about you," and I responded, "I am waiting." That became our mutual code for "I love you."

***

May 8, 1996, Emma left for London. Jay and I took her to Hartsfield and we all hugged and cried together before seeing her off at the gate. We had not always seen eye to eye, but still, I considered her one of my closest friends and I did not envy her having to move home.

Emma had already planned on going home for the summer, but had expected to return for her senior year. Those plans were dashed when the call came that her father had pancreatic cancer and her mother needed help caring for him and her younger brothers. If it had been a matter of money, I would have helped her without hesitation, but her father had so little time left by the time the cancer was discovered that the only thing to be done was for her to go home to be with her family.

Jay took her leaving especially hard. They had been inseparable for three years. It was as if one of his family members had died that day. I tried to assure him that we would get our passports and go to visit her, but he was beyond convincing.

Jay hardly spoke the entire ride back and it was a slow ride. We had taken my truck because between us, it was the only vehicle that would hold the three of us to get Emma to the airport. There was no air conditioning in the C10 and when Jay finally spoke it was to comment on the heat.

"I think if there is such a thing as my own private hell, this will be it. I will spend eternity roasting in this truck, having lost one of my best friends."

"Who knew the fiery pits of Hell were made by Chevy?" I tried to lighten the mood without making fun of his pain.

It worked and Jay's mood shifted just enough to keep him from full blown depression.

"I still have you," Jay said as he reached over and put his hand on my shoulder.

"You will always have me, so you will be among friends while trapped in your version of Hell."

***

On May 23rd, I wrote the first check from the George and Andrew Anderson Scholarship Fund. The following day I drove to Green County High School in Greensboro and presented the check at Honors Day. The check was made out to the University of Georgia in the name of Rudolph Alton Allen, Jr.

The ceremony was held in the gymnasium. The students filled the bleachers and the seniors were in the back left corner, farthest from the stage. Folding chairs holding parents, teachers and visitors who were presenting scholarships and awards covered the basketball court. The first two rows of folding chairs nearest the stage were reserved for those presenting awards. I was in the second row, third from the end. On the stage were seats for the school administration as well as a hand full of teachers.

With his grandmother and siblings in attendance, Rudy hardly realized it when his name was called. All of his life, he had been Rudy Allen and no one ever called him by his whole given name. Few people even knew his given name. So, not only did it take a minute to register his actual name, he also had no idea that he was one of the students receiving a full ride scholarship to college that day.

As he stepped to the stage, so did I. I was the youngest of those presenting scholarships and Rudy was the most shocked of the students receiving one. He was equally shocked to see me.

Most of the other male students had dressed in suits and ties for the occasion. I gather those were students that knew in advance that they had won scholarships. I don't know if it would have made a difference in his attire if he had known in advance as Rudy likely did not have the money for special occasion clothes beyond that of church. He arrived at the stage wearing second generation jeans and a Button Your Fly t-shirt. He was clean, but anyone could tell he was not as fortunate as half of the kids in the gym.

Once on the stage, I did as those who had gone before me. I held out the check to him in my left hand and offered my right to congratulate him. "On behalf of the George and Andrew Anderson Scholarship Fund, it is my distinct honor to present you with this full ride scholarship to the University of Georgia. Congratulations and I hope you continue to make everyone who knows you proud. Best of luck to you."

I was immediately pulled in from the handshake to a giant bear hug lifting me off my feet. I was only three years older than Rudy, but he referred to me as Miss Millie and he said, "Miss Millie, this is the kindest thing anyone has ever done for me and I will never forget you! I promise I will not let you down!"

"I know you won't and if you need anything else you let me know."

The seniors were released after the ceremony and Rudy had to get to Port Honor for work since it was a Friday. I was on my way to my car when Rudy's grandmother, with three small children in tow, chased after me.

"Miss Millie, Miss Millie," she called as she struggled to run to catch me.

I turned to see Mrs. Allen carrying one child and holding the hand of another and pulling it and another along. This was the sight of a woman who was doing the best she could to get by and I was nearly brought to tears at the sight of her. She was likely wearing her Sunday best complete with pink floral dress and matching wide-brim hat, the size of a golf umbrella. I had managed to get word to her through the school letting her know what today would be about.

I put on a smile and tried not to let on that I felt sorry for her. "You must be Rudy's grandmother."

"Yes-um. I just wanna thank you for what you did for my Rudy," Mrs. Allen said to me.

The Allens were a hugging bunch. She had hardly finished speaking before her, the toddler and I were wrapped in a group hug. She was a large lady and that child was riding on one breast and I was lifted onto the other during the hug. It was sweet and awkward all at the same time. I felt myself blush with embarrassment from the contact with her boob.

"You are ever so welcome," I squeaked out as my oxygen was being cut off by the hug.

When she finally turned me loose, which came just as I am sure I was turning blue in the face, I asked her, "Mrs. Allen, have you any plans for what to do once Rudy leaves for college?"

I hinted at her financial circumstances although ultimately I knew they were none of my business.

She handed me the child while taking a handkerchief from her purse and dabbing off the sweat on her brow. "I am hopin' his mama will take these young-uns to live with her and then we'll all get by. She gets the welfare ..."

"I know it's none of my business, but you mean to tell me that the mother gets welfare for the children, but you are the one raising them?" I was astonished.

"I took 'em from her cuz of the crack 'n all. Made a deal to raise 'em, let her keep the money if I could have 'em. Theys pitiful when I found 'em. Ain't eatin in days."

I felt she could not count on the mother, but I did not want to let on about my suspicions. At the same time, I had never intended my good deed toward Rudy to leave the rest of his family in the lurch. "Until she comes for them, do you have anyone at all that can watch the children if you were to get a job?"

"I got a sister that lives down the way, but what job could I do? Ma'am, I ain't e'er been more than a housewife."

"You can cook and clean like nobody's business I bet."

Mrs. Allen blushed in answer. I was still holding the child and she was again wiping her brow again as we carried on our conversation in the parking lot of the high school.

"Go see Mr. Hewitt, Rudy's boss at the club. When Rudy leaves for school, he will need a replacement. Tell him I sent you and that I am calling in a favor. If you want the job, it's yours."

No sooner had the words left my mouth did another idea pop into my head. "Or, if you would like to get a jump on things, he is going to be in need of a nanny come mid-June. Do not deal with the mother of the child and never mention me to her, only deal with Mr. Hewitt. I am sure you are aware through Rudy that he is a kind man. He is going to need all the help he can get with a baby."

***

Mid-June came and went and I had received no word that Beth had had the baby. I also had not heard from Gabriel in a while. I tried not to dwell on things I could not control and instead focused on things that I could.

I decided to spend my summer getting started on Seven Springs. Jay was taking classes the last half of the summer, but the first half he was mine. We spent a great deal of time staying at Aunt Gayle's. Since Emma had gone, Jay and I had been constant companions. Unfortunately, I think our living alone and constant togetherness was reinforcing old ideas that his parents had of us ending up together.

There was so much for us to do at Seven Springs. Aunt Gayle and I had not come to terms on a General Contractor who could fit us in anytime soon, so Jay and I started on the land. We cleared the meadow and prepped it for building a pergola just as I had described to Gabriel when I nearly lost my virginity there. In fact, I planned to build the pergola in the very spot where we had laid down the blanket that day.

Cousin Dixon was between jobs, so I hired him to help us. Our first task together was to build the pergola and plant wisteria around it. We accomplished it with little effort, thanks to Dixon. It appeared I had underestimated him all these years. His mentality was simple, but he was quite good with tools and building. The pergola was absolutely everything I had dreamed it would be.

We decided to take the weekend off and go back to The Jefferson. Jay wanted to call Emma and check in with her. The last we had heard it could be any day for her father so there might very well have been a message waiting on our machine when we arrived.

We were no sooner up the stairs before Jay was on the phone with Emma and there was a knock at the door.

"Millie!" It was Cara. She had stayed on in her apartment for the summer though her roommate had gone home. Stella and Travis had stayed as well.

The knocking was quite impatient and she knocked again just as I was laying a hand on the door knob to open it. I opened the door to find Cara all in a fit. She appeared to have run in from her car or beyond even. She came right in when I opened the door. She grabbed my hand and led me to the couch.

"You may want to sit." Cara said before she flopped down on the couch and continued. "You are not going to believe it, Beth has insisted that Gabriel marry her or she will take the baby away once it is born."

I took a seat next to her as I made my reply. "And you are shocked by that?" I believed I expected such a grand ultimatum from Beth from the moment I first saw her rise from the bar stool on New Year's Eve.

"Aren't you?" she gasped.

"Not particularly." I tried to remain calm.

"Gabriel has moved her in the house with him and agreed to her terms."

Now that was a bit shocking to me and I felt as if I had been gut punched. "Did he now?"

"I think he may have given into her." Cara appeared as mad as I at the situation.

What was I to say? I hid my real feelings as best I could. "I am sure he has his reasons. You know what they say, keep your friends close and your enemies closer."

"Well if that's the way of it, then you should be the one living with her." I never thought I would laugh at the situation, but Cara and I had a great laugh at her statement.

"Could you just imagine? I would surely smother her in her sleep." I laughed.

531

"You're a better person than me. I don't think I could wait for her to go to sleep." Cara paused. "I can't believe you are taking this so well."

"Whatever will be will be, right?"

"I heard that even though she has demanded for him to marry her and even though she is so pregnant she is about to bust, she has refused for her wedding photos to be of her pregnant. Can you imagine?"

"That sounds about par for the course with her." I shook my head in disgust. "I have forgotten my manners, forgive me. Could I get you something to drink or anything?"

Cara looked at me in disbelief. "Are you kidding me? I have just told you what would be Earth shattering news to me and you ask that I forgive you because you forgot to offer me a cold beverage?"

"I don't want you to think I am a fool, but I just have a feeling that everything is going to work out the way it is supposed to." I did not know how to fully describe it, but I did my best. "You know people say when bad things are going to happen they can feel it like a storm brewing?"

"Yeah," Cara replied, but I could see skepticism written all over her face.

"It's not a storm that I feel coming for me. It's more like a vacation, a day at the beach on my horizon. I can't tell you why and I know what you are seeing going on with Gabriel, but perhaps something is going to work out for me or something else is out there for me. I just have to have faith."

Regardless of what I said to Cara, the idea of Gabriel moving Beth into the house with him and the potential for him to marry her ate at me. I finally broke down and called him about 9:30 p.m. at the club.

I had not even told him why I was calling; in fact, I had barely gotten the word "hello" out of my mouth before Gabriel abruptly told me he would not be able to talk to me for a while. He hung up without saying anything further. My head was spinning.

I admit it was not Pearl Harbor or anything, but July 3, 1996, would be my day that lived on in infamy. At least that's the way I felt at that time. It was the day that Gabriella Grace Hewitt was born and the day I got completely shit faced drunk. I got so drunk that I woke up the next afternoon not just hung over, but still drunk. I had never been drunk before and if this was what it was all about I knew I would never be drunk again.

As soon as we found out that Beth had given birth, Jay whisked me away to the Juniper Street Pub in Macon. That is not exactly where one would think a straight girl would go to mend a broken heart, but it sure made a dent for me. Jay was a regular there and I had been once or twice as his DD, but this was the first time he was mine.

The Juniper Street Pub was the gay bar of choice for the Macon area. Dark, loud and full of everything your mother ever warned you about and things she probably did not even know existed.

Jay picked out my outfit and did my hair and make-up and away we went.

"Whew! You're a sight!" Jay exclaimed as he finished with his master piece.

Jay had picked out the shortest dress I owned. It was a pink chiffon baby-doll dress with black trim and it barely covered my behind. He had matched it with my black stilettos and no stockings. He teased and sprayed my hair before rolling it in the tiny hot rollers. By the time he was done, I had the biggest pageant hair of my life.

I had not realized before we left home that I looked a little like a fifteen year old boy dressed in drag thanks to the heavy make-up Jay had caked on me. I had more drinks bought for me that night than Imelda Marcos had shoes. Jay was over the moon that I could have had my pick of the lesbians or the boys that were into queens. I was not sure how to take that.

I was propositioned all night long. Jay held his own keeping the majority of the riff-raff at bay. Most just sent drinks over and waited for us to acknowledge them, but anyone that approached us that Jay did not know were promptly thanked for the drink, told we were an item and sent on their way. Jay and I danced and danced.

The drinks kept coming and I kept accepting them and by midnight I did not know my own name let alone that of Gabriel's daughter. We would likely have kept dancing and drinking, but the night came to a screeching halt just after 1:00 a.m. when one of Jay's conquests approached us.

"Who's this bitch?" Marcus said as he put his hand on my shoulder and snatched me back from Jay.

Marcus was about six foot three and a dead ringer for Alec Baldwin, if Alec Baldwin was about thirty pounds heavier and had a swishy limp when he walked. He stood there waiting for an answer with one hip propped out and a hand resting on the other.

Marcus addressed Jay when talking, but Jay did not dignify him with an answer. Jay just pulled me back to him and we went back to dancing. All of the sudden it was Jay who got spun around by Marcus.

"Girlfriend, I am talking to you!" Marcus huffed. Marcus had thought he and Jay were more of an item than they were and it ended badly. From the looks of things, he was still not over it.

Jay did not have time to react when liquid courage took hold of me and I stepped between them. I stretched up on my tip toes in my heels and did my best to go nose to nose with Marcus.

"He's my man now, BITCH!" I screamed at him with emphasis on the B-word while I did my best to chest bump him.

My best chest bump amounted to my chest to Santa's belly. Needless to say, I bounced off and my feet went out from under me. I went flat of my behind on the slick, slushy cocktail covered floor of the bar. The smell of the floor was pungent and liquid courage was replaced by the stomach churning rise of all of the concoctions I had swallowed that night. Marcus gave a big belly laugh at my demise and Jay offered a hand to help me up, but I waived him off. I regained my footing in a matter of about three minutes, at which time I puked all over Marcus Brisby's coral colored shirt and white pants.

Marcus screamed like the big girl he was.

I did not remember much else of the night beyond Jay carrying me out of the bar and yelling back to Marcus, "That's what you get when you wear a blouse the color of vomit, hooka!"

According to Jay, I vomited two more times out the window of his car on the ride home. I also threw up in the kitchen trashcan, which Jay sat outside on the back porch of the building, but could still be smelled all the way inside.

The next day, I awoke face down on my bathroom floor to Jay prodding me. It was noon and Aunt Gayle was on the phone. I could not move my arms, so Jay held the phone to the ear that was not still plastered to the tile floor.

"Where are you?" Aunt Gayle demanded to know.

"Don't yell at me!" And the room spun with the vibration of my words. I tried to lift my head, but my neck was not getting the message.

"I am not yelling! Now why aren't you here yet?"

"B- E- C" pause... "A- U- S- E."

"Millie, are you alright?" So many questions.

"Oh.....yeah," apart from the fact that I just spelled the word "because" since I could not think of a better cover story to try to hide the fact that I was still shit-faced. I finally mustered the strength to put my arms out and try to brace the floor to stop the room from spinning only to realize when the room stopped I started. The tilt-a-world at the fair paled in comparison to the way things were spinning for me in the bathroom.

At that point, Jay took the phone and went into my bedroom with it. He proceeded to explain to Aunt Gayle that everything was under control, but I would not be attending the annual Wilkes' bar-b-que this year.

I figure she responded something akin to, "Pray-tell why not?"

Jay tried to keep things to a whisper, but I could still hear him tell Aunt Gayle that Cara had reported the not so happy news of Gabriel and Beth's baby's arrival. Again, I could not hear Aunt Gayle's side of things.

"Yeah, I think three weeks past her due date was very odd as well. I was actually starting to think that she had had the baby and folks saw fit to spare Millie the details. We weren't so lucky. We found out yesterday."

"No, it wasn't exactly my solution to the problem to get her drunk. It just sort of happened.... alright. I will have her call you later."

Shortly thereafter, Jay returned to the bathroom to check on me. I had not moved a muscle, but tears were running down my face and onto the floor.

"Are you going to lie there all day?" he asked.

"I am going to lay here forever."

***

I tried to get on with my life and forget about Gabriel, "tried" being the key word. Jay started back to summer school and I took a break from my work at Seven Springs. I could hardly stand to look at anything as everything reminded me of Gabriel. He had touched every aspect of my life, including my dream of the hotel at the springs. Each morning I awoke it was only to be reminded that no one slept on that side of the bed anymore. Immediately after that thought, I vomited like clockwork. Initially, I thought it was a stomach virus, but then Jay and I just figured it was nerves or something and it would pass.

Banging on our door became a faithful act of Cara's. She was at it at least every other day. I explained to her shortly after the arrival of the baby that I could not take hearing about any of it any more. She respected my wishes and from then on, she did not mention a word unless I asked; which I rarely did.

The Olympics started on July 19 and on July 26, Cara was again banging at the door. The German Equestrian team had given some of employees of the club tickets to come to their event. Cara was given two tickets for Saturday. Everyone else she knew had to work but me.

"Come on, Millie, it will do you good to get out. It will be something to tell your grandchildren, 'I went to the Olympics when it was held in Atlanta.' It will be fun!" Cara made a pretty good argument and reluctantly I agreed to go with her. "Plus you need to get some sun. You are looking rather Casper like."

Shutting the door to Cara's 1996 Thunderbird behind me, I asked, "So, how are the Germans?"

"The men are quite nice, but most of the women, some wives, some girlfriends, they kind of treat us like we are trying to steal the men," Cara responded as she started the car and put it in gear.

"And is there anyone trying to steal the men?" I could not help but ask.

"Well, maybe, but I am not one of them," Cara insisted.

"Really?" I kind of drew out the word for emphasis.

"Really, but I cannot say the same for Katie. That girl is after everything that moves. I mean everything. I think she may be try-sexual." Cara was full of gossip and this was going to be a fun ride to Atlanta.

536

"I lived with a gay man so naturally I have heard of homosexual and thanks to my recent trip to The Juniper Street Pub, I have now been exposed to some bisexuals and transsexuals, but the term try-sexual, is a new one for me." I probably sounded like such a hick.

Cara snickered a bit prior to giving me the definition. "That girl will try anything sexual hence the word 'try-sexual'."

"Oooohh, okay then. Wow!"

"Seriously, I think she went home with Kimmie and Mr. Marvin the other night."

I screamed in shock and Cara jerked the wheel of the car in response to my scream. \

"Shit-fire! Don't scream like that! I thought we were about to die!"

"Yeah, that's probably what Mr. Martin said too!" And I squealed with laughter at my own joke. Cara just looked at me and shook her head.

By the time we arrived at the Georgia International Horse Park in Conyers, my face hurt from laughing. So far this was proving to be the most fun I had had in recent memory. I was glad Cara twisted my arm into coming with her.

As we entered the gates, Cara mentioned that she had heard the equestrian events had been sold out so we were lucky to be given these tickets. I wholeheartedly agreed with her.

"This might not be Churchill Downs, but I feel as if I am at the Kentucky Derby!" I was a bit star struck by the passing horses and riders.

"I know, right? All I am missing is a big floral hat! Dang it! How could I forget the hat?" Cara exclaimed as we took in our surroundings.

Our tickets were for the conclusion of the Mixed Dressage team competition, which had begun the day before. Our seats were pretty good, almost dead center of the bleachers and five rows up from the bottom. We could see everything including the Olympic ring topiaries. Where I was from, the big thing was going to the Masters golf tournament in Augusta, but I had never been. This was essentially my trip to the Masters.

I had been around horses all my life. I had even trained for a little barrel racing when I was much younger, but I had never seen horses do anything like they were doing here. The way they moved to the music, they were dancing. They kept with the beat and it was just extraordinary.

Cara pointed out the riders from the German team that she had met at the club. Even though she was USA all the way, she figured the next best thing to the home team winning was when the German's won. She stood and cheered as if they were her team and I stood with her. We clapped until our hands were sore.

We stayed until the medal ceremony was over and on the way to the car Cara asked if I wanted to go to the Olympic Park. She had heard of the band that was playing and just thought it would be fun to be a part of all of the celebration.

"We have come this far and we are having such a good time, we might as well," I responded.

"I don't particularly like to drive in the city, so do you mind taking MARTA?" Cara asked.

"I don't know, I have never taken MARTA before. Should I mind?" While responding, I rolled down the window of the Thunder-chicken because the air conditioning left a bit to be desired.

"I think we will be fine." Cara assured me we had nothing to worry about and that MARTA was safer in the city than her driving.

Apparently this was something that Cara had done before because she had no trouble at all finding the Indian Creek MARTA Station. It was getting dark by the time we parked the car there and hopped the train. The train filled nearly to seated capacity at the Indian Creek Station, but that did not stop it from taking on more and more passengers at every stop. This would not be the last of my evening's packed to the gills experiences.

I followed Cara's lead and we got off at Five Points Station. The streets of Atlanta were crowded that night and there was no need asking directions to the park as everyone was moving in that direction. We just went with the flow.

"This is like being on Bourbon Street in New Orleans the Saturday night before Fat Tuesday." I did not know exactly what Cara meant by that since I had never been to New Orleans, but I assumed that everyone there was body on body and moving like waves in a sea of people. I feared getting lost from Cara, so I took her hand. I did not care what people might think especially since we would have been about the tenth same gender couple I had seen holding hands since we got on the train in Clarkston.

I was amazed at just the people watching aspect of everything. There were people from all walks of life and from what appeared to be all nations. There were thousands upon thousands upon thousands of people and I was reminded just how small I was, just one girl from Avera, Georgia. I was impressed with what I had accomplished that day. I had seen people from the homeland of one of my great-grandparents win a gold medal in the Olympics in person and now I was standing among the tallest buildings I had ever seen, with the night lit up like day and I could hear the roar of a hundred different languages being spoken all around me. I struggled to take everything in and keep up with Cara as she pulled me along through the crowd. There were people there who had probably traveled five thousand miles to get there and I had traveled less than a hundred, yet I felt as foreign as they probably did. This was the first time I truly felt alive in weeks.

"Look, there's the Swatch Pavilion. Remember those?" Cara pointed to the all glass building.

"Yeah, I had two Swatch watches. My favorite was my giant yellow Pop Swatch." I was wondering for a moment where I had last seen my Swatch watches when a reporter and his camera man approached us.

In very slowly spoken English, he asked, "May I interview you ladies?"

"Ok," Cara answered.

The band around the microphone indicated he was a reporter for Channel 11 out of Atlanta. We did not get Channel 11 in Milledgeville, so neither of us recognized him. He turned to the camera and did a lead in regarding all the different people from around the world that were here in the greatest city in the South.

After his lead in, he turned and stuck the microphone in our faces and asked, "Where are you ladies from?"

"Avera, Georgia," I answered.

Cara was quick to answer right behind me. "Woodstock, Georgia."

The reporter's face fell. He turned and motioned cut to the camera and the camera man immediately lowered the camera. The reporter was so clearly disappointed that we were not from some place far away or exotic. It left me questioning what was it about us that would have led him to suspect we might have been from anywhere else. Before I could ask him just that, he turned his sights on some other very American looking college boys that were passing by.

Cara and I continued on past the Swatch Pavilion. We pushed on through the crowd toward the stage. It was the largest party I had ever been to and it was beyond words. There was so much to see that I could have been there a week and still felt as if I had not seen everything. I am sure I would never see everything in one night, especially since I was careful to keep an eye on Cara. I was a little terrified of getting separated from her and not being able to find her in the sea of people. I kept my hand tight to hers.

"Are you getting hungry?" I screamed so Cara could hear me.

"Yeah," Cara nodded her head.

There were so many food vendors that we ended up eating at the one with the shortest line. It was next to the Georgia Office of Tourism where two guys from Sweden bought Cara and I glasses of peach iced tea, invited us to the House of Blues with them and tried to get our numbers. I would have never given them my number and them only being in town for the Olympics was the cherry on top of that decision. Cara on the other hand, looked as if she were contemplating giving her number when I thanked the guys for the drinks and pulled her back into the crowd.

While moving through the AT&T Global Village, I looked down every now and then to see if I could find the brick we had purchased in the name of my dad and Granddaddy. I wanted to find their bricks, but in this chaos, it was hopeless. Still, I glanced down every so often just to check. I could hardly see the bricks at all for everyone's feet.

We were walking alone when suddenly the group in front of us parted. I was looking up at the night sky and all of the signs and billboards around the park so I did not see why they parted.

"Millie, watch out!" Cara jerked my hand and tried to pull me out of the way, but it was too late.

I was sprayed with water and completely drenched from the Olympic Rings fountain. I jumped back, but the damage was done. I was soaked to the bone and cat calls were already starting. Cara moved to help cover me since my white t-shirt and bra were wet to the point of being see through.

"How do you feel about a souvenir t-shirt?" Cara asked.

"I feel pretty good about that and luckily I brought spare cash for emergencies." I replied while trying to shield myself and make my way to the closest vendor. I ended up buying a shirt with the Olympic mascot on it, Izzy. It was the cheapest shirt on the table, purple and tacky, but a means to an end.

It was getting later and later and the night was humid, but I had no complaints. Normally I would have been tired, probably dead on my feet at that time of the night. That night I felt nothing beyond the energy coming from the crowd. It was that energy that kept me going, dancing even. The entire place was an outdoor nightclub.

It was well after midnight and the band Jack Mack and the Heart Attack took the stage. We were near these giant speakers, sound towers actually, and I could hardly hear myself think let alone what Cara was saying to me. I finally made out that she was trying to tell me that we would leave in another thirty minutes.

No sooner had Cara spoke did one of the security guards, a portly man, start trying to clear everyone from the area near the speaker and the stage. Within minutes, other security guards joined in and pushed us back. We did not move without a bit of reluctance. We had worked so hard to make our way through the crowd to get to the stage that we weren't readily going to give up our spots.

"Seriously, Miss, it's for your own safety," the portly man with the mustache insisted as he gave me a little nudge to move along.

"Our own safety? It's just a concert." Cara protested, but it did not do any good.

We moved as we were directed and the security guards moved on to other visitors. From our new vantage point, about fifteen yards from where we were, we could see men digging at what appeared to be a back pack beneath a bench near the stage. One man was wearing an ATF windbreaker which struck me as odd for two reasons. The first oddity was that anyone would be wearing a windbreaker in this heat and humidity and the second was that the ATF was taking an interest in something under that bench. I knew what ATF was and what they did from watching weeks and weeks of the news on their stand-off with David Koresh and the Branch Dividians a few years before.

I was standing closer to the area being inspected than Cara. I turned to Cara with my back to the site, "Get a look over there. I wonder what's going on that the ATF and FBI would be looking under a bench?"

"I am sure it is nothing," Cara said as the men disbursed a little and other men came to push us back further.

Suddenly, there was a flash of blue light that came across her face and Cara screamed. It was a blood curdling scream from her and from a great many of the people around us.

A wave of heat hit my entire back. Accompanying the heat was a thousand bee stings. I gasped and I slapped at my neck as if I were actually killing the bee to make it stop. I went to my knees and I think Cara did her best to catch me as I pulled my hand back around in front of my face. There was more blood than I had ever seen and the stinging. Oh, God, the burning stings were everywhere.

"Millie! Millie! Dear Lord, Millie!" Cara saw the blood on my hand and fell as my weight shifted on to her. I could hear Cara calling me as if I was in a well and she was calling down to me. She sounded frantic and so very far away, but she wasn't. I could feel her trying to hold me up, but there was nothing I could do to help her. There was something terribly wrong.

There was pounding in my head and it wasn't from the music anymore. I could hear the screams of others near me, screaming through the wrong end of the mega phone.

I heard Cara one last time, "MILLIE!" She screamed as people, complete strangers, bumped into her forcing her to loosen her hold on me. They grabbed her and forced her to move with them as they fled the chaos. She tried to hang on to me, but between my weight and their pull it was too much for her.

And then nothing. Silence. Deafening silence, the very opposite of how things had been just moments before.

"Ma'am, ma'am, you have to move. You have to get back."

"But my friend was injured in the blast and now I can't find her."

"Ma'am, I am sure your friend is fine, but there is nothing you can do here. You need to move so the professionals can get through."

"No! She was not alright! She fell and she had blood... She's hurt and I can't find her! Oh my God! Her name is Millie and you have to help me find her. We have to find her!"

"Ma'am, you are going to have to trust that the emergency personnel will find her and get her help. For now, you need to go home."

"Go home? I can't just leave her! Here, I will give you all of these collector pins and all of the money I have on me if you will just help me."

It was still dark and I struggled to come to. It was as if all of the bells of Saint Peter's Cathedral were going off in my head all at once. I did not know whether to answer the alarm clock or hit the snooze on the phone. The only source of the noise that I could rule out was a crying baby.

All of the sudden, I did come to and realized it was indeed the phone ringing. A cold chill rushed over me as I noticed the red numbers shining in the dark signaling what time of night it really was. No one calls at 3:00 a.m. unless someone is dead or on the way to the hospital. Not to mention, I had only been asleep for a little over an hour.

In the pitch black, I searched the nightstand with one hand for the cordless phone and with the other I tried to find the pull cord for the bedside lamp. The phone stopped ringing just shy of the answering machine kicking on. As quickly as the ringing stopped, it started again and I was no closer to finding the lamp switch or phone than I had been when it stopped.

Scores of obscenities rolled under my breath and off my tongue. I feared the ringing would inevitably wake Gabby. Just as I spouted off the third "mother-fucker" under my breath, I finally had a hand on the phone.

"Hello!" I demanded as quietly as I could still trying not to compound whatever problem the caller was about to lay on me with the whaling and screaming of my three week old daughter.

A sobbing voice on the other end of the line gasped my name, "Gabe! Gabe! You have to help me!"

I recognized the voice. It was Cara, one of my employees at Port Honor. I could hardly understand her words through her crying.

"I will do what I can, but you have to calm down and tell me what is wrong." She was clearly upset, but if she did not calm down there was no way I would be able to understand or help her. I shuttered to think what was going on as displays of emotion like this were uncharacteristic of Cara. She was the tough one of the bunch of servers at the club and I had never seen any customer even slightly ruffle her feathers.

I had been walking through the hall toward Gabby's room to make sure she had not woken up when Cara said the words, "I can't find Millie."

I may not have understood too much else that Cara had said, but those words came across the line as clear as day. My heart dropped and I could feel the blood drain from my face. My voice was stern and I responded with a touch of panic, "What do you mean, you can't find Millie?"

I leaned against the door jam of the hall bathroom as my knees went a little weak. As soon as Cara had said the words, I remembered two things all at once. I remembered that Cara had been given tickets to the equestrian events by the German Equestrian team members who were staying at Port Honor during the Olympics. I also remembered glancing at a breaking news report that was there was a bombing at Centennial Olympic Park that night before I left the club.

My mind was quickly headed toward the conclusion that Cara verbalized. "Gabe, I can't find Millie." Cara repeated herself and continued through tears, "I could not hang on to her. It is complete chaos here and I can't find her. I don't know what to do. I tried calling Jay..."

"Calm down and tell me what happened." I was telling her to calm down, but I was struggling to remain calm myself.

"They are saying there was a bomb. We were just standing there. Talking. A flash, a boom and suddenly people were running everywhere. Millie was injured. Shit, Gabe, the pay phone's about to cut off. I don't have any more change. Shit!" Cara snorted and cried and the volume of the phone was already starting to go.

"Cara, call me back collect. I will accept the call," I instructed her.

I anxiously awaited Cara to call back. I checked on Gabby and she was still asleep. My mind raced. All of my regrets and fears were coming to the surface. Where was Millie? I told her I would come for her, but I had not sorted out everything with Beth and Gabby yet. I had a plan and I was working on that plan, but I had been so busy since Gabby was born and things had been derailed by the business at the club with the Olympics. I could think of a hundred reasons, but they were just excuses for self-preservation. I was terrified to tell her that I needed more time. Terrified I would lose her for good and now what if I never saw her again? What if something had happened to her and she did not know how I felt about her? Dear God, when is the phone going to ring again?

My mind raced and I took the cordless phone and the baby monitor to the garage. It was the only place I could think to go so that I could speak freely without risking waking Gabby. I paced back and forth in the space along the side of my car and the garage wall. It was nearly five minutes between hanging up with Cara and the phone ringing again. Those five minutes were an eternity.

"You have a call from, caller say your name," the operator instructed.

"Cara Price."

"Sir, will you accept the..." I completely cut off the operator.

"Yes! Yes, I will accept the charges," I responded urgently.

The operator was gone and Cara spoke again. She was still crying and she sniffled in between her words and sentences. "Gabe, I don't know what to do or where to look. There are police everywhere and FBI. They told me to go home, but I can't leave her. I know she is injured."

"Cara, you are no good to her as long as you are hysterical. Are you sure she was injured and you did not just get separated from her. Have you gone back to where you all parked to see if she is just waiting on you there?" I tried to comfort both Cara and myself with thoughts that they had just lost one another in the rush of everything.

"No, Gabe, she got hit with stuff from the bomb or whatever it was," Cara explained before starting to fully sob again. "Millie got hit and blocked me from getting hit. There was blood everywhere on her back, on her hands from her back. I have her blood on me. Oh, God, I have her blood on me! I tried to hang on to her, but the people just kept pushing past us. I tried Gabe, I swear."

I was sick to my stomach. Thoughts of Amelia being alone scared and hurt were nearly more than I could bear. I did not know what to do, but I knew I had to go and help try to find her. I had to do more than try, I had to find her.

I said I would come for her and I hadn't. My God, what would I do if it was too late?

...

Dear Reader,

Thank you so much for giving your time to my book. I sincerely hope you enjoyed it.

I just wanted to assure you that I am not finished with Gabriel and Amelia yet. There is more to come in the next book, In Search of Honor, which I intend to release soon. Please check my website, www.tsdawson.com, for upcoming release dates and events. Also, I ask that if you did enjoy my work, please pass the word. I cannot be successful without you and I appreciate all that you do.

Thank you again.

Sincerely,

TS Dawson